THE
PHOENIX
AND THE
SPIDER

Benny Charles and Alex Robinson

Content Warning:

This novel contains topics and descriptions that some readers may find confronting or distressing. These include violence, murder, torture, sexual assault, suicidal ideation, self-harm, and mental illness.

∞∞∞

This is a work of fiction. Names, characters, places, and incidents either are the product of the author's imagination or are used fictitiously. Any resemblance to actual persons, living or dead, events, or locales is entirely coincidental.

For more information, address: pennedupemotion@gmail.com.
First Print Book edition April 2022
Cover design by Xenoyr

www.xenoyr.com

ISBN 978-0-6454464-1-8 (paperback)
ISBN 978-0-6454464-0-1 (ebook)
www.childrenoftheaether.com

Penned Up Emotion Publishing

In memory of
Maureen Packineau
1956-2021

The Mind's Eye

It was a day like any other. Sunlight streamed across the city, scattered clouds intermittently blocking its path as they rode on the gentle breeze drifting in from the bay. The temperature was mild, pants and shirt weather, with a jacket just in case; it was Melbourne after all. Everything was serene and calm. Everything was as it should be. In a matter of moments, though, everything changed.

The bustle of people weaving through the streets stopped and turned to each other in confusion as a low hum started to echo all around. It was as if a thousand subwoofers had been turned on and placed next to each other, creating a feedback loop that radiated outwards. To the east, a beam of black light shot upwards, piercing the clouds and bisecting the sky. The air contorted around it, creating a swirling gale, and the hum turned into a roar that drowned out all else.

Then, as suddenly as it had appeared, the beam vanished, and a heavy silence engulfed the city. Slowly, sounds began to reappear: pops like firecrackers, the snap of a tree splitting, a deep rumbling, then another long pause. Office workers gathered at their windows, searching for the source of the commotion. As they looked down at the streets below, a scene unfolded that defied belief, flouting every shred of sense and science.

A figure landed in the middle of an intersection, traffic screeching to a halt. Its form was shrouded in smoke-like darkness, and legs like those of a giant spider protruded from its back, black as obsidian yet strangely ethereal. The haze around it faltered, and its features became clear. It was not some fantastical creature but rather a man. What appeared at first to be spiders' legs were more like blades that rose and fell with each breath, alive and eager for violence. There should have been eight, but a gap on the right side spoke of an ancient wound.

Ashen trails flowed behind him as he paced in a circle, waiting, and bystanders on the street stared at him in disbelief, holding their breath

1

with nervous anticipation. A minute later, a second figure landed gently nearby. He, too, was human, obscured by the same darkness as his foe, but instead of blades, wings of pure shadow and electricity stretched out behind him, unearthly and intangible.

The Spider mockingly christened his opponent Phoenix, and the title rippled through the crowd in hushed whispers as they watched on with trepidation and curiosity. It seemed an appropriate name to those who could see the battle, the power emanating from his wings licking the air like flames.

The Phoenix unleashed a booming war cry, his very being pulsating as the air pressure increased. The pair charged towards one another, and a swirling fog of otherworldly dark energy encompassed them both as they collided, the two opponents deflecting shadowy blasts into nearby buildings, fracturing stone and shattering glass. Dust and debris filled the streets, and from amidst the mayhem came the screams of onlookers seeking to escape the escalating fray, their fascination swiftly giving way to terror.

Eventually, there came a lull in the combat, and the few spectators who remained could just make out the two figures through the haze. The Spider picked up the Phoenix by his throat, holding him aloft as though he were weightless before the quiet was broken by a sharp crack.

The Phoenix shot upwards, his wings fading away as he grazed the top storeys of a skyscraper rising from the corner of the intersection, glancing off the building and starting a long arc to the hard concrete below. He seemed defeated, his limp form falling towards inevitable death. The battle was over; the Spider had won.

All hope seemed lost, when suddenly, his wings reappeared, radiating energy as he swooped around a low-rise building and out of sight. There was a long, drawn-out scream of rage, and the Phoenix emerged, barrelling into the Spider, his ethereal blades disappearing like smoke on impact as he was carried skyward. They ascended into the clouds until their outline was just a faint speck, and the two foes hovered there for what seemed like an eternity.

Without warning, the Spider began to fall, blades sprouting once more from his back as he plummeted. Seeking to avoid his imminent fate, he unleashed a torrent of energy, sending himself careening into the twin skyscrapers that rose from the eastern side of the cityscape. His blades gripped the stone facade like an axe biting into rock as he leapt between the two buildings, slowing his descent towards the busy atrium below. Blasting through the roof, the Spider hit the ground hard, the impact fracturing the concrete tiles of the courtyard and sending plumes of dust billowing as rubble fell all around. He paused to recover slightly before moving onto the street, his gaze focused on the skies, his blades twitching impatiently.

The Phoenix dived earthward with wings spread wide, streaking towards his target like a missile, a deafening whine echoing across the city as he sliced through the air. There was a thunderous detonation as he struck the Spider, and the shock wave shattered every window in a five-block radius. Fearful shouts rang out from those caught in the pandemonium as they struggled to make sense of all that was befalling them, ducking for cover to avoid the glass raining from above.

A low hum permeated the city once again, reverberating through the chests of everyone within earshot, buildings shaking from its power. A second hum joined it, both growing in intensity and volume as people dropped to their knees, desperately covering their ears in a feeble attempt to block it out. Resonating with each other, the two sounds amplified until they created a tangible darkness that lanced through the streets like the bastard child of lightning and fire, scorching everything it touched.

The chaos reached a crescendo, then ceased abruptly, the energy that had previously filled the air seeming to race back to its creators. A sphere of darkness sprang to life between the Phoenix and the Spider, expanding outwards until it engulfed the two grappling foes entirely in its inky, impenetrable embrace. It hung there for a long moment, its mere existence a testament to powers far beyond mankind's comprehension. Then, all at once, it burst, the ensuing explosion destroying all in its path.

In the aftermath, nothing remained of the once-thriving metropolis. Every hidden laneway, towering skyscraper, and unsuspecting soul was simply erased from the world. A pale blanket of dust and ash settled over the now barren landscape, and from amidst the desolation, something emerged. It was the Spider, yet his form had no substance, his essence composed entirely of transparent black energy. Seven blades stretched out behind him, and he held out his hand, turning it over as he regarded it. Throwing his head back, he let out a triumphant cry. At long last, he had achieved the goal he had long been striving for.

He was free.

Theo

Chains swayed to her left, their menacing clink against stone walls rousing her slowly from unconsciousness. There was no breeze here, though, not even a draught, only a terrible darkness that sought to consume her. She hung in place like a carcass in a butcher's shop, her hands strung up around a long hook, her legs dangling loosely, her feet resting limply on the ground.

More than anything, she wanted to stand, to take the pressure off the shackles biting into her wrists, but she knew she couldn't. The last time she'd tried, the pain had been so intense she'd passed out.

The clinking stopped, and the room fell deathly silent. Her racing heart pounded in her ears, born of a terror she knew was there, hiding in the dark, watching.

"I think it's time to start again," a voice declared from the shadows, the words travelling in circles around her, sinister and disconcertingly calm. "What do you think, my dear? It's been so long since we've had a chance to play."

Panic gripped her, clamping its claws around her chest, her short, sharp breaths robbing her of oxygen until spots appeared in her vision.

A snicker echoed around the room. "Yes, yes, we will play now."

Something cold brushed against her leg, and she shuddered, not from its icy touch but from memories of the agony it had inflicted. Closing her eyes, she searched for the strength to survive the ordeal when a vision flashed before her, a shadowy figure with rippling wings of jet-black lightning. It was her sentinel, the Phoenix, the one who would come to save her. She called out, pleading, but something gripped her hair, yanking her back to reality.

Hot breath wafted past her ear. "No! You stay here with me. I don't want you to miss all the fun."

Something sharp dug into her back, close to her spine, and she clenched her jaw, not wanting to give him the satisfaction of a response.

5

The blade twisted deeper as blood ran down her leg, pain tearing through her body. Unable to contain it, an ear-piercing scream escaped her lips, the image of the Phoenix shattering into a thousand pieces.

∞∞∞∞∞∞∞∞∞∞∞∞∞∞∞∞

Theo jolted awake, her lungs gasping for air as if making up for lost time. The dream, the pain, the fear, it had all felt so real. A few long minutes passed before she managed to shift it to the back of her mind to hopefully be forgotten. She knew it wouldn't, though. If there was one thing Theo could rely on, it was her memory, her emotional memory doubly so.

She lay back on her pillow, staring up at the ceiling as her heart found a calmer beat, and pondered the one image that stood out above all others: the dark figure of the Phoenix. This ethereal shadow who seemed such a source of hope amidst the terror, where had it come from? And even more importantly, why did it feel so familiar? It was an image she'd seen in her dreams countless times before, but this was the first time she'd been able to give the figure a name.

Looking over at the clock on her bedside table, Theo squinted, trying to make out the numbers while cursing her damnable short-sightedness. It was 8:14 am, and her first alarm was about to go off. Right on cue, it began to beep, and she grabbed her phone, dismissed her wake-up call, and proceeded to spend the next fifteen minutes mindlessly scrolling through social media. She cared for very little of it, but it allowed her brain to slowly reboot enough for her to function as a human being. Finally, her second alarm sounded, and she slowly clambered out of bed, heading to the bathroom to put in her contact lenses. It was time to get ready for work.

She slipped into a pair of jeans and a black tank top, shoved her uniform in her bag, and returned to the bathroom to fix her unkempt mane of shoulder-length, chestnut hair. It had an unnatural ability to frizz and wave of its own volition, as though it were stuck in the eighties despite postdating the decade, and it required attentive wrangling to make it presentable to the outside world. Pulling it into a tight bun, she layered it with hair spray to hold the flyaways in place for the long shift ahead before brushing just enough mascara onto her lashes to hide her fatigue.

With her lacklustre beauty regime out of the way, she stared at herself in the mirror for a moment. Theo liked to think she was passably pretty, not model beautiful by any stretch but good enough to get by. She was tall, with kind, grey-blue eyes, high cheekbones, and lips that, depending on their curl, told you exactly what she was thinking, good or bad. Unfortunately, her anxiety and depression often warped this self-image, forcing her to see only flaws, and despite her best efforts, it was a battle she had been in the midst of for as long as she could remember.

Still bleary-eyed, she trudged into the kitchen and half-heartedly downed a couple of spoonfuls of yoghurt and a handful of blueberries. It was a meagre meal for someone about to dive into another hectic double shift, but it was far too early for her to stomach anything more substantial. Checking her watch, she noted the time, sliding on a pair of black flats, grabbing her backpack, and heading out the door right on schedule.

It was through sheer luck that Theo had found her East Melbourne apartment. The real estate had forgotten to post the ad online, but she'd seen the listing on a visit to their office. She didn't quite fit the key demographic for the area, which tended towards society's older and wealthier spectrum. Still, with a steady full-time job and an excellent rental history, the rest had taken care of itself. It was expensive and a little on the small side, but she was happy to pay for the convenience of being so close to work, the extra sleep it afforded her helping to mitigate the fact she was living alone for the first time in her life.

That's not to say she had a problem with being alone, but she did get lonely, and in her loneliness, she had a bad habit of getting inside her own head. Solitude often allowed the demons in her mind to venture forth, but there was nothing else for it at the moment. Her choices were either to live with strangers or to live by herself. As much as she didn't always enjoy the latter, interacting with people she barely knew in an enclosed space for extended periods was not something she wanted any part in. She was a classic introvert who relished her privacy.

The sun was out that morning, its light reflecting off the water trickling playfully in the central fountain of the courtyard as she emerged from her apartment tower, squinting. Theo liked sunlight about as much as she liked the morning, in that she saw the point of it but preferred not to partake. Of course, that was primarily due to her pasty white skin's tendency to burn almost instantaneously. In truth, she was more of a night person; she found solace in the darkness, the stillness, the quiet.

With a sigh, she began the five-minute walk to Porphura, a classy, upmarket restaurant situated across from Fitzroy Gardens. It sat proudly on the ground floor of a luxury apartment complex inhabited by people with far more wealth than she would ever have. The building was elegantly designed, with an impeccably clean, ivory exterior and sleek, dark tinted windows that bestowed enviable garden views on both the apartments and the two hundred seat dining room below.

More dollars than sense, she mused with her usual morning disdain as she passed the bright red Porsche sitting illegally in the loading zone at the rear of the restaurant, its parking fine flapping in the breeze.

Theo had no apprehension about going to work. She disliked the time of day she had to roust herself out of bed to get there, not the job itself. Slipping in the back door, she passed through the loading bay and wandered to the locker room, changing into her neatly ironed uniform with an efficiency that only comes from having done it thousands of times before. Without even having to think, she drew tight the drawstrings of her chequered pants, double cuffed the sleeves of her well-worn chef's jacket, tied her black apron snuggly around her waist, pulled on her shoes, grabbed her knife wrap, and crammed her backpack into her locker. Clicking the lock shut, she spun the numbers out of alignment and took a breath, her mindless, automated morning routine at an end.

As she walked past pot-wash and into the kitchen, Theo smiled at the comfort her job offered her. It was the kind of comfort that can only be found in doing a job you enjoy, and sometimes, it was the only thing keeping her going.

At eight years old, she'd proudly announced she wanted to become a chef. Neither her teachers nor her parents had succeeded in discouraging her from that path, even when she'd scored high enough grades to study medicine. No amount of snide comments about wasted intelligence or strategically placed university brochures had managed to sway her. She didn't want to be a doctor; she wanted to cook, and

8

she was smart enough to know that a life spent following her passion would not be a life wasted. Besides, she'd always figured if she wanted to work horrible hours in a demanding environment, cut things up, and have the ability to kill people with her mistakes, why not be able to eat while she did it?

Theo had only ever worked in restaurants, and although she was twenty-six, she had more than a decade of experience under her belt. She'd studied for four years after high school, on top of working part-time, and had come out the other end with papers for cookery, patisserie, and management. To her, becoming multi-qualified had been a way of over-achieving in a role she'd constantly been told was beneath her.

Now, she was the head pastry chef of Porphura, a position that was both arduous and rewarding in equal measure. The kitchen tested all within it, and the world of extremes it harboured meant a good day felt like pure magic, but a bad day could leave her feeling battered and bruised. In spite of its pitfalls, though, positive feedback from customers or getting a knowing nod and a wry smile from Peter, her head chef, could make it all worthwhile. He was a man of little praise and a hard taskmaster, but that only made his compliments all the more satisfying.

Peter waved as she made her way around the kitchen circuit to the pastry section at the back, and she nodded at him, too tired to speak. She was always like that in the morning. It took her a good two hours to reach the point of effective communication; unless the question was work-related, it wasn't getting an answer. Until then, she simply prepped away on autopilot while waiting for her brain to stop lagging.

In a perfect life, she would wake up at midday and start work at one. Unfortunately, the world didn't function that way, particularly in hospitality. Theo arrived at nine, prepped for lunch, did lunch service, prepped for dinner, did dinner service, cleaned the kitchen from top to bottom, and somehow found the time to create new desserts, specials, and any other request that was thrown her way. More often than not, she didn't walk out before midnight. Just a lazy fifteen-hour shift; pretty standard, really.

Down the bench from her, Justin was studiously shelling peas for larder, the birthplace of salads and cold entrées. They'd worked together long enough for him to know small talk at that time was futile, and so he continued in relative quiet. Justin was Vietnamese, with short, jet-black hair, deep brown eyes, and a babyface that made him appear almost pre-pubescent. He'd immigrated with his family as a child, and despite growing up in a household where English was firmly the second language, he possessed an Australian accent broader than anyone in the kitchen.

Slipping her knives from her wrap and starting on her first task for the day, Theo's mind conjured up the faces of the countless cooks she'd worked with over the years, Justin included. They'd come in all shapes and sizes, but as long as they were reliable and hardworking, those shapes and sizes had mattered very little. Kitchens were a place of sanctuary for the outsiders, the loners, the quirky. They were a place where a sharp wit was almost as important as a sharp knife, and they were the only place where Theo didn't feel like the odd one out.

As dissimilar as her peers seemed to be to one another, her experience had found one consistent truth about almost all of them. They all had some sort of psychological issue and some sort of addiction, whether it be depression and alcohol, anxiety and coffee, bipolar and drugs, or plain old superiority complex and adrenaline. It was a twisted game of 'name your problem, pick your poison', and the two rarely played well together, especially when exacerbated by the stress, pressure, and culture of the kitchen. Still, in the space between the chopping boards and the stovetops, these traits found somewhere to call home, although that wasn't what drew them all to cooking, nor was it what kept them there.

The thing people rarely understood about being a chef was the joy that came from taking the most basic of products and creating art in its edible form. It was one of the few jobs in the world that required the finely tuned use of all five senses, and there was a beauty in its science, in the discoveries just waiting to be made. Beyond that, though, there was a unique calm that came from blocking out one's demons and focusing fully on the food. Cooking was all-consuming, and in being so, became a temporary cure to life's perpetual problems.

Suddenly, a head poked around the corner. "Your brain functioning yet?"

"Sort of," Theo replied with a shrug as Ruth sauntered over.

Ruth was the sous chef, second-in-charge to Peter. This often meant she was stuck doing prep for both of their sections while Peter worked in the office, even when said 'work' involved him whiling away the afternoon playing mobile games or going on internet tangents. She had a strikingly unconventional appearance, with cropped hair dyed a washed-out shade of blue, a sleeve of seemingly unrelated tattoos up her right arm, a smile that reeked of mischief, and hazel eyes that somehow appeared both perpetually fatigued and ready to rumble simultaneously.

On top of that, she was quite possibly the most lesbian person Theo had ever met. To Ruth, the penis was the most foul, disgusting thing ever invented, and, in her mind, all women would be better off if they moved to an island where men were shot on sight. She was fun to be around, and even though they weren't particularly close, she was the nearest thing Theo had to a friend. Besides, they had some common ground.

"You seen the new waitress yet? The blonde, British one?" Ruth asked.

"No," Theo replied, raising an eyebrow inquisitively. "Should I?"

"You should. She's quite the babe. I'll even let you have first go at her if you want."

Theo rubbed her brow with one hand, shaking her head at Ruth's sheer tactlessness when it came to pointing out attractive waitstaff and customers. The woman called out 'chicken in the oven' more than the guys did, and it was a trait she shared with an alarming majority of other chefs, although Theo lacked any enthusiasm for joining in.

"There are so many things wrong with that statement," Theo said, rolling her eyes.

"Like what?"

"Firstly, she's not a piece of meat for you to raffle off. Secondly, you're assuming she's my type. And lastly, and most importantly, you should never date people you work with. It always ends badly." Theo smiled knowingly, picking up her knife and pointing the tip at Ruth like it was an extension of her hand. "Don't shit where you eat."

"You can't live that way. We don't get a social life outside this place. If we don't use work to get laid, what other choices do we have?"

Theo waved her free hand around in sarcastic frustration. "Literally *anything* else! Flirt with an unsuspecting checkout chick at the supermarket. Wink suggestively at someone on the tram. Hell, go on Tinder!"

"Tinder? Even *I'm* not that desperate," Ruth mocked.

"Do you even know if she's interested in chicks?"

"Doesn't matter! All you need is enough alcohol, and you can have any girl you want," Ruth laughed.

Theo chuckled despite herself. "Well, I'm not interested, so have at it, if that's what you want."

"Yesss!" Ruth said with a pump of her fist, scurrying back to her section before Peter noticed the conversation was far from professional.

Theo stared at her knife for a moment, then finished slicing the core off the pineapple on her board, placing the quarters in a tray and rubbing them with brown sugar.

From down the bench, Justin chimed in. "Did I hear that right?"

"What, two women can't talk about wanting to have sex with another woman?" Theo asked, feigning indignance.

He stared ahead blankly for a moment before recovering his faculties. "No. It's not that. It's just ..."

Justin's family was quite conservative, and when he'd started as an apprentice at Porphura, his eyes had been abruptly opened to a world he hadn't known existed. Chefs were an indiscriminate bunch when it came to language, and those with delicate sensibilities usually found other professions before too long.

At times, the kitchen was a lot like being aboard an unruly pirate ship. You drank like a pirate, swore like a pirate, got yelled at by your captain for daring to question even their most outrageous commands, and if there was even a whisper of mutiny, you were tossed unceremoniously overboard. The fact that Justin, who was a clean-mouthed teetotaller, was still around was a testament to his fortitude. Nevertheless, he did ask some adorably naive questions sometimes.

"Do girls really get other girls drunk for ... you know?" Justin asked sheepishly.

Theo stared at him for a second as an impish grin crossed her face. "All the time, Justin. All the time."

"But I thought only guys did that."

"Nope. Ever since booze was invented, we've been using it to try and get laid. Man or woman, it's just human nature."

Justin seemed to consider that for a second. "What about you, though?"

Theo's eyebrow arched. "What about me?"

"Well ... with you being ... I mean ... because you're ...," he spluttered like an old car in need of a service.

"Bisexual?" she said, finishing his sentence with amusement.

Justin nodded innocently.

Theo smirked. "I have sex with guys and girls, Justin, so I get everyone drunk, just in case. Maybe one day I'll get *you* drunk and see what happens!" And with that, she gave him a long, exaggerated wink.

Justin took one look at her, his face turning pale, and went back to shelling his peas without another peep.

Trying not to laugh at the absurdity of the conversation, Theo sliced open a vanilla pod and placed it in with the pineapple before covering the tray with foil and sliding it in the oven. She wasn't like that, of course; in fact, she could still count the number of sexual partners she'd had on one hand. Justin was just fun to stir.

∞∞∞∞

It was just past midnight when Theo stepped through her apartment door, exhausted. Dumping her dirty uniform into the hamper and setting her backpack aside, she shuffled into the bathroom, turning on the shower faucet and peeling off her clothes while steam began to fill the space around her. As tired as she was, she knew she'd be awake for a while yet, her mind still buzzing from the adrenaline of service.

With scalding hot water flowing down her body, she slowly scrubbed the sweat of the long day away, trying her best to let her long list of work-related thoughts wash away as well. Shutting off the shower, she lingered in the warm air, breathing it in deeply before towelling herself dry and slipping into a pair of plaid purple pyjama pants and another of her countless black tank tops.

As the steam dissipated, Theo found herself wrapped in a far less fleeting mental fog, and she wandered over to her bed, perching on its edge. Hunched over, she let her head hang low, her damp hair clinging coldly against her neck, and, for the briefest of moments, she contemplated her existence. It only led to dark thoughts, though, and unwilling to wallow in them, she set them aside and went to the fridge, filling up a glass with mineral water and slumping onto the couch.

As usual, her body and mind were a good few hours out of sync, and although she was physically drained, she wasn't mentally ready for sleep. With nothing else for it, she flicked on an episode of a reality show she'd watched a hundred times before, sipping her water as she sought to replace her cavalcade of thoughts with the familiar voice of a celebrity chef verbally abusing incompetent cooks. Even in her spare time, away from work, the sounds of the kitchen were comforting. They were her white noise.

At times like these, living alone wore on her. She was isolated, all alone in a city full of people, and with no friends to call upon and a distant and disconnected family, Theo lacked anyone to confide in about her struggles. As a result, there were days when it took every ounce of her strength just to get out of bed, to take one more step, one more breath. In the absence of a support system, her depression became malignant.

For Theo and all those like her, life was not a smooth road stretching towards some golden sunset. Instead, it was a treacherous, winding mountain trail cloaked in dark forests filled with the howls of creatures hungry for blood. It was an unbeaten path pelted by unceasing rain, which, without warning, fell away to sheer cliffs. Her way ahead was all but obscured, muddling her sense of direction and feeding her anxiety until her gait shortened to little more than a cautious tiptoe.

Lost and fearful, she began to question every choice and dread every turn. Each fork in the road became an irreversible ultimatum at which a single misstep would inevitably spell certain doom. Unable to see any other option, though, she simply gritted her teeth and kept moving forward, clinging to the hope that she would eventually emerge into a clearing of calm contentment.

As futile as her journey felt at times, her stubbornness kept her holding on. It wasn't as though she was always miserable. There were happier times, when the light seemed to almost surround her, but they were always fleeting. In her heart, she knew the shadows were lurking just out of sight, waiting for the opportune moment to lead her back down darker paths, back to the cliff's edge. She'd teetered there more than once, and at times, she wondered why she even bothered pulling herself away. It would be so easy to let go, to float away into the abyss. After all, there was no pain in death, only peace.

The episode ended, and she was stirred back to reality by the silence, her mind continuing to whir, but her body demanding respite. With another early rise and long shift on the cards for the next day, she was forced to turn in for the night, switching off the television and heading to the bathroom. As she brushed her teeth, Theo stared at her reflection in the mirror, despairing at the dark circles under her eyes until she removed her contacts, her features becoming an indiscernible collection of smudged shapes and colours.

Collapsing into bed, she pulled the covers over herself, tucking them under her feet as she settled gratefully into the embrace of her mattress. The room was dark, but beams of moonlight seeped in through the Venetian blinds. They cast a faint, banded pattern across the ceiling, and Theo stared at the blur as she lay there.

On the one hand, she wanted to go to sleep, to recharge, but on the other hand, part of her was stricken with a deep sense of trepidation. Sleep meant dreams, but far too often, it also meant nightmares. They were a constant in her life, and there were times when they came with frightening regularity, tormenting her for weeks on end every time she closed her eyes. Images of everyone she knew betraying her; images of her successes turning to failures; images of her own death.

All at once, the nightmare she'd had that morning came flooding back, and she turned it over in her mind, examining it closely. Even now, it felt real. What was wrong with her, that she could remember every detail of such a terrible dream? For most people, it would have dissolved from consciousness soon after waking, but for Theo, those kinds of images rarely faded, staying with her always.

Each one weighed on her, and she feared the weight would eventually become more than she could bear. There was only so much adversity and pain a soul could endure before it caved in to the call from the shadows and disappeared into the eternal night. Was that what the dream meant? Was she reaching her breaking point? Was the darkness close to claiming her? Her eyes grew heavy, closing until the light of the moon was hidden from view, and she continued to ponder the final question. As she fell asleep, there was still no answer.

Auryn

Streaks of prismatic colour swirled around him, strange and otherworldly. There was no floor beneath him, no gravity to bind him to a time or place; he just moved through empty space, floating like a bubble caught on the breeze. Despite the surrealness of his situation, though, he was not afraid.

Finding nothing distinguishable in the haze of hues racing past, he moved onwards, propelled by mechanisms beyond his comprehension, until finally, he reached something and stopped. Before him stood a wall of darkness, stretching out endlessly in either direction, bisecting the universe and barring his way. He searched for some clue to unravel its mystery, but the barrier seemed to exist both without and beyond reason. Its surface was smooth and glassy, yet somehow it failed to reflect any of the technicolour palette behind him.

Pounding on it with his fists, he tried to force it to open, but it was impenetrable, seamless. Eventually, he turned around in defeat and floated away. It was a puzzle he would have to decipher another day.

∞∞∞∞∞∞∞∞∞∞∞∞∞∞∞

Soft rays of light crept across Auryn's face, and his nose twitched. He lay there for a moment, willing himself back to sleep, but it was no use. Reluctantly, he opened his eyes, his body still aching from the rigours of work the night before. Staring up at the ceiling, drained and exhausted, he pondered what he was doing with his life. As he swung his legs off the side of the bed and sat up, he thought of the people who lived around him. They all seemed content to merely traipse along with no discernible purpose. Auryn could find no joy in such a passive existence, though. He wanted to make a difference, to be special, to mean something.

Dragging himself into the bathroom, he was met by his reflection in the mirror, realising despondently that time had caught up with him.

If he looked closely, he could see a smattering of silver peeking out from amidst his short, dark brown hair, and on his face lay the unwelcome marks of his life. The faint acne scars on his temples sat as a memento of his pain-filled youth, the ever-deepening lines on his furrowed brow offered a glaring reminder of his own mortality, and the weariness in his grey-blue eyes stood as clear evidence of his dissatisfying present.

He bent over with a sigh, splashing water on his face and running his fingers through his hair before wandering to the kitchen. As he opened the pantry to a scant view, the bare shelves served only to hammer home his overwhelming sense of internal emptiness. Eating in the morning was more of a mechanical routine than anything else; he did it because he was supposed to, not because he wanted to. It could wait.

Scraping together enough energy to leave the house, he changed into a pair of jeans and slipped on a black t-shirt bearing the faded logo of a metal band he'd seen in concert years ago. Then, with shopping bags and wallet in hand, he laced up his shoes and descended the narrow stairwell to the street.

Auryn lived in Footscray, a large suburb just to the west of Melbourne. It wasn't an affluent place by any means, but rather one of the last bastions of affordable housing close to the city, filled with an eclectic mix of the lower middle class: immigrants, young families, and older people who'd lived there their entire lives.

It looked run down for the most part, bereft of the money needed to afford sleek exteriors and manicured gardens, but he could already see the gentrification happening all around. Small businesses closed to be replaced by big brands and corporate franchises, while large old houses which sang of bygone eras were demolished to make way for soulless, concrete apartment complexes.

The late morning air was cooled by an autumn breeze that drained some of the bite out of the slow waning summer sunlight awaiting him outside. Nearing his vacant parking space, he stopped, a pang of sentimental sadness piercing his chest as his eyes fell on the smudge of motor oil at its centre. In his darkest times, he'd sought to fill his emotional void with a physical object, and as such, he'd purchased a second-hand, black Jeep Cherokee, similar to one his parents had briefly owned in his adolescence and of which he held fond memories.

For seven years, it had helped keep him from the brink, and it had been with great reluctance that he'd sold it after its growing myriad of problems made it prohibitively expensive to maintain. Adjusting to its absence was proving difficult, though, not simply for transport reasons but because the space sat as a stark embodiment of his position in life. There he was, thirty-eight years old, living in a tiny, rented apartment with no car, no partner, and mired in debt. How had it come to this? Most people his age had families, houses, and careers; they had debt, but at least they had something to show for it. Auryn had nothing.

Leaves floated past him, equal parts autumnal and sun-scorched, as he tore himself away and began the now familiar walk to the supermarket. The streets were quiet midweek, and his thoughts whirred uninterrupted until he reached the main strip on Barkly Street. The thrum of people there was wildly juxtaposed to the rest of the suburb. Young parents wrangled toddlers and groceries alike. Petite, elderly Vietnamese women tottered along with canvas shopping trolleys overflowing with Asian vegetables from the market. And on the corner, two men harassed passers-by for spare change, their haggard, gaunt faces a clear indication of what that money would be used for.

Weaving through the hubbub, Auryn reached the supermarket and grabbed a basket, immediately cursing himself for not bringing his headphones. Monotonous lo-fi pop tunes seeped through the aisles as he strolled up and down, aimlessly browsing the shelves as his mind wandered once more. His internal monologue soon drowned out the music, and he found himself wallowing in the broken dreams of his youth: dreams long since buried under fear of rejection and crippling self-doubt.

In his twenties, he'd wanted to be a writer, to start a band, to DJ in clubs; he'd had plans for his life, but he'd failed on all counts. Writing had been put on the back burner after his laptop and hard drives were stolen in a burglary almost a decade ago, his countless stories irretrievable in a time when the cloud was not around to be his digital insurance policy. Playing guitar and songwriting had always been a soothing creative outlet for him, but he'd never had the courage to put his music out into the world or try to form a band. As for his DJing career, it had at least feigned possibility when his previous job had given him a regular gig on Fridays, but it had never progressed any further than that.

Although he'd once had great optimism about the last dream, if he were to be completely honest with himself, it would never have come to fruition. To be a successful DJ, especially when starting out, you needed to bring a crowd to watch you play, friends who would show up and make a bar or club look busy until the other party-goers arrived. Auryn didn't have any, though, no real ones, at least.

He had plenty of acquaintances and workmates, people who spoke to him provided it benefitted them, but he had no one he could truly rely on, no one who was there when he needed them. Like most people wrestling with mental illness, he found it hard to maintain relationships in a world where anything less than happy was seen as weak, inconvenient, and contagious. In the end, he simply stopped following up on the few connections he did have, putting up walls to prevent anyone from growing close enough to cause pain. He did not wish to be a burden on those he cared about, so, in response, he removed his weight from their lives altogether, isolating himself before they had a chance to forsake him.

Not only did his deep-seated fear of rejection rule his personal life, it governed every aspect of him. It stunted his confidence, paralysed him socially, and, in a twist of self-fulfilment, ensured his rejection by forcing inaction. Behind him lay a trail of failed ventures, unfinished projects, and abandoned aspirations, and in wishing not to repeat the pain of past failures, he now remained stagnant. He stumbled through life as a bartender because it was the only job he'd ever had, and despite his efforts, he'd never managed to get a job doing anything else.

Auryn had always found a dark humour in the way his life had evolved. How, just like everyone else, he'd started on a path to his idealistic future, his heart filled with reckless abandon and a blind confidence that, in spite of the fact no one else had managed it yet, *his* life would go perfectly to plan. As time passed, though, he watched his path crack and warp, each misstep having a knock-on effect, each crest and unforeseen corner taking him further from his dreams. Eventually, regardless of his best intentions and carefully laid plans, he'd ended up in a place that looked in no way like the perfect picture he'd painted all those years ago.

An overwhelming hopelessness enveloped him as he walked down the confectionary aisle and paused. There were discount signs everywhere: a dangerous situation for anyone foolish enough to go shopping on an empty stomach. He stared at the shelves for a moment, considering the plethora of options before picking up a block of peppermint chocolate. Auryn knew the consequences of a poor diet. Every article on health could give him a million reasons why he shouldn't buy it, but like so many others in the grip of depression, feeding his soul often came at the sacrifice of nutrition.

As the two sides of his conscience grappled with the decision, he despaired at how society peddled the belief that obesity was a choice made by those lacking in self-control when, more often than not, it was a symptom of a far more complicated problem. The surge of serotonin provided by 'bad' foods satiated a great need, filling the void and dulling the ache of internal anguish. They were a temporary bandaid over a gaping wound, soothing self-hatred, treating trauma, and alleviating anxiety. They were cheap, neatly wrapped, affordable medication for the mentally ill: edible therapy, if you will.

Wielding cutlery against the encroaching darkness, wounded souls just like his wagered their weight in return for a few moments of peace, for a fleeting lull in the storm, for survival. Although music had always been Auryn's personal crutch through hard times, he understood how easily sugar could replace songs. If his demons were to lead him down that path, though, he knew he would find nothing but further rejection, and that knowledge troubled him greatly.

Emotion kept his hand clamped on the block of chocolate until he conceded, placing it in his basket between the packet of salt and vinegar chips and the bottle of soft drink. Continuing haphazardly, he flitted between aisles, mindlessly guided by the whims of his stomach until he reached the fresh produce section. Feeling a vague obligation to include something of notable nutritional value in his shop, he picked up a few small bags of fruit and vegetables, disheartened he couldn't purchase more. That was hospitality, though. Long hours and sporadic home cooking meant anything fresh had a habit of withering away long before he had a chance to eat it.

Heading over to the self-service checkout, the introvert in him once more revelled in the fact he could complete his trip with no need for human interaction. His current state had stripped him of the energy required to swap superficial pleasantries in exchange for convenience, and he scanned his items in grateful silence. A few minutes later, he was on his way home, his wallet empty and groceries straining his weary arms, so lost in his thoughts that he scarcely remembered the journey at all. In truth, he only zoned back into reality when he found himself jamming the key into the lock the wrong way around.

Hit with a wave of exhaustion as he stepped inside, Auryn abandoned his bounty on the kitchen counter, one of the bags toppling to release a stray orange which rolled off the edge and thudded onto the floor. He sagged onto his ageing couch, the springs creaking as he sank into the familiar embrace of its indented cushions, their threadbare fabric a tacky brown colour that was probably last popular in the seventies. Collapsing over, his head landed on the pillow stashed at one end, its form crumpled from too many nights when his depression made the short walk to his bed seem like a marathon.

As he closed his eyes and took a deep breath, the memory of his grandmother sprang to mind. It was a natural association; he was lying on her couch, after all. Scenes of childhood visits played out before him, of eating homemade cakes and consuming a Frankenstein concoction of lemonade, lime, orange, and cola because when you're eight years old, you can do things like that. He'd always been happy as a kid, but a long succession of bullies coupled with the intense competition of attending a private high school had eventually crushed his spirit and drained all the fun from his once carefree life. Auryn had never really forgiven his parents for that.

To make matters worse, when he was sixteen, his family had been forced to move away from Melbourne after his father was promoted and transferred to Sydney. Auryn had loathed the change and returned to his home city five years later, while his parents, brother, and sister had remained in their new home. The distance had created a rift between them, and their interactions had gradually decreased over time until he'd stopped bothering altogether.

Both siblings were married now, with kids of their own. They were caught up with their own families and thus had very little time for their older brother anymore. His life was so wildly different to theirs that any common ground they'd once shared had long since eroded. To them, Auryn's struggles were inconsequential to their blissful existence, and they held no desire to listen to his troubles in place of bragging about their children's micro-achievements in a never-ending game of one-upmanship. They found his mental illness tiresome, and he found their self-absorption equally so. Of course, they saw his ostracism as his own fault, a lack of effort on his behalf, a conscious choice to elect sadness over joy. Regardless of where the fault lay, though, the result was the same. Auryn was alone.

The breeze blowing in through the window rustled the curtains, and he watched the shadows dance across the ceiling. As he did, he wondered if there was a parallel universe where he had a different family: one that cared about him, nurtured him, loved him. Shaking his head to dispel the wistful daydream and the painful memories that triggered it, he checked his watch, realising an hour had slipped by unnoticed.

His stomach grumbled as he begrudgingly stood up and headed to the kitchen, squeezing a slapdash cheese and Vegemite sandwich into the jaffle iron. Rescuing the escapee orange from its hideout between the foot of the pantry and the bin, Auryn packed away his previously forsaken groceries. As his sandwich cooked, he straightened the cans and aligned the packets on the shelves in some vain attempt to create order in his otherwise frazzled mind, although it offered little relief.

Snack in hand, he schlepped over to his desk, turning on his computer and scrolling through the abyss of the internet as he ate before leaning back in his chair. His mind was hazy and withdrawn. He considered playing a video game, but he didn't have the concentration for it. He thought about watching a movie, but none appealed to him. Even the notion of playing his guitar wasn't enticing. Nothing seemed powerful enough to push back the melancholy, all the hobbies that usually brought him pleasure seeming devoid of their lustre.

Suddenly, his phone rang, and he glanced over at it, a pang of unease stabbing him just below his ribs. He groaned as he saw the name on the screen and picked it up. It was Tony, his assistant manager at Benzin, the bar in the CBD he'd been working at for five years, and while they got along well, he knew this wasn't a social call.

"Hey, man," Auryn said with little enthusiasm as he picked up.

"Hey, buddy. Sorry to bug you on your day off, but I need to clean the beer lines, and I can't find the chemicals."

Racking his brain, he tried to recall where he'd put them. It was at times like these that he cursed being the manager. He was always on call should something go wrong or missing, making switching off virtually impossible. Agitated, he paced over to the window, staring at the skyline of Melbourne sprawled out in the distance, when he finally remembered.

"They're in the cleaning cupboard, right up the back. You'll have to dig them out from behind the boxes of paper towels."

"Oh, okay, I thought they were in the keg room. Sorry."

Auryn stifled a sigh. "It's fine, dude, don't worry about it."

"No, no, I'll have to make it up to you," Tony said in his usual bright tone, trying to lighten the mood. "How 'bout I tickle your balls a bit tomorrow after work? Should help to ease the pain."

Auryn laughed despite himself. They'd been working together for years now, and sometimes their jokes erred on the side of ridiculous. Still, if nothing else, it made life a little more entertaining.

"Yeah, probably not, but I'll think about it," Auryn replied, feigning consideration.

"Well, the offer's always there," Tony chuckled. "See ya tomorrow."

"See ya."

Auryn put his phone away, smiling for the first time all day as he glanced around his apartment. The fog of depression wasn't gone, but the distraction of the call had dispersed it enough for him to function again, and sometimes that was all he could strive for. He plonked himself down in front of the television, flicking it on and mindlessly binge-watching anime for the remainder of his singular day off, pausing only to make an uninspired bowl of reheated spaghetti bolognese.

As the daylight dwindled and midnight drew closer, he decided to forgo another back-aching sleep on the couch, brushed his teeth, peeled off his t-shirt, and crawled into bed. Rest didn't come willingly, though, and he rolled over, fidgety and frustrated. A faint orange glow seeped past the sheet he used to cover the blinds on his bedroom window. It was there to block out most of the morning sun, the bane of all night shift workers, but the muted illumination creeping in at its edges left his nights shrouded in a veil of shadows.

Auryn had never liked the dark. It had terrified him as a child, and he vividly remembered going to the toilet in the middle of the night, then sprinting back to bed and diving under the covers, holding his breath in case anything had followed him. He'd always seen monsters and murderers in every silhouette and hiding behind every door. Although it wasn't quite that bad now, something about it continued to set off a primal fear in him, a fear that no amount of rationalisation could dispel, his imagination filling his head with all sorts of strange and hellish scenarios.

In the silence, he pondered the absurdity of being afraid of the dark as a grown man when he knew full well the true monsters of the world walked in broad daylight. Still, an errant feeling in his gut gave him pause for thought, as if a part of him was trying to send a warning to be wary of the shadows and the creatures that lurk within. Shaking it off, he closed his eyes, his conscious mind remaining somewhat optimistic, even if his subconscious disagreed wholeheartedly. The day had been a struggle, but there was always tomorrow.

Birtha, Mesopotamia, 424 BCE

Ashur perched atop the roof of his small mudbrick house, as he did every morning, watching the sun rise over the Tigris River. Its warmth rid his mind of the loneliness and uncertainty of the night and filled it with the rekindled hope of a bright new day. The soft rays of light shimmered on the river's surface, the turquoise water reflecting the cloud-dotted sky above, and he found himself lost in thought.

The gentle lapping against the banks calmed him, and he allowed his gaze to follow the current as it flowed south to join the shores far beyond the horizon. Sometimes he dreamt of the sea, its crystal blue expanse, its powerful waves that shaped the coast with their perpetual motion, and the peculiar creatures that lived in its depths. He'd give anything to leave his home behind and see it for himself, to feel the waves wash over his feet.

Shaken from his daydream by the sound of his neighbour trying to corral her children inside, he looked around at Birtha. Sitting stoically on the northern bank of the river, the fortified city offered respite to those who journeyed across Mesopotamia, a place of trade for wandering merchants, and a protected home to those who resided there. With a deep breath, he closed his eyes and basked in the sun for one final moment before rising. He couldn't sit around all day; there was work to be done.

Ashur's job was a simple but arduous one. The wealthy residents would send a servant to the markets to purchase items for the household, and it was his job to haul the goods back to their estates on the other side of the city. Despite the intensity of the labour, the pay was decent, if at times unsteady, and the merchants he worked with would often provide him with wares as a show of gratitude for his assistance.

Arriving at the market, he collected his first delivery. It was for one of the most prominent families in the city, and although he'd never actually seen them in the flesh, he could often hear the sounds of music and laughter carried on the wind from the extravagant parties they so often hosted. Such luxuries were beyond Ashur's reach, but in all honesty, it didn't faze him; nothing did anymore. He had plans for his life, and none of them involved the godforsaken city of Birtha.

Legs of goat and sides of pork filled the basket strapped to his back, and the ropes cut into his shoulders from the weight. By the time he reached his destination, he was sweating profusely, slowing to catch his breath as he approached the front gate. Two men with short swords hanging from their belts waited for him, their brown leather chest armour scaled with shining bronze plates, their matching bronze helmets conical and not in the least bit tarnished, their facial expressions overly serious.

Ashur had nothing but contempt for men like this. He delivered there at least once a month, but his was a face they never deemed worthy of remembering. They thought of themselves as soldiers, but they were nothing more than status symbols for the wealthy: polished baubles with weapons. Ashur had been a soldier years ago and knew their type all too well. They wouldn't last two seconds in a real battle; they would either be the first to die or the first to flee. Still, he tilted his head respectfully as he reached them, knowing he would be greeted as a stranger yet again.

"Delivery for the feast," Ashur announced, straightening himself.

One of the men nodded, stepping forward to block his way. "Leave it here. We'll take it to the kitchen."

Ashur knew all about the scam they were attempting. The soldiers would take the meat, keep some for themselves, then blame him if anyone noticed. It wasn't going to happen, not on his watch.

"I'm sorry," he said, putting out a hand. "I must deliver it personally so I can collect my fee."

The soldier glowered at him, but Ashur stood his ground until the other man tapped his partner on the shoulder and motioned with his head. "Let him through."

Nodding reluctantly, the soldier stepped back. "Turn left and go around the house. The servant's entrance is at the rear. Don't go wandering, understand?" he grunted, his hand resting on the pommel of his sword.

28

Ashur strode through the gate, a smug grin tugging at his lips. As much as he wished to disregard the guard's warning, he knew the consequences of being caught where he shouldn't be. Thus, with every intention of keeping his head and hands firmly attached to his body, he followed the most discreet path to the kitchen.

Walking slowly around the house, Ashur marvelled at the tall columns lining the exterior. He snuck a sidelong glance through a window and spotted a small, ornate table up against a wall, its legs carved into the shape of winged lions. On the table sat a large vase, glazed in white, with a bright red, geometric design around its centre and a bunch of delicate flowers sprouting from its mouth. Everything oozed extravagance, and no matter how many times he laid eyes on the residence, it never ceased to amaze him.

Hearing heavy boots crunching into the dirt at the front of the estate, he hurried around the corner to the far more unassuming kitchen, delivering the meat to one of the cooks, who yanked it from his hands gruffly and walked off. As he waited patiently for the head servant to arrive and pay him, he swiped a couple of bread rolls that sat unattended on a bench to cool, stuffing them inside his tunic while no one was looking.

A clipped step could be heard nearing the door, and the room fell silent as every underling hyper-focused on their work, not wanting to incur the wrath of, as Ashur liked to call him, His Haughtiness. Moments later, the head servant entered, coin purse in hand and nose in the air, as if to glance at anyone below him would invite death and dishonour. Regardless of his thoughts on the man, though, Ashur did his best to act deferentially. After all, he was a good client.

Ashur collected his coins, nodded his thanks, and made a swift exit, all the while trying desperately to hide the bread tucked in his tunic. Quickstepping past the soldiers, he waited until he was out of sight before retrieving the rolls and stuffing them into his mouth one at a time. They were freshly baked, their centres warm and yielding, their crust crisp and golden: a rare treat, if somewhat questionably obtained. In a matter of seconds, they were gone, the crumbs on Ashur's chest the only evidence of their existence.

The delivery had taken most of the morning, and as the sun rose higher, he wandered slowly back towards the market, taking in the sights, such as they were. Birtha wasn't a pretty place. Most of the houses were made of coarse mud bricks, with the only stone structures being those of the wealthier families and administrators who could afford to purchase them. Even the city walls were constructed of worn, old bricks that Ashur was convinced a stiff breeze could easily blow over. His home was destined to fade into oblivion; he knew it in his heart. It survived for now, but just as the great empires of the past rose and crumbled, so too would Birtha eventually return to rubble.

As long as the city stood, though, the market was its beating heart and a feast for the senses. Tents lined the road, and the place hummed as people rushed around, trying to buy what they could before the best offerings were gone.

Merchants hollered their wares at anyone who would listen, the thoroughfare a cacophony of products and prices. Donkeys pulled laden carts up to stalls to unload goods, and burly men hauled crates up from the boats docked on the riverbank. The air was thick with intermingling scents: the rich smell of freshly tanned leather, the aquatic odour of baskets of fish fresh from the morning's catch, the stench of nervous goats bleating as they were bought and sold, and the sweet aroma of dates piled high in earthenware bowls. At the far end stood stalls manned by wealthier merchants from distant lands. Some displayed fine fabrics that delighted the eye with their bright pops of colour, whereas others spruiked shining trinkets of Egyptian gold, intricately carved Indian ivory, and delicate beaded jewellery.

Ashur stopped at the crossroads that led to his home in one direction and into the thrum of marketgoers in the other, absentmindedly fondling the small pouch of money hanging from his waist. He was trying to decide whether to call it a day or look for another job when someone he'd never seen before caught his attention. Her lack of veil outed her as a maidservant, and her unshrouded olive skin, vivacious brown eyes, and braid of long dark hair draped over her shoulder left Ashur awestruck.

Of course, although their social standing was compatible, he knew he stood no chance with her. He was far from a handsome man: his nose slightly askew from where it had been broken in battle years earlier, his dark hair hacked short with no real finesse, his chin wrapped in an unkempt beard, and his face weathered far beyond its thirty years. As he gazed through the crowd, watching her haggle with a merchant over a sack of barley, he once again became painfully aware of his loneliness.

Seemingly frustrated from dealing with her, the merchant threw his hands up in exasperation. The woman looked unfazed by him, though, flicking the braid off her shoulder, dropping a few coins on the table, collecting the sack of grain, and marching off into the sea of people.

Ashur stood there, longing to follow her, when he felt a tap on his shoulder and turned around to find Niku, one of the local merchants who often employed his services.

"Ashur! Thank the gods I found you! I have a delivery you need to make."

"Sorry, maybe tomorrow," Ashur replied, shaking his head, his motivation gone.

Niku grabbed his arm. "Even for this?" he asked, retrieving a gold coin from the pouch on his belt and holding it out.

Ashur eyed it in disbelief. He'd never seen a gold coin that close before. It was easily more money than he would make in a year. Picking it up, he turned it over in his hand.

"It's real. I've already checked," Niku said with a grin. "A man paid me three pieces of gold for supplies, but only on the condition I paid you one to deliver them to him."

"He asked for *me*?"

Niku nodded. "He did. Will you do it?"

Ashur smiled, his loneliness and self-loathing suddenly banished. "How can I say no?"

He followed Niku back to his stall, shouldered the sack of goods, and set off quickly. It was only later, as Ashur neared his destination, that he began to have second thoughts; after all, gold had no value to the dead.

There was much affluence in Birtha, but there was also much poverty, and he found himself amidst the slums. It was a dangerous part of the city to wander, even in broad daylight, where only the desperately poor and sick lived, sequestered away out of sight of the wealthy and far from the river and market. Refuse lay on the side of the narrow dirt streets, and the smell grew worse the further he ventured. Grubby-faced children stood shoeless in the shadows

31

watching him, tattered, ill-fitting clothes hanging from their scrawny frames. From the darkened doorways of dilapidated dwellings, Ashur felt eyes follow him down the street as he passed, and he tucked his coin purse into the folds of his tunic and out of reach of sleight hands.

None too soon, Ashur reached the house he had been tasked to deliver the package to, although 'house' was far too kind a word for the ramshackle hovel standing before him. Its walls were made of plaited reeds, the clay that plastered them falling away in patches, but, rather unusually, it had a solid wood door which seemed a more recent addition. As he reached the entrance, he glanced back over his shoulder to find the streets still and silent.

Ashur knocked and waited, but there was no answer. Tentatively, he opened the door and stepped inside. The space was dim, illuminated only by what light could pierce the two small slits cut into the wall, the floor nothing but well-trodden dirt.

"Hello?" he said, his voice wavering slightly. "I'm here to make a delivery."

Again, he received no answer. His instructions had been to bring the goods to the house and leave them in the centre of the room: a request he had found rather odd. The only reason he could fathom was that the occupant was perhaps a rich man, struck with leprosy or some other unfortunate malady, and this was the only way he could get food.

Looking around the bleak interior, Ashur spied no furniture save for a stool in the centre of the room and a wooden chair against the far wall, sheathed in darkness. He placed the package down atop the stool, examining it for a moment. Its contents were meagre, just a tiny roasted pigeon, a chunk of cheese, and a round of flatbread. Who would pay three gold pieces for such a minuscule amount of food? Even if they *were* rich and sick, it was still an exorbitant amount to pay. And why had they asked for him when anyone else could have easily made the delivery? None of it made any sense.

Ashur's neck tingled as though someone was watching him, and he spun on his heel, peering into the dark, but there was no one there. Unsettled, he turned to leave when something gave him pause for thought. Perhaps he should just keep the food for himself. The idea floated around in his mind briefly before he dismissed it and left the hovel. He had been paid generously to do a job, and he was going to do it properly, no matter the temptation. He was better than that.

∞∞∞∞

It was late afternoon by the time Ashur weaved his way back to his house. Sitting down on the mat of woven reeds that constituted his bed, he retrieved the gold coin, playing with it mindlessly as he gnawed on a strip of dried goat meat and a staling piece of bread.

From its place of safekeeping beneath his tunic, he pulled out the small pouch hanging from his neck by a thin leather strap. Dropping the coin in, he heard it clink against the only thing in the world that held any real value to him: his mother's ring. Her face appeared in his mind, and a pang of longing lanced through his chest. He couldn't linger on the past, though; he needed to clear his mind and rest. Lying down, Ashur concentrated on the warbling of birds coming up from the riverside, breathing slowly until he finally fell asleep.

The sun had just dipped below the horizon when he finally awoke, and a feeling of excitement swelled in his stomach. It was almost dark, and that meant only one thing: practice. Before he could begin, however, he first had to cross the Tigris. A bridge upstream led to the main gate, but soldiers were posted there day and night, and Ashur preferred his escapades to remain secret. Instead, he chose to sneak out of the city through an inconspicuous breach he'd discovered in an alley near his house a few years back.

In these peaceful times, the guards cared little for the maintenance of the ageing perimeter, and Ashur had managed to keep his private entrance disguised by way of a stack of broken crates he'd amassed from his numerous deliveries. Once outside the wall, he simply made the short jaunt to the small, weather-beaten kuphar he kept moored on the riverbank.

There were times when the river raged, making the crossing treacherous, especially on moonless nights, but the winds were calm that evening, and his journey went without incident. Disembarking at his customary spot some ways downstream, he tied the boat to a stake he'd hammered in amongst the bulrushes, retrieved his waterskin, clambered up the bank, and headed off across the plains.

The land was harsh, all compacted dirt and sparse, grey shrubbery, and in the distance, a crop of rocks jutted from the ground. Spotting them, his pace quickened to match his growing anticipation. As Ashur neared his practice grounds, he replayed in his mind the events that had led to his strange nightly routine.

At eighteen, he'd become a soldier, hoping to travel the world and make his fortune at the same time. Starting off as a novice, he'd spent a year or so guarding bridges and gates, itching for action, before the orders came for the army in Birtha to mobilise and march south. He hadn't known who the enemy was, nor had he cared. Like all the other men in his battalion, he'd just wanted to fight.

Two weeks later, his company met their foe in the blazing heat of the desert, the midsummer sun scorching everything it touched. They had gone into battle full of confidence, arrogant and cocky, but within minutes they fell back, retreating as fast as they could from a force far more experienced and battle-hardened. In the naivety of his youth, he'd pictured war as some glamourous endeavour, but when he'd seen the man beside him almost cleaved in two by a sword, all such thoughts had forsaken him.

The enemy cut them down like a scythe, men lying dead all around, the dirt painted red. What few survivors there were had fled, leaving Ashur trapped, blood running down his face from an errant shield that had shattered his nose. He remembered kneeling down, not ready to die. The will to survive had swelled within him until finally, he screamed, releasing his fear and anguish.

Energy had burst forth from the centre of his very being, obliterating all who surrounded him, their bodies torn asunder by the fury of his attack. Amidst the chaos, he'd managed to escape, but when he'd returned to Birtha, he'd told no one of what happened. Besides, who would believe him?

In the years that followed, after much introspection, Ashur had reached the conclusion he'd lived before, his soul travelling to a new body after death. At times, he would dream of different lives in different eras and places, but they were too vivid and realistic to be mere fantasy. They were memories; he was sure of it. Spurred on by his revelation, he'd subtly asked others if they had ever experienced similar feelings or memories, but he'd received only strange looks in response. As far as he knew, he was one of a kind.

The plains stretched out before him, the light of the crescent moon safely guiding him to the secluded ring of rocks that hid him from prying eyes. Bandits had once used the spot as a secret base to waylay travellers, but Ashur had 'persuaded' them to move elsewhere. He smiled at the thought as he gazed up at the monolithic stones haphazardly fashioned around him, as though a giant had been carrying them and dropped a few on its journey. There was no green here, only yellowing tufts of grass and lichen spotting the boulders, its colour bleached by the constant battering of the sun.

Glancing up at the sky, he paused to admire the stars gently twinkling. Ashur didn't know where his power had come from, but he reasoned it had to be linked to his soul's ability to live on when his body expired, although its deeper complexities confounded him. The strangest thing about his power was that he couldn't see it; he could only sense it inside him and feel it when released. Sometimes, if he concentrated hard enough, he thought he saw wisps of energy appear around him, but it was never for long.

He peered one final time between the rocks towards Birtha, glimmering in the distance, but nothing stirred. Content that he was alone, Ashur closed his eyes, focusing as he drew his power inwards, then pushed his palms out, unleashing the energy through his hands, the air crackling as he thrust them back and forth. There were small detonations, and sparks shot off the rocks as they were hit.

Breathing deeply, he watched the dust settle before he closed his eyes once more, the energy growing in his chest. He held it there, letting it build until he thought he might explode, and then unleashed it with a shout that echoed through the night. There was a larger detonation, and when Ashur opened his eyes, he saw dirt flying through the air all around him. Walking over to the epicentre of the explosion, he examined the ground. Every blade of grass in the area was gone, incinerated by the blast, nothing but ash remaining as the smoke dissipated into the cool night air.

Taking a few minutes to compose himself, he sat down on a low-lying boulder and swigged from his waterskin. When he felt ready, he rose and closed his eyes. The power built again, but he didn't try to contain it as he usually did. Instead, he let it swirl around him like the wind, his skin prickling, the hair on the back of his neck standing on end as he tried to stabilise it. He'd done this before, but he decided to try something new. Using all of his strength, he pushed the energy downwards, focusing it into the ground. His stomach lurched, and a strange feeling came over him. Opening his eyes, Ashur stared at the rocks ahead. They seemed different somehow, shorter, almost as if …

He looked down to find himself floating in the air. With a shriek of surprise, his concentration broke, and he collapsed to the ground, his legs propelling him forward and depositing him face down in the dirt. Slowly, he pushed himself up onto his knees, dusting himself off as he stared at the ground in disbelief. He'd used his power to levitate!

In an instant, Ashur's thoughts turned to Birtha and the countless small birds who called it home, darting around the markets in search of food, then taking off, using the air currents to soar up and away. He allowed himself a small smile at the realisation he was close to what he wanted most: to escape from his accursed homeland and explore the world. It would take time, but he was sure now that he could do it. Every night he would practise, and every night he would become more controlled, more focused, more powerful.

Standing up, he propped himself against a rock, the brief stint of hovering significantly more taxing than any of his regular attacks. Finding himself spent, he decided to bring the night's training to an end. He would need to build up his strength before tomorrow.

Ashur's body ached as he walked back to the river, exhaustion slowing his pace. Reaching the banks, he downed the final dregs of his waterskin and threw it into the kuphar before launching out into the current. As he rowed sluggishly, he wondered what he would dream of that night. Sometimes he had horrific nightmares that bathed him in a cold sweat, while other times, he dreamt of his family, loneliness surrounding him like a thick fog when he awoke. Sometimes though, he would be gifted with memories of other lives.

The night before, he'd dreamt about travelling through a lush forest on horseback: the sky blue, the air heavy with moisture, the trees a shade of green he could scarcely believe was real. It was all so vivid that the mere thought of it left the smell of foliage clinging to his nostrils yet again.

Those dreams were a gateway to his past, and Ashur cherished them above all others. As far as he could tell, he'd lived all over the world, from snow-covered mountains to seaside villages, and it was the source of his wanderlust.

The lure to explore was so strong, in fact, that some days he found himself driven mad by it. It would lead him into incredible rages over nothing or leave him hopelessly depressed about being stuck in such a small, insignificant place in the middle of nowhere. Now, all of a sudden, he had hope. Freedom was within his grasp.

Slipping back within the city walls and disguising the breach once more, he arrived home before the fishermen and bakers began to stir. Fatigue won out, leaving his stomach's pleas for sustenance unanswered, and he collapsed into bed, falling asleep almost instantly.

As the new day dawned, he dreamt not of the past but of the future. He dreamt of flying.

∞∞∞

Ashur awoke exhausted, his muscles aching, his mind numb. What had begun as joyous dreams eventually morphed into warped visions of his family, and the dark mood they invoked lingered all around him. He sat up slowly, ignoring the call of the sun and the river, preferring instead to stare mindlessly at the wall, contemplating all he had lost over the years.

A decade ago, while he'd been off playing soldier, bandits had stormed the very house he now sat in, following a rumour of gold but finding nothing. In their anger, they had murdered his parents in cold blood. Two years later, in his father's absence, Ashur had been tasked with finding a suitor for his younger sister. Barely eight months into their marriage, though, while his sister was ripe with child, her husband had run the baby through with a dagger before brutally beating and strangling her. Ashur had scoured every inch of Birtha, within and without, searching for justice, but to no avail.

The image of holding his lifeless sister in his arms flashed before him, and he remembered the power pulsing through his chest as he had placed her, his only remaining relative, on the funeral pyre. Never had he felt so helpless. He should have been there to protect her, to protect his parents, and the mantle of guilt hung heavy on his shoulders still.

Closing his eyes for a moment, he felt the rage threaten to consume him, its power swelling, then stopping abruptly. He held out his

37

shaking hands, staring at them before clasping them tightly to his chest. Taking a few deep breaths, he resolved to go to the market and buy a leg of goat and some vegetables to roast over the fire. Fresh food was an extravagance he couldn't usually afford, but he was craving it after the night's efforts, and the gold coin was still safely tucked in its pouch. While the sun was up, he would rest and gather his strength, then under cover of darkness, he would go back across the river and attempt to levitate again.

Soon he would be able to leave Birtha and all its painful memories behind. Even if he had to fly to the ends of the earth, he vowed he would find the places from his dreams and others just like him. He would find a soul that mirrored his, and he wouldn't be lonely anymore, in this life or the next.

The sun was high overhead as he stepped out onto the street, and he was barely halfway to the market when sweat began to drip from his brow. A few clouds drifted slowly across the sky, but their effect was negligible as waves of midday heat battered the city. He thought about soaring through the air, the cooling wind flowing past him. Out of the corner of his eye, he saw two birds dart up above the houses as if it was the simplest of feats, and Ashur paused to watch, knowing he would join them one day.

He continued walking, lost in his own world, but as he neared the first set of stalls, he saw something that startled him out of his reverie. A group of soldiers flanked either side of the road, observing Ashur as he approached. Avoiding eye contact, he attempted to blend into the bustle of people ebbing and flowing along the street, but the sights of the eagle-eyed mercenaries remained locked on their target, oblivious to all else. He quickened his pace to try and duck past them, only to find the hand of one of the men blocking his path.

"Are you Ashur?" the soldier asked, his voice stern.

"I am," he replied casually, although his heart pounded in his chest. "Can I help you?"

The soldier gestured back towards the centre of town. "Your presence is required. You will come with us."

The men on either side of the soldier moved their hands to their hilts, their faces unflinching.

Ashur looked around, scanning the crowd for aid. No one would help him, though; only fools crossed armed men. It occurred to him that he could simply obliterate them all and walk away unharmed, but he wasn't a murderer. Besides, he had no enemies, and he was on good terms with his neighbours and associates. There couldn't be anything malicious about this, could there? Maybe they simply wanted him to re-enlist as a soldier.

"Can you at least say who sent for me?"

The soldier shook his head. "Come. Your questions will be answered soon enough."

Seeing no alternative, Ashur nodded. "Lead the way."

Five soldiers encircled him as though he were a criminal en route to answer for his sins. As they continued through the city streets, he realised he wasn't being led to the barracks or even the quarters of the higher officers; he was being led into the slums.

There was no one lingering on the streets this time, the sight of the soldiers sending those who lived there scattering. They approached a ramshackle hovel, and Ashur realised with trepidation that it was the very place he'd visited the previous day. He stopped in his tracks, his blood turning to ice, before a firm hand shoved him in the back, propelling him to the door.

The leading soldier knocked loudly, waited a moment, then opened it, gesturing for Ashur to enter first. He complied, albeit hesitantly, stepping over the threshold and into the poorly lit room. The soldier followed behind him, shutting the door and leaving the remaining men outside to stand guard.

Ashur looked around, his eyes slowly adjusting to the darkness, then turned back to the soldier, puzzled. "Why did you knock? There's no one here."

Unexpectedly, he heard an ominous voice behind him. "Oh, but there is, and it was a necessary action. I am not a man you burst in on."

Ashur spun around to see a figure shrouded in a dark cloak that allowed him to melt seamlessly into the shadows. His breathing grew heavier as he realised with a start that the man must have been there the day before, watching him deliver the package.

"Who are you? Why have you brought me here?" Ashur demanded, bolstering himself to prevent his voice from shaking as he tried to quell the barrage of questions running through his head.

The figure ignored him and instead approached the soldier, placing a small leather pouch into his hand.

The soldier opened it, taking out a single gold piece and holding it up to the light. Satisfied, he dropped it back in. "Is there anything else we can do for you, sir?"

"No, your services are no longer required. Thank you for your assistance," the figure replied, his accent foreign and almost musical compared to the harsh guttural dialect of Birtha.

The soldier nodded, turned on his heel, and marched out, shutting the door quietly behind him.

Ashur took a step forward, desperate for answers. "Who are you?"

The figure calmly gestured towards the wooden stool, which now stood against the wall. "Please, sit."

Ashur abided, dusting it off and perching on its edge as the figure took up his place on the high-backed wooden chair in the shadows. The man peeled off his hood to reveal shoulder-length, brown hair, eyes so dark they almost appeared black, and a paler complexion than any who called Birtha home. His skin was weathered, and, going by the lines on his face, he seemed to be in his mid-forties. Men like him were rare in the city but not unheard of; they came from across the sea to the west.

The man clasped his hands in his lap, relaxing back into his chair and regarding Ashur with a smile. "To be honest, I wasn't sure if you'd come. You could have defeated those soldiers and escaped if you'd wanted to. Isn't that right, Ashur?"

Ashur stared back, dumbfounded, an inexplicable feeling of familiarity washing over him. "Who are you?" he asked for a third time.

"I have been known by many names over the centuries, but in this time and place, you may call me Alû."

Struck with a sudden realisation, Ashur jumped to his feet. "You're like me, aren't you? You've lived before!"

"Very good! I didn't even have to explain it to you this time. Although you can't really compare yourself to me. I have walked this earth for millennia. You are but a babe in comparison."

Ashur's mind whirled as Alû's words sank in. He wasn't alone; he wasn't the only one. Heart fluttering with unbridled excitement, he

40

paced back and forth. "I have so many questions. How did this happen? Are we part of a higher order? What is our purpose?"

Alû remained silent until Ashur stopped to look at him, and he directed his guest back to his seat with a wave. Only then did he speak.

"It is unclear why some are reborn, and others are not. I believe stronger minds are able to bind themselves together in death and seek out new bodies in which to return, whereas weaker minds simply dissolve into the aether, the unseen world around us where souls reside." Alû rose to his feet, his eyes boring into Ashur as he continued. "As for your other questions: there is no higher order, nor is there some pre-determined purpose for our existence. We are not tethered to unchangeable fate by divine hands. All those worshipping pieces of clay and stone, blaming their misfortune on the whims of fickle gods, are naught but fools. They spend their time praying for ascension into some upper echelon while failing to realise that it is their own lack of mental fortitude that binds them to their lesser existence. Our purpose, Ashur, much like theirs, will be of our own making, our own design."

There was something about the way Alû watched him that made Ashur uneasy. His words were calm and his answers forthcoming, yet the look in his eyes was that of a predator, vigilant and cold.

"I believe," Alû continued, "that it is my destiny to leave this world one day, to transcend this cycle of rebirth and decay and travel the universe as a being of pure energy and thought."

"And what is my destiny?" Ashur asked.

"The same as the rest," replied Alû with a nonchalant tilt of his head.

"The rest?"

Alû laughed. "Ashur, Ashur, Ashur, you didn't *really* think you were the first, did you? In every generation, there are a handful of people who harness their inner power and return. They do not do it on purpose, of course. They merely possess the innate strength to bind their mind and soul together in death and, in turn, transfer their complete being into a new body."

Ashur leant back in stunned silence, his head resting on the wall behind him, eyebrows raised as he let out his breath through puffed cheeks. The urge to leave Birtha swelled in his chest to almost unbearable levels as he considered the fact that there were countless others just like him out there in the world. If only he could track them down.

"Where are they now?" he asked with childlike impatience. "Can we travel to meet them?"

"No, my dear Ashur, we cannot," Alû snickered. "They are all dead."

"What? How?!"

A broad, self-satisfied smile crossed Alû's face. "I killed them."

Cold fear gripped Ashur, a feeling he had not experienced since his days as a soldier.

"You see," Alû continued, wandering casually around the room as he spoke. "Every time someone is reborn, I can sense it. It is like a bell going off that only I can hear. Over time, I have attuned this sense to the point where I can locate their souls regardless of where they are in the world."

"And then what? You kill them in cold blood?"

Alû shrugged. "Occasionally. Although I usually let them kill themselves. I reach into their subconscious, influencing their thoughts from the shadows, burdening them with guilt and pain until they become devoid of hope and fall into despair. It's a talent I've perfected over the centuries," he said with an air of pride. "Despair is the key, really. A mind that despairs is a mind that does not wish to live again. In the end, their will crumbles, and they all just fade away."

He stopped and turned to meet Ashur's gaze intently. "All except for you, that is. You are my greatest and only failure."

Thoughts surged through Ashur's mind with such force and speed that he had to close his eyes to regain any semblance of balance and perspective. His whole world had just been turned upside down, and, in the tumble, he had lost any idea of his next move. He opened his eyes to find Alû's still firmly fixed on him.

"I don't understand," Ashur finally blurted out. "You've tried to destroy me in past lives?"

"Probably. I couldn't really say for sure. Nothing set you apart from the rest, but I can only assume your past deaths were by my hand. Provided nature did not reach you before I did, that is." Alû flashed a menacing smile. "After all, I've dispensed with every other reborn soul, haven't I?"

"If you have no memory of me, how can you be so sure I've lived before?" asked Ashur.

"When I reached you in this life, I sensed something different, an energy that surrounds and flows through you, an energy that can only come from multiple rebirths. I realised in that moment that, despite my past efforts, I had failed to disperse your soul. Still, I remained undeterred by the challenge," Alû said, a twisted satisfaction contorting his features.

"I decided to take a different approach this time around. I did not simply toy with your mind; I eroded the very world around you. Every move I made was part of a grand design to isolate you, to tear those you love from your grasp and drive you to the brink. It was I who convinced the bandits there was gold hidden in your family home, knowing that when they found nothing, they would punish those inside. It was I who manipulated your sister's husband into believing the child she bore was not his, knowing he would not stand to endure such dishonour on his name. And it was I who hid him from your vengeance so that it might fester and consume you."

Alû sat back down in his chair, sighing contently, his hands clasped once more in his lap. "Every dark and turbulent nightmare of your misfortunes, every haunted thought that eats at you in waking, grew from a seed *I* planted. All of the misery in your life was my doing and mine alone."

Ashur's mind reeled. All of his pain was the result of one single person? It didn't seem possible. If it was true, though, then every second of loneliness and despair in his life was this man's fault.

Anger crept into his throat, and his face hardened as he glared back at Alû. "Why are you telling me this? Why not just kill me and be done with it?"

"Because I've reached an impasse, my dear Ashur," Alû replied, his expression grim. "I have taken everything from you, and yet you prevail. Not only that, you become stronger. I have seen you practise each night across the river. Your power is growing. I could destroy you here and now, but you would simply come back, and all my efforts would have been in vain."

When Ashur spoke next, it was through gritted teeth. "So, what do you plan to do now then?"

"The question is not what *I* plan to do, Ashur," Alû replied, leaning forward. "It is what *you* plan to do."

Ashur flexed his fingers, balling them in and out of fists impatiently as he rocked back and forth on the stool. He knew in his gut it was a trap; Alû wanted him to attack, but that knowledge did nothing to suppress his fury.

Images of his parents and sister flitted through his mind, their youthful shapes transforming into lifeless bodies crackling amongst the pyre flames. Everything he lost, he lost because of the monster sitting before him.

In an instant, Ashur was on his feet, grabbing Alû by the shoulders and throwing him to the ground. He was too angry, too unfocused to use his power, so he simply whaled on him with his fists until Alû grabbed his right wrist.

"Is that all you have, Ashur? Fists? I'm disappointed. I expected more," he mocked with a bloody grin.

Ashur glared at him, his all-consuming rage feeding the energy coursing through his veins, demanding release. He wrenched his wrist free and pinned Alû down. "If that's what you want, have it! Have it all!"

Power exploded from him at full force, channelling into the man beneath him, and he continued until his energy was spent, plumes of dust dancing in the rays of light pouring through the cracks that appeared along the walls. He looked down, stunned. His foe lay completely unharmed.

"You are weak, just like your memory," Alû taunted. "You have known me over centuries, yet you stand perplexed. Deep down, you know my true name, the one that has endured through the ages."

Ashur felt the hair on his arms and neck stand on end, his ears popping as the pressure around him surged.

"I am Anasazi! I am power incarnate!"

There was a sudden detonation, and Ashur was blinded by a flash of darkness, his ears pierced by a high-pitched whining sound. He felt his stomach lurch as he was flung backwards by the force, his body slamming into something hard, the breath knocked from his lungs. Pain washed over him, and Ashur groaned as he opened his eyes to find himself out on the street, surrounded by crumbled clay and reeds.

The hovel was no more.

Chest burning and breathing ragged, he righted himself and peered through the settling dust to spy Alû standing where the building had been only moments ago, the air crackling with energy.

"Only now, at the bitter end, do you see. You should have given up like the rest. Now you must suffer!" Alû boomed, his voice seeming to resonate through the streets.

A bolt of energy lanced towards Ashur, who dove out of the way just in time. He heard the wall behind him explode and felt fragments of clay rain down on his back. Knowing he only had one chance to flee, he clambered to his feet, unleashing a string of energy at Alû, who flicked it to one side in annoyance. What his foe didn't realise was that he wasn't the target; the ground was.

The energy drove up plumes of dust as it raced past Alû, obscuring his vision and cloaking Ashur as he made his escape, staggering as fast as he could down the street. Adrenaline kicked in, his hobbled gait morphing into a full-pelt sprint as his body went into flight mode, and he searched desperately for a place to hide. It was fruitless, though; there was nowhere safe to go. He could run for the barracks, but he didn't trust the soldiers after the day's events, and he questioned if they'd even be able to hurt Alû.

Ashur managed to make it another street over before a second detonation sounded behind him. A wall exploded, sending debris rocketing into the adjacent building, and he dropped to his knees for a moment, his hands slamming down hard into the ground and propelling him back to his feet. Snatching a quick glance over his shoulder, he couldn't see Alû anywhere, only destruction. Fear choked him, his anger turning to panic as he realised he might not survive this encounter. Alû had killed his entire family, all because he had lived before. Had this been the fate of his loved ones in the past? Would this be their fate in the future?

The question haunted him as the hair on his neck prickled again. He dodged to the left, darting down an alleyway, another explosion just steps behind confirming that his foe was at his heels. Men and women alike cried out in alarm, snatching up their children and scrambling out of Ashur's way as he raced through the chaos.

Careening around the corner of the alleyway, he joined the wide street that led out the city gates and across the bridge. The rocks, his practice grounds: they were his only chance of survival. Not only did he know the area better than Alû, but luring his enemy away from Birtha meant he could ensure no more innocent lives were lost on his account.

Ashur felt something strike his back, and he toppled sideways, twisting as he did. He scanned the street as he scurried to stand up, but his hunter was not amongst the sea of faces staring at him with consternation.

A flicker of movement caught his eye from the rooftops, and he looked up to find Alû bounding along them with ease, the air rippling around him. Acting on instinct, Ashur sent a wave of energy crackling towards him, shards of brick showering the people below as Alû disappeared into the subsequent dust cloud that billowed upwards. Ashur attempted to track him in the haze but gave up and sprinted off to the left, away from the bridge.

Racing past his house and weaving through the shortcuts he knew so well, he finally reached the broken crates guarding his secret exit. Blasting them out of the way with his power and diving through the splinters, Ashur tumbled head-first through the breach.

He made a beeline for the riverbank, ignoring the handful of fishermen mulling around, their eyes trained towards the bridge and the sounds of commotion coming from just out of sight. In a matter of seconds, he had reached his kuphar, torn it from its moorings, and begun rowing like a madman in the vain hope he'd make it across before Alû appeared.

As his arms pulled hard on the oar, his muscles straining to command the vessel in its battle against the current, he thought about his family again. Their faces reappeared in his mind's eye, and his fear turned back into anger and determination. It would take time for Alû to cross the bridge and follow him to the rocks, and by then, he would be ready.

Reaching the centre of the river, Ashur scanned the bank to find Alû standing there, shaking his head and smiling smugly. His entire posture was one of satisfaction, as though everything was going perfectly to plan. Straightening his shoulders, Alû unleashed a torrent of energy that singed the air as it shot towards its target. Ashur barely had enough time to raise an arm to shield his face before it reached him, his own energy springing forth to encase him in a sphere of protection.

The force of the impact sent the kuphar skipping across the water and into the far bank, a massive hole appearing in its hull as it slammed into a submerged rock. With water rapidly pooling around him, Ashur scrambled out, clutching at the bullrushes as he dragged himself up the embankment. Regaining his feet at the top, he turned to face his foe, feeling safer now that the mighty Tigris stood between them.

Alû met his eye across the river, a shroud of dark energy building around him until his features were all but invisible. Ashur expected him to run for the bridge or dive into the water in pursuit, but he did neither. Instead, he crouched down, a low hum emanating from him before he launched into the air, soaring higher and higher until it became apparent he would clear the river. The sense of safety Ashur had felt shattered instantly. Alû did not require manmade methods to overcome the vast expanse of water; he simply jumped over it like a puddle in the street.

Ashur turned before Alû had reached the apex of his trajectory, sprinting off across the arid land, his breathing laboured and sporadic as his panic returned with a vengeance. With each step away from the river, he scoured his brain for a way to gain the upper hand, but it didn't seem possible; Alû was too powerful.

Despair weighted his shoulders as he reached the rocky outcrop. Was this his future? To constantly be reborn, only to die in fear and agonising pain at the hands of this madman? He dropped to his knees, his mind reeling with thoughts of his family, his dreams of other lives, and his hopes for the future. None of it would mean a thing if he died here.

Ducking behind a large boulder at the far edge of his practice grounds, he noticed the marks on its surface, evidence of the power contained within his own life force. He slowly traced the scarred stone with his fingers, energy building inside him. If he was going to die, it wouldn't be without a fight. In his next life, he wanted Alû to have a moment of pause, to think twice before he dared hunt him down again. Closing his eyes, Ashur steadied his breath and tamed the power swelling in his chest as the hairs on the back of his neck prickled. His foe had arrived.

He stepped out from his hiding spot to find Alû standing atop the tallest rock on the opposite side of the outcrop, the air around him shimmering, almost tangible.

"Have you seen your future yet?" Alû asked with a cruel grin. "Life after life, your family slaughtered, your own soul experiencing the most exquisite pain before death."

Ashur stood silent, determination written all over his face, his energy swirling around him. There was no point in talking, not anymore. The die of fate was already cast; all that was left was to see how it landed. He unleashed his power in one burst, aiming not for Alû's head but for his feet. Alû managed to deflect the attack, but in doing so, he slipped and fell to the ground.

He was barely on his knees by the time Ashur reached him, a forceful fist striking him square in the chest. The connection of flesh was all that was needed to send Alû flying, his back cracking against a rock on the far side. Ashur charged forward, not wanting to give his foe a chance to recover, but as he drew near, the air around them fractured and pain lanced through his body. He staggered backwards, his legs collapsing under him as Alû stood up, wiping blood from his face with the sleeve of his cloak.

With a grimace, Alû spat onto the ground before lunging forward, cannoning into his prey at full force.

Trying to clear the fog of the impact from his mind, Ashur shook his head, but his vision was still blurry as Alû grabbed him by the throat, hauling him to his feet. Another blast of energy slammed into Ashur's chest, sending him twisting slowly into the dirt, dust burning his nostrils as he lay there, face down.

He heard Alû take a step backwards, his mocking laugh reverberating off the stone. "Fool. You think because you have discovered an iota of power that you can challenge me?"

Another wave of adrenaline surged through Ashur, and his mind became lucid despite the pain. It contained only one thought: escape.

"You shall die today, Ashur, as you have always died, and as you shall always die. In horrific agony."

Ashur lumbered to his feet, his head down as he glared up past his brow at Alû, power building up inside him once more. He resisted the temptation to release it, though. Instead, he focused through the pain

48

and directed it downwards with every shred of strength in his body. There was a pause as if time itself stopped to watch, then he shot into the air, the wind whistling past him as he rose into the sky, his fear replaced with overwhelming joy. He was flying!

In an instant, he reached a small patch of cloud overhead, ploughing through it, his skin dampening before he breached the top and emerged above, the sun shining all around. With his power waning, his ascent stopped, and for a long moment, he gazed down in wonder at a sight no human had ever witnessed before. It was a view so surreal that Ashur could scarcely believe it. The world stretched out before him to the impossibly distant horizon, and Birtha sat as an almost insignificant speck just below, its people invisible from such a height.

His energy spent, Ashur began to descend, picking up pace as he dropped back through the clouds. Trying to turn sideways, he became disorientated and started spinning, exiting the clouds entirely out of control. He attempted to right himself but overcorrected, each movement causing a chain reaction that only worsened his predicament. Finding the ground in his tumbling view, Ashur tried to turn around, to climb upwards again, but his downward force was too great. He didn't have the energy to stop his fall to earth. He was going to die.

A deep shame filled Ashur as he realised that in escaping Alû's grasp, he had condemned himself to the most inglorious of deaths. The wind grew stronger, tugging at him mercilessly, and giving up his fight against it, he stopped trying to turn, plateaued, and finally gained some stability. Gliding forward, he scanned the ground, and from the corner of his eye, he spied the rocky outcrop where Alû waited for him. He had two options: crash into the desert or use all his momentum to deliver an uncounterable strike to his enemy. The choice was easy.

Managing a sharp, banked turn, Ashur aimed himself directly at the rocks, his speed building exponentially as he hurtled towards Alû, who stood watching, patient and unmoving. He gathered what little power he had left to muster, which, when combined with the speed of his descent, produced a ball of kinetic energy around him. Death was inevitable, Ashur knew that, but at least he could take Alû with him. With one single act of self-sacrifice, he would ensure that no others fell prey to that eternal monster, not in this lifetime.

His eyes watered from the air roaring past as he drew closer. Suddenly, Alû did something unexpected. He leapt upwards, meeting Ashur mid-air and wrapping his arms around his prey, their combined energy dissipating harmlessly. Their eyes met, and Alû gave a sly grin before pivoting and tossing Ashur to the ground like a sack of spoiled vegetables.

Landing hard, he rolled over several times before coming to a stop against a rock. As he heard Alû touch down softly off to the side, Ashur clambered onto his hands and knees, his lungs burning as he gasped for air. He coughed deeply, blood spraying across the scarred rock as he clawed at it, trying desperately to stand, scarlet saliva dripping to the ground and staining the dirt.

Alû sighed with satisfaction as he approached. "I want you to remember this in your next life: how powerful you became, and how little it mattered in the end. It is important that you understand the futility of the course you have chosen. You stand at a forked road. Down one path lies eternal emptiness, the aether; there is no pain, no misery, and no sadness there, only peace. Down the other path lies nothing but ruin, for you and all those you love. I am not your equal, Ashur. I, Anasazi, am and always will be your superior. Think on this as you take your final breaths."

Ashur doggedly pulled himself to his feet, determined to die with dignity. Alû just smiled at him, eight blades, black as obsidian, emerging from his back. They were jointed at the centre such that they almost resembled the legs of a spider. Ashur tried to fight back, drawing on his energy for one last attack, but Alû grabbed him by the throat, lifting him effortlessly into the air as his blades rose behind him.

"Goodbye, Ashur."

Dipping his shoulder, the blades on Alû's right side leapt forward, skewering Ashur through the chest. He hung there for a moment, numb from shock, a trickle of crimson escaping from the edge of his mouth. Alû slung him to the ground and watched him gulp a few tortured breaths as blood slowly pooled around him.

The afternoon sun shone from behind Alû, painting him as nothing more than a featureless silhouette to the misting eyes of the man dying at his feet. As Ashur looked up at the Spider, a sudden and overwhelming rush of recognition swept over him. A series of images flashed through his mind: the same scenario playing out again and again, in different times and different places. Was he seeing the past or the future?

"Anasazi," Ashur whispered unwittingly, his voice almost inaudible.

With a triumphant smirk, the figure simply turned and walked away.

Ashur felt the hair on his neck prickle and heard a rush of wind, then all fell still, and he slowly closed his eyes. As his life ebbed away, he made a solemn vow. He would never fade away into the abyss of the aether. He would come back to challenge Anasazi in the next life, and all that followed it. He would choose righteousness over eternal peace. He would never give up, not until Anasazi was destroyed.

Theo

The air was crisp. Cold enough to awaken the senses but not so frosty as to be a burden; the perfect time to delve into nature. She wandered amongst the towering conifers, her feet crunching on fallen cones and bracken as she journeyed through the forest. The vivid green and intoxicating smell of pine needles elicited within her an overwhelming feeling of calm. There were shadows everywhere, but she was not afraid. This was her home.

Birds sat chirping on the branches above, and she paused, listening as their merry tune harmonised with the sough of the trees. Now and then, travellers would come through her village, playing music in exchange for money, but to her mind, their ballads paled in comparison. Nature was a symphony she never tired of; it was her soul song.

Suddenly, the birds fell silent, and she continued walking until she reached the edge of the treeline, where the land fell away into a deep valley. Off in the distance, an imposing castle stood buttressed against the base of a cliff. Soldiers with long pikes and thick armour guarded the entrance, barring the way to any seeking entry. Their presence was of little consequence to her, though; she had no intention of going there. The forest was all she needed.

As she turned to head back, she stopped. A deer, deep umber and speckled with white, stood gazing out at the castle below, just as she had. It looked up, and neither of them moved as they locked eyes, the pair entwined in a lingering moment of pure connection. Then, just like that, the deer flicked its tiny puff of a tail and bounded away, leaping dextrously through the bracken, and disappearing amongst the maze of trees.

She stared ahead blankly for a minute, imprinting the encounter into her memory with a smile before meandering into the embrace of the forest once more. It was time to go home.

The first sensation Theo experienced upon waking was not wonder from her dream but the painful prickle of pins and needles in her right hand. She closed her eyes and groaned, shuffling across to dangle her arm off the side of the bed and flex her fingers. Twisting her wrist around, blood flowed back to restore normality in her fingertips, and she opened her eyes again with a grimace.

One of the fun side effects of her job was having permanent knots in her shoulders that pinched her nerves and wreaked havoc on her hands, especially while she slept. She could have used a weekly massage to help ease the strain, but she couldn't really afford it, not on a chef's wage. Besides, when would she find the time, and how could she book an appointment with her everchanging roster? That being said, the thought still crossed her mind each time she woke to find her arms burning and numb, but in the end, she always decided against it. After all, she had more important things to save for: travelling.

As she swung her legs around and stood up, walking towards the bathroom to begin her morning routine, she finally took a moment to consider the dream, each replayed image sparking within her a pang of sadness. Her longing to see such wonders in real life pulled at her in a way she couldn't quite describe. It was as though her soul demanded she seek them out: the ancient forests, the centuries-old castles, the places where the whispers of history were tucked behind every leaf and hidden beneath every stone.

Saving for her dream trip had been in the works for years, fuelled by a deep yearning seeded in her heart half a lifetime ago. She'd been born in the suburbs of Melbourne, but her mother had decided on a tree change while Theo was in primary school. As a result, they'd moved to the country town of Benalla, some two-hundred kilometres away. The feeling of being trapped and isolated in the small town, far from her friends and family, had grown and festered until it transformed into a burning desire to escape as far away as possible. That singular childhood upheaval had planted the seed of wanderlust within her, and finding comfort in its presence, she chose to nurture it rather than prune it.

In her angsty teen years, she'd held great resentment for her mother's choice. As she'd matured, though, she had begun to understand the reasoning behind her decision and found forgiveness, albeit to the point of indifference. After all, her mother had single-handedly taken care of her and her older brother since they were infants, and despite being somewhat cold, she was never neglectful. Theo held a deep respect for her, but now that she'd moved back to Melbourne, they barely spoke at all. The same sentiment applied to her brother, who was busy with his own life and career. It was like a wall had sprung up between them, distance causing a rift and life filling the gap. There was no ill-feeling; they had simply grown apart.

As for her father, he'd moved to another state around the same time they'd moved to Benalla, and with visits suddenly changing from fortnightly to annual, their relationship had withered. In adulthood, with the structure of her youth removed, they stopped communicating altogether. As far as she could tell, her existence mattered very little to him, and with each unattended event and forgotten milestone, she cut another cord until she was no longer tethered.

Snapping back to reality as she realised she was trying to cram the wrong foot into her shoe, Theo attempted to pack away her depressing thoughts, grabbing her backpack with a sigh and walking out the door.

∞∞∞∞

The kitchen was quiet when Theo arrived, and the tension hanging in the air confirmed that Peter was likely in a foul mood. Ruth and Justin grunted hello as she made her way around to her bench, all dour faces and frown lines despite only being an hour into their respective shifts. As the pastry chef, she started a little later than most, which suited her circadian rhythm far better. Still, as lingering tables took their time deciding whether to splurge on a third course, she often found herself the last to leave, so it all evened out in the end.

Surrounded by the wordless workings of her colleagues and with the general unease triggering her own negative emotions, her thoughts turned once more to the failed relationships in her life as she began her day's prep. Outside of her strained family ties, Theo didn't really have any friends, no close ones, at least. She got along with the other chefs, but none of them were anything more than workmates. They talked, they laughed, they bonded over the trauma of working in the often brutal environment that was hospitality, but there was no deep connection. They were friends of convenience, and when the time came for her to leave her job, she knew their relationships would not endure.

As painful as that knowledge was, it was not unfamiliar. Every friendship Theo had attempted in her life had eventually failed. Most were eroded by the constant flow of time, while others crumbled when the black dog of depression came to lay at her feet. Despite the pain it caused her, though, she found herself unable to detach from those she connected with, even when their interest waned. While they shrugged off the warmth of her friendship in favour of newly sparked fires, she remained cold and alone, fanning the embers in the hopes they would one day return.

She knew it was masochistic, that she should let them go, yet she found such a severance impossible, as though waiting was an innate and indelible part of her soul. That's not to say the constant rejection and indifference hadn't affected her; she had all but given up on trying to organise catch-ups, and being the sole instigator of conversation was wearing away her self-worth. Still, her birthday sat as the one remaining candle she refused to let her sense of abandonment snuff out.

Every year, Theo would swallow her fear and invite those she missed to celebrate with her, and every year, the vast majority of them would make empty promises or simply wouldn't respond at all, the number of attendees dwindling the older she got. Her birthday wasn't for another seven months, but, caught in the slipstream of her current train of thought, a sense of dread washed over her. What if no one came at all?

"What the hell are you doing?" Theo heard Peter shout from across the kitchen. "We're not serving *that!* And clean up your section, or I'm gonna kick off!"

Shaken abruptly from her internal monologue, she raised her eyebrow, poking her head around the corner to find Peter standing at Ruth's bench, his half a foot height advantage seeming all the more evident in his anger.

Ruth did not shrink at his words, though. Instead, she nodded at him with military precision as he stood there glowering at her. "Yes, Chef."

Without another word, he shook his head in disgust and stormed off.

Ruth looked over at her, rolling her eyes, and Theo chuckled despite herself. It was going to be one of those days.

As she turned back to her bench, Theo found Peter standing beside her, his expression stern. He was a prime example of a time wearied and strung-out chef, a chef desperately trying to keep his business afloat in an industry of almost negligible profit margins. His dark brown hair was short and dishevelled, his chin was covered in a shadow of stubble, his physique was sculpted by skipped meals and late-night takeaway food, and his arms and hands were a canvas of ancient battle wounds.

In the furrows carved into his forehead like fault lines, you could almost see every special occasion he'd been forced to miss, every family milestone captured in a photo from which he was absent. Each morning he left before his children rose, and each night he arrived home after they were tucked into bed. His burden was a cross he himself had chosen to bear, but as she regarded him, Theo found it hard not to offer some measure of forgiveness for his short temper.

"Yes, Chef?" she said, quickly wiping the smile off her face and composing herself.

"Gino needs you to make a cake for his son's birthday," Peter said with a sigh. "Pick whatever flavour you want, but not chocolate or coffee. Maybe try one he hasn't had before."

Theo groaned internally. "When does he need it by?"

"Tomorrow morning."

"Tomorrow?! That's going to take me all night!"

Peter shrugged. "We've all got a lot of work to do, Theo. If you don't like it ..." He left his words hanging there as he walked away.

Theo cursed to herself and gripped the bench in frustration. Gino co-owned the restaurant, acting as the primary investor, but he didn't have any idea of how it ran. He was the money, whereas Peter was the talent. He was rarely around, only showing up when he wanted to either impress his Z list celebrity friends or use it as his personal catering service. He couldn't name a single kitchen staff member; in fact, he probably couldn't pick one out of a lineup. Still, that didn't stop him from swanning in and expecting to be pandered to. Consideration was not a word that sprang to mind with that man. If it did reside in his brain, it was buried somewhere in the darkest reaches, most likely under the words decency and forethought. Last-minute orders were his signature move.

Completely exasperated, she stood there for a moment, scrambling to mentally rearrange her day. As the initial shock wore off and she entombed the anger deep in her stomach, ideas started to come to her, and she left her bench for the coolroom. There were two punnets of raspberries and a few passionfruit sitting on her shelf, and while the tiny file clerk in her brain flicked through her internal cabinet of recipes, flavour combinations began to solidify into a plan of action.

Picking up the fruit and a container of caramel buttercream she had left over from her latest batch of cupcakes, Theo returned to her bench, taking down the recipe folder she had stashed above her section. She was back in her comfort zone, and with a slow, soothing breath, she allowed the calm of cooking to take over. It was never the food that was stressful; it was always the people.

Porphura could be a struggle to work at sometimes, but it was a damn sight better than many other restaurants. Head chefs, especially the old school ones, were often egotistical and narcissistic, using their power to abuse their subordinates as if their title excused their behaviour. Peter, on the other hand, despite being a royal dick sometimes, at least had enough redeeming qualities to balance things out. For all the yelling he did, he offered Theo something many other chefs hadn't, something that garnered him her loyalty: appreciation for her work, respect for her opinion, and equal treatment in a typically male-dominated profession.

As she began weighing out the ingredients for a tonka bean cake batter, Theo couldn't help but muse on all the head chefs she'd encountered over the years, shaking her head as she pictured them one by one. As she considered her experiences, a single, unmitigated fact bubbled to the surface: blatant sexism was still alive and well in far too many kitchens. That's not to say there weren't undeniably more female chefs nowadays, but she knew as well as anyone that there were still plenty of places where being a female meant degradation or sexual harassment on a regular basis. It took a thick skin and a liberal sense of humour to survive at the best of times, and this was doubly true for women. It was hard to get a foot in the door and even harder to get to the top, especially when the men's proverbial ladder was far sturdier.

Theo had more firsthand experiences of sexism in practice than she cared to admit, and each one stung just as acutely as the last. Each time she'd turned up to an interview only to be greeted by a puzzled look, it had chipped away at her confidence. With a name like Theo, people expected to see a man walk in the door, and the grimace of disappointment they bore upon her introduction was equal parts disturbing and tiresome. Needless to say, she'd never been offered those jobs.

The old guard of antiquated head chefs who led those establishments saw women as weaker both physically and emotionally, a liability destined to leave in pursuit of childbearing. In their eyes, women were, by their very nature, wholly incapable of outperforming their male counterparts in commitment, skill, or endurance. Overall, Theo found their assumptions laughable. Not only because they all seemed to be made entirely out of false bravado and glass ego, but because she'd personally surpassed and outlasted more male chefs than she could keep track of and had absolutely no desire to reproduce.

Ruth popped her head around as Theo poured the now finished cake batter into a tin and slid it in the oven. "Urgh, I heard Gino slapped a cake on you. Tough break."

"Yeah. There go all my grandiose plans for working on a new soufflé," Theo replied with a shrug, flipping through her folder again in search of her passionfruit curd recipe. "What was Peter yelling at you about?"

"He told me to create a new beetroot side dish, but he didn't like it, so he wants me to go back to the charred broccoli. It's ridiculous. He was the one that suggested the new dish in the first place. The man is so fucking bipolar, I swear to God. Sometimes I think he escaped from a mental asylum and somehow convinced Gino he's a master chef."

Theo laughed at the thought as Justin came up behind them. "Are you two talking about sex again?"

Theo and Ruth both rolled their eyes.

"That's right, Justin," Theo said. "All we talk about is sex, and breasts, and vaginas."

Justin's cheeks flushed. "You don't have to tell me stuff like that, you know."

"Then why did you ask?"

"I don't know," he shrugged. "I was curious."

"About what? Vaginas?" Theo asked with a smirk.

"You don't have to keep saying that word."

Ruth smiled at him. "Vagina."

Theo looked at Ruth before they both took a step towards him. "VAGINA!" they said in unison as he scurried off to the safety of his bench.

Ruth pointed at the spot where Justin had just been standing. "That boy has some serious sexual repression going on."

Theo shrugged indifferently. "Maybe he's gay."

Ruth nodded slowly before winking at her and disappearing around the corner.

Sometimes the banter was what made the day bearable.

∞◌◌∞

Dinner service was chaotic. There weren't any functions, but the restaurant was fully booked, with groups of people being seated at the bar while the waitstaff frantically endeavoured to turn tables. On top of that, as always seemed to be the way of things at Porphura, every order managed to hit the kitchen at the exact same time.

The number of dockets staring Theo in the face was daunting, and the fact that she still had to finish the cake for Gino was quickly shifted to the backburner of her brain. As she started mentally preparing herself and grouping orders to speed things along, a new docket popped out of the printer. It was for a table of eight, but one of the guests had extensive dietary requirements: vegan, gluten-free, and fructose-free.

"Oh, for fuck's sake," she muttered to herself in annoyance as she read it.

Random dietaries arriving without warning in the middle of a busy service was the bane of every chef and a spanner in the works that Theo could really do without. Checking the name on the docket, she waved down the waitress responsible: Katie, the new one that Ruth was so infatuated with. She was cute, in a blonde, bubble-headed kind of way. Not really Theo's type.

"What's this?" Theo asked, sliding the docket across the pass to her.

Katie shrugged. "Sorry, she only told us when she got here. What can we give her?"

A glass of water or directions to the door, Theo's inner monologue silently screamed.

She didn't have time for this, there were three soufflés in the oven, and she had four other desserts to finish before the timer went off. Closing her eyes for a split second to repress her rage, Theo opened them again to find the doe-eyed newbie staring at her.

"A plate of very specific sorbets, I imagine," Theo finally replied sarcastically. "Seriously. With that combination of dietary requirements, that's all I can make her. You'll need to ask her what fruit she can eat, apologise, and suggest she call ahead next time."

The waitress nodded and disappeared into the gaggle of tables as Theo went back to her dockets. Laying out plates, she hustled to make up for lost time, flinging open fridge doors and snatching things out with the sightless precision only muscle memory can provide. Seeing a shadow appear on the stainless steel of the pass, she looked up to see that Katie had returned.

"Make it quick!"

"So, apparently, she can have a little bit of gluten. And fructose. She mainly just insists that it's vegan," said the waitress meekly.

Theo suppressed the urge to smash her head against the wall in frustration. Customers and their kinda-sorta dietary requests were precisely why so many chefs didn't take them seriously anymore.

"Fine. Tell her I'll put something up in a minute."

"Sure thing," Katie said, disappearing again without another word.

Eleven minutes later, with ice cream on the plates and the oven timer sounding, Theo called for service, but no one came. Taking the soufflés out and putting the finished dishes up on the pass, she called again to no response. Sometimes, she swore her voice must be the exact same pitch as exhaust fans and inane dinner conversation. Her pass was sporting three different tables worth of dessert, the vegan customer included, and so she yelled in earnest for the third time, watching as the soufflés began to settle down into their moulds. Suddenly, Peter appeared from around the corner, took one look at the situation, and stepped forward.

"PASTRY SERVICE!" his voice boomed across the restaurant.

Every waiter stopped simultaneously and bolted for the pass, Theo watching in amusement as they scurried to take the desserts while actively avoiding eye contact with Peter.

As she put the finishing touches on the next wave of dockets, Theo was met by a voice from across the pass. "Just so you know, the vegan lady said the sorbets are delicious."

Without looking up, she gave Katie a small smile and nod, the compliment of a satisfied customer making the stress at least partially worthwhile.

∞∞∞

It was midnight by the time Theo finished the cake. She'd cooked it hours ago and made the other components, but she'd had to wait until after dinner service to stack and decorate it. With a sense of relief, Theo took a step back and admired the fruits of her labour. The light layers of tonka bean sponge were perfectly sandwiched with passionfruit curd and raspberry mousse, then encased in caramel buttercream. On top lay a jumble of passionfruit macarons, fresh raspberries, and white chocolate truffles. She knew Gino wouldn't appreciate the effort that had gone into it, but as she put it in a cake box and placed it in the coolroom, Theo was content to claim her own self-satisfaction.

By the time she'd cleaned down, the rest of the kitchen staff were long gone, and she paused at the office door on the way to the locker room to find Peter finalising the next day's seafood order.

"I finished the cake. It's in the coolroom," she said, kneading her knuckles into her aching lower back as she spoke.

Peter put down his pen and smiled. "Thanks, Theo. I always know I can count on you."

She didn't react to his praise outwardly except for a slight nod, but a little ball of pride swelled in her chest. "No worries. Do you need anything else before I head off?" she asked, her weary body hoping for a negative response.

"Just one thing,"

Theo sighed quietly. "Yes, Chef?"

"You and Ruth need to let up on Justin a little bit. He's having a hard time adjusting to our ... language."

62

"Like when you said you'd stick a rolling pin up his arse if he didn't hurry up during service?" she jibed, arching an eyebrow.

Peter started coughing uncontrollably, grabbing his glass of wine and taking a gulp to calm his throat. "Yeah, something like that," he replied with a smirk.

"No more vaginas. Got it," Theo nodded as she turned to leave. "Night, Chef."

∞∞∞∞

Opening the door of her apartment, Theo dropped her bag down and kicked off her shoes. Glancing around the space, she felt almost disconnected from it, like she was walking into a hotel room rather than her own home. The bedroom remained undisturbed other than her ruffled sheets, and the kitchen was spacious but sat idle most days. As for the living area, the three extra dining chairs at the table and the two unused cushions on her three-seater couch only served as stark reminders of her solitary existence.

Very little spoke of the soul who occupied the place save for the antique, wooden bar cart, the alphabetised DVDs in the cabinet holding the television, and the bookcase housing her jumble of cookbooks and fantasy novels. Food and fiction had always been her escapes, and she found a soothing calm in letting her mind wander to imaginary lands or the creative realm of the culinary world.

The walls sat bare aside from an eclectic collection of pictures that spoke of her past. On one wall hung a poster of a woodland fairy in a flowing white dress and autumn leaf shoes she'd had since her tween years. On another hung a relatively generic canvas of Buddha from her late adolescence when she'd hoped to find a little peace anywhere she could. And tacked up beside the bookshelf sat a small picture painted in purple glitter glue that she'd made when she was eight years old and towards which she was strangely sentimental. She wandered over to it, tracing the strands that snaked across the paper like tendrils. It had always made Theo feel strong when she looked at it for some reason, and thus, despite its shedding glitter and tattered edges, she kept it.

Trying to shake the feeling of being a stranger amongst her own things, she reverted back to her routine, systematically having a shower and collapsing onto the couch. Flicking through the channels, she stumbled on a documentary about wolves and let the soothing voice of the narrator fill the silence.

On the screen, two wolves came together, nuzzling each other in the frozen forest, and her thoughts veered unwittingly to something she desperately wanted to forget: her last partner.

She'd been a bartender when Theo had first met her, vivacious and carefree, picking up Theo at a time when she'd been at her lowest. They were together for two years, and while at times she'd been a kind and generous person, she'd often taken advantage of Theo's naivety and trusting nature. Her bipolar disorder had made for a volatile relationship when mixed with Theo's depression, and when both were at their worst, the environment was nothing short of toxic. It was your classic narcissist and empath coupling, and Theo had found herself to be the collateral damage in the implosion of someone who could not see beyond their own needs. When it had ended, Theo had been left a shell of her former self, shattered beyond recognition.

The biggest issue had been her ex's alcohol addiction. She would start drinking when she woke up and wouldn't stop until she fell asleep on the couch in the early hours of the morning. It was the cause of a lot of tension between them, and she would punish Theo when they fought by disappearing for hours on end, refusing to respond to her calls or messages.

On top of that, she'd previously been a drug user, but in a rare moment of clarity, she'd decided to shave her head and go cold turkey just a month before they'd met. Theo had been there through the residual drug-induced psychosis and paranoia and cared for her despite it all. She'd been knowingly self-destructive, violent at times, hurtful towards others, manipulative, and dismissive of Theo's feelings. In the end, though, it was the fact she'd lied and cheated in their final months that had brought things to a head.

Love had made Theo blind, and it had cost her much of her mental stability. When she looked back on it now, only one phrase ever came to mind: through rose-coloured glasses, all the red flags just look like flags.

The two wolves trotted through the snow together, equally strong, equally loyal. To find the other half of her pair was all Theo wanted, but as she examined her scarred heart, she wondered if she was capable of that kind of love anymore. Maybe she was destined to be alone with her broken pieces and her baggage.

Turning off the television, she slowly readied herself for sleep as she tried to cram the painful memories back into their boxes and bury them once more. When she switched off the light and lay in bed, her head swirled with dark thoughts of death and emptiness. She knew that if she died then and there, the only reason anyone would notice would be due to her absence from work. No one would care that she was gone, only that they would have to pick up the slack. Her family would be the only ones who attended her funeral, more so out of a sense of obligation than sorrow. She'd be as lonesome in death as she was now in life.

Tears fell silently down her cheeks, and she curled into a ball. She knew the nightmares that awaited her should she fall asleep in such a depressed state, and so she steeled herself and tried to envision a happier existence. In her mind, she imagined herself arriving in London, her joyous heart buoying her into a black cab at the airport. She fantasised about being in Paris, breaking open a croissant on the Champ de Mars, the shadow of the Eiffel Tower passing over her as the day marched on. She pictured herself in Mexico, a tequila in one hand and a taco in the other, clinking glasses with someone she loved on a long sandy beach. She painted herself the scene of standing outside a centuries-old temple in the picture-perfect mountains of Japan.

Smiling for the briefest of moments, she felt her breath slowing as she started to sink into sleep's embrace. One day she would go on her dream trip. She would fly far from the pain of these shores; she just needed to find someone to share it with first.

Auryn

In the darkest days of his twenties, when his depression had been at its worst, Auryn had always clung to one motto: homicide before suicide. While it seemed like the epitaph of a deranged serial killer, it was, in actual fact, his final promise to himself. A promise that he wouldn't just fade away from existence but instead use his death to accomplish some good in the world. Besides, it rhymed, and he'd always wanted to use it in a song one day.

The reason it had come to Auryn's mind in that instant had to do with the large graffiti tag he'd found as he did his morning walk through at work: a strange pseudonym penned in marker all over the wall of the men's bathroom. It was at times like these that he hated humanity with a passion. More than anything else, it was the lack of empathy and foresight that bothered him. When people drew on a wall, they knew full well someone would have to clean it off, yet they did it anyway, wantonly and without remorse.

Taggers were a constant bane of Auryn's existence, and the most frustrating thing was he'd never caught one in the act. He had, however, promised himself that if he ever *did* manage to, he'd make them pay for all the people who'd eluded him. Dabbing some more methylated spirits on the tea towel balled in his fist, he gritted his teeth and scrubbed the wall with vigour, watching as the marker started to lift. When it was almost gone, he fetched a new cloth and wiped off the remainder with a little water. With the graffiti removed, Auryn breathed a sigh of relief and walked back behind the bar, dumping the towels in a bucket. Now to start the actual work.

Benzin was a small bar located in the heart of Chinatown in the middle of the city. Ironically enough, though, despite the fact it was surrounded by Asian restaurants and karaoke on all sides, it had no ties to Asia at all. It was owned by two Australians, who had designed the bar to reflect their European heritage. Each corner had its own theme, although none of the four meshed together. One sported a raised square platform bordered almost entirely by banquette seats, their cushions upholstered with dowdy red velvet. Another was home to a long wooden table flanked by bench seats and stained by years of coasterless cups. The third was furnished with a series of plush, French-style booths, the leather misshapen by constant use. The last boasted a jumble of the kind of white, wrought iron outdoor furniture that elicited images of aristocratic English garden parties.

It was hideous and gaudy but, for reasons Auryn could never quite comprehend, people commented on how great the place looked almost daily.

There's no accounting for taste, he often mused to himself, sure that they would feel differently if they saw it sober and with the house lights up.

As he looked across the room, he saw one of the owners standing at the far end of the bar: Carlos, a middle-aged man of Croatian heritage with thin, reedy, brown hair; a long, broad nose; and a barrel chest. His raging alcoholism had weathered him by at least ten years, and it was also the reason why, at that very moment, he was hunched up against the bar top cradling a beer.

Carlos smiled up at him, swaying a little from the effects of another all-night bender. "Hey! You get it off?"

"Yeah, it's gone," Auryn replied with a nod.

"Good, good! Wanna shot?"

"No thanks. It's a little early for me," he said with quiet sarcasm, glancing down at his watch and noting that it was barely two in the afternoon. "You want me to pour you one?"

Carlos shrugged sheepishly and grinned. "Why not? Give me that nice rum you showed me last week."

Auryn grabbed the rum from its place on the top shelf, filling a shot glass and sliding it down the bar to Carlos, annoyed that he couldn't afford a bottle for himself while his inebriated boss probably wouldn't even remember drinking it. What a waste.

Carlos raised the glass in a toast, then downed it in one gulp, a streak of it splashing down his chin and dripping onto his sweat-stained, white shirt. He drew in his face as the alcohol flooded his palate and then shook his head, smiling again.

"Now that hit the spot!" he exclaimed in a voice quite a few decibels louder than was necessary in an empty bar.

Carlos's job, when he actually got around to doing it, was to organise the DJ's and promoters, and as his phone lit up with the name of one of their regulars, he slapped the counter and answered it.

"Johnny boy! How ya doin'?" he said with drunken enthusiasm as he wandered off, flinging open the front door and stepping out into the laneway.

Auryn rolled his eyes, clearing the glass away as his own phone buzzed. It was the other owner, Adam.

Unlike his flamboyantly social counterpart, Adam was much more of an introvert, and he had a bad habit of sitting in the office upstairs, watching everything from the cameras while he lent his fastidious hand to the bookkeeping. He never came down into the bar, especially while it was open, and his interpersonal skills were less than tactful. If he wanted to see you, he simply sent you a text message. It was impersonal, passive-aggressive, and had the distinct vibe of a king in his tower surveying his subjects.

Slowly walking up the stairs, Auryn wondered for the millionth time why he stayed. He'd been there for five years, working his way up from bartender to venue manager, but he didn't enjoy it anymore; in fact, sometimes, he flat out hated it. There was a comfortable nature to it that was hard to ignore, though, and like many hospitality workers, he was inexplicably loyal. He knew every facet of the venue, every bottle, every piece of equipment, and he could sort out any problem that came up with ease, except for the ones that involved people. They were the problem that never really went away.

Sighing as he reached the office door, Auryn braced himself and knocked, entering to find Adam sitting at his desk, frowning at a piece of paper. He had a classic, broad, European face and short, brown hair that he constantly dyed blond like he'd never quite outgrown his youth despite being in his early forties. The look was rounded off with a shadow of stubble that stretched across his face like greasy sandpaper. Owning a business had certainly taken its toll on him.

Auryn stood there awkwardly for a moment, not wanting to sit down in case he'd only been summoned for a quick word, but when Adam looked up, he waved Auryn in.

"Take a seat," he said, gesturing at the chair across from him.

Auryn sat down with a sense of dread, preparing himself for what he assumed would be another of Adam's non-sensical suggestions. The man wasn't an accountant, although he liked to think of himself as one. He constantly nit-picked at small things to try and save money, even if the implementation of such measures ended up costing more than he expected to save. In short, he was the epitome of penny-wise and pound-foolish.

Adam lifted up the piece of paper in his hand. "I'm not liking these staff costs, Auryn."

The bar had been quiet the previous week, the city unexpectedly devoid of the people needed to make any decent money. Because of that, though, staff costs had been high. After all, you still needed to pay staff to be in the building, even if there weren't many customers, and until someone invented a way of reading the future, it remained necessary to roster for the busy times, not the quiet ones.

Auryn shrugged. "It was quiet. They'll be better this week."

"That's not good enough. I need you to make some changes to the roster to save on costs."

Maybe if Carlos stopped drinking all the stock, you wouldn't be so strapped for cash, Auryn thought to himself with disdain before he opened his mouth again.

"That's not workable, though. What happens if it gets busy? I won't have enough staff on. Plus, I need to give everyone enough hours so they can survive. If I cut their shifts, they'll start looking for other jobs, and then when we do get busy again, we'll be screwed!"

Adam eyed him sternly. "That's not my concern. It's your job to ensure that the venue isn't wasting money on staff. If it gets busy and you all have to work a bit harder, that's fine by me."

Auryn's temper flared. That was easy for Adam to say when he wasn't the one in the trenches. "You realise that if we don't have enough staff on when it's busy, you'll lose money, right? I need X amount of staff to maximise our profits. If I cut that, it cuts your profit."

"If you're not willing to do it, I'll find someone who will," Adam snapped, folding his arms.

Auryn held his gaze, realising his earnest pleas would afford him no leniency, before slowly nodding. "I'll go downstairs and sort it out."

Adam placed his hands back on the desk, pleased. "Good."

As he left the office, Auryn suppressed the urge to punch a hole in the wall. That was Adam to a tee; he cared more about numbers than people. He didn't have the scope to see that the old adage, 'you have to spend money, to make money,' applied doubly to hospitality, where profits weren't linear and could not be viewed on a week-by-week basis. He wanted to see savings now, basing snap decisions on the previous week's performance even if doing so cost him more in the long run. Shaking his head, Auryn reached the bottom of the stairs, leant over the bar to gather his phone, a pen, and a piece of paper, and plonked himself down in one of the booths. The new roster wasn't going to write itself.

Outside, Carlos was still talking loudly on the phone, gesturing left and right as if he was conducting an invisible orchestra. They were an odd pair, the two owners. Carlos, quite obviously, had always been a party animal, but one thing you wouldn't pick about Adam, the creepy office hermit, was that he also loved to go out, especially in the days before purchasing the bar.

That was how they'd met. They'd been at a dive bar, both hammered to all hell, having a drunken conversation about what they'd both do with a bar if they had the chance. Once they realised they had similar ideas, an agreement was struck to open their own place together. By some miracle, they both remembered the conversation the next day: some money was borrowed, an old warehouse in Chinatown was found, and twelve months later, Benzin was born.

After it opened, though, the two started to diverge in their habits. To the surprise of no one, Carlos's alcoholism worsened, while Adam, after a few big nights following the opening, decided it was wise if he didn't drink there at all, so he could keep a more lucid eye on things. Naturally, that seemed like a sensible idea, right up until the severe micro-management began.

That was the state of play now; Carlos was a careless drunk, and Adam was a sober grinch. The once close friends now sat as polar opposites, both with traits that irritated the other and both unable to escape the business they'd locked themselves into together. The dynamic made for a highly stressful work environment and resulted in a venue that was nigh on impossible for Auryn to manage effectively.

By the time three o'clock rolled around, Auryn was knee-deep in his usual Tuesday tasks, flitting between putting away deliveries and churning through random office work: organising functions, checking emails, fielding calls from liquor company reps, and redoing the roster. It was tedious, but the solitude of the work offered him private calm. As such, it was with great reluctance that he chocked open the doors two hours later, turning on the music and standing at his post, ready but less than eager to serve.

The bar itself was poorly designed and prohibitively impractical when it was busy, the design clearly the brainchild of someone who had never actually worked behind one before. It was a tiny space that could barely fit three people, with glass racks underneath the benches, premium spirits lined up on shelves along the back wall, and beer fridges below that made the space even smaller every time they were opened. Two small wells with no drainage held the ice, which ran out constantly, forcing the staff to swim through the crowd each time they needed to fetch more from the ice machine out the back.

To top off the lunacy, all the house spirits were arrayed on either side of the venue's singular cash register, the draw of which was simply left open during the busy periods so the bartenders could keep up with the demand for service. Of course, it was far from best practice to have staff handling money without keying in a single transaction. Still, with the alternative being lengthy wait times and dissatisfied customers, Auryn had been duty-bound to choose the lesser of two evils. Adam used to tear his hair out trying to reconcile the tills on Mondays, but now he didn't bother; he just counted what was there and took it to the bank. It was a questionable accounting method, to say the least, but the only alternative was to buy another register, and true to his nature, Adam didn't want to spend the money.

As he polished a rack of glasses, Auryn despaired at his predicament. Technically, he was the manager, but Adam robbed him of authority, and when coupled with the constant call for lower wage costs, he was stuck forgoing the problem solving of management he thrived on for more menial tasks. Although he'd worked his way up to a higher position on paper, Auryn simply found himself in the same old role with a few additional responsibilities thrown in. He couldn't better the business and supervise the venue whilst tethered to bartending duties, but his hands were tied. It left him feeling chained and restless, and for the second time that day, he contemplated why he stayed. After being there for half a decade, the place was starting to feel stale. It was time for a change, but to what? The question troubled him.

An older man walked in and asked for a pot of beer, pulling Auryn from his thoughts. As the drink was placed in front of him, the man flicked a twenty dollar note on the bar top, and Auryn grabbed it, biting his tongue. Fetching his change, Auryn carefully placed it in the man's hand, trying to show through actions how to function as a polite member of society, but the man just grunted and wandered off to find a seat.

There would be no bars without customers, but they could be a trial at times. Some were a pleasure to serve: those who had good manners, good taste, or good sense. On the other end of the spectrum, though, there were plenty who ground Auryn's gears. Those who put their money on the bar top instead of the hand outstretched to them definitely fell into the latter group, but they weren't even the worst breed, unfortunately. No, the top spot was reserved for the kind of people who saw bar staff as servants rather than servers, those who seemed to take sick pleasure out of antagonising staff and who clicked or whistled for service as if beckoning dogs. Auryn had been working in bars for almost twenty years, and his patience and empathy for his fellow man had worn down to a nub.

He thought about that as he walked the floor, wiping down tables and straightening furniture. He hadn't always carried hatred for humanity in his heart. Even when he'd been bullied as a teenager, he'd still believed deep down that people were inherently good. Over the years, however, that view had changed, and alcohol had a lot to do with it. Auryn theorised that being drunk was a window into a person's soul. Whilst there was usually a civilised politeness to normal society, that thin veneer often disintegrated after a few drinks. Even the most unassuming people had a habit of becoming rude, arrogant, and unkind when inebriated, caring little for the problems and injuries they caused.

With their inhibitions lowered, people's sense of self-entitlement shouldered its way to the forefront, stamping out moral duty and convincing the intoxicated that the world revolved solely around them. These same people considered themselves above animals, seeing them as creatures of instinct who survived without thought or consequence, but in reality, they were exactly the same.

Left unchecked, they would consume everything around them with no shred of remorse, the same way a group of rabbits in a vegetable patch would eat everything within reach if given the opportunity. When it came down to it, though, they were worse than animals. They had the power of human reasoning and yet chose to blatantly ignore it. That's not to say Auryn didn't believe there were a few redeeming people left in the world. They were just unquestionably drowned out by the rest of the population who demanded praise for the mere act of existing, like they were God's gift to man.

The customer downed the rest of his drink and departed as Tony sauntered in for his shift. He was, of his very essence, the epitome of a laid-back hospo employee, his slapdash combination of black tank top and tan cargo shorts showing off the various anime and superhero-inspired tattoos dotting his limbs. Couple those with spiky, brown hair, glasses, and an almost unshakable grin, and you had yourself Benzin's assistant manager.

Unlike Auryn, Tony still viewed hospitality with fervent optimism, as a way to rise through the ranks to manager before scrounging together enough money to open his own little dive bar. The lure of such a goal had waned for Auryn over the years, and at times, he envied Tony's seemingly unsnuffable flame.

Casually removing his headphones, Tony waved and cleared the empty glass from the now vacant table. "Hey, mate. What's cracking?"

"Not much," Auryn replied with a shrug. "The usual shit. Adam wanted me to cut staff costs, so I had to cancel Janet's shift tonight."

Tony groaned, placing the glass on the bar top. "Dude, you're ruining my good mood. What if it gets busy?"

"Don't stress. I'll stay back 'til it quietens down."

"Thanks, man," Tony said, leaning over for a fist bump.

"All part of the service," Auryn laughed with a mimed tip of the cap.

Being a manager meant being on call twenty-four hours a day, seven days a week, and it was starting to grate on Auryn's nerves. If someone was sick and no one else could cover, he worked. If there was a special event on his day off, but he was needed at the bar, he abandoned it and came in. If the owners wanted to have a meeting bright and early, he turned up, even if he'd finished his last shift at four in the morning. If he was told he had to cut staff costs but had too much common decency to leave his colleagues in the shit, he stayed back. It was the hardest facet of the job, never getting to unwind properly, and the worst part was, he was only paid for forty hours a week; everything else was unpaid overtime.

Despite having to give up his early finish, Auryn had to admit that he did enjoy slinging drinks with Tony, and the pair spent the next two hours serving the occasional customer whilst talking movies and comics. They dissected films, discussed ones yet to be released, and debated the stories they would create if Hollywood was stupid enough to give them a hundred million dollars and free reign. In short, the kind of outlandish conversations that offered escapism to idle minds.

Auryn had always loved superhero stories. As far back as he could remember, they had captured his imagination and sung to him on a deep level, and it wasn't hard to understand why. Beneath his outward distaste for humankind, he yearned to have those same powers himself, to be able to help people and impact the world in a positive way, to restore good to a world that had not always been good to him. When his thoughts had time to wander, he often daydreamed of the abilities he wished he had, the fantastical what-ifs that pander to the whims of struggling souls. Without prompt, an image flitted into his mind, but he dismissed it as Olivia showed up for her shift, the short, feisty, young bartender tying her long, black hair into a messy bun as she stepped through the door.

It was Tuesday, which meant it was Uni Night, and with drink specials ready to roll out and a DJ booked to start in a couple of hours, all that was left to do was hope the students of Melbourne were in a partying mood. Some weeks it was quiet, but more often than not, it was perpetual chaos, and with the city buzzing just outside the door, it looked like they were in for the latter.

The clock had barely ticked past seven when people began to pour in, large groups of friends arriving in bursts, ready to make the weekly choice of booze over Wednesday morning lecture attendance. As Auryn started to pump out drinks, ducking and weaving around Tony and Olivia as they did the same, he cursed internally at the realisation that they really could have used that extra pair of hands Adam had forced him to remove from the roster. Usually, he'd be free to head home at ten or eleven, once all the other staff had turned up and everything was chugging along comfortably, but he already knew he was destined to be in it for the long haul.

The flow of customers was constant, and by the time the DJ started playing, the place was a madhouse. Inebriated students stumbled around the venue, alternating between sculling drinks and gyrating against each other in what could only loosely be described as dancing. Sweat melted into the air, forming a fog over the dance floor and turning the space into a veritable sauna, and although the air conditioning tried its hardest, it barely made a dent in the wave of heat suffocating the room.

When a bar was that busy and hot, there was really only one course of action for the staff: take a swig of water, put your head down, and keep serving until there was a lull long enough to escape outside for a few minutes. It was the only way to survive.

Niceties went out the window when the crowd waiting at the bar was three deep, and there was no time for friendly chit chat. If a customer reached the front not knowing what they wanted or without the means to pay ready at hand, the bartenders simply moved on to the next. In the midst of such chaos, being systematic was the only defence, and service became a robotic process of take order, fill order, process payment, repeat.

It wasn't until two in the morning that the drink orders dwindled to a mere trickle, and seizing the opportunity, Auryn stepped outside, the early morning air cooling the sweat on his shirt and sending welcome chills through his aching body.

He glanced across at the two security guards standing watch over the front door. "All good?"

One of them shrugged. "We kicked out a couple of drunks, but apart from that, no problems."

Auryn nodded, closing his eyes and taking a deep breath, a wave of exhaustion crashing over him as he crouched down, goosebumps appearing on his arms. His mind begged him to stand up, walk down the alleyway, and never look back, but he knew in his heart that he couldn't. Instead, he slowly rose to his feet and headed back inside to allow his colleagues their turn at a brief reprieve.

As the clock finally reached three, the new hour brought with it what was arguably every bartender's favourite pastime, turning up the house lights. That glorious moment when the facade of customer service could be shaken loose and squinting, dishevelled customers pleading for one last drink could be directed to the door without remorse. In the single turn of a dimmer switch, adrenaline gave way to relief, and freedom drew closer by the second.

It took a good fifteen minutes after the music stopped to herd everyone out, and with security gone for the night, Auryn was finally able to lock the door. Turning back to the stark remains of the now empty bar, he was quickly reminded that the job was still far from over. With Olivia left to finish cleaning the bar, Tony and Auryn darted around the venue, playing the inevitable game of stray glass hide and seek, retrieving cups from the strange and almost impressive places people felt compelled to cram them when drunk.

"You want to count the cash?" Tony asked, pulling a glass filled with a slurry of half-finished beer and semi-dissolved napkin from between the cushions of the banquette.

"Nah, I'm too tired. You do it."

"Okay, well, I'll do the toilets before I start then. Fair?"

Auryn nodded, more than pleased he wouldn't have to deal with the unmentionable surprises he was sure lay waiting to be discovered.

Turning on some dance music and cranking the volume until the bass could be felt through the floor, Tony disappeared to face the bedlam of the bathrooms.

With a sigh, Auryn picked up a cloth and started wiping down the tables, retrieving an errant earring that had somehow become lodged between the planks of the wooden table. What he really wanted to listen to was some metal, something with blast beats and crushing riffs, something that mirrored his own raging soul. That was his lot as a metalhead, though. He was one of the small bunch of people who appreciated an artform the majority of the world found too coarse and abrasive to revel in. You could put on pretty much any other genre at the end of the night, and no one would object, but put on some heavy music, and suddenly everyone was up in arms. He understood why, but that didn't help him in that moment, more than fourteen hours into his shift.

Fetching the broom, he swept the remnants of the night into a pile in the middle of the dance floor, the monotonous loop of simplistic dubstep beats pounding him back into his own thoughts. Music had always been a crux for him, and its effect was difficult to describe. Ever since his teen years, he'd relied on music, especially metal, to stabilise his mood and get him through the day. For Auryn, it gave him energy and power he otherwise wouldn't possess, it gave him the strength to deal with the weight of his depression, and above all else, it gave sound to his silent sorrow. As it was for so many others, music was fuel for his soul.

As he filled the mop bucket, the air stinging his nostrils with the familiar smell of synthetic citrus, an image came to mind of a New Year's Eve many years ago, when he was in his early twenties. He hadn't had anyone to celebrate with, so he'd just stayed home, music his only companion. With midnight approaching, he'd started playing one of his favourite songs on repeat, the beat hammering over and over again, louder and louder until it began hurting his eardrums. He didn't stop, though. He kept listening to it as the start of another year came and went, that single song the only thing stopping him from hurling himself out the window and ending it all. That was the power of music.

It was almost five when they finally finished cleaning, the fatigue of working another understaffed night stripping them of their desire to linger over a knock-off drink and sending them each on their respective ways. With his headphones blaring, Auryn walked past the countless Asian restaurants surrounding Benzin, the jump between nationalities and cuisines little more than a few steps.

Turning left off Little Bourke Street, he left Chinatown behind, the streets suddenly filled with convenience stores that never closed and retail stores that would open again soon. He snaked his way towards Flinders Street Station, passing a string of fast-food joints filled with people searching for sustenance before they went home to sleep off the booze and bad decisions. Across the road, he saw a scuffle break out between a group of drunken teens, and he quickened his pace, wishing as he so often did that he still had his car.

Auryn was always on edge at this time of day, when those not in complete control of their faculties made up the majority. There was an unpredictability about it that triggered unease in him and a need for vigilance. One bump, one look, one angry remark was all it took to set some people off. As he reached the steps of the station and passed under the clocks, he breathed a sigh of relief, making his way down to the platform and waiting for the first train of the morning to deliver him home. By the time he arrived and crawled into bed, it was six, and he fell asleep to the sounds of the world waking up.

∞∞∞∞∞∞∞∞∞∞∞∞∞∞∞∞

It was dark, as if all the light in the world had been snuffed out. Blind to his surroundings, he slowly crept forward, hearing them all around him: shadows that stalked with sinister intent. As his eyes adjusted, he began to see shapes, indistinct yet menacing. He whirled around, trying to find a way out, but there was none. He was trapped in the void with nothing save the enemies who waited for their opportune moment to strike.

A rustle of movement came from behind him, and he turned on his heel just as one of the shadows leapt forward. Fighting with everything he had, he sent it flying backwards into the abyss, its shriek echoing through the darkness. More of the shadows pressed forward, and he retaliated again, dispatching his foes one by one. As he glanced around, though, he realised his triumph was short-lived, his defeat inevitable.

There were howls and cries in every direction, the creatures scraping and shuffling as they circled him, waiting. Suddenly, the shadows paused, silence falling before they lunged forward as one, attacking from all sides. He tried to beat them back, but their number seemed infinite, their hands clasping at his limbs and face until he was dragged to the ground, unable to move.

He struggled, his muscles straining as he tried to wrench an arm free, but it was useless. Overwhelmed, he screamed out, but there was no one to help him, no one to rescue him from his fate. As he died, one truth reverberated through his mind, inescapable and resolute: the darkness always won.

∞∞∞∞∞∞∞∞∞∞∞∞∞∞∞∞

When Auryn awoke, he found himself in no way refreshed. He desperately wanted to go back to sleep, but his bladder had other ideas. Venturing out to relieve himself, he clambered back beneath the covers, shutting his eyes and trying to convince his brain to return to its previous state while flashes of his dream paraded through his head.

He lay there feebly attempting to clear his thoughts and sink back into much-needed slumber, but it was to no avail. His body might have been exhausted, but his mind was well and truly awake, and he knew from experience that there would be no more rest. Groaning, he glanced over at his watch sitting on the bedside table. It was eleven. He'd only been asleep for five hours.

Reluctantly, Auryn rolled out of bed again, abandoning the idea of dozing and going to the closet to fetch a t-shirt. Slipping it on, he wandered out to the kitchen in search of a glass of water, downing it and pouring himself another before slumping onto the couch. As he stared into the middle distance, he wondered if this was the sum of his life: working in a crappy job for minimal pay while suffering from a constant state of inextinguishable exhaustion. He was tired of being tired, sick of the struggle that came with pushing through the haze in his mind just to exist. He wanted to feel fresh and composed when he woke up, happy and healthy, but that never happened. Not even once.

He'd been in a fog his entire life, and as it grew thicker, he was finding it hard to come up with reasons why he should keep fighting. Dark thoughts inched forward as his unblinking eyes lost focus on the world. What would happen if he ended it all? Would the world even notice the departure of a loser bar manager with more dreams than achievements? In his heart, he knew the sad truth already.

Shaking himself back to the present and rubbing his eyes, he unwillingly stood up, forcing himself to cobble together a breakfast he had very little will to eat. He had to work again that afternoon, a depressing thought in and of itself, but there were still a few hours he would need to struggle through before that distraction began. Watching television to try and banish the shadow that hung over him ended in restless abandonment, as did his attempt at playing his guitar. He had yet again found himself in a cycle of indeterminable want, too uneasy about his approaching shift to settle into any particular task.

Returning to his bedroom and sitting at the computer, Auryn turned on some music, sliding on his headphones and cranking up the volume as he skimmed mindlessly through cyberspace on a tangent only achievable by someone trying to avoid reality.

He opened a playlist he had for times like these, its contents made up exclusively of songs that spoke to his soul and kept him grounded in a world that seemed to desire nothing more than to tear him down. It may have been labelled 'A+ Favourites,' but in his mind, he knew what it should be called: 'Music for the Clinically Depressed'. Outside the four walls of his apartment lay a city of over four million people, yet there he sat, shrouded in a feeling of complete disconnection from humanity as a whole.

As driving guitar riffs rang in his ears, he leant back in his chair, an unwelcome memory surfacing of a day back when he was twenty-one and attending university in Sydney. His high school teachers had told him he needed to do something with his intellect, pushing him into an applied science course against his better judgement. That's not to say he disliked science, but no part of him longed to be a scientist. His heart wanted to play music, to write screenplays, to pen novels. His heart cried out for art in place of science.

Auryn's time at university had been a difficult one. He hadn't been good at making friends with the kind of vapid people he found himself amongst, and the course load was relentless and unrewarding. In the rare moments of freedom he was afforded, he dreamt of creative writing, but the combination of work and study stripped him of the time and mental energy required to pursue it. Left with no outlet for his emotions, he found himself consumed by them.

One day, between lectures, the loneliness and pain had reached an unbearable level. Whilst walking through campus to his next class, he'd suddenly stopped on a staircase, physically unable to go any further, his depression threatening to overwhelm him completely. He hadn't been suicidal, though; instead, he'd found himself filled with a boundless rage born of constant rejection and eroded self-worth. Its power exceeded anything he'd experienced before, and it coursed through him, lingering just beneath his skin.

Harsh vocals growled in Auryn's ears, and distorted chords crashed over him like waves as he closed his eyes tightly, reliving the moment as though it were yesterday. The power that had swelled inside him on that staircase had begged for release. In that moment, he'd felt like he had the power of an atom bomb harnessed within his very being. It wasn't real, of course, but even now, he could feel it surging through his veins: a power so terrible that if he unleashed it, it would kill everyone around him. An entire city annihilated, all because of the pain of one man.

Alexandria, Egypt, 139 CE

It was another hot, dry day on the plains in the south of the great African continent, and the air hung still around Madkodi as she crouched down. Hearing a lark call, she glanced across, noting the position of the other warriors in front of her and slowly moving towards them through the sparse brush and long grass that dotted the landscape. Her tribe, the Naolo, had been enduring raids on their camp by the Tsia for weeks now, and the time had finally come to fight back.

Wodasa, the leader of the hunting party, mimicked the whistle of a lark once again, and Madkodi crept over to him, shuffling in alongside her tribesmen. There were four of them in the party, including herself, all armed with sharp, bone-tipped spears and wearing short, woven grass skirts, their rich, dark skin glistening with sweat as they huddled in close. Wodasa motioned for her to stay and guard the rear before gesturing to the others, the three men moving off silently, spreading out as they went. She bristled at being left behind, but there was nothing for it. They had accepted her as a warrior, but that didn't mean they trusted her in combat.

Madkodi had always felt like a stranger in her tribe, uncertain of her place within it. Born a female, she had been expected to fulfil her role alongside the other women, but growing up, she had preferred play-fighting and catching lizards with the boys over weaving and cooking with the girls. On top of that, as she'd matured, Madkodi had found she lacked any interest in sexual or romantic relationships of any kind and refused each offer of union laid before her.

The path she was expected to follow was one she did not wish to walk, and eventually, her resistance had caused issues with the tribal elders. Desperate to keep herself from being forcibly married off, she'd pleaded with them to allow her to become a warrior: something women were expressly forbidden to do in the Naolo tribe. After much discussion, they had acquiesced, although their allowance was not without condition. In return, she was required to renounce her place amongst the women of the tribe whilst also holding no place amongst the men. She would become a permanent outsider, allowed to stay only if she contributed by hunting and defending the tribe from attacks. Should she fail to provide for her people, she would face exile.

Despite the harshness of their demands, the decision had been an easy one for Madkodi. Freed from the constraints of her gender, she had shed the feeling of abnormality that had haunted her youth. She was a warrior, a hunter, a provider, and unweighted by expectations she had no urge to fulfil, she became more than the sum of her parts.

In the months since her transition within the tribe, she'd proven her prowess, helping take down gemsbok and pulling her weight in transporting them back to camp. Her tribesmen may still have been wary of her, but her actions had gained her some modicum of respect, and that respect had bought her a place in today's hunt: a hunt not for food but for revenge.

From a distance, she appeared almost identical to her companions. Her head was completely shaved, with little more than a thin shadow of hair covering her scalp, and her broad features and slender physique varied very little from her male counterparts save for the curve of her hips and fullness of her chest.

Her weapon, on the other hand, was unique. Her spear had small grooves running down the shaft to improve her grip, and both ends were bone-tipped and honed to sharp points that she took great pride in maintaining. Looking down at it, she smiled softly. The other warriors used the blunt end of their spears as walking sticks when returning from a hunt and thought her modifications foolish, but Madkodi paid them no heed. She had always enjoyed walking, and besides, the edge the dual tips gave her in battle more than made up for the minor inconvenience of being tired after a long day.

Surveying the area, she caught sight of the enemy they sought. Barely fifty paces away, two Tsia tribesmen with stripes of deep yellow ochre painted on their skin stood bent over the carcass of a freshly caught young zebra. Their weapons lay beside them in the dirt as they lashed the beast to a long, sturdy branch for transportation. Suddenly, a guttural cry rang out, and Madkodi's tribesmen leapt up from their hiding places with spears in hand, charging forward and cutting down their foe before they could arm themselves.

As her companions finished off their grisly business, Madkodi saw something out of the corner of her eye. Peering through the long grass to her right, she spied another Tsia warrior twenty paces away creeping towards her tribesmen, and she shifted to face him. Her movement betrayed her, and the warrior turned tail to run, but Madkodi was faster, her long strides closing the gap in a matter of seconds.

Stopping short, the warrior turned to meet his inescapable fate, thrusting his spear at her with a shout. Madkodi parried it away, but he adjusted quickly, leveraging his weight and forcing the point of her spear into the ground.

Without a second of hesitation, she spun on her back foot, yanking her spear around her in a wide arc and impaling the man in the throat with its hind tip. He held her gaze in a frozen moment of disbelief, his weapon dropping to the ground with a clatter, a trickle of crimson cutting through the ochre on his chest. Twisting the shaft, Madkodi pulled the spear out, blood spurting from the wound as the man crumpled to the dirt, a desperate gurgle escaping him before he fell still.

A rustling came from behind her, and Madkodi whipped around with racing heart to find Wodasa standing there, his face stern. Beside him, her other two tribesmen shouldered the young zebra between them, the weapons of their fallen foe grasped in their free hands. Nodding in acknowledgment, he motioned for her to follow him. It was time to head back and report their victory.

∞∞∞∞

Dusk was falling as the tribe gathered around the central fire of the camp, each member eager to hear the recount of events. Madkodi knelt in deferent silence alongside her fellow warriors while Wodasa described their successful expedition to the three elders: Jakaba, Lefa, and Banele. It wasn't the way of the Naolo to praise individuals, so he simply relayed the fate of the Tsia men with neutral frankness.

With the report complete, Jakaba, the most revered of the elders and the only one to oppose her transition to warrior, glanced over, his eyes boring into her.

"Did Madkodi perform its duty?" he asked Wodasa.

His choice of the word 'it' stung her pride a little, but in truth, it was more a limitation of language than anything else; the Naolo had no word for people like Madkodi. She'd forsaken her place amongst both the women and the men, and as such, Jakaba had stripped her of their titles. Of course, she wasn't entirely sure what her preference would be even if given the option, and so, for the moment at least, her self-identity remained female.

"It chased down a fleeing warrior and killed him."

There were mutters from the crowd, but Madkodi tried to ignore them.

"That is good. All must contribute for the tribe to survive," said Jakaba, his eyes shifting to look more kindly over the tribe. "Let us hope that this show of force is enough to deter the Tsia from encroaching on our territory again."

Raising his hands, Jakaba gestured that those gathered were free to leave before turning to his fellow elders in private discussion. The crowd began to disperse, and Madkodi watched as Wodasa and the other warriors were beckoned over to the fireside and congratulated on their victory, laughter filling the air around them. No one approached her, though, and she stood up, dusting the dirt from her knees with a sigh. She may not have been exiled from the tribe, but shunned to its peripherals, she often struggled to see much difference.

"So, you're a warrior now, huh?" a voice asked from the shadows.

Spinning around, Madkodi found the shaman, Mlamulla, standing behind her with a wide smile, his lips peeled back to reveal his three remaining spaced-out teeth. He was a strange old man, his face like leather from decades of exposure, his clothing nothing more than a tattered zebra hide secured around his waist with a cord of dried grass.

Mlamulla drove the tribe crazy. He was a constant burden and would wander off for days at a time, forcing men to be sent out in search of him. Madkodi, like most of the Naolo, had always wondered why the elders put up with him at all, but there were rumours he had the ability to find water when no one else could, to see portents of the future, and to detect deceit in others.

When Madkodi had approached the elders to become a warrior, she'd first had to enter the shaman's tent and undergo a ritual to determine her worthiness. Although she had no idea what his obscure hocus pocus had proven, she had apparently passed with flying colours, and Mlamulla had enthusiastically recommended she be given their permission and their blessing. As much as she appreciated his help, though, she had little patience for his eccentricities.

"I hear you killed a fearsome warrior with that nifty spear of yours," he chortled to himself, the joke apparent only to him.

"Yes," Madkodi replied, forcing a polite smile. "An enemy tried to flee, but I was able to hunt him down."

"Did you enjoy it?" Mlamulla asked, gazing deep into her eyes as if searching for something.

"No. I did it because I had to. I did it to protect the tribe."

"Good. The enjoyment of violence leads a warrior down a dark path," he responded, nodding slowly before slapping her on the shoulder. "Rest now, young one. I have a feeling the fight has only just begun."

And with that, he walked away, disappearing back into the shadows.

∞∞∞∞

The attack came four nights later, when the moon was hidden from view. Madkodi was woken by the sound of footsteps, her eyes opening just as the tip of a spear started its descent towards her head. On instinct, she rolled out of the way, feeling for her own spear in the dark. Looking back up at her attacker, she noticed the signature yellow paint of the Tsia marking his face, the weapon she sought already held lightly in his free hand. As he lifted his spear to thrust it at her again, she raised her foot, kicking him square in the crotch and diving past him out of the tent as he crumpled to the ground.

Emerging into fervent and unmitigated chaos, she scrambled to her feet, ripping a nearby intruder off one of the children, cracking his wrist against her leg to disarm him before knocking him out with a blow to the forehead. As the child scurried away, Madkodi glanced around quickly at the devastation. There was fighting all around, but it was more a massacre than a battle. Her fellow tribesmen were being cut down on all sides, children lay on the ground in pools of blood, and women were being dragged kicking and screaming into the darkness.

Taking a short moment to refocus, she heard an enemy behind her and whirled around as a short blade sliced at her abdomen. She jumped back nimbly, but quick as lightning, the warrior thrust it at her heart, her reflexes the only thing saving her as she twisted to her right and grabbed his wrist with both hands.

With more Tsia warriors closing in to attack her, she used her weight to wrench the man to the ground, ducking under the first strike from behind and hitting her next assailant in the face with an elbow. A third man charged at her, but she thrust her heel into his knee and sent him toppling before she took off running.

Desperately, Madkodi tried to put some distance between herself and the enemy, but something caught her foot in the dark, and she tumbled to the ground, her pursuers closing the gap as she clambered to her feet. The leading warrior approached at full speed, spear in hand, and she waited until the last second to leap aside, the man losing his balance from the continued momentum and stumbling. As he turned to come back around, Madkodi kicked him full force in the side, dispatching him into the dirt as more Tsia reached her.

Finding herself surrounded, a sense of defeat and failure washed over her, and Madkodi closed her eyes, her frustration and anger building at the indignity of her imminent death. As the emotions swelled in her chest, they morphed into a pure rage that boiled beneath her skin, threatening to overwhelm her. Her foes lunged forward as one, and she threw her head back, letting out an almighty war cry. She wanted to show them that she too was a warrior, not some easily slaughtered prey, but what her cry unleashed defied explanation.

Out of nowhere, a whirlwind sprang up around Madkodi, dirt whipping at her attackers and forcing them back as its intensity grew, their determination quickly replaced by fear. At the centre of the maelstrom, Madkodi stood in sheer ecstasy, her newfound power coursing through her veins and pouring out around her unencumbered. She cried out again, this time in jubilation, and she watched with satisfaction as the Tsia warriors retreated into the night.

Reluctantly, she drew the power back inside her, the wind dying down in an instant, the dust settling once more. Madkodi fell to her knees in exhaustion, her breathing ragged but her mind triumphant as she basked in her unexpected victory.

Her reverie was short-lived, though, and she was torn back to the present by a rock striking her cheek. Glancing up, she found Wodasa standing before her, another rock already in hand.

"Demon," he hissed at her with contempt.

She moved to stand up, but more rocks flew at her from every direction, forcing her to shrink into a tight ball as the remaining members of the tribe joined in the assault, pelting her with whatever they could find.

Part of her wanted to lash out, to release the power still churning inside her, but they were her own people, the only family she had. The barrage continued as she shielded her head with her arms, and she gritted her teeth with a heady mix of shame and resentment. Finally, she heard a sound and peeked up to find Mlamulla in front of her, his arms outstretched.

"Stop! Stop!" he shouted. "Madkodi is no demon! She acted only to protect us all!"

Wodasa raised his hand, signalling for a cease to the onslaught.

"Where are the elders? I must speak with them," Mlamulla demanded.

"They have all fallen," replied Wodasa, his face hard and vengeful.

Mlamulla nodded solemnly. "Then you must lead us, Wodasa. The Naolo are yours now."

Wodasa glanced around, uncertain, but the other warriors all nodded their assent, and, turning back to Mlamulla, he inclined his head. "As you wish. Do you have any advice for us, shaman? Why did you not foresee this attack?"

Wodasa's tone was accusatory, but Mlamulla brushed it aside with a flick of his hand. "I cannot see what will be, only what might be, but two things are certain. In order to survive, the Naolo must leave this place and find new lands. The Tsia will not stop this war, and we are not strong enough to defeat them."

Wodasa considered this, then pointed at Madkodi, who remained crouched as she watched. "And what of *it?* It used demon magic. It must be destroyed before it kills us all."

Mlamulla looked over his shoulder at Madkodi before answering. "That is the second thing I know for certain. Madkodi is no demon. The spirits of our ancestors came to us in our time of greatest need.

They used her as a vessel with which to protect the tribe and win the battle." He paused for a moment as whispers began to titter amongst the gathering. "She has been tainted by the spirits' magic, though. She must remain here, and I with her. I must help cleanse her soul before I can rejoin you."

Wodasa nodded before addressing the chattering group around him. "Gather only what you can carry. We must put distance between us and the Tsia before daybreak."

As the other warriors led the tribe back to the camp, Wodasa walked over to Mlamulla, placing a heavy hand on his shoulder. "Thank you for helping us once again, shaman. As chief of the Naolo, I ask that you honour our elders and grant them a proper burial."

"It would be my privilege," replied Mlamulla. "I will see to it that they find their way to the next life."

Wodasa bowed his head, then made haste to join his people.

Left alone, Mlamulla turned to Madkodi as she rose to her feet, drops of blood trickling from the places hardest hit.

"You, come with me," he said, heading away from the camp.

Before she followed the shaman, Madkodi took one last look back at her tribe. As she watched, the shapes of those she knew moved in the dim light of dying fires, some gathering supplies while others knelt beside their slain kin to bid a final farewell.

Mlamulla had always insisted the camp interfered with his ability to communicate with the spirits, and thus he chose to set his tent some distance away. Despite his claims, however, Madkodi suspected that the strange man simply preferred his privacy. Ducking in through the flap, she was met by the lingering smell of smoke and the commingled scents of medicinal herbs emanating from the earthenware jars scattered around. In the centre of the space lay a lion pelt, worn from years of use, and atop it stood Mlamulla, who handed her a small scrap of impala hide doused in an oil pungent with the aroma of ginger, motioning for her to dab it on her cuts.

"Thank you," she said as she blotted at a seeping wound on her forearm. "If you hadn't stopped them, they would've killed me."

Mlumulla shrugged. "Seems like I should be the one thanking you. You saved what is left of our tribe from destruction, myself included."

"The spirits saved us, like you said."

"Don't believe that nonsense," Mlamulla snorted. "That was just to stop them attacking you. Nothing scares them into submission more than the wrath of their ancestors."

"What are you saying? I don't understand," Madkodi said, surprised by his sudden change of tone.

He glanced past her and out the gap in the tent flap, ignoring her completely until he snapped back to attention and met her eye again. "I would've thought it was obvious. Stay here," he said before disappearing outside.

Madkodi looked around, more confused than ever. As she stood there, wiping the blood from her cheek with the scrap of hide, her emotions caught up with her: the fear of battle, the exhilaration of unleashed power, the shame of rejection. She crumpled to her knees as the weight of it fell heavy on her shoulders, her chest constricting, her breath coming quick and fast, her eyes welling with tears.

It felt like an eternity before Mlamulla poked his head back in the tent and tore her from her thoughts. "Come on, they've all gone," he said, waving her after him.

He led her back to the camp, the crescent moon escaping its confinement behind the clouds and lighting the way. All that remained in the aftermath were broken belongings, abandoned embers, and fallen fellows. Every tent had been dismantled and removed save for her own, which sat askew in its segregated place at the very edge of the encampment. Running over to it, she pushed back the flap to find her spear laying in the spot she had been soundly sleeping only a short time ago. Hefting it in her hand, it brought her a strange sense of comfort, as though all was not lost. It was an extension of her being, and its presence calmed her.

When she returned to Mlamulla, she found him standing over the blood-stained body of Jakaba, his bare chest pierced with countless stab wounds, his eyes ajar and lifeless. Regarding her former elder, Madkodi couldn't help but think he looked much smaller in death, and something about his vulnerability stirred pity in her.

"Stupid old fool," said Mlamulla, poking the body with his foot. "I told you your stubbornness would be the death of you. But would you listen? No. And now look, here you are, half of your tribe slaughtered, and more holes in you than a cheetah has spots."

Madkodi stared across at the shaman in disbelief. This man, who had been so deferential to the elders in life, now stood taunting Jakaba in death. It was as though his former persona was nothing more than a false shroud he'd slid out of, like a snake shedding its skin.

"Don't look at me like that," he said, glancing at her. "If he'd had his way, you would be bearing your fourth child by now. He didn't deserve your respect when he opposed your desire to become a warrior, and he certainly doesn't deserve it now."

A thousand questions raced through her head, but only one sat on the surface, refusing to be ignored. "If the spirits didn't come to our aid, does that mean I can rejoin the tribe?" she asked, her voice hopeful.

Mlamulla shrugged. "You can rejoin them anytime you want. They'll never trust you, of course, but feel free to waste the rest of your life in pursuit of their acceptance if that's what you desire."

"You lied to Wodasa when you said you would find them, didn't you?" Madkodi asked as things slowly began to make sense to her.

His lips curled into an almost imperceptible smile. "Very good. This tribe was only ever a marriage of convenience. As long as they protected me, I was happy to stay, but that is no longer necessary." He let the words linger before continuing. "We are both tired, but there is still much to do. We must leave. Now."

Madkodi looked around at the bodies of her tribesmen. "But what about the dead?"

"What about them? Leave them to the jackals and hyenas. Humans are not exempt from the cycle of life."

She couldn't believe what she was hearing, his lack of empathy jarring. "But you said-"

He cut her off with a wave of his hand. "I said what I needed to in order for them to move on. The tribe is not our future, it is our past, and we need to leave them and this place behind. There are things I must show you, and I can only do that somewhere we will not be disturbed."

Without another word, Mlamulla turned on his heel and walked briskly away, leaving Madkodi alone with her unsatisfied curiosity, her mind reeling from the change in the shaman. In the stillness of the night, she could hear the chirp of insects, the rustle of grass, and the sough of the wind. He was right; there was nothing left for her here.

Following in his stead, she found him waiting outside his tent, a small pouch slung over his shoulder.

"Come, we must walk," he said.

Mlamulla led them east, setting such a brisk pace that any attempt at conversation was impossible: an impressive feat for someone his age. Finally, just as the sun began peeking up over the horizon, they arrived at a giant baobab tree and stopped. In the distance, she could hear the flow of a river and the calls of waterbirds waking up to a new day.

"Rest now," Mlamulla advised, placing his pouch down and taking a seat against the tree trunk. "I will explain all when you wake."

Madkodi yearned for answers, but exhaustion muted her questions and beckoned her to the ground, sleep embracing her almost instantly.

∞∞∞∞

The sun was already on its descent by the time she finally stirred, her mouth parched. Mlamulla smiled at her from beside the small fire he was tending and held out a clay bowl of water. Taking it from him eagerly, she drained its contents in a matter of seconds.

It wasn't until she put the bowl down in front of her that the shaman spoke. "The river is a short walk from here," he said, gesturing over his shoulder, behind the baobab. "Fetch some more water and bring it back."

Madkodi opened her mouth to speak but promptly closed it again, standing up and taking the bowl and her spear with her. She knew the answers she sought would only come when the shaman was good and ready.

The afternoon was hot and sweat beaded on her forehead as she reached the banks of the river, kneeling amongst the lush green reeds. Aside from a few lanky ibis wading in the shallows, Madkodi found herself alone, the day still too warm for predators to begin their hunt.

Resting her spear on the ground, she dipped her cupped hands into the cool, flowing water and splashed her face, the sweat washing into the cut on her cheek and leaving it stinging. She looked down at her arms and sighed, the welts and scabs her only keepsake of a tribe that had left her behind without a second thought. Dejected, she filled the bowl and grabbed her spear, turning from the river and marching back towards the baobab and the wisp of smoke that marked her only companion's position.

Mlamulla snatched the bowl from her hands impatiently, stray droplets hissing as they splashed the glowing coals. Without a word, he opened his pouch, taking out a small jar and pouring its powdered, grey-brown contents into the bowl before placing it into the heart of the fire. He stirred the concoction diligently with a carved bone spoon until the water began to bubble at the edges, the steam laced with a strange, acrid odour. Madkodi sat cross-legged opposite him, each revolution of the spoon seeming to take a lifetime to her racing mind.

"You seek answers about what happened last night." he finally said, glancing up at her as he scooped a measure of the liquid and passed her the spoon. "Drink. Through this, everything will become clear."

She eyed it suspiciously, the smell worsening as she brought it to her lips. Before her mind could convince her otherwise, though, she swallowed it, recoiling as an intense woody bitterness flooded her palate and sent her tongue tingling.

"Your story will become clear soon, young one, but before it does, let me tell you mine. My earliest memory is one of building a stone temple in a faraway land, in the time of our ancestors. Since then, my soul has lived in countless bodies. I have seen things that would baffle and amaze the small-minded Naolo, and I have done things they could never dream of. I hoped against all odds that I would one day find another like me." He leant forward. "And last night, that time came."

Madkodi stared at him dumbfounded, her head starting to spin, his face going in and out of focus. "What are you talking about, shaman?" she asked, her words slurred and distant.

"It is time for you to go on a journey," he said, gesturing south. "Walk until you find the darkness. Only then will you uncover your truth."

His words made little sense to her; he was speaking in riddles. Still, she rose to her feet, swaying as her balance faltered and bolstering herself with hands on knees until the spots cleared from her vision. Taking one last look at Mlamulla, she followed his unwavering finger and stumbled off.

The sun neared the horizon to her right as she picked her way along between tufts of hardy grass, eventually glancing back to find the baobab little more than a speck in the distance, Mlamulla nowhere to be seen. Her brain swirled, her thoughts becoming indistinct and sporadic as flashes started to appear before her: forests so green they seemed otherworldly, strange creatures bounding across endless red deserts, and mountains so tall they defied reality. More and more images came to her, surprising her not with their existence but rather how familiar they felt. She moved through these landscapes as though they existed all around, immersive, albeit only to her.

As the sun slipped out of view, painting the sky with the day's final fanfare, the wonders she basked in began to dissipate. It wasn't until the last vestiges of warm orange gave way to duskening skies, though, that she began to perceive something following her. It was far away, hiding in the shadows, but Madkodi could sense it.

With alarm, she remembered she'd left her spear behind, her heart racing as she debated whether to run or fight. After a steadying breath, the warrior in her quashed the internal conflict. She had never been one to shirk a battle, and she wasn't about to start now. Allowing that part of her to take over, she found a good patch of solid earth, clear of any obstacles, and waited.

By the time her stalker finally emerged, the night wore a veil of shadows, and Madkodi could only just make out a figure approaching her by the faint light of the stars. She stood frozen, her fists and jaw clenched, her muscles wound tight like coiled springs. Its footsteps, slow and methodical, could be heard as they fell heavy on the dirt. With a gust of wind, the waxing moon popped out from behind its mask of clouds, and she beheld her foe's true form. It appeared as a spider but impossibly large: human-sized. As it drew closer, she noticed it had human features as well. Before she could register anything else, it attacked, spiders' legs slicing towards her like blades, hands reaching forth as she ducked and weaved out of harm's way. She twisted from its grasp, trying desperately to escape, but she felt something icy take hold of her right wrist, her entire body going numb.

Unwittingly, she screamed, releasing her pain and fear in a burst of strength, the wind swirling around her and creating a vortex that forced the creature of darkness backwards. She knew her opponent was too powerful, but she attacked anyway, thrusting her hands out and unleashing a devastating torrent of dark energy towards the creature.

Stepping to the side, it evaded her assault with ease and then retaliated, its own energy burning her skin as she desperately tried to shield herself. It dove forward, its blades slashing to the left and right of her, and she stumbled backwards, falling to the ground. As it leapt at her to deliver the final strike, she reached deep within her soul, closing her eyes and releasing all she had left.

When she opened her eyes again, Madkodi found herself alone, the Spider returned to the darkness from whence it came. She knew it would return, but as she scrambled to her feet and whirled around, she could neither see nor sense it. Suddenly, something different emerged from the shadows: a figure with wings of jet black, ethereal and resonating with power. As it stopped in front of her, an innate knowledge surfaced. The being was not a new threat; it was a reflection of her own soul.

Catching sight of something in her peripherals, she glanced over her shoulder to find the very same wings flowing from her own back. In an instant, she knew how to escape. She built up her power, holding it tightly beneath her skin, before releasing it downwards, her stomach lurching as her feet slowly lifted off the ground. Taking a deep breath, she launched herself into the air, feeling the wind rush past her, the sense of euphoria clouding her vision with tears of joy.

As she blinked them away, she was met with a view of the plains stretching out beneath her. Holding out her hands, her ascent slowed until she hovered in the air, allowing her a moment to catch her breath before the downward pressure on her body began to take its toll, her muscles aching as she realised she could not stay in the sky indefinitely. She began to glide downwards, scanning the land below for any sign of the Spider, and, finding none, she searched for a place to land. A large body of water to the south caught her attention, so vast that she could see no end to it, and she aimed for the coast, pulling up as she reached a spit of land stretching out from the foot of a cliff.

Her landing was rough and graceless, and she lost her footing as she hit the earth, tumbling head over heels until she came to rest flat on her back. As she slowly found her feet, rubbing her throbbing spine, she felt the hairs on the nape of her neck prickle. Rolling her head back to try and shake the feeling, she spotted the Spider streaking through the air, poised to strike.

Madkodi jumped out of the way without a second to spare, her opponent landing nimbly before lunging to attack. She grabbed his wrists, feeling the ice that ran through his veins as she desperately tried to fend him off. Pressure built up around them both until there was an explosion of energy, and she was thrown backwards, slamming into the rocky shore and tumbling away, the breath shooting out of her lungs.

As she gasped for air, rough hands gripped her shoulders and pulled her up slightly. The Spider stared at her with dead eyes before his blades sprang forth, sinking into her side, her entire body going cold as she lost consciousness.

∞∞∞∞

Madkodi awoke with the dawn, the sound of gull calls overhead stirring her. The icy feeling in her chest remained, but the sun's gentle rays soothed her as she sat up gingerly, her head aching. Looking around, the spit of land she had set herself down on the previous night came into focus.

She sat atop a mound of sand blanketed with soft, low-lying shrubs sprouting vibrant magenta flowers, steep cliffs towering behind her. The shore was edged with stones over which the waves crashed, leaving their caps of seafoam to dissolve softly in the crevices. The morning sun glinted off the deep blue expanse before her, meeting the far horizon and disappearing beyond. She stared at the sight in wonder, mesmerised by the constant ebb and flow. It was more water than she'd seen in her entire life.

Snapping back to reality as a gull dove in and re-emerged with a fish in its beak, the evening's nightmare returned to her. Mlamulla must have given her the draught of waking dreams: a concoction he usually reserved only for the elders or great warriors. She'd heard tales of its ability to send its recipient into a trancelike state in which visions would surface and certain truths would become apparent.

Madkodi shook her head to try and clear the internal fog as she stood up. If they were simply visions, though, how had she come to be in this strange place? Stumbling over to the water's edge, she knelt down, splashing her face, the chill of it awakening her senses in an instant. As it dripped down her cheeks, she licked it from her lips, then spat it out. Why was it so salty? Yet another mystery she had no answer to.

Closing her eyes, she tried to reconcile the images swirling in her mind: the visions, the dreams, the reality she found herself in now. Without thought, she clenched her left hand, feeling something beneath her skin itching to be released. She tensed her muscles as it coursed through her body, the air pressure rising around her before she unleashed it. She felt the pressure drop again as the energy raced outwards, a booming sound echoing along the cliffs, water spraying out in all directions.

When Madkodi opened her eyes again, she looked over her shoulder and blinked in disbelief. Ethereal black wings stretched behind her, their substance equal parts shadow and dark lightning. All at once, the pieces fell into place, and it felt as though a veil in her mind lifted. The visions may have been intangible fragments, but they had served to deliver an innate awareness she'd been lacking up until then. As she let the knowledge unfurl, she found the answers she had been seeking.

Just like Mlamulla, Madkodi had lived before, in other lands and other times. Those lives had allowed her to gain ever-growing power over each iteration, an energy she could use to protect herself and soar through the air. That was how she'd come to be on that spit of land; she'd flown. If that part of the vision was real, though, did that mean her enemy was real as well? Deep down, she knew he was.

Ever since she was a child, Madkodi had been tormented by nightmares of a shadow that hunted her, intent on her death, and last night, that shadow had shown its face. She knew now that he was not a figment of her imagination or a subconscious personification of her own fears. He was a memory of what had been and a harbinger of what would be.

Part of her wanted to just fly away, to see how far the expanse of water that lay before her stretched, to escape from her otherworldly foe. After all, if her nightmares had proven to be true, then surely her dreams of fantastical lands and magnificent beasts were too. Why shouldn't she explore the world? Why shouldn't she seek out her dreamscapes?

She knew in her heart that she couldn't, though, not while the Spider lurked in the shadows. She was a warrior; she had a duty to confront her fears and the threats they posed. Besides, she was certain Mlamulla had known the truth destined to be revealed to her. He had sent her on this journey on purpose, and she was keen to find out why.

Madkodi focused inwardly, trying to remember what she'd done in the midst of the vision. The air crackled around her as she felt her power spring to life in her chest again, and she started to slowly rise upwards. She pushed down with all her might and shot into the air. As her stomach lurched, she banked sideways, swooping down, and sailing arm's length above the surface of the water. Beneath the waves, she spied a strange creature, mammoth and majestic, gliding through the water with as much ease as she flew above.

She continued, revelling in the sensation, before she angled herself vertically and rocketed high into the sky, twisting back towards land. The air was thinner there, and only delicate wisps of cloud surrounded her. Aside from knowing she'd come from somewhere vaguely north, she had little idea of how to return to Mlamulla, and as such, she flew on instinct, travelling until the sun was directly overhead, the heat battering her body despite the cooling wind.

Finally, as exhaustion was about to force her back to earth, she spotted a small trail of smoke floating up from a fire below a giant baobab, a lone figure sitting patiently beside it.

Descending slowly, she looped around to lose speed until she landed softly in front of the shaman.

"So, you have found yourself and returned," he said with a satisfied smile.

Madkodi took a moment to catch her breath before replying. "You knew all along, didn't you?"

"I had my suspicions. To see such power in the flesh, though ..." He stopped, staring at her for a moment before regaining his composure and standing up. "I always suspected there might be others like myself."

"So, you sought me out?"

"Sought you out? No." Mlamulla laughed, putting his hand on her shoulder. "I think perhaps pure luck has brought us together."

"Your powers as a shaman, are they like my power?"

"Most of my 'powers', as you know them, are fake, merely products of the knowledge I've acquired over the course of my many lives. I can find water because, if you know how, it is easy to find. I appear to be able to see the future because, for the most part, the happenings of humans vary little and repeat often. And I can sense deceit in others because I've learned to listen to people's actions rather than their words." He paused. "There is one true power I hold, though, one that courses through me, that feeds from my soul: a silent sense that can detect the enemy who stalks us, even across vast expanses."

Madkodi felt a cold pang of dread pierce her stomach as she realised who he was talking about. "The Spider."

"You saw him in your vision, didn't you?"

"I did," she replied, grimacing at the memory. "He hunted me down and killed me."

Mlamulla sighed softly to himself, his face pensive. "That is the fate of us all, I'm afraid. It always has been. He tracks down those who dare to return, punishing them for having the audacity to cherish life and share this gift."

In that moment, Madkodi's mood grew dark but determined. She knew exactly what she had to do.

"Do you know where he is now?"

Mlamulla nodded hesitantly. "I do, but you should not confront him. He is too powerful. You would be best-served hiding, the way I have throughout my own lives."

"No disrespect to you, shaman, but I am a warrior. I cannot run from this fight. I must meet it head-on. Where is he?"

Mlamulla knelt beside the fire and drew a series of strange symbols in the dirt. "I, too, had a vision last night, and in it, the Spider's location was revealed. AL-EX-AN-DRI-A," he said, drawing a line under the word as he pronounced it.

"Alexandria? Is that the name of his tribe?" she asked, leaning in to inspect the symbols despite them appearing meaningless to her.

"No. It is not a tribe; it is a city. Like a camp, but with far more people. They do not move like our tribes either. They live in solid houses that rise from the sand. It is within that flock of humanity that our enemy hides. The city lies far to the north, where this land melds into another, where a great river meets a vast sea, and where a fire high above lights the way in the darkness. To walk there would be perilous and would take many moons, but for someone with your abilities ..." He left the last part unsaid.

Madkodi straightened up and paced back and forth without speaking, questioning the wisdom of what she was about to do. Her uncertainty was fleeting, though; she knew it was the only way. The real question was whether she should rest and regain her strength or leave immediately, and even that was answered quickly. There was no point wasting any more time.

"Is there anything else you can tell me, any other wisdom you can offer?" she asked as she picked up her spear and turned to face him.

"Only that when you find him, you must not hold anything back. It will take everything you have to evade defeat, and the odds lie with him."

"How will I find him once I get there?"

Mlamulla gave her an encouraging smile. "You're a hunter, are you not? I'm sure you'll figure it out for yourself." After a pause, his smile became grim, and he shifted uncomfortably. "Failing that, if you linger long enough, he is sure to find you."

"That won't happen," she replied resolutely. "Farewell, shaman. I hope to see you again, to regale you with my victory."

The wind swirled, embers from the fire dancing around them both, and Madkodi slowly rose into the air. She hovered there, her eyes holding Mlamulla's gaze for a moment before she shot skyward, ascending until the shaman and the baobab were nothing more than a speck.

∞∞∞∞∞∞∞

When Raemka arrived back in Alexandria, he didn't receive quite the homecoming he'd expected. The Roman soldiers guarding the gates all knew him by sight, if not by name, and would usually greet him with a grin as he passed through. Of course, that was due mainly to the fact he often brought back gifts for them: barrels of red wine from their homeland and trinkets from distant places. That night, though, Raemka found unfamiliar faces staring at him with distrust as he approached, and he glanced back at his cart. It was empty, for the most part, but a few barrels of red wine from Umbria were there for the taking, or the bribing.

It was a shame his welcome was lacklustre because the trip itself had been a raging success. He'd travelled across the Roman Empire and beyond, selling his wares, buying more, and selling those as well. Every task on his agenda was tended to, and he'd felt a deep sense of satisfaction as he'd come down the road, finally returning home.

His donkey, Grey, snorted as the smell of leather and oil reached his nostrils. Grey was, well, grey, dumb as a stump, and slow to boot. The reason Raemka kept him was entirely based on his dependability and his calmness in the face of chaos. Two armies could be battling by the side of the road, and Grey would just keep plodding on, only changing course to move around the bodies. A most nonchalant beast.

As they reached the gate, two soldiers held out their pilum, commanding him to stop, the torchlight glinting off the metal tips of the towering spears.

Raemka looked at them with an amicable smile. "What is the issue tonight, my friends?"

A third soldier stepped forward armed only with a gladius, the sword of choice across the Empire, his ornate helmet denoting his higher rank.

"Are you a resident of Alexandria?"

"I am indeed. My name is Raemka. I have a house close to the market."

The soldier eyed him sternly. "How long have you been away?"

Raemka shrugged. "Two years, give or take. I wasn't really keeping track, to be honest."

He was about to make a joke but caught himself as the soldier marched forward to search the cart, his face officious and unmoving.

"Where are your wares?" the soldier asked, peering into the half-empty cart.

"I don't generally import things to Alexandria," Raemka explained in the most patient voice he could muster, "I can't compete with the Roman merchants. Instead, I take local products and sell them abroad, returning home with a few keepsakes and hopefully some well-earned money."

"How much money?" the soldier asked, his interest piqued.

Raemka assessed the situation quickly. There was a hefty cache of gold and silver beneath the false bottom of the cart, hidden only by the barrels of wine, some hay, and a few flimsy planks. If the guards decided to tear it apart, things would go south quickly.

He gave the soldier a mournful smile. "Well, when I say hopefully, I mean that this time it didn't work out so well for me. I had just enough money to buy some Umbrian red to drown my sorrows."

The soldier looked at him suspiciously before tilting one of the barrels on its side.

"Of course," Raemka added hastily, "I know how much the great Roman legions enjoy a taste of home, so I'm more than happy to donate a barrel. My gift to you."

Technically, the attempted bribery of a soldier was in and of itself a death sentence for a non-Roman citizen, but he was gambling on their love of wine to overcome their sense of duty.

Eyeing him for a moment, then looking at the wine, the soldier picked up the barrel with both hands and placed it on his shoulder, motioning for another soldier to come forward. "We're taking two!"

"Please, be my guest," said Raemka, waiting as the barrels were deposited out of sight before gesturing at the gate. "May I pass now? I'm aching to lie down in my own bed after such a long journey."

The soldier nodded, and Raemka yanked on Grey's reigns, driving him onward.

Trotting through and heading for home, Raemka already knew he wouldn't be getting any sleep just yet. Something was afoot in Alexandria, and he intended to find out what it was.

With Grey tucked away in his stall and feeding eagerly on some hay, Raemka made his way back across the rear courtyard of his meagre mudbrick house, past his own familiar front entrance, and down the street to a large house a few blocks from his own, knocking sharply on the door. It was the home of Khul, a fellow merchant whom he'd known for years. They weren't friends by any means; in fact, Raemka saw little benefit or point in expending time and energy on relationships of any form. Still, associates like Khul were useful, both for information and favours.

"Raemka! How are you, my old friend?" Khul bellowed with great mirth as he swung the door open, enveloping him in a hug and thrusting him inside.

Khul was a large man, almost perfectly round, with dark olive skin, shoulder-length black curls, rich brown eyes, and a thin wispy beard that flowed down his chin and was held in place by an ornate gold clip. His knee-length silk tunic was bright red with hammered gold triangles sewn around the hem and was cinched at the waist with a thick leather belt, and on his feet, he wore pristine leather sandals. From his neck hung a broad collar woven with blue and gold beads that matched his gold arm cuff and ring, both of which were inlaid with lapis lazuli.

He was a man who liked to wear his wealth, and he stood in stark contrast to Raemka, whose own black hair was hacked short while his face was framed by a neatly trimmed beard. Even his clothing was simple: a coarse, white linen tunic worth next to nothing and worn leather sandals that had seen better days. The pair were like chalk and cheese, and yet they had kept in good stead for nigh on two decades.

"When did you return?" Khul asked, slapping him joyfully on the shoulder.

Raemka smiled. "Just now. I had a rather unpleasant experience with the soldiers at the gate, though, so I thought I'd come over and see what's happened since I left."

"Wise decision," said Khul with a thoughtful nod. "Much has changed, and none of it good."

Raemka stepped inside, once again taking in the fine furniture, intricately decorated pottery, and fresco-painted whitewashed walls that filled Khul's opulent home. Most merchants lived in lesser dwellings, but Khul had done well for himself and was widely regarded as the city's most highly respected silk and spice trader.

He waved Raemka into the next room, guiding him over to two low, wooden chairs with lion's heads carved into the ends of the armrests. They were seamlessly crafted from contrasting timbers and set pride of place on either side of a matching table in the centre of the room. Raemka sat down, and almost instantly, a servant appeared bearing a platter overflowing with dates, grapes, and a few small cakes smelling sweetly of honey and orange blossom, which he set down on the table, along with two pewter goblets of red wine. Graciously, Raemka took a sip, nodding his thanks to Khul. In spite of what he'd told the soldiers at the gate, he didn't generally drink, preferring to keep his senses unimpeded. The only occasion he consumed wine was when being social and only to be polite.

Khul drained half of his drink in one go and sighed. "It started about a year ago. Rome installed a new prefect in the city, and his first action was to increase taxes on all native-born Egyptians." He snorted as he took another swig from his goblet. "You can imagine how that went down."

"Not well, I take it?"

"Not well at all," replied Khul, cramming a handful of grapes into his mouth and continuing to talk around them. "Wealthier merchants, such as myself, are able to absorb the costs, but it's driving the masses to the brink and causing civil unrest. The taxes have continued to rise, and there are murmurs of a revolt, but so far, no leaders have emerged. The Romans are aware of what's happening, and another legion arrived a month ago to stamp out any dissent. I'm sure you spotted their camp on your way to the gate."

Raemka swirled his wine pensively, ignoring his host's gesture to eat as he considered the ramifications of what he'd just been told. With the Roman legions looking for any excuse to crack down on the local populace, it would be much harder for him to conduct his own affairs. For a moment, he contemplated leaving, but he was too invested in Alexandria. It was central to much of the civilised world, afforded him all the benefits he needed, and provided a stable income while allowing him to travel widely to attend to his other ventures.

"We can talk more on this later, though," Khul said, breaking the silence. "Tell me, were your travels successful, and more importantly, did you bring home any good wine?"

"Despite what the gatekeepers now think, it was very successful," said Raemka with a chuckle, raising his goblet and pointing it at Khul. "As for wine, I do have a few barrels of Umbrian red that I could sell to you. At a discount, of course."

"Excellent!" Khul guffawed, slapping his knee. "That's the best news I've heard all week."

Finishing off his drink, Raemka placed the goblet back on the table and stood up. "I best be off. I'll make sure the wine is delivered tomorrow."

"Take care, my friend," said Khul, shaking his hand and leading him to the door. "The streets are far more dangerous than they once were."

∞∞∞∞

There was a disquieting mood in the streets of Alexandria as Raemka walked them the following day. They were still bustling and frantic, but there was an added tension in the air. He had seen it before, in other cities, but he never thought he'd see it in his hometown. Eyes flitted furtively, hands clutched at coin purses, and muscles tensed as people went about their daily business.

The agitation was worsened considerably by the increased presence of heavily armed Roman soldiers patrolling the streets and setting up roadblocks at random intersections to harass passers-by. It was only the Egyptians they victimised, though. Visitors and merchants from other lands could travel unhindered, and Roman citizens could do as they pleased, although that had always been the case. Everywhere Raemka turned, he saw his countrymen being persecuted, not that it bothered him that much. He viewed it simply with a sense of apathetic detachment: something to be wary of only because it may interfere with his own dealings.

Weaving between carts and pedestrians alike, he eventually came to a small square, planting himself inconspicuously in the shadows cast by the mid-morning sun and watching silently as the comings and goings continued around him. Raemka was adept at surveillance, he'd done it all over the world, but it felt strange in his own city, amongst his own people. Normally, Alexandria served as a safe haven for him to stop and recharge before departing on another adventure, but with things such as they were, he knew he couldn't leave now. He had to be sure there would be somewhere to come back to before he could do that.

The surrounding buildings were all uniformly beige, their walls a jumble of ageing mudbrick. The square itself was merely an unadorned patch of dirt, compacted into a solid mass by the steps of countless people. There was no greenery there, but that was the standard in most of the city. The only plants that clung to life were in the homes of the wealthy, close to the water's edge, or in the gardens of the Roman higher officers. He surveyed the people who wandered past him silently, their clothing ragged, their heads down. Moving from place to place, they struggled to find a way to survive in a city they called their home, but which was fast becoming inhospitable towards them.

Raemka heard them before they even reached the square: the clinking of armour, the whine of swords being unsheathed, the heavy, regimented footsteps. As he looked through the crowd, he found nine Roman soldiers marching in his direction, their weapons at the ready.

"What is your business here?" the leading soldier demanded.

Raemka was careful not to make any sudden moves. "Just people-watching. I was bored at home and decided to see how the city was faring. I returned from a long journey only yesterday."

The soldier motioned to the others, and they lowered their swords. "Let me tell you what's happening, Egyptian. Your people aren't paying their fair share and are plotting against the great Emperor Antoninus Pius. You would be well advised to go to your home, pay your taxes, and keep to yourself. If we catch you spying from the shadows again, we'll make an example of you. Understand?"

Raemka nodded deferentially. He did not feel threatened by the soldiers, but there was no advantage in forcing a confrontation now. Raising his hands and trying to look as unassuming as possible, he backed away until the soldiers turned on their heels and marched off. In that moment, one thing became clear; if the city continued on this path, he wouldn't be able to stay much longer.

∞∞∞∞

A week passed by uneventfully, despite the unrest in Alexandria continuing to simmer just beneath the surface. When Raemka opened his eyes that particular morning, though, he could sense that something had changed. It was only a feeling, but he had learned to trust those over the years.

He rose to his feet, shaking away the cobwebs of slumber from his mind as he pulled on his tunic, looping a leather belt around his waist and slipping on his sandals. Eager to find the source of the change, he made his way out into the early dawn to find a steady stream of people hurrying down the street, away from some unseen horror.

Intrigued, he headed in the opposite direction, swimming through the stampede as they shouldered past him, eventually finding himself in a side street amongst the dwellings of the poorest Egyptian citizens. The space usually brimmed with animated chatter and the hum of life, but it now stood eerily quiet. People turned onto the street or poked their heads out of doorways in curiosity, only to retreat in haste, and small huddles of people stood dotted around, talking in fearful, hushed whispers before scurrying away.

It only took a quick glance over their heads for Raemka to discover the reason for the commotion. In the centre of the street, a man hung from a makeshift crossbeam of worn wood, his lifeless form swinging slowly from side to side, his eyes bulging, his face a dark shade of purple. The clothes he wore were finely made but stained and scuffed as though he'd been roughhoused, and from his hip dangled an upturned leather purse.

Taking a step closer, Raemka realised that it was not the man's gruesome appearance that had frightened the locals away but rather the series of scrolls that sat tucked along his belt. Each one bore a red wax seal, and Raemka grimaced as the gravity of the situation hit him; the man was a tax collector. Whoever was responsible was making a statement, not only to the Roman prefect but to all the residents of Alexandria as well, and in doing so, they had set in motion events that could not be undone.

No one wanted to be there when the soldiers arrived on their morning rounds, and Raemka dispersed along with the last few onlookers, eager to put distance between himself and the body. He knew the modus operandi of the Romans: detain anyone nearby, interrogate, and repeat until the perpetrator was found. He needed to lay low, but more importantly, he needed to decide whether to stay and hope things improved or leave before they got worse.

In the safety of his home, far from the morning's monstrosity, Raemka spent his day contemplating his predicament. As he pondered his next move, something else began to bother him, an anxiety that had droned in the back of his mind since his return. It had nothing to do with the situation brewing outside, though; it was different, and it grew with every passing hour. As he sat there silently meditating, casting his mind out, the answer came to him, and he smiled. He knew exactly what he had to do.

Suddenly, there was a knock, and Raemka's eyes snapped open. It was late evening, and long shadows hung over the house as he rose to his feet and approached the door, opening it tentatively.

"Yes?" he asked the simply-dressed young man he found there.

108

"Excuse the interruption, sir, but the famed merchant and favoured son of Alexandria, Master Khul, has requested your presence at his house to attend a meeting of great importance to the city."

Raemka sighed internally; he didn't have time for such distractions right now. Still, something gave him pause for thought.

"Am I the only one receiving this invitation?"

"No, sir, Master Khul has called all the loyal sons of Alexandria to this gathering. Will you attend?" the servant asked, waiting patiently for a response.

Raemka nodded his assent, and, with that, the servant dashed off into the shadows.

Closing the door in annoyance, he frowned. He didn't want to go, but he didn't have a choice. To refuse Khul now would cause issues he couldn't afford, and he still needed time to gather what he required for the next part of his plan. With nothing else for it, and reasoning that he need not bother satiating his hunger beforehand, Raemka headed off to see what his associate had to say.

Upon arrival, he was led through to the same room he had been entertained in a week prior, only it appeared different. The elegant furniture and decorations that had previously adorned the space had been removed, and in their place, there stood a select group of local men abuzz with conversation. The other striking omission was the sheer lack of food and fine wine that usually flowed so freely in Khul's home. Everything about the scene was restrained, dressed down, and entirely out of character, and it confirmed only one thing: this was not a social gathering.

As he scanned the crowd, he spied a number of local merchants dotted amongst the flock of otherwise unfamiliar faces. There couldn't have been more than fifteen of them in total, all talking in hushed voices. Raemka nodded greetings at those he knew but made no attempt to speak with anyone. Interacting with humanity was a necessary facade he tried to avoid whenever possible.

A lull fell over the room as Khul entered, walking down the stairs from his living quarters above. His usual red and gold tunic was replaced with a shorter, unembellished, dark brown version that barely ran halfway to his knees, his beard was cropped and bound with a leather strap, and his hair was slicked back behind his ears. As he walked to the centre of the room, the men splayed into a semi-circle to face him, eager to know why they'd been summoned. Stony faced, Khul swept his gaze over the group before offering them a sombre smile.

"Normally, I am a happy man, my friends, but today is different," he said, his voice serious and booming. "Over the past year, our Roman rulers have seen fit to persecute our people, to treat us lower than dogs on the street! They take and take but never give back. Rome cares only for the Romans. It cares nothing for we Egyptians, we who were building great monuments while they were still scratching for sustenance in the dirt!"

There were rumbles of agreement, and Khul nodded before waving for silence.

"I have a confession to make, brothers. It was I who killed that tax collector and hung him on display. He stood right where you are now, demanding more and more from me, determined to bleed me dry in the name of the Roman Empire!"

Outrage and shock rippled through the gathering.

"I choked him to death right there," said Khul, pointing at a spot on the floor. "Then my men and I strung him up for the Romans to see, so they would know we will no longer stand for our money, our wares, and our lives being stolen!" There were shouts of support from the men around Raemka, as Khul stood tall, pointing skyward. "I say to you, brothers, the time has come to take a stand and reclaim Alexandria for its own people!"

A unanimous cheer came from the rest of the men, their fists raised in the air, while Raemka remained silent.

"I will lead you, brothers. I have painted the target on my back in Roman blood, and I bear it with pride. Will you join me? Will you stand with me against our oppressors? Will you help me show that never again may they threaten the lives and livelihoods of the great Egyptian people?"

The assent from the men grew from a rumble to a roar, and they gathered closer around their newfound leader. Raemka, on the other hand, hung back, cursing to himself. The last thing he wanted was to get caught up in a political uprising.

Before the knock on his door that evening, he'd made the decision to leave, to gather some wares and set off again until the unrest had ceased. That option was no longer on the table, though. The Romans would suspect he was a guilty man trying to flee should he head for the gates now, and even if he managed to slip through, they would hound him to the ends of the earth, just to make an example of him. The best he could aim for was to distance himself from this mob and wait for them to offer enough of a distraction for him to escape unseen.

Glancing over his shoulder, Raemka spied a doorway hung with a papyrus covering towards the rear of the room that led to Khul's food storage. Suddenly, a plan began to form in his mind. The food storage was accessible by a back door, the same door he had delivered Khul's wine through a week ago, a door he could use to slip out of unnoticed and return home. He took a couple of steps backwards and was about to beat a hasty retreat when he heard a commotion by the front entrance.

A flood of soldiers poured into the house led by their heavily armoured centurion, their brandished gladii and sharp-tipped pilum glinting in the torchlight.

"The Romans are here, brothers!" Khul shouted over the chaos. "Fight through them for your freedom! Show them the courage of the Egyptians!"

Raemka made a break for the rear exit, but before he could reach it, he heard clattering and banging coming from the other side of the papyrus. Backing up into the corner of the room, he slunk into the shadows as more soldiers burst through, their weapons already drawn.

Caught between two forces, the Egyptians' will to fight disappeared quickly, the shouts of rage and anger from the unarmed men soon replaced with pleas for mercy and forgiveness. It didn't matter what they said, though; they were cut down ruthlessly and systematically, their screams of agony echoing around the room. As Raemka watched the massacre, his back pressed up against the wall, he noticed Khul using the mayhem as a cover to sneak upstairs to his living quarters.

In the space of two minutes, not a single one of the loyal sons of Alexandria were left alive, and as the last of them fell, the centurion finally took notice of Raemka. With a simple gesture of his finger, the soldiers began to surround him in an arc, their weapons dripping with blood.

Holding out his hands, desperate to avoid a confrontation, Raemka met the centurion's eye. "I did not know what Khul intended here. If I had, I would not have come. I pay all my taxes gladly to the Roman Empire and its most glorious ruler, Emperor Antoninus Pius. I am not a traitor."

The soldiers hesitated as their centurion stepped forward. "That may be, Egyptian, but an example must be set. No one leaves this house alive."

Raemka lowered his eyes to the floor in resignation, his fists clenching. "So, that is your command? All must die?"

"It is the only way."

Snapping his eyes back up, Raemka stared at him grimly. "So be it."

All at once, the air pressure spiked, and Raemka released the energy pent-up inside him, unleashing it like a tidal wave that knocked the soldiers to the floor. As the able few struggled back to their feet, eight blades emerged from his back, like the legs of a spider.

Before the men could react, Raemka rushed forward, sending three of them flying as he expanded the air around him, detonating it with a sonic boom. As they hit the walls and collapsed to the ground, unconscious, he brought his blades around, slicing his way through the ranks like a knife through butter, maiming more than killing, his opponents howling in pain as blood gushed from their mangled limbs.

The soldiers' weapons offered little defence, passing through his otherworldly appendages as if they were made of smoke. One of them tried to cleave him in two with his gladius, but Raemka dodged to the side, sending the man flying with a concentrated burst of energy.

Finally stepping into the fray, the centurion took a wiser approach than his underlings, bringing his gladius around sideways, so his foe couldn't evade the attack. Before the blade reached its target, though, it stopped dead, wavering in the air as if caught by an invisible force.

Raemka grabbed his wrist, energy rippling across his skin like black lightning and surging into his prey, and the centurion screamed. Smoke started to seep from the man's eyes and mouth, his cries continuing until he was released from the Spider's grasp and dropped to the ground, dead.

Only two soldiers remained standing, and both froze in fear as Raemka looked across at them. Their only intent was to withdraw, but

112

as they turned to flee, he lunged forward, thrusting his blades into their backs. They hung there for a moment, blood dripping onto the floor, before the blades disappeared, and the men collapsed into a heap.

Hearing moans of pain from the incapacitated soldiers, Raemka extended his hands, two beams of darkness shooting out, a whining sound echoing through the room as he turned full circle, slicing through the injured soldiers and putting an end to their misery. Drawing his power back inside, a silence fell over the house, and Raemka took stock of the damage dealt. All of the soldiers were dead, as were the merchants. That only left ...

"Raemka! What happened?" Khul said, coming down the stairs slowly, his eyes wide as he surveyed the scene. "You did all of this?" A wide grin crossed his face. "Surely you were sent here by the gods to help us dispense with the Romans and recapture our freedom."

Charging forward, Raemka grabbed Khul by the throat and thrust him against the wall. "Fool! There are no gods, only me. I did not attack these men for the freedom of Alexandria. I attacked them only because they gave me no choice."

"B-but, Raemka, you could help us," Khul pleaded with him. "Together, we could force the Romans back and retake the city for its people."

"For yourself, you mean. You don't care about the people. You wish only to increase your own wealth and power."

"And you care about the people?" Khul scoffed before noticing the blades that had emerged from Raemka's back and falling silent.

"I care nothing for them, nor for you. Whether the people of this city live or die makes no difference to me. I have lived for thousands of years, and I shall live for thousands more. As for your paltry attempt at rebellion, it will be nothing but a tiny footnote in history, if it's even remembered at all."

Khul heaved for breath as Raemka's chokehold grew tighter. "Then let us both forget about the Egyptian people and speak the truth. You have power, but so do I. Together, we could not only rule Alexandria but build an empire that surpasses the Romans, one so powerful that no one would dare to cross us. We could rule the world!"

Raemka smirked as he lifted Khul by his throat until his feet dangled in the air. "Rule the world? What a pitifully small scope you have. In time, this world will cease to exist at all. It shall crumble to dust and every living thing along with it. But I, I shall endure until the end of time itself."

The four blades on his left side suddenly thrust forward, impaling Khul, who jerked in place before falling still. Raemka examined him emotionlessly as he felt the man's soul dissipate into the swirling aether that surrounded them, unseen. The blades disappeared into thin air once more, and Khul's heavy frame thudded to the ground, a pool of blood slowly expanding beneath it.

With a shake of his head, Raemka strode across the room towards the papyrus door, passing through the food store between barrels of wine and reed baskets of produce destined to rot. Casually grabbing a handful of dates, he popped one in his mouth before slipping unseen out the back entrance and turning for home.

∞∞∞∞∞∞∞

Madkodi loved flying. She felt the most incredible ecstasy whenever she took to the skies, and it often took great effort to convince herself to continue on her quest rather than veer off and explore the great unknown. In truth, the only thing that brought her back down to the ground at the moment was fatigue or hunger. She'd been making her way north for over a month, travelling by night to avoid attention and spending her days recuperating in the hidden safety of rocky outcrops or banks of trees. As much as possible, she avoided people, and the further she went, the more foreign they seemed to become, all strange clothes and unfamiliar faces.

The skies were clear that night, and Madkodi had an unobstructed view as she hovered above the dunes. Golden sand undulated forth as far as the eye could see, giving little indication of distance or direction. The only landmark she had to guide her was the river she had found a week earlier, carving its way through the otherwise arid and lifeless scenery, its banks lush and green. She knew it must be the great river Mlamulla had seen in his vision, and so she followed it along, stopping beside the water from time to time to cool off and recover her strength.

Up ahead, she saw something protruding from the desert and

114

descended, landing on the sand and staring upwards in disbelief, her mouth agape. A giant triangular mountain rose before her, impossibly tall but too perfect to be a creation of nature. There were others scattered around as well, their sides crumbled and decaying, as if they'd been built thousands of years before and then forgotten. As she examined them closer, Madkodi discovered they were made entirely from massive blocks of perfectly cut stone stacked one on top of the other, and she ran her hand across them, unable to fathom how such a marvel had come to exist.

Passing around the base, she finally took notice of the equally impressive sight just beyond. Sprawled out over the seemingly uninhabitable desert stood the biggest camp she had ever seen, similar to the towns she'd passed along the banks of the river but on an unfathomably large scale. The buildings appeared innumerable, their walls sand coloured, almost as though they had grown there organically. It was just as Mlamulla had described except for two small details; there was no sea here nor a fire high above to guide her.

Setting herself down on the bottom block of the stone mountain, Madkodi sat mesmerised by the lights blinking at her like eyes from within the dwellings until they began to fade and burn out. Something caught her attention from the corner of her eye, and she jumped to her feet with a start, turning to find a young boy peeking around the corner.

He snuck out from his hiding place, speaking meekly and pointing at her chest, but Madkodi shook her head, unable to understand him. She was about to respond when she realised her words would be equally as unintelligible. After a long moment, she placed her spear down on the stone block and knelt on the sand beside him, trying to seem as unthreatening as possible, and spoke the only word she thought he might understand.

"Alexandria?" she asked, pointing at the city.

The boy followed her finger with his eyes before looking back and shaking his head, pointing further north. He drew his arms out, and Madkodi realised he was trying to tell her she still had a way to go. Craning her neck to find the moon, she reasoned time was on her side. If she hurried, and the distance wasn't too far, she might be able to make it to Alexandria by dawn.

115

With racing heart, she stood up, looking down at the boy with a smile and nodding her thanks. She wanted to repay him somehow, and she knew just the way to do it. She spread her arms out wide, energy igniting around her, her dark wings appearing from her back. The boy stared with the kind of wide-eyed wonder only children seem to possess as she soared up into the sky. Cutting a low circle around his head, Madkodi caught sight of his grin, and as she darted off, she wished everyone could share his reaction to her power instead of the fear she'd seen in the eyes of her tribe.

The river led her past the city, and as she continued to follow it north, she discovered something Mlamulla had not prepared her for. Far below, the sand gave way to swathes of green, and the river branched out like the limbs of a tree, stretching away in different directions. Unsure of which branch to follow, she scanned the horizon for a sign until her eyes met something unusual to the north-west, a light shining the way in the darkness. Buoyant, she banked left and shot off towards the beacon. She'd found it: Alexandria.

As the sun began to paint the horizon a warm amber, the city came into view, the shaman's vision brought to life. Before her, she saw the buildings rising from the sand; she saw the river reach the end of its long journey; and, atop an impossibly tall building, she saw the light that had guided her, its flickering flame reflected outwards like the sun's rays off water.

The vast sea beyond was dappled with strange floating shapes like those she'd passed countless times along the river, controlled by men with skin much fairer than hers. There were people everywhere, bustling between the buildings and gathering on the shore, their sheer number both frightening and galvanising her.

Swooping down, Madkodi landed quietly and ducked out of sight in a thick tangle of reeds. The wall surrounding the city was guarded by armed men, and she knew that landing in the middle of so many people in broad daylight would be far too dangerous, and so she settled in to wait for the cover of darkness once more.

∞∞∞∞

Alexandria was interesting, to say the least. Madkodi had been there for almost a week but was still no closer to understanding it or the

116

people who lived there. On the night she had entered the city, she'd managed to snatch a long, beige tunic hanging from a line outside a house by the river, casting aside her familiar grass skirt and pulling the garment on, its coarse fabric irritating her skin as she pulled it down. As a hunter, she knew the importance of blending into her surroundings to capture her prey, and thus, although it was uncomfortable and restrictive, she understood the tunic was her best chance at remaining undetected.

Walking the perimeter of the city in the shadows, she had found a quieter spot along the wall, waiting until the moon had hidden its face behind a cloud momentarily before leaping over and landing softly in an empty street. All at once, she'd felt entirely out of place, and looking down at herself, she'd realised that she could not go unnoticed while still wielding her spear. With little other option, she had found a narrow gap between the large building she'd stood beside and the wall, reluctantly entrusting her spear to the safety of the shadows. Taking a deep breath and one final look around, she had begun the next stage of her hunt unarmed.

It had proven challenging for Madkodi to gain her bearings in the days that followed. She was used to finding her way by distant landmarks or the movements of animals, but that was not possible in Alexandria. Instead, confined to the city's endless mess of narrow streets and identical buildings, she was forced to rely on the subtle differences between houses and the residents' daily routines to keep herself from walking in circles.

Trapped within the manmade maze, even judging the time became a trial, the sky cut down to little more than slivers overhead. On top of everything, the habits of the people were entirely foreign to her, and she'd been forced to mimic them as best she could to remain inconspicuous. Of course, she need not have worried so much about trying to blend in. Aside from a few sideways glances, a thick tension in the air left most people with their eyes glued to the ground and minding their own business.

Amongst the sea of faces, Madkodi had seen only a few who shared her skin colour, but they seemed to struggle more than most and often appeared to be under the command of the fairer-skinned men. She had also seen a few beaten by the warriors who stalked the streets like

117

lions, wearing hard, shiny clothes and bearing blades and spears with tips made from the same gleaming material.

Day and night, these warriors would search for prey in every nook and cranny, although she could never understand why they preyed on some and not others, as though the city were made up of different tribes. Even stranger to her was the fact that most of these warriors seemed to come into their hunting grounds from a camp set up a short distance from the gate. They did not even live within the city, yet they held the most power. Unable to decipher how the order of things worked, she simply tried to avoid them.

By day, Madkodi explored the streets and searched for sustenance, but food was scarce, and she'd been reduced to stealing what she could to survive. It was a harsh reality she loathed more than anything. She was a hunter, able to take care of herself, but there was nothing to hunt in Alexandria. The people there had blocked out nature with their walls, making food a commodity that could only be gained by sleight hands or in exchange for small, shiny discs.

There was a juxtaposition in this city she could still not understand, and it was one that grated on her. In her tribe, everyone did their part to ensure each person was fed and cared for, but in Alexandria, people seemed divided. While some starved on the streets, others ate to excess and threw the rest away. It was selfish and naive, but above all, it lacked any sense of humanity.

At night, she would find a quiet corner and sleep, albeit never well. The streets felt claustrophobic, and she was wary of the people skulking in the shadows. Even in the short time she'd been in the city, she'd seen more than a few bodies dumped in laneways, and, even with her power, she felt vulnerable without her spear.

With each passing day, the search for her mysterious foe continued, but in each place she looked, she found no trace. As Madkodi sat in a darkened doorway on the seventh night, tucking her knees up into her tunic to keep the evening chill at bay, she did so with great despondence. How would she ever find the Spider amongst such a plethora of people? And what if she couldn't? What if he found her first?

∞∞∞∞∞

It was late the following evening, and Madkodi kept to the shadows as she moved through the streets. The day had brought strange happenings, the movements of the locals appearing more frantic than usual. Something had frightened them, but she thought better of seeking out the cause with so many warriors roaming the city, deciding instead to lay low and continue her search for the Spider by night.

As she passed through the centre of Alexandria, she suddenly heard shouts and turned left to investigate, coming across a crowd of people gathered outside a large house. The front door was closed, and several people were huddled beside it, whispering in ardent tones as the rest of the crowd chittered nervously behind them. Intrigued, Madkodi sidled around them, turning down a narrow lane and stumbling upon a side door. Something in her soul beckoned her to enter, and she slipped silently inside.

The air was still, and she moved cautiously, her senses pricked for any sign of danger. She seemed to be in a room filled with barrels, the pungent smell of the liquid they held mixing with the alluring aroma of the food piled up in reed baskets along the walls. Unable to resist temptation, she grabbed a handful of small brown fruits and quickly shoved them in her mouth, their yielding texture and intense sweetness answering her stomach's call as she devoured them, pits and all.

Snapping back to her senses, she crept towards a door hung with a thin covering and pushed the edge aside to peek into the next room. Before her lay a scene of utter carnage. Bodies were strewn across the ground, and pools of blood filled the spaces in between. Some of them were warriors, while others were ordinary people, like those she saw swapping things for small discs in the open space across town.

As she edged out into the room and tiptoed between them, she found herself horrified. She had seen the dead many times before, but although the ordinary men had been stabbed or slashed, the warriors had died in ways she could barely fathom. A few had been split almost in two, others were missing limbs, and one was smouldering like he'd been burned from the inside out. Madkodi stared at the singed corpse in disbelief. Who had done this? *What* had done this?

Crossing to the stairs on the far side of the room, she reached the bottom and stopped. At her feet lay the body of a rotund man, his eyes open and glazed, his arms outstretched, his hands curled like claws.

As she knelt beside his torso, she gently touched the wounds that had killed him, the blood seeping from them still warm. There were four holes down his side, in an almost perfect line. Without thinking, she traced her own side, closing her eyes to replay her encounter with the Spider in her vision. The man's injuries matched her own.

Madkodi's skin went cold at the realisation, her mind reeling. Had she finally found evidence of the Spider's presence in Alexandria? She fought to control her breathing as she stood up, taking another look around the room and trying to decipher the series of events. The ordinary men seemed to have been slaughtered at the hands of the warriors, who were, in turn, slain by the Spider, yet the scenario failed to answer an important question. If the Spider was on the side of the ordinary men, why not save them, and why kill the rotund man who looked to be their leader? Of course, the Spider's reasons mattered very little to her in that moment; she had a much more pressing question. If the bodies were still warm, did that mean the Spider was close?

Suddenly, a shout came from outside, and Madkodi glanced up to find a group of warriors flinging open the door and storming in, blades pointed at her. Turning on her heel, she sprinted for the door she'd entered through, barrelling past the covering hanging from the frame as footsteps thundered in pursuit. As she reached the storeroom, she released a blast of energy behind her, the covering billowing into the faces of the warriors, the force of the attack throwing them backwards.

Madkodi leapt back out into the narrow lane, this time turning away from the crowd and following the side streets, twisting and turning until she was thoroughly lost. Slowing to a walk as she caught her breath, she spotted a familiar building on the corner and turned right, heading back towards the house, resolving to stake it out until the warriors left. She knew it was dangerous to return, but it was her only lead in her search for the Spider.

Drawing closer, she slunk into the shadows of a nearby laneway and scaled a neighbouring rooftop, carefully walking along the ledge until she secured a clear view. There were warriors everywhere, brandishing their weapons to disperse the crowd. As she surveyed the scene, her attention turned to a man with cropped black hair and a plain tunic who stood watching the commotion from the far end of the street, his arms crossed. There was nothing special about him, nothing to differentiate him from the thousands of other people who lived in Alexandria, but Madkodi couldn't take her eyes off him.

Finally, after what felt like an eternity, the man turned and walked away. Without a second thought, Madkodi took off after him, keeping to the rooftops to stay out of sight. As she stalked him, what started as a vague niggling in her mind, grew to an irrefutable belief that drowned out everything else. He was the one she'd been seeking; he was the Spider. All that was left was to hunt him down.

∞∞∞∞

She tailed the man from the shadows for three days, learning his habits. In the morning, he would cross the city to swap discs for food, but the rest of the days were spent with what appeared to be a stripeless, grey zebra and a wooden contraption the beast pulled behind it. They traipsed back and forth between his house and a larger building near the eastern gate, seeming to move very little with each trip: a few small wooden boxes on one journey, a pile or two of animal pelts and clothing on the next. By the looks of it, he could have taken it all in one trip, yet, for reasons she could not understand, he dragged it out.

His movements weren't the only strange thing she discovered. Once, when he'd left on yet another trip across the city, Madkodi had snuck into his house. Apart from a small bed topped with a reed stuffed sack, there was no other furniture; in fact, there wasn't much of anything. He had no possessions, no trinkets, nothing of substance. The place barely looked lived in at all.

At night, he would travel back to the large building near the gate, go through the door, and disappear inside, only returning home as dawn began to break. Madkodi couldn't figure out what the door led to or why he stayed there rather than in his house, but, in the end, it didn't matter. By going there every night, he'd established a pattern, and she fully intended to exploit it.

∞∞∞∞

Night fell over Alexandria, and Madkodi moved stealthily through the laneways until she reached a building on the city's southern edge. Checking her surroundings and noting the position of the fire burning

121

high above, she crept over to where the building abutted the city wall and pressed her cheek against the stone.

With a sigh of relief, she slipped her arm into the darkened gap she found there, wiggling her way forward until her fingers clasped the familiar notched shaft of her spear. A sense of comfort swept over her as she pulled it from its hiding place and gently felt the tips at either end, their sharpness digging into her flesh.

Tearing a strip from the hem of her tunic, she tied it around her waist, pulling the loose-hanging fabric tight against her body so that it wouldn't hinder her before she weighed the spear in her hands and thrust it back and forth to limber up. The time had come.

Armed and bolstered, she made her way back towards the eastern gate. Scaling a nearby building, she nimbly moved from roof to roof until she reached the laneway of the man's nocturnal visits, settling down on the ledge opposite the door.

The full moon illuminated the street, but it lay undisturbed aside from a few stray cats stalking the streets in search of mice. Closing her eyes, she allowed her other senses to take over her search as she waited patiently. Little noise disrupted the evening air: steps off in the distance, dust swirling, muffled voices echoing down empty streets. The ledge felt smooth to the touch, but as she caressed the surface, imperfections revealed themselves. Strange smells wafted past her, carried on the cool breeze blowing in from the sea, the pleasant, spice-filled aroma of evening meals mixing with the undesirable odour of rotting food and refuse.

Suddenly, her eyes shot open as the sound of approaching footsteps reached her, and she froze, her breath becoming a mere whisper. As she peeked over the ledge, she saw the man she sought step up to the door and stop. Madkodi lifted her spear as quietly as she could, slowly building up the power inside her. When she was ready, she leapt down, focusing all her energy into the spear, aiming to deliver one devastating strike. As she closed in on her target, she thrust the spear forward, pointing the tip at the centre of his back, knowing that in a moment, her enemy would be no more.

Without warning, though, her prey slid sideways, spinning around and grabbing her by the throat with his right hand, his other hand wrapping around her wrist, her spear clattering to the ground. He said something in a language she could not understand and thrust her against the far wall, pain shooting through her skull like someone had reached inside and set it aflame. The pressure in her head grew as she writhed in agony under his grasp. Then, abruptly, the pain ceased, and he released her, stepping back as she collapsed to the ground.

Madkodi held her throat and gasped for air, her ears ringing, when, through all the noise, she heard something.

"So, it *is* you."

On hearing familiar words, Madkodi looked up at the man in disbelief. "How?" she croaked.

The man looked down at her with a cruel smile. "I have learned, over the centuries, to use my power to enter the minds of those I hunt. It's quite useful, really. I can use it to bring them grief and sadness, I can use it to turn their friends and family against them, and I can use it to learn their language." Tilting his head, he looked her up and down. "Strange, I've never seen you as a woman before. It perplexes me why you would choose the weaker sex, but perhaps you didn't have a choice. Your spirit never *has* been as strong as mine, I suppose."

Madkodi did not reply, coughing as she tried to catch her breath.

The man paced around her, regarding her from every angle before clicking his tongue and chuckling to himself. "You really thought you were the hunter this time, didn't you?" He paused for effect as she looked up at him. "I suppose you congratulated yourself when you spotted me from the rooftops, thinking you had caught me off guard admiring my own chaos. I wasn't watching the soldiers or the crowd at all, though. I was waiting for you, waiting to start the game that has led to this very moment."

Her stomach turned as she realised he had known where she was all along. The Spider had laid his web, and she hadn't even noticed she was caught in it. Desperately, she tried to regain her composure as he knelt beside her, his breath hot against her ear.

"The game is at an end," he hissed before rising to his feet again, eight blades slowly appearing behind him. "Remember this as you die: this fear, this pain, this defeat. Remember it, and let your soul dissolve into the aether. Should you return, you will succeed only in damning yourself to yet another torturous life and inglorious death. I, Anasazi, promise this."

Madkodi shivered at the sound of his name. It evoked a strange reaction in the depths of her very being as if a warning bell had been struck.

All at once, a wave of memories flooded her mind: memories of pain, of death, of misery. Adrenaline surged through her as she pushed them aside and scrambled to her feet, all intentions of destroying the Spider shattered as she grabbed her spear. Only one thought remained now: escape.

Energy bloomed around her, black, ethereal wings emerging into existence as she threw out her free hand, sending Anasazi careening backwards with a short, sharp attack. Before he could rise, she shot upwards, flying past the rooftops and into the sky, knowing instinctively he couldn't follow her.

As she reached the cloud line, she stopped and stared down at the city. It looked surreal, like it had been etched into the sand by deft hands. Desperately, she tried to formulate a plan. Flying as far away as possible crossed her mind, but what kind of life could she lead under the constant threat of his reappearance? Her other option was to fight him head-to-head, but that seemed equally as futile. Their powers were incomparable; she wouldn't stand a chance.

Despair was beginning to creep in when she looked down at the beacon that shone over the city, one small light piercing the darkness unwaveringly. She took a deep breath, determined to find a better solution. After all, he was still just a man. Anasazi could be killed. She just had to figure out how.

Her eyes surveyed her options below, and she caught sight of the camp outside the city walls that housed the warriors of Alexandria. Suddenly, an idea sprang forth. She might not be able to defeat him alone, but if she fought him there, he would have to contend with the warriors as well, and that might be all the distraction she needed to gain the upper hand.

Not wanting to waste any more time, she started to descend, circling wide, before quietly landing just inside the wooden perimeter in the rear corner of the camp, far from the guards posted at the gates. Her wings dissipated as she edged forward between the tents, glancing around cautiously, her spear held lightly behind her back. Small torches lashed to poles were scattered here and there, their dull light casting long shadows that Madkodi flitted between until she found a large open area, its edges lined with weapons resting freely on stands.

A group of warriors were gathered on the far side, and Madkodi sidled closer, wanting to be as near to them as possible when her foe arrived. Her eyes darted around, searching for him in the darkness, her muscles tensed for battle. As she moved closer, though, the group parted to reveal a man standing in the centre, pointing directly at her. Her heart pounded in her ears as she recognised him. It was Anasazi, one step ahead of her yet again.

There was no more time for thought as the warriors charged forward with a shout, their shining armour glinting in the torchlight as they ran, their blades drawn. Madkodi didn't have much experience fighting with her power, but feeling the energy flow through her, she channelled it into her spear, trusting her instincts to do the rest.

The first man reached her in a rush, his blade held high, but before he could bring his arm down, she whipped the spear across his throat, blood spurting off to the side as he twisted to the dirt.

A second came at her from behind, but the butt of her spear rammed into his neck, angling upwards. He collapsed as two more men appeared on either side of her, the first swinging his blade in a circle only for Madkodi to parry it and thrust her spear into his foot. As he cried out and tumbled to the ground, the other vaulted in to attack, but Madkodi dodged to the side, thrusting her spear forward and piercing the shining plate on his chest, its tip sinking deep into his flesh before she kicked him away.

Another wave of men approached, and Madkodi spun around, her spear now blazing with black energy, its dual tips slicing through anything they touched with ease. The men reared back, screaming as their blood sprayed the nearby tents, more warriors appearing on all sides, this time armed with the same shiny-tipped spears and large shields she often saw the guards of the city bearing.

They quickly surrounded her, but Madkodi stood her ground. The first group she'd fought on instinct, but she didn't want to hurt any more of them if she could help it. They were not her quarry.

She tried to hold them at bay, whirling her spear high above her head, but row upon row of men gathered until she could see nothing around her but a wall of shields. They inched forward as one, closing the circle tighter, and Madkodi knew she had to act now or risk being overwhelmed. Not knowing what else to do, she stopped whirling the spear and abruptly thrust it into the ground, releasing her pent-up power into the earth.

A shock wave rippled through the men, sending them flying backwards, and instantly Madkodi was airborne, seeking to find refuge in the sky once more. She had only risen a few metres, though, when a figure crashed into her, riding her to the ground. She looked up to find Anasazi on top of her, blazing with energy, his blades poised to strike.

"You know," he said, greeting her gaze with a mocking smile, "the strangest thought came to me as I watched you fly out of that laneway. I was reminded of the tales I heard in Greece of the mythical bird they call the phoenix." Unpinning her arms, he stood up. "It is said the bird dies in a blaze of fire, only to be resurrected from the ashes."

Madkodi scrambled to her feet and saw the warriors closing in on them, quickly forming a new circle around the pair, although their actions were tentative and fearful. Madkodi noticed they had their weapons trained not only on her but on Anasazi as well, and with a feeling of relief, she realised that no matter what happened to her, her foe would have to fight his way to freedom.

Anasazi completely ignored the threat as he continued. "That's what you are, I think. A foolish little phoenix, returning from the ashes of your miserable past, scratching and clawing your way to a new life only to find yourself in ashes once more."

Madkodi brought up her spear, energy swirling around her as she prepared to defend herself. "And what does that make you then?"

Anasazi gave her a grim smile. "The fire that kills you."

There was just enough time for her to throw up a shield of energy before Anasazi's blades disappeared back into his body, a beam of energy shooting out from his hands. He swept it in a wide arc, cutting through the warriors like a scythe, death taking them so swiftly that no sound escaped save for the gushing of blood.

The majority of those who had survived the reaping turned and ran, honour falling to the wayside in the face of certain doom. Those who hesitated regretted it immediately as Anasazi leapt into the air, blades re-emerging behind him as he sliced into the backs of those bringing

126

up the rear of the flood of escapees. As for those who were too brave for their own good, they were swiftly gutted and impaled.

Trying to pick the opportune moment, Madkodi waited until Anasazi was occupied with the last two survivors and approached him from his blind spot, lunging forward to stab him in his right flank. Instantly, he turned to face her, taking out the men with his blades as he did so, his hand grabbing her spear near its tip. Attempting to tear her weapon from his grasp, Madkodi felt it shudder and dissolve, the entire spear turning to ash and blowing away in the breeze.

She tried to seize him by the shoulders, seeking to throw him aside and create some distance between them, but Anasazi was too quick. He snatched hold of her wrists, the air erupting with a deafening boom, the shock wave tossing her backwards to the ground.

Madkodi tried to get to her feet but found she couldn't move her limbs at all. Dropping her head back down onto the dirt, she knew she was going to die. It wasn't a sad realisation, merely an acknowledgment of fact. The air pressure rose, and she looked up to find Anasazi walking towards her, the air around him crackling with power.

"And now, Little Phoenix, we end this dance," he said, crouching beside her. "Let me leave you with a final thought before you go. In the bliss of non-existence, you can find your freedom."

Anasazi's face grew stern as he grabbed her head, black electricity lancing through his hand. Madkodi smelt something burning only to realise it was her own body, cooking from the inside out. The agony grew too much to bear, and she screamed until her lungs ruptured, the sound choking off to silence.

∞∞∞∞∞∞

It was almost dawn when Raemka arrived home. Slipping calmly into a clean tunic, he tossed his singed and blood-stained one on the floor before fetching Grey and leading him to the warehouse he'd leased out almost two weeks prior.

With his stash of small chests safely secured under the floorboards of the cart and covered with piles of clothes and animal pelts, he harnessed Grey, trotting off towards the eastern gate. The soldiers stationed there were so engrossed in their heated debate over the cause of the previous night's incident that they didn't notice the humble departure of yet another merchant as he passed them by.

There was a crisp wind off the sea as the first rays of dawn painted the sky a delicate shade of blue, and Raemka smiled as he left behind the chaos brought about by his own hand. Grey plodded along stoically, the chests shifting slightly with each step, bumping into each other with tiny thumps. Muffled by the pelts and fabric, his small fortune of gold and silver clinked merrily, each coin a reminder of the lives he had destroyed.

Raemka felt no pity for them, of course; after all, does a spider feel pity for the fly? His mind turned back to a memory he often dreamt of, its details dancing around his head. It was long ago, back when he'd made a conscious decision to follow his current path, to keep the power of rebirth solely for himself. In the subsequent passing of time, he had only grown more formidable while all his potential rivals had been snuffed out. All except for the Phoenix, that is. He smiled to himself at the name. He would have to remember that for the next life.

The sun rose higher into the sky, bathing the hard beaten road in its morning warmth, and Raemka squinted. The Phoenix would be hard to defeat, but it wasn't impossible. It might take a dozen lifetimes, but he would succeed; he would find his foe's Achilles' heel and use it to shatter his spirit.

The thought buoyed him as he travelled along. He'd decided to head east in search of the fantastical lands of colour and intrigue he had heard tell of on his travels. Somewhere along the way, he would find a new place to make his base, and his quest to eliminate those who had returned from the aether would start anew. Flicking Grey's reigns, Raemka spurred him on, Alexandria disappearing into the distance behind them.

∞∞∞∞∞∞∞

When the Roman soldiers finally returned to the camp, they found the body of a dark-skinned woman at the centre of their fallen comrades, her skin charred, her face contorted with pain. There was

128

much debate over the foe their brothers in arms had faced. Some swore it was a demon, while others were convinced it was a demigod descended from Jupiter himself. Regardless, they burned their own with full honours for the bravery they had shown in the face of the unconquerable. As for the woman at the epicentre of the mystifying massacre, they buried her in an unmarked grave before shifting camp to a new, larger location. More Roman legions were en route to quell the unrest in Alexandria, determined to not only stamp out the dissent but erase it from history altogether. The rebellion, much like Madkodi, was destined to be lost in the annals of time.

Theo

The hut was small but well kept. There was a place for everything, and everything was in its place, just the way she liked it. Rising from her hay-stuffed mattress, she straightened the pelts atop it, stoked the dwindling fire in the clay oven in the corner, and walked the goodly distance down the winding trail, through the forest, to the creek.

The water was pristine, as clear as crystal and glacially cold. Kneeling into the dirt, she scooped it up with cupped hands and brought it to her mouth, drinking deeply. When her thirst was quenched, she filled her two waterskins and a wooden bucket, hauling them back down the path to her tiny abode. She lived a solitary life, challenging but carefree, if such a thing existed. She was at peace: alone but in no way lonely.

Pouring feed into the trough for her cows, they lumbered over, lowing, and she greeted them cheerfully. As she surveyed her garden, the sun shining off the morning dew, she noticed something that made her heart sing and wandered over to her apple trees for a closer look. Along the branches, tiny, pale pink flowers were starting to appear. Another harsh winter was at an end.

With the apple blossom heralding the beginning of spring, it was time for her to carry out her own quiet ritual. Draping a wool cloak around her shoulders and hanging a waterskin from her belt, she placed another log on the fire and left her hut, heading into the trees once more and ascending the nearby hill to its bald peak.

Sitting down on the grass, she crossed her legs and looked out over the landscape, waiting patiently for the sun to reach its zenith and melt the stress from her soul, basking in the warmth as she welcomed the new season in her own small way. All around her, the world was waking up from its hibernation, and she smiled as she listened to the cycle of life begin anew.

It was in such moments, when the world was at its most tranquil, that she could visualise the Phoenix: her silent sentinel, its form sheathed

131

in shadows, wings of darkness flowing from its back. At times, the figure would simply stand before her, while at others, it would take off into the air, circling the skies overhead. As she watched its familiar shape, memories came back to her of happier times: times when they had been together, in different lands and different lives.

She remained on the hill with her daydreams until the sun slipped below the horizon, and the moon emerged to illuminate the night sky. Reluctantly, she succumbed to the chill of the evening and surrendered her seat, heading home to her hut but carrying with her one incontrovertible truth. One day, she would be reunited with her soulmate; she would find her Phoenix again.

∞∞∞∞∞∞∞∞∞∞∞∞∞∞∞

Images flashed through Theo's mind as she slowly sat up, turning off her alarm and swivelling out of bed. As she readied herself for another double shift, she was overcome with a sudden sense of great emptiness, a feeling that everyone had abandoned her. The disconnection she felt from her life was worsening alongside her depression. It was like a curtain had been drawn between her and the rest of humanity, segregating her from the land of the living and placing her in a dystopic, insular purgatory. The days all blurred into one, and she struggled to find the will to go on when she did naught but work and sleep. She needed a break, something to reset her life.

Picking up her keys from the bowl next to the front door, she stared at them for a minute. Part of her wanted to throw down her bag, march into work, and quit her job, and as she reached for the door handle, the voice in her head dared her to do it. In the end, though, just as it always did, routine won out.

It was another long day at Porphura, anxiety and stress fuelling the fire of each and every staff member. Theo was behind on prep, and lunch had been unexpectedly busy, which only served to make the predicament worse. By the time the tail end of lunch service bled into the early start of dinner, she had resigned herself to the fact that her already cold staff meal was going to remain half-eaten. With a sigh, she scraped the rest into the bin, clearing her bench as she hurried to pack away a batch of macarons to the sound of the first docket for the night coming in.

It seemed almost ironic that she could be surrounded by food all day and still go hungry, but aside from obligatory tasting, she, like so many other chefs, had little time to actually consume complete meals, let alone healthy ones. Still, with a function for eighty people on top of a fully booked dining room, at least she was too busy to dwell on her grumbling stomach, or her troubles.

In keeping with the chaotic nature of the day, the function desserts were called away at the precise moment a wave of a la carte orders were simultaneously being spat out of the printer, and Theo swore under her breath. With a hundred plates littered throughout the kitchen, service ground to a halt as the other chefs stopped to help clear the backlog. The symbiosis created by countless hours of working together resulted in the seamless dance of four chefs in a space designed for one. They ducked under arms and dodged hot trays, then promptly dispersed back to their original sections to continue the symphony of a standard Saturday night in hospitality.

With the last plates served and the clock ticking past midnight, Theo found herself exhausted, and as she listlessly finished cleaning up, Ruth poked her head around the corner.

"I don't know about you, but I need a drink or five after that clusterfuck. Wanna come, babe?" she asked.

Theo hesitated; her muscles ached, and her urge for sleep was teetering somewhere between mild narcolepsy and pre-hibernation bear. That being said, the idea of going back to her empty apartment and sitting alone with her thoughts wasn't exactly enticing.

Maybe spending some time with other people is exactly what I need right now, she thought, pondering the offer. *And if not, at least there'll be alcohol.*

Of course, binge drinking was hardly the best coping mechanism. Still, given her current state, Theo was happy to settle for anything that would loosen the vice of anxiety clamped around her chest and sweep her dark mood under the rug, if only momentarily.

"Sure. Why not?" Theo finally replied.

A sly grin appeared on Ruth's face. "Excellent. Now I can force Justin to come. We'll get him drunk and find some woman to take advantage of him!"

Theo smirked. "Or man. Whatever floats his boat."

"Of course! Now hurry up. I'm keen to get fucked up."

"Aren't you working tomorrow?" Theo asked, raising an eyebrow.

"What of it?" Ruth replied with a wink, scurrying off to get changed.

Theo packed away her knives, checking over her section for the umpteenth time to make sure it was set up for her absence the following day before leaving the kitchen with a relieved sigh. As she slipped out of her uniform and shouldered her backpack, she lingered for a second in the quiet of the locker room, mentally preparing herself to don a more affable social facade. Bidding a quick farewell to Peter on her way past the office, she stepped out the back door to find her colleagues waiting for her. Going by the butts at her feet, Ruth was clearly halfway through her third cigarette, and just upwind, Justin shifted awkwardly from one foot to another with an expression of unwilling participation.

Setting off towards the CBD, they made a quick detour to her apartment building, and Theo peeled off temporarily to dump her backpack and leave herself a light on. She knew full well how a night out with Ruth had the potential to end, and it was unlikely to involve her being able to flick on a light switch on the first attempt.

By the time she got back downstairs, Ruth was on the phone trying to pinpoint where her friends were, and Justin had gone from looking slightly put out to borderline flight mode.

"Don't stress. I'm sure they're as harmless as she is," Theo said to him with a comforting smile as the trio set off again.

They were turning onto Little Bourke Street when four of Ruth's friends came frolicking across the road to meet them, their swagger the kind only achievable by hospitality workers who'd just slammed three knock-off drinks after a double shift. Brief introductions were bounced around like pinballs, and the group resumed their aimless wander down the street, crossing the next intersection and passing the arch that marked the start of Chinatown.

"So, where to?" asked Ruth, her voice drenched in an enviable amount of energy for someone who had just worked sixteen hours straight.

Despite plenty of bar names being thrown around, there was little consensus on a destination, with Ruth and Co. rejecting each one in quick succession for anything from 'Nah, What's Her Face's ex works

134

there' to 'I'm pretty sure I'm banned for life.' Stopping at an open car park as the debate continued, Theo looked past the squabbling rabble, her eyes inexplicably drawn to a pair of wooden doors flanked by bouncers. As she watched on, a group of scantily clad girls entered, the sound of bass-heavy dance music escaping onto the street before being muffled again by the closing doors. It was hardly the ideal choice for enjoying a quiet after-work drink, but something about it called to her. Of course, that something was probably the fact the place sold alcohol and offered a solution to the circular deliberation of her companions.

"What about there?" Theo asked, the chatter ceasing as she pointed over to the doors.

"Benz? Fuck it, why not! I haven't been to Benzin in years," replied Ruth.

Finally escaping the cold, the group wandered past the bouncers and entered the curiously segmented decor within. Theo glanced around, thinking as she did that the non-sensical jumble of styles seemed to be the work of a deranged mind. Either that or it was the collaboration of four separate people who were all given a corner to decorate but were in no way allowed to interact with one another while they did so.

Ruth and her friends danced their way across the room to snag a spot on the recently vacated platform of gaudy, red velvet banquettes. Instead of following, though, Theo grabbed Justin by the shoulder, shoehorning him over to the bar.

"What do you drink?" she asked him over the music.

Justin shrugged. "I dunno. Not beer."

As she looked across at the back bar, she tried to calculate the best option for a kid whose conservative parents likely didn't condone him drinking much, if at all. Two female bartenders flitted around the far end, the two of them seemingly polar opposites: one a small, feisty looking woman with dark hair, and the other tall and slender, with short, platinum blonde hair and a wildly alternate wardrobe. The pair handed out drinks and forced smiles to a bunch of lecherous uni bros, while just below the bottle shelves, a heavily tattooed man in his mid-thirties crouched at the beer fridge, restocking it.

Flagging down the taller of the bartenders with a knowing smile, Theo ordered herself a gin, lime, and soda, and Justin a vodka and cola.

"Give that a go," she said, handing him his drink and lifting her glass. "To being socially awkward."

The next hour went quickly as Ruth and her friends chatted at ever-increasing volumes, occasionally straying onto the dance floor to carry out some less than graceful moves before swanning back with another round. For the most part, Theo just downed her drinks, smiling politely when the others looked over at her, the music too loud to engage in proper conversation without having to lean in uncomfortably close and shout 'What!?' several times before any progress could be made.

She was about four drinks in when she looked over to find Justin, red-cheeked from the alcohol, picking at the corner of the cushion and cradling a beer one of Ruth's friends had forced into his hand. As the first decent song of the night boomed out of the speakers, Theo drained her glass and tapped Justin's foot. Gesturing her head towards the dance floor, she rescued him from the ongoing peer pressure to scull a beer he so obviously didn't want.

Underneath his penchant for asking naive or tactless questions, Justin was a good guy, if a little socially stunted. As they bopped along to the tune, Theo was surprised to find that, given a handful of vodkas, the kid had some smooth moves. She watched him loosen up with a satisfied laugh, and for a short moment, they shook off the stress of the day amongst strangers before rejoining the group.

At that point, Justin begged off to go home, his decision eliciting no surprise from Theo. He was well past tipsy, which was to be expected given his slight frame and lack of alcohol exposure, and with his next shift less than seven hours away, the last thing he wanted was to give his colleagues any extra ammunition for a good ribbing. Sympathising with his concern, Theo walked him out, bundling him into a taxi and sending him on his way.

Turning to go back inside, she found Ruth and her friends stumbling out into the laneway.

"Oi. We're off!" Ruth shouted, as only inebriated people can.

"Where are you going?"

Ruth waved vaguely. "Coburg. A mate's having a party. Wanna come?"

"Nah, I'm 'right. You guys have fun."

"All good. Catch ya later, babe!" Ruth replied with a shrug, and just like that, the group disappeared around the corner.

Theo sighed, resigned once more to being by herself. She had no desire to join Ruth at some unknown suburban house party, but by the same token, she didn't want to go home, not yet at least. Instead, she resolved to sit near the bar, have one more drink, then head home. Possibly two drinks. Outside chance of three. Okay, it would probably be three.

Weaving her way back through the crowd of sweaty people gyrating amidst flashing lights and artificial smoke, she found two empty stools at the end of the bar, deliberately sitting on the first in the hopes that no one would spot the second and think to join her. It seemed a juxtaposition, but despite not wanting to be alone, she also did not want company. She was out of energy for frivolous socialising and just wanted to forget about the shitty rut in life she'd found herself in whilst indulging in some quality people-watching.

"Can I get you something?" a voice asked from across the bar.

Looking up, she found the tattooed man she'd seen stocking the fridges earlier, his general demeanour leading her to assume he was the manager.

Before she could answer, he grabbed a glass, waving it at her. "Gin, lime, and soda. Fresh lime, no cordial, no straw, and not the house gin. You had Four Pillars Navy Strength last time, right?"

Theo gave him a small smile and nodded, a little surprised he remembered her drink. He must have served hundreds of people over the course of the night, and Theo could only recall him serving her once.

The glass appeared in front of her, and she quickly paid before taking a sip. As the alcohol reached her stomach, she took a deep breath, letting the tension of her long day fall away. The venue was designed so the bar was quieter than the dance floor, and it was a fact Theo was immensely thankful for in that moment. Pumping house music, with its mindless, repetitive thumping, wasn't exactly her thing. It was fine for dancing, but that was about it. She preferred music with a decent melody and lyrics that actually meant something, music to distract her from the woes of her own life or empathise with her pain.

She was just bringing the glass to her lips again when a figure appeared beside her. "Is this seat taken?"

Theo looked up to find a man with short, bleached blond hair standing uncomfortably close and ogling her. She shrugged and indicated he could sit if he wanted, regretting the invitation immediately.

He pushed past her, plonking himself down and giving her a wide smile. "So, what's a pretty girl like you doing at a bar all by herself?" he asked, his voice drenched in smarm.

Theo made a concerted effort not to roll her eyes at the terrible pick-up line, doing her best to stare ahead at the bottles on the shelves. Trapped in an unwanted situation and finding her tolerance work-wearied, she decided there was only one way to get rid of him: sarcasm, her speciality.

"Drinking," she replied in a blunt, monotone voice.

Even without looking, she could tell he was a bit put off by her response. Yet another alarmingly overconfident, drunk guy surprised a woman wasn't immeasurably grateful for his attention. He was expecting her to turn and take the bait, but what he didn't know was that Theo would rather saw off her foot with a rusty blade than engage in a conversation with him. Men like him were the same as wolves, though; once they'd caught the scent, they always came back, no matter the obstacle. To them, 'No!' meant 'Try harder, mate. She's totally into you and just playing hard to get!'

"Well, a pretty girl like you shouldn't drink alone. Mind if I join you?"

"What do you mean?" she asked, feigning confusion.

The man looked stumped. "Huh?"

Theo finally turned to him, thinking as she did that comparing the man to a wolf was doing wolves a terrible injustice. A seagull was probably a more apt comparison, which meant Theo was the chip: a depressing thought if ever there was one.

"You're already sitting here. How else did you intend to join me?"

"Oh ... well ... I thought we could talk a bit," he spluttered.

Theo stared at him, her eyebrow raised. "We are talking."

The man blinked as she watched him try to figure out what the hell was going on before standing up abruptly. "I, uh, think I left my drink on another table. Excuse me." And with that, he beat a hasty retreat.

Theo shook her head, rolling her eyes and turning back to her drink to find the manager looking at her, a massive smirk on his face.

"What?" she asked, taking a sip and regarding him.

He started laughing. "Sorry, I couldn't help overhearing. It's always satisfying to see a girl skewer a guy like that. It doesn't happen nearly enough, in my opinion."

Theo smiled despite herself, a part of her pleased that her wit wasn't completely wasted. "So, what usually happens?"

"The girl sits there awkwardly while the guy tries to chat her up, completely oblivious to the fact she's not interested, then she makes up an excuse and leaves."

"Well, I'm not going anywhere. If he doesn't like my conversational skills, he can leave," she retorted.

"So I see," the manager replied with a chuckle before producing two shot glasses. "You like tequila?"

"What's the catch?" Theo replied as she watched him grab a bottle off the shelf and fill the glasses.

"No catch. I'm just rewarding you for being the only entertaining person in here." He grinned and held up his shot glass. "Cheers!"

With a clink, Theo downed her shot in one, the alcohol burning a little on the way down and almost immediately charring away the unease caused by the attempted suitor her brain had aptly dubbed Prince Alarming.

"Thanks," she said with a wry smile.

"No worries."

Theo waited for him to introduce himself, to try his own luck, but instead, he cleared the glasses and peeled off to serve another customer. She watched him for a moment, intrigued. She wasn't used to guys who didn't think with their dicks first. As he reached for a bottle from the top shelf, she finally took full notice of the tattoos running down his arms and spilling onto the backs of his hands, their appearance almost tribal in nature but with a flow more akin to fire and smoke.

When coupled with the cute, dorky vibe he had going on, his intimidating body art seemed almost conflicting. She couldn't figure him out. On the surface, he carried an air of anger and simmering discontent, but when he'd smiled at her, it was with a gentle warmth she hadn't expected: kind eyes on a coarse canvas.

Time ticked on, but Theo decided to stay all the same. She was enjoying the calm that being drunk brought to her noisy thoughts, and the manager occasionally wandered over to chat before flitting away again. It was just the right amount of socialising for her current mood: enough to stop her sinking into melancholy, but not so much as to be draining.

He would tell jokes, most of which were amusingly terrible, but beyond the light-hearted banter, he had a depth of cynicism and mild antipathy for the world that mirrored her own. Of course, if there was one thing every person in hospitality had, it was a deep-seated distaste for humanity as a whole. Bars and restaurants exposed you to the worst of people. More often than not, they were selfish and condescending beings who never gave a thought to anyone or anything around them unless it directly affected their own existence.

As if on cue, a drunk man stumbled over and leant on the bar top beside Theo, his eyes glazed.

"Hey, babe, can I buy you a drink?" he said.

Internally, she recoiled. He was the epitome of everything that was wrong with humanity wrapped in a drink-stained shirt, his crumpled jacket slung haphazardly over his shoulder. His words stank of cheap bourbon and privilege, just another man viewing a lone woman as an object they were entitled to possess due to the mere fact no one else had laid claim to her yet. The predatory look on his face relayed two wildly ill-founded beliefs. The first, of course, was that buying a woman a drink equated to entering into a watertight agreement in which he was assured sexual gratification. The second, and probably more disturbing of the two, was that any woman he extended this contract to was required by some unspoken law to accept his drink, along with its terms and conditions.

Theo shook her head, swallowing her disgust and holding up her glass, clinking the ice with a sharp shake. "Sorry, already have one."

The man waved the comment away and motioned the tall, blonde bartender to come over. "Nah, you need another one. And a shot! I'm Clyde, by the way."

She looked at him with an expression somewhere between a half-hearted smile and a grimace. "Theo."

"Thea?" he asked.

She shook her head. Every. Single. Fucking. Time. "No, it's Theo," she repeated, over pronouncing the 'o' as much as possible.

The man stared at her blankly as she watched the singular cog in his brain attempt to turn.

"Your parents gave you a boy's name? Tough break!"

That's the sperm that won? she marvelled silently to herself as she took a long sip of her drink, wanting more than anything to punch him in the face.

The man turned back to the bartender, who was watching the interaction unfold with a look of uncertainty. Luckily, it was at that point the manager appeared.

"It's all right, Janet. I've got it," he said, tapping her on the shoulder and pointing her towards the other end of the bar before addressing the man. "Can I help you?"

"Yeah, one of whatever this girl's having, a Jim Beam and Coke, and two shots of Sambuca."

The manager glanced over at Theo for a moment with the look of someone who was far too well versed in this exact interaction before responding to the man. "I don't think she wants a drink, mate."

The man balled his hand into a fist. "That's for her to decide. So, until she tells me to get lost, I suggest you just make my drinks and shut up!"

Theo watched the manager clench his jaw, clearly trying to hold in all the wildly inappropriate things he was yearning to say, contempt dancing in his eyes. That look decided it for her.

Slowly, deliberately, she turned to Clyde. "Hey!" she snapped, and he looked at her, confused. "Get. Lost."

"What?" he hissed, leaning in angrily. "I try and be nice to you, buy you a drink, and this is the thanks I get? You ungrateful fucking bitch."

He was little more than an inch from her face, and while most women would start to understandably freak out at this point, Theo didn't flinch, rage growing in her chest. She'd dealt with the same intimidation tactics from a good handful of egotistical male chefs before and knew that, beneath their paper-thin bravado, there really wasn't much substance to them. She longed to slap him as hard as she could, but of course, that would be a terrible idea. Drunk men rarely responded well to rejection and even less well to being hit, no matter how much they probably deserved it.

There were several ways to put the douchebag in his place, and Theo played each one out in her mind as she tried to settle on the best approach. She could throw her drink on him, but that would be a waste of a perfectly good shot of gin. She could get up and leave, but she didn't want to give him the satisfaction. In the end, she decided a short, sharp, scornful reply was probably the safest course of action. As she opened her mouth to speak, though, she heard a voice beside her.

"HEY!" Theo turned to see that the manager had come out from behind the bar, his hand outstretched. "You're done for the night, buddy. I think it's time you went home."

Clyde moved away from her, his attention diverted. "Whatever, mate. Go clean some glasses and mind your own business."

The manager just smiled at him grimly and disappeared out the front door. Clyde, convinced he'd won the battle, gave a smug huff and leered back at Theo for a moment, swaying a little as he propped himself against the bar top again. Before either of them could get another word in, the manager marched back inside and pointed towards her unwelcome companion, a satisfied look painted on his face.

The two security guards from the entrance appeared, motioning for Clyde to follow, and he reluctantly stormed off through the crowd and out the door, mumbling obscenities to himself as he went.

Theo looked across the bar at the manager, who had resumed his post, her eyebrow raised. "You know I was handling that just fine until you came and interrupted me."

"Yeah, you were doing great," he said with a sly grin. "I'm surprised you don't work as a hostage negotiator or a mediator for the UN."

"I was fine," she repeated stubbornly. "I don't need your help."

The manager regarded her for a second, then smiled. "You have a hard time saying thanks, don't you?"

Theo didn't trust herself to speak; he was telling the truth, after all. She had never been good at accepting charity or unsolicited assistance, and the idea of people doing good things with no expectation of reward was completely foreign to her. His actions seemed to denote a baseless belief that she was some helpless damsel in distress, and the thought sat uneasily beside the fierce independence she was so proud of. She had spent years building an armoured shell of strength and fearlessness around her anxious and fragile heart. Constructed of scars and trauma, it was a shell she used to disprove the weakness assigned to her while walking a male-dominated career path, and to protect herself from those who would seek to damage her empathetic soul.

The side effect of her endeavour, though, was that saying 'thank you' often felt tantamount to admitting she wasn't as formidable as she believed herself to be. On top of that, her past experiences had proven time and again that accepting help rarely came without cost. More than anything, she hated the feeling of being indebted to people: a feeling which, over time, her depression had twisted to include owing gratitude.

The manager sighed, grabbing down a bottle of tequila from the top shelf. "Here, I'll make it easy. I'm going to pour you a shot of this insanely good tequila, and if you want to say thanks, drink it."

Part of her wanted to tip it over his head, but the other part of her, buried deep beneath her kneejerk indignance, did actually want to thank him. Besides, her nerves could do with a salve.

Slowly, she picked up the glass. "To Clyde, the aptly named jackass," she toasted before downing the shot.

He laughed to himself, nodding his agreement and following suit. "Hey, listen, I'm about to put up the lights and close the bar, but you don't have to leave if you don't want to. It'd be nice to have another sarcastic individual here to rip on the stupidity of mankind with while I clean up."

"Sure," she chortled.

"I'm Auryn, by the way."

"Theo."

∞∞∞∞

It was just after four in the morning when the other staff clocked off, dispersing to venture home or out to drink at another of the city's late-night haunts. At her perch at the bar, Theo swirled the melting ice in her otherwise empty cup, its effortless movement and gentle clink mesmerising her as she sat lost in her thoughts. Shaken by a sound beside her, she looked up to find Auryn taking a seat on arguably the

143

most hotly contested stool of the evening, sliding her a drink as he did.

"I have to say, you've made this one of the more interesting nights I've had here."

"Oh really?" Theo asked with a smirk.

"Yeah, you don't often get to see a woman brush off two douchebags in the space of an hour. It was quite the sight."

Theo watched him, his face lighting up as he laughed and took a sip of his drink. There was something different about him that disarmed her: a natural sense of comfort and ease she hadn't felt before. As they stared at each other in silence for a long moment, Theo did not find the usual pang of awkwardness she was accustomed to, and so she shooed away the superfluous words obligation tried to hand her.

"So," she eventually said, shifting her focus to her glass and gesturing it towards him, "Auryn's a pretty random name. Don't think I've ever met an Auryn before. Where's it from?"

"It's Welsh apparently," he said in the derisive tone of someone who's had to explain his name a few too many times.

"Your parents are Welsh?"

"Nope. They're classic Aussie mongrels: a mix of Irish and English from a few generations back. I don't think I have a drop of Welsh blood in me."

Theo couldn't help but laugh at that. "Why the name then?"

Auryn shrugged. "I don't know. Originally, they were going to call me Brandon, but once I was born, they decided to give me a more 'unique' name. To be honest, part of me thinks they were just flicking through baby name books and got bored before they got to the end of the 'A' section."

"Would Brandon have been any better?" she asked with some scepticism.

"Who knows. I'm stuck with it now, though."

"You could always change it."

"No," he said, taking another sip of his drink, his face changing to a more considered expression. "Changing it would change who I am."

There was a profound silence as they both pondered that sentiment.

"So, what's with your name? There aren't many girls named Theo."

"Who knows," she replied. "My parents would never admit it, but I think they, not so secretly, wanted a boy and couldn't be bothered thinking of a new name when they realised I wasn't. Plus, they love to argue that technically Theodora is a girl's name, and people would have shortened it anyway. I mean, obviously, they ignored the fact that 'Theo' wouldn't be most people's initial choice for a nickname in that scenario."

Auryn winced. "Ouch. And here I thought there'd be an interesting story behind it."

"No, just questionable parenting decisions," she said with a resigned smile.

"Parents really shouldn't be allowed to name their kids these days," he said with a laugh. "Everyone should just be called 'It' for the first eighteen years, and then they can choose their own name."

"That would make for an interesting roll call at school, don't you think?" Theo chortled, polishing off her drink. "And let's be honest, imagine how bad the names would be if we let teens pick their own. Not that it would matter anyway, I'd probably still be Theo."

Auryn put down his glass, gazing at her as he leant his arm on the bar top. "Let me guess. It's a part of you now?"

"Pretty much," she replied, quietly enjoying that he was giving her his full attention. "Besides, it suits me."

"What do you mean?"

"Because I'm bi," she said, waiting tentatively to gauge his reaction.

Auryn processed this for a second, then nodded. "Cool! Makes sense, I guess. So, can I ask you something?"

"Sure," she said, dreading the sleazy or homophobic statement she was sure he was about to make, her mind thumbing through all the responses she'd heard before. What would he go for? 'So, you'd be up for a threesome then, yeah?' or perhaps the more traditional 'It's just a phase, right?' or maybe it would be her personal favourite 'I bet *I* could change that!'

He took a sip of his drink, then tilted his glass towards her as he continued. "What do you think of rounding up all of the rude, arrogant, and self-entitled people, putting them on a deserted island, and nuking it? It seems like a perfect solution to the world's problems if you ask me."

Theo couldn't hold back the laugh that came blurting out. That was not what she was expecting, not by a long shot. "I don't know. I don't think there'd be many people left in the world once we were done."

Auryn grinned at her and shrugged. "Would that be such a bad thing?"

∞∞∞∞

It was very late or very early, depending on your outlook on things. Normally, Theo would be home, trying desperately to catch restless snatches of sleep between nightmares, tossing and turning her way into one of her precious days off. Instead, she and Auryn were still entrenched at the bar, drinking and talking, the sheer lack of windows shielding them from the sunlight that had sprouted from the horizon over an hour earlier.

As the time passed, Theo found it impossible not to trail off in thought about Auryn. Beneath his goofball exterior, he was a serious, intelligent man, and in spite of his deeply rooted distrust of humanity, he had a caring nature that defined everything about him. They'd been talking for hours, but it seemed like mere minutes. It was as if they were old friends catching up after spending years apart, the conversation easy, comfortable, and calm.

"Theo?"

She snapped out of the tangential ponderings playing out on the floor in front of her and smiled up at him guiltily. "Sorry."

"It's okay. Maybe we should go. It's pretty late."

He was right, but she didn't want the night to end; it had been perfect so far, in a roundabout sort of way. With a feeling of defeat, she nodded, hesitantly rising to her feet, the alcohol in her system making her unsteady.

She felt gentle hands wrap around her shoulders, and she looked up to find Auryn watching her with a warm smile. Turning away, she felt his hand touch her chin and guide it around to face him again, realising as he did that he was barely an inch taller than her. Her eyes traced the laugh lines on his face and the shadows cast by his small dimples before lingering on the soft grey-blue of his irises. Tilting his head, he swept the stray wisp of hair that had escaped her bun behind her ear, her face inching closer to his as a flutter of butterflies sprang to life in her stomach. It seemed like both an eternity and an instant before they kissed, and with that, everything around them faded away.

146

Auryn

It was always slightly disconcerting falling asleep in the warm glow of morning only to wake up to the same light. Auryn had never liked it personally, but as he lay staring at a ceiling he didn't recognise, he found himself less bothered than usual. The clock on his phone read midday, which meant he'd only managed a few hours sleep, but surprisingly that didn't bother him either. It was funny how insignificant his problems felt in the light of a new flame.

He rolled over to find Theo resting on her side, her eyes closed and mouth slightly open, and he couldn't help but smile. Slipping silently out of bed, he pulled his clothes back on and snuck out of the room. Her apartment was small, but it had a balcony just off the lounge room with a small wooden table and a couple of chairs. As he opened the door to it, a cool breeze washed over him, and he approached the railing, looking across at the surrounding apartments. A sliver of sunlight had managed to find its way down through the concrete jungle, and basking in its warmth, he marvelled at how peaceful it was. Given his proximity to the city, he expected to hear cars rushing past, horns blaring, and people shouting as the rat race raged on, but a near-silent calm filled the air.

Taking in the small measure of tranquillity afforded to him, Auryn allowed his thoughts to lead him back to that first moment, only hours ago, when he had spotted Theo across the bar. She hadn't been dressed to the nines and plastered with make-up like so many of the other women there. In fact, it had been evident from her slapdash outfit, tight bun, and wearied demeanour that she was there for a stiff drink after a long shift. Still, when he'd caught a glimpse of her laughing, he could have sworn she'd lit up the entire room.

As he continued to reminisce, his mind tugged him along to the moment she'd sat down at the bar, replaying her witty disposal of unwanted suitors and the wry smile that had left him yearning to know

147

everything about her. He relived the flip of his stomach when she'd agreed to stay after close and the effortlessness of the ensuing conversation. Then, all at once, his mind delivered him to the serendipitous second of anticipation before their lips met, when he held her gently in his arms, her broad frame filling the space as though it were made just for her.

Closing his eyes, his memory repainted her in that perfect freeze-frame. Her soft, pale skin that made him forgive the world its sharpness. The shadows caught in the hollows of her collarbones that struck down his fear of the dark. The all-consuming depth of her grey-blue eyes that he lost himself in willingly.

Torn from his reverie by the sound of shuffling, he looked over his shoulder to find Theo standing in the doorway, a blanket wrapped tightly around her, her hair still in a bun but slightly unkempt, her mascara smudged unceremoniously beneath her eyes.

"Hey," he said, a grin bursting onto his face.

Theo gave him a small wave, stepping outside with a yawn and leaning on the railing to watch the world with him. "Did you sleep okay?" she asked

"Yeah. I'm still tired, though."

"Me too."

He looked across at the dishevelled beauty beside him, and she smiled, the curl of her lips stoking the fire in his chest.

Auryn had never been a fan of one-night stands. A single encounter wasn't enough to pass judgement on another human being, and meaningless throes of passion had always seemed too vapid and empty for his taste. Even if he hadn't felt that way, though, there was something about Theo that drew him in and demanded he stay. They'd only spent the briefest time together, most of it mixed in a swill of alcohol, but there was a connection between the two of them that made him feel like he'd known her for years, the strings between them attaching organically like re-fusing bone.

Theo shifted her stance, blowing a few stray strands of hair off her face with a puff of breath. "Do you have to work today?"

"No. You?"

Theo shook her head, the potential of the situation hanging in the air.

More than anything, he wanted to spend the day with her, but social etiquette meant he couldn't exactly invite himself to stay. He considered taking her out for lunch, but he didn't quite feel up to venturing out in his current state of sleep deprivation. The other option was to invite her to his apartment instead, but he feared it might come off as too forward. Finding the best way to request her company without seeming overeager was quite the conundrum, and he scrambled anxiously in the silence until he hit upon a plan.

"So, what do you normally do on your days off?" he asked.

"When I'm this tired, I tend to just curl up on the couch, eat junk food, and watch horror movies. Tragic, I know, but something about watching idiots being killed soothes me," she chortled.

"Sounds pretty similar to what I do, except I usually go with action movies instead," said Auryn, trying to sound as nonchalant as possible.

"Do you like horror?"

"Yeah. I have a decent collection at home. You're not the only one who likes to see idiots get their comeuppance. I think it's a hospo thing."

Theo laughed, pulling the blanket tighter around her as a gust of cool wind whistled between the buildings. "You want to stay here for a bit and watch a movie? I can make breakfast."

"Sounds great," he replied, quietly pleased his plan had worked.

"I just need a quick shower first. Make yourself at home. I'll only be a minute," she said, kissing him on the cheek before he knew what hit him and scurrying inside.

∞∞∞∞∞

When Theo had first told him she worked as a pastry chef, Auryn had simply been happy to have someone to share hospitality war stories with. As she placed a plate on the table before him, though, he found a deeper appreciation for her career choice. A stack of fluffy, raspberry-studded pancakes drizzled with caramel sauce awaited him, and as Theo sat down opposite and gestured for him to eat, their alluring smell mixed with the scent of coconut lingering in her damp, tousled hair. Without hesitation, he grabbed his fork and tucked into the first breakfast in years he wasn't eating mechanically or out of obligation. Every mouthful brought with it a satisfaction he had

149

forgotten food could offer, and as such, it was with much disappointment that he devoured the final morsel and leant back in his chair.

"Those were insanely good!" he said with a contented sigh.

"Eh, I've made better," Theo deflected before reaching to gather the empty plates.

Auryn shooed her away. "Not a chance. The cook doesn't wash up. You go pick a movie."

Placing the plates in the sink and flicking on the tap, Auryn couldn't help but think how natural things felt with Theo. It was almost like falling back into a long-forgotten routine, each action comfortable and familiar. Amidst the bubbles, his brain attempted to reconcile the fact that only yesterday she had been all but a stranger, and as he set the last fork onto the draining rack, he shook his head at how inconceivable that seemed.

The afternoon was whiled away in a nest of pillows and blankets on the couch, Theo bundled in his arms as horror movies played one after the other. Her choices teetered the line between cult classic and craptastic: the kind so bad they almost circled back to being good. Well, maybe not good, but certainly amusing. Regardless of their quality, though, they served as the perfect remedy for a pair of weary souls in need of mindless entertainment.

As another villain's tragic backstory was revealed, Auryn couldn't help but admit he empathised with the antihero far more than their privileged victims, and to his pleasant surprise, he discovered Theo's sentiments mirrored his own. The idea of being pushed to madness and revenge by an uncaring world was one they could both understand, and the desire to wield one's pain as a weapon resonated so profoundly that they missed the remainder of the film while they discussed the matter.

It wasn't until the soft purple of dusk hung around them, about five movies into their marathon, that they managed to untangle themselves long enough to order pizza. As they ate, Auryn looked over at Theo, who was battling with a string of mozzarella refusing to break away and be eaten. He was starting to fall for her, and as warming as that realisation was, it brought with it a dilemma. He had an unshakeable habit of latching onto people too quickly and driving them away with his eagerness. The idea of that happening with Theo terrified him, and so, taking a deep breath, he swallowed all the things he wanted to say to her and took another bite.

With her cheese-based struggles overcome, Theo glanced across. "So, do you have any family?"

"Yeah," he shrugged, finishing his mouthful before continuing. "I don't really talk to them much, though. Besides, they all live in Sydney. You?"

"Same. Not the Sydney bit; the not talking bit," she replied, separating her next slice before steering the conversation away from the obviously contentious topic. "Do you have to work tomorrow?"

"Unfortunately, yes," he nodded. "It's my admin day. I have to go in and see the owners, go over the reports, do the ordering. You know, boring shit."

"Sounds like fun," she said, raising a sarcastic eyebrow.

"Pays the bills, I guess."

"So apart from watching movies, what else do you do on your days off? Hang out with friends?"

"No. I stay home for the most part. Watch television, play video games, that sort of thing," Auryn replied, picking at the toppings on his last slice of pizza. "I don't really have any friends."

Why the hell did I say that? She probably thinks I'm a fucking loser now, he thought to himself, cringing inwardly as he braced for what he was sure would be merciless mocking, or at the very least, a burst of laughter.

Much to his surprise, however, she met his eye with a half-hearted smile. "I don't really have any friends either. I mean, I have work friends, but I don't have anyone ..." she broke off, losing focus in the middle distance just over his shoulder.

Auryn reached across and took her hand, waiting patiently as she returned to him in the present. "Well, you have me now. I know it's not much, but at least I have decent taste in movies, right?"

Theo laughed despite herself, and Auryn, temporarily losing control of his inhibitions, leant in and kissed her, his self-consciousness melting under the warmth of her lips.

∞∞∞∞

151

As the clock ticked past ten and the credits rolled on another movie, Auryn looked down at Theo curled up against him, her head on his shoulder, his heart sinking as he acknowledged the fact he'd have to go home. He didn't want to; he wanted to stay in that apartment forever with the amazing woman that he'd somehow managed to convince to spend time with him. In a perfect world, he would just blow off his job and live out his whims without consequence, but reality didn't work that way.

Determined to savour the moment, he closed his eyes and ran his fingers through her hair, enjoying the sensation before it was gone.

The movie flashed back to its title screen, and he reluctantly opened his eyes again. "I'd better go. I've got work really early tomorrow."

"What time?" she asked, tilting her head back and looking up at him. "Ten."

Theo raised an eyebrow. "Ten is not early."

"It is for me!" he replied with a grin.

She smiled back, and he kissed her before standing up.

"You okay to get home?" she asked, rising to see him out.

"Yeah, I'll catch the train," he replied, a loaded silence filling the space. He yearned to say more, to pour his heart out, to put into words the feelings pounding in his chest, but it was too soon. "So, I, uh, guess I'll message you tomorrow."

"Okay," Theo nodded, her eyes full of her own unspoken feelings.

Auryn glanced down at his shoes for a second. "Thanks again for the pancakes. They were amazing."

"You already told me that," she said, the impish smile that made him weak crossing her face. "But you're welcome. And thanks for paying for pizza."

Auryn chuckled. "Considering how good those pancakes were, I think I underpaid!" Theo rolled her eyes, and he put his arm around her waist, kissing her tenderly. "Bye."

She stared into his eyes, her hand resting on his neck. "Bye."

Pulling away slowly, Auryn turned and opened the door. As he stood on the threshold, he looked back and waved, the pair sharing a meek smile before he slipped away to begin his journey home, laden by his heavy heart.

∞∞∞∞

It was a weird sensation, returning to his apartment, mainly because it didn't feel like his anymore. It held his possessions but not his soul; he'd left that behind. Changing into a pair of tracksuit pants and brushing his teeth, his mind flitted to Theo, and he had to fight the urge to march out the door and go straight back to her.

The feeling was strange, profound, and sudden, and he struggled to understand it. Their kinda sorta date that had somehow managed to span most of the day was essentially the relationship version of cramming for a test: intense, but you came out of it knowing a lot more than you had before you started. It wasn't normal by any standards, but he didn't necessarily see that as a bad thing; rather, he saw it as a positive. He could now confidently say that he'd never met anyone he connected with as seamlessly as Theo.

She was unique: sarcastic and disdainful, but underneath that guise, sweet and caring, with a deep empathy that surprised him. She hated humanity as a whole in the same way he did, but simultaneously, she ached from all the suffering those around her had to endure, bearing their grief as her own. As paradoxical as it was, she appeared capable of both rational detachment and immovable emotional entanglement all at once, but Auryn understood it. Humans were a blight on the Earth, full of an overpowering greed and boundless apathy that was slowly destroying the planet, but he still had hope for them. He believed that, given the opportunity, humanity would rise above its petty squabbles and unite as one, committed to saving the world instead of razing it to the ground. That was, of course, if they could ever get past their own selfishness and focus instead on personal sacrifice for the greater good.

For the first time in his life, Auryn had finally found someone who vibrated on the same obscure wavelength as him, and as he slid between the cold sheets of his bed, he plugged his phone in and stared at it. He felt compelled to text her, but the fear of seeming desperate paralysed his hand. For all he knew, she was lying in bed staring at her phone for the exact same reason, but then again, she might just as easily be falling asleep unfazed by his absence. Sighing, he closed his eyes, wishing as he did that his bed didn't feel so empty.

∞∞∞∞∞∞∞∞∞∞∞∞∞∞∞

There was just enough light to vaguely make out the walls surrounding him. He ran his fingers over the cold, damp stone of the cave, its jagged texture clearly Mother Nature's handiwork. Tunnels led off in every direction, each shrouded in the same inky darkness.

Fear gripped him as he tried one path after another, searching in vain for a way out when, without warning, he slipped on the slick rock, collapsing to the ground as pain shot through his leg. He clambered to his knees, feeling around for something he might have missed, but there was nothing: no cracks, no seams, no draughts, no pinholes of light. His despair swelled as he sat back on his feet, ready to give up, the chill of the stone seeping into his bones as desolation began strangling his soul. He was trapped. Death was inevitable.

Suddenly, something wafted past him: a cool, gentle breeze that cut through the stagnant air. He held out his hand, feeling the breeze ripple across his body, and scuttling around on all fours, he tracked it to a small opening hidden behind a boulder. Crawling through, he emerged into a slightly wider passageway, the fresh air renewing his spirits and leading him onwards until he reached the mouth of a large chamber.

After a few moments, light began to fill the space, a pale haze permeating the darkness from an unknown source. It bounced off the dust particles, growing brighter until he was surrounded by a soft white glow that cast out the shadows with its ethereal splendour.

Certain now that he was on the right path, he quickened his pace, crossing to the tunnel on the far side and heading down it until he reached a corner and stopped. Yet again, the way ahead was steeped in stale, musty darkness, and he stood there dejected for a moment, glancing back over his shoulder to the glowing chamber. With a sigh, he returned, stepping back into the safety of the light and taking a deep breath. He might still be lost, but the chamber offered something to carry him through all the trials ahead: hope.

The Humber, Britain, 567 CE

Only a few families had settled along the banks of the Humber in the small kingdom of Lindsey. While living there offered them freedom, they'd quickly learned it was a difficult place to survive. Brigands lurked along the secluded roads looking for easy prey, the weather was always against them, and the land was harsh and unforgiving.

Despite the hardships, though, the shared trials knitted the community together. The women were all sisters by blood or by choice, the children were as close as siblings, and the men were as thick as thieves. Only Ingram stood apart, but then, he'd always been strange.

Leila sat waiting for him on the riverbank, staring out over the water. Her thick, wavy, chestnut locks danced across her shoulders in the wind, framing her soft features and contrasting starkly with her fair skin and green eyes. Wisps of hair were constantly falling across her face, and she tucked the strands back behind her ears, her thoughts ebbing and flowing in time with the waves pushing their way upstream.

The Humber was an estuary, a meeting point between two rivers and the sea, where the water level followed the tides. It offered fish for the taking, although the expanse beyond the mouth of the estuary could be rough and treacherous at times, and the fishermen of the village moored their boats further down the banks, taking them out on the high tides in search of food.

As for the land, it was fertile in places but boggy in others, and farming in such conditions proved to be somewhat of a precise art. Still, generations of farmers, including her father, Arlys, continued to yield enough produce to sustain them all. It was a hard existence, but those who resided there were proud to call that slice of the world their own.

Arlys loved to recount, with ever-growing gusto, the story of how her great-great-grandfather had come to the region by boat after the

Roman Empire collapsed, braving perilous seas, only to be set upon by Britons looking to defend their territory. Her father would sit, tankard in hand, regaling anyone who would listen with the tale, his narration so fervent that by the time he was through, there was often more mead sloshed on the table than remained to be drunk.

Leila must have heard the story several dozen times over her sixteen years of life, and she'd noticed the story seemed to grow more elaborate and outlandish with each retelling. In its current iteration, the legend had her great-great-grandfather single-handedly beating back the Britons, armed only with a wooden paddle and a flagon of wine. She was sure he had been a tough and honourable fighter, but she was equally sure the other men on the boat must have helped out as well. After all, they'd driven their foe all the way back to the other side of the island.

The Britons were still a threat despite her kin's historic bravery, though, and sortie parties were constantly raiding throughout Lindsey, attacking small, vulnerable villages on the fringes as they tried to reclaim their land from the Angles. Luckily, the Humber sat a considerable distance from the Britons' territory, and Leila's home was yet to be raided. Regardless, it was something that played on the minds of all who lived there, a constant fear that permeated their entire existence. They were farmers and fishermen, not fighters.

Hearing gulls screech overhead, Leila looked up, watching as they glided effortlessly against the dreary canvas of unbroken clouds blanketing the sky. Such weather was far from uncommon, and she drew her knees up to her chest, pulling her pale green, woollen dress taut around her legs and hugging her cloak tighter as the wind whipped off the water, cold and biting. There were almost no trees along the banks to break the barrage either, the land instead covered in coarse, straw-coloured grass.

When the tide was in, as it was now, the water came right up to the edge of the village, but when it was out, it revealed a sandy beach dotted with tiny pools and jumbles of pebbles and shells. It wasn't the most picturesque landscape, but for Leila, it was all she knew.

The sound of splashing drew her attention back to the water, and she caught sight of a small, wooden boat gliding towards her, propelled by two oars that rose and dipped through the waves in unison, watching as it came to rest on the bank of sand. A hooded figure alighted the weather-beaten vessel, pulling it firmly onto land, before glancing down at her. Pale hands pulled back the cowl of the grey cloak to reveal the cold, refined face of a man in his early twenties, his hair dark brown and hanging to his shoulders, his eyes a piercing grey.

"What are you doing here, Little Butterfly?" he asked.

Leila couldn't remember when or why he'd started calling her Little Butterfly, but she had no recollection of him calling her anything else, not that it irked her.

"Waiting for you, of course," she replied with a wry smile.

He shook his head as he started walking towards the village, Leila quickly jumping to her feet and jogging to catch up.

"Surely you have better things to do with your time," he retorted as she reached his side.

Leila shrugged. In actual fact, she had a multitude of chores to do; she'd just chosen to wait for Ingram instead. Each day he set out in his boat and disappeared for hours. When he returned, he brought nothing back with him. Where did he go? What did he do? His routine fascinated her no end, but then so did everything about him.

Everyone else in the village was friendly, jovial, and eager to help out, but Ingram kept to himself. He rarely talked and never joined in on anything social. In short, he was a mystery, and Leila wanted to be the one who solved it.

She glanced across at him as they walked. "Can I ask you something?"

Ingram stopped, meeting her eye.

"Where do you go every day?" she asked, waiting eagerly for an answer, her heart pounding.

There was a moment of pause, but he did not reply. Instead, he set off once more, completely ignoring her.

Leila scurried after him. "Why won't you tell me?"

Sighing, he stopped again and turned to regard her. "Because it is none of your business, Little Butterfly," he said before continuing up the gentle slope that abutted the north-western edge of the village.

"Hey! Wait!" Leila called after him.

By the time she drew caught up, though, he'd reached his hut and disappeared inside. Leila scowled in frustration but lowered her hand, which hung poised to knock on the door, deciding she was best served heading home before her father flayed her. There were still many chores to be done, and she clearly wasn't getting any answers out of Ingram today.

∞∞∞∞

It was nearing midnight, and Leila lay nestled in her blankets, staring up at the rafters. Shaken from her thoughts by a voice outside, she realised her father was still awake, mumbling to himself as usual. She shuffled out, still wrapped in her blanket, to find him sitting on a log beside the fire, a tankard of mead in his hand.

Arlys was a short, stout man, but years of hard work in the fields had made his muscles tough and wiry, his hands calloused, and his face weathered and worn. Although his appearance was coarse, his eyes were gentle and kind, identical to his daughter's but framed by deep laugh lines which spoke of happy times despite hardship.

As she approached, he looked up, the tufts of grey speckling his thick hair and bushy beard shining in the firelight. "What are you doing up?"

Leila shrugged. "I couldn't sleep."

Arlys nodded and gestured at the log beside him.

As she sat down, she turned to him. "Can I ask you something?"

"What is it, Sprout?" he asked, a patient smile accompanying the pet name he'd bestowed upon her before she was even born.

"Everyone here has a job, right? The men tend the fields or go out fishing. The women look after the huts, cook, and take care of the children. Everyone has to do their part."

"Of course. It's what holds our little village together."

Leila looked into the flames for a moment, watching them dance in the darkness before she continued. "What about Ingram then? He never seems to do anything useful. Why do we let him stay if he doesn't help us?"

Arlys took a long sip of his mead. "Why are you asking?" he enquired, his brow furrowed.

"It's just, I see him leave every day and return every night empty-handed. You always make sure everyone in our village does their part, even the children. I don't understand why he isn't expected to help."

Arlys stared into the fire pensively before answering. "That is a

158

complicated question, and the answer even more so."

"What do you mean?"

"The thing is, Sprout, Ingram's father died in an accident before he was born, and his mother fell ill just after his sixth birthday. You were too young to remember her, but she was very close to your mother and I, like a sister. By the end, she was racked with fever and delirious with pain, but before she passed, she grabbed my arm and begged me to take care of her son, to keep him safe." He took another sip of mead, the emotion of the memory clear on his face. "It was a solemn promise I made that day, and it is one I have kept. I helped take care of him; we all did. He was always a strange child, though. He would disappear for hours at a time, and we'd often find him staring at the sea or gazing into the fields. I remember asking him why he didn't play with the other children, but he wouldn't answer me. He just shrugged and walked away. The only child I could ever get him to spend time with was you."

Arlys paused, his thoughts swirling in the contents of his tankard. "As he grew older, I gave him jobs around the village, and he did them, for a while at least. Eventually, he stopped and began disappearing every day. Remembering my promise, I let it go, but it started to cause discontent with the other families, so I sat him down to talk about it. I explained that although the village had loved his parents, their pity for him was fast-fading in the wake of his idleness, and he needed to pull his weight. I reminded him that I had made an oath to his mother, but I could not extend the grace it had bought him forever. He sat in silence for a long time before he finally spoke. He asked me what would happen if the village was attacked. I told him we would be devastated, that we didn't have the means to fight back against brigands or bandits. I remember him looking up at me with a sternness I hadn't seen in him before. It was then he asked me to make him a deal."

Leila leant forward. "What deal?"

"That as long as the village and its people remained safe, he could stay. He vowed that we wouldn't be attacked by anyone while he was here, and if we were, he would leave on his own."

"I don't understand."

"Neither did I," Arlys said with a frown, "but Ingram wouldn't say anything else. I thought about it for some time and spoke with the others. In the end, we decided to take him up on his offer in honour of his mother. To this day, we've never been attacked by anyone, and so he remains."

Leila shook her head. "I still don't understand."

Arlys finished off his mead and put the tankard down beside him. "I don't know how, but he's protecting us. The only thing I can think is that he's learnt to track dangers and lead them away. That would explain why he disappears every day."

"You really think that's where he goes?" Leila asked sceptically.

"I don't know. It doesn't really matter, though. He's held up his end of the deal, and I am satisfied with that." He stood up slowly, holding out his hand to her. "Come on, Sprout, it's time for bed. We've both got a lot of work to do tomorrow, and only one of us finished our chores today!" He flashed her a cheeky grin, his warm smile melting the tension as they both walked back inside.

∞∞∞∞

Leila's week was consumed with chores: there were clothes to wash and repair, flax to weave, wool to spin, meals to prepare, and huts to maintain. Her mother had died giving birth to her, so the responsibility of maintaining the household fell squarely on her shoulders. By the end of the week, through sheer determination and the drive of curiosity, she finished her tasks early and asked her father if she could take their small boat out onto the river. The tide was on its way in, so he acquiesced, albeit grudgingly, and only on the proviso that she return before dusk.

It was a rare sunny afternoon as she set out on the Humber, slowly crossing the estuary. She had no fear of the craft she travelled in or the current she battled against. Everyone in the village had experience with boats in one way or another; it was part of their way of life.

Leila put as much strength as she could into each stroke of the oars, slicing through the water with determined efficiency. What she hadn't told her father was that this wasn't a casual trip; she was in search of Ingram, who'd been absent from the village all week. She didn't know where he'd gone, but she swore to herself that today was the day she found out.

As she rowed, Leila revelled in the sunlight bathing her skin, enjoying it while she could. Scanning the shore for signs of Ingram's boat, she travelled to the end of the estuary and stopped. To go any further would mean venturing onto open waters, and Leila wasn't game to do that. One rogue wave and her tiny vessel would likely capsize or, worse yet, be dragged out to sea.

Instead, she paddled alongside the peninsular that jutted out from the tip of the far bank, narrowing the mouth of the Humber and offering safety from the incoming tide. As she neared the curve where the peninsular sprouted from the mainland, she found a semicircular, sandy beach and ran aground gently, hauling her boat further ashore so the waves couldn't reclaim it.

Glancing around, unsure of which way she should go, she finally decided to just close her eyes, pick a direction, and follow it. She started on her way, heading for the coastline on the other side of the narrow spit of land, then turned left and followed the shore. It was flat but treacherous, with sinkholes and hidden rocks everywhere. After carefully picking her way along for a quarter-hour or so, she saw something on the beach and stopped. It was a boat.

Leila walked over, bending down to examine it, and realised it was Ingram's. She surveyed the area, a little puzzled, when she remembered the partially submerged stretch of land she'd spotted just down from where she'd disembarked on the peninsular. Suddenly, it all made sense. Instead of travelling out the mouth of the estuary where the fishermen would easily spot him, Ingram must have been using that temporary tidal passage to reach the coast in secret. But why? She turned full circle, scouring her surroundings to no avail. Where was he?

Bolstered by her newfound knowledge, she marched on, hugging the water's edge until the beach ended. Leaving the sand behind, she prowled the top of the eroded cliffs, searching for any clues of Ingram's whereabouts in the bleak landscape, the trees just as sparse as around her village, the land blanketed with the same hardy grass that refused to die despite the wild, salt-laced winds.

Almost an hour later, when she was on the verge of admitting defeat and heading home, the air fell still around her. A strange thrumming sound came from inland, and Leila turned on her heel, trying to locate its source. In an instant, it stopped, and the air pressure seemed to drop. She peered out across the swaying grass and spotted a crop of tall rocks in the distance.

With excitement swelling in her chest, she hurried towards them, drawing closer to find them laid out in a tight circle, almost as though they'd been placed that way by human hands. Creeping forward as quietly as possible, she reached the edge of the outcrop and peeked between the towering stones.

What played out before her eyes was mesmerising. Ingram stood with his back turned, the ground beneath him nothing more than compacted earth, his tunic resting on a rock off to the side. He raised his hands, and the pressure rose, Leila's ears popping as the same strange thrumming sound from earlier echoed around her.

Tiny specks of dirt began to tremble and ascend upwards, and her breath caught in her throat, her mind reeling. The very air itself seemed to dance around his body, waves of invisible energy bursting forth as he stood there, his arms outstretched. She felt the hairs on the back of her neck stand on end, then all of a sudden, everything stopped.

Ingram stood perfectly still, the only sound within earshot that of the wind as it whistled past, its natural flow restored. Leila spun around and closed her eyes, trying not to move as she pressed her back to the stone that concealed her.

"What are you doing here, Little Butterfly?" he asked with a sigh.

She poked her head around sheepishly to find him facing her. "How did you know?"

He breathed slowly, his chest flexing as he did so. "I felt your presence."

"You felt my presence? What are you talking about?"

Ingram didn't answer as he grabbed his tunic, slipping it back on and squeezing out of a gap in the circle.

"What are you talking about, Ingram? You could feel me watching you? Can you always feel people who are out of sight?" she asked, a million questions flooding her mind.

"No. Only you," he said, actively avoiding eye contact by fiddling with the lace of his tunic. "I can always feel where you are."

With that, he turned and started walking towards the shore, his pace so brisk that Leila practically had to run to catch up with him.

"Hey! Don't run away!"

Ingram stopped, meeting her eye with knotted brow. "Why are you here? Why did you follow me?"

"I hadn't seen you all week," she shrugged meekly. "I wanted to find out what you do every day and what's so important that you neglect the village."

He looked down at the ground for a moment, considering his response. "Tell me, Little Butterfly, why are you so insistent on knowing what I do with my time? Why do you seek me out at every opportunity?"

Leila opened her mouth to answer, but no words came out, and she frowned. The honest truth was, she didn't know why. Suddenly, Ingram smiled at her. As far as she could recall, it was the only time she'd ever seen him smile, and it completely changed the dimensions of his face. Gone were the cold, stern features that made up his icy facade, and without them, he appeared almost warm and approachable.

"It seems we both have questions to ask ourselves," he said, tilting his head as he regarded her. "Maybe we should continue this conversation when we have the answers."

Leila nodded mutely.

Ingram went to leave but paused. "You won't tell anyone what you saw today, will you?"

There was an air of concern in his voice that she'd never heard before, and she quickly shook her head.

"Thank you," he said, giving her another small smile before turning and walking away.

∞∞∞∞

Months passed, another summer drawing to a close, and yet Ingram and Leila did not speak, avoiding one another as they tried to sort through their intentions. Leila saw him leave in his boat every day, but she never told anyone what she'd witnessed, not even her father. At night, she'd lie in bed and ponder the questions Ingram had posed. Why *did* she follow him around so much? She'd always been intrigued by him, even as a child, but what was it that drew her to him exactly? Much sleep was lost in the pursuit of answers, but none came to her.

The fields were good to them that year, and the harvest was bountiful. In fact, they had more than enough food for their small community. A vote was held, and Arlys was nominated to take the excess produce to a neighbouring village and trade it for supplies. To Leila's surprise, he decided to take her with him, although he was vague about his reasons when she questioned him. In the end, she simply put it down to his usual overprotective nature.

It was a two-day trip to the nearest market, and with the wares loaded into the sturdiest cart they could find and a horse borrowed from one of their neighbours strapped to it, the pair took off down the long dirt path. The countryside rolled past them at a snail's pace as they plodded along at their leisure, making their way west alongside the Humber before veering south at the juncture of a smaller river.

They met no other travellers on the road, and the first day passed without incident, the mild weather and jovial conversation making for a pleasant journey. By nightfall, the tree cover along the roadside had grown denser, and they set up camp under a large oak, a small fire keeping them warm as they slept.

When Leila awoke the next morning, it was to find ominous clouds hanging overhead, and she looked at them nervously as they continued down the road.

"Should we find shelter?" she asked, looking across at her father, who seemed unfazed.

"No, a little bit of rain won't hurt us, and we need to get these goods to the market before day's end. If we stop, we won't make it. The fresher the food looks, the better the trade."

"But I hate getting wet."

"I know, Sprout," he said, laughing heartily. "I remember the time I threw you into the river when you were seven. You wouldn't speak to me for a week."

She couldn't help but chuckle at the memory.

Arlys glanced at her for a second before returning his eyes to the road.

He'd been giving Leila the same look since they'd left the village, and she'd finally grown sick of it.

"What is it?" she asked. "You've clearly got something you want to say."

"Tell me, Leila," he said with a soft smile, the sound of her name sounding foreign coming from his lips. "Have you given much thought to your future?"

"Not really. I imagine it involves taking care of you, old man," she laughed, poking him in the side as she tried to deflect the imminent discussion.

"Taking care of me is no way to spend the rest of your life. You're growing into a beautiful young woman."

"Where are you going with this?" she asked, eyebrow raised.

"I'm talking about you finding a husband and settling down."

Leila rocked back in her seat. The thought of marriage had been one she had pushed aside whenever it arose. She'd always considered herself somewhat unattractive, with a face only a father could love. Others in the village had told her time and again that she was beautiful, like her mother, but she'd never believed them. Besides, she liked being independent, and her free spirit despised the idea of being tied to another.

Out of nowhere, the image of Ingram smiling popped into her head. Why was she thinking of him now? She shook it off, turning back to her father. "I'm happy taking care of you, though."

"That's very kind, but you have to think of your future. There's no one suitable for you in the village, and making a better life might mean moving away."

Once again, the image of Ingram crept into her thoughts, and once again, she shook it away.

"I care about you, Sprout, more than life itself, and I wish you could stay my little girl forever, but the time has come for you to look at starting a family of your own. I just want you to find the right person, to be happy. I want to know there is someone to care for you when I'm not around anymore."

Leila glanced down at her hands in her lap, blinking away the tears welling in her eyes, her heart not ready for the thought of a life without him in it. "I don't want to leave."

"What if I take you to the markets and introduce you to some of the young men there? You might find yourself having a change of heart," he asked, his warm smile speaking of a father who only wanted the best for his child.

"No, I won't," she said, crossing her arms with adolescent petulance. "There's no one that interests me in that way, and no one ever will."

"No one, eh? Somehow I doubt that. But if you're sure, I guess we can just sell these goods and return home. Perhaps when we get back, I should sit down and speak with Ingram."

"Why would you speak with him?" she snapped.

He regarded her for a moment, then burst out laughing. "I'm sure you'll figure it out in due time, Sprout. Let's leave it be for now."

Leila didn't want to leave it, though, but as she grabbed her father's arm to push the conversation, she saw his face and stopped. Arlys was looking down the road, his skin drained of colour, his eyes wide.

"What is it, father. What's wrong?"

The horse snorted nervously, and she spun around to find a man standing in front of the cart. His face was hard, with welts dotting his forehead and cheeks, and he wore tattered clothes that barely covered his body. Leila swivelled in her seat as the cart ground to a halt, catching sight of five more brigands surrounding them, dressed in similarly shabby attire. All of them wielded clubs that were little more than large branches with the twigs ripped off, but they hefted them slowly and deliberately, leaving little doubt as to their intentions.

They spoke to each other in a language she didn't understand, and her breath quickened as fear began to take hold. The man in front gestured at them, motioning for them to leave the cart. Leila looked across at her father, who nodded stoically, and they climbed down, being careful not to make any sudden moves, the man beckoning them over. A chill swept through her body as she saw another of the brigands walk behind her and stand guard.

The man in front waved his club at them, his shouting unintelligible, but Arlys understood his meaning regardless and grabbed her arm, leading her off the road. The men were going to steal their cart and their food, but at least they'd survive.

Suddenly, Leila felt sinewy arms grab her from behind, picking her up off the ground, a hand clawing its way up her leg as she screamed in terror.

"GET AWAY FROM HER!" Arlys yelled, lurching forward to protect his daughter.

Before he could get more than a step, though, another of the men

166

interceded, smashing him over the head with his club.

Arlys tumbled to the ground as Leila was pulled backwards, clawing for release. "FATHER!"

She pleaded for them to stop as the man swung downwards once more, clubbing her father in the head, again and again, his body twitching slightly as blood pooled beneath him, seeping into the dirt.

Leila was carried away kicking and screaming into a nearby grove and thrown down at the foot of a towering oak tree. Sobbing in pain and fear, she looked up as all six men surrounded her, each one sporting a predatory grin.

The ringleader shouted something, and the others laughed, one grabbing at his crotch while another started to undo the rope that held up his trousers. Two men came in from either side, grabbing her shoulders and pinning her to the ground. She didn't know what to do. She was frightened and alone, but as the fear turned to rage, she allowed her adrenaline to take over and did what came naturally.

Yanking her arm free, she snatched up a fallen branch in her right hand, driving its point into the neck of the man on her left, blood spurting into the air as he grabbed at his wound. She pulled her arm back, smashing her fist into the face of the man on her right, who yelped in pain as he gave up trying to restrain her and instead clasped his now disjointed nose.

Scrambling to her feet, Leila swung the branch in a wide arc, trying to fend the others off, but a large, meaty hand grabbed her wrist, ripping the weapon from her and tossing it aside. She fell backwards, hitting the ground hard, the air shooting out of her lungs.

As she wheezed for breath, her eyes flitted between the men, their faces grim as they glared at her. The two she had injured nursed their wounds, their blood dripping onto their tunics to mix with that of her father's. The ringleader let out a shout, and they all lunged forward, seizing her and holding her down as she felt hands tearing at her dress.

Time slowed in that moment, her entire life hanging from a precipice as she strained under the weight of the band of brigands. Her efforts would make no difference in the end, but she refused to go down without a fight. She thrashed around, inflicting as much punishment with her knees and elbows as she could, writhing in the grasp of her assailants until something blunt struck her temple.

All at once, her vision blurred, her limbs no longer obeying her commands as she vaguely felt her dress being ripped open. Cold air flowed across her body, the chill on her skin matching the fear that rippled down her spine as her legs were held apart by rough hands.

She closed her eyes, not wanting to see what happened next, when suddenly, a thunderous detonation shook the ground, the air vibrating from the shock wave. The men released their grip, scrambling to their feet to find a figure standing on the road behind them, black energy shrouding its form like smoke. Blinking to try and steady her swirling vision, Leila propped herself up, but she was unable to make out any details through the darkness.

The men picked up their clubs from the dirt, brandishing them as they left her behind to encircle their new enemy. Slowly regaining her faculties, Leila clambered to her knees, pulling the tatters of her dress tight around her with shaking hands, a trickle of blood dripping down her cheek and onto her bare, bruised shoulder. As she stared at her saviour, the energy parted for a moment, and she saw who it was: Ingram.

Rushing in, the ringleader swung his club to deliver a crushing blow, but Ingram brushed aside the attack with his left arm before striking the man in the chest. The impact sent the ringleader careening through the air and crashing into a tree some distance away, his body curling around its trunk with an unsettling crack.

The remaining five brigands paused for a moment, and it was the last mistake they would ever make. Ingram stepped forward, shooting a stream of energy into one of the men, knocking him backwards to the ground, his skull taking the brunt of the landing. Another man attempted to grab Ingram from behind, but he simply flexed his back, energy exploding outwards, dispatching the assailant into a thicket.

The remaining three men approached from all sides, swinging their clubs in unison, beating Ingram over and over. He crouched down, absorbing the blows until finally, he reared up, the air crackling all around him. There was a detonation, and a ripple of darkness expanded around Ingram, catapulting the men upwards, past the treetops, and leaving them to fall to the ground like hapless hailstones.

Turning full circle, Ingram surveyed the aftermath. All of the men lay still, save one, who clambered out of the thicket and rose to his feet defiantly. Ingram strode forward, shafts of black energy flowing from his back, the power emanating from them arcing like lightning. He grabbed the man by the throat, his sole remaining foe attempting one last desperate attack, swinging his feet and fists but missing the target on all counts.

Leila felt the air pressure rise, and she watched Ingram hold him at arms-length, energy swirling around them as the man began to cry out in excruciating pain. The pressure intensified along with the screams, the noise reaching a crescendo then stopping abruptly as the man fell limp. Ingram tossed him to the ground, and Leila blinked in horror and disbelief at the lifeless body of a man who had threatened her innocence only moments earlier, his skin singed, smoke pouring from his eye sockets.

A deafening silence surrounded Leila as she stood up, her eyes moving to Ingram, who drew several slow, deep breaths before turning to her mournfully. She staggered towards him, shock controlling her movements more than free will, and he stepped forward, catching her before she tumbled to the ground and putting her back on her feet.

"Are you hurt?" he asked, removing his tunic and helping her slip it on.

She was, but her mind was far too numb to register it.

"I'm okay," she said, looking around at the carnage as she fashioned the remains of her dress into a skirt, securing it at her hip with its broken straps. "How did you...What did you...?" she spluttered, unable to pick out a complete question from the flurry in her head.

"That is a conversation for another time," he said, dipping his head to try and get her to make eye contact with him. "We should tend to Arlys first."

All at once, the grief hit her, his name piercing her chest like a dagger and stealing her breath in one fell swoop. Turning on her heel, she spotted her father's familiar form beside the road and stumbled over, falling to her knees at his side. Tears poured down her cheeks as she lifted his head onto her lap, his skin already growing cold, his stare vacant.

She brushed the hair from his blood-caked forehead and kissed it. "Wake up, Father. It's me. It's Sprout," she cooed as her tears fell on his cheek and cut rivers through the blood. "Please, wake up."

Rocking back and forth, she begged for one more moment, pleading for the fire in his eyes to be rekindled. As she patted his hair, though, her fingers found the concave indent on the back of his skull, and her heart broke.

Time marched on all around: the trees soughed, the birds chirped, and Ingram righted the cart that had tipped over in the fight, spilling its contents over the road. The horse had broken free of its tethers and bolted, and thus, pulling a knife from his belt, he cut away the snapped ropes and tossed them aside.

In the midst of everything, Leila sat frozen, trapped in the vacuum of horrific loss. Outside of herself, she heard nothing, saw nothing, felt nothing.

After what seemed like an eternity, gentle hands weighed on her shoulders.

"Wait here, Little Butterfly. I'll put him in the cart so we can take him home."

Leila nodded mutely, and Ingram crouched down beside Arlys, pausing for a moment, bowing his head in respect for a father who had cared for him in the absence of his own. Reluctantly, Leila yielded her grasp, instead clutching at the grass as she watched Ingram lift him carefully from her lap and place him in the tray of the cart, propping his head up on a small sack of rye. With a quiet word of gratitude, Ingram delicately closed Arlys's eyes one last time and covered him with a blanket.

Moving to the shafts the horse had once been lashed to, Ingram picked them up and swivelled the cart homeward. As he turned to fetch Leila, he found her standing beside him, her jaw clenched, her brow knotted, her eyes fixed on the road.

"You should ride in the cart, Little Butterfly. You're hurt. You need the rest."

Leila shook her head. She needed to walk, to focus on the movement instead of the trauma threatening to overwhelm her.

He nodded in understanding, and so they set off, the tragedy rendering them both incapable of speech as they travelled through the rain and the night, neither of them willing to stop on their solemn funeral march.

∞∞∞∞

It was almost light when they finally arrived at the edge of the village, a delicate amber glow appearing on the horizon. No one was stirring yet, at least not outside, and Leila looked across at Ingram as he put down the cart shafts, his chest beaded with sweat from the exertion.

"Thank you," she said, her voice barely more than a whisper.

Ingram nodded, rubbing his arms thoughtfully. "This is where I must leave you."

"What?! You can't go. Not with father gone!" she exclaimed frantically, hurrying over to block his path.

"I'm sorry, but I made a deal with your father to keep the village and its people safe," he said, looking down, his face full of regret. "I failed him, and so I must go."

Leila shook her head, trying to deny the inevitable. She knew in her heart that she couldn't stop him, though.

"Will I ever see you again?" she asked, her voice quavering.

"Perhaps. I will not leave this land, but I will find somewhere I can live with my failure in peace, away from others." Ingram paused at her side for a moment as he moved past her. "Goodbye, Little Butterfly."

He went to take another step, but Leila grabbed him by the shoulder. "Wait! I have to know something before you go."

"What is it?" he asked, meeting her gaze.

"How did you find me? How did you know I was in trouble?"

Ingram stared at her for a moment, a wince of pain crossing his face. "I always know where you are, Little Butterfly."

And with that, he turned and walked away, his form melding into the shadows. Leila went to follow after him, getting as far as the village edge before she heard the shouts of folk emerging from their huts and approaching the cart to find their fallen kinsman. Her eyes flitted between the shadows and the torchlight of the villagers calling out her name, her curiosity daring her to continue. In the end, though, duty called her back to her father's side.

∞∞∞∞

True to his word, Ingram did not return to the village, neither to retrieve his few meagre possessions nor to attend Arlys's burial. In spite of his absence, Leila lay two stems of bluebells on the grave, sitting beside it in the early autumn sun that blessed the day, telling her father of Ingram's bravery, of his regret, and of his promise kept. She lingered there, between the twin resting places of her parents, lost in her memories until the day waned and the night's chill set in.

In the months that followed, Leila insisted on taking her father's place tending the fields, trying to fill the void he had left with actions that made her feel close to him. Initially, the men had objected, but they respected her father too much to disallow her, and as she proved her worth, those opinions faded away. In the evenings, she would visit Arlys's grave, bringing him a tankard of mead and telling him of the happenings in the village and the bounty of the crops. It was small comfort, but comfort, nonetheless.

The village prospered, and people from neighbouring areas started to move in until it almost resembled a town. The roads grew more pronounced, and the houses became larger and more numerous. Despite the growth, though, Leila felt more isolated than ever, her days blurring into one, her nights lonely.

With her father and Ingram gone, the strings tethering her to her home snapped one by one, and as the second summer since Arlys's passing came to a close, Leila made a decision. After the crops were harvested, she would leave. She'd given her all to the village for the sake of her father's memory, but there was nothing left for her there. The time had come to follow her own path: a path that led to the man she'd thought about every day since he'd left.

Leila departed just after nightfall, taking only a few belongings with her. She left the hut and everything in it to a young family who had sought refuge in the village after their own was raided and burnt. All she'd asked in return was that they reassure everyone she'd gone to find Ingram and that no one need come after her.

Bidding them a kind farewell, she walked one last time to the grave of her father, running her fingers gently over the letters of his name carved into the wooden cross.

"You were right, you know," she whispered, "that I would figure things out in due time. I just never thought I would have to do it without you. I love you, father, but I must leave now. Rest peacefully."

Just as she had so long ago, Leila climbed into the small boat tied up on the shore, wiping a tear from her cheek as she took one last look back at the soft glow of the village. With a deep breath, she pushed the boat out onto the water and rowed across the Humber to the narrow peninsular by the pale moonlight of a rare cloudless night. Pulling the boat beyond the reach of the tide, she travelled on foot until she found the rocky outcrop where she'd first seen Ingram use his power, but there was nothing to be found there except dust and wind.

Returning to the coast, she followed it further north until she came to a spot where the waves smashed into the base of the sheer cliffs she traversed. The sea danced in the light, the tips of the waves glinting like stars, and she glanced out over the water, her eyes drawn by an inexplicable feeling she couldn't quite comprehend towards something just out of sight. She stayed the night there, bundled up in her father's thick, brown cloak, sleeping beneath the stars and thinking of Ingram.

As the dawn broke, she was roused by the sun peeking between the clouds and streaming onto her face. Still tired, she rolled over, jolting awake with a start as her eyes met the familiar shape of Ingram crouched beside her, a barely perceptible grin on his face.

"You know, I feel like I ask you this a lot, but what are you doing here, Little Butterfly?"

She swivelled onto her knees, her heart still pounding against her ribs from the surprise as she stood up, her eyes never leaving him for fear he was a mirage. His face seemed more weathered than before, but apart from that, he hadn't changed at all, his dark brown hair still softly resting on his shoulders, his eyes the same piercing grey she had seen in her dreams each night.

"You've dodged my questions long enough. I think it's about time for answers, don't you!" she said matter-of-factly, brushing the dirt from her cloak and failing miserably at her attempt to look stern.

"Of course," Ingram laughed, his smile softening his features. "I suppose that's fair. Ask away."

"Um ... Okay. Well, ahh ..." Leila spluttered, taken aback by his willing cooperation. "How do you do the things you do? You know, the thing with the darkness and the...?" She mimed the explosion of energy with her hands in the absence of suitable words to explain it. "Are you some sort of god, or demon, or ...?"

"Nothing as exciting as all that. I'm just a bit different from everyone else," Ingram replied. "You see, Little Butterfly, my soul has lived countless times before, in different places, different times, and different bodies. My abilities stem from those lives, like a power carried over from one existence to the next, growing along the way. When I was younger, I could feel it flowing through me in times of great emotion, lingering beneath my skin. One day, I snuck out of the village to a quiet spot on the far side of the fields, and I found that if I focused, I could release the energy outside of myself and use it to influence the world around me. The power itself comes naturally, but it takes practice to control it. That's why I disappeared every day."

Leila raised her eyebrows in amazement. It all sounded utterly ridiculous, and yet something in her heart assured her that he was speaking the truth.

"How do you know this?" she asked. "Did someone tell you?"

Ingram shifted in place. "I think I always knew, deep down. Do you remember when I used to tell you stories when we were kids?"

"Yes," Leila replied, smiling at the memory. "I always liked the one in the desert with the winding river, the giant pyramids, and the black-skinned woman who could fly. You never would tell me how it ended."

"Well, those stories, they weren't made up. They came to me in my dreams." He paused for a moment, gauging her response before he continued. "As I got older, though, I realised they weren't dreams at all; they were memories. Over time, they became clearer and more frequent, until finally, the truth became something I couldn't deny. Every time I die, my soul holds together, finding a new body to inhabit. In this way, I continue living. As soon as I understood that, I knew my destiny wasn't to stay in the village."

"So why did you stay?"

"Because of you."

"I don't understand," she said, shaking her head.

Ingram closed his eyes, swallowing nervously before looking up at her meekly. "I stayed because I love you, Leila. I always have, ever since we were young."

Stunned by his admission, Leila's reeling thoughts left her nothing to offer but a look of silent confusion, her voice muted by the emotion swelling in her chest.

"Remember that day you found me in the rocks not far from here, and I sensed you behind me? You wanted to know how I could do such a thing, but I wouldn't answer you. It wasn't because I was unsure.

It's because I was a coward. I was afraid you'd reject me." Ingram took a step towards her, meeting her gaze intently. "My love for you is the reason I can always sense your presence. You're like a beacon only I can see, a fire in the night, a guiding star. When you were attacked, I knew you were in danger; I felt it in my very being. I only wish I'd reached you sooner. Arlys was a good man. He didn't deserve to die like that."

Lifting his hand, Ingram cupped her cheek gently. "I'm sorry I left you. I was ashamed of my failure. It pained me to walk away that day, but I didn't think you'd ever want to see me again."

"Of course I did," she blurted out. "I thought about you every day as I worked, and your face was the last thing I saw every night before I fell asleep." Her heart bounded with relief as she admitted the truth she'd tried so hard to deny. "I love you, Ingram."

He swept her hair from her face and tilted her chin up, leaning down and kissing her with the passion of a heart set free, the weight of secret affection lifting from both their shoulders. When their lips finally parted, they lingered in the afterglow, forehead to forehead, nose to nose.

"So, what now?" Leila whispered.

Ingram pulled back, flashing her a grin before pointing over the waves in the direction that had captivated her the night before. "I live on a small island just out there. I built a cabin, and there's a little garden as well. It's not much, but it's yours if you want it."

Leila beamed. "How do we get there?" she asked, looking along the shoreline for a boat.

"The same way I got here," he answered, taking a step back.

Pressure built up all around her, and slowly, a pair of wings emerged from Ingram's back. Each one was made of three shafts of darkness dancing with ethereal, pitch-black lightning and appearing translucent in the sunlight that shone down from another break in the clouds.

Incredulous, Leila crept forward, her eyes fixated on them as she inched closer. She reached out her hand to touch them, only to find there was nothing there *to* touch, her hand drifting straight through them. The only feeling they elicited was a gentle tingle of energy that caused the hairs on her arm to stand on end as it rippled up towards her shoulder.

"Come on," he said with open arms.

She hesitated for a moment, then stepped into his embrace, wrapping her arms around his neck, his mouth close to her ear.

"Hold tight, Little Butterfly," he whispered, hugging her close, "and don't look down!"

Closing her eyes, she pressed her cheek to his chest, the unseen energy around them crackling, the pressure change making her ears pop. All at once, her feet left the ground, her stomach lurching into her throat as she felt air rushing past. She dared to peek for a moment and saw nothing but water below, quickly burying her face into Ingram's neck and clinging tighter until her feet touched the earth once more.

Blinking into the sunlight flooding her vision, Leila glanced around, the shore they had left behind now little more than a thin line on the horizon. Gulls glided overhead, squawking their disapproval at their unwanted visitors, and the waves pummelled the large, jagged boulders that encircled most of the island. She stood at the edge of a meadow swaying with golden grass and dotted with a few gnarled, windswept trees. On the far side, she spied a small, wooden cabin with a thatched roof, the sight of it making her glow inside. It had been so long since she had felt at home.

Ingram took her hand, an excited smile still painted on his face. "Let me show you around."

As he took her by the hand and guided her from one site to the next, Leila saw in his face a look of youthful joy that sparked a fire in her soul. If she had asked him, he would have told her that he felt as though he was seeing everything for the first time. He would have explained how the trees seemed stronger in her company and the ground softer underfoot. He would have declared with unbridled confidence that the cabin felt bigger, warmer, and happier with her inside it. And he would have thanked her for bringing his world into focus. She didn't need to ask him, though; she already knew.

Eventually, Ingram led her to the small stony beach hidden on the north side of the island, and they sat watching the seals gambol in the waves as the ocean's symphony played on. Side by side, hand in hand, the day slipped away around them.

As the sun set, she ran her hand along Ingram's arm, which was wrapped gently around her waist. "Can I ask you something?"

"Sure," he replied with a casual shrug.

"You said you left every day to practise, but why dedicate so much time to it? If you'd spent more time in the village, you could've spent more time with me."

She'd meant it to be a playful question, but as his face dropped, Leila realised she'd struck a nerve. "I'm sorry, I didn't mean to pry."

Ingram shook his head. "Don't be sorry, Little Butterfly. The reason I practise so often is complicated."

She could see the concern on his face as he pondered what to say next and decided to spare him. The day held so much joy, and dredging up answers to painful questions would only spoil it.

"I'm not little anymore. You do realise that, right?" she jibed, poking his chest with a grin. "And you know, I never really understood the whole butterfly thing. Why did you start calling me that anyway?"

Ingram watched the waves lapping at the shore as though replaying the memory in his head before he spoke. "When you were young, maybe eight or nine, I heard a couple of the older girls teasing you, calling you an ugly moth."

Leila remembered the events vividly, their words and heartless laughter echoing around her mind. The night after it had happened, she'd laid in bed, her knees tucked up to her chest, sobbing so loud it had woken her father. He had sat holding her hand and humming a lullaby for hours until she'd finally fallen asleep.

As Arlys's comforting expression reappeared in her mind, Leila blinked away a tear.

"I remember thinking how pretty you were," Ingram continued, taking her hands in his and pulling her back to the present, "not like a moth at all. More like one of the beautiful butterflies we'd see every spring fluttering between the bluebells. After that, I made sure to always call you Little Butterfly. I can stop if you'd like."

Leila just shook her head, leaning in and kissing him tenderly. Everything around them swirled into a haze of insignificance as they moved deeper into their embrace. Never have two people cared less about a sunset.

∞∞∞∞

177

Ten years passed, give or take a few days. Leila and Ingram made their home on that tiny, secluded island, revelling in their peaceful privacy, cut off from the outside world, just the way they liked it. They were almost entirely self-sufficient: the vegetables Leila grew were able to sustain them, their few chickens provided them with eggs and feathers, and Ingram quickly became an adept fisherman. Although they didn't have a lot, they were happy.

Once a year, on the anniversary of Arlys's death, Leila would return to the village. She'd leave a sheath of wheat from her small garden on her father's grave and assure him that he need not worry about her, and she'd trade what she could in return for the supplies their little island could not provide them. Each year, the village seemed to grow larger and more prosperous until it no longer resembled the quaint little community from her youth. It was a thriving town, bustling with faces she didn't recognise, and each year, leaving it behind hurt less.

One day, Leila woke to find Ingram gazing at her, the gentle morning rays creeping in around the door and lighting his face. As she reached up to sleepily caress his cheek, his lips curled into a contented smile, and she couldn't help but think how love had softened him over the years, remoulding him until he bore no resemblance to the cold, distant boy she had grown up with.

"Good morning, my beautiful butterfly," he said, brushing the hair from her face. "Did you sleep well?"

With a grin, she pulled him towards her, kissing him passionately. "What do you think?"

"I'll take that as a yes," he said, rolling out of bed and slipping on a pair of trousers and a long-sleeved tunic. "I'm going to practise, but I'll come back and help you dig up the parsnips in a little while, okay?"

"Don't take all day. I'll miss you."

"I won't be long," he said with a wink, grabbing an apple from the table and disappearing out the door.

Leila sighed, rousting herself from the warmth of the blankets and shuffling over to stoke the fire before pulling on a dress, sliding on her shoes, and clasping her father's cloak around her shoulders. Even after all these years, the cloak still felt like one of his hugs, and a sentimental pang tugged at her heart each time she donned it.

Stepping out the door to face the new day, she took a deep breath, letting it out slowly. The sun, somewhat uncharacteristically, was free of its usual veil of clouds and intending to make the most of its warmth, she decided to wander along the rocks.

Ingram still practised every day without fail, and she had given up trying to stop him. It was important to him, although he'd still never tell her why, so she let the matter lie, not wanting it to interfere with their otherwise blissful life together. If nothing else, she took solace in the fact he was less obsessive about it than he used to be, and it was rarely an all-day affair anymore. He'd set up his practice grounds on the other side of the island so as not to disturb her, and she reasoned that by the time she reached him on her walk, he would be finished and could accompany her back.

The air was thick with sea spray and the wind cold as she picked her way from one boulder to the next. Coming to a large crop of tall rocks, she clambered up. Leila always loved watching the waves from above and looking out over the undisturbed vastness of the ocean. As she reached the top that morning, though, she spotted something in the distance that perplexed her. It was a tiny boat heading slowly towards the island from the mainland.

She observed it for a moment to see if it changed its course, but it held true, heading straight for the small stony beach a short walk from where she was. No one had ever come to visit them, but she assumed it was someone from the village, and she hurried to meet them, jumping down and jogging over as the boat came ashore.

She reached the beach just in time to see the lone passenger plough the vessel into the rocks with little care for the damage it caused to the hull, and she stopped short. A hooded figure alighted and stepped onto the beach, shrouded in a dark cloak with a grey tunic peeking out from underneath. They straightened up to an alarming height, pulling back their hood, and Leila gasped in shock. It was a man with skin as black as the night sky, skin like the woman in Ingram's stories when they were children. She had never seen such a person.

The man smiled at her, his teeth in bright contrast to his dark complexion. "Hello!" he said, his accent deep and guttural.

Leila waved, intrigued.

"My apologies for not announcing my arrival, my good lady," he said, walking forward and bowing his head politely.

Leila nodded back, studying the man's face. He had eyes of rich brown, a broad nose, full lips, and a shaved head. Each feature seemed more striking than the next, but none more so than the series of eight scars that ran over his skull in two rows of four, beginning just behind his ears and coming to a point between his brows like the tip of an arrow, scars clearly placed there with purpose and meaning.

"My name is Uduak. I have come a long way in the hopes of speaking with your husband."

"We're not married," she replied politely.

"You have made a commitment to each other for life, have you not?"

Leila nodded.

"Then you are married," he asserted. "You do not need others to do this for you. It is already done."

She smiled at him. He had a strange charm to him that eased her fears. "I suppose you're right. But why do you wish to speak with him?"

"I mean no disrespect, ma'am, but that is a private matter between myself and your husband. Where is he now?"

"He's foraging on the far side of the island," she lied as casually as she could.

Uduak tilted his head in acknowledgement. "I see. May I wait for him at your home perhaps? I do not wish to intrude on his work."

"I don't see why not," she said, waving him after her. "This way."

"Excellent! Thank you," he replied with a smile, following her up the beach and over to the cabin.

Inviting him in, Leila watched Uduak remove his cloak and set it down on one of the chairs, looking around in admiration.

"This is quite the home you've made for yourselves here," he said, brushing the creases from his tunic.

"It is, isn't it. You know, you're actually the first person to ever visit."

"Really? You don't entertain guests?" he asked.

"No, we quite enjoy the solitude."

"Something that is in short supply in this day and age, what with people spreading around the world like rats," Uduak said solemnly before abruptly changing tack, gesturing around the cabin. "So, your husband built all of this?"

Leila beamed with pride. "Yes, before I came to live with him."

"Unbelievable! Such fine workmanship. I look forward to meeting him. He must be a remarkable man."

Offering her guest a seat, Leila sat down opposite. "You've never met him?"

"No, I only know him by reputation, I'm afraid. I must admit, though, I was surprised to find out he had a wife."

"Why is that?" she asked, puzzled at how the strange man had come to know of Ingram, or her for that matter.

"I suppose it's just not something I ever imagined for him. He's always been a recluse," he said with a laugh, running a hand over his shaven scalp and leaning back in his chair. "Still, I can see why he had a change of heart. You are a most beautiful woman."

Leila blushed. "Oh. Thank you."

"No, no, it's never any trouble to speak the truth," he said, waving away her bashfulness as a sound came from just outside the door. Uduak's eyes narrowed. "It seems your husband has returned."

Ingram walked through the door, saw the unexpected visitor perched at the table, and stopped.

"What's going on?" he asked, turning his attention to Leila.

"This is Uduak," she said, rising from her seat. "He came all the way to our island just to talk to you."

Uduak chuckled to himself. "Well, not talk exactly."

As Uduak moved to stand up, Ingram dove forward, pushing Leila to the ground and knocking the table over in the process. She hit the floor hard, protesting, but quelled her objections as she looked past Ingram to see Uduak approaching, his hands shooting forward and gripping Ingram by the throat, lifting him up as if he weighed nothing.

"It's nice to see you again, Little Phoenix. It's been so long since we've had a chance to play!" Uduak said, his voice's soothing tone making way for malice.

The air around him began to shimmer, and Leila rolled behind the table as a detonation ripped through the cabin. Suddenly, she saw Ingram go flying into the air, bursting through the thatched roof and turning it to splinters that rained down around her as she crouched with her hands over her head.

She peeked from behind the table as the destruction settled to see Uduak near the door, watching her intently. He strode forward, grabbing her by the throat and pinning her against the wall. As Leila gasped for breath beneath his grip, eight blades of black energy appeared from his back like the legs of a spider, wavering on either side of her, threatening to strike.

Uduak looked over his shoulder and out the now doorless frame before turning to face Leila again with a cruel grin. "It's a shame, really. I was so lost in the moment I forgot to rip you to pieces in front of him," he said with an unsettling calm. He let go of her, his smile only growing wider as she slumped to the ground, coughing. "A pity, but there's no point in killing you now, is there? I guess you'll have to be the one who watches him die."

Without another word, Uduak leapt into the air, wisps of smoke and clouds of dust the only thing left in his wake. As her eyes lingered on the space he'd vacated, she suddenly realised why Ingram had always been so obsessive about practising.

Adrenaline called her to action, and she grabbed a broken chair leg from amongst the debris, clambered out the door, and began to sprint towards the other side of the island. In the distance, she could see Ingram patiently awaiting the imminent battle, his black wings blazing, his face skyward as his foe descended upon him.

As she ran, Leila watched Uduak crash into Ingram, sending him flying backwards and skittering across the grass until he came to a stop in a pile of dirt while Uduak himself landed lightly on his feet. Ingram jumped up, power surging through his body as he threw out his hands, unleashing it towards his enemy, but Uduak conjured a shield, deflecting the attack before launching his own.

Black energy smashed into Ingram, who was pushed back by the sheer force of the assault. Steadying himself, he leapt into the air, seeking to attack from above. Uduak was too quick, though, hitting Ingram with another burst of energy as he descended, sending him hurtling sideways into a large rock, the force of the impact cracking it in two.

Leila rushed towards the fray, brandishing the broken chair leg, her heart racing as Ingram slowly stood up, shaking his head. Uduak charged at him, his blades transitioning from ethereal to tangible in an instant as he leapt into the air. Diving to the side, Ingram dodged the attack, but Uduak recovered and launched himself forward, his blades slashing across Ingram's chest, the advance inescapable.

Ingram cried out, dropping to his knees in pain as blood poured from his wounds, dyeing the tatters of his tunic a deep scarlet.

"You fight hard, Little Phoenix. It's almost a shame it has to end in your death," Uduak said with a satisfied laugh, his voice booming across the island. "Almost."

The blades arched from Uduak's back, preparing for a parting blow, but before they could so much as twitch, Leila leapt between the pair in a desperate attempt to save Ingram. She swung at Uduak with the chair leg, but he batted it away, grabbing her arm and holding it tightly, unfazed by her struggles.

He looked down at her with contempt. "You are a fool to attack me, girl. Can you not see the power I possess? I am Anasazi. You are nothing, an ant under the foot of an elephant."

Retracting his blades, he grabbed her by the throat with his free hand. Leila thrashed fruitlessly, attempting to wrestle free of his vicelike grip as she felt the pressure surge, the hair on her neck standing on end. Out of the corner of her eye, Leila saw Ingram launch himself forward, trying to take Uduak by surprise, but he flew backwards as if struck by an invisible force, and Leila lost sight of him.

Amidst the thrumming that flooded her ears, Leila heard one last thing. "Let this be a lesson to you. Something to take with you to your grave, so you never return!"

There was a flash of darkness, and pain hammered into Leila's chest, several of her ribs cracking from the impact. All of a sudden, she found herself airborne, shooting over the island like a rock from a catapult, an involuntary scream escaping her lips, her cloak billowing around her. Her vision came in flashes that matched her heartbeat until finally, she smacked into the sea and sank beneath the waves.

∞∞∞∞∞∞∞

Ingram cried out in rage at the sight of Leila sailing through the air, and he leapt after her, his wings blazing behind him as he soared upwards. Below, Uduak stood watching him, his blades once again emerging from his back, flexing hungrily. A cold smile crossed his face, and he crouched down, building up his power before springing into the air like a spider towards its prey.

He caught up to Ingram mid-air, grabbing the back of his foe's neck with both hands, all eight of his blades sinking into his torso, his wings disappearing like smoke. Uduak drove him back down, blood flowing after them like twisted crimson rain, and Ingram hit the ground hard, tumbling through the long grass and skidding to a stop in the middle of the meadow. Landing gently beside him, Uduak flipped him over with his foot. Ingram grimaced in pain, blood oozing from the puncture wounds as Uduak dug his heel into his chest, eliciting a groan.

"Do you understand now?" Uduak asked. "Do you finally comprehend? Every life you live will end with the same slow, painful death, for you and everyone you love. Give up now, Little Phoenix, and spare yourself the suffering."

He removed his foot, walking off into the haze of dust before springing into the air and disappearing in the direction of the mainland.

Ingram cried out as he strained to roll over, using his elbows to inch his way towards the shore, towards Leila. With each passing second, he could feel his strength draining away, but he refused to stop as he edged closer to the sea, a trail of blood left in his wake.

∞∞∞∞∞∞∞

When Leila hit the water, it was as though the world had ended. She couldn't tell which way was up, the muffled silence of submergence causing her to flit in and out of consciousness.

Her soul battled the darkness until her legs finally began to work again, kicking desperately as she tried to propel herself towards the light. The weight of her father's cloak hung heavy on her shoulders, though, dragging her towards the inky depths. With her lungs screaming out for air, she clenched her jaw and did the unthinkable; she unhooked the cloak pin, watching for a frozen moment as the last remnant of her father sank into the shadows.

As she breached the surface, she gasped for air, her stinging eyes just able to make out the island some distance ahead. Her chest burnt like fire, and her limbs felt like dead weight, but she didn't care. She had to make it to shore. She had to reach Ingram.

The waves propelled her forward, the tide bringing her closer and closer until she finally felt sand and pebbles beneath her feet. She dug her heels in, trying to stand up, only for the next wave to topple her over again. Eventually, the sea released its grasp, and she hauled herself on hands and knees out of the water and across the stony beach. She collapsed to the ground, exhausted, when she spotted Ingram, his body lying prone at the foot of the rocks a short distance from the beachhead.

With every ounce of strength she had left to muster, Leila scrambled to her feet, stumbling over and slumping down beside him. His laboured breath whistled from his mouth, and she rolled him onto his side, stroking his cheek as his eyes fluttered open.

"I knew you would ... survive ... my beautiful butterfly," he croaked between breaths, reaching up a shaking hand to brush a strand of damp hair from her face.

Blood dripped from his mouth, and Leila saw the deep puncture wounds running down his side, his once pale tunic now almost entirely red.

She lay down in the dirt beside him, her face only inches from his, and leant in, kissing his nose gently. "We both survived, my love," she whispered, wiping away the blood from his lips.

Ingram shook his head. "No. My time ... in this body ... has come to an end," he said, wincing as he swallowed. "You can ... follow me. You can find me ... again."

Tears ran freely down Leila's face, dripping onto the dirt as she grasped his hand tightly in hers, kissing his fingers.

He smiled at her. "You will always be ... my beautiful butterfly."

Ingram's chest fell still, and his hand went limp. Leila called out, pleading with him to get up, telling him he was strong, but in the end, it made no difference. He was gone.

"I love you," she whispered, her voice cracking as she kissed his forehead, closing her eyes and pressing her nose to his. "I will find you again. I promise."

∞∞∞∞

In the aftermath of all that had happened, when she had healed enough to bear weight and endure exhaustion, Leila rebuilt her house without the person who made it feel like home. She rehung the door, righted the furniture, and repaired the roof. As for Ingram, she buried him beside their cabin, planting bluebells atop the grave and marking it with a circle of stones she had gathered from the beach they had watched the sunset on every evening for a decade.

At night, she would lie in bed and think of Ingram. She wondered if there was a baby out there somewhere bearing his soul, its eyes flickering with a light its parents did not understand, and if there was, she wondered how long it would take for the memories of their life together to emerge. When she finally fell asleep, she dreamt of seeing him again.

Uduak never returned to the island, but Leila spent many a night thinking about him as well. It was clear that he, too, had lived before, but so many questions still remained. What inspired him to spend every lifetime killing others like him? What threat did Ingram pose to him by simply existing? Why waste his gift pursuing hatred? Why not live? Why not love?

Life grew harder as time went on, but Leila never had any intention of leaving. To leave the island would mean leaving Ingram, and that was something she could not bring herself to do. Her ribs never healed properly after that fateful day, and the constant pain left her struggling to breathe, her constricted lungs a sharp reminder of all she had lost. As a result, maintaining the garden became a chore, but in the absence of her partner, it served as her only source of sustenance. It wasn't enough, though. After three years, her body finally gave out, developing a fever that left her bedridden for days. Leila died in her sleep, her arm outstretched towards Ingram's grave, and her soul rose from her body, strong, determined, and whole, disappearing into the aether in search of a new life.

As the years marched on, the cabin succumbed to the ravages of time, falling away until there was nothing left of it or the woman within. The only thing that survived was the circle of stones, weathered with age: a monument to a promise that would never be broken.

Theo

It stretched out all around him, flat and endless, heat radiating off the earth in waves and causing the way ahead to warp and shimmer as he trudged along. He knew of deserts, of towering dunes and blinding sandstorms, but there was no sand here, only barren isolation.

Small, spindly shrubs poked defiantly from the dirt, but they were little more than tufts, each one trying vainly to cling to life just long enough for the rains to come, their colours muted by the constant assault of the sun. There were no other signs of life in his bleak surroundings. Any animals still living were hiding underground or sleeping in some unseen refuge, waiting for the cool of night. He wanted to stop, but he knew he would perish if he didn't find water soon. To stop now would be to forfeit his existence.

The sun hung directly overhead, the treeless landscape offering no shadows to provide shelter from its onslaught, so when he saw a silhouette flash across his peripheral vision, he paused for a moment, shading his face with his hand as he looked around. It kept moving, maddening him as he turned full circle, trying to catch a glimpse of the elusive shape, but it had fled. He'd seen enough, though; he knew what it was.

With rekindled determination, he continued onwards. This land was unfamiliar, but he knew there must be water somewhere; he just needed to find it. The intense heat battered him, each step growing harder than the last, his muscles aching, his head heavy. He was so dehydrated he could no longer perspire, and the heatstroke was making his vision blur and pulse race. For two days, he'd been walking, and every part of him screamed in protest, calling for rest, no matter the cost. In spite of it all, his mind remained strong, and thus he carried on, undeterred.

Raising his eyes to the horizon once more, he spotted a crop of rocks in the distance, trees dotted around its base. His heart leapt at the sight.

There could be a spring there; even a puddle would suffice. A wave of adrenaline buoyed him along, and he hastened his pace, knowing the silhouette had somehow led him there. In the shade of the trees, he could rest and build up his strength, then when night fell, he could continue.

As his eyes plotted the path ahead, he spotted a furrow in the earth, cutting through the terrain towards the rocks. It was a stream; it had to be. As he reached it, though, his hopes were dashed. If there ever had been any water, it was long gone. All that remained was dust. A wave of dizziness overcame him, and he fell to his knees, nausea swirling in his stomach. Rising to his feet again, he forced himself to press on. He wouldn't fail; he couldn't.

The sun was halfway to the horizon by the time his legs finally gave out beneath him. He tried to stand, willing himself up, but his limbs wouldn't cooperate, and he could feel his body begin to shut down. Wiping his lips with his hand, he noticed they were cracked, the blood glistening on his dark skin. Rolling onto his back, he finally realised the truth. Hope was an illusion: a mirage in a desolate landscape. No one would come for him. He would not be saved.

Just as his spirit prepared to give up its fight, a shadow fell over him, the harsh light of the afternoon sun obscured by a figure standing at his side, wings flowing from its back. Blinking, he watched as the image drifted in and out of his vision. Deep down, he knew it wasn't real, but it didn't matter. His life was finished, but his journey had been a success. He'd set off on this walkabout to discover his true purpose, and he'd found it. His quest would continue in another life.

∞∞∞∞∞∞∞∞∞∞∞∞∞∞∞

Theo opened her eyes, feeling more than a little disjointed as she re-entered the waking world. Stretching her hand out before her, she almost expected to find her skin dark and blood-stained, and she wondered whether anyone else ever had dreams of being a different race and gender, dreams in which they could recognise neither time nor place.

Although she could not understand it, Theo found an odd sensation lingering in her heart. It was a feeling of familiarity akin to déjà vu, as though what she had seen was less a dream and more a strange memory from a life she'd never had. Shaking her head, her mind flitted to another image, that of the winged shadow, the Phoenix. Its presence in her dreamscapes was becoming more frequent, and the mystery it posed irked her greatly. Where had it come from? What was its purpose? And why was it imprinted so firmly on her subconscious?

Rolling over onto the other side of the bed in frustration, she was met with the faint odour of sweat and alcohol lacing the pillowcase. Her nose wrinkled in distaste, dark memories of fights with her ex invading her thoughts, triggered by the smell that had engulfed them. Echoes of cruel words and broken glass seemed to fill the space around her, plucking her heartstrings in offkey chords that set her teeth on edge, their tempo matching her racing pulse. Then, all at once, Auryn's face appeared in her mind, dispelling the anxiety and replacing it with a quiet calm, a small smile creeping across her face as the ghosts of old love yielded to the memory of new beginnings.

It had been a week since they'd met, although the days felt longer without him in them, and they'd both been working solidly in the interim. Hospitality had its perks, but the ability to socialise on a nightly basis was not one of them. Fifteen-hour shifts barely left enough time to breathe, let alone anything more substantial, the industry serving far too often as a relationship death sentence for anyone but the most committed and understanding. Still, hope sprung eternal.

Theo climbed out of bed, slipping in her contact lenses before stripping the pillow of its case and throwing it in the washing machine alongside her uniforms. As the wash cycle began to dissolve the shadows of her past, she grabbed her phone and flopped down on the couch. There was no message waiting for her, but she knew Auryn was likely still asleep after another long night shift, and so she scrolled back through those he'd sent previously, basking once again in the sweet nothings they held.

It had taken him a day to finally message her after their first goodbye: a fact Theo still shook her head about. His want to not seem clingy made perfect sense to her rational mind, but her anxiety did its best to override such thoughts and seed uncertainty about the almost tangible connection between them. As the hours had ticked on, her overthinking had tended her garden of self-doubt with expert hands.

She'd wanted to contact him herself, but her own insecurity had been paralysing, her feeling of inadequacy holding her hostage. When he'd eventually broken the silence, her fears had lost their foothold, and in their wake, the space was filled with almost constant messaging, their conversation akin to two old friends who were never short on a topic.

Venturing out onto the balcony, she looked out at the apartments across the way, the sunlight bouncing off their windows to warm the tiles beneath her feet. Work had been brutal that week, and her body ached, her mind floundering in a pool of exhaustion. By some miracle, though, she had managed to find herself rostered off for two consecutive days. Not only that, but those days just so happened to mirror Auryn's, and thus they had made plans to meet.

The excitement of seeing him again rekindled the embers of her spirit, although she'd be lying if she said her excitement was not tempered by a subtle sense of apprehension. The brief time they'd shared together had been so easy and unencumbered she feared it could not continue. The thrill of new love meant she'd built up an image of Auryn in her mind that almost didn't seem real, and their messages to one another only served to bolster her affection for him, everything they said synching on a profound and deep level. Still, her scarred heart was afraid of being blind to red flags again. Surely she was missing something.

As critical thinking wrestled the wheel from the hands of her anxiety, she reminded herself that, over time, she would discover his flaws, and the perfect image of him she was so wary of would be swept away. Eventually, she'd realise he was just like everyone else, not that that was necessarily a bad thing. A person's faults could be a joy, some could even be endearing, and as long as he accepted hers, she would happily do the same.

You can be perfect for someone without being a perfect person, she assured herself as she picked at the peeling paint on the railing and watched it float gently to the jutting balcony three floors below.

Suddenly, Theo found her inner monologue inundated with a barrage of intrusive thoughts that ousted her mindful optimism. What if he grew tired of her? What if, after getting to know her, he decided she wasn't worth the hassle? What if he abandoned her like everyone else?

The sunlight, revealing itself from a brief curtain of clouds, hit her pale skin, and she was shaken back to reality to find she was unknowingly holding her breath. Letting it out slowly, she repeated to herself, for the thousandth time that week, an indisputable truth: Auryn had walked into her life eagerly and of his own volition.

Despite her feeble attempts at positive affirmation, the anxiety swelled within her unimpeded as she stepped back inside. She thought about eating, but her stomach was churning far too violently for the addition of food. Instead, Theo concentrated on wrangling herself into something that resembled a functioning human being: straightening her unruly hair, pulling on a pair of jeans and a singlet, and applying just enough mascara to appear rested.

Standing before the mirror, she micro-analysed every part of herself. The shade of her eyes and shape of her nose. The smattering of freckles and moles that dotted her skin like paint splatter. Even the trio of faint pockmarks on her face that stood as a testament to her childhood bout of chicken pox.

As she twisted and turned, Theo saw only flaws, her body carrying on its surface the evidence of fifteen years of seesawing weight, crash diets, and self-harm. Sucking in her stomach, then letting it out despondently, she tried to remind herself that she was not overweight anymore, despite how she felt. Still, she lamented the skin hanging far more loosely than she'd like from her upper arms, and she found it hard not to feel self-conscious as she studied the slow wear on the inseam of her jeans. In that moment, regardless of her best efforts, her mind seemed to forget that kilograms were a measurement of weight, not worth.

The clock ticked over to eleven fifteen, and she sighed, practising a fake smile in the mirror in the hopes it would spark an honest one. She'd organised to meet Auryn at midday to see a movie in the city, but as the hour drew closer, Theo found it hard to breathe. Gripping the side of the basin, her irrational fears grew from a whisper to a roar, constricting her chest and making it impossible to think about anything else. Finally, she clenched her fists and took a deep breath, slipping on her leather jacket, grabbing her keys and bag, and marching out the door before she could stop herself.

As she hurried down the stairs, she beat back the demons in her

191

head, striding through the front entrance and onto the street wearing a well-rehearsed facade of confidence. Pausing at the bottom of the stairs, she hoped against hope that Auryn wouldn't let her down like all those before him had. All at once, her mind conjured forth the look of longing he'd worn as he'd left her apartment, and she started walking again, knowing in her heart that he wouldn't.

They'd agreed to meet outside the cinema at the shopping centre above Melbourne Central Station, but Auryn was nowhere to be seen when she arrived. After scanning the crowd in a futile attempt to find him, Theo gave up, plonking herself down on a bench near the entrance with a defeated sigh.

She checked her phone, but there were still no messages, and her doubts and fears flooded back, clawing at her until she finally registered the time; she was ten minutes early. Reasoning that she should at least give him the chance to be late before manning full panic stations, she scrolled through social media in search of distraction.

It was barely five minutes later when she glanced up and saw Auryn escape from amidst the throng of strangers, his headphones in to drown out the bustle of the city. He was hardly the most dapper looking man in the crowd, dressed in a black concert t-shirt of some obscure metal band she'd never heard of and cargo pants that looked like they'd been stolen from an army surplus store in the mid-nineties. Still, she was glad to see him, even if his dress sense left a little to be desired.

"Hey," he said with a smile, taking his headphones out and tucking them into his pocket.

Theo smiled back. "Hey."

"You been waiting long?"

"No," she replied casually, trying to disguise the anxiety she'd been bathed in all morning. "Only five minutes or so."

He held out his hand, and as she took it, he pulled her up into his embrace and gently kissed her, her fear losing its grip and falling away.

"Sorry. Couldn't help myself," he said, looking in no way apologetic.

Theo couldn't help laughing; he was such a dork. "Did you still want to see that superhero movie you were talking about?"

"Yeah," he said, taking her hand and leading her over to the ticket queue. "I don't know about you, but I could do with watching

192

something that involves minimal concentration, and as far as I know, the entire film is just indiscernible plot and unnecessary explosions."

"Sounds perfect."

Reaching the front of the queue, Auryn paid for their tickets, and they quickly settled into their seats. As they waited for the lights to dim, Theo couldn't help but survey the eclectic selection of people filling the auditorium. Two rows in front of them sat a cute, little, old couple who looked like they'd been together since before the creation of film. Behind them, a rowdy group of university students flicked popcorn at one another. And dotted around the place were several couples appearing to range anywhere from 'awkward blind date' to 'way too comfortable showing affection in public'.

The trailers started, and Theo felt Auryn reach out and take her hand. It was warm and strong, and she intertwined her fingers in his, the anxiety in her chest finally easing as the movie started. It was far from a cinematic masterpiece with its myriad of plot holes and characters so paper-thin they could probably slide under doors. Still, what it lacked in logic, it more than made up for in extravagant special effects and epic action sequences.

As the credits rolled, Auryn leant over. "So, what did you think?"

"It was okay," she said with a nonchalant shrug. "Did *you* like it?"

"Meh, I like movies where you can just turn your brain off and enjoy the visuals or get lost in another world, but the plot for this one was so simple it was irritating. I mean, I know it's supposed to have no plot, but this bordered on negative plot territory."

Theo nodded in agreement and turned back to the screen, watching the names scrolling by.

"What?" she asked, spying Auryn staring at her from the corner of her eye.

"Sorry, I just thought you'd want to go."

"No way. Sometimes watching the credits is the best part. Some of the names are spectacular! I was watching an awesome horror movie a while back, and the assistant director's name was Pants McFadden."

"Pants McFadden?!" Auryn snorted with laughter. "Amazing!"

Settling back into their chairs, the hunt for obscure names continued as the other filmgoers made their way to the door. By the time they finally left, the only other person in the auditorium was the unfortunate staff member who'd been tasked with sweeping up the flurry of popcorn sprinkled along the back row.

The smell of food met them as they exited the cinema, and Theo's stomach grumbled at being denied breakfast, Auryn's joining in the chorus for the same reason. Following the alluring aroma of grilled meat, they wandered over to a nearby burger joint, filing in at the back of the queue and scanning the menu.

Theo looked across at the fridge beside her as they waited, tossing up drink options with her usual indecision, her anxiety's need to constantly ask 'but what if we make the wrong decision?' extending its reach to include arbitrary beverage selections. In the end, she fell back on the safety of the familiar and settled on cream soda, but before she could reach over and grab one, Auryn opened the fridge, pulling out a bottle for himself.

He glanced back to ask what she'd like when he saw the look on Theo's face. "What?"

"That's what I was going to get!"

"So, you have good taste in movies *and* soft drinks? I might have to marry you!" he said, grinning and handing her a bottle.

With their order placed, Theo opened her purse to pay, half-expecting Auryn to object, but to her relief, he stood back as she handed over her card. Some women fancied the spoilt life, but Theo took pride in paying her own way. She was not some damsel in distress waiting for a white knight to swoop in, nor was she a pompous princess demanding she be doted on for merely existing. They had organised the date together; she was not his guest. Besides, he'd bought the movie tickets. It was only fair that she bought lunch.

Finding a quiet table towards the back of the restaurant, they sat down, eager to discuss the finer details of the shambles of a film they'd just endured. As they settled in, though, Theo spotted a man sitting behind Auryn, her eyebrow rising in a mixture of confusion and mild contempt.

"Auryn," she snapped under her breath.

He looked up. "What?"

"Turn around. Slowly."

He gave her a quizzical look before doing as she said. The man was eating his burger with a knife and fork, painfully attempting to skewer the pieces of meat and bread before shovelling them into his mouth.

Auryn's eyes went wide, and he quickly turned back to Theo, his voice a whisper. "What the hell is he doing?"

"I don't know! Who uses a knife and fork to eat a burger?" she asked with exaggerated mock outrage.

"No one does. No one," Auryn replied, shaking his head forthrightly. "Except maybe sociopaths."

Theo stifled a laugh. "It's literally designed to be eaten with your hands. Why does this place even have cutlery?!"

They both grinned, their hands reaching across the table, clasping gently. The tender moment was only broken by the arrival of their food, and they let go reluctantly, grabbing their burgers and taking a bite. The rest of the meal was eaten in relative silence, but it wasn't awkward; it was the comfortable kind of quiet that exists between people who are at peace with each other. There were no knives or forks involved.

∞∞∞∞

It was just after four when they hopped onto a train and began the journey to Auryn's apartment. A person's home was a window into their personality, and Theo was intrigued to see what Auryn's would reveal about him. The walk from the station was serene, autumn leaves floating gently to the ground as they wandered hand in hand. Reaching the ageing building, they passed the car spaces, and Theo looked over at him.

"Do you have a car?"

Auryn let out a deep breath with such force it was almost a hiss. "I used to, but I had to get rid of it. It was costing too much to maintain."

Theo heard the pain in his voice and decided to drop the subject.

Climbing the two flights of stairs, they found themselves at the front door, Auryn hesitating before turning the key and jerking the door open.

"After you," he said, gesturing inside with a meek smile, apprehension written on his face as she stepped inside.

The first thing that struck her was how tidy it was. There was no mess in the lounge room; in fact, there wasn't very much there at all. A few guitars and amps sat neatly tucked in the corner; a rather ratty, old couch faced a small cabinet topped with a television, a gaming console, and a handful of games; and a trio of tall wooden bookcases filled with books and DVDs lined the wall. Scanning the shelves for a second, Theo noticed immediately that all the movies were alphabetised, and all the books were separated by author and genre, a smile creeping onto her face as she realised he was just as pedantic and particular as her.

"What do you think?" Auryn asked, shutting the door behind him.

She walked up and kissed him on the cheek. "Your orderly bookshelves please me," she quipped with a grin.

"You know, I once had a girlfriend whose best friend used to swap them around just to piss me off."

"People like that should be spayed," she said, shaking her head in disdain.

Auryn nodded his agreement with a smile. "You wanna watch a movie?"

Theo didn't respond, instead pointing at the games console. "You have any good two-player games?"

He looked at her for a second as though he'd never met a woman who enjoyed playing video games, then knelt down, searching through his collection. "What are your thoughts on running around killing people with swords?"

"Good by me," she replied, putting her handbag down on the kitchen counter and settling into the threadbare cushions of the couch.

And so the day passed around them, their knees touching as their characters flitted around the screen, wreaking vengeance upon every foul creature they encountered. Swear words were thrown at glitches and untimely deaths, and tiny dances of celebration marked the triumph of good over evil.

The stiffness and fatigue of not moving, or seemingly blinking, for hours on end eventually caught up with them, and with night long since fallen, Auryn rose creakily from his spot to throw together a stir fry. To be fair, it actually wasn't too bad, but some of his kitchen techniques made Theo cringe as she watched on, Auryn insistent he didn't require assistance. That's not to say she didn't struggle to bite her tongue a few times as he awkwardly chopped carrots and put chicken into a pan that wasn't nearly hot enough. Still, she smiled to herself as she ate. At least he was willing to cook for her, and when you spent your entire life in a kitchen, that was something to be thankful for. Food almost always tasted better when she didn't have to make it herself.

The horror movie marathon they had begun the previous week resumed over dinner, cult classics filling the time until midnight struck. As they walked into the bedroom in search of sleep, Theo noticed the room's stark difference from the rest of the apartment. The order of the lounge room gave way to a more dishevelled space: an old doona thrown haphazardly on the bed, papers stacked and strewn awkwardly on the desk around his computer, and clothes scattered on the floor, which he promptly scurried over to pick up and squirrel away.

Beside the wardrobe sat another small bookcase, its upper shelves lined with a mix of fantasy novels and non-fiction titles, most relating to filmmaking. As her eyes reached the bottom shelf, though, she spotted something a little more obscure: a stack of screenplays from what she could only assume were some of his favourite movies.

"What's with all the screenplays?" she asked, looking over at Auryn, who was midway through changing into a pair of tracksuit pants.

"When I was younger, I wanted to get into scriptwriting, so I used to collect them."

"What happened?"

"It was a pipe dream, so I gave up on it," he replied, slipping off his t-shirt and tossing it onto a shelf in the cupboard, revealing once more the tattoos that covered most of his upper body.

Sensing that she'd touched on a sore subject, she quietly walked forward, gently tracing the inky black shape on his back with her finger. It almost resembled a cross, which seemed strange given that he was most fervently non-religious, and at its centre sat a shape similar to a yin yang but lacking the dark shading on one half.

"What does it mean?" she asked, trying to both shift the topic and unravel the mystery of the art he'd chosen to paint himself with.

"Nothing really."

Auryn sat down on the bed, and Theo pulled her hand back, disappointed with his clipped response.

"Sorry. Reflex answer," he said, seeing the look on her face and patting the bed until she joined him. "Everything has a meaning; I just don't like to explain it to people. The yin yang represents balance, and the cross pays homage to an anime series I loved when I was younger. It was in my mind for years before I finally had it done."

"What about all this?" she asked, her fingers running along the tattoos that began just above the cross, crept over his shoulders, and flowed down his arms to his hands. "It almost looks like fire and smoke."

"It represents my energy. It's a reflection of the pain in my past and a reminder of my determination to survive."

Something about their meaning resonated with her, the deep, unspoken connection between hurt and hope making her think of her own body art, both professional and self-inflicted. In the absence of words to describe the emotion stirring in her chest, she did the only thing that made sense to her. She put her hand on his neck, kissing him passionately as their clothes fell away, their bodies as intertwined as their souls.

∞∞∞∞

Night morphed into the wee hours of the morning, and as Theo rested in the nook of Auryn's shoulder, an image suddenly entered her thoughts: one of dark skin, dry riverbeds, and an otherworldly shadow.

"Do you ever remember your dreams?" she asked, looking up at him, his face a blurred silhouette in the dim light.

Auryn thought about it for a second before shaking his head. "Not usually. Even when I do, they fade pretty quickly. Why?"

She lifted her head from his shoulder and propped herself up with her elbow. "I have these strange dreams sometimes, and they never fade. They stay with me, like memories."

"Interesting. When was the last time you had one like that?"

"Last night," she said, running her fingers through her hair as she recalled the landscape in her mind. "I dreamt I was wandering through this barren wasteland. It was flat, with nothing but scrappy little bushes everywhere. Kind of like the photos you see of the road through the Nullarbor, but there was no road."

Auryn leant over and kissed her on the forehead. "That's not so strange."

"I wasn't me, though. In the dream, I was a black man. I was

198

staggering around, on the verge of death, and I kept seeing something," she said with a frown, the figure darting through her mind.

"Seeing what?"

"A winged shadow. I've seen it before in other dreams."

He cocked his head. "A winged shadow?"

"Yeah. It's called the Phoenix, but it's not an actual phoenix. It's a person with these big, black wings. Well, not so much wings, more like shafts of energy surrounded by black lightning, and it's always shrouded in darkness, so I can't see its face. Sometimes I feel like it's there to protect me, like a sentinel or a guardian or ... I don't know."

"So, just to recap, you're protected in your dreams by a shadowy creature with lightning wings called the Phoenix?" Auryn said, his tone a mixture of amusement and confusion.

Theo shrugged, a little disheartened by the levity of his response. "I know it sounds insane, but I dream about it a lot."

"Sorry, that came out wrong," he said with a wince before caressing her cheek. "If you have any other dreams, let me know, okay?"

"You sure?" she asked.

"Well, your dreams already sound more riveting than the drivel we saw at the cinema, so yes, I'm sure," he said with a chuckle before relaxing onto his pillow again.

Lying back down in the nook of his shoulder, she rested her hand on his chest, and as its steady rise and fall eased her into sleep's warm embrace, she thought about Auryn and the Phoenix, their shapes blurring into one as she drifted off.

Auryn

There was a strange and wondrous feeling encompassing Auryn of late. It was hard to explain, but it was almost as though he was floating through life, oblivious to the problems around him. The feeling shielded him from his usual dark moods and placated his annoyances, not just in his personal life but at work as well.

When he'd arrived at Benzin that morning, Carlos had been propped up on the bar, predictably drunk and demanding a mid-morning shot, but pouring it didn't seem to bother him for once.

Likewise, Adam was being his usual relentless self, complaining about the cost of stock and badgering him to try and lower it by cutting uncuttable corners. It was something that would typically have driven Auryn mad, but instead, he found it simply slid off his back as he agreed to follow Adam's doomed directives.

Once both his bosses had been mollified, they'd eventually left, and Auryn stood alone behind the bar, wiping down bottles as he waited for the first customers of the day. His quiet introspection involved only one person: Theo. He'd been thinking of her almost incessantly since they'd first met a few weeks prior. The more he thought about her, the more he realised she was someone special, someone he wanted to spend as much time with as possible, someone -

"Who or what are you fantasising about?"

Snapping out of his reverie, Auryn looked across to see Tony standing beside him, grinning like a kid who had snuck out of school early and was ready to cause mischief.

"Oh, nothing," he claimed unconvincingly as he wiped the bar top.

"Bullshit. Out with it!"

Auryn tilted his head from side to side. "It's nothing. I was just thinking about that girl I hooked up with a couple of weeks ago."

As he saw Tony's grin grow wider, he knew his strategic choice of words had done little to downplay the situation.

"You saw her again?" Tony asked, eager for gossip.

"Yeah. We spent two days together, just hanging out."

"Nice one," Tony exclaimed, clapping him on the back. "You gonna see her again?"

Auryn thought about brushing off the question but lying about it didn't feel right. "As often as time and work allows," he eventually replied, a broad smile crossing his face.

Before Auryn knew what hit him, Tony wrapped him in a bear hug. Although the two of them weren't much more than workmates, he was probably the only person who understood Auryn's trouble with women and the isolation he resided in.

"I'm glad you finally found someone as twisted as you are, man," Tony laughed, pulling back slightly and winking at him. "May the Fourth be with you."

"And also with you," he replied with an almost tangible amount of sarcasm, chuckling to himself at Tony's shameless Star Wars reference.

As they began to set up the bar, they talked more about Theo, and Auryn found that he couldn't stop once he started. The words just seemed to flow out, and he found himself armed with neither the will nor the desire to silence them. Just the thought of her filled him with joy: a feeling he'd been somewhat estranged from up until that point.

Customers started to pour in by late afternoon, and the rest of the night went quickly. In fact, the entire weekend seemed to fly by. Auryn practically swanned around the bar, remedying any issues that came up without a flicker of irritation. The work was challenging and unrelenting, as always, but like everything else, it didn't seem to bother him so much. This was, of course, primarily due to the fact he and Theo messaged each other at every opportunity. They exchanged rants about their respective workplaces and planned their time off together, hope for the future pushing back the darkness that so often threatened to swallow him up.

By the time he locked the door to Benzin behind himself at five on Sunday morning, Auryn was exhausted. Still, as he turned the key and headed off down the laneway, he found a second wind, buoyed along by the knowledge that, for once, he wasn't destined for his miserable, lonely apartment. He was going to see Theo.

The sun was not yet visible above the horizon as he turned onto Little Bourke Street, but that didn't stop it from painting hues of warm amber across the early morning sky. As he walked, the cool breeze revived his spirit, and he felt like he was seeing the world for the first time.

Making his way to Lonsdale Street, Auryn followed it until he reached Fitzroy Gardens, the green space flanking the city's eastern edge. On the left, there were towering corporate buildings that slowly morphed into smaller offices and the odd heritage house before finally giving way to a jungle of stunted apartment complexes. The roads were deathly quiet, and nothing stirred in the gardens aside from a few flitting birds and the trickle of the fountain. It felt as though he was the only person left in existence, and that thought stayed with him as he crossed the final intersection and walked up the stairs to the entrance of Theo's building.

Punching fifty-three into the dial pad, he sighed contently as he waited for her to drag herself out of bed and buzz him up. The doors slid open beside him, and Auryn quickly dashed through, crossing the courtyard and taking the lift. As he emerged into the bright light of the fifth-floor landing, he turned to find Theo standing with the door open, leaning her weary head against it as she waved at him sleepily.

"Howwaswork?" she mumbled, her words slurred and semiconscious.

"Okay. I'm just glad to be here with you again. Come on, back to bed," he replied with a smile, planting a kiss on her cheek and guiding her by the shoulders to the bedroom.

Theo flopped back down on the mattress and quickly crawled under the covers, sleep reclaiming her willingly, and Auryn smiled again as he peeled off his work clothes and slid in beside her.

In the gentle glow creeping in around the blinds, he took a moment to admire her: the soft slopes of her face, the arch of her brows, the faint freckles that dusted her cheeks. He caressed her arm before kissing her on the forehead and settling into his pillow, basking in her presence until his eyes grew heavy and he joined her in the Land of Nod.

∞∞∞∞

When Auryn woke, it was to find Theo lying on her back, flexing her fingers and grimacing in pain.

Instant concern pierced his chest, and he propped himself up. "What's wrong?" he asked, his expression one only available to those whose anxiety leads them to the worst-case scenario in every instance.

"Ergh, nothing. Work just does a number on my shoulders, so my hands feel the need to wake me up with pins and needles most days. Fear not; you won't be rid of me that easily."

"I hope not," he replied with a silent sigh of relief. "Sit up."

He prodded her playfully until she did, scooting over and rubbing her shoulders, the knots he found there crackling under his fingertips.

"You're the best," she said when he finished, leaning back onto his chest and looking up at him with a smile, "I might keep you."

He kissed her forehead, his heart swelling at her words as he watched her disentangle from his arms and disappear into the bathroom.

Work had been strenuous and exhausting for both of them that week, and, as such, their inner hermits demanded they stray no further than the couch. If they were honest with themselves, though, staying in was always their preferred option, tired or not.

Three movies later, Theo wandered off to rummage through the fridge in search of enough odds and ends to scrounge together a slapdash evening meal. That's how she described it, at least. To Auryn, however, the risotto she placed before him was possibly the best he'd ever had. Of course, she waved away his praise as if his admiration was completely misplaced. Her inability to accept compliments was a quirk he was not used to in a partner, but he heaped them on her all the same. Sometimes he was sure it was the love she put into her food that made it taste so good; then again, it was just as likely to be the love he had for her that swayed his opinion. Either way, he relished every mouthful.

As the evening rolled on, they found themselves snuggled around a tub of choc peppermint ice cream he'd ventured out to grab from the convenience store around the corner. His spoon clinked against Theo's as they fought for dominion over a small cluster of chocolate chips, and he couldn't help but think that the world often had a warped view of hospitality life.

Sure, for some, it was all about partying or splurging on going out; it was rolling into work hungover in the same clothes as the day before; it was sex, drugs, and rock and roll. For most, though, especially those in relationships, it was comfort food and binge-watching until ungodly hours; it was proposing 'Netflix and chill' with no hidden agenda; it was work hard, rest hard.

Auryn groaned with satisfaction as he ate, and Theo raised an eyebrow.

"Enjoying that, are we?" she laughed.

He nodded, sighing as he took one last spoonful. "I'm a sucker for ice cream. It's helped me through some tough times." He smiled at her, meaning it as a joke, but he immediately saw that his words affected her. "You okay?"

"Yeah," she shrugged as she put her spoon down, "It's complicated."

"What do you mean?"

"My depression and food have a somewhat complex relationship. Emotional eating and all that jazz, you know," she said, picking at the sleeve of her hoodie. "Food's a simple joy. I mean, look at ice cream. Have you ever been unhappy because of ice cream? Of course not. Unfortunately, my relationship with food means I've had some ups and downs when it comes to my weight. It's hard to be a pastry chef and maintain a healthy diet, especially when you chuck mental illness into the mix. I'll put on weight when I'm depressed, and I'll lose it when I'm anxious. I'll eat to band-aid how I feel, but then I'll end up at a weight society tells me is 'unattractive', so I'll restrict my food and lose weight. Unhealthy, I know."

She paused for a moment, but Auryn didn't interrupt, waiting patiently for her to continue. "Going on crash diets with my mum when I was a teen didn't help much either. I have a lot of guilt when it comes to eating, and I get pedantic over what I eat, especially in the bad times. I think it's because I can control food, even when I can't control my feelings. Food is consistent, predictable, reliable." Theo looked up at him and cringed. "Sorry, I'm waffling."

"Don't be sorry. I get what you mean. Everyone needs something to help them get through the day, something to hold onto when they can't get a grip on anything else. Mine's music. It's the thing that makes me feel like I can get control back in my life when it's spiralling away from me. Like you said, it's a simple joy."

"I still don't understand how listening to screaming and growling helps," she said with a grin.

"I'll have you know that growling is very rhythmic, and screaming can be quite soothing to a damaged soul," he retorted. "In all seriousness, though, finding solace in music taught me it's about the journey, not the destination. You don't listen to music for the final note; you listen for everything that came before it."

"That sounds like a good mantra in theory," she replied. "Ironically enough, though, my destination *is* a journey."

"Your destination is a journey? How cryptic. Do tell."

"Travel. Travel is my end goal," Theo said, her face lighting up at the mere mention of the word. "I want to see the world. I want to go exploring without worrying about when I should come home."

"That sounds epic. Do you have the money for a trip that big?"

"Yeah," she said, a frown creeping into her face. "The problem is, I want to share it with someone, but no one's ever wanted to come with me before. I could go by myself, but that just seems so lonely, and solo travel isn't exactly the safest option for a woman. My wanderlust eats away at me a lot of the time, and I end up feeling stuck and stagnant, like I'm not achieving anything. Do you want to travel?"

Auryn sat back, sinking into the couch cushions as he took a deep breath. He'd been to Europe a few years back and longed to return. In fact, he longed to see the entire world just as Theo did. What little travelling he'd done had brought him joy, but she was right; it wasn't as much fun when you had no one to share it with. The sudden notion of exploring every corner of the globe with someone he cared about held massive appeal, but there was only one problem: he was entrenched in debt. It would be years before he'd be able to afford such a prolonged trip. The thought of admitting that, though, scared him immensely, the knowledge he might lose her over his shortcomings paralysing his tongue.

He didn't know what to say, staring ahead with pounding heart until Theo grabbed his hand. "Does playing guitar help with your depression?" she asked, changing the subject.

"Yeah," he nodded, trying to dispel the negative self-talk droning in the back of his mind. "I write songs to help deal with the pain. When I was younger, I wanted to start a band, but ..."

He left it hanging, throwing his arms up in the air and letting them fall back down in defeat.

Theo grabbed hold of his hand again, squeezing it gently. "Are we going to your place tomorrow?"

"If you want to. Why?"

"Could you play me something?" she asked with a warm smile. "One of your songs?"

He looked down at the floor, unsure of how to respond. The thought of playing her something he'd written was terrifying. Her opinion held great weight to him. What if she hated it?

"I don't think you'll like it. My music is very heavy and full of angst."

"Maybe, but you wrote it. If it means something to you, it means something to me. I want to hear it."

Taken aback, he glanced up at her. Her plea was so earnest, so heartfelt, so different from all those who'd come before her. Auryn was certain she'd regret it once he started playing, but in that moment, it didn't matter. He finally had someone who supported him unconditionally.

"Thank you," he said, stroking her cheek.

"It's okay. It'll be like catching a glimpse inside your head. I'm curious to see what's rattling around in there anyway," she laughed, poking her tongue out and grabbing the remote. "Movie?"

∞∞∞∞∞∞∞∞∞∞∞∞∞∞∞

The shadows seemed to stretch everywhere, so much so that the bar top itself appeared to be constructed of pure darkness, each figure before him lit as though by spotlight.

Tony stood quietly polishing glasses, ignoring him as he held each one up to the light and wiped away its watermarks. Janet and Olivia bustled around the room, straightening furniture, the sound of chairs grating on the floor only adding to the discomfort of the scene around him. Carlos leant at his usual post at the end of the bar, uncharacteristically sober, sternly shaking his head, disappointment clearly evident on his face. As for Adam, he stood at the bottom of the stairs, his brow knotted, his finger pointed towards the front door.

He looked to his co-workers for support, but none lifted their gaze. He pleaded for them all to see reason, but his words fell on deaf ears

207

as though they were lost in a vacuum. Suddenly, they all raised their hands in unison and pointed at the door, which creaked open of its own volition, light swirling around it.

The rejection settled over him, and he stepped through, his head hanging despondently. Looking back, the door slammed shut behind him, the sound echoing down the unfamiliar street he found himself on, skyscrapers towering above. As strangers passed, he was met with more shaking heads, as if he'd failed them. He stumbled through the crowd, confused. What had he done wrong? He called out, demanding an answer to the haunting question, but each figure simply walked away, melding into the shadows.

Anger surged through his veins, the city dissolving around him and transforming into a small, empty room. A man stood before him, backlit, his face hidden from view. All he could make out was long, dark hair and eyes that seemed to pierce to his very core. He begged the man for forgiveness, for a shot at redemption, but he just shook his head. No one would forgive him. There would be no second chances.

The figure stepped backwards, melding into the shadows, and he crumpled to the ground, the cloak of failure growing unbearably heavy on his shoulders. As he shrunk into himself, the darkness descended, enveloping him until there was nothing left but the emptiness of his soul.

∞∞∞∞∞∞∞∞∞∞∞∞∞∞∞

Auryn had awoken haunted by his nightmare, and breakfast had been a quiet affair as he retreated into his own thoughts. The first time Theo had asked what was wrong, he'd brushed it off, not wanting to burden her with his mood, but as they sat down on the train to Footscray, she'd asked once more, determined to extract an honest answer. Initially, he'd tried to fob her off again, to assure her it was nothing to worry about, but he could see the concern on her face, and he eventually relented, relaying to her the details of the scene eating at him.

"It's probably just because you're unhappy at work," she said, trying to ease his mind.

Auryn tilted his head indifferently, knowing in his heart that it had nothing to do with his job. He wanted to tell her; he did. He wanted to voice the real root of the nightmare, to be open and honest, but the fear of ruining things between them was such a gamble. Still, he couldn't fend off the discussion forever; he owed her the truth. Swallowing the ball of anxiety in his throat, he steeled himself and rolled the dice.

"I don't know. It might not be that," he replied, trying to ease himself into the inevitable as if it were scalding water.

"Well, what is it then?"

Auryn hesitated, but there was nothing he could do. He had to tell her. "I think it's about my guilt."

"Your guilt?"

"You told me you want to travel," he said, looking down and taking hold of the kind, gentle hands he wished so very much to hang on to, "but I'm not going to be able to make that dream come true for you."

"I thought as much. Your reaction last night said it all," she replied, her words pensive. "Why don't you want to travel?"

"It's not that I don't want to travel. I do, Theo. Travelling the world with you is the best proposition I've ever heard. It's just ..." He paused, knowing the pain he was about to cause her. "I don't have any money. I have debts I need to pay off. It would be years before I could afford the trip you're dreaming of. I'm sorry."

"It's okay," Theo said quietly, her hands slipping out of his and back into her own lap, her leg jiggling as she turned and looked out the window.

Auryn saw a single tear roll down her cheek, and his heart broke. He tried to think of something to say, something to ease her pain, but his guilt kept him from any intelligible thought. After all, how do you say sorry for destroying the dreams of someone you care about? How do you offer hope in a hopeless situation? There wasn't much left to say after that, and silence filled the space between them as they pulled into Footscray station.

The walk to his apartment was slow, and he saw on her face a look of disconnection as if she were staring at the world but seeing none of it: a look he himself was no stranger to. Lifting her hand to tuck her hair behind her ear, Theo's top came up over her jeans, and Auryn caught a glimpse of the tattoo he knew inked her left side. She only had the one, but it was hardly a minute, dainty piece; it ran from halfway up her ribs all the way down to her hip. Despite the tattoo's size, though, the two roses it depicted had a refined elegance to them. The upward-facing one was inked in rich purple, and the downward one in black, their deep green stems intertwining in the middle.

Conversational inspiration came to him, and he touched her arm gently.

She looked across as though shaken from an alternate reality. "Hmm?"

"You know, you've never told me about *your* tattoo," he said, a wave of relief sweeping over him as she took the bait willingly.

"I've always loved roses. They can subsist off very little care, but if you don't handle them right, they'll shank you," she said with a completely deadpan expression.

Auryn couldn't help but laugh as he watched her try and hold back the smile tugging at her lips. "Beautiful but a bit stabby, just like you."

The tension lifted slightly, and as they stepped through the door of his apartment, he continued his inquiry. "Why two of them, though, and what's with the colour scheme? Is the black one because of your deep love of metal music?" he asked with a cheeky grin.

"No, you dolt," she replied, rolling her eyes and unconsciously rubbing her side. "There are two to represent the internal battle between mind and soul, and they're intertwined to show the connection between them. As for the colours, purple has always been my favourite, so it's there to represent the good times, while the black represents the bad. It helps remind me that without darkness, there would be no colour in life. The balance of ups and downs, you know."

He went to envelop her in a hug, but she pushed his arm down and punched it.

"Ow! What was that for?"

"For suggesting I like metal," she said, feigning outrage.

Auryn pouted, rubbing his arm despite lack of injury. "So, I guess you don't want me to play you a song anymore then?"

"Of course I do. You're not getting out of it that easily. Fetch the guitar! Mush!"

He'd been secretly hoping she wasn't in the mood anymore, but she was as insistent as ever. So, desperate to keep her from wandering back to her sadness, he picked up his seven-string guitar from its stand, plugged it in, and sat down on the couch. With shaking hands, he strummed it to check the tuning, his eyes falling on the Evangelion stickers dotting its crimson surface, the faces of characters who had seen him through the dark days of his twenties triggering uncomfortable memories.

That guitar, amongst all those he owned, held the deepest meaning. As he tuned its low B string down to an A, his mind flitted back to the moment, some ten years prior, when he'd arrived home to his old apartment to find the front door hanging on its hinges, its lock smashed in. He plucked the string again, remembering how he had crept down the hallway to the lounge room to find his world turned upside down. All of his most valuable possessions had been stolen, all except one. The guitar he now cradled on his lap had remained propped on its stand, its broken string the only reason it had been afforded mercy. With one last strum, he found the deep note he'd been searching for, and with a loud sigh to steady himself, he pressed the distortion pedal with his foot and began playing, a discordant minor chord leading the way.

Theo sat on the floor cross-legged in front of him, and he tried not to look at her as he gripped the pick tightly and plucked at the strings, the song growing heavier as it progressed. It was a song written from pain but also reassurance: a personal affirmation that he would prevail no matter the obstacle. Reaching the last chord, the final lyrics burst through his mind.

He let the chord echo around the room until he brought down his fingers, cutting off the sound and turning tentatively to Theo. "What do you think?"

"I like it. Very broody. I wish I could've heard those lyrics you were mouthing to yourself, though."

Auryn squirmed. "I can't really scream."

"Why don't you sing then?"

"I can't sing either," he said, grimacing at the idea. "Not that it matters anyway. The lyrics would sound weird if you sang them. They're written from a place of pain that only really translates to screaming."

He turned to put down his guitar, but Theo reached out, grabbing his knee. "Will you play me another one?" she asked.

211

As he reset the guitar on his knee, he watched her lay back on the floor and close her eyes as though waiting to get lost in the sounds of his emotion as a way to soothe her own. He tilted his head as he considered how calm she looked as she waited for him, and without thought, new notes poured from him, notes for her.

∞∞∞∞

It all started out innocently enough. However, a simple phrase contrived to bring everything to a sudden flashpoint. The day had given way to night, as it was wont to do, and they were well into their third horror movie when Theo suddenly whacked him on the shoulder. It wasn't completely unprovoked, of course. Auryn had just questioned her intelligence after she'd told him about her love of musicals. To him, musicals were possibly the stupidest thing mankind had ever conceived. A story where everything has to stop every ten minutes so people can run around and sing a song. What complete and utter nonsense.

Theo, on the other hand, thoroughly enjoyed them: a fact that struck him as odd, considering her love of horror movies and fascination with death in general. The more he thought about it, though, the more it showed off the juxtapositions within her personality and the way in which she dealt with her depression. At times, she seemed to choose music that empathised with her emotions, and at others, she chose the exact opposite. Either way, her choice was almost always based more on the emotion of the lyrics than the instrumentals. When coupled with her admission that she enjoyed singing, he could see why musicals held an appeal to her. She desired songs with a story to be told, tales she could relate to, feelings she could croon. Whereas Auryn found comfort in the music, Theo found comfort in the verse.

Although he understood her reasoning, he had still taken the opportunity to gleefully stir the pot, calling into question her ability to think clearly. The statement had bought him a swift strike in response, and he'd made a show of being upset, but he wasn't. In all honesty, he enjoyed her playful punches: it was part game, part attention-seeking.

"Ow! That really hurt!" he cried out in faux agony, trying hard to keep the grin off his face.

It was what she said next, though, that had floored him.

Theo just waved away his cries of pain before exclaiming, "It's fine. I know you still love me!"

It was the first time either of them had said the L-word around each other, and although she'd said it flippantly, it still made him stop. Barely three weeks had passed since they'd met, but a feeling had been brewing in Auryn from the second she'd sat down at the bar. As it had grown, he'd tried to suppress it, fearful of scaring her off, as so many often were, with a premature declaration of love. He knew the word was often thrown around far too freely at the start of relationships, but it was different with Theo. His feeling wasn't just lust posing as something more; it was far too intricate and deep-rooted for that. Although he knew it sounded ridiculous, it felt to him like they'd been destined to find each other, as though what they shared was old love masquerading as new.

The emotion swelling in his chest was an ocean being held back by a dam of twigs, and as he pulled out the first stick, he felt it give way. "Theo, I need to tell you something."

Her grin fell away, and she turned to regard him, pressing pause on the movie. "What is it?"

Auryn knew that no one in the entire world would recommend what he was about to do, but he didn't care. It needed to be said. In truth, he should have said it earlier.

"I love you."

Theo sat silent for what seemed like an eternity as Auryn's heart hammered in his ears.

Slowly, she slipped her hand into his and met his gaze with a smile. "I love you too."

In that moment, all other words became superfluous, and he leant in, cupping her neck with his hand and kissing her tenderly. All at once, she sprang into his arms, toppling him backwards onto the couch cushions, her arms wrapped around him so tightly he thought he might burst. Never had he been hugged that fiercely before. It made him feel special, it made him feel needed, but more than anything else, it made him want to live.

Sogn, Western Scandinavia, 986 CE

There was no rain that day, a godsend for the men toiling ceaselessly along the edge of the fields, hauling large logs into position whilst others with mallets hammered them into place. Nimble young boys in ragged clothes followed behind, their arms as slender and limber as the yew branches they bent and weaved between the fence posts. It was hard work, backbreaking at times, but compared to the alternative, it wasn't so bad.

In fact, if they concentrated on nothing but the task at hand and the breathtaking landscape surrounding them, they could almost imagine they were free men, building a fence on their own property. As Einar snatched a glance back, though, that illusion was shattered. It was impossible to miss the axes held lightly in the hands of the guards supervising the construction, looking down their noses at them as though they were loathsome pests. Their constant presence reinforced the inevitable truth; Einar wasn't free, nor would he ever be.

In this corner of the world, there were four classes of people. At the top of the pecking order sat the king: empowered to rule over all within his domain. Beneath him were the jarls: noblemen, wealthy in both property and influence, elected by the king to watch over their assigned regions and ensure they prospered. Lower down still were the karls: freemen who made their living as farmers, merchants, seafarers, or any other profession they elected for themselves. At the bottom of the food chain sat Einar and all those like him, the thralls: slaves by another name, either born into suffrage, enslaved to repay debt, or captured during wars or raids on foreign lands.

As far as Einar knew, he had been born into his place in the world, although he had no recollection of his parents. They sat as nothing more than blank faces in a faded memory, and with no one able to recount when he'd arrived or where he'd come from, his origins remained a mystery. In spite of his intriguing past, he himself was

215

unremarkable. His face was plain and weathered beyond its twenty-four years; his dusty brown hair was hacked short and, more often than not, infested with lice; his rich brown eyes were dull and sunken from far too many restless nights; and his body was thin, malnourished, and sporting the scars of servitude.

His home, as much as it could be considered a home to a man unable to own property or possessions, lay on the western shores of Scandinavia, amid the fertile valleys winding between the dense forests of the mountains and the icy water of the fjords. It was a place of great tranquillity; at least, it would have been if it weren't for the jarl who ruled over it.

Unlike most other jarls, Ove was neither a great warrior nor an accomplished diplomat, and he did little to pander to the whims of his karls, taking far more from his people than he gave in return. The region, however, offered much to the kingdom, largely by way of its quernstone quarry and highly successful raiding parties. As such, the king left Ove to his own devices, and so it had remained since he was charged with the jarldom some nineteen winters ago.

There was nothing formidable about Ove's appearance: he was quite short, his stomach stout and ever-growing, and his face was round, ruddy, and covered in a thin, reedy, greying blond beard which sat in perfect contrast to his bald head. In addition, he carried no weapons save for his knifr, a short blade that sat tucked in its sheath at all times as he steadfastly avoided any conflict outside of terrorising his own people.

Despite his less than inspiring presentation and relatively small jurisdiction, though, Ove was infamous across the lands as a man you would do well not to cross. Those in the surrounding areas were deathly afraid of him, and whilst he seemed averse to conflict, tales persisted of people challenging his power and authority only to die shortly after in cruel and unusual circumstances.

Einar had once heard the story of a young warrior from a neighbouring land who'd come to the gates of Ove's compound not long after he'd been made jarl, calling him a coward and demanding he engage in a fight to prove his courage. Ove had refused the challenge and insisted his would-be opponent return home. The young man, insistent on proving his mettle, had camped outside the walls for twenty-seven days, demanding each morning that Ove fight him. On the twenty-eighth day, the guards had opened the gate to find him dead, his body covered in puncture marks as if he'd been stabbed multiple times by a long blade. Rumours swirled, with some saying Ove had slain him in the dead of night as he slept, while others claimed he'd paid warriors to kill the man in his stead. Either way, the message was sent out across the land: to challenge Ove was to forfeit your life.

As Einar looked up at the unfamiliar face of the man hammering the stump in his hands, he knew it mattered very little whether the rumours held water. To him and his peers, Ove was a contemptuous master who revelled in the suffering of others, the kind of man who could, unflinching, eat his dinner as a thrall died at his feet.

He may have avoided violence against the free folk, but amongst those bound to his service, he did not hesitate to mete out punishment with his fists and boots or order death on the disobedient. Without a flicker of remorse, Ove worked them to their graves in the fields or, worse still, in the nearby quarry. When their numbers dwindled, he simply used his wealth to fund raids to the hapless southern lands in order to refresh his expendable herd. Einar had seen so many arrive and perish over the years that he didn't even bother to befriend them anymore; it was pointless.

Reaching to collect the next post from the cart, he felt the butt of an axe handle crack into his back as one of the guards passed on his rounds, shouting for them to pick up the pace. To the guards and warriors under his rule, Ove was considered a fearless leader. The men swore black and blue that if faced by the gods, Ove would simply stand with his trademark smirk and dare them to challenge him. The reason for their belief was plain to see, of course. What Ove lacked in brawn, he more than made up for in bravado. In his ice-blue eyes, there sat only cold, unquestionable self-assurance.

The closest Einar had ever come to seeing anything remotely resembling fear on Ove's face was when a man from far away had come to visit a few years back, a day he remembered all too well. While mucking out the horse stalls, he'd spotted the man striding through the gates of the compound: a strange, short figure, dressed in clothing of foreign fabric and design, with eyes that seemed almost cut into his face. Some of the thralls whispered that he was a wealthy trader

217

from a distant land to the east who'd come to seek council from Ove, but Einar had never bought into that idea himself.

Ove hadn't been afraid of the strange man exactly, but he'd been unusually deferential, almost fawning as he'd shown him around. Einar remembered finding the man's piercing gaze upon him as they'd passed, but he'd looked away quickly, not wanting to invite trouble. The feast Ove held that night was the most extravagant he'd ever witnessed, with tables overflowing with food and music that carried on into the early morning. Upon the departure of his guest the following day, Ove had been so uncharacteristically elated he'd gifted the abundant leftovers from the feast to the thralls. Einar was not to benefit from his master's sudden good mood, though. As the others had scrambled for scraps, he had been marched to the quarry yet again.

As far back as he could remember, that had been his lot in life. More often than not, he was assigned to long periods at the quarry, toiling with pick and chisel to shape quernstones from the bedrock, prying them free and hauling them to the carts. It was a horrible place, full of disease and danger, lacking in both adequate food and adequate sleep.

He had almost died there several times, but each time he became too weak to work, he would be returned to the compound, spending the following weeks performing lighter duties. The luxury was always short-lived, though, and as soon as he had regained his strength, he would be sent back to labour in the pits once more. Einar didn't know what Hel had in store for him in the afterlife, but some days he was sure it was a quarry.

His most recent stint in the pits had left him racked with fever, and it was the reason he was, at that very moment, straightening another post into its position. Unfortunately, the day's efforts were sure to prove his health had returned. That's not to say he was ungrateful that his fate was unlike those around him, but Einar had never been able to figure out why he, and he alone, was spared from death. Ove let thralls expire willingly; after all, more were coming off the ships every day. So what was it about him that was worth keeping?

A hand thumped Einar on the back of the head, and he stuttered forward, shaken from his dismal thoughts to find himself crouching motionless beside a stump long since hammered in, the other thralls continuing their work around him. Looking up, he met the gaze of

Gunnar, one of Ove's best warriors, who was glaring down at him.

"Stop staring into space, Einar, and get back to work before I skin you!" he commanded.

Nodding mutely, Einar scurried over and grabbed another post, plonking it into position. As he waited for the hammer to fall upon it, a crisp wind swept through the valley, chilling him to the bone and reminding him that summer was well and truly over. The thin, ragged clothing hanging from his meagre frame offered little protection, and as he shrunk into his moth-eaten cloak, he wondered whether he would survive another harsh winter.

With a pang of envy, he snatched another look over at Gunnar, clad comfortably in sturdy woollen trousers, a thick, long-sleeved tunic, and a heavy bear pelt cloak. He was everything you would expect of a warrior: broad-shouldered, barrel-chested, and rippling with muscle. His blond hair hung well past his shoulders, the top half tied out of the way with a thin leather strap, and his long beard was plaited into a thick braid that ran down his chest.

For the most part, he appeared just as coarse and cold as his counterparts, the scar running through his left eyebrow and across his nose giving his appearance a somewhat menacing quality, but his steely blue eyes had a good-natured mischief to them. It was that single feature that had prompted Einar to dare ask a question of him the previous week, the exchange replaying in his mind as he sidled across to hold the next log.

While still recovering from his fever in the compound, Einar had been helping unload a wagon of plundered foodstuffs from the season's final raid under Gunnar's supervision. When they'd finished and the others had dispersed, he'd finally bolstered himself for the attempt.

"Gunnar, can I ask you something?" he'd inquired meekly, testing the waters.

Normally, a thrall daring to speak to a warrior would result in a beating. Still, Einar's curiosity had grown beyond containment, and he'd hazarded a guess that Gunnar, of all the men, was the one person less likely to punish him. He was a fierce warrior but a little unconventional. He had a habit of talking to the thralls in a colloquial way most of the other men avoided, and over the time he'd known

Einar, he'd seemed to have almost grown to pity him like he was a stray puppy.

Gunnar had stared at him for a moment, almost amused he would be so bold. "All right, one question, but make it quick, or you'll be in for a thrashing."

Einar had nodded and plunged ahead before his nerves got the better of him. "Why am I always brought back from the quarry when the others are left to die?"

"I don't know, Einar," he'd said with a shrug of indifference. "Orders are orders, and Ove has made it clear that you're not to die. We're to punish you freely and regularly, but he has threatened a fate worse than death to anyone who kills you."

And with that, Gunnar had walked away, leaving Einar with far more questions than he'd had to begin with.

Even as he reconsidered the answer, it continued to puzzle him. Why was Ove so insistent on keeping him alive, but more than that, why did Ove despise him so much he instructed the guards to terrorise him? It didn't make any sense. He wasn't any different from the countless other thralls. Of course, he could never ask Ove himself. Thralls who even dared look at him the wrong way had a habit of dying slow, painful deaths, and Einar didn't want to tempt fate.

Taking a deep breath to steady his racing thoughts, he basked in the beauty that existed all around him. It seemed so surreal to live a life of such misery in a place of such peace. On the far side of the fields sat the fringes of a dense birch forest that ran up the steep slopes of the mountains beyond, their peaks dusted lightly with the year's first snowfall. It was a view that made even the most detestable life more tolerable, and thus he sought to enjoy it before he was plunged back amongst the stone dust and echoing coughs of the quarrymen.

A hand slapped Einar's chest, and he glanced across at Kjell.

He resembled most of the other thralls, with a weather-beaten complexion, sinewy frame, tattered clothing, and unkempt hair and beard. The two of them often worked together in the compound and the fields, although Kjell was spared from the trials of the quarry: a fact that undoubtedly explained why he'd achieved such longevity compared to his peers. Amongst all the sorry souls around them, Kjell was the closest thing in the world Einar had to a friend.

"Come on, it's time to go," said Kjell.

Einar nodded, and together they joined the march of weary thralls being led back to the compound.

∞∞∞∞

Dusk was swiftly enveloping the land by the time they arrived back, the torches at the gate already lit and the nightwatchmen standing to attention at their posts. Unlike most other settlements, Ove did not reside amongst his people but in his own barricaded compound some distance away. Within the high wooden fence surrounding his isolated abode sat Ove's hulking longhouse, along with a large mead hall to entertain guests, the warriors' training ring, a series of stables and storehouses, and several huts to house his personal thralls.

As they marched through the gate, Einar could see the dull orange glow of fire coming from the windows of Ove's house, thin wisps of smoke escaping the opening in the lush, turf-covered roof. Sighing quietly to himself, he followed the others behind the stables to the cold, dark, dilapidated huts, rubbing his hands together to try and fend off the chill of the evening.

A few moments later, one of the guards arrived, throwing a bucket of food scraps onto the dirt in front of them all. The thralls fell over themselves to snatch what they could, and Kjell emerged from the pile of flesh with a crust of bread. He tossed some to Einar, who had abstained from the scrum, and sat down.

"You know, you'll have to get your own food one of these days," Kjell jibed.

"I'd rather starve," Einar replied, shaking his head in disdain at the thralls continuing to wrestle over rotting vegetables and gnawed bones. "This is what Ove wants from us. To act like the animals he thinks we are. If we were smart, we'd divide it evenly, so everyone got more."

"You're right," Kjell said, talking around the mouthful of stale bread he was still struggling to chew, "but these people *are* animals. I mean, look at them. They don't care about sharing. They just want to survive a little longer in case they can find a way to escape."

"There *is* no escape. The sooner they accept that, the better."

Einar turned the bread over in his hand. It was hard, at least three days old, and covered with flecks of mould. Picking off the spoiled

221

parts, he cringed as he crammed what was left in his mouth, chewing slowly.

The hushed mutterings of those milling around outside filtered in through the open door, and Einar looked over at Kjell. "You have any idea what's going on?"

"Yeah. So, you know how Ove isn't married? And you know how sometimes other jarls like to send their daughters to meet him, hoping he'll take a fancy to them? Rumour is, one's arriving tomorrow."

"Don't these idiots know by now that Ove's never getting married? Women and thralls are all the same to him. He takes what he wants from them, then throws them away. These other jarls want an alliance, but Ove isn't going to share his power with anyone; it doesn't matter how pretty their daughters are," Einar said, rolling his eyes. "So, who's the lucky lady this time?"

Kjell shrugged. "No idea."

"A lady from the north, from Nordmøre," an old woman croaked from her perch in the shadows. "A skjaldmær."

Einar and Kjell stared at each other with surprise.

"A shield-maiden?" said Kjell, his eyebrows raised in surprise. "That's a new one."

Einar sat back, nodding pensively, pulling his cloak tight around him and blowing a puff of warm air into his clasped hands. Whoever the woman was, she obviously didn't know a thing about Ove.

∞∞∞∞

It was just past noon when she arrived, riding through the gates of the compound atop a majestic, pure white fjord horse that looked to be a gift from the gods themselves. She travelled alone, with not a single thrall or handmaiden to tend to her needs: an unusual situation for any jarl's daughter.

Despite the lack of entourage or fanfare, though, there was a regal bearing to her that demanded attention, every soul she passed stopping to gawk as she made her way towards the longhouse. The intrigue around her was only bolstered by the fact that she was shrouded in a thick, grey, wolf fur trimmed cloak, the hood pulled up to obscure her face, the amethyst studded silver brooch clasping it together glimmering in the sunlight.

222

Hearing the commotion and seizing the opportunity it presented, Einar and Kjell snuck away from their work repairing the compound wall to peek around the corner of the stable and steal a look. She was wondrous: tall and broad, her strength clear as day in the surety of her movements, the rumours of her being a shield-maiden proving truer by the minute.

As she pulled up beside the stable, they caught a glimpse of the clean, white sleeves of her undershirt accenting her pale skin and the deep purple riding dress that sat over it, its straps fastened to the bodice by ornate silver clasps, its fabric hugging tightly to her figure. Throwing her leg over, she landed nimbly on the ground, her long, black leather boots barely making a sound as they hit the dirt. Whispering something to her mare and stroking its neck, she pushed back her hood, her long, ashen blonde braid tumbling down her back.

As she smoothed down the flyaways of her long journey and straightened the thin leather strap tied around her forehead, Kjell took a sharp breath inwards. "That is the most incredible woman I've ever seen. She's a Valkyrie come down from Valhalla. She has to be. I mean, look at her horse. Do you think I could convince her to take me back with her?"

Einar could only nod, deaf to Kjell's question as his eyes traced the delicate lines of her jaw and the soft angles of her cheekbones, his mind ever more convinced she had been carved by Freyja's own hand.

Surely only the goddess of beauty herself could have created such a woman, he thought to himself, his heart despairing at the knowledge he would never have the honour of her company.

The pair watched on as she handed the reins of her horse over to the stablehand. Suddenly, as she was shaking out her travel-ruffled cloak, she looked up and spotted them staring at her, her brooding blue eyes catching them off-guard and sending them ducking back behind the stables in a panic.

Kjell looked around, frantic. "Do you think she saw us?"

"Of course she fucking saw us!" Einar snapped. "If she tells Ove, we're dead men."

Desperate for an alibi, they bolted back to their place repairing the compound wall, luck favouring them as they returned to find the guards deep in discussion and neglecting their duties.

Never have two thralls been so engrossed in the finer details of a wooden fence than those two friends that afternoon.

∞∞∞

By nightfall, it seemed the danger had passed and left the pair unscathed, the usual air of fear and discontent in the huts dulled by the feast being hosted in honour of the newly arrived guest.

Aside from the gatekeepers, all of Ove's men were gathered in the mead hall, giving the thralls a rare moment of semi-freedom. As the sounds of drunken, jovial ruckus carried on the breeze, the otherwise sequestered souls were afforded the luxury of wandering the compound at will. If nothing else, the ability to warm themselves beside the fire pits lifted their spirits, if only for the night.

Einar and Kjell decided to stick together, creeping around the back of the mead hall to see if they could get their hands on any decent scraps from the thralls attending to the feast. Acting as a distraction, Einar struck up a conversation with the old woman filling flagons of mead as fast as they could be served. Meanwhile, Kjell used the opportunity to snatch a leftover beef shank and a nub of bread from the platters being cleared to make way for the next round of food. Begging off as Kjell ducked back around the corner, Einar scurried away, meeting his accomplice behind the stables to share their spoils.

They were huddled together in the relative dark of the new moon, midway through taking turns ravenously gnawing the few tantalising chunks of meat left on the shank, when Gunnar rounded the corner, drinking horn in hand and a little unsteady. The startled pair sat bolt upright, scrambling to conceal their meagre meal behind their backs as Gunnar loosened the belt on his trousers and began relieving himself into the bushes.

Looking over to find them attempting to look casual, Gunnar let out a hearty laugh. "Don't worry, boys, don't let me spoil the party," he said, shaking himself off and plonking down next to them, mead sloshing to the ground as he did so. "What a woman that Alva is! A proper shield-maiden. If I had the right forebears, I'd marry her myself."

Einar knew they shouldn't risk being caught fraternising with a warrior, but he longed to find out all he could about this captivating

224

woman, and Gunnar was drunk and eager for conversation, so he took the bait.

"Why?" he asked.

Gunnar swigged his mead, belching loudly before answering. "Most of the women who come, they bat their eyelids and spew flattery. They use their charms to try and appease Ove. You know, pander to him and the like. Not this one, though!" Gunnar roared with laughter, slapping his thigh in glee. "She starts on about how great the northern warriors are and how even *she* could defeat our best. Of course, we were all up in arms about it when, you wouldn't believe it, she goes and lays down a challenge to Ove: her against his champion. Ove took it in jest, said he didn't want her getting hurt. Well, she didn't like that, did she! Said he'd 'besmirched her honour' and demanded he fight her himself!" He took another long gulp, still snickering as he wiped his mouth with his sleeve. "What a woman!"

"What happened then? Did Ove accept?" asked Einar, all sense of restraint thrown to the wind.

"Pfft, course not. You ever seen him fight? I reckon that knifr of his is rusted in its sheath. He goes and tells her he has no interest in battling a woman, but if she insists on a fight, he'll pick her an opponent. Boy, did she rip into him! Called him a coward and everything. Once she'd run out of insults, she grudgingly accepted on the condition she could take a thrall of her choosing when she wins."

Einar stared at him incredulously. "A thrall? Really?!"

"That's right. One of you lot are on the table. The battle's tomorrow at noon," Gunnar replied, finishing off his mead.

Einar stared into the middle distance, his mind reeling at the ramifications of what he'd just been told. Deep down, he knew that even if she won, she would never choose him. There were plenty of bigger, stronger, and more skilled thralls who would serve her far better. As futile as the situation was, though, a flicker of hope burst to life in the depths of his soul.

"I wonder who she'd take?" Kjell piped up, "I'd gladly follow that beauty 'round."

"No point getting your hopes up, my feeble friend. There's no way she'll win," Gunnar mocked, lumbering to his feet. "Ove chose me as his champion. She'll be begging for mercy before she can get a swing in." And with that, another booming laugh burst from his lips, and he disappeared back towards the hall in search of mead and merriment.

Einar and Kjell looked at each other, their hearts pounding at the potential the next day held, their excitement dampened only by the announcement of Gunnar's election as champion. They'd seen him fight in the training ground. He was a fearsome warrior who took pleasure in toying with his opponents and was more than adept at splitting open a man's head with a swing of his axe. He wouldn't kill Alva, of course, only humiliate her. Still, it was no way for a woman of her standing to be treated.

The night wore on, and the sounds of raucous laughter and singing slowly gave way to the snores of the men slumped on the tables of the mead hall and sprawled in a drunken stupor beside the fire pits. Yielding their place behind the stables, Einar and Kjell threw the shank bone over the fence to hide the evidence of their stolen feast and reluctantly made their way back to the huts, sandwiching themselves in amongst the jumble of limbs and mouldy hay.

As he settled in for another uncomfortable night, Einar wrestled free a corner of one of the few rat-gnawed pelts the thralls were forced to share, tucking it under his shoulder to keep it from being reclaimed while he slept. It might have stunk, but that sliver of worn, hairless cowhide was the only protection he had against the seeping cold, and so he nestled it up to his chin, his head resting on his hand.

"Do you think she could win, Einar?" Kjell asked him in a hushed whisper, his friend's face so close he could feel the warmth of his breath.

"I don't know. Have you seen Gunnar with an axe?"

"If she's smart, she'll apologise to Ove and back out of the fight," Kjell said, pausing to consider the alternative. "Imagine if she won, though. Imagine if it were you or me finally escaping this place."

Einar smiled at the thought, although it went unseen in the darkness. Closing his eyes, he allowed himself a moment to do just that, to imagine. In his mind's eye, he saw Alva defeat Gunnar, her beauty unmarred by the battle. He saw her claim him as her prize. He saw freedom.

∞∞∞∞

As noon neared and the last remnants of the night's revelry were cleared away, the orders came down that all thralls within the compound were expected to attend the fight. Ove, ostentatious as ever, desired as large a crowd as possible to witness his champion beat the upstart shield-maiden who'd dared to challenge him. As such, Einar and Kjell eagerly put down their tools and joined the horde of thralls vying for the best view on the far side of the rope-lined circle of dirt that served as the warrior's training ring. Jostling in through a sea of hips and shoulders, they managed to tunnel their way to the front, much to the distaste of those behind them, the tempting smell of roasting meat lacing the air as it rode on the breeze from what Einar assumed was a victory feast in the making.

The throng of warriors opposite parted, and Gunnar entered the circle, his bare chest thick with hair, his beard braided as it always was, his usually loose mane tied in a tight knot. He wore no armour; instead, he was clad in simple woollen trousers and a pair of short boots, his outfit making it abundantly clear that he did not expect much of a fight. A roar of applause came from his brothers in arms, most looking a little worse for wear after the evening's escapades, and the thralls joined in the cheer more out of obligation than admiration. He waved confidently, shouldering his well-worn, two-handed axe and grinning as the crowd chanted his name.

All of a sudden, silence fell, and the men parted again as another figure entered the circle. It was Alva, her grey cloak tight around her body, her hood casting a dark shadow over most of her face. As the two opponents nodded their acknowledgement at each other, Ove appeared wrapped in a black cloak lined with ermine pelts and fastened with a large gold clasp. Swanning over like royalty, he settled down into an ornate wooden chair that had been set up at the edge of the circle, its high back carved into the shape of two dragon heads, its arms etched with intricate knotwork.

"My lady," Ove said, gesturing at Alva, "there really is no need for this. Surely you'd much rather join me on my ship to admire the beauty of the Sogn. The fjord is truly spectacular this time of year."

Alva pulled back her hood and delivered him a disingenuous smile. The top half of her ashen blonde hair was braided in four tight rows along her skull and fastened at the back with a leather strap. The rest was draped over her shoulders, the loose locks dancing in the wind around the brooch securing her cloak. At its centre, the single oval amethyst caught the midday sun and dappled the tiny silver flowers that surrounded it on either side with glimmers of purple. As Einar stared at it in awe, he couldn't help but think the brooch, much like its wearer, was far too delicate a jewel to be caught in such a coarse situation.

"I'm sorry, Ove, but I must insist. I cannot go back to my father with my honour marred," she replied, a hard edge creeping onto her otherwise refined face.

"Of course, my lady. I can assure you Gunnar is one of my best warriors. He'll give you quite the contest," Ove said, his trademark smirk appearing on his lips. "Once battle commences, though, it will continue until one of you either yields or dies. I simply do not wish for you to be injured. It would be such a waste of Freyja's fine work."

"My safety is a matter of my concern, not yours," she said, her tone sharp and clipped. "Will you uphold our agreement? Will I have one of your thralls when I win?"

"By all means. I am a man of my word, after all."

Alva's expression lost a fraction of its sternness, and she smiled warmly. "Excellent. Perhaps after lunch, I could take you up on your offer of sailing the Sogn."

Ove nodded his assent, then looked over at Gunnar. "Try not to hurt her too much, my friend."

"Only bruises, you have my word," Gunnar said, grinning as he turned to Alva. "I'll try not to hurt you, my lady. My sincerest apologies if my axe cuts off some of those fancy clothes of yours."

The warriors all shouted their encouragement at his threat, their jeers and laughter only half-heartedly mirrored by the thralls.

Alva smiled back at him with amusement, her expression devoid of fear. "Let us begin then. I'm eager to see if the blood of the southerners is as impure as they say."

Gunnar sneered viciously at the insult and hefted his weapon off his shoulder, the warriors egging him on as he lunged forward, his axe sweeping down to cleave Alva in two. It wasn't meant to hit her, of course, only scare her, but Alva watched the axe swing its arc with calm indifference. As it drew closer, she shifted to the side, letting the blade cut into the dirt with a heavy thud.

Gunnar bent over to lift it again, but as he did, Alva brought her foot down, cracking the heel of her boot into his wrist. The next kick, which struck him in the chest, sent him flying backwards, his axe toppling over.

Sounds of disbelief rippled through the crowd, and Alva watched Gunnar slowly stumble to his feet. Glaring up at her as he wiped dirt from his cheek, Gunnar gave a sudden roar and barrelled towards her. Alva didn't flinch, standing perfectly still as he swung to punch her, dodging to the side just before impact and ramming her elbow into his sternum. He threw out another backhanded punch, but she ducked beneath it and kneed him in the stomach. It was her first mistake.

Gunnar grabbed hold of her leg, trapping her on one foot. As she struggled to free herself, he wrapped his other arm around her neck, locking her head in place as he released her knee and punched her twice in the stomach. Alva doubled over in pain, and he kneed her in the chin, sending her sprawling to the ground.

The warriors whooped in appreciation as the power balance fell back in their favour, and under the stern eye of their master, the thralls joined in as well.

Alva was barely on her knees when Gunnar moved towards her again, his forearm connecting with her head before she had time to escape, sending her crashing into the dirt once more.

"You have some fine moves, I'll grant you that, but I've won the fight," Gunnar snarled as he retrieved his weapon, the cheers growing louder from the edge of the ring. "Grovel at my feet, my lady, and I promise not to use my axe."

The thralls held their breath as Alva rose slowly to her feet.

"The battle isn't over yet. I'm not afraid of you or your axe," she said, spitting blood onto the ground as she leered back at him. "Here is my counteroffer. Kiss the hem of my cloak, and I promise not to cut you."

Gunnar let out a booming laugh. "Cut me with what? Your brooch?"

"Come and find out," Alva replied, a sly grin creeping across her cheeks.

Gunnar shook his head and lunged forward, swinging his axe, not to harm her but rather to force her back. Alva responded by stepping into his advance and kicking him square in the ribs. He grunted with pain, swinging again in anger, left then right, before finally charging ahead and ramming his forearm into her chest. Alva staggered backwards but kept her feet, coming to a stop as she grabbed her brooch, pulling it out and sending her cloak billowing away in the wind, her hidden attire finally revealed.

The base of her outfit comprised thick woollen trousers and a long-sleeved tunic woven of fine linen, both dyed dark grey. The rest, however, was made up entirely of jet-black leather, embossed with intricate knot patterns: a heavy corset with thick straps pinned by silver clasps; tassets hanging from her belt and resting lightly against her thighs; bracers laced snuggly around her forearms; and a pair of sturdy, knee-high boots.

The entire ensemble was hardly the garb of a jarl's daughter in search of a husband but rather a wealthy and hardened warrior, a shield-maiden. The armour was clearly crafted for her and her alone, well-maintained but bearing the scars of battle, the sight of it eliciting only gasps and gaping jaws from the crowd.

Reaching up, she secured the brooch above the leather strap in her hair before lowering her hands to the two short scabbards that sat at her hips, her hands hovering just above the leather-wrapped hilts of her seaxes: the large battle knives she wielded as her weapon of choice.

"You are most certainly a worthy opponent. May Valhalla welcome the one who falls," Gunnar called out.

"Indeed," Alva replied with a nod.

Gunnar barrelled forward again, but he was smarter this time; he didn't try to use brute force, instead opting for finesse. He swept the axe low, trying to take out her legs, but she dove to the side, somersaulting over and springing effortlessly to her feet.

In one fluid movement, she unsheathed her seaxes, twirling them in her hands as she stood at the ready. He came at her again, his axe aimed at her stomach, but Alva stepped inside his attack, slicing at his chest with her right seax. Gunnar screamed out in pain as the blade bit into his bare flesh, and he quickstepped back in search of safety. Alva disallowed him the privilege of distance, though, darting forward in pursuit, slashing his stomach and left thigh before retreating.

The noise of the crowd grew with the turn of events, calls in support of Gunnar echoing around the ring, Einar's heart leaping into his throat as he watched Alva circle her opponent.

"This is your last chance, woman. I've gone easy on you so far, but no more," he threatened as he straightened up and pointed his axe at her, blood sheeting from his wounds. "Throw down your weapons. If you don't, I will have no choice but to kill you."

Alva just smiled grimly, twirling her seaxes again, before diving forward, slicing his left arm as he brought up his weapon to defend himself. Gunnar whirled around, the axe growing heavier as the weight forced blood from the cut. With a heave, he brought it to bear, but Alva lunged low, ripping open his calf. He cried out in pain, dropping his axe and collapsing to the ground.

Those watching fell silent as Alva stalked around Gunnar, who forced himself to one knee, his chest hair matted with blood and sweat.

"Hear my final warning, Gunnar. Stay on the ground, allow me to retrieve your axe, and I will let you live. If you rise, it will be the last thing you ever do. The choice is yours."

Gunnar grimaced as he lumbered to his feet, his eyes darting across to Ove, who sat gripping the arms of his chair white-knuckled, his face a picture of disappointment and seething anger.

"You'll die, wench, by my hand!" he said through gritted teeth, turning back to meet Alva's eye with a glare.

Staggering over, he fetched his axe from the dirt, its handle slick with blood, hefting it above him with a grunt. He stepped towards his foe, putting everything into one final attack: a beautiful swing born of countless battles. It started high and angled downwards, so there was no way his opponent could avoid the strike without leaving herself open to a secondary attack.

Alva didn't try to avoid it, though, once again stepping into his advance, her right seax flashing in the sunlight as she reversed her grip on it. The axe connected near the shoulder of her left arm, carving through the flesh but narrowly missing the bone as she twisted, bringing up her seax and neatly slicing his throat.

She stopped just past him, her blade held high, shimmering crimson at its tip. As for Gunnar, he stood frozen, his axe tumbling to the ground barely a moment before he did, a halo of blood pooling around his head as he lay splayed at unnatural angles, his eyes vacant.

Silence echoed around the compound as Alva knelt beside Gunnar's body, wiping her blades on his trousers before sheathing them and standing up. She clutched her arm tenderly, dark blood oozing between her fingers as she walked towards Ove, who was swiftly trying to compose himself.

"My apologies, Ove. I did not wish to kill him, but he insisted on a warrior's death."

"He died with honour. There is no shame in that," he replied calmly before addressing the warriors to his right. "Olav, Tarben, see to your brother's body. Prepare him for his journey to Valhalla."

The two men nodded slowly and peeled away, walking solemnly over to their kinsman, lifting him gently and carrying him from the ring.

After a second of contemplation, Ove turned back to Alva. "Would you like me to send for a healer to tend to your wound?"

"Perhaps later. For now, I wish to claim what is rightfully mine. A thrall, as promised."

"Certainly," Ove nodded. "The battle may be lost, but I will not lose face by reneging. You may choose a single thrall to take with you when you depart. Unless, of course, you choose to stay," he finished with a grin.

Alva nodded politely, ignoring his lingering intentions.

"Very well. Who shall you pick? A house servant, a field hand, or perhaps you'd prefer one of our strong quarrymen. I can send for one easily enough."

"I think I'll just pick someone from the crowd. After all, it doesn't really matter who I take, does it?"

Ove tilted his head knowingly, gesturing for Alva to make her choice from amongst the thralls encircling the far side of the ring.

Alva walked slowly as she surveyed the sea of weathered and weary faces opposite her, examining each in great detail. Einar's heart felt poised to stop beating, his stomach churning nervously. She passed along the inside of the rope, each step measured and calculated, her gaze lingering on Einar for a long moment before flitting to the next.

Finally, she stepped to the centre of the ring and turned back to Ove. "I'm not sure who to choose, so I think I'll simply pick one at random."

Before Einar knew it, she'd flung out her hand, her blood-smeared finger pointing in his direction.

"That one," she said, much to his disbelief.

Ove suddenly bent over double, coughing loudly. He stood up, taking a swig from the tankard of mead being held by his attendant. "I'm sorry, my lady, but that is not possible. You may take any thrall you desire, except him."

"Are you reneging?" she challenged.

"No, of course not, but that thrall is not on offer. You cannot take him. I'll allow you to take two thralls in his place. That is more than generous compensation."

Einar stood confused. Why wouldn't Ove let him go?

"Are you reneging?" Alva asked again, her voice unwavering.

For the first time, Einar saw true fear cross Ove's face as he left his chair and walked up to her. "Three thralls! One quarryman, one field worker, and one house slave. Surely that will satisfy you, my lady!"

"It will not," Alva asserted, "You promised me a thrall of *my* choosing."

Ove fell unceremoniously to his knees, grasping at her hand, pleading. "Ten thralls! Please! Anyone but him!"

"No, Ove, I have made my choice. Your compromise will not satisfy the terms of our agreement. So, I ask one last time. Do you renege?"

Not a single sound escaped the crowd as Ove picked himself up, his demeanour switching from defence to offence almost instantaneously, as though he'd finally become aware of his surroundings again.

"I will not sully my good name. The thrall is yours," he declared, glowering at her with cold eyes.

"Excellent," she said, flashing him a warm, satisfied smile. "Would you still care to escort me along the Sogn?"

Ove shook his head, storming back to his chair and sinking into it like a petulant child. "No, I don't think I'm in the mood anymore," he sulked before quickly regaining a scrap of diplomacy. "I wish to rest, for tonight we shall feast to honour Gunnar and celebrate your great victory, Lady Alva."

"An event I shall attend with pleasure."

Ove breathed a sigh of relief and waved over two of his men. "Take the good lady's thrall and secure him in the stable. We don't want him escaping now, do we?"

Einar looked at those around him as if to verify his new reality, and Kjell met his eyes with a strange mix of excitement and sadness. Before he could say a word, though, the two men crossed the ring and grabbed him gruffly by the shoulders, Alva watching on dispassionately as he was hauled away.

∞∞∞∞

Einar sat lashed to a pole in the centre of the stable for the remainder of the day, the two men who'd secured him guarding the door. Left alone with his thoughts, he pondered the future.

He tried to be positive, to convince himself that any life was better than one bound to Ove's service, but the truth was, he was anxious. He didn't know what lay before him. Alva, although beautiful, was most clearly a warrior with a killer's instincts. What would she do with him? His life was tough, brutal at times, but he was afforded respite. For all he knew, she might very well march him north and work him into his grave or sacrifice him in pursuit of the gods' favour.

Desperate to stave off panic, he considered the other possibility. There was a chance she might use him as a simple house slave or perhaps even see it in her heart to set him free. She might offer him a better life.

Dusk grew nigh, as did the feast, although both made little difference to Einar's circumstance. The rays of light slowly turned orange as the sun sunk behind the mountains, the torch above him flickering but offering little warmth, horses sighing and nickering in their stalls the only sound piercing the otherwise deafening silence.

Suddenly, the door to the stable opened, and Einar looked up to see Ove walk in, motioning to one of the guards as he entered. The burly man untied him as instructed, hoisting him up and dropping him before Ove, his stomach clenching in fear as he watched puffs of dust rise around each approaching footstep. Einar kept his eyes fixed on the ground, frozen in a bowed huddle until he realised Ove was waiting for his attention.

"Yes, master?" he said with deference, looking up slightly but avoiding eye contact.

Ove crouched down in front of him, the wafting smell of mead on his breath. "Tell me, Einar, and be honest, did you put the wench up

234

to this? Did you contact her somehow? Sneak an audience with her in the dead of night? It's okay; the game is done. I just want to know."

Einar's mind raced. "I don't know what you mean, master. I've never spoken to her."

Tilting his head, Ove searched Einar's face for any hint of falsity, then stood up, laughing. "You know what the crazy thing is? I believe you. The question remains, though. How did she know?"

Einar didn't move a muscle, didn't make a sound, didn't blink.

"HOW DID SHE KNOW?!" Ove bellowed, his foot flying out and cannoning into Einar's stomach.

He bent over double as the breath exploded from his lungs, and he wheezed. The next kick hit Einar square in the temple, sending him toppling onto his side and causing his vision to spin. The world had still not righted itself when the third kick connected with his face, his nose clicking as Ove's heavy boot realigned it, blood spurting onto the dirt.

Lifting his arms, Einar covered his face to protect against the next blow, only to have it strike him in the chest. There was another kick, then another, and he heard a crack as two of his ribs fractured.

He felt Ove's footsteps reverberate through the ground, but the blood in his eyes blinded him from tracking their approach, a boot ramming down on his head a second later, crunching his skull into the compacted earth. Einar yelped for the first time, but Ove didn't let up. He unleashed another flurry of kicks, connecting with his chest, stomach, and back in quick succession, until finally, he stopped.

Einar curled into a ball, his lungs afire as he gasped for air, his brain a teeming mess of pain and confusion. He coughed violently, and through swollen eyes, he could just make out a dark pool of blood stretching out before him. A laugh echoed all around, and he braced for the next attack, but he remained untouched.

"Fool. You are needed alive. Don't you realise that yet?" Ove said, circling his victim. "Your torment serves a purpose. It will never cease. Not as long as I live."

Einar began to sob, his tears stinging each cut they found on their journey over his nose and down his cheek.

He felt a hand grip his shoulder, and warm breath flowed past his ear. "You will never leave this place, Einar. That wench is in for a surprise at the feast. Somehow, I don't think she's going to survive the night."

The hand released its hold, and he heard Ove rise to his feet and stride over to the guards. "Keep an eye on him. No one comes in. No one. Do you understand?"

The men grunted their assent, and Einar closed his eyes, his heartbeat hammering in his ears. He lay there for what felt like an eternity, his pain lengthening each minute beyond measure, when all of a sudden, he heard movement outside the door.

"Halt! By order of Ove, no one is allowed in, not even you," one of the guards called out.

There was no reply, only the sound of drawn blades, exclamations of surprise, and then a pair of long groans followed by two thumps. Einar opened his eyes as much as he was able, his vision still clouded, and as the door swung open, he saw a cloaked figure step into the dull torchlight. The figure pushed its hood back, and amidst the blur, he recognised Alva's unmistakable ashen blonde hair.

She crouched beside him, touching his cheek tenderly. "I'm so sorry, Einar. If I'd known he was going to do this, I would have come sooner."

He opened his mouth, but little more than a croak escaped his lips. "Don't speak. You'll strain yourself."

Einar shook his head. "Ove ... kill ... you ..." he panted.

"I know, I know. Shh," she cooed. "We're going to leave now, while we still have a chance. Can you stand?"

He nodded, sucking a sharp breath through his teeth as he propped himself up, Alva wrapping a strong arm around him and attempting to help him to his feet. Unable to keep his balance, though, he promptly crumpled to the ground again with a moan.

"I guess we'll have to do this the hard way then," Alva said. "Wait here while I saddle my horse. I'm going to have to lash you to the back while we make our escape."

Einar's head was spinning, and he coughed violently, blood splattering onto his lap as he leant forward over his crossed legs, resting his head in his hands. Alva hurried over to her mount, slipping on the saddle and fastening it firmly, the ivory mare whinnying softly as she prepared it for the long ride ahead.

"Hush, Skaði," she whispered, stroking the horse's neck.

Einar wiped the blood from his lips, only managing to smear it further with his already slick hand. He watched her intently, her movements swift but meticulous as she marched outside, coming back a minute later with two leather packs and strapping them across the saddle.

Grabbing a blanket from where it hung between the stalls, she lay it over the horse's hindquarters, tying it down firmly. As she pulled the blanket taut, Einar saw her wince, touching the spot on her arm where Gunnar's axe had struck, her clean tunic bulging around the bandages binding the wound.

She took a deep breath before returning to him, holding out a leather strap. "You might want to bite down on this," she said with a grimace.

He nodded, placing the strap in his mouth, and clenching his teeth, dreading the pain to come but desperate to flee. Alva slid her right arm around him, and on the count of three, helped heave him to his unsteady feet again. Bearing most of his weight, she guided him over to Skaði, boosting his sinewy frame up until he lay atop the blanket. She draped a reindeer pelt over him for warmth and lashed him down, being careful to avoid his ribs, the acuteness of his agony evident in his eyes as he panted through the pain.

"I know it hurts, but it's the only way. I'm sorry." She took his hand in hers, squeezing it softly, her warm strength bolstering him. "It'll be okay," she promised with such conviction he almost believed her.

Einar groaned in response before a sudden wave of nausea hit him, and he vomited, his head hanging limply as his vision swirled, the beat of the mare's heart beneath the blanket the only thing grounding his senses. Alva placed a comforting hand on his shoulder, then grabbed the reins, leading Skaði out of the stall and past the two slumped guards at the door. The crisp evening air brought Einar a jot of clarity, and he heard Alva drag the bodies into the stable and shut the door, kicking dirt over the pools of blood left behind. As she swung her leg over the saddle, Skaði snorted and began to walk towards the gate of the compound, each step sending waves of pain through Einar's tortured body.

Finally, they stopped, and he heard Alva dismount as two men approached.

"I'm sorry, my lady, but Ove has ordered that no one be allowed to leave the compound. Even you."

"I understand."

There was the sudden sound of scuffling, two loud thuds, then silence. Einar heard the gates open, and Alva remounted quickly, goading Skaði forward. Through swollen eyes, he saw the shapes of the guards on the ground: one with a clean incision to the left side of his chest and the other with his throat slit. Turning northbound, they continued down the path running alongside the compound at a casual pace, desiring not to draw any further attention until they reached the wider track cutting between the fields.

Alva pulled up and turned to him, touching his shoulder tenderly. "We must hurry now. We need to put distance between us and Ove before he discovers we're both gone. Are you ready?"

Einar nodded, sinking his teeth deep into the leather strap as he braced himself. He heard Alva thrash the reins, and Skaði bolted off down the track. As the mare's gait lengthened, each heavy fall of hooves jolted his broken ribs, his semi-clotted wounds reopening and dripping crimson down the horse's ivory thigh, the excruciating pain sending him in and out of consciousness.

They rode through the night, only stopping for moments at a time by creeks or rivers to allow Skaði to catch her breath, drink, and feed from a bag of grain stashed in one of the leather packs. Occasionally, Alva would give Einar water and dab trickles of blood off his face, but there was no time for anything else: no food, no rest. Daybreak came, but still, they didn't stop, Einar continuing his cycle of varied awareness, time passing around him in nauseating bursts until he realised night had fallen once more.

Alva pulled up again, Skaði breathing heavily, and he felt her hand brush his cheek, its warmth soothing him, if only a little. "I'm sorry, Einar. I know you're in pain, but we can't stop yet. Ove will have sent men after us. Our best defence is distance. We'll be travelling like this for a week or so, as far north as I can take you. You can hold on, can't you?"

The surety in her voice gave him courage, but if he was honest, he wasn't convinced he could. Still, the idea of being recaptured by Ove struck far more fear into his heart than the idea of his pain continuing, and so he nodded slowly.

"Have strength, Einar. You're free now. Once we're safe, I will explain everything."

The hand left his cheek, and he heard her climb back into the saddle. Even as they rode away, Einar could feel her warmth lingering on his skin, and in his haze, he wondered how she'd come to know his name. Suddenly, what she had said registered in his mind, and a sense of calm washed over him. He was free. Before he could truly appreciate the gravity of her words, though, Skaði transitioned to a gallop, and as pain lanced through his body, darkness once again flooded his mind.

As it turned out, Alva was wrong. The terrain proved harder to traverse than expected, and when coupled with frequent stints of doubling back, switching trails, and covering their tracks to confuse and delay their pursuers, a week or so quickly morphed into a month or so. The only saving grace was that the further they ventured, the more frequently they stopped to rest, finding shelter amongst the veil of trees.

Alva did her best to reset Einar's broken nose, protect his fractured ribs, and clean and bind his countless cuts, but with few supplies and little food, his recovery was slow. She supported him as best she could, but she was growing weak herself, sleep only coming in snatches, her hunger left unsatiated. As for Skaði, the mare's pace only grew slower as she pushed on relentlessly.

Einar's pain took its toll, and as they advanced north, he spent far more time out of consciousness than in it. He found it hard to keep track of time, his only marker being the ever-declining temperature and the changing landscape. In his lucid moments, Einar saw the fertile fjords give way to rocky, snow-capped cliffs, and the silver trunks of the birch forests yield in favour of fragrant, needle-covered pines.

Finally, as the sun reached its peak on the thirty-second day, their journey came to an end. Einar felt the ropes that lashed him loosen and come away, but as Alva slipped him off Skaði's back, another wave of pain shot through his ribs, and he passed out.

Fevered dreams plagued him: flashes of vivid green woods, of endless sand and winding rivers, of ice and mountains, of huts and castles. The last image that passed before him was of rowing a small boat through choppy water towards the shore where a young woman waited for him, a wry smile crossing her face as he drew closer. A small part of his heart fluttered at the sight of her. He was always so disappointed when he returned and she wasn't there.

∞◦◦◦◦∞

When Einar awoke, he found himself propped up against a rock and draped with a thick reindeer pelt. As he opened his eyes, the world slowly coming back into focus, he was met with the welcoming sight of a crackling fire. Its warmth melted away the cold that had seeped into his bones, its flames fending off the night's chill breeze creeping in the mouth of the cave in which he found himself. Out of the entrance, he could see nothing but stars and the thin arc of a crescent moon.

A figure appeared to his right, touching his forehead gently. "You're awake."

He looked across and saw Alva crouched beside him, smiling.

"Where are we?" he asked, his voice a hoarse whisper.

"North. Well, as far north as I dare take us. Travel much further, and we'd likely not make it through the winter. Don't worry, though. We have everything we need to survive. You've been in and out since we arrived a week ago. You had a fever at one point, but it's passed now. Here, drink this. It'll help," she said, passing him a carved, wooden cup, the steam wafting off it greeting him with the heady smell of mint.

Einar took a sip, peering over the lip of the cup at the woman who had seemingly risked everything for the life of a lowly thrall. Only one question came to mind.

"Why did you save me, my lady?" he asked.

"Call me Alva," she replied, "and let me make us some food first. You need to eat."

Alva didn't say another word until the meal was ready, sitting down beside him and handing him a wooden plate topped with a few turnips she'd cooked in the coals, a torn piece of flatbread made from ground oats stashed amongst the supplies stacked along the wall, and the leg of a small animal she'd roasted diligently over the flames. It was delicious, and although meagre, it was far more food than Einar had ever been given by Ove's men.

240

"What is this?" he asked, holding up the bone he was gnawing on, unable to decipher the flavour.

"Wolverine. Not much else can survive up here, I'm afraid, and there doesn't seem to be any reindeer in the area," she replied, finishing her turnips before picking up a leg and chomping down.

"Where's your horse?" he asked, glancing around. "Shouldn't she be out of the cold as well?"

Alva's face fell. "Skaði collapsed soon after we arrived. She waits for me in Valhalla now."

"I'm sorry," he said, shifting uncomfortably and placing his plate on the ground beside him.

Alva watched the flames absently for a long moment before responding. "My father, Úlfr, gave her to me when she was only a foal. I raised her and trained her to ride. She was strong and brave and loyal, but the journey was long and unforgiving."

Einar looked down at his hands, picking at his nails to distract himself from the sinking knowledge that saving his life had cost her a companion surely worth ten times his own value. "I don't understand. Why did you sacrifice so much for me?"

"We should start at the beginning," she replied, looking over at him. "Tell me, do you ever have dreams of the past? About other lives?"

"What do you mean?"

"Have you ever dreamt about a small island with a wooden hut, an island you shared with a woman with green eyes and chestnut hair?"

Einar frowned. "How do you know about that?"

"Because I have the same dream," Alva replied with a smile. "I've dreamt about you all my life."

"They're just dreams," he said, shaking his head. "I have plenty of others. Sometimes I'm in these hot forests full of strange trees and animals or on hills of sand that go on forever. It's my mind making up stories, that's all."

"They're not just stories, Einar. They're memories."

He stared into the fire as her words began to sink in. It was impossible. They were just silly dreams: a way to escape from the harsh reality of his existence. They'd always been vivid, but it had never occurred to him they might be anything more than fantasy. They couldn't be.

"I ..." He looked back over at Alva, shaking his head, words deserting him.

"It's a lot, I know. Let me tell you my story. Perhaps that will help you to understand yours. I have memories of a place where a river meets the sea. A place where I met a man who touched my soul in ways no one else ever had. It was you, Einar. We fell in love and built a home for ourselves on an island off the coast, the island we both see in our dreams. I'm not sure where or when it was, but before you died, we vowed to find each other again, in a new life."

She paused as though basking in her thoughts before she continued. "Unfortunately, it would seem our souls fell almost completely out of sync after that. We were both reborn, but we were almost always separated by untraversable distance or found ourselves at misaligned times in our lives. When one of us would be in our prime, the other would be elderly and frail. No matter where you were, though, I could feel your existence, like an invisible thread tying us together. I never knew where the end of it was or what would be there when and if I reached it. All I knew was that it led to you. This continued for what must have been centuries until I was born in this land twenty-eight years ago."

Einar's mind raced, his thoughts going back to the dream he'd had just before he'd woken up.

"I came into the world again as the third daughter of a jarl," she continued. "A lowly rank, despite my father's position, and one that meant I would be wedded off to a warrior when I came of age, as some sort of prize for his victories. When the dreams started, though, and I realised what they were, I knew I couldn't waste my life as a trophy. I begged my father to train me as a shield-maiden, and, after a fair number of arguments, my stubbornness wore him down, and he agreed."

She paused, closing her eyes as she relived the memory with a smile. "While I trained with him, I started to dream of the island and of the man I'd fallen in love with so long ago. I became determined to find him, to find you, no matter the cost. I would spend hours alone at night, trying to follow the thread with my mind, to find where it led so that I might begin my journey. Finally, last winter, I succeeded."

Alva opened her eyes again. "When spring arrived, I took Skaði, left my home, and travelled through the mountains and between the fjords, following wherever the thread led. I kept heading south until I came to the fringe of a birch forest beside a field and found you working there amongst the other men."

"But how did you know it was me?" he asked. "It could have been any one of us."

"It's hard to explain. It was like the pull that little thread had on my soul, the pull that had been there for as long as I could remember, continued right up until the moment I saw you, then it stopped. As I looked at you, I felt this overwhelming sense of calm, like I'd found a piece of me I didn't know was missing."

"I bet you were disappointed when you realised I was a thrall."

Alva pursed her lips and tilted her head side to side. "I'd be lying if I said my heart didn't sink a little. Not because it mattered to me, of course, but because I knew what it meant for your life. I didn't know what to do, so I just watched for the first few days, trying to come up with a plan to reach you. I mean, I could hardly walk over and strike up a conversation. In the end, luck fell in my favour, and I followed a few of the men guarding you as they headed to the Midsumarblot feast in the village mead hall. The jarl was absent, which seemed strange until I actually met Ove. Anyway, I couldn't ask *him* anything, so instead, I dressed down as a karl, waited for the guards to get drunk, and plied them for information with my –ahem– charms." She arched her eyebrow at him, a wry grin creeping onto her face. "It proved easier than I expected. Apparently, you're quite infamous amongst Ove's men. They had all sorts of theories about you and why he kept you alive."

"Like what?"

"That you are the son of one of Ove's enemies, and he kept you alive to torture your family," she replied. "Or my personal favourite, that you're Ove's child with a thrall, and although he despised you, he couldn't bring himself to kill his own flesh and blood."

"Midsumarblot was almost three months before you came to the compound, though," Einar said with a look of confusion.

Alva poked the fire with a branch before throwing it on top. "I know. I'm sorry it took me so long, but it wasn't as easy as marching in and taking you. The men, in their drunken spill, had been laughing about the fact you'd been returned to the quarry. I knew there was no way I could rescue you from there. Realising I needed to figure out a solid plan and prepare somewhere safe to house us if it worked, I returned home and spoke to my father. I told him I needed to take my leave permanently, to go out into the world on my own."

"Didn't he ask where you were going?"

Alva laughed. "My father is a great fighter and was proud of the fact I could outmatch even our best warriors. By the time I first left home, I was more capable in battle than even him. When I told him I needed to take Skaði, a bank of supplies, and my weapons, he didn't ask questions. I think he knew it would be futile to try and sway me, so he simply gave me his blessing and told me to honour his name and those of the gods. He said that even if I didn't return, he knew he would see me again sitting beside Odin at his table."

Einar grinned with amusement.

"After I left, I headed north until I found this cave. I set it up and ensured the area could provide for us, then returned to Ove's domain. When I got back, I staked out the road leading from the quarry. When you emerged a week later, I swung my plan into action, dispatching a message to Ove, purportedly from my father, stating that he was sending me to meet him with the intent of a marriage between us."

"Why did you challenge Ove to a fight, though? Couldn't you have just stolen me in the night?"

"It was too risky to steal you. All eyes were on me from the moment I entered the gates. I knew he wouldn't fight me himself anyway, so I had the leverage to ask for a thrall. He didn't think I'd win, and he certainly didn't know I'd ask for you if I did. To him, I was just some jarl's daughter, a woman easily beaten by his best warrior. I tried to keep up the ruse afterwards, but once I'd elected you as my prize, Ove knew something was up. I wouldn't have survived the night if I'd stayed, but I wish I'd acted sooner. I should have watched the stable. If I had, I could have saved you from your pain and killed Ove in one fell swoop."

Alva glanced over at him, regret painted on her face, but Einar looked away. "What if you're wrong about me?"

She grabbed his shoulder, twisting him around to face her. "I'm not wrong, Einar. I can feel your soul resonating with my own. We were

244

meant to be together. We always have been. I was destined to save you."

Einar remained silent as Alva stood up, moving to the other side of the fire and taking a log from the stack, embers fluttering into the air as she dropped it into the coals. "Why don't we leave it at that for today. It's a lot for you to process, and you need to rest."

Einar nodded, lying down and covering himself with the pelt. He tried to close his eyes and relax, but one question persisted in tormenting him until he couldn't hold it in anymore.

"Alva, do you ever have nightmares?"

"About what?" she responded from the other side of the fire.

Einar hesitated. "A man with eight blades growing from his back like spiders' legs."

There was a long silence before Alva replied, her voice so low Einar almost didn't hear her. "He's hunted us for centuries. I don't know why he does it, only that he does and that many of our lives have been ended by his hands. When he can find us, that is."

"That's why we're in the cave, isn't it? It's not to hide from Ove. It's to hide from him, from the Spider."

"Einar, you need to understand something important," she said, propping herself up on one elbow and looking through the flames at him. "It's possible that Ove *is* the Spider. I don't know how he found you or why he kept you alive, but I won't let him take you again, not now."

Her words echoed around the cave, haunting him as she lay back down to her own thoughts. Einar closed his eyes again, but sleep only came to him in fits, his dreams corrupted by the image of the Spider bearing Ove's face, coming to abduct him, to return him to the dust and rubble of the quarry.

∞∞∞∞

In the weeks that followed, they focused solely on surviving in a land that consumed almost all life that dared enter it. Each day, Alva would venture out with bow and hatchet to search for food or gather wood, ever vigilant for any signs of Ove or his men. She seemed almost certain they'd never be discovered so far north, but doubt persisted in both their minds.

Einar's wounds slowly began to heal, and he did what he could to help. He was not strong enough to stray far from the cave or hunt and gather for the fast-approaching winter, but he made himself useful where he could. Under Alva's patient tutelage, he quickly became adept at the finer points of skinning Arctic foxes and wolverines, plucking and gutting wood grouse, prying out pine nuts from their cones, smoking meat, tanning pelts, and fletching and tipping arrows.

To keep the thoughts of his twisted nightmares at bay, he would try to focus on his memories, striving to recall his former existences. No matter how hard he tried, though, the snippets were hopelessly vague and incoherent, and he could never place them in order or connect them to one another. When all else failed, he would think about Alva.

He'd been sceptical about her story at first, but as time went on, it was hard to deny the bond that existed between them. Every day he spent with her seemed to pass in a blip, and when she left him alone, he felt incomplete. Still, his sense of inadequacy kept him from voicing his feelings. He may have been freed, but in his mind, he remained a lowly thrall. To even contemplate being with a woman as highborn and beautiful as Alva was something he couldn't reconcile in his heart, and so he made no attempt to act on his emotions.

In the evenings, they would speak in depth about the Spider, trying to piece together his motives from amongst their disjointed and muddled memories, but nothing ever came of it. No matter which way they looked at it or how many times they turned it over, they could find no clear reason why he sought to destroy them. Nor could they understand why, in this life, he'd chosen to hold Einar as a hostage rather than simply strike him down.

Eventually, they conceded to the fact that, despite living so many lives, they never seemed to be able to remember the details of their own deaths, the events either hidden behind a veil of fog or snatched away in waking. This unknowing did nothing to quell the trepidation rumbling in their hearts, the fear only growing as each dusk fell earlier than the last, plunging them into the depths of yet another long winter's night.

It was on one such night, as Einar sat beside the fire fantasising about what he would say to her if he ever had the courage, that Alva's voice rang out excitedly from the mouth of the cave.

"Einar, come quick!"

He scrambled to his feet, wrapping his reindeer pelt cloak around him as he scuttled towards her.

"Come on, you have to see this!" she said, beckoning him with fervent hands.

As he reached her side, he stopped, and from the top of the steep embankment that led up to the cave's entrance, Einar looked out at a sight that never ceased to amaze him, a sight that seemed all the brighter in Alva's presence. Across the sky drifted mesmerising sheets of blue and green light, undulating like curtains rippling on the breeze, the glow reflecting off the thick blanket of snow dusting the top of the pine forest that stretched into the distance below.

He felt something warm touch his hand and realised Alva had grasped it tightly.

"You know, they say the norðrljós is the light reflecting off the armour of the Valkyries as they lead fallen warriors to Odin in Valhalla," she said pensively, "but I like to think they're souls like ours, searching for new bodies. The lights were the only thing that kept me going on the journey here. When I began to lose hope, they appeared, and I knew I had to keep going. I had to make it here so we could watch them together, so we could make this memory for us to find in the next life."

Einar glanced up at her, dumbstruck, wishing he could say something even half as eloquent. Unable to find any words, he just entwined his fingers in hers. The longer they lingered, watching the lights twirling overhead, the more a memory tugged at him. He closed his eyes, trying to find the image in his mind. Glimpses came to him of standing on a mountain with the same moody hues lighting the sky, and then wings and floating.

He opened his eyes to find Alva watching him. "What is it?" she asked.

Einar turned his gaze to the sky again, shaking his head. "I'm not sure. The lights just reminded me of something, but I …"

"It's okay. I know it's hard for you to remember."

Einar regarded her again, the brooch that fastened her cloak glimmering. "Where did you get that brooch?"

Alva touched it gently and smiled, tracing the stone at its centre and the flowers surrounding it with her finger. "My father gave it to me the day I left. He told me the amethyst brought out the colour of my eyes, and its shine would light my way to Valhalla should I fall. The winter roses were to remind me of my mother, who passed away three winters ago."

"You know, every time I see it, I always think the flowers are going to turn into wings," he said.

Alva gave him a curious look.

"I know it's silly," he shrugged. "It just reminds me of a butterfly."

Alva turned to him and grabbed his other hand, drawing him towards her. "And why might that be?"

Einar felt her warm breath wash over him, the norðrljós glinting off her eyes as he met them nervously. "Because you're a beautiful butterfly."

Alva leant in closer, their noses almost touching. "Your beautiful butterfly," she whispered, before pressing forward, their lips meeting, their arms winding their way around each other as the sky continued its dance, illuminating their rediscovered love.

∞∞∞∞∞∞∞

The seasons passed quickly, and to Alva, it seemed like months became years in an instant. Time was a strange concept so far north. The days were short at times and endless at others, weeks blurred together, and the seasons often meant very little; there was only cold and colder.

As the years came and went, her relationship with Einar grew stronger, their shared memories and experiences deepening the bond that started centuries ago. At the same time, their fears of Ove finding them began to fade, their nightmares coming less frequently until the image of the Spider grew vague and inconsequential, and they were left with nothing but their hard but joyful existence.

When the first spring had arrived, she'd taught Einar to hunt; although, much to her amusement, he remained an amateur with a bow. In truth, he spent far more time retrieving his arrows from tree trunks or amongst the undergrowth than from prey.

Still, he was growing more capable with axe and knifr, and so he bumbled along beside her with those. To help rebuild his strength after his injuries had healed, she had also begun to teach him to fight. No matter how much he improved, though, she beat him hands down, every single time.

It was another spring day, two winters later, when Alva awoke to find Einar sitting at the mouth of the cave, basking in the warmth of the morning sun as it glinted off the slowly thawing blanket of snow that covered the land.

Shuffling over with a bear pelt wrapped tightly around her shoulders, she sat down beside him.

"Good morning, my beautiful butterfly," he said, turning to her with a smile before taking her hand in his and kissing it.

She returned his smile and squeezed his hand, looking out over the forest below and sighing with contentment. "Should we go for a walk? It's such a nice day. It seems a shame to waste it."

"You read my mind," he replied, standing and pulling her up into his embrace.

With another harsh winter over, it seemed to them that they had earned a day of rest from the rigours of survival, and thus they decided to forgo both fighting and hunting and simply enjoy each other's company. Alva took with her little more than her bow and a handful of arrows, should they accidentally stumble into the path of a bear awoken early from its hibernation, and Einar tucked his knifr into his belt more out of habit than necessity. They scurried down the embankment, and, with snow crunching beneath their boots, they indulged in the luxury of a stroll without purpose, hand-in-hand and happy.

It was an hour or so by the time they reached the side of the lake they so often skipped stones on in the summer, the paper-thin layer of ice still capping its waters reflecting the blue sky like a mirror. As she gazed at the beauty surrounding her, Alva heard a rustle and looked over to see Einar cutting a small stem of tiny white flowers sprouting from the thawed bank. With a grin, he brought it over to her, tucking it into her brooch before taking her arm in his and turning for home.

The walk back was tranquil, the chirps of birds the only sound breaking the silence as they wound through the dense pines, two lone figures amongst a thousand tree trunks, the midday sun trying its hardest to reach them through the branches. They hadn't seen another human since they'd arrived, and they felt safe in their solitude. As such, the pair were more than surprised to find a hooded figure standing motionless atop the embankment to their cave when they stepped out of the forest.

Alva and Einar exchanged a worried glance as she took a step forward. "Can we help you with something, stranger?" she called out.

"You can, but I'm hardly a stranger, am I, my lady?" said the figure, peeling back his hood.

"Ove," she said, her hands instinctively moving to her hips, only for her to curse under her breath as she instantly regretted leaving her seaxes behind, on this of all days.

She was about to reach for her bow when she saw movement in her peripherals and turned to spot two of Ove's men creeping out from their hiding places amongst the pines on either side of her, nocked arrows trained on both of them.

Hearing a branch breaking underfoot, she spun around just as another two men appeared from the forest, the first grabbing Einar from behind, relieving him of his knifr and holding it to his throat. As she watched Einar's panic grow, the second man strode forward, tearing the arrows from Alva's quiver and snapping them over his knee, tossing them idly into the snow.

"I remember these," said Ove with a satisfied laugh, Alva's attention drawn immediately to the two leather sheaths he'd pulled from under his cloak and was holding aloft. "You killed one of my best men with them and swindled me out of my property."

"We had a deal, Ove. You kept your end of the bargain, and with it, your honour. Let Einar go. You have no claim over him."

"I said you could *take* one of my thralls, dear Alva, not that you could keep him forever. Besides, if you're dead, I think he should return to his former owner, don't you?" he snickered. "How does that saying go again? Ahh, yes, a knifeless man is a lifeless man, or woman, in your case."

"So, it *is* you," she replied, her voice resolute. "You won't kill us. Not without a fight. Not this time."

Ove tilted his head, narrowing his eyes in confusion before flashing her a vicious smile. "I don't know what you're talking about, my lady, but rest assured, I am not here to kill you. I am simply here to reclaim what's mine."

A shout rang out, and she looked back to see Einar being dragged into the trees, his arms and legs flailing as he tried to break free and return to her side. She went to pursue him but stopped at the sound of bowstrings flexing, the archers keeping their aim locked on her as they sidestepped around until they blocked her path. In the gap between them, she saw Einar wrench an arm free and strike the man hauling him off. Before he could get in a second blow, he was hit in the temple with the butt of his knifr and fell limp, the man slinging Einar's slight frame easily over his broad shoulder as they disappeared amongst the trees.

Two more warriors came into view from her right, stepping before her as the archers peeled off and followed the others into the forest. As she sized them up, she couldn't help but think that their stern faces seemed strangely familiar, their steely blue eyes sparking a memory.

"Do you remember the man you killed?" Ove said, reaching the bottom of the embankment, her seaxes tucked in the belt lashed around his rotund waist. "His name was Gunnar, an excellent warrior, much loved by his family. These two gentlemen are his brothers: Olav and Tarben. I made a promise that I would allow them a chance for vengeance, and as you well know, I'm a man of my word."

Olav was markedly the older of the two, with long sandy blond hair and a coarse beard braided just as his late brother's had been. His barrel chest was encased with leather armour that was pockmarked and worn, his shield dashed and scarred, the handle of his axe gnarled and notched.

Tarben, on the other hand, was taller but far younger, the blotchy stubble of his beard barely covering his chin, his identical blond hair shaved at the sides and back, the rest knotted tightly into a bun. Despite his likeness in appearance, his weapons and armour couldn't be any further from Olav's: his shield freshly painted, his axe shining in the sun, the newly-tanned leather strapped to his lanky adolescent form pristine, not a single mark marring its fawn lacings.

Alva eyed the men, edging back a couple of steps to put some space between herself and her assailants as her mind raced to form a plan.

Aside from the bow hanging across her chest, she was completely unarmed, and without arrows, it offered her no advantage.

There were other weapons hidden in the cave, but she couldn't risk being cornered should she enter in search of them. She considered tackling Ove and retrieving her seaxes, but in her hesitation, he'd already disappeared amongst the trees, his footsteps in the snow the only sign he'd been there at all. In the end, her only real option was to fight with what she had; to flee would be to condemn Einar to his fate.

The two brothers stepped closer, their boots crunching in the snow, their breath coming out as a hazy fog that dissipated into the frigid air. Alva's eyes flitted between them. She needed to act quickly before Einar was carried out of her reach, but it was clear that her opponents planned on dragging things out.

The pair looked across at each other for a moment, Olav giving a knowing nod and resting his axe on his shoulder, gesturing for his younger sibling to take his turn at vengeance. Tarben swung the weapon in his hand as if testing its balance, his eyes tracking Alva as she arced around him in a semicircle.

All at once, his impatience won out, and he raised his axe, charging forward and bringing it down to strike her. Nimbly, she leapt to the side, the blade cutting through the air beside her stomach. He stumbled a little on the follow-through before coming back around, swinging at her again wildly, left and right. His movements lacked both control and precision. They were the actions of a rage-filled teen, not a seasoned warrior, and it was that fact that she planned on exploiting.

Alva retreated further, dodging until she found herself amongst the protection of the trees, the light battling the shadows as it filtered through. Edging closer to the thick trunk of a towering pine, she waited for him to advance. As he began to charge, she slipped her bow off over her head, holding it against her chest. Tarben swung again, just as she expected, and she ducked under it, the axe head cutting into the tree and sticking.

Seizing the single moment of opportunity, Alva twisted the bow around so that the string faced her foe, bolstered the wooden arch against her shoulder, drew it towards herself, and released it.

The string snapped back against Tarben's forehead and cheek, biting into his skin and stunning him. He staggered back as blood began to drip into his eye, and Alva grabbed her bow at either end. Looping the arch over his head, she yanked it down with a heave, slamming his face into her knee. With a crack, the bow broke in two, and Tarben tumbled to the ground in an unconscious heap.

One down, one to go, she thought to herself as she looked up to find Olav standing amongst the pines, blocking her path.

His brow was furrowed, but his axe and shield were held lazily at his side. Her opponent knew full well that her only chance at rescuing Einar was in catching up to Ove's men before they reached the horses. Time was on his side, not hers, and it was fast running out.

A shout echoed through the trees, Einar's familiar voice growing ever more distant, and panic began to rise in her chest. She looked at Olav, gauging the distance and obstacles around her as she considered trying to make a run for it. Peeling off her quiver and tossing it aside, she reasoned that he was bigger and heavier than her. It was likely she could outrun him, and with her knowledge of the forest, she could likely outmanoeuvre him as well. All she had to do was make it past.

Without wasting another breath, she darted to her right, sprinting forward, her boots grinding through the snow until they found traction on the frostbitten heather beneath. Olav's reaction time was almost instantaneous, though, and she realised too late that she had misjudged his gait, her foe reaching the gap she was aiming for a split second before she did.

He raised his shield to meet her and slammed it into her chest, the clasp of her brooch breaking from the impact. Alva's legs shot out, and she landed flat on her back atop her now detached cloak. Dazed, she had just enough sense to roll over, Olav's axe cutting through the fabric still occupying the spot she'd vacated half a heartbeat before.

Alva tucked her legs underneath herself, scrambling to her feet, and she brought her arm back, winding up to punch him. Before she could, though, he crashed into her again with his shield, driving her back against a tree and pinning her there.

She strained to free herself and succeeded just long enough to wriggle out and spin around him. Catching him from behind, she leapt onto his back, her right leg curled around his arm so he couldn't use his axe. One hand locked his head in place against her torso, while the other was wrapped around his throat, her fingers pressing in on the

253

right side of his neck. She knew if she could just maintain her hold, he'd lose consciousness and collapse. It was a move she'd used a lot against warriors back home, something her father had taught her to give her an advantage against bigger opponents.

You won't always be the strongest, so you need to be the smartest, she heard her father's voice repeating in her mind.

Olav struggled for a second, dropping his shield as he tried to wrench her off to no avail. Despite her grip on his right arm, his hand was free enough to be able to toss the axe across, catching it in his left with ease. Flipping it around, he swung it over his shoulder with all the strength he could muster, and as it bit into Alva's side, she released him, landing on her feet and staggering backwards, the axe still lodged in her ribs.

As Olav reached down to grab his shield, Alva knew what she had to do. She grabbed the axe handle, gritted her teeth, and ripped it out, a yelp escaping her lips as pain rippled through her body. Hefting it, she swung the axe as hard as she could, Olav raising his shield to protect his head. She wasn't aiming for his head, though, and instead, she slammed it down into his foot, the blade slicing through the leather like butter, the bones of his foot crunching audibly.

Olav dropped to one knee with a scream, and Alva raised the axe one final time, bringing it down with a roar and burying it in his neck. They stayed like that for a long moment before Alva planted her boot in his chest and kicked him away, the axe coming free, blood spurting from the wound in an arc and staining the snow.

Suddenly, she heard a shout behind her and turned to find Tarben barrelling in, his face half crimson, his axe held high, his shield forgotten in his rage. In one fluid movement, she brought up Olav's axe and threw it as hard as she could, the toe of the blade hitting him square in the face. There was a choked off scream, and he fell to the ground, half disappearing into the snow, the axe protruding upwards as though he were nothing but a fallen log.

Mist rose into the air as the ebbing warmth of the brothers slowly melted the ice surrounding their lifeless forms. Heaving for air, she pressed her hand into her wound, her side throbbing, blood flowing slowly down her right leg and pooling in her boot. She staggered forward and retrieved Tarben's axe, steadying herself against a tree as she tried to regain her bearings. She was running out of time.

Alva had just spotted the footsteps leading into the trees when, out of nowhere, an unfamiliar voice rang out. "You're too late, you know."

She spun around, the world swirling as she did, but there was no one there. The voice was strange: masculine but higher pitched, with a peculiar lilt that made it difficult to understand.

"Ove and his men are already at the horses. Einar is beyond your reach," it continued, the words laced with a disconcerting calm.

Alva turned full circle again, raising the axe in her hand, but still, the source of the taunts remained hidden. "Who are you?" she called into the wind as it whistled past her, chilling the blood soaking her clothes and sending shivers down her spine.

"Just an interested bystander."

The pain in Alva's side was worsening, and she faltered over to her cloak in search of warmth, dropping to her knees beside it. Her heart pounded in fear and panic, and she clutched at her wound, her racing pulse pumping blood through her fingers.

"Your prowess in battle is impressive, my dear. The men you killed were both formidable warriors. The fact you were disarmed and still defeated them says much about you."

The words echoed around her, but Alva was having a hard time keeping her eyes in focus, let alone finding the mysterious man.

"You may have won the fight," he continued, "but you have still been defeated. Your wound is deep. You are not long for this world."

Alva forced herself to her feet with a groan, brandishing the axe. "Show yourself, you coward. If I'm to die, I plan on taking you with me."

Laughter rang out. "Not today. Today you shall die, and I shall live."

The axe grew heavier by the second until it finally dropped out of her hand, her head spinning as she lost her balance and fell forward, landing face down on her cloak. As she turned her head, she saw someone land beside her as though they'd leapt there from a great distance. Their shoes were as foreign as their accent, and the hem of their dark green robe was embroidered with golden thread in a pattern she'd not seen before.

"You wasted so much time fearing Ove, my dear, but he is little more than a puppet dancing beneath my hand. I am the figure who stalks you in your nightmares. I am the spider spinning the web. I am

Anasazi," the man said, his name ringing familiar in her ears. "It was I who bound Einar to his cursed life. When I discovered him, he was little more than the young child of thrall parents in Vestfold, easily bought from his master, no questions asked. As for Ove, manipulating him proved rudimentary. He desired nothing more than wealth and power, and I gave him both in abundance. In return, all he had to do was keep Einar alive and in turmoil. Normally, I would just hunt him down and kill him, but I was curious to see if a life of misery and hardship would break his spirit; if keeping him in a constant fight for survival would alter the outcome."

He paused, crouching beside her. "It's interesting, don't you think? In this lifetime, he knew only anguish, pain, and, thanks to you, love, and yet none of those emotions unlocked his true potential. The Little Phoenix lived with clipped wings. Without his rage, he remained powerless."

Alva felt a hand grab her shoulder, pain shooting through her as she was rolled onto her back. Through the haze blurring her vision, she looked up to see a small man with grey hair tied in a tight knot, a thin wispy beard, and dark brown eyes that seemed almost cut into his face. He stood up, the folds of his robe seeming endless, the sleeves made of the same silken green fabric, wide and draping, his hands neatly clasped in front of him.

"I must admit, much to my regret, that in my endeavour to stunt him, I have underestimated you. I made a mistake on the island, you see, all those lifetimes ago. I assumed you were dead, consigned to a watery grave, your soul destined to disperse amongst the others in the aether, but I was wrong. Even when you were reborn, I failed to realise who you were or the strength you carried. To me, you were just another sapling to be cut down, another afterthought to be swatted away like a fly, another tinkling bell to be silenced."

He lifted his foot and pressed it hard into her chest, constricting her breathing, her cry of pain coming out as a mere whimper. "Only now do I see the true threat you represent to my plan. While you exist, I will never defeat him."

As he removed his foot, eight blades emerged from his back, black as obsidian. "Know this, though. It would serve you well to commit yourself to the aether, for in it sits your only chance at peace. Should you return again, the same fate awaits you; both of you. In the next life, just as in this one, I will be there. To strike terror in your heart, and to kill you."

"Do it then," Alva hissed through her teeth, "I'm ready."

His blades reared behind him, and he regarded her with a small smile. "No, I think not. You will bleed out soon enough, and who am I to cut that suffering short. As for your phoenix? Don't worry. I have plans for him too. Slow, excruciating plans," he said before turning his back to her. "Goodbye, Alva."

Feeling the hairs on her neck prickle, she watched as he leapt into the air, disappearing up over the treetops. She searched the sky for him, but he was gone. With a heave, she rolled onto her side, hoping to numb her wound in the cool of the snow beneath her cloak, but the pain proved too much, and she tumbled onto her stomach again.

As the dappled sunlight crept along the ground, the amethyst of her broken brooch cast a band of purple across her face, and looking over at it, her eyes welled with tears. Beside it lay the stem of white flowers so lovingly affixed to her by hands she could not save, its blood-flecked petals blurring as her breath grew shallow, her heart slowing until it could beat no longer.

Her last thoughts were of Einar.

∞∞∞∞∞∞

It was four long weeks before Einar began to recognise his surroundings; four long weeks of being gagged and bound, of being shuffled between horses like a sack of turnips, of realising all hope was lost. At Ove's command, he was taken to a small clearing just past the quarry and thrown into a deep, narrow pit, its sides too steep to climb, its width too constrictive to even crouch down.

Looking up, his eyes wide with panic, he was met by the smug smile of Ove. "I have a message for you from Anasazi." He paused theatrically, the name sending the image of the Spider flashing through Einar's head. "It would serve you well to commit yourself to the aether, for in it sits your only chance at peace. Should you return again, the same fate awaits you; both of you."

Ove nodded at someone out of sight, and one of his men appeared beside the pit, upending a large bucket and raining rocks down upon Einar. His screams were muffled by the wad of cloth still gagging him as he raised his arms in a feeble attempt to shield his head, the stone smashing into him, equal parts sharp edges and blunt force.

In an instant, another man appeared, then another, each wielding a bucket they were all too eager to unload. One by one, the waves of rubble struck him, weighing him down until he became pinned, a huddled mass of fractured bone and trickles of blood. Eventually, the barrage stopped, and Einar found himself in the most terrifying position. He was trapped, only able to draw in enough breath to stay alive, but not enough to extinguish the feeling of suffocation.

Ove left without another word, taking his men with him and leaving Einar alone to his fate. Tears slowly rolled down his cheeks as he realised he was destined to die in that pit, his body interred in a most inglorious unmarked grave. Ove's words echoed in his mind, but as despair began to creep in, an image pushed its way to the forefront of his consciousness: Alva.

Above all else, he hoped that she'd made it out alive, that she wouldn't risk her safety to try and rescue him again, that she would escape to somewhere she could thrive, somewhere the Spider would never find her. He envisioned her as she was beside the lake, the wisps of blonde hair tugged from her braid by the breeze fluttering around her, and he recalled the look in her eyes as he'd tucked the stem of flowers into her brooch. It was those eyes that calmed him, those eyes that eased his pain, those eyes that carried him to his final breath five days later.

His last thoughts were of Alva.

Theo

Only a few faint stars managed to pierce the thick clouds that hung overhead, the moon hidden. The mountain ranges were harsh that time of year, full of sleet and danger, but his concerns lay with the men chasing him, not his environment. He couldn't outpace them forever, especially on foot.

A shout echoed down the trail behind him, and he turned on his heel to see a troop of men galloping towards him, clumps of mud flinging off hooves as the horses churned the path into a slurry. Pulling up, the troop split, half remaining in place to block the track, while the rest continued around him to obstruct the way ahead. Their silhouettes appeared like shadow puppets in the dim light, their mismatched weapons held lightly in their hands.

He stood tall, gauging his surroundings, preparing himself for a final stand. His thoughts turned briefly to the blades he'd been forced to abandon, and he grimaced, his heart aching from the knowledge he would have to fight this battle without his partner.

Their well thought out plan had descended all too swiftly into chaos, and in the aftermath, they'd been separated, his partner taking their prize out of reach of these men while he lured them away. Now here he stood, alone and unarmed.

Suddenly, his foe called out, pointing to the sky as their horses shifted beneath them. Following their fingers, he looked up to spot the shape of a winged figure against the softly glowing clouds. His partner, his friend, was here.

The Phoenix slammed into the ground, energy rippling through the air, the horses rearing up and tossing their riders to the ground before bolting away. His partner flashed him a grin, his dark wings dancing with power behind him, and despite the danger, he couldn't help but smile in return. With their backs to each other, they pivoted to face their enemies, who rose to their feet with weapons held high. He didn't fear them, though; he feared nothing with the Phoenix at his side.

As the men charged forward in unison, their battle cry echoing all around, a rush of energy surged through him, and ten dark purple tendrils of light appeared from his back, arching like wings and undulating slowly. A smirk crept onto his face. He'd never been as sure of victory as he was in that moment.

∞∞∞∞∞∞∞∞∞∞∞∞∞∞∞∞

Theo opened her eyes with a start, the upbeat tune of her alarm tinkling from her phone as sunlight seeped in through the blinds. Fumbling to silence it, she relaxed back into her pillow, taking a deep breath to calm her startled heart. On the out-of-focus canvas of her ceiling, the dream replayed on a loop, her imagination painting around her the tendrils she'd sported on that all too distant mountainside. Closing her eyes again, she envisioned the Phoenix landing beside her when a realisation struck. For the first time, he was not her protector but her equal. For the first time, she had her own power.

Every facet of the dream puzzled her, not least of which being that it had played out like some Hollywood blockbuster. Concentrating, she tried to remember the finer details, but they were hazy at best. She had found herself as a man once again and had been wearing the kind of archaic armour she'd only ever seen before in samurai films. Outside of that, she remembered very little. The question was, why was she dreaming about fighting in feudal Japan with supernatural power? And why was the Phoenix there yet again? What was her subconscious possibly trying to tell her? Was she missing something?

Get a grip, Theo. It's just a dream! she reassured herself as she snapped back to reality with the sounding of her secondary alarm.

Still, as she fumbled through her routine, the dream stayed with her, clinging to her coattails as she stepped out the door. It wasn't real, she knew that, but there was a truth to it that resonated with something deep inside her, as if her mind was trying to divulge something fundamentally important about herself. Her rational mind attempted to make sense of it all, but to her frustration, she was no closer to unravelling the mystery than she was when she awoke. Shaking her head as she crossed the road and stepped through the back door of Porphura, she chuckled at her own audacity to think she could pick apart the intricacies of her very being in the space of five minutes.

Although Ruth was uncharacteristically quiet yet again, her morning progressed smoothly, with no surprises to add extra stress to her already stressful job. All was calm as she checked the temper of her dark chocolate and began dipping the lemon coconut truffles she'd rolled the previous afternoon. Losing herself quietly in her work, she allowed the rhythm of it to guide her back to the ongoing hunt for meaning in her dream.

Before she knew it, lunch service was over, afternoon prep was out of the way, and Justin was sliding staff meal under the heat lamps. As she wandered over to grab a plate, she despaired a little at seeing pasta for the third day in a row. The day's offering consisted of a haphazard carbonara that would make any Italian nonna shake her head, sitting alongside a slapdash salad masquerading as a healthy side dish. It was a meal that spoke of a lack of time, ingredients, and inspiration.

As with so many other kitchens, the chefs rarely had time to sit and eat, so the five minutes they paused to lean on their bench and shovel in food constituted a brief moment of social time. Seizing the opportunity, Theo decided to get to the bottom of Ruth's ongoing strange behaviour since she'd started seeing Auryn.

"How are you?" Theo asked, planting her plate on the bench beside Ruth and twirling the pasta on her fork.

"Yeah, okay," Ruth replied, poking at her salad. "In the weeds a bit, but I should be able to handle it. How about you?"

"Same. Prepping for that ninety pax function on Saturday, but otherwise all right."

Ruth nodded, and Theo took a mouthful as an awkward silence developed.

"Is this because of Auryn?"

"Of course not. I don't know what you're talking about," Ruth said, the tone of her voice making her words ring hollow.

Theo put down her fork and poked her until she made eye contact. "I'm bi, Ruth. You know that. Yes, I like girls more, but occasionally I do meet a guy who manages to pass muster."

"So, you're official now?"

"Yeah. Somehow, despite all common sense, his personality makes up for the fact that he doesn't have breasts," she said with a smirk.

261

Ruth laughed despite herself, snorting in the process, and that, in turn, started Theo laughing as well.

When they'd both pulled themselves together, Ruth looked back over at Theo. "Well, I'm glad he's making you happy. You deserve it. Sorry I acted so weird about it. I guess I felt like you were abandoning the sisterhood."

"Don't be sorry. I picked a person, not a side," she said with a smile. "Besides, who else am I going to point out attractive customers to, if not you? I can't do that with the others. They don't understand admiring the breasts *and* the bra. Nor do they know what it's like to want to ask a girl where she got her dress from, but also whether she'd like to tell you over a drink sometime."

"True. The struggle is real."

"Hey, look, why don't the three of us go out some time so you can meet him properly. You know, when he's not the one getting us drunk."

Ruth feigned shock, clutching imaginary pearls around her neck. "What? But that's his only redeeming quality!"

With a snicker, they both returned to their meals, the silence enveloping them one of comfort and warmth.

∞∞∞∞

On every level, it had been a good day. Not only was the awkwardness with Ruth cleared away, but dinner service had gone off without a hitch, and Peter had given the go-ahead on her new dessert without wanting to change a single thing.

Those little victories buoyed her home, and yet, as she walked through the door of her apartment, she found a low hum of anxiety continuing to vibrate in her chest. A sense of dread accompanied it, settling in the pit of her stomach and assuring her all the good was sure to crumble away at any moment. To her troubled mind, it felt as if she was clinging to a pendulum at the apex of its upswing. All that was left was to wait for it to fall. It was a feeling she loathed, but no matter how hard she tried to dispel it, it had been her companion since childhood.

Turning on the shower, she stripped out of her clothes and examined herself in the mirror with a sigh. Pinching and prodding the bulges and curves the models and movie stars never seemed to have, she despaired at the stretch marks on her arms, hips, and breasts that her teenage growth spurts had gifted her. As she turned around, she cringed at the cellulite dimpling the backs of her thighs like sound dampeners tucked beneath stubbled skin.

In the rising steam, the voices of her past found their way to the forefront of her mind: 'If you eat any more, you'll be as big as a house!', 'You could do with a few laps around the block!', 'Run, Fatty!', 'You're not at skinny as you used to be!', 'Do you want to be the fat kid when you go back to school?'. These familiar words gifted to her by acid-tongued family and schoolyard bullies were lined with the same disdain she, in turn, bestowed upon herself. Suddenly, the shame of her youth resurfaced, and the sound of the water hitting the tiles morphed into the tittering of laughter.

Shaken from her thoughts by her phone buzzing beside the basin, she leant over to find a message from Auryn lighting up the screen:

> *Hope work was okay, beautiful. Can't wait to see you tomorrow! I'm working late, so I'll be over whenever I wake up. Love you.*

With a small smile, she stepped into the shower. Usually, she was resigned to standing beneath the cascade of hot water, wishing that by some magic, it would melt away her imperfections, but having Auryn in her life was beginning to change the script in her head. The way he looked at her made her feel differently about herself. He made her more confident. He made her flaws feel like assets.

She longed for tomorrow to come faster, for Auryn to arrive at her door with a smile, ready and willing to fill the empty spaces of her home and her heart with love and laughter. So, for the first time in a long time, she forwent her routine of winding down on the couch with her worries, settling straight into bed instead, her mind flitting from thought to thought until the buzz of work finally wore off and she slipped into sleep's gentle embrace.

∞∞∞∞∞∞∞∞∞∞∞∞∞∞∞

Far behind her, the snow-capped mountains stretched upwards into the clouds, and to her right, through the trees, the sun glinted off the placid waters of a crystal-clear lake, its banks dotted with tiny white wildflowers. Birds chirped in the distance, but they remained hidden from view as she tugged on the reigns of her ivory mare, guiding her mount carefully through the pine forest.

Eventually, they stepped out of the trees and found themselves at the base of an embankment that rose to meet the sheer side of an immense crag of rock. Shading her face from the sun, she spotted the mouth of a cave carved out of the rock at the top, and she knew she had finally found what she was looking for.

With a smile, she dismounted, patting the neck of her mare, who whinnied gently in reply. Clambering up, she stepped into the cool, still air of the cave, her hand hovering over the hilt at her side as she ventured down as far as the light would reach. To her relief, she found nothing but shadow and stone, and she closed her eyes, letting out a slow, satisfied sigh. It was perfect.

∞∞∞∞∞∞∞∞∞∞∞∞∞∞

Theo awoke to the gentle sound of rain pattering against her window, the cave still clear as day in her mind, the scent of pine needles seeming to linger in her nostrils, although it had no right being there.

Once again, she had found herself waking from a dream that had felt unsettlingly real and was left with a strange feeling of familiarity, as though she had not been dreaming but rather remembering. As absurd as the notion was, she allowed herself a quiet moment to revel in the idea of being in such a beautiful place, just her amongst nature, with none of the pressures and worries of life to disturb her peace.

Rising from beneath the covers to find the house filled with the chill of early winter, she shrugged on a hoodie, popped in her contacts, and shuffled to the kitchen to fix herself a proper breakfast for once. As she settled cross-legged onto the couch to the soothing sound of the continuing downpour outside, she cut into her steaming omelette with the side of her fork and smiled.

Perfectly baveuse, she thought to herself in the thick French accent of her old cookery instructor as the slightly runny centre of the omelette oozed out, strands of melted cheese and flecks of bacon riding the slow-moving wave.

By the time she placed her empty plate on the coffee table, her mug of tea had finally reached a drinkable temperature, and she cupped her hands around it, snuggling it close as the steam wafted up and warmed her face. Sipping it slowly, she allowed her eyes to blur into soft focus as she stared out the window, her mind returning to her dream. It was the vividness that ate at her, and as she played out the scene again, she found herself, as was so often the case, yearning to see the world, her unfulfilled wanderlust dampening her mood and laying heavy on her shoulders.

She was so lost in her thoughts that when the doorbell blasted its unnecessarily loud warble, she almost dropped her mug. With her heart hammering in her chest, she scurried over and buzzed Auryn in, planting herself at the peephole and waiting for him to step out of the lift.

"Hey," he said as she opened the door, his weary expression softening into a grin upon seeing her.

Theo waved him in, closing the door and turning to find herself being wrapped in a hug she melted into eagerly.

"How was work?" she asked, taking his hand and ushering him over to the couch as he set his backpack down beside it.

"The usual shit. Nothing too bad. You?"

"Ehh, same same," she replied, plonking herself beside him and leaning into the crook of his shoulder.

Auryn sighed with contentment, kissing the top of her head and wrapping his arm around her. "So, any more interesting dreams? Anything to top that samurai one you messaged me about yesterday? I'm starting to get jealous of all these adventures you have with this Phoenix guy."

Theo looked up at him with a raised eyebrow. "I'm afraid it was a solo adventure this time. Sorry to disappoint. I was riding through this pine forest on a horse. There were massive snow-covered mountains in the distance and a picture-perfect lake with white flowers around it. It looked like New Zealand or Norway or somewhere epic like that. Anyway, I ended up finding this cave, but I woke up before I figured out why I was there. I mean, it's not the most exciting dream, but it was so realistic, I swear I could smell the trees."

"Still sounds more interesting than mine."

"What was yours about?"

"No idea," Auryn shrugged. "All I remember is that it was weird and didn't make any sense. That's pretty standard for me, though; it's either nightmares or nonsense."

"You have nightmares too? What about?" she asked, absentmindedly tracing the tattoo on his arm with her finger.

"Monsters in the dark mostly. You know, zombies and shit."

"Creepy."

"Hey," Auryn said with an air of hesitation, taking her hands and guiding her around until she faced him. "I've been thinking about something."

"Yeah, and what would that be?"

"Travelling. I know it's your dream to go, and I feel guilty that I'm holding you back."

A wave of emotions hit her so hard she thought she might drown, and she desperately tried to suppress the tears that threatened to emerge against her will. She had postponed all thought on the subject since he'd mentioned it on the train last month, as if burying it would somehow change the reality that they were standing at a crossroads in their relationship. All at once, flashes of her first boyfriend appeared in her mind, and an old scar reopened.

Theo's desire for travel had been just as alive and well back then, and although her high school sweetheart had been tentative on the topic, she had been young and dumb enough to think she could change that. She'd even deferred her tertiary studies for a year for the cause. Fearing the loss of someone he loved, he had made empty promises, as all in his position did. He swore he wanted the same things for his life, but when push came to shove, he'd crumbled and admitted his falsity. They had tried to make it work for a year or so after she'd moved back down to Melbourne, but the distance only widened the gap between them. Whereas he was happy with his country life, she longed to explore the far reaches of the world.

Eventually, her dreams had pulled her down a path he would not follow, and the bond between them severed. With a single text message, he had walked away from a relationship that had lasted almost four years. Now here she stood again, at the same crossroads bearing the same signs: in one direction, travel, in the other, love.

Returning to reality and finding herself muted by her emotions, she simply nodded.

"I've had a lot of debt build up over the years; jobs that didn't pay well, mistakes I've made in the past, things that have happened to me. It's all taken a toll. I'd need to pay off those debts before I could even think of starting to save for a trip," he said defeatedly.

She nodded again, two tears freeing themselves from the precipice of her eyelids and slowly rolling down her cheeks.

Auryn squeezed her hands in a feeble attempt at comfort. "Have you ever been overseas?"

Theo shook her head. The furthest she'd ever ventured was Queensland on a childhood holiday almost two decades ago, but that didn't count for much when her heart begged to experience new cultures, to taste foreign foods, and to search for the kinds of places she only ever saw in her dreams.

"Well, I've travelled a little bit. It was amazing. I wish I could do more of it." He stopped, punching his thigh with one hand, realising he was only salting the wound with his words. "I guess what I'm trying to say, in the most awkward way possible, is I would love to go overseas with you. You'll have to be a little patient with me, is all." He tilted her chin until she looked at him, meeting her eyes in earnest. "I just want you to know I'll get you there, Theo. I promise."

It was not a promise made from desperation or fear, the sincerity in his face unmistakable, but it did nothing to halt the slow shatter of her heart as she grieved her dream slipping through her fingers. He watched her, waiting for her to say something, but for Theo, there was nothing to say. Auryn meant well, she knew that, but deep down, she also knew her wanderlust would remain unfulfilled. Something would always keep her from going, whether it was money, or fear, or circumstance. She was choosing the path of love this time, but each step from that crossroad felt like self-betrayal.

She opened her mouth to speak, but the lump in her throat only grew larger, her mind screaming emotions she was unable to articulate. The tears flowed freely down her cheeks as she slid her hands from his, pulling up her hood and burying her face into her knees as she hugged them tightly to her chest.

"I'm sorry. I thought this would help, but I think I made it worse," he said, wrapping his arms around the bundle she'd curled herself into.

267

They stayed like that for ten minutes, words offering little balm and so going unspoken as the pair encompassed the ball of sorrow bouncing around Theo's core. In that moment, the pressure of his tight embrace felt to her as though it was the only thing stopping her from bleeding out.

When she finally lifted her head, her eyes puffy and red, Auryn was there to wipe her cheeks with his sleeve. His expression was one of helplessness, but she could offer him no comfort, nor could she relieve his guilt.

"You wanna watch a movie to take your mind off everything?" he asked, desperate to distract her from her pain.

Theo shrugged, too numb to care, the cuff of her sleeve becoming a conduit for her depression as she gritted her teeth into the fabric.

The sounds of a Z-Grade horror film began to fill the silence, and although she was looking at the screen, she registered nothing. In search of comfort, she took one of the throw cushions and buried her chin into its yielding softness, tucking her legs up as if making herself smaller would shrink her overwhelming feeling of paralysis.

In the haze, she was dimly aware of Auryn sitting beside her, his hand delicately caressing her arm at intervals to try and lure her back to the present. It was no use, though. In her mind, all she saw were images of herself at the airport in London, floating down a tranquil fjord on a ferry in Norway, and eating at a tiny restaurant in Japan.

She was lost amongst the ghosts of what might have been.

∞∞○○○○

Each movie blended into the next, and time flew past her, nightfall undistinguishable in her swirl of dark thoughts.

Auryn shifted off the couch, kneeling beside her and ducking his head to catch her eye. "What would you like for dinner, my love?"

Once again, she shrugged with disinterest, her grief stealing her appetite as it had her words.

"I'll go and get us some pizza, okay?" he said with a meek smile, squeezing her hand softly. "I'll be back in a minute."

If she was honest, she was thoroughly sick of pizza. It was her staff meal at work at least once a week and had lost its appeal months ago. Still, she didn't have the strength to complain, nor did she have the energy to make decisions on an alternative. So, when Auryn set it down on the arm of the couch beside her and wandered off to choose another movie, she just opened the box and picked at it with indifference, peeling off a slice of salami and chewing it listlessly.

"How's the pizza?" he asked, trying to get her to say something, anything, but to no avail. "What would you like to watch?"

She could sense Auryn's frustration as she responded with a shrug, but in spite of it all, she couldn't fake happiness.

"Well, I'm not really feeling like a fifth horror movie. Maybe a comedy or something?"

Another shrug.

"How about we just watch something random on TV?" he said, plonking himself back down on the couch and sitting his pizza on his lap.

Theo managed a non-committal nod, and Auryn picked up the remote, flicking through the channels as he ate until he stumbled upon a documentary on Vikings.

"This okay?"

Nodding again, she pulled a piece of crust away and nibbled on it, Auryn glancing across at her before digging into another slice with a sigh.

For the first time that day, her attention was drawn away from her pain, and she watched in silence as re-enactors began to play out the construction of a village beside a winding fjord, a historian with a clipped British accent narrating the scene enthusiastically. As she watched it take shape, something about it tugged at her, but she dismissed it.

Beside her, she could hear Auryn tapping on his phone, his concentration divided between both screens as the historian continued. The topic moved to the hardships the Vikings faced in the harsh weather of Scandinavia, the camera panning through a pine forest to a nearby lake as the seasons changed around it. In a matter of seconds, the landscape morphed from the snow-blanketed trees and ice-capped lake of a freezing winter to the lush green foliage and wildflowers of a sun-warmed summer.

"Hey, it's like your dream," Auryn said, putting his phone down and smiling at her. "Maybe you were a Viking."

The idea seemed to snap Theo out of her trance, the memory of the cave springing forth to oust her despair.

"Maybe."

Auryn sidled over and put his arm around her, drawing her towards him as the historian began speaking of raids on British soil over images of Viking ships sailing down the fjords and out onto open water.

"I wish it were true," she said quietly, her eyes remaining glued to the screen. "It would be nice to think that in another life, I was a Viking warrior. I wish I was strong and brave like that."

"Tell me about it. Who wouldn't?" he chuckled to himself. "I think you would've been a kickass warrior."

"And you would have been my faithful servant," she replied with a smirk, her sense of humour finally managing to claw its way back to the surface. "You would have carried my weapons for me."

Auryn's mouth fell open in mock outrage. "I would have been a warrior as well, thank you very much!"

"Nope, definitely a servant."

"Well, as long as I'm your servant, I guess that's okay."

She looked up at him, pausing for a moment before she spoke. "Sorry I was shit today."

Auryn frowned at her. "Hey, you weren't shit. You were sad, and there's nothing wrong with that. I'm the one who should be apologising to you. I thought it would make you feel better if you knew I wanted to go with you. Instead, I made it worse."

"It does help," she said, trying to reassure him. "It was just a bit out of the blue, you know. I wasn't quite mentally prepared for it. We had to talk about it at some point, though. At least it's out of the way now. I guess I'm frustrated that everything's so far away. I feel like I'll never get there. Like I'll keep putting it off and wake up one day to realise I've missed my chance. It'll be years before you can come away with me, but I have the means to go now. It's suffocating being stuck waiting. Plus, when I have dreams like last night, it's a cold reminder that there's a whole world out there that I'm missing out on."

"I know, but unless I rob a bank, I don't see any other way to make it happen."

Theo shrugged. "It's not your fault, but it still makes me sad, and there's always going to be times when I'm upset or frustrated about it.

270

I hope that's okay."

"Of course it is," he said, kissing her on the forehead. "I just wish I could do more. I feel really helpless."

"Join the club."

There was a short silence between them before Theo threw out her fist and punched Auryn lightly on the arm.

"What was that for?"

Theo pointed her finger at him. "No more pizza. I eat it every week at work. I'm sick of it."

"Sure thing, beautiful. No more pizza," he said with a grin as the credits of the documentary began to roll. "What do you wanna do now?"

Sliding off the couch, Theo took the games console from its place in the cabinet under the television, setting it up and handing a controller to Auryn, who seemed entirely surprised by its appearance. She hadn't played it since she'd moved in, but a sudden urge had struck her in that moment. As the title screen of the fantasy hack and slash game popped up and she flicked the joystick away from single-player mode, she looked across at him and smiled. She'd finally found her player two.

Auryn

The house was sparsely lit, shadows steeping its corners in darkness. He pushed open the door and crept into the bedroom. A solitary candle in a tarnished brass chamberstick flickered on the nightstand, lighting the dark wood of the four-poster bed which stood there unmarred, its fading, damask sheets still pressed neatly across its body. He looked around, but there was no one there. The room appeared as though it hadn't been touched in eons, everything in it covered with a thin layer of dust, as if someone had once taken great care to clean it and then disappeared without a trace. The air was still and silent, with not even the whisper of a draught to disturb it. He felt guilty for even breathing as he slowly moved across the room, checking for clues but discovering none.

Reaching the door on the far side, he gently turned the glass knob and opened it to find himself at the top of a steep, mahogany staircase. With no other way forward, he tentatively descended, each step creaking beneath his feet. The stairs delivered him to the middle of a long corridor that ran off into the distance in either direction, their ends imperceptible in the darkness. What little light could be found was provided by the withering candles tucked inside the widely spaced sconces dotted along the walls. The air was just as stale down here, and as he stood in its cloying stillness, he knew something was wrong; he wasn't alone.

He felt the figure move before he saw it, and he turned as it inched closer and entered the halo of light seeping from the candle to his left. As its features were revealed, he recoiled in terror. It had been a man once, but it wasn't anymore. Half of its face had been ripped away, leaving only tendons and blackened flesh clinging to its now visible skull. Its clouded eyes met his, and it lunged forward, snatching at him with decaying hands.

Ducking to the side, he managed to evade it, and he spun around,

273

moving quickly down the corridor. As his gait grew wider, he realised that he hadn't escaped, his heavy footfall succeeding only in attracting more of the hellish miscreations. From shadows left and right, they lurched at him, moaning mindlessly. Weaving his way past them, he finally came to the end of the corridor, throwing open the heavy double doors and leaping through.

The room beyond was lit by a dying fire in the hearth at the far end. A long, varnished wood table ran the entire length of the space, twelve matching Chippendale chairs tucked in along its length, the fabric of their cushions dull with age and fraying at the edges. The top was set meticulously for a three-course meal that would never come, the fine china and silverware blanketed with dust but otherwise undisturbed. A series of ornate silver candelabras sat down the centre, their arms draped with the fine filagree of spiders' webs, the candles unlit. Passing along the left side, he reached the hearth and stopped, mesmerised by the glowing coals for a moment before he remembered himself and hurried on. He needed to find a way out.

The next door led to an antechamber, bereft of any signs of use save for a small side table covered with photos, their images paling, their edges motheaten. The only other feature was another door on the far side towards which he headed, stepping through and closing it behind him.

Looking around, his eyes fell on a small, wooden cot against the wall, a mobile hung with tiny painted animals reaching out over it, tinkling like a windchime in the wake of his sudden entrance. At the foot of the cot sat a neatly packed toy chest, and at its head, a nursing chair draped with a baby blue blanket. Without warning, another rotting figure lunged forth from the shadows, and he scurried backwards to avoid its grasp, stumbling over an antique rocking horse and falling to the ground. Scrambling to his feet, he made it to the next door, rushing through and slamming it shut with a kick.

He was met with the smell of old books, leather, and whiskey as he peered around at the library before him, the walls lined with towering bookcases filled with dusty tomes, the centre of the room set with dark green Chesterfield sofas encircling a glass table. Atop the table rested a brass oil lamp emitting a soft glow which glinted off the crystal decanter on the wooden bar cart across the room, a nip of amber liquid sitting undrunk in one of the glasses beside it. Within seconds, more figures slunk from the shadows, and he darted for the door on the far side, vaulting over the sofas and hurdling over the table to flee their clutches.

He managed to make it through the door unscathed and began sprinting down the corridor on the other side, trying to put as much distance between himself and the monsters as he could. The corridor led to a set of stairs, and he bounded up, taking the steps two at a time as he sought safety.

Bursting through the door at the top, he stopped in disbelief. The footprints on the dusty floorboards confirmed the horrifying truth; he was back where he started. Across the room, the perfectly made bed seemed to mock him, the candle flickering as if to laugh at his predicament. His mind whirred with confusion, but the feeling was soon displaced by fear. Spinning around, he descended the stairs once more, this time setting off down the other wing of the corridor, zig-zagging through the shadows as hands emerged to steal his life. He ran because there was no other choice. He didn't want to die.

∞∞∞∞∞∞∞∞∞∞∞∞∞∞

Auryn woke feeling foggy. The zombie-filled nightmare had disturbed him greatly, but then again, they always had. For some reason, the grasping hands of the undead had been a recurring theme for him since he was a child. He reasoned their regular appearance was simply the residual imagery of horror films or video games. Somewhere beneath that rationalisation, though, there was a feeling that they represented a buried truth, something deep within him that his subconscious was trying to warn him about. Then again, maybe it was just his anxiety.

Sitting on the train to work, he could feel the stress building inside him. He stared out the window at the sea of grey and beige rushing past, the backs of dilapidated buildings displaying a cobbled collection of graffiti tags and legitimate street art. As for the tracks, they were being enveloped by an unkempt tangle of weeds that mirrored his jumbled thoughts.

The journey from Footscray to the city wasn't the most picturesque, but that wasn't what troubled him in that moment. No, the issue

275

plaguing him was his urgent need for money. His mind had been fumbling through the calculations for a few days now, and no matter how many times he reran the figures, the answer was the same. Even if he were to cut his expenses back to the bare essentials of food and rent, it would still take him six months to pay off his debt. After that, it was just a matter of saving enough money to travel.

That sounded easy enough, except Theo's dream was far more extensive than a few weeks of globe-hopping here or there. To grow a nest egg that large would take him at least two years. The unchangeable reality tore at him. Years, he was setting her plans back by years. With no other way to ease his guilt, he made a mental note to go through his belongings in search of anything he could sell. It didn't matter what it took; he was going to make Theo's dream come true.

As he looked at the bank balance sitting on the screen of his phone, a familiar feeling of discontent settled in his chest. Managing Benzin paid the bills, but he knew he should be earning more, especially considering his ever-growing list of responsibilities. Still, his bosses refused to pay a single cent more than they could get away with, and given there were plenty of others out there willing to do his job for less, Auryn wasn't left with much leverage to ask for a pay rise, no matter how much he deserved one.

Docklands flashed past the window, modern and sleek, yet a bastion of emptiness, and as it did, he considered seeking a second job. As practical as that solution sounded, though, it would be nigh on logistically impossible. He was already clocking more than fifty hours a week as it was, and he was often called in on his days off or forced to change the roster at Adam's whim. There was no way he could organise another job from such a structureless position.

The train pulled into Flinders Street Station, and he stepped off with a sigh, walking along the platform to the escalator at the end. What he really wanted was to miraculously find a bag full of money or discover he was the sole beneficiary of some eccentrically rich relative's estate, but life didn't work that way. He joined the queue of people lining up to pass through the turnstiles, the scene around him far too closely resembling lambs being funnelled through to the slaughter, fleeces replaced by suits and briefcases.

Thoughts of Theo filled his mind entirely as he waded through the throng of people on the streets, muscle memory guiding his steps. The bond he felt with her was so strong, so all-encompassing, that he was struggling to remember life before she entered his world. Their relationship was only a few months old, and yet the urge to turn his life upside down to fit her dreams into it came naturally. She'd had a lonely life so far, full of pain and disappointment, much like his, and no matter what it cost him, he was determined to protect her from that from now on.

∞∞∞∞∞

The first thing he saw when he walked through the door of Benzin was Carlos, perched on a stool and slumped onto the bar top, a half-empty bottle of expensive rum sitting beside him.

"Hey! Come have a shot with me," Carlos slurred, lifting his groggy face from its resting place on his arm, grabbing the bottle and waving it like a flag.

Auryn didn't particularly want a shot, but Carlos had a habit of being offended when you didn't take up his offer. It was as if refusing him reinforced the fact he was an alcoholic, whereas if people joined him, he was just being social. Of course, Carlos was an alcoholic regardless of the actions of others, but he endeavoured to deny that to himself wherever possible. Still, you had to pick and choose the moments you rebuffed him, and given that Auryn had turned down the same offer the past two mornings Carlos had graced the bar, he knew it was probably best to oblige in this instance.

"I'll have *one* shot with you, and then I need to start setting up," Auryn said, walking behind the bar and grabbing himself a glass.

Carlos nodded, a lopsided grin spreading across his face. "No worries! I got a meeting soon anyway."

Auryn shuddered at the thought of Carlos attending anything vaguely professional in his current state as he pried the rum and empty glass from his sweaty hands. Pouring them each a shot, he wiped the bottle and put it back in its rightful place on the top shelf to prevent Carlos from taking it with him when he left.

The pair clinked glasses and downed it in one gulp, the shot warming Auryn's chest on the way down. Hints of vanilla and spices lingered on his palate as he closed his eyes, enjoying the momentary pleasure of

277

indulging in a luxury well outside his current budget. When he opened them again, he finally registered the state of the bar. There were used glasses everywhere, and as he ran his hand along the bar top, he recoiled at how sticky it was.

"How long have you been here?" he asked, looking across at Carlos, who was smacking his lips loudly and dabbing the stray drips from his chin.

"I dunno," Carlos shrugged. "I was out with friends, and we came back here for some drinks. They all left, and then you turned up."

Auryn could feel the rage build up inside him as his eyes flitted from table to table, each one somehow dirtier than the last. "You've been here for hours?! The place is a pigsty! It's going to take me at least an hour just to clean up the mess."

"That's what I pay you for, isn't it?" he said with a laugh.

"I don't get paid enough to deal with this kind of shit!" Auryn snapped, throwing his hands up in frustration. "You could have at least made them clean up after themselves a bit. I won't be able to open on time now."

Carlos waved his anger away. "It's fine. I'll make it up to you later."

Naturally, that translated to, 'I'll give you a couple of shots when I come back.' After all, alcohol was the currency he used for everything, from favours to forgiveness.

Hoisting himself off the stool, Carlos staggered over to the storeroom, grabbing a bottle of red for the road and casually heading out the front door. "See ya later," he called out over his shoulder as he disappeared down the laneway.

Auryn watched the door swing closed, the rage subsiding a little with Carlos's departure. He knew from experience that had he stayed much longer, things would have gotten ugly. Carlos had a habit of becoming irrationally angry when staff didn't obey his drunken requests or reprimanded him for his actions, regardless of how unreasonable they were. In his mind, it was his business, and he could act however he wanted within it.

Auryn had worked for him for five years, and in that time, he'd seen Carlos fire two people for standing up to him in that state. Trying to find the balance between expressing your frustration and saying something that would get you fired was often a fine line to toe.

I need a new job, he thought to himself as he picked up a tray and began collecting the plethora of dirty glasses scattered around the room.

All at once, though, Theo's face popped into his mind, and he realised he couldn't quit; he couldn't fail her. As much as it pained him, he was going to have to stick it out until he'd saved up enough money. Either that or somehow miraculously find a job that paid better. As he scanned the room again for any glasses he may have missed, he couldn't help but notice it resembled his own emotions; both were a mess.

∞∞∞

Theo's apartment door opening was Auryn's favourite part of the week, and he smiled as it swung ajar. Despite it being early afternoon, she looked like she'd only just rolled out of bed, her plaid purple pyjama pants crinkled, her hoodie slightly askew, her hair a tangled mane around her slightly flushed face. Everything about her said, 'it's been a long week', but she was a picture of beauty in his eyes.

"Come on," she snapped with a smile, gesturing inside.

He'd barely had time to drop his bag and turn around before she enveloped him in a deep embrace, both of them breathing a long, contented sigh.

All the stress of his week melted away, and he kissed her forehead. "Miss me?"

Her only response was to hug him tighter.

"So, what's it like out there?" she asked, pulling back slightly and nodding towards the window, her arms still around his neck.

"You'd hate it. There are people jogging and everything," he laughed, their usual schtick of hating on the 'normal people' making him once again grateful that her profession mirrored his own.

"Ergh. Shouldn't they be off eating avocado on toast or drinking cold-drip coffee or whatever it is morning people do on Sundays?" she said, rolling her eyes. "Tea?"

"Let me," he replied, wandering into the kitchen and brewing them both a cup.

The day was uncharacteristically sun-drenched for mid-winter, and as such, they enjoyed the mild weather on the balcony. Decompressing in the safe comfort of non-judgement, they lost themselves in conversation, debriefing on the gossip, war stories, and battle wounds of another work week. The sunlight crept along the apartment building opposite, expressing the slow march of time by redirecting beams of blinding light off its windows until they eventually came to land on Auryn's face. Distracted by them, he looked down at his watch to realise three hours had slipped away unnoticed.

Theo begged off to start dinner, leaving him to dabble in his thoughts as the sun sank lower, the signature chill of a Melbourne cool change compelling him to head back in. Stepping through the balcony door, he was met with the enticing smell of spices wafting from the kitchen and an insatiable urge to discover the source lured him into a space Theo usually shooed him out of.

"What are you making, beautiful?" he asked, sidling up behind her and wrapping his arms around her waist, peeking over her shoulder into the pot she stood stirring on the stove.

"Food," she replied with a smirk.

"I know that. I was after a slightly more in-depth answer."

"Hot food."

"Not going to tell me what it is, huh?"

"Nope. You'll find out when it's on the table. It's not like you won't eat it," she said, poking her tongue out.

He put his hands up in defeat, backing out of the kitchen. "Whatever you say, my love. How long will it be?"

"It's nearly ready."

"Want me to make us a drink?" he asked, in search of a distraction from the irresistible aroma of food making his stomach growl.

"Gin, please. There's a bottle over on the cart," she shot over her shoulder.

As he picked up the gin from the antique, wooden bar cart in the living room, his eyes fell on the crystal decanter resting beside it, a small etched plaque reading whiskey hanging from its neck, five matching crystal glasses sitting upturned around its base. That singular vintage piece of furniture seemed so out of place amongst the mishmash of cheaper objects that made up Theo's belongings, and given she didn't drink or even like whiskey, the whole set-up seemed strange.

"Where'd the cart and crystalware come from?" he asked, taking two glasses and fixing them each a gin, lime, and soda from the scant supplies.

"It was my grandfather's. I always remember it being in his office when I used to visit as a kid, so when he passed away, I made my plea for it during the division of his estate. Luckily, no one else wanted it."

"It's very old school," he said, placing their drinks on the table.

"What can I say? I'm an old soul," she replied with a smile as she emerged from the kitchen with two bowls of food, a plate of warm bread balanced on her wrist.

"Thanks for dinner, beautiful," he said, lifting his glass and clinking it against hers. "Are you going to tell me what it is yet?"

Theo smirked as she picked up her spoon. "Just eat it."

Taking up his own, he eagerly shovelled a steaming spoonful into his mouth, sucking in air around it as the hot liquid scorched his tongue, Theo raising an eyebrow at him as she sensibly blew on hers. After the initial shock wore off, his tastebuds were flooded with the moreish flavours of cumin and smoked paprika, the piece of chicken he bit into meltingly tender. Closing his eyes for a moment, he let out a gargling groan of pleasure.

"You right there?" Theo asked with a chortle.

"This is delicious, whatever it is!" he mumbled, his mouth half-full. "Is it Cajun or something?"

She gave a small smile in response to the praise. "It's kinda-sorta gumbo, I guess."

"Well, it's more than kinda-sorta amazing."

"You're laying it on a bit thick now, don't you think?"

He shook his head emphatically. "I'm going to praise you until you learn to accept it."

As they sat there, mopping up the last of the sauce with the bread, she looked at him. "You up for another horror movie night?"

"Sure. No zombies, though," he replied, grimacing as the decaying face from his nightmare flashed into his mind again.

Theo frowned. "How come?"

"I had a weird dream a couple of nights ago."

"What about?" she asked, picking up her glass and leaning back.

Auryn finished off his drink before he answered. "I was in an old house, with shadows everywhere, and I was being chased by zombies."

"Interesting," she said, swirling the last drops of her drink pensively, then downing them.

"Yeah. It's the one monster that seems to always lurk in my nightmares."

"Why do you think that is?"

Auryn shrugged as he reached over and grabbed the gin, pouring them both another nip. "Who knows. I've always been fascinated by zombies, but then, I'm fascinated by Batman too, and he never swoops into my subconscious."

"When you say 'fascinated', are we talking sexual fetish or...?" she asked with an impish grin, gathering the plates and dumping them in the sink.

He couldn't help but laugh, rising from the table to top their drinks up with soda. "It's nothing like that. To be honest, I'm probably more fascinated with the darkness than anything else. My nightmares are usually in pitch-black or full of shadow."

She wandered over and took her glass from his hand. "So, you're scared of the dark?"

"I like to think of it as more of a healthy distrust than a fear, thank you."

"Sure. Sure," she said, taking a sip of her drink. "Why zombies then?"

"No clue. I guess my brain had to put something in the dark to lunge out at me. At one point, I started writing a novel to get them out of my head. I thought if I used them in a story, my subconscious might finally forget about them. Clearly, that didn't work, though."

"You started writing a novel? Why am I only hearing about this now? When can I read it?"

"You can't," he replied, looking down into his glass. "It's gone. Years ago, long before internet backup existed, my house was robbed. They stole my laptop and my hard drives. I lost everything I'd ever written."

"I'm sorry," Theo said, squeezing his arm. "Didn't you ever start over?"

"My motivation disappeared after that," he said, his shoulders sinking in defeat. "Losing my work really affected me. It was as if they'd stolen a piece of my soul. I haven't really had the urge to write since."

Theo took his hand and guided him to the couch. "Why don't you write something now? You could do your zombie idea. It's obviously still on your mind. Maybe if you tried again, the motivation would come back, and you could finally banish the nightmares for good?"

Auryn considered her words in silence. Before the robbery, writing had been one of his greatest joys. It was an outlet that offered him infinite freedom, a way to escape into worlds of his own creation, worlds where he had ultimate control, worlds that brought him hope when life felt hopeless. As his heart swelled with excitement at the prospect, though, his anxiety reared its head, filling his mind with thoughts of failure and rejection.

"Maybe. It seems like a lot of work for no gain. No one would ever publish it."

Theo raised her eyebrows and looked down her nose at him like he'd just said something truly idiotic. "I don't know how to tell you this, but it's not the 1980s anymore. You don't need the approval of a publishing house like you used to. You can just put it online yourself."

"What's the point. No one would buy it!"

"I would," she said, grinning at him. "Plus, you'd give me my own signed, leather-bound copy, so I could put it on my bookshelf."

"I would?"

"Yep!"

Her confidence dampened the self-doubt in his head, but there was still a feeling of uncertainty pulsing in his chest. "I don't know. Maybe," he replied, picking up the remote and going in search of a film to allow him the space to process his rush of emotions.

To his relief, Theo dropped the subject, and they settled down to scenes of a supernatural creature hunting down hapless humans with seemingly no survival skills or common sense.

It was about halfway through the film, after he'd seen Theo responding to a few messages, that he noticed her glancing in his direction as if she wanted to say something, and he pressed pause in search of answers.

"What?"

"Nothing," she said, the upward inflection of the last syllable giving her away.

"Is it about the writing thing because I need time to think about it?

283

It's been years since I've even considered it properly."

"No, it's not that. It's just that your birthday is tomorrow, and you still haven't told me what you want to do."

If he was honest, he didn't want to do anything. If he could, he would rather pretend it wasn't happening at all.

Turning thirty-nine was nothing more than a cold reminder of everything he hadn't accomplished. It was just another year in which he was stuck in the same monotonous rut. He'd gone out of his way to avoid mentioning it around her, hoping she would treat it like any other day, but it seemed his efforts had been in vain as he looked over at her, her face full of eagerness.

Auryn sighed slowly. "What do you want to do?"

"It's *your* birthday! You're supposed to be telling me!"

Auryn thought about it for a moment, realising he only wanted one thing. "I want to spend the day with you. Can we just hang out here?"

Theo shook her head with a frown. "I wish we could, but I have to do the day shift in larder now because someone called in sick. Justin's away for the next few days and can't fill in, so I'm it, unfortunately." She considered the options for a second. "Why don't you head home in the morning, have a nice relaxing day, and I'll come 'round after I finish? I shouldn't be too late."

"Sure, that sounds good," he said, thankful he'd finally found someone who didn't insist on making his birthday a massive deal for their own entertainment.

"What do you want for your birthday dinner?" she asked. "I can make you something if you like. Obviously, nothing too fancy given the woeful lack of equipment at your place, but I could whip you up a nice steak or something."

"Sounds perfect."

"Consider it done then," she said, grabbing the remote from his hand, pressing play, and snuggling into his arm.

He looked down at her as the light from the screen flashed colours across her face and smiled. Maybe it wasn't birthdays he disliked after all. Maybe he'd just never met someone he wanted to grow old with before.

∞∞∞∞

There were no dreams that night, at least none Auryn remembered, his mind affording him an uncommon night of peace, free from zombies and shadows. He awoke to the light brush of Theo's lips on his cheek and the gentle whisper of 'happy birthday' before she slipped quietly off to work. Blinking his way back into the waking world, he allowed himself the luxury of rising slowly, breathing in the still calm he was left to.

By the time he began to walk to the station, his mind was free of its usual undercurrent of anxiety. In its absence, his thoughts wandered back to Theo's suggestion of trying again with his writing. The very notion of it used to carry only the painful reminder of all he'd lost, but that morning, it carried something he hadn't felt in a long time: motivation.

Suddenly, his mind burst to life with questions, firing in quick succession. If he restarted his zombie novel, what would it be about? Should he scrap the outdated plot he'd had originally, or were there parts of it that had stood the test of time? Could the conversations he'd had with Tony about the best way to survive a zombie apocalypse help guide the story? What flaws irked him in existing zombie tales that he could rectify with his own work? His mind swirled until ideas started to form amidst the chaos, emerging from the mental soup like primordial creatures, rough in nature but bearing the potential to evolve into something greater.

As he turned the key in his apartment door and shoved it open with his shoulder, the thin veil of a plot had begun to form. Reasoning that much of his best creative work was often seeded under the hot cascade of the shower, he threw his bag down on the couch, stripped off his clothes, and flicked on the tap.

Surrounded by the symphony of splashing water, characters and scenes appeared to him thick and fast, his mind scrambling for a fifth gear just to keep up. He was at the point of information overload when he finally hung up his towel, leaving his shadow of stubble unshaven as he slid into clean clothes and plonked himself at his desk. Stirring his computer from its hibernation, he allowed his tidal wave of thoughts to tumble out onto the screen.

The world moved around him, but he was deaf to everything but the sounds of his own feverish keystrokes, too engrossed to even notice

285

the half-hearted birthday wishes from his family appearing on his phone. Over the years, their willing calls had regressed to brief text messages flung to him from a place of social obligation, but for once, he was too entangled in the joys of rekindled creativity to be depressed by them.

It was almost five o'clock when a knock at the door startled Auryn out of his frenzy, and he opened it to find Theo standing there, a large box balanced in her arms, a wide grin on her face.

"What's that?" he asked, guiding her inside and clearing a space on the kitchen bench for it.

"I made you something," she said, putting it down, opening the lid, and pushing it towards him. "Happy birthday!!!"

Auryn's mouth fell open as he looked down at the cake before him. It was the kind of cake he'd only ever seen in expensive patisseries, its flawless coating of shiny chocolate icing reflecting the light like a mirror. It wasn't the icing that had made his jaw drop, though, but rather what sat on top of it: two cartoon zombie figures, their hands outstretched, a tiny amount of blood dripping down from their mouths, while in between them sat a small, green book with 'Z.A.' written on the cover.

"Wow," said Auryn, his brain still trying to process what he was seeing. "How the hell did you do all of this?"

"I crammed it in during my prep time this week, and Peter let me decorate it today while I was doing my larder shift. Unsurprisingly, it's a lot quicker to make with commercial equipment."

Auryn leant down to examine the zombies closer up. "How did you do these? Are they edible?"

"They're made of sugar paste, so yes, but if you keep them somewhere dry, they'll last for years. They're not my greatest work. I just sort of threw them together in between serving entrées. If I'd had more time, they probably would have looked a lot better," she said, making a face. "Maybe not, though. I suck at artsy things."

Auryn looked up at her. "What are you talking about? They're amazing! The whole cake is amazing! You're amazing!"

"Going a bit fast there, aren't you? You don't even know what flavour it is yet!"

"Please, madam, enlighten me," he said with an overly dramatic bow.

"It's chocolate fudge cake layered with peppermint choc-chip mousse and covered in choc peppermint glaze."

"See, amazing! Change of plans. I think we should eat this for dinner," he said, reaching for it.

"Hands off! You're having a proper meal first," she shouted, smacking him away. Auryn pouted, but Theo shook her head and pointed at the couch. "Sit. You have presents to receive."

"There's more?" he asked as he sat down, dumbfounded.

She ruffled around in her backpack and produced two neatly wrapped gifts, which she placed in his lap with a satisfied smile, sitting down next to him. "Happy birthday, old man!"

Auryn cocked an eyebrow at her, but she just poked out her tongue.

The first present was a stack of three notebooks, a pen tucked in the ribbon tying them together.

"They're for your music. I noticed you have all these loose pieces of paper on your desk with songs and lyrics written on them. I thought these would be more practical," she said as he flicked through them.

"They're perfect. Thanks, beautiful."

"NEXT PRESENT!" Theo yelled out with fervour.

He stared at the other rectangular package for a moment before carefully opening it to reveal a dark brown leather notebook cover. It was fastened shut by a leather strap attached to an old-fashioned key which wrapped around it and tucked into a small loop on the front. Slipping the key out, he opened it to find another notebook already in place.

"It's to protect them. The key is from an abandoned nineteenth-century warehouse, and look," she said, pointing at the bottom right corner of the cover where his initials were embossed into the leather, "A.B. for Auryn Berenger."

"It's incredible," he said, enveloping her in a tight hug. "No one has ever given me something so personal before. Thank you."

"My pleasure," she said, kissing him tenderly. "I know you don't like fuss on your birthday, but I wanted to get you something special. You ready for dinner?"

He nodded enthusiastically before going back to poring over his gifts, turning the century-old key over in his hand and getting lost in his thoughts as his mind wandered off on another zombie-based tangent.

It seemed like only a moment later that Theo was handing him the steak dinner she had promised, and as Auryn relished another perfectly cooked meal, he glanced across at her and smiled to himself, quietly revelling in the obscure idiosyncrasies he found so adorable.

She ate each item of food on her plate separately, starting with the green beans before moving on to the baby carrots, then the drool-worthy, butter-laden mashed potatoes, and finally digging into the porterhouse steak. Something about it just felt so familiar to him, like he'd watched her do it a thousand times before.

"You know," he said, smearing the rest of his mash onto his last morsel of steak and balancing the final bean on top of it, "I started writing again today. I think I'll use my notebooks for writing ideas instead of music. After all, I probably wouldn't have tried again if not for you."

"That's amazing. I'm going to be your biggest fan," she said with a smile, taking his empty plate over to the sink. "Why don't you pick a movie, birthday boy?"

Selecting one of his favourites from the shelf, he slid it into the player and sat back down as Theo returned bearing two slices of his most highly anticipated gift, the wafting smell of peppermint meeting him as he brought the first bite to his lips.

It was just as good as he'd imagined. In fact, he had to stop himself from grabbing the entire cake, barricading himself in his room and consuming the whole thing single-handedly. Luckily, Theo was there to be a model of restraint.

As the epic orchestral notes of the opening scene began to blare from the speakers, he shot a glance over at Theo, who was winkling out dimples of cake from her slice with a teaspoon. She always told him that eating with a smaller spoon made it last longer, and as he thought about it, he couldn't help but wish every moment with her lasted longer.

Not only did she make his world better, but she made him want to be a better person. She gave him the strength to clamber up out of the mire he found himself in and aspire to do more. She'd given him something over the last couple of months he hadn't had in a long time: hope, not just for their relationship but for his entire life.

London, England, 1349 CE

They were just past Maidstone when she saw them. Corpses piled high on carts, one on top of the other, their faces contorted in pain, their skin blotchy and discoloured, their necks swollen with boils. Hardened men with rags tied over their noses and mouths moved the carts to the edge of a deep pit and unloaded them, tossing the bodies in like sacks of garbage.

No sunlight shone there, the sky blanketed with thick clouds, the air reeking of death. Pulling up her horse, she watched as they worked.

Another horse stopped alongside her, and Edward motioned with his head. "We should keep moving. It's not safe here."

Adaeze stared at the men for a moment longer, then turned back to her travel companion. Edward was as white as they came, with short, light brown hair and kind blue eyes. In Niani, he'd turned bright red whenever he was in the sun for too long: something that had always greatly amused her family. Having ventured from England to Morocco seeking knowledge and adventure, he'd traded a portion of his family inheritance and bought passage south on the caravan of a gold merchant, straying further from his home until he came to find himself amongst her people.

He'd lived at the palace with them for seven years, teaching her and her siblings English at the behest of her father, the Mansa of the Mali Empire. Edward taught them his language and, in turn, attempted to become versed in theirs; although, by his own admission, he remained terrible at it. Still, he knew more of their language and culture than any outsider before him.

Adaeze pulled back the hood of her cloak, letting the cool breeze wash over her. Her skin was the rich brown of fertile soil and smooth as satin, her nose broad, her lips full, her eyes dark and lively. Running her hand over her hair, she could feel her once tight and tidy braids becoming looser as they grew out from the long journey, a few of the gold clasps which adorned them lost along the way. As a child of the court, the intricacy of her braids had long been a symbol of her status, but they meant nothing here, and she knew she would soon have to opt for a more maintainable style plaited by her own hand.

Edward grabbed her arm. "We need to go, now! They've seen you."

Adaeze looked over to find the men had stopped their grisly work and stood glaring at her from beside the pit. "So? Have they never seen a woman before?"

"Adaeze!" he said in earnest, his mouth tight as she turned back to him. "They've seen women before, but I doubt ever one from Mali. The people here are as superstitious as they are back in Niani, especially during trying times. We must leave!"

Clicking his tongue at his horse, Edward began to canter down the road, Adaeze reluctantly following him. Once she'd caught up, she dared to take one final look back. The men had returned to work as another cart pulled up, a mound of corpses piled upon it.

∞∞∞∞

The first thing that struck them when they entered the outskirts of London was how empty it seemed. The city was home to more than seventy thousand people, yet the streets stood all but deserted. As they rode between the towering, ramshackle houses, it seemed that every other door was painted hastily with a red cross. The foulest stench met Adaeze, and she turned her nose up at the filth all around. Rotten vegetables and festering entrails squirmed with maggots, and excrement-filled water pooled in the crevices, soaking into the dirt.

"Why are these streets so dirty? My father would never allow this," she asked Edward.

"I can think of two reasons," he said, looking around grimly. "Either the muckrakers are too afraid to go outside, or they're all dead."

There was silence between them after that.

She had expected to find a buzzing metropolis when she arrived in London: a city which, despite its flaws, Edward had often spoken of fondly. All she saw, though, was misery and death. As the day wore on, the clouds thickened overhead and a bitter chill set in. Cold like this was unheard of in her sun-drenched homeland, and Adaeze hugged her cloak tightly, looking down at the dull, unfamiliar clothes Edward had purchased for her when they arrived.

Everything about London seemed to be painted in a palette of grimy browns and washed-out greys, from the sky to her heavy linen dress, even her horse. She knew he'd chosen her outfit to help her blend in, but in that moment, she missed the bright, vibrant colours of Niani; she missed the sun.

Edward reigned in his horse outside a crossless door. A wooden sign hung from the building bearing the image of a bed, and although Adaeze didn't recognise the words accompanying it, she understood their meaning.

"We need to find somewhere to sleep," Edward said, sliding off his horse and cringing as his boots squished into the ground beneath him. "This place looks as good as any. Come on."

Dismounting, Adaeze handed her reigns to him, and he secured them to a nearby hitching post. Inside, the air was dank and stale. Almost no light pierced the cracks in the shutters, drawn tight to keep the stench of pestilence out, a rushlight the only source of illumination in the narrow entryway, which contained little more than a staircase along the right wall, and a series of rooms branching off further down.

As they closed the door behind them, a woman descended the stairs until she was just low enough to see them.

"What do ye want?" she asked tentatively.

"Lodgings for the night, good woman, and maybe more after that. I have money," said Edward, producing a small leather coin pouch from beneath his cloak and jingling it.

"Are ye both well?"

"We are both perfectly healthy. You need not worry."

She came down another couple of steps. "Show ye faces."

Adaeze looked over at Edward nervously, but he nodded, and they both peeled back their hoods.

As soon as the woman saw Adaeze's skin, though, she fell pale with fear. "A black witch!" she cried, taking a few steps back up the stairs.

"I can assure you, good woman, she is no witch," he replied calmly. "She is the esteemed daughter of a great ruler, who travelled here with me from-"

"She's a witch!" the woman shouted, waving her hand and cutting him off. "A bringer of the plague. A harbinger of death. Away with ye!"

Edward stepped forward, arms outstretched, but the woman screamed and disappeared up the stairs.

"We should leave," he said, glancing back at Adaeze, who had already drawn her hood back up.

Unhitching their horses, they climbed back into their saddles and continued.

"What now?" she asked with concern, realising rather despondently that her royal blood held no clout in this land.

"We keep trying. Someone will take us, eventually," he said, trying his best to reassure her.

The word 'eventually' turned out to be more accurate than they'd expected. Three other innkeepers demanded they leave after a single glance at her skin. One shooed them hastily into the street with a straw broom when a speck of dust caught in Edward's throat and induced a coughing fit. One barred them entry altogether, threatening violence. And four more lodgings were closed up completely, all too familiar red crosses marking their doors, 'Lord have mercy upon us' written in the same hue beneath them.

Finally, they stopped outside a door with a carved wooden lion's head topped with a crown swinging above it.

"This is not like the other places," Adaeze said, seeing no signs bearing beds adorning the building.

"It is a tavern, a place to drink. Sometimes they have lodgings upstairs, though, and with our options wearing thin, it might be worth enquiring."

The interior was dark and gloomy: a reality Adaeze was fast becoming accustomed to. Two scruffy men sat at a table in the far corner, tankards in hand, their faces weary and grim. They glanced over as the newcomers stepped through the door but soon turned back to their drinks in silence.

A stout man, looking to be in his mid-forties, with greying hair and a stubbled chin, stood behind the well-worn, wooden bar, drying tankards with a rag.

"Stop right there 'n' remove ye hoods, the pair of ye," he said.

With a sigh and a fair measure of anxiety, they slipped them off.

The man tilted his head, regarding Adaeze with a frown. "Where's she from?"

"Far across the deserts to the south, good sir," Edward said, trying his best to sound as cheerful as the situation would allow. "My name is Edward, and this is Adaeze. She is the esteemed daughter of the ruler of the great Mali Empire, and she is here to visit our famed city of London."

"A princess? Well, I'll be," the man said with a laugh, looking over at her. "No offence, Highness, but ye've picked a poor time to visit, what with everyone dyin' of the pestilence and all. Anyway, how can I help ye both?"

"We seek lodgings for the night, possibly longer," replied Edward. "To be perfectly frank, we have been having trouble finding somewhere. You are the first not to turn us away on sight."

"That's 'ardly surprisin', sir. Ye both look well enough, but most people see black skin these days 'n' think only o' death. Doubt anyone'll take ye 'round 'ere."

"Do you have any rooms you would be willing to let?"

The man shrugged. "Might 'ave. Depends what ye're offerin'."

"I do not have much, but what I have is yours if you will help us," said Edward, trying to conjure a reassuring smile.

He stepped up to the bar, opened up his coin pouch, and emptied its meagre contents into his hand: a shilling and a half dozen pennies.

"No offence, friend, but that won't buy ye a bed anywhere with things such as they are."

Edward looked to Adaeze, who nodded reluctantly. When they'd left Niani, she had taken five small bars of gold to help fund their journey. Four of them were already spent, but with little choice, she reached for the pouch hanging at her waist and handed it to him.

"I can give you this," Edward said, taking the pouch and turning back to the tavern keeper. "It is worth far more than a single night's accommodation, though."

The small bar dropped into Edward's hand, and upon seeing it, the man's eyes grew wide. "That what I think it is?"

"It is. And it is yours if you can offer us safe lodgings and food."

The man snatched the bar eagerly from Edward's outstretched hand, putting it in his mouth and biting down, his crooked teeth marks clear in the corner as he looked at it, satisfied. With disbelief still painted on his face, he tucked the gold out of sight in the pouch at his hip, checking over his shoulder that the two men in the corner were unaware of its existence, and turned back to his unlikely benefactors with a grin.

"There's a room upstairs, sir. It's nothin' fancy, but ye can both stay as long as ye like," he said, stepping out from behind the bar and gesturing towards the stairs. "Follow me."

The narrow, well-trodden steps creaked beneath them as the man took a rushlight and led them to a room in the eastern corner of the building. Although small, it held two hay-filled mattresses set atop rope strung bed frames, a chamber pot, a somewhat rickety-looking stool, and a plain, wooden side table set against the wall, topped with an earthenware bowl.

"So, 'ere's the deal," said the man, ushering them inside before fussing over tightening the ropes of the beds. "The apothecary 'round the corner, 'e told me 'e reckons the sickness is bein' spread by rats, so I keep the place as clean as I can. I'd appreciate it if ye did the same. Ye welcome to food 'n' ale when 'n' as you like. As I said, I've nothing fancy to offer, but I'll share what I 'ave. If ye need pennies for sundries, I'll kindly oblige ye. Lord knows ye've afforded 'em. I'd advise ye stay indoors as much as possible, though." Standing up, he took a broom from the corner of the room and used the handle to strike the hay mattresses, a couple of roaches scurrying out across the floor. "Only condition is that ye remain in good 'ealth, o' course. If either o' ye become ill, ye'll be out on ye rears, 'n' ye won't be gettin' that gold bar back neither. Agreed?"

"Agreed," said Edward with a smile, offering his hand to the man, who shook it gruffly. "What of the gentlemen downstairs?"

"I'll head down and shut up shop. I've only been open so I can earn a penny or two to get by, but with me lil bar o' gold, I don't need to no more. Ye've free reign of the place."

"Thank you ..." Edward said with a warm smile, hesitating as he fished for the man's name.

"Kole. The name's Kole."

"Well, thank you, Kole. Would we be able to trouble you for some food and drink, perchance?"

"O' course. I've only pottage 'n' bread, but I'll bring ye some up, along with some ale 'n' extra blankets," he said with a nod, closing the door behind him as he hurried off downstairs.

Adaeze walked over to the window, opening the shutter slightly and peeking out to see a cart overflowing with bodies trundling down the street below. "What does pestilence mean? You never taught me that word," she said, pulling the shutter closed tight as the fetid smell of death drifted up to meet her.

"It means a disease that spreads widely and kills many people. This is far worse than any I have ever heard tell of, though. They are calling it The Great Pestilence. I spoke about it with the captain of the ship that ferried us from Tangier to Dover. It seems they believe it may have come to Europe from the Far East. Apparently, it first appeared in the south of England mid last year and has since spread across the entire country."

"Is that why everyone is scared of me?" she asked, sitting down on the bed. "Because they think I brought the pestilence here?"

"I am afraid so. As I said, the people here are superstitious. They are looking for someone to blame, and foreigners are an easy target. They are scared, and most have seen their family and friends die already. It's killing people in their tens of thousands, and from what I have heard, it is not a pleasant way to go."

"Why? What happens?"

"They say the sick come down with a horrible fever and chills, then large, swollen boils appear under their arms, on their neck, and around their groin. They don't last long after that."

"Do you think it will reach Mali?" she asked, her brow knotted with concern as she sat down on one of the beds. "Do you think my family is in danger?"

"I cannot know for sure, Adaeze, but Mali is a long way away, and there is an ocean and a desert in between. We can only hope the distance protects them," Edward said, taking the stool, placing it in front of her, and sitting down. "Now that we have made it to London, I think it is time you finally explain to me why you were so insistent we come here?"

"I do not know why we are here," she replied, tucking her legs up onto the bed and picking at a stray straw poking out of the mattress.

"What do you mean you do not know?" he snapped at her, straightening up. "Six months ago, you came to me in confidence,

295

pleading with me that although your father had refused to grant you leave, you *had* to travel to England. You told me that your life depended on it, that you would explain the reason when we arrived, but I had to trust you until then. I betrayed your father by stealing you away: a man who treated me well for seven years."

His hands clenched as his voice grew more exasperated with each word. "I can never go back there, Adaeze, on pain of death. Do you understand that? Even if I returned you to your father, he would kill me. As for you, well, I do not know what he would do." He abruptly rose to his feet, the stool tumbling over as he did, his hands animating his words. "You begged me to bring you here, to a city rampant with disease, where stepping outside is fraught with peril. So I ask you again. Why did you insist I bring you here? What is so important that you would risk both of our lives for it? Please. I need to know."

"I cannot give you the answer you want, Edward," she said, meeting his eye, her expression timid like a chastised child. "I have always felt a strong pull north, for as long as I can remember. I never knew why until I met you. When you spoke of England, of the bustle of London and the rolling green countryside, I just knew it was England pulling my heart north. I had to come, I had to answer the call, but I do not know what called me here yet."

Edward let out an incredulous laugh and ran his fingers through his hair, clasping his hands together and resting them on top of his head. "We came here for a feeling? We came here for a feeling," he said to himself.

A knock on the door broke the tension hanging in the air, and Kole walked in bearing a loaded tray, a pair of woollen blankets draped over his arm. Shifting the earthenware bowl aside with his laden hands, he placed the tray down on the side table, two wooden bowls of pottage steaming atop it, alongside two tankards of ale and a jug to refill them.

"There anythin' else I can do for ye?" he asked, in his gruff but hospitable tone.

"Yes, actually," said Edward, composing himself and righting the stool. "Our horses are hitched out the front. Would you be able to shift them into your stables?"

"There aren't no stables 'ere, I'm afraid, but there's a laneway out back. They'll be safe there, 'n' I'll make sure they're fed 'n' watered."

"Thank you, Kole."

"G'night, sir. Ye Highness," Kole nodded to them both as he left.

Edward headed straight for the tray, ignoring the food and snatching up one of the tankards, taking a long swig and wincing as he wiped his chin.

"God, he was not lying. This ale tastes like gnat's piss," he exclaimed, although that didn't stop him from downing the rest of it in one go.

Adaeze walked over to him and placed a gentle hand on his arm. "I am not trying to deceive you, Edward. I honestly do not know what called me here. It is difficult to explain. All I have is a pull tugging on my soul. It has grown more intense during our journey, as if I am nearing my destiny. I plan to follow it tomorrow to find out what it is that led me here."

He glanced over at her, unconvinced of her sincerity, before refilling his tankard. "A tug on your soul? Do you know how insane that sounds? I risked my life, my wealth, my reputation, all because you listened to a few of my stories and had a feeling? I ..." he stopped himself, pursing his lips and letting out a measured sigh through flared nostrils.

She looked away, removing her hand from his arm, and he turned his back to her, his frustration almost palpable as he took another long draught of ale.

Unable to soothe him, Adaeze picked up one of the bowls and a wooden spoon from the tray and sat down on the stool to eat. He needed time to process, and nothing she could say or do would offer him comfort in the meantime.

∞∞∞∞

The morning came, and Adaeze rose with the sun. Edward was still passed out on his bed, the top few buttons of his dark green cotehardie unfastened to reveal his pale chest beneath, the jug and both tankards sitting empty on the floor beside him. She smiled at him as she shook the creases out of her dress and fastened her cloak around her shoulders.

He needed the rest. The trip had been arduous for him, its coordination falling squarely on his shoulders. From finding a merchant willing to smuggle them out of Niani and north along the trade routes to bartering for safe passage to England with the captains in the port of Tangier, he had risked his safety and wagered what money he had to help her. She knew the trip would have been impossible without him, and for that, she was immeasurably grateful.

Knocking the dried muck off her shoes and slipping them on, she crept out the door, closing it quietly behind her.

"Good morning, Kole," she said politely as she reached the bottom of the stairs to find him sweeping the empty tavern, a small fire crackling in the hearth.

"Mornin, ye Highness," he said with a cheerful smile. "I'm sorry to say, but there's no breakfast 'cept for the scraps of yesterday's bread. Truth be told, food's a lil hard to come by at the moment. I'll head out shortly to try 'n' buy some if I can."

"Please, call me Adaeze," she said with a smile. "When Edward wakes up, will you tell him I have gone out but that I will be back before dark?"

Kole raised an eyebrow. "Ye goin' out?"

"Yes. No need to worry, though. I do not intend on meeting with anyone; in fact, I plan to avoid people altogether. I just wish to see the city."

"Well, if ye insist, I can't stop ye, but do be careful now, won't ye, miss," Kole said with a sigh. "Head left out the door. There's more to see that way. Oh, 'n' there's some pattens by the door if ye don't fancy sloshing through muck all day."

She nodded her thanks and walked to the door, slipping her boots into the leather loops of the wooden overshoes beside it before stepping out.

The wind was brisk against her skin, and she pulled up her hood, holding her cloak tightly around herself. She let her senses guide her as she walked, turning left and right at whim, taking note of landmarks as she went so as not to get lost amongst the maze of buildings. She didn't pass a single soul as she wandered, the only sign of life being the sound of groans and coughing from behind cross-painted doors.

Finally, she reached a small square and stopped. A well, built of rough-cut stones, stood at its centre, an ageing thatched roof perched above it, a weathered bucket hanging from the winch swinging in the breeze. On the far side, four men slowly piled bodies onto a cart, and

Adaeze watched them from the shadows before quickly returning the way she came.

She spent the next hour or so in the same vein, strolling around the city from one muddy street to the next until she turned down a laneway and found herself at a dead end. Staring at the wall blocking her path, she wondered what lay beyond. Was it hiding the strange force that had pulled her across the world?

A stone skittered along the ground behind her, and Adaeze spun around with a start. At the end of the laneway stood four men, all of them dressed in fraying tunics and ratty hosen, their tangled hair peeking out from beneath their stained linen coifs. They leered at her with grime-covered faces, the one on the left cracking his knuckles.

"Is that 'er, Gil?" one of them asked.

"Yeah, that's the one what was staring at us," the man on the left answered, absently wiping his bulbous nose on his sleeve.

The one on the right, who was notably shorter than the rest, took a step back. "She got black skin, Gil. She's sick!" he exclaimed.

"Yer an idiot, Sheldon. She's not from round 'ere. That's why she got black skin."

"I dunno, Gil, it's not natural to 'ave skin like that," said Sheldon, screwing his face up in disgust. "She might not be sick, but she's prolly the reason the rest o' us are."

"Yeah," said the other two men, nodding and looking over at Gil.

"Good point, Sheldon. She must be one o' them filfy foreigners what brought the pestilence 'ere. It's 'er fault our families are dyin'. I think it's time we returned the favour, don't you, boys?"

"I can assure you I did not bring this plague to your shores," said Adaeze, raising her hand and gesturing for them to wait. "I only arrived in London yesterday, and this sickness does not exist where I am from."

The men looked at each other, ignoring her plea of innocence completely, and started to advance. In their eyes, she saw only pain and anger. They'd experienced the full devastation this disease inflicted, and now they sought vengeance; they didn't care if it was just or not.

Adaeze took a step back, her hands held ready at her sides, poised to defend herself.

As the men drew closer, though, a voice rang out from behind them. "Stop!"

The men turned around warily, but standing at the beginning of the laneway wasn't a constable or a soldier, but rather a short man wearing a tattered, long-sleeved robe of unfamiliar design, crossed over at the front and tied with a series of strings at the right hip. Its fabric was so threadbare that it was held together largely by patches of mismatched cloth from some unknown source.

He walked around the men casually, positioning himself between them and Adaeze, and she studied his face as he did. He was different to anyone she had ever seen before, with wide-set, narrow, brown eyes and an almost bridgeless nose set on a round, flat face. His skin was far whiter than hers, but in contrast to the men behind him, he appeared brown, and his black hair was cropped short, its unkempt nature matching his similarly scruffy goatee.

"Leave her alone," he shouted, his words laced with a strange accent.

"Or what?" Gil sneered at him.

The man smiled softly, but Adaeze stepped forward before he could respond, calling out to her unsolicited saviour.

"Excuse me, sir, but I do not require your help," she snapped.

The man looked over his shoulder at her, shocked, as the four men chuckled to themselves.

"That's right, stranger, you can get out o' 'ere. We 'ave business wif this woman, 'n' it don't involve ye," one of the ruffians mocked.

"My apologies," the strange man said, turning to Adaeze and bowing before giving her a quick wink and disappearing out of the laneway.

She smiled despite herself, wondering who on earth the man was, when reality intruded.

"Looks like it's just us again," Gil jeered, cracking his knuckles.

Adaeze turned her attention back to the situation at hand, unable to keep the contempt out of her voice. "Leave now, and you will not be harmed. I did not bring the pestilence here, and I am not responsible for the deaths of those you love."

The four men glared at her, their faces hard, her warning falling on deaf ears.

"Get 'er," growled Sheldon before the four of them began their advance again.

They expected her to run down the laneway towards the dead end, thereby allowing them the opportunity to grab her from behind. Much to their surprise, though, she stood her ground unwaveringly.

As the first man reached her, she stepped into him, ramming her elbow into his jaw and sending him stumbling away. The second man approached with arms raised, and she bent down, ramming her weight into his bottom half and sending him flipping over her and tumbling to the ground. The smaller man, Sheldon, swung a punch at her, but she dodged his short reach with ease, grabbing his neck and slamming him hard into the wall, once, twice, then a third time, before dumping his unconscious body in the dirt.

The pack leader, Gil, grabbed her from behind, encircling her in a bear hug that pinned her arms to her sides.

"Come on, boys, grab 'er!" he yelled. "She can't figh' us all."

The two other men groped at her chest and shoulders as she desperately tried to break free, wrenching from side to side until suddenly, she stopped struggling, her eyes closing, her body falling limp.

The men grinned to themselves, thinking her defeated, when out of nowhere, her fists clenched, and the air around her fell deathly still. Before the men could do anything, there was a surge in pressure and a cracking sound resonated down the laneway.

The force that exploded from Adaeze was so great it sent all three of the men flying backwards into the surrounding walls, collapsing to the ground as wattle and daub crumbled around them, their ragged breathing the only sign they were still alive.

As for Adaeze, she just stood there silently, dark purple energy pulsing around her body as ten long tendrils emerged from her back. She looked around cautiously, but all the men were subdued. Breathing a sigh of relief as the tendrils dissipated, she walked to the end of the laneway, expecting to find her would-be hero waiting there. When she rounded the corner, though, he was nowhere to be found, the street devoid of people, a stray cat the only sign of life as she turned full circle in search of him. There was something about him, something that tugged at her soul. The only problem was, she couldn't figure out what that something was exactly.

∞∞∞∞

The buildings were casting long shadows across the street as Adaeze headed back towards the tavern, her mind still turning over her encounter with the strange man. A clicking sound brought her out of her reverie, and she spun around to find him leaning against a wall at the entrance to a small alley, grinning.

"You know, that was very rude of you," he said.

"I'm sorry?" she asked, peeling back her hood as she scrambled to decipher his words through his accent.

"I said, that was very rude of you."

"Like I told you, I did not need rescuing," she snapped back. "I can take care of myself, thank you very much."

The man laughed, clapping his hands on his legs. "I can see that, but that's not what I meant. You defeated all those men by yourself, and you didn't leave any for me." He shook his head in mock anger. "It's very rude. You should have shared."

"Who are you, and why are you following me?"

"My name is Nergüi," he said, stepping forward and bowing his head slightly. "I come from the Mongolian Empire to the east."

"You speak English quite well for a Mongol," she sniped.

"I learnt it from a merchant we captured on the trade routes. Nervous talkers make good teachers," he said with a laugh. "And where might you be from?"

"I am Adaeze, from the great Empire of Mali across the sea and the desert to the south."

"You have travelled far," he said, making a clicking sound with his tongue.

"I could say the same to you."

Nergüi shrugged. "Yes and no. I fought alongside the other Mongols as they attacked the edge of Europe. By the time I deserted them, the journey was already halfway done."

"Deserted? That is not very noble of you," she said, an air of royal superiority creeping into her voice.

"We all have shame in our life. I fought for my country for a long time, but there were things I needed to do for myself, places I needed to see."

Adaeze regarded him for a moment. "And why did you come to London? What is your business here?"

"I don't know. I just felt a pull on my soul and followed it until it led me here," he said, laughing as he saw the look on her face change with his words.

"What?" she asked defensively, ironing the furrows from her brow.

"Go on, say it."

"Say what?"

"Why you came here," he replied, waiting for an answer he already knew.

She hesitated, taking a deep breath to steady her racing heart. "I ... I felt a pull as well."

He made the clicking sound again. "Well, perhaps we came here to find each other?"

Nergüi grinned at her once more, and she couldn't help but smile back, the pair regarding each other in silence for a moment. There was a roguish quality to him that was both endearing and irksome at the same time.

Adaeze broke his gaze, looking down at her cloak and fussing with it. "I should go."

"Yes, it's getting late. Can I see you tomorrow?" he asked with a wink.

Her kneejerk reaction was, of course, rejection. After all, Edward had told her of the Mongol hordes. For all she knew, he meant her harm. Still, something gave her pause for thought, a mixture of emotions picking at her until, all at once, she realised that the pull was gone. Could Nergüi be the reason she abandoned her home and family to come to this godforsaken city?

Yielding to her curiosity, she nodded. "I suppose so. Where do you wish to meet?"

He tilted his head to the side. "Do you remember how to reach that square with the well in the middle, where you first saw those men?"

"I think so," Adaeze replied, somewhat perturbed by his detailed knowledge of her movements.

"I will meet you there tomorrow before noon. Until then..." And with that, he turned and disappeared down the alley, melting into the shadows.

Adaeze stared after him, resisting the urge to follow and demand answers about what had drawn him to London and how long he had been following her. Prudence prevailed, though, and instead, she continued on her way.

∞∞∞∞

By the time she reached the tavern, it was nightfall, and Edward was waiting impatiently for her in their room.

"Where have you been?" he asked, standing up as she entered and beginning to pace, his voice laced with a combination of concern and annoyance.

She lay down on her bed with the casual calm of a teen being interrogated by a parent. "Out exploring."

"Have you forgotten that half the people here are dead or dying! What were you thinking?"

"I was trying to find my purpose," Adaeze said, glancing over at him.

"And did you find it?"

"Perhaps," Adaeze responded with a distant smile. She didn't mean to, but the thought of Nergüi's cocky face had suddenly appeared in her mind, and she hadn't been able to help herself.

Edward stopped and sat down, stunned. "You did? What is it?"

"I'm not entirely sure yet. I must go out again tomorrow to be sure, but if it is true, you will be the first to know," she reassured him.

There was a knock on the door, and Kole appeared with a tray of food and ale, along with another bundle of rushes for the light.

"Evenin'. I guessed ye must both be starvin'. Haven't neither of ye eaten today," he said, placing the tray down on the side table. "I got a scrap o' beef from the butcher 'n' made a stew, so eat up. There's more downstairs if ye be wantin'."

"Thank you, Kole," said Adaeze sitting up. "Would I be able to trouble you for some warm water? I wish to wash my hair."

"O' course. I got a pot on for the linens. Gimme two shakes," he replied, scurrying off, returning a few minutes later with a steaming pail and filling the earthenware bowl before bidding them goodnight.

After ravenously devouring half her bowl of stew, Adaeze rustled around in the small pouch she carried at her hip. From it, she pulled out the only personal trinket she'd taken with her from Niani: a small, wide-toothed, ivory comb carved from elephant tusk, the top etched with delicate patterns.

As Edward continued to eat, she moved the stool over to the side table, sat down, and began the slow, tedious process of unravelling her grown-out braids, placing each of the golden clasps she removed into her pouch for safekeeping.

Edward persisted with his inquiries between mouthfuls, fishing for answers, but she refused to divulge anything. Instead, she tried to shift the conversation to other topics, their discussion skewing back and forth to both of their dissatisfaction.

Eventually, they simply gave way to silence as Edward sat drinking his ale and Adaeze, having unfurled all of her hair, washed and combed it fastidiously. Parting it into five thick rows along her scalp, she began to braid it once more, closing her eyes to concentrate on the movements of her hands, which up until that point had very rarely had to perform the task on her own head. As she paused periodically to move the rush in its holder, shake out her tired arms, and redo the parts she was unhappy with, she thought about Nergüi.

When she finally snuffed the light and lay down for the night, Adaeze was in such a state of anxious anticipation that hours slipped by before sleep took her into its arms. When at last it did, she dreamt of an island and of a man with wings as dark as night.

∞∞∞∞

Her eyes opened to the uncommon appearance of soft rays of sunlight filtering in through the shutters and falling on her face. It was mid-morning, her pleasant dream enticing her to linger in her subconscious far longer than usual, the island staying in her thoughts as she sat up to find Edward's bed empty. She'd dreamt about this distant place numerous times over the years, and the dark-winged man was becoming clearer and more ever-present with each iteration.

As she reached the bottom of the stairs, she found Edward sitting at the table beside the fire, nibbling at a piece of coarse barley bread and a nub of cheese, while Kole fussed around behind the bar. She sat down opposite him, reaching her hands out to warm away the residual chill of a frosty night.

"Good morning, Edward," she said, meeting his tired eyes as he pushed the plate of bread and cheese to the centre of the table and gestured for her to eat without a word.

She looked towards Kole, waving him over. "Please, join us. It is your breakfast as much as it is ours."

"Thank ye, miss," he replied, coming over with three tankards and filling them from the pot of cider he had warming on the hearth.

They ate in relative silence, Kole trying as best he could to cut the tension with comments on the day's fine weather and the tale of his successful endeavour to find the meagre meal before them.

As Kole cleared away the plates, Adaeze made ready to leave, but Edward grabbed her arm. "You are leaving already?"

"I have to meet someone before noon," she said, snatching her arm back and straightening her sleeve.

His eyes narrowed. "What? Who?"

"I cannot tell you. Not yet. I do not really know myself. I am just following the same feeling that brought me to this place."

"No. It is not safe," he said, stepping between her and the door. "You cannot just go meeting with strangers at a time like this, in a city you barely know."

"That is not your choice, Edward. Please do not try and stop me," she pleaded as she ducked past him and reached the door.

He went to follow after her when she glanced back at him, a look of headstrong immovability in her eyes.

"Just ... be careful, Adaeze. Please. I do not wish for you to get hurt."

"That is not my fate, Edward," she said with a comforting smile.

"When will you return?"

"I do not know. I am sorry for being so secretive, but I will explain everything tonight. I promise."

He nodded slowly, brow knotted, and she slipped on her overshoes and bounded out the door with the energy of an excited child.

∞∞∞∞

Adaeze found herself lost several times, but after an hour or so, she finally reached the small square. The stone well, with its rickety thatched roof, sat unattended, much like the rest of the space. Relieved there was no sign of her attackers from the previous day, she wandered over to its side, flicking a loose shard of rock from its edge and watching it fall down into the darkness, eventually splashing into the unseen water at the bottom.

Sitting down on the edge of the well, she scanned the streets for Nergüi but found each direction deserted. The sun was almost at its peak, and she began to wonder whether she'd made a mistake coming when she felt a presence behind her, a familiar click reaching her ear.

"I didn't think you'd come," he said.

She turned to him, eyebrow raised. "You know, that is an incredibly annoying habit you have."

Nergüi grinned widely at her, revealing as he did several missing teeth at the back. "I know," he said, sitting down beside her. "I use it to distract my enemies."

"Is that what I am?" she retorted. "Your enemy?"

"No," Nergüi laughed before his face grew earnest. "I've travelled my whole life, never feeling at home, never finding my purpose. All I ever felt was a pull, a longing I couldn't understand until I met you. You are the pull, Adaeze."

She stared at him, her mind whirring with his words. All her life, she'd felt that same pull: a pull she had often dreamt was guiding her to her true purpose, her true love. Still, she had never genuinely believed it to be more than mere fantasy. Even as she crossed land and sea in search of its source, she was unconvinced she would uncover anything of substance. To her rational mind, the pull she felt was just the wistful yearning of a discontent princess to whom fate had handed a unique opportunity.

"I don't know what to say," she blurted out, finally managing to find her voice.

"Sometimes, there is nothing to say. Sometimes, the energy that flows between two souls is enough."

Adaeze surveyed his face in detail, reassessing him with her changing emotions. On the surface, he appeared a rootless vagabond, a mischievous nomad of little means, but beneath that lay something greater. She found in his eyes a purity she'd not seen before.

Her gaze fell to her lap. "I just ... I never imagined the pull would lead to ..."

Nergüi chuckled as her sentence trailed off. "What? A dirty Mongol?" He waved the comment away nonchalantly with his hand. "It's okay. I didn't expect to be reborn in this body either! But then, I'm often surprised where I end up."

She was caught off guard by his words. She'd long had a sense her soul had lived before, her dreams actually memories of other times, but she'd never allowed herself to believe it. Until now.

"Do you really think it possible?" she asked, her voice suddenly alive with excitement.

"What?" Nergüi asked, scratching his armpit before continuing. "That we've been reborn? Why not?"

Adaeze couldn't help but smile. It was difficult to explain the feeling that swept over her, but comfort was the closest she could come, although it was a wholly inadequate description of the warmth settling around her heart as all her wild beliefs were validated.

He smiled back softly before fumbling beneath his robe and pulling something from around his neck: a necklace of silver, its pendant hidden in the curl of his fist.

"What is it?" she asked, craning her head to try and snatch a peek.

Nergüi opened up his hand, revealing a gleaming piece of obsidian intricately carved into the shape of a butterfly. "I was pillaging a small town somewhere in the east of Europe when I found this. Something about it called to me, and I remember standing there staring at it for the longest time."

He held it out, and she leant in to admire its finer details, its beauty haunting, its glossy midnight black seeming to both absorb and reflect all light in equal measure.

"I put it around my neck that day, and it's stayed there ever since."

Adaeze ran her fingers across its glassy surface. "It is remarkably crafted. I can see why it would enchant you."

"It was more than just its beauty that drew me to it," said Nergüi, looking down at it serenely for a moment before clasping it back around his neck. "Tell me, Adaeze, did you dream last night?"

"I did."

"Of what?"

She looked wistfully past him as she drew forth the memory. "An island and a man with dark wings."

Reaching over, Nergüi took her hands gently, their eyes meeting as his lips curled ever so slightly, softening his features, his voice thick with emotion. "I, too, dreamt of an island and the woman I shared a life with there. My beautiful butterfly, I called her."

From the shadows of a narrow laneway, Edward watched Adaeze as she spoke with the stranger beside the well, jealousy clenching his jaw tight and furrowing his brow. So intent was he on the scene playing out that he did not notice the person behind him until a hand covered his mouth. Strong arms dragged him backwards, a meaty forearm pinning him against a wall by his throat.

The hand left his mouth, and he looked at his attacker, whose features remained largely obscured by the dimness of the laneway.

"What is the meaning of this?!" Edward croaked, trying to stifle his fear. "Who are you?"

The man released his arm from Edward's throat and took a step back, bowing his head slightly. He wore a spotless, brown woollen cloak clasped at his left shoulder, the front flap flung back over his right. Beneath that, he was clad in a crisp, dark blue cotehardie woven of fine linen and clean, tan hose tucked into long, polished leather boots. Despite his immaculate attire, though, his face betrayed his true calling: it was coarse and hard, with a long scar running across his right cheek.

"Forgive me, sir. My name is Tucker, and I have been sent here for the purpose of obtaining your personage on a matter of some urgency," the man replied, his accent far more boorish than the words he had so obviously been assigned with relaying.

Edward straightened his cloak, composing himself. "And who is it that calls for my attendance in such a forceful manner?"

"A merchant named Abbott, sir. He's eager to make your acquaintance."

"I am afraid if this Abbott wishes to meet me, he should make the journey himself. I have no intention of accompanying you on your fool's errand. Good day, sir," Edward said, turning to depart.

Tucker took a step to block his path, pulling his cloak back, a speck of sunlight dancing off steel at his hip. "He was quite insistent, sir. Shall we?" the man jibed, gesturing down the lane, away from the square.

The blood drained from Edward's face, and he nodded awkwardly, setting off as directed, Tucker following close behind.

As they walked, Edward's mind reeled from the events of the day; however, the overwhelming emotion he felt at present was no longer jealousy but fear. After an hour of trudging east through muddy streets, they eventually arrived at the gate of a two-storey manor at the edge of the city surrounded by lush lawns and manicured gardens. Its walls were built of dark timber framing, the wattle and daub filling the spaces painted in a bright white coating of limewash. Its steep roof, unlike most in London, was not thatched but instead tiled in slate, wisps of light smoke dancing up through an opening at its peak.

"He must be quite the merchant," said Edward, trying to break the tension as they reached the threshold, but Tucker did not respond, simply opening the heavy wooden door and ushering him through into the large hall beyond.

The fire crackling in the central hearth offered the only light outside of the waning rays of dusk creeping in the small windows, and Edward looked around the mammoth space. The cruck-framed roof hung the full two storeys overhead, and a long, dark wood table ran along the far end bearing twelve chairs. Tucker left him to warm himself by the fire, walking over to the door on the right wall, knocking sharply, and disappearing into the next room.

After what felt like an eternity to Edward's pounding heart, the door opened, and Tucker emerged, crossing the room and leaving without a word. A moment later, a large man stepped through the same door dressed in a bright crimson cotehardie with shining gold buttons down its front and fastening its sleeves, jet black hose, and pristine, brown leather boots. He looked to be over six feet tall, his chest broad, jawline sharp and clean-shaven, and hair a neat crop of dark brown waves streaked at the sides with greys. As he walked forward, the piercing gaze of his striking green eyes unsettled Edward, who shifted in place as he straightened himself in an attempt to look taller.

"Good evening, Edward. My name is Abbott. Thank you for coming," he said in a calm, congenial voice.

Edward gave him a half-hearted smile and shook his hand, not wanting to offend the man who'd so forcefully demanded his attendance. Abbott clicked his fingers twice, and a servant appeared from behind a screen in the far corner bearing two glass goblets of red wine on a tray. The humbly clad man scurried forward, Abbott taking his glass without so much as a nod of acknowledgement, Edward following suit more out of a sense of duty than want.

The servant disappeared silently, and Abbott turned back to his guest. "My apologies if Tucker was a jot brusque with you. He is fabulously effective at his job, but tact is a skill I fear he will never learn."

"That is quite all right," Edward replied, bowing his head slowly in acceptance and taking a small sip of wine. "I was just startled, is all. I do not normally receive invitations at knifepoint."

"How very true!" Abbott laughed before walking over to a pair of beautifully carved oak chairs set in the corner beside a small matching table, their seats topped with luxurious, crimson silk cushions stuffed with goose feathers. "Please, sit. I suppose you are wondering why I have called you here."

"I imagine it must be quite urgent given your methods," Edward said, feeling a little more at ease as he sat down. "I must say, though, I am confused as to how you have come to know of me and my whereabouts. I have not been in London for many years."

Abbott smiled at him in the disquieting way a cat smiles at a mouse before it pounces.

"I am not interested in you, Edward. It is Adaeze who has drawn my attention, or more specifically, the man she seems to have taken a fancy to."

Edward eyed him with suspicion. "How could you possibly know of her?"

"I make it my business to know everything," Abbott replied, sitting back in his chair and taking a long draught from his glass. "The man seducing your friend is named Nergüi, a fierce Mongol warrior who deserted his own horde to travel here."

"Why has he come?"

"Of that, I am unsure. What I do know is that Nergüi has made a lot of powerful enemies. Enemies who wish him dead."

"And how does this concern me exactly?"

Abbott looked over at Edward with a knowing expression. "Because you love Adaeze. You want her for yourself, and this man poses a great threat to that desire."

"That is absurd! An Englishman and a black princess. What makes you suggest such a thing?" he retorted, although his sudden paleness spoke the truth.

"Nothing, I suppose. Aside from the fact you risked your life, fortune, and reputation to bring her to a city overrun with pestilence simply because she wished it so. And, of course, the fact that when Tucker located you, you were lurking in the shadows spying on her."

"I suppose it would appear obvious," Edward admitted, "except to her."

"The objects of our affection are often the last to know," Abbott chuckled. He took another sip of his wine, swirling the remainder. "I want Nergüi gone, and you want Adaeze. It seems we have a common goal, does it not?"

Edward sat back in his chair, his mind such a mess of emotions he didn't know what to think. Finally, he shook his head. "I cannot be a party to murder."

Abbott drained his glass and set it down on the table beside him. "Of course not, and I have made no mention of it. I want your help to oust him, to make him so unwelcome, so vilified, that he will be forced to leave not only London but England in its entirety."

Edward raised an eyebrow. "You do not wish him dead?"

"Killing is a messy business. By forcing him to the mainland, he will have two choices: go back to the Far East or risk being slaughtered in Europe for bringing the pestilence to our lands."

The request did not sit right in Edward's mind. To ruin a man he knew very little about seemed immoral, but as he thought about Adaeze, he found himself nodding in spite of himself.

"What would you have me do?" he asked, his jaw clenching as he wrestled with his eternal conflict.

Abbott rose to his feet. "Come, Edward. I will explain everything over dinner."

∞∞∞∞∞∞∞

Adaeze and Nergüi talked all day beside the well, time passing around them inconsequentially. As they retold their most vivid dreams, the

312

pair found they could regularly finish one another's tale with snippets of their own, like matching cards without seeing the other's hand. The more they spoke, the more they came to realise that not only were these dreams actually memories of their past lives, but many were lives they had lived together, as partners, as lovers, as soulmates.

In the memories they could not align, the details seemed more clouded, as though the other's absence faded the ink on those pages. It was frustrating, but Adaeze felt confident that, united, they could uncover all the answers.

Between recounting their memories of the past, they recounted memories of their current life. Nergüi was far too amused to discover she had been reborn a princess, and Adaeze couldn't help but see his present existence as one grand adventure. They spoke of anything and everything, their conversations easy and comfortable, but most of all familiar. For the first time, she had found someone who felt like home, and it painted on her face an indelible smile.

It was almost dark by the time she bid him farewell, promising to meet him again the next day. When she arrived back at the tavern, Edward was nowhere to be seen, her day's joy dampened by concern as she sat by the hearth with her bowl of pottage, waiting for his safe return. It wasn't until she was slipping into bed hours later, though, that he stepped through the door. He offered no explanation or apology, simply kicking off his boots and collapsing into bed. Adaeze did not press the issue. After all, she was in no position to judge; she had been keeping her movements secret for days now. Still, the sudden change in him troubled her.

∞∞∞∞

The sound of a raven cawing on the window ledge woke her the following morning, and she rolled over to find Edward's bed already vacant. When she went downstairs in search of him, Kole could shed no light on where he'd gone, only that he had left at dawn in a dark mood. Her concern remained, but she set it aside as she remembered her plans, assuring herself there would be plenty of time that evening for discussion and resolution. With her heart buoyed by anticipation, she wrapped her breakfast of barley bread, cheese, and smoked pork in a cloth and hurried out the door.

313

Nergüi was already at the well when she arrived, sitting cross-legged on its edge, his eyes closed. As she approached and sat beside him, he roused from his meditation, meeting her with a warm smile and plucking a small, white flower from the fold in his robe.

"A daisy," he said, reaching over and tucking it behind her ear. "Just like your name, you see. A-dae-ze."

She couldn't help but smile at his boyish charm as she placed the cloth parcel between them and opened it up.

"You brought food! What a marvellous creature you are."

She beamed at his praise as she tore off a piece of bread and topped it with a scrap of smoked pork. Gnawing on it, she noticed he seemed cleaner: his face clear of its usual smudges of dirt, his robe seeming at least a few shades lighter and less soiled, his hair kempt, and his previous lingering odour notably absent.

"You washed," she said between bites.

"Better a Mongol than a dirty Mongol. Besides, you keep yourself so well; I thought I should follow your example." He took a small knife from its place at his hip and winkled off a piece from the chunk of cheese. "Did you dream last night?"

"Not that I can remember. Did you?"

Nergüi's expression grew distant for a second. "I dreamed, but of nothing important," he said as he pressed the cheese into a nub of bread and bit into it eagerly, continuing to talk as he chewed. "Where did you find all this food? I've barely been able to find a scrap in London, and no one will sell to me."

"You would have to ask the man who runs the tavern. He is the one who found it."

Nergüi pondered that as he helped himself to some of the pork, clicking his tongue as he cut off a slice with his knife.

Adaeze raised an eyebrow at him. "I very much want to know if the annoying sound you make is something you did in previous lives."

He made the clicking sound with his tongue again, grinning. "I don't remember being this annoying before," he laughed. "I'm fairly sure it's something I picked up in this life."

"And hopefully, something you'll forget in the next."

They ate until they'd had their fill, wrapping up the last morsels and setting them aside for later.

Nergüi licked his fingers and sighed contently. "Now that's the way to start the day. Breakfast with a beautiful woman."

"You think I am beautiful?" she asked, a little taken aback.

Nergüi gazed at her affectionately. "Inside and out, my princess."

He leant forward to kiss her, but she pulled back on instinct. After a second, though, she moved forward again, her lips meeting his for a long, tender moment. When they finally separated, Nergüi's face bore a serene smile, and he began to lean in for another when she put a finger across his lips.

"One is enough, Mongol. You try that again, and you will get what I gave those men the day we met," she warned with a playful smirk.

"You truly are marvellous," he said, chuckling to himself before his smile faded and a knot rumpled his brow. "I thought of something last night, you know."

"What?" she asked, troubled by his paling joy.

"I think I know why there are holes in our memories."

Adaeze took his hand, her eyes meeting his, the slight rise in her eyebrows prompting him to continue.

"I believe it's trauma. We must have suffered deaths so full of pain and despair our very souls were damaged, our memories pushed aside to make room for agony. I believe our souls had to heal before they could find each other, and that healing took many lifetimes."

She considered his words before she spoke. "I suppose that makes sense. Perhaps the trauma had to recede before we could feel the pull towards each other again. Do you think now we are reunited, we will be able to mend the holes and make some sense of all this?"

"I don't know. I suppose only time will answer that question," he said, his contemplation eliciting another involuntary click of his tongue and a subsequent guilt-filled apology. "We can't keep meeting like this, though. The threat of pestilence is too great in London. The streets are too narrow and the people too many. We should leave. Come away with me, Adaeze. Come away, and we'll figure it out together."

"Where would we go? I do not know this land."

"Where do you think?" he replied with a grin.

"The island," she said, her words escaping as a whisper as her dream came back to her all at once. "You know where it is?"

"I do."

Adaeze stood up, brushing the crumbs from her dress as her heart raced with excitement. "I must find Edward and bid him farewell before we go. I must explain that I have found my purpose. I must thank him. Without his help, I never would have made it here. I owe him that much."

"Let me escort you. I don't think we should be apart anymore ..." he replied, his voice trailing off as he caught a glimpse of something over her shoulder.

"Adaeze!" a familiar voice shouted as a man in a dark green cotehardie stepped out from the shadows of a laneway adjoining the square.

She turned, running towards him and enveloping him in a hug. "Edward! What are you doing here? I have so much to tell you."

Edward hugged her tight, then pulled back, his eyes full of love and regret. "I am doing this for your own good, Adaeze."

"What are you talking about?" she asked, her eyes growing wide as she saw a stocky, bearded man appear from the shadows.

The man motioned at Nergüi. "Is this him?"

Edward ignored Adaeze and nodded. "That's him, Constable. I overheard him boasting about bringing the great pestilence to our land. He is the reason so many are dead."

The man drew his short sword from its sheath and pointed it at Nergüi. "Don't move. You're under arrest!"

Adaeze stumbled back from Edward in shock as Nergüi stood up from the edge of the well, his open hands before him as to placate the man.

"I have no wish to fight you, sir," he said, eerily calm, "or your men."

Adaeze whirled around and saw more men melt out of the shadows in every direction, some armed with short swords, others with knives and clubs. "What have you done, Edward?" she asked, her voice wavering.

"Something I had to do, to save you. One day, you will thank me."

Edward reached out to her, but she backed away, turning to return to Nergüi's side.

"No, Adaeze. Stay back," said Nergüi, holding up his hand to stop her. "This is my fight. They're not here for you."

Adaeze glanced back at Edward, who nodded, beckoning her over.

She shook her head, backing up against a wall instead as the men surrounded Nergüi, who stood stoically still, his eyes flitting between his assailants.

Finally, he spoke, his words booming around the square. "You are all angry. This I understand. But do not confuse anger with righteousness. This path will only lead to regret. I'll give you one chance to turn back. Leave now, or I will be forced to defend myself."

The constable strode forward. "Every man who stands before you, myself included, has lost their entire family to the sickness you brought to our lands. They will give their lives willingly to ensure you receive swift justice."

Nergüi snickered, clicking his tongue. "This isn't justice," he called out, turning in a circle as he spoke, surveying the faces of the men. "This is vengeance. I did not bring the pestilence. It was already here when I arrived. This is your last warning. I don't want to hurt any of you."

The constable shook his head in disgust before rushing in to attack, his sword held high. Nergüi didn't flinch until, at the last moment, he brought his hands together, a bolt of pure black energy shooting out and slamming into the constable's chest. The man was hurled backwards by the impact, skittering across the ground until he hit the wall beside Adaeze and slumped over motionless.

Looking at the other men, Nergüi's expression grew grim. "I have given you all fair warning," he said, bringing his arms in close to his body. "I will not be held accountable for what happens next."

As he held out his hands, Adaeze felt the pressure rise, and she crouched down, covering her ears. Six shafts of shadow dancing with black lightning appeared from his back like wings, and the men hesitated, dumbstruck by the supernatural sight.

Nergüi let out a deep, guttural cry, the air crackling as power erupted from him, encasing him in a churning eddy of shadow. The men stopped in their tracks, and Nergüi crouched down momentarily, energy exploding outward as he sprang back up, the shock wave sending the men flying in all directions. They hit the ground hard, mud spraying up around them, the square filled with groans of pain.

The least injured of the men scrambled to their feet, grabbing their weapons and advancing once more. Nergüi stood tall, his hands poised

317

at his hips as they approached, their faces dirt-smeared and bitter. All at once, he thrust his hands out, ribbons of energy lancing forth, piercing their chests and eliciting screams before they toppled over and fell still.

Nergüi glanced over at Adaeze, his face full of regret as he crouched down, a swirl of darkness building around him until suddenly, he was airborne. Craning her neck, she watched him shoot upwards towards the clouds, his wings the only thing visible by the time he reached them and disappeared.

A cold pall hung over the square, and with shaking hands and pounding heart, she stood up and surveyed the destruction. The splintered thatching of the well's now non-existent roof floated gently to the ground, coming to rest between the crumpled men writhing in the mud, the bucket dangling precariously from the snapped winch which sat askew in its unstable stone footings.

Everyone around her was either incapacitated or in shock, each of them as fractured as the walls surrounding the square. Those who were able, clambered to their feet, dragging their wounded compatriots away until the scene stood deserted of heartbroken vigilantes, their vengeance abandoned in the aftermath.

Steadying her breath, she spotted Edward slowly propping himself up where he lay, and she hurried over, helping him to his feet.

"Do you see now?" he asked solemnly, straightening his cotehardie and wiping the mud from his cheek with his sleeve. "Do you see what he is?"

"You are the one who does not see, Edward," she said, a flicker of contempt glinting in her eyes.

"Indeed," a cold voice responded from the shadows, the words reaching them just as four dark blades pierced Edward's chest, blood spurting into the air and sending Adaeze stumbling back in shock.

Edward looked down at the blades in disbelief, his hand passing through them like they were little more than smoke. Then, all at once, they were gone, and he collapsed to the ground, pawing at his chest as blood oozed out and pooled beneath him. Adaeze rushed over, kneeling beside him and lifting his head onto her lap as his mouth gaped for air his lungs were too punctured to accept.

She brushed the hair from his face, her contempt replaced with grief as his eyes met hers with the unmistakable ache of love unspoken and unrequited. Their gaze lingered for a heartbreaking moment before Edward's attention flitted to the figure who had stolen his life, his eyes growing wide with realisation.

Adaeze glanced up to find a tall, broad man with piercing green eyes dressed in a crimson cotehardie circling around them until he stopped in full view of his victim, eight black blades stretching out from his back like spiders' legs, a look of deep satisfaction on his face. She felt a shudder in her lap and looked down as Edward fell limp, eyes she had trusted for seven years glazing over as he slipped away from the world.

In an instant, her grief morphed into unbridled anger, and she lowered her friend's head to the ground, rising to her feet to face his murderer. Something about the stranger disturbed her soul, and as she took in his obscure silhouette, a deep-rooted knowledge surfaced within her. This man was the source of all her misery, all her anguish, all her pain, not just in this life but in all that had come before it.

"That never gets old, you know," the man chuckled. "The moment of recognition. The wide-eyed realisation that I, Anasazi, have arrived." His blades flexed behind him menacingly. "I shall never tire of the hollow expression of death inevitable."

He charged forward, catching her unawares, but as he swung at her with his right blades, she ducked underneath his attack, responding with one of her own. Purple energy cannoned out of her body and into Anasazi, sending him careening across the square.

Adaeze balled her hands into fists, and she stayed the power in her chest, purple tendrils emerging from her back as she watched Anasazi stand, wiping blood from his lip and smiling viciously.

"Well, well. It seems the butterfly finally sprouted wings. How fascinating. I did wonder how long it would take you to transcend the barrier between this world and the aether and harness its power for yourself," he said, walking towards her, his smile yielding to a more serious facade. "Unfortunately, your progression only makes you a bigger target."

He lunged forward, his blades arcing around him to catch her in the middle, but she leapt back before launching herself at him, slamming her hands into his chest and unleashing a blast of energy. Anasazi stammered backwards, grunting with pain, then, recovering quickly, thrust his blades at her head. As she ducked underneath, though, Adaeze realised her mistake.

Anasazi snatched her wrist, grinning. "Got you."

Searing pain coursed through her, and she lashed out on reflex, the ensuing detonation sending them both flying backwards to the ground. Anasazi rose to his feet, but when Adaeze tried to do the same, she found her limbs uncooperative.

"It's okay. There's no rush," he said with a smirk. "I've got all the time in the world."

Gritting her teeth, she forced herself to her feet, defiance squaring her jaw as her tendrils billowed behind her.

Anasazi's smile waned, and he tilted his head as his eyes turned cold. "You think now you have discovered an iota of power you are a match for me? Fool," he said, his voice booming, the air around him beginning to ripple as his power surged. "You have enthusiasm, I'll grant you that, but you lack control." He brought his hands up in front of him as though to clap but paused. "Now, I want you to remember this pain, the agony of finding your love, only to lose him again. I want you to remember it was I who consigned you back to the aether in this life, and it is I who will consign you in the next. Ad infinitum, my dear, to infinity."

With that, a glistening orb of pitch-black energy sprung up between his hands, and as he brought them together with a thunderous clap, the orb shot towards her. She knew it was futile, but she rallied her last shred of energy and encased herself in its faint aura in a desperate attempt to ward off impending death. As she braced for impact, though, a figure dropped from the sky, a dark shield enveloping them both. The orb struck the shield with a deafening crack that reverberated through the city, the combined energies neutralising one another as they dissipated harmlessly into the air.

As the darkness cleared, Adaeze looked across to find Nergui by her side, his wings blazing. With a wink, he wrapped his arms around her waist and in an instant, they were airborne. Clinging to him for dear life, the wind shearing past her face and snatching away the involuntary scream escaping her, she looked down through the shroud of energy at the ever-shrinking square. She expected to see Anasazi poised to pursue them, but instead, his eight blades simply dissolved, and he turned from them, disappearing amongst the shadows of the narrow streets once more.

∞∞∞∞

By the time they landed, Adaeze's mind was racing, her stomach tied in knots of terror and exhilaration in equal measure. A wave of nausea crashed over her, and she sat herself down on a nearby rock, gripping its sides as her body reaccustomed itself to ground level.

"Don't worry," said Nergüi, crouching down in front of her. "I was the same my first time as well. It will pass soon."

After a few deep breaths, she managed to collect herself. "Thank you," she said with a flustered smile.

He let out a small chuckle. "No need to thank me. You didn't think I would just run away and leave you, surely?"

"There have been a lot of surprises today. I barely know what to think," she replied, looking around and registering, with a fair amount of disbelief, where they were. "We are here? The island. But how?"

"When I first arrived in England a few months ago, I travelled the country, following the pull on my soul until it led me here. I stayed for a few days, exploring it as my memories of our life together came back to me. Eventually, I realised that although part of the pull had disappeared, the other part of it had only grown stronger. It was then I knew where it would lead me, and I left in search of you."

"It is perfect," she said, her eyes tracing the outline of the jagged boulders guarding its edge and flitting between the windswept trees dotting the golden grass of the meadow filling its centre.

"It's home."

Without warning, the image of Edward's lifeless eyes flashed through her mind, and her grief hit her so hard in the stomach she doubled over. Not a moment later, his eyes were replaced with the cold, heartless green of the man who'd killed him.

Adaeze looked up at Nergüi, her eyes welling with tears. "Anasazi. He is -"

"I know," he replied, taking her hands and squeezing them gently. "I was surprised to find you had no memories of him yet, but I thought we could just bask in our joy for a while. I thought I would have more time to warn you about him. I'm sorry, my beautiful butterfly."

321

"Butterfly," she said to herself, her words vague. "You have always called me that, haven't you? That is how he knew."

"You must be strong, Adaeze. Look at me," he said, ducking his head and catching her eye. "We can't escape him. I could fly us to the other side of the world, but we'd be watching our backs every day."

His words weaved their way in, and she was struck with a paralysing fear. The man she had faced had been so powerful, so sure of victory. She could see no way to defeat him. Despair caught in her throat, choking her, until the image of the orb and the shield dispersing replayed in her mind's eye.

Anasazi was relentless, yes, but he was not infallible. Together; together they stood a chance.

"We have to fight," she said, her resolve dispensing with her fear and replacing it with vengeance. "We have to end this once and for all."

"And we will," he said, offering her a comforting grin. "But how about I give you the grand tour first?"

∞∞∞∞∞∞∞∞

Abbott sat at the head of the table in his hall, carving the leg off a roasted duck, when Tucker walked in.

"What is it?" asked Abbott, irritation lacing his words, his eyes not rising from his meal.

Tucker kneaded his hands together nervously. "Ahh, one of the servants is sick, sir."

"And why would that interest me? Surely the others can pick up the slack."

"She has a fever, sir, and is coughing up quite a lot of blood."

Abbott stopped dead, the duck leg halfway to his mouth. He didn't mind if the whole of London fell to the devastation of the pestilence so long as he himself did not succumb. Its appearance in his own household, especially this most deadly variant, was of grave concern. While his soul was strong, he was not immune to the ravages of disease, and with his foe within his reach, to take ill now would thwart his plans.

He lay down his food, wiped his hand on a torn piece of bread, and turned to face Tucker. "Has she been isolated?"

"Yes, sir, she's been moved to the loft above the stables."

"Are any of the others showing symptoms?"

Tucker shook his head firmly. "Not yet, sir, but they're being monitored."

Abbott brushed the crumbs from his lap and nodded. "Good. I'm leaving town for a few days to attend to something. While I'm gone, I expect the servants to stay out of my private quarters. Keep them confined to their rooms until we can be sure this has passed. Is that clear?"

"As you wish, sir," Tucker nodded in deference before turning on his heel and leaving in silence.

Abbott looked down at his supper again, but he'd lost his appetite. Pushing the plate away with a sigh, he rose and retired to his bedroom. Tucked in the corner of the room, behind a folding screen, was an inconspicuous wooden door to which only he held the key. It opened to a narrow wooden staircase, and he climbed it slowly, emerging onto the small, inset balcony on the roof of his manor.

As the cold air of the evening flowed past him and clarified his thoughts, he closed his eyes, reaching out with his senses. The energy of every soul in every person rang out in his mind, but they were mere blips, inconsequential. He quietened their din, concentrating as he cast his net further until he heard two familiar chimes sounding in unison to the north. Opening his eyes, he smiled. He had found them.

∞∞∞∞∞∞∞

As the sun stretched its first gentle rays from the horizon, Adaeze opened her eyes and looked out from the alcove of rock they were sheltering under at the swaying grass of the meadow. A large bird glided overhead, squawking its salutations to the new dawn, the ever-constant waves crashing into the shore behind her. She rose to her feet, brushing the dirt from her dress and looked down at Nergüi, snoring softly, completely dead to the world.

With her cloak pulled tight around her, she wandered pensively along the stone guarded border of the island, passing a sheltered pebble beach and coming to an oddly flat patch of earth dotted with a smattering of bluebells. Bobbing down, she plucked a stem and twirled it between her fingers as she paced the area, staring mindlessly out to sea, the clouds above glowing a gentle shade of pink.

Without knowing why, she stopped, brushing the topsoil away in front of her with her boot, unwittingly uncovering a circle of small flat pebbles underneath. As she stared at them, contemplating their meaning, she heard a noise behind her and turned to find Nergüi standing there.

"What are you looking at?"

"I'm not sure," she shrugged, crouching and tracing the circle with her finger. "I was just drawn to it. Do you think we could have put it here? In another life, I mean."

"It's possible," he said, squatting beside her to inspect the stones. "If only our memories were clearer."

Adaeze gave him a small smile. "Let us just concentrate on the present then. There will be time for understanding when the battle is done."

He took her hand in his, leaning in and kissing her gently until a rumbling noise from his stomach interrupted the tender moment. "Sorry, my stomach practises its war cry when ignored for too long," he joked.

Adaeze just shook her head. "What will we do for food? There doesn't seem to be anything edible growing here, and I know nothing of fishing. There is not even any fresh water."

"Good question," he said, clicking his tongue and scratching at his goatee as he assessed the situation.

"You have stayed here before. What did you eat and drink then?"

"I had supplies with me. I was somewhat less prepared for today's journey," he replied sarcastically. "The few things I have are still hidden under a barrel in a laneway in London."

"Well, that is not overly helpful now, is it?

"Forgive me, princess," he said with an exaggerated bow. "I suppose I could always fly back to the mainland. I have a few coins left to use if I can find anyone to sell to me. If that fails, I can steal us what we need." He looked around the island with a frown. "I wish I could remember how we survived here in the past."

"You have travelled across the world. How is it you have survived with so little knowledge?" she jibed.

"I was a fighter, not a farmer. We pillaged as we went, taking food and supplies from those in our way. Our survival came from the use of force, not knowledge."

"What about before that? When you were young?" she asked.

"In Mongolia? It's mainly desert and grassland there. Food is scarce. Most of us move around a lot, finding what we can, where we can. We raise animals for milk and meat, and trade for everything else," he replied, remembering the challenges of his youth. "It's a terrible place. It's no wonder Genghis Khan raised an army and left in search of other lands."

Suddenly, a large wave crashed into the nearby rocks to their right, catapulting water high into the air, the droplets catching on the breeze and showering over them.

Nergüi laughed as the spray hit his face. "Okay, okay, I take the hint. Enough talk, more action," he called up into the sky as if addressing nature itself.

Adaeze laughed, wiping the droplets from his face with her sleeve. "Do not take too long. It looks like it might rain soon."

"I won't," he said with a wink, the hair on her neck prickling as he took off into the sky, banking and skimming low across the water.

∞◦◦◦∞

The evening's drizzle had cleared by the next morning, the soft sunrise turning the meadow into a glistening sea of swaying dewy grass. Adaeze woke slowly and reluctantly, stretching out on her damp cloak, her muscles tired and aching from her cold, stony resting place, the fire at her feet long since burnt out. Nergüi was still asleep beside her, but at least, for once, he wasn't snoring.

A familiar voice reached her ears from just outside the alcove. "And here I thought I was going to have to wait until the sun was at its zenith before you stirred!"

Adaeze jerked around, adrenaline flooding her system as she saw Anasazi perched casually on a small boulder.

"Good morning, Adaeze," he said politely.

"What are you doing here?" she snapped, scrambling to her feet.

325

He threw her a contemptuous look. "Why do you think I am here? Certainly not for the scenery."

Nergüi snorted, scratching his arm before falling back to sleep.

Abbott just shook his head, looking down at him. "How far you have fallen, Little Phoenix. You truly are pathetic."

Adaeze glanced at Nergüi, about to kick him awake, when he slowly opened his eyes and winked at her.

She quickly turned her attention back to their unwanted visitor. "You killed Edward!"

"I did. The naive, lovesick fool, risking his life to bring you here simply because you asked him to. And you, too self-concerned to even recognise his feelings."

Adaeze looked down, ashamed, the look of pain in Edward's eyes in his final moments replaying in her mind for the thousandth time.

"I did him a favour, to be honest. He never stood a chance against your 'eternal' love, did he?" Anasazi mocked. "Don't you realise it yet? Your love makes you weak. You waste your lives, your energy, on an endless quest to find one another, hoping each time you won't find them too young, too old, too far away. Instead of holding onto your knowledge and power, you fritter your memories away on emotion: weak, fickle emotion."

"You're wrong!" she said, feeling her power swelling in her chest. "Our love makes us strong. *You* are the one who is weak. Loveless, heartless, soulless you."

"You truly are delusional, aren't you?" Anasazi snickered to himself as he stood up, fiddling with the gold buttons at his cuffs before rubbing his hands together. "What do you think, shall we finish this?"

When the response came, it didn't come from Adaeze.

"Let's!" Nergüi said, rolling over and unleashing a torrent of energy.

The blast pummelled into Anasazi, sending him flying backwards, whipping through the tall grass as droplets sprayed around him, then thumping into the mud. As Nergüi tried to press the attack, though, Anasazi got to one knee and brought up his hand, energy lancing through the air, hitting his opponent and sending him twisting to the ground.

Anasazi hoisted himself to his feet with a grimace, his stance unsteady as he brought his hand to his forehead and wiped the beading sweat from his brow, eight blades emerging from his back.

"I'll make you both suffer for that," he hissed.

Nergüi gritted his teeth, righting himself. "Don't you see? We're not afraid of you."

"You never have been," Anasazi replied, a subtle smirk creeping onto his face. "That's always been your mistake."

Dark energy lanced across the ground, but Nergüi dove out of the way just in time, the air crackling. Anasazi strode forward, his blades flashing in the sun, and as Nergüi glanced across to make sure Adaeze was all right, he found her launching herself at full pelt towards their foe, her body shimmering with energy, purple tendrils flowing from her back.

She was almost upon him when Anasazi hit her with a sharp blast to the shoulder, but she managed to roll as she hit the ground, using the momentum to spring back up with ease. Wasting no time, she charged to meet him, grabbing his forearms and releasing a potent attack that slammed into his stomach. The force allowed her to twist and toss him over her head, his blades disappearing as his concentration broke.

Anasazi was barely on his feet when Nergüi hit him with a burst of energy, knocking him back down, Adaeze doing the same and sending him skittering away through the grass. The pair approached his prone body from either side when, out of nowhere, Anasazi laughed.

"Do you want to know why I always defeat you?" he asked, hefting himself to his knees.

Neither of them replied as they neared.

He turned to Adaeze, smiling at her viciously. "Because I've spent my entire existence devoted to one thing and one thing only. Power!"

Leaning back, Anasazi arched his spine, energy erupting from him and entrapping them in a domed cage of lightning, pain coursing through their bodies. Anasazi rose slowly, wisps of darkness dancing around him like smoke as his blades emerged from his back once more.

"Do you understand now?" he called out. "The pain you endure life after life? You can end it all. You can be free. You can find peace. All you have to do is let your souls disperse. Embrace oblivion."

Adaeze glared at him defiantly. "We will never give up on life. A thousand deaths would not stop us."

"Then you are doomed to an eternity of misery and pain. Tell me, is your love really worth that?"

Before she had a chance to reply, Nergüi leapt forward, giving his answer in the form of a punch to the face. Anasazi reeled, then flew backwards as Nergüi hit him with a bolt of energy.

Gathering her power inside her for a moment, Adaeze crouched before vaulting into the air. She came down on Abbott from above as he struggled to regain his footing, his feeble shield barely strong enough to deflect the attack, the impact sending him crashing back into the mud.

They watched as he wrestled himself onto one knee, shaking his head and blinking quickly as he tried to refocus, and Adaeze looked across to see Nergüi building up his power. The air rippled around him as his wings flared, misty black energy engulfing him in a swirling gale.

He waited until Anasazi began to stand, one hand still on his knee for balance, before he attacked. Darting forward, Nergüi charged at his enemy, but as he closed in, Anasazi threw his arm out and grabbed him by the throat.

Nergüi pawed desperately at the vice-like hand choking him, trying to free himself as his energy surged out of control, but Anasazi lofted him off the ground, revelling in his advantage.

Adaeze tried to advance, but she could not pierce the vortex of energy. Trapped on the outer, she could only watch on helplessly as Anasazi drew Nergüi close to his face.

"Farewell, Little Phoenix," he said with a contemptuous smile. "If you're smart, you won't come back."

There was a thunderous detonation, the ground rumbling as Nergüi careened through the air like a sack of turnips before crashing to the ground on the other side of the island in a heap, his clothes smouldering, his body limp.

Adaeze looked at his crumpled form with pounding heart, turning back to Anasazi just as he attacked, a barrage of energy cannoning into her, driving her backwards, her feet struggling to find grip in the mud. She was barely standing her ground when the next attack swept across her torso, connecting with her chin and snapping her head back.

Collapsing flat onto her back, she lay there barely conscious, her neck aching. Unable to move, she stared up through the grass surrounding her, harmless puffs of cloud drifting leisurely across the sky as though they could not see the devastation below.

The figure of Anasazi appeared above her, his mud-stained clothes smoking, his expression menacing as it spun in her vision. "Do you see what you've done? You have brought this fate upon yourself. I must kill you slowly now. Only through a long, agonising death can I make you accept the truth. This power is mine and mine alone. I am Anasazi. I am unconquerable."

His blades arched back behind him as he prepared to attack, but then, out of the blue, he coughed: a deep, bracing cough that racked his entire body. He faltered backwards, away from Adaeze, who watched as he raised a hand to his mouth, another cough exploding from his lungs. Anasazi lowered his hand, and she saw blood-tainted spittle seep through his fingers.

His eyes widened as he looked at his palm in disbelief. "No! NO! NOOOOOOOOOOOO!"

Adaeze felt the hair on her neck prickle as the pressure increased, and Anasazi leapt into the air, landing atop the boulders along the western edge of the island. A moment later, he was airborne again, shooting towards the mainland and disappearing out of sight.

With a groan, she heaved herself onto her knees and stood up. As she looked across the island, her heart raced at the sight of Nergüi propped up on his elbows, and she stuttered unsteadily over to him.

"What happened?" he asked, his voice straining as she helped him regain his feet.

"He started to cough up blood, then ... he ran away."

"The pestilence," Nergüi said, staring ahead grimly. "He's dying."

"Dying?"

Nergüi stretched out his neck and rolled his shoulders back and forth. "He's still only human. As frail as the rest of us."

"So, it is over?" Adaeze asked, her question tinged with hope.

"For now."

∞∞∞∞∞∞∞

For all his assurances, Nergüi couldn't erase the image of Anasazi from his thoughts, unease haunting him in waking and sleep. They camped on the island for two days, washing themselves and their clothes in the bracing cold of the ocean and tending to their wounds by the fire.

With aching neck and bruised fingers, Adaeze had tried to comb out and rebraid her hair, hands shaking, jaw clenched. Watching her suffer had pained him greatly, and with much insistence, he had convinced her to show him how to do it. It had been cathartic for them both, his nimble fingers taking to braiding with ease, the time spent in that simple act of service only bringing them closer.

Nergüi was already awake when the sun rose on the third day, his mind still troubled. Gazing down at Adaeze as she slept, a deep sense of protectiveness swelled in his chest. He knew he'd never gain any peace until he knew for sure.

"You want to go and find his body, don't you?" she asked, opening one eye and looking up at him.

"I need to know. I need to be sure it's finished. For this life, at least."

Adaeze sat up. "I thought you said it was over already."

"It is. I just ..."

"Let's go then."

"No, it's quicker if I go by myself."

Before she could object, he took the obsidian butterfly from around his neck and placed it around hers.

"Look after this for me, my beautiful butterfly," he said, taking her hand and kissing it gently. "I'll be back for it soon. I promise."

Stepping out into the open, he took off. He knew she would be upset, but there was nothing for it. It was something he needed to do for himself. Carrying her would have slowed him down, and if, by some cruel twist of fate, Anasazi was still alive, he didn't want to risk her life in another battle.

It proved easier than expected to find traces of his foe on the mainland. A long scar marked his landing place on the coastal clifftops, the earth scorched like it had been sliced with a hot knife. He followed its direction inland, flying over a small copse, the trees cracked and bent as if a massive explosion had ripped through the area, the epicentre marked by a deep crater, a splatter of blood staining the freshly turned soil.

The signs after that grew less damaging and harder to spot, but he eventually tracked them south until he came to the gate of a large two-storey manor on the eastern edge of London.

It was dusk when Nergüi landed quietly on the doorstep, his wings disappearing into the wind. Hearing nothing beyond, he pushed on the door, and it swung open. He poked his head inside, the smell in the air ripe, the hearth cold, the amber glow of the setting sun creeping in the windows the only light.

Stealing into the large hall, breathing through his mouth to mitigate the smell, he almost tripped over what he soon discovered to be the body of a well-dressed man with a scar running along his right cheek, his chest slashed with four deep incisions. Remaining vigilant for movements or sounds, he tiptoed around the space, exploring the adjoining pantry, buttery, and servants' quarters, finding three more unfortunate souls, all slain in the same manner as the first.

Moving back through the hall, he snuck into the private rooms of the manor's owner, finding the study and the sitting room on the bottom floor deserted. With only one area left, he crept up the stairs to the room above. As the door creaked open, Nergüi found what he had been searching for.

Anasazi lay lifeless on the bed, the fine white linen beneath him stained with a smattering of dry blood. Nergüi neared the body cautiously, examining it in the dim light and recoiling at the sight. His enemy's once piercing green eyes sat clouded but just as cold as ever, and his mouth hung open, its cavity coated in crimson as to match his cotehardie. At his throat, his hands sat poised as though he'd been clawing for air in his final moments.

With a sigh of relief, Nergüi stepped back. The threat was finally over.

∞∞∞∞∞∞∞

In the months that followed, the island served as a safe haven for Nergüi and Adaeze. The pestilence continued to rage across England until it eventually burnt itself out and subsided, but they were safe from it all on their little spit of land, their needs somewhat questionably filled

331

by Nergüi's sleight hands. With the pull on their souls satisfied and the threat of their enemy removed, a serene feeling of contentment filled the space, and they were left to decide how they would use the remaining time they had been gifted. Their lives were being lived on different pages, though, and thus the debate continued often and at length.

"This place is special to us, yes, but I do not wish to stay here forever," Adaeze argued unequivocally as they sat wrapped in their cloaks on the small, pebbled beach, watching the sunset. "I want to explore the world with you. I want to show you where I grew up. I want to see the lands you hail from. I want to find the other places from our memories."

"I know, my love," he replied, taking her hand in his, "but I've been travelling all my life. I'm sick of the dust, the weariness, the danger."

"Would travelling with me be so bad?" she asked with an impish smile. "You wouldn't even notice the dust or the weariness, and there is no danger, not anymore."

"Travelling is arduous and time-consuming. I'm not as sprightly as I once was, and I'd much prefer to spend what time I have left concentrating on one thing and one thing only. You."

Adaeze sat in silence as she pondered his words. Although he would never tell her his age, she knew enough to guess he was easily twenty years her senior, and he was not always in the best of health. In the end, the fear of pushing him too hard and losing him too soon won out, and she conceded, much to his ecstatic joy.

In the spring, when the snow thawed and the bluebells sprang up once again, they began to build themselves a proper home. They dismantled their makeshift abode in the alcove, and, with diligent application of their powers, they blasted rock from the boulders bordering the shore and built themselves a house. At the expense of a windswept tree, they constructed a slapdash roof to top it, making thatching from the meadow's long grass. It wasn't the prettiest or even the most watertight, but that single room, with its simple bed and its small but ever-burning fire, became the most beloved of homes.

They traded Adaeze's gold hair clasps for a small boat to help keep their powers a secret, and they set up rain catchers to supply them with water. Beside the house, they planted a hazel tree to offer shade and sustenance, and on the other side, around the circle of stones, they tended a small garden of vegetables, berries, and barley.

For ten years, they called that island home, filling it with love and laughter, in the good times and the hard, in sickness and health, until one day, Adaeze woke to find Nergüi had passed once more into the aether. His long ailing heart had finally lost its battle to keep beating.

She lay beside his body the entire day, the rain falling outside as though to join her in her sorrow, and she cried until there were no more tears. When the sun dawned again, and the sky cleared itself of clouds, she took the driftwood they had gathered for the winter and built a pyre. Just as he had asked, she placed him upon it, sitting silently as she watched the flames burn away the remnants of her now soulless soulmate.

When the fire died, she collected the fragments of bone and buried them beneath the circle of stones, replacing the ring and sprinkling the ashes at its centre. She found a tall, flat jut of rock amongst the boulders and fashioned it into a headstone, using her power to etch the likeness of his wings into it: a monument to their love that she hoped would stand the test of time.

Finally, she took the obsidian butterfly from around her neck and kissed it. Part of her wanted to keep it, but deep down, she knew it belonged on the island, as a beacon.

"Until we meet again, my phoenix," she whispered, burying it at the foot of the stone.

With nothing left to bind her, she gathered her things and closed the door of their house behind her one last time. With a heavy heart, she rowed their boat to the mainland, pulling it up onto the sand and pausing for a moment to look back over the waves, her heart bidding its final farewell. For Nergüi, life's adventure was over, but as Adaeze turned from the shore, she knew hers was just beginning.

Theo

It looked like either a prison or an industrial factory; she wasn't sure which. The walls were built of old, weathered concrete, the doors of thick iron with barred windows. Hulking, rusted machines sat arrayed all around her, but she knew not of their purpose. It was cold and dark, and aside from the unsettling creak of the slumbering contraptions, it was deathly silent.

Fear rippled through her, and she shuddered as she moved through the space, uncertain of what to do or where to go. Very little light illuminated the way, and what little there was seemed to come from some unknown source. Long shadows stretched across the floor, swallowing up corners. Finally, she reached a door at the far end and stopped. It seemed to be locked, but on closer examination, it was only jarred shut. Peering inside, she saw nothing but an empty room.

She pressed her shoulder into the door, and it popped open, creaking loudly as it swung inwards on its ageing hinges. Rust covered everything, as if the entire room was rotting away, the floor covered in pits and scratches. As her eyes adjusted to the dim, unnatural light, she realised something else was with her in the room. Her heart pounded as she looked left and right, yet she saw no movement amongst the formless shadows.

Suddenly, she heard a noise and glanced up. In the far right corner of the ceiling, it sat watching her: a being of darkness and death. Their eyes met, and it shifted, falling to the ground. She stumbled backwards, her breathing fast and heavy as it coalesced into a humanoid figure, eight legs sprouting from its back like those of a spider. It stood motionless as she ran for the exit, almost as if it was savouring the chase to come.

Gripped by terror, she bolted out the door, slamming it shut behind her, the echo reverberating all around as she ran for her life, weaving between the haunting machines on either side. As she reached the far end of the room, she dared to glance back and found the shadowy figure staring at her through the barred window with gleaming black eyes.

All at once, there was a crashing sound, and the door buckled in the middle, its hinges snapping. She screamed, turning the corner into a long corridor as it slammed onto the floor, shooting across until it came to rest in the position she had just vacated, spinning lazily.

Heaving for breath, she kept running, but she couldn't hear any footsteps in pursuit as she raced around another corner, venturing further into the gloomy labyrinth. She approached a crossroads, hesitating slightly while she decided which direction to head, when, out of nowhere, she felt spiders' legs whipping past like blades of steel, and the darkness appeared in front of her.

A shriek of surprise escaped her lips, the piercing note ringing down the corridor as she spun left, racing past a series of open doors that led to nothing but barren emptiness. Her pace quickened as she sprinted onwards, not bothering to look back. She knew he was at her heels. He would never stop, not until she was dead.

∞∞∞∞∞∞∞∞∞∞∞∞∞∞∞

Theo jolted awake, her lungs burning as she gasped for breath. She contorted into the foetal position, closing her eyes tightly in an attempt to banish the horrors from her mind. Everything seemed to spin around her, and when she finally dared to open her eyes again, her bedroom appeared spliced together with a long, dark corridor. Taking long, deep breaths, she blinked a few times until the ghosts of her nightmare faded, and she was released into the safety of the waking world once more.

She rolled onto her back, staring wide-eyed at the ceiling, the cold sweat lingering on her skin sending a shiver up her spine as images of the dark, spiderlike being remained at the forefront of her thoughts. It wasn't the first time she'd dreamt of him; in fact, he'd been a recurring figure for as long as she could remember, although she didn't know where his imagery had sprouted from. She'd never been afraid of spiders, nor had she ever seen his likeness anywhere outside her nightmares: not in movies, or books, or art, not even in the endless abyss of the internet.

She turned the creature over in her mind: his shadowy human form, his eight bladelike legs stretching out behind him, his soul-piercing eyes. The Spider, as she called him, mystified her, much like the Phoenix did, and just like with the Phoenix, she detested the inexplicability of his presence in her life.

As her alarm sounded the beginning of another monotonous day, the Spider seemed to follow her. The unease he brought crept beneath her skin and settled there, his nimble legs wrapping her anxiety in a web and feeding on it.

Arriving at work with a churning stomach, Theo did her obligatory lap of the kitchen for morning greetings before settling quietly at her bench. The previous day had been busier than expected, and although good for business, it left her with an almost impossibly long list of jobs. With another fully booked Saturday night service looming, and two functions on top of that, her mental load was near breaking point as she prioritised her prep list and got to work.

It was half an hour later when Peter turned up beside her, freshly printed sheets of paper in hand. A head chef wielding paper almost exclusively meant extra work, and with her prep list such as it was, it would be pushing the realm of physical possibility to add more.

Whisking a large batch of lemon curd over a double boiler, Theo groaned internally at Peter's arrival.

"How are you going, Theo?"

"Good, Chef," she replied with a somewhat forced smile.

She wasn't good, of course. She was depressed, anxious, and exhausted, but she couldn't say that. The options for acceptable replies were 'good' or 'fine'. Anything even vaguely more negative put her at risk of being pulled aside for a lecture on leaving personal issues at the door. That being said, Peter held himself to a completely different standard on that front. He often took out his frustrations on the staff when he was struggling emotionally, then became angry at them for having the audacity to be upset by his actions. The man really could be the poster child for hypocrisy at times.

"So, we've picked up a last-minute sixteen pax VIP function, and they want a cake for lunch tomorrow. Just one off our list, chef's choice, no dietaries. You'll be fine with that, yeah?" he asked, despite there being no acceptable answer other than yes.

337

Theo wanted to beat her head against the wall and/or cry, mentally scrambling to figure out where in her day she was going to fit it in such a labour-intensive request. She wanted to bitch and moan about the extra work, to try and explain to Peter she already had an ungodly amount to do that day, but there was no point. She was in the weeds, yes, but then again, weren't they all?

"That's fine. I'll get right on it," she replied, removing the bowl of tempered curd off the boiler and whisking in chilled butter, cube by cube.

"Thanks, Theo," he said with a small smile, handing her a copy of the function sheet before hurrying off to deliver the extra workload to the other sections.

Theo let out a long sigh as she slipped the sheet into the docket rail beside her prep list. If nothing else, at least she was free to choose the least complicated cake. Still, the biggest issue wasn't cake type but rather cook time. With all three of the conventional ovens being less than reliable, the singular combi oven was arguably the kitchen's most in-demand piece of equipment, its use requiring a delicate and well-orchestrated schedule of tag-teaming between the sections. Given the amount of baking Theo already had lined up, trying to pry an extra hour or two away from the others threatened to throw a spanner in the well-oiled machine.

She would just have to make it work, though; there was no Plan B. After all, she was the only pastry chef at Porphura at the moment. There used to be two of them, a junior keeping the boat afloat on the quiet days, but finding a replacement after the last one quit two months ago was proving difficult. Those they'd trialled turned out to be little more than a parade of people with pieces of paper but no actual skills or knowledge. As a result, chefs from the other sections filled in when Theo was off, but their knowledge only extended to plating whatever came on order.

All the prep work was her responsibility and something she had to squeeze in around service. Essentially, she was left trying to fit seven days' worth of work into four, but Peter wouldn't pay her to work extra days to keep up, and given that she already worked more hours than her salary covered, she was unwilling to come in on her days off and work for free. With her workload only growing the closer they got to

338

year's end, she was unsure how long she could keep up with the demands, and she was burning out faster by the minute.

Deciding to get the cake out of the way first, if only to shake the weight of it from her mind, she took down her recipe folder and headed to the dry store in search of pistachio meal. As she pried the container from the stack on the shelves, she turned to find Craig, the front of house manager, standing in the doorway.

He had hazel eyes that screamed of forced conviviality and short, dark brown hair fastidiously styled into an unmoving quiff that appeared to take far too much time and product to achieve. Generally speaking, Theo didn't interact with him outside of service, but even she would admit he was more than adept at preventing the dining room from descending into utter chaos. Still, he had one nagging flaw; he was a bit of a dick.

"Theo, have you got a minute?" he asked, his mouth crafted into a smile far too serene for his surroundings.

She didn't; that was blatantly obvious to even the most untrained eye. In fact, at that point, she had negative minutes to offer him. His question was clearly rhetorical, though, and she knew well enough that letting him say his piece was the path of least resistance.

"Sure, what do you need?" she replied as she ducked past him and made a beeline back to her bench.

Craig scurried after her. "I just wanted to talk about your desserts."

"What's wrong with them? Have there been complaints?" Theo asked with a frown, taking out the scales and weighing the ingredients for a pistachio dacquoise.

A pang of anxiety lanced through her stomach, her heart pounding hard against her chest. Peter hadn't mentioned any problems, and the plates always seemed to come back clean. Why was she only hearing about this now? Peter was sure to go on a rampage if the news reached him at his current stress level.

Craig laughed nonchalantly, oblivious to the panic he'd induced. "No, there's nothing wrong with them. I've heard nothing but good things from customers. It's the presentation I want to talk to you about."

"What do you mean? They look fine, and Peter approved the plating on all of them."

"Yeah, I know, but I've been watching some videos online, and I think our desserts could do with a bit more pizzazz. You know, to help us gain more followers on social media."

Theo suppressed the sudden urge to grab the nearest utensil and strike him upside the head with it. "Is this something Peter wants?"

"I can't see why he wouldn't," he replied with almost enviable self-assurance. "I saw the most spectacular thing last week. It was a video where they built a chocolate lotus flower around a dessert that slowly unfurled when you poured hot sauce into the bowl at the table. Wouldn't that be exciting for customers to see?"

"I know the dessert you're talking about, but it wouldn't work here," she said, trying to rein in her growing frustration. "What you're describing would take too long to prep and is far too fiddly and temperamental for Porphura, especially given I'm the only pastry chef at the moment. It works for high-end, fine dining restaurants where you have a separate pastry kitchen and only feed thirty guests a night, but we seat two hundred plus functions."

"It seemed simple enough," he asserted, dismissing her with a wave of his hand.

"Everything looks easy online where it's all prepped, and you don't have to watch the hours of work that goes into it beforehand. Besides, this kitchen sits at forty-five degrees most of the time during service. That flower would unfurl before it even got to the pass."

"Yeah, well, you can't not do something just because it's not practical. You need to at least try it, okay?" he snapped, desperately trying to save face by pretending he was in a position to dictate her job to her.

Theo was about ready to rage quit, and she took a deep breath to steady her words. "Sure, Craig. I'll have a play around with it when I get some spare time."

His only response was to smile smugly before disappearing around the corner and out of the kitchen.

Of course, her final words meant very little. She had no spare time, and any that she could miraculously find would not be assigned to the whims of a man in no way involved with the inner workings of the kitchen. There were mountains to deal with, and she was not about to be bothered with the unnecessary molehills of others. If Craig wanted to take his non-sensical idea to Peter and argue his case, that was his own grave to dig, but she was having no part in it.

Shaking her head, she poured the egg whites into the mixer and flicked it on. The rage lingering in her stomach lured the Spider out from its temporary hiding place in her mind, and it brought with it a stormy mood she knew was destined to taint the remainder of her day.

She could not afford to allow her dark emotions to overwhelm her, though, and so, like so many times before, she immersed herself in her work, making sweet things from a place not of love but of spite.

∞∞∞∞

It was almost one in the morning when Theo finally turned the key in her apartment door. By some miracle, she had managed to snag three consecutive days off, although preparing her section for such a long absence had come at its own cost. Eating staff meal had been forgone in return for the few extra minutes it bought her, and she had bid farewell to her colleagues long before she'd packed up her own things.

As a result, she was drained to the point of feeling hollow by the time the latch clicked shut behind her. Dropping her backpack and leaning against the door, her pent-up emotions broke their banks and surged forth. With tears streaming down her face, she slid into a crumpled heap on the floor, her head resting in her hands.

After the wave eventually passed, Theo composed herself and began her usual end of week ritual. Grabbing a few ciders from the fridge and selecting a playlist of angsty songs from her youth to fill the silence, she peeled off her clothes and hopped into the bathtub, pulling her knees to her chest as the scaldingly hot water slowly rose around her. The mix of ice-cold cider and warm steam soothed her as she reclined with eyes closed, her skin reddening from the heat, the music harmonising with her churning emotions.

As she set the first empty bottle down beside the bath, her mind buzzing from the swift effects of alcohol on an empty stomach, she ran her finger over the thin scars that crisscrossed her upper thighs. The sudden urge to reopen them pulsed in her chest, but she resisted it. Instead, she settled on simply digging her nail along the well-worn letters nestled within the sea of other cuts: **IHMSYC**. Those six letters she had first carved into her skin over a decade earlier denoted the

341

pain-filled motto she'd clung to in her most helpless times. I hurt myself, so you can't.

To Theo, self-harm had always served as a release. When depression and anxiety threatened to consume her, when the call from the dark sounded like siren song, the physical pain of running a razor across her skin grounded her. The blood-tinted bathwater she'd so often soaked in stood as an undeniable reminder that she was still alive. Even in the times when it had veered into the realm of addiction, cutting had provided her with a sense of control in the face of unsurmountable powerlessness. In place of death, she found life in those thousand cuts.

When she had first shown her scars to Auryn in the cold light of day, she had done so with a deep sense of trepidation. They had already proved, more than once, a gale too strong to foster new flames, visible proof of a soul too fractured to elicit love, odds too high to gamble on. She had revealed them, heart pounding, to the internal screaming of her first love's final question: 'How can you love someone who wants to kill themself?'

As she'd braced for the recoil, she had instead been met with a response wholly unfamiliar. Instead of disgust, Auryn had responded with unbridled empathy, kissing them gently and reminding her of the beauty she held in spite of her flaws. He had told her if that was what she needed to do, he would be there to help clean up the mess and care for her in the aftermath. For the first time, she'd found someone who saw them as she did: as a symbol of strength, of resilience, of survival. With that one simple act of acceptance, Auryn had unknowingly cured the need for them to be there at all.

The track changed, and a heavier melody filled the room, an earnest male voice belting out heart-wrenching lyrics of pain and defeat. As it did, Theo's mind returned to the creaking, rusted machines of her nightmare and the cold, dead eyes of the Spider peering at her through the barred window. He was the reason she so often dreaded sleep. For every excitement filled adventure she was granted, there was another in which she was running for her life in dark places.

Placing a second empty bottle beside the first, she couldn't help but envy Auryn his zombies: their familiarity, their obvious source material. If she could just find the root of the Spider's existence, then maybe she could tear him from her mind. Maybe if she knew where he had sprouted from, she could drag him back there and find a way to destroy him.

With the bath beginning to cool, Theo drained a little, watching the water swirl before stopping the flow and replacing it with hot. Transitioning to a soundtrack less melancholic, she shooed the Spider away, closed her eyes, and sent her mind in search of more pleasant places.

Eventually, she found herself outside a large country manor, like the kind you see in Victorian period dramas, its front facade ivy-clad, its flower beds overflowing with a sea of purple pansies. She allowed herself to wander across the manicured lawns, jumping over a puddle and strolling through the hedged garden until the bath grew cold again. Flicking the tap on with her foot, she felt the hot water disperse around her and took a deep breath. She wasn't ready to get out just yet.

∞∞∞∞

It was fast approaching noon when Theo finally roused from her slumber, exhaustion and alcohol leaving her sleep dreamless and unbroken. She had little will to crawl out of bed at all, except Auryn was en route to her apartment, and she felt obligated to at least appear semi-functional when he arrived. Through a fair measure of strategic shift swapping, he too had managed to finagle himself a three-day weekend, and with her mood still on the weightier side, she was grateful he would be around to offer buoyant distraction.

She was just brushing the crumbs of an uninspired slice of Vegemite toast from her hands when the doorbell warbled down the hallway, and she stood with door open as she awaited his emergence from the lift. As soon as he was inside, she nestled herself into his embrace, breathing a sigh of relief, as though the burden she carried seemed lighter in his presence.

"You okay, beautiful?" he asked, kissing the top of her head.

Theo nodded as she felt her bound up nerves uncoil at the sound of his voice, disentangling herself and looking up at him with a smile. "It's just been a hard week. You know how it is."

"Well, the weekend is ours. What would you like to do?"

"I don't know," she shrugged, walking over to the couch and

collapsing onto it. "I feel a bit blah, to be honest."

"Is there anything that would make you feel better? Build a fort and gorge on junk food? Run away into the woods and become hermits?"

All at once, a random urge struck her. "I wish we could go camping and get away for a bit. I don't have any gear, though," she said with a sigh and tumbled over, resting her head in Auryn's lap and looking up at him.

"Lucky you," he said, a grin creeping onto his face. "I just so happen to have just what you're looking for collecting dust in a cupboard at mine. So, what do you say? Spontaneous camping trip?"

Theo arched an eyebrow. "What, right now?"

"Why not? We'll pick a spot, grab some food and booze on the way, and stay for a couple of nights. We could both do with an escape from reality. What do you think?"

When she'd mentioned it, she'd meant it more as a wistful projection with no real expectations of fruition. Routine was the cornerstone of her existence, the constant that kept her from imploding; no part of her functioned spontaneously.

Her anxiety mixed with spontaneity like oil and water, and not in an 'if you shake them together, they temporarily mix' kind of way, but rather a 'pouring a cup of water into a deep fryer' kind of way; they were volatile. Still, as the idea settled over her, it started to sound less like impulsiveness and more like freedom.

"You know what, let's do it!" she said, suddenly filled with excitement, her mind floundering for control by offering a familiar location for their ad-lib adventure. "How about we go to Beechworth? I've always liked it there."

"What are we waiting for?" he replied, prodding her off the couch.

∞∞∞∞

It felt like barely a moment later that they were leaving the tightly packed roads of the suburbs behind and merging onto the wide lanes of the Hume Highway, Auryn behind the wheel of Theo's sky blue 1995 Toyota Camry, lovingly dubbed Tits McGee.

Although the car was on its last legs, it trundled along defiantly, as it had been for years now. It had trouble starting sometimes, especially in cold weather, and it had a tendency to overheat in traffic if the

344

radiator wasn't constantly topped up. However, given that Theo hated driving and avoided it wherever possible, she saw no point in wasting money on repairs that would exceed the car's value.

The hastily gathered supplies in the boot clunked as they settled into more permanent positions, and the three-hour journey north-east began to the sounds of the very few bands they both enjoyed. Soothed by the motion, Theo sang softly to herself and watched the scenery fly past: golden brown paddocks dotted with livestock interspersed with patches of tall eucalyptus trees swaying in the breeze.

She smiled as she looked over at Auryn, his fingers tapping the beat onto the steering wheel. Something about his willingness to go camping spoke to a deeper commitment and solidified his assurances about travel in her heart.

He'd been saving like crazy over the past few months, swearing blind he would have everything paid off by her birthday, and each time he handed her another debtless credit card to cut up, they grew closer. His effort was conscientious and self-propelled, but above all, it was consistent. She had never had that in a partner before, and it was something she appreciated beyond measure.

When they finally arrived at the lakeside campground, the shadows were growing long, the off-season providing them with a neighbourless site, much to their joy. The only other visitors appeared to be a few stray caravanning enthusiasts across the water, the playground by reception sitting devoid of raucous children. The afternoon sun warmed the late winter air as they pitched the tent and lay down for a moment to drink in the serenity of birdsong in place of car horns.

Stirring at the sound of their own stomachs, they emerged into the quick-settling dusk, retrieving the esky and a bag from the boot and meandering over to the communal barbeques. As the well-worn hotplate heated up, Theo dug out a packet of burger patties from the ice and glanced over at Auryn, who was, at that point, struggling to cut open the buns with the abysmally blunt knife they'd thrown in.

"You sure this is a good idea?" he asked with a playful look of scepticism. "Shouldn't we have just bought beef like normal people?"

"Of course it's a good idea," she replied with a forthright nod, taking their rather obscure meat choice and placing it on the barbecue. "Come at me, camel!"

Walking back over to the esky, she rummaged for the packet of bacon, turning around to find Auryn, spatula in hand, preparing to turn the burgers.

"No!" she snapped, doing what any self-respecting chef would do and batting his hand away like he was a toddler reaching for a naked flame.

"What? I was just turning them."

She shuffled him aside, laying the strips of bacon on the hotplate. "Once. You turn a burger once. They'll dry out if you keep playing with them."

"Are you sure?" he asked with uncertainty. "I thought it made them cook evenly. People always seem to flip them at barbecues."

Theo sighed and pointed at herself, motioning up and down her body. "Chef," she said before performing the same gesture at Auryn. "Not a chef. I don't tell you how to make margaritas, do I? Just trust me on this one. Inexperienced men manning backyard barbecues are not a solid point of reference."

"Fair enough," he chuckled, handing her the spatula and backing away. "I should probably stick to what I'm good at. Drink?"

Theo couldn't help but smile as she nodded, flipping the patties, just the once, as he tottered off to the car.

She had just finished constructing the burgers when Auryn reappeared bearing two large plastic cups. In them swirled a concoction that managed to remind her of both childhood and adulthood in equal parts: cream soda and vodka.

"Voila! Dinner is served," she said, gesturing towards a lakeside tree with her head. "Let's eat over there."

Auryn looked at her as they settled onto the grass. "Here we go then, I guess," he said, taking a bite out of his burger and chewing slowly as he considered the flavour. "Well, who knew? Camel's pretty fucking good."

"Shh. Eating," she mumbled around her mouthful, both of them grinning as talk ceased.

When the food was eaten, the drinks refilled, and the mess cleared away, they took a blanket from the car and returned to the tree, snuggling together as the cool evening swept in and painted the sky a haze of orange and red.

346

"It's a beautiful sunset," Auryn said softly as he lay back in the grass, pulling her into the crook of his shoulder.

"Yep."

"This is why I love you. You're such a sterling conversationalist."

Theo responded with a raised eyebrow.

"See," he said with a laugh. "I can't get that wit anywhere else, can I?"

"Hey, I can say more with one eyebrow than most people can with a heavily rehearsed ten-page monologue," Theo retorted indignantly, poking out her tongue.

"I can believe that," he chortled before pointing up at one of the puffs of cloud gliding overhead. "See that? It looks like a duck."

"No way. That's clearly a T-Rex. See its stubby little arms?"

"Nah uh, it's totally a duck," he replied with fervour. "What about that one beside it?"

She followed his finger and saw a bulbous cloud topped with two triangular peaks. "Wolf's head."

Auryn looked across at her in exasperation. "What are you talking about? It's *obviously* a pig! See, that pointy thing is its tail!"

"Are you on crack? That's the wolf's ear," she laughed.

"I don't know. Looks like a pig to me."

"I think you just have bacon on the brain," she said, jabbing him in the side playfully.

"You might be right," he snorted. "What about that one then?"

The cloud was shaped like a body flanked by what appeared to her to be two wings. Only one answer came to her mind.

"It looks like ..."

Auryn looked over at her. "Like what?"

"Nothing," she replied, shaking her head.

"No, go on. What were you going to say?"

"It looks like the Phoenix from my dreams."

"So that's what the creeper looks like," he jibed, shaking his fist at the cloud. "You leave my girlfriend alone."

"They're not a creeper. More a protector if anything," she said defensively.

"Are they in your nightmares too?"

"No, there's a different one in those."

"A different one? You sure do have quite the cast in your head, Theo Shaw," he said, wrapping his arm tight around her and hugging her close. "So, what does this other one look like?"

"It's hard to explain. I just call it the Spider. It's kind of like a human, same as the Phoenix, but with these eight long blades sprouting from its back like spiders' legs and these dark, soulless eyes. It lives in the shadows, and no matter where I am, it's always chasing me."

"Wow. And I thought my nightmares were bad. Maybe I should ditch my idea for a zombie novel and start writing about this Spider guy!"

Theo could tell he had meant it as a joke, but even the thought of the creature sent shivers down her spine, and she stared into the middle distance as flashes of it appeared in her mind.

"Sorry," he said, taking her hand in his, its warmth drawing her attention. "I didn't mean to make light of it."

She looked up and flashed him a fleeting grin. "That's okay. I just don't like dwelling on it. The Spider unsettles me."

"I think it would unsettle anyone." There was a silence between them before Auryn shuffled out from under her and stood up, holding out his hand and drawing her into his arms. "How about we move this drinking session to the tent?"

Theo nodded, the chill starting to seep through her clothes and into her bones, her mind in desperate need of warmer surroundings and warmer topics.

They spent hours talking in their tiny makeshift sanctuary, the night slipping away around them until they fell asleep in each other's arms.

∞∞∞∞∞∞∞∞∞∞∞∞∞∞

As soon as the sunlight hit her face, her eyes shot open. She'd always been a light sleeper, but at that moment in time, with danger all around her, she was jumpier than usual. Rising to her feet, she refastened the cloak she'd been using as a blanket around her neck, stretching out her stiff muscles as she scanned her surroundings for signs of movement. Seeing none, she took a quick swig from her waterskin before sluicing her face with the dregs and patting it dry.

She had spent the night away from the main road, concealed from prying eyes behind a bank of trees and shrubs, her weapons stashed

348

amongst the tight foliage of the boxwood to keep them safe from any would-be thieves. Extracting them from their various hiding places, she affixed them to herself with leather straps. With everything secure and tucked out of sight beneath her cloak, she pulled up her hood to obscure her face and set off.

The main road, though well-trodden, was nothing more than compacted dirt weaving through the fields and forests. Occasionally, she would pass other travellers, but no one attempted to speak to her. Even the group of soldiers passing on patrol ignored her, assuming she was a simple beggar. Her stomach rumbled, but she had no food to satiate her hunger as she walked onward with undampened purpose, eager to complete her trek. She'd gone days without food before; another wouldn't kill her. Besides, there would be plenty to eat when she reached her journey's end.

Finally, she crested a hill and stopped, staring down over the landscape before her. A city bisected by a winding river sprawled outwards, its streets bustling with life and activity. To the east, a crumbling colosseum rose amongst the ruins of the ancient power that once ruled there. With a deep breath and a satisfied smile, she marched on, her hand lightly brushing the blade at her hip. She had a job to do.

Auryn

Auryn was sick of waking up feeling the same: tired, listless, despondent. Just once, he'd like to wake up refreshed and energised, but today was clearly not going to be that day. He rolled over with a groan, wishing he was at Theo's, her morning disdain for the world resonating with his own. Another long shift the night before had left his muscles weary and aching, the person outside mowing their lawn oblivious to the disturbance they were causing to the night shift workers of the world.

With no hope of sleep returning for an encore, he swung himself out of bed and shuffled to the bathroom, splashing water on his face and gripping the side of the basin as it dripped off. His depression was weighing heavily on him at the moment, corrupting his mood and turning his sadness into slow-burning anger. Desperate for distraction, he sat down at his computer, opened his web browser, and, although likely ill-advised, scrolled through the morning news.

As usual, it made for demoralising reading. Each article seemed more reactionary and inflammatory than the next, those penning them seeking to elicit disgust, fear, or hatred with each poke of the bear. There was no call to change in the words, no desire to improve the world or rectify gross injustices. Within the paragraphs on his screen sat only a call to chaos, the venting of spleen of uninspired and uninspiring writers in search of clicks, and it served only to stoke the flames of his discontent.

Feeling his anger reaching boiling point, Auryn turned off the screen and leant back in his chair with a sigh. The selfishness of the world was slowly but surely eating away at his soul. Watching the vacuous masses seek naught but their own personal gain, even if it meant stepping on others to do so, was infuriating. Worse than them, though, were the politicians charged with their leadership. These corrupt cronies chose the economy over empathy at every opportunity, dangled carrots of short-term comfort at the expense of long-term security, and wilfully looked no further than their own temporary time in office. They peddled smoke and mirrors just well enough to stay in power while they lined their pockets, distracting the public with minor favours in the hope they remain blind to the deceit and not seek to oust them from their throne.

Power corrupts; absolute power corrupts absolutely, he thought to himself as he ran his fingers through his hair and tried to quell his rage.

It was a maxim he believed in fiercely. To his mind, the most effective way to find a benevolent and just leader would be to simply ask everyone to raise their hand if they held a desire to lead in the first place. Those people should subsequently be banned from running for the position, and a candidate chosen from the remaining group. Although less willing to lead, Auryn was convinced these reluctant recruits would be far better suited to the job. After all, if history had proven anything, it was that the people who rule over humanity were, more often than not, the exact people who shouldn't be allowed to.

With his agitation only growing from his current train of thought, he slipped on his headphones and sought to lose himself in a more concordant world until reality demanded his attention once again.

∞∞∞∞

By the time Auryn began his shift that afternoon, his mood was no less turbulent. He was there at the bar, but at the same time, he wasn't there at all, moving more mechanically than consciously. Orders were taken and drinks delivered, yet it seemed to him that all the pleases and thank yous of the world had fallen by the wayside. The actions of the customers he served were nothing more than a personification of the self-entitlement portrayed in the news, and it seemed to only be worsening as the years passed. His ability to endure it was reaching new lows with each shift, forced smiles and polite nods becoming harder to muster, as if his body was developing an intolerance to intolerance.

Benzin was fast filling up as eleven o'clock rolled around on another intense Saturday night, and the bar was starting to get slammed. Auryn, Janet, and Olivia were all slinging drinks at breakneck speed while Tony worked the floor, hoping desperately it would quieten down

352

enough for him to knock off. Naturally, it was at that point in the night, when the tension and pressure was at its peak, that trouble reared its ugly head.

A middle-aged man in an expensive suit with slicked-back hair and an air of superiority stood at the bar waving a fifty-dollar note in the air like he was hollering for a lap dance at a strip club. Of course, that was quite possibly the worst way to get a staff member's attention aside from whistling or clicking, and seeing the brazen display, Auryn's blood boiled.

At the best of times, it was difficult to tolerate being summoned like an indentured servant, but with his patience evaporating, Auryn chose the diplomatic approach. He simply ignored him, purposefully skipping over him and moving on to the next customer. Usually, that small act of defiance was enough to get the point across to even the most clueless of patrons. This particular man, however, appeared to be especially feeble-minded and instead began waving the money more fervently than before, seamlessly progressing from strip club attendee to flagman at a racetrack finish line.

After a solid ten minutes, Auryn addressed him. "Hey mate, I'm not going to serve you until you stop waving that money around."

"I didn't come here for attitude, *mate*. Now get me a drink, or I'll have you fired," the man sneered, flicking the note across the bar where it landed in a small puddle of water beside the ice well.

Auryn stared at him for a long moment, his skin prickling as his rage resurfaced. He looked down at the fifty-dollar note and slowly picked it up, wiping it dry on his jeans and holding it out in front of the man.

"Here's your money back. Go and get your drink somewhere else," he responded calmly.

The man glared at him. "What are you talking about? Get me a drink. Now!"

"Not going to happen."

"Get your manager! I want to speak to him!"

Auryn leant forward, his face hard. "I *am* the manager, and I have the right to refuse service. Now please leave the venue."

He wanted to add a giant 'Fuck off!' as well but managed to restrain himself, holding out the note once more to the dumbfounded man who glowered at him, snatching it out of his hand and storming off.

Tony appeared beside him with a stack of glasses running up his arm. "What's going on? You all right?"

"Yeah. Just dealing with a fuckwit. I'll tell you all about it later. Can you do the bar for a bit? I need to get away from people before I go postal."

Tony nodded, chuckling to himself as he dumped the glasses in the sink and pointed at the next customer.

Auryn walked out from behind the bar and started circulating around the room, picking up glasses and avoiding human contact, his teeth clenched as he seethed internally about the heated encounter. The man had been so condescending, and if there was one thing Auryn couldn't abide, it was being talked down to.

Although not ideal for wage costs, the night continued at full pace, and Tony stayed on until close. Auryn was sure he would hear about it from Adam, but as the pair of them sat down for a knock-off drink, he was thankful for the company, Tony offering welcome distraction with his animated opinions on the latest comic book and movie releases.

Returning with another round of drinks, Tony put his hand on Auryn's shoulder as he sat back down.

"You okay, man?"

Auryn nodded. "Yeah, just tired."

"Everything okay with Theo?"

"What are you talking about? Me and Theo are fine," he snapped defensively.

"Sorry," Tony shrugged. "You've been in a funk all weekend. I figured something was up."

Auryn took a long sip from his drink. "No. We're all good. There's just a lot of stuff going on in our lives at the moment. Her dream is to travel, but I can't because I have debts to pay off. It's stressing me out."

"Are you making a dent in it, at least?"

"Slowly. This job pays the bills, but it's not enough."

"Welcome to hospitality!" Tony scoffed sarcastically, trying to lighten the mood.

Auryn rolled his eyes. "Yeah, I know, but trying to save on my salary is making me re-evaluate my life choices, and it's pretty depressing."

"What do you mean?"

Auryn drained his glass and set it down. "I feel trapped. I'm sick of working in bars. I'm sick of serving people. I'm sick of Benzin. I'm sick of everything. I want to get out, but I can't."

"You should ask for a raise, man. You're the backbone of this place. Adam and Carlos couldn't run it without you."

"They won't give me one. Have you met Adam?" he asked, his voice laced with disdain.

"Probably not, but there's no harm in trying. Besides, you deserve it."

"Thanks, bud," he replied, slapping Tony on the shoulder. "Should we jet off?"

Tony grinned, dumping the glasses in the sink before throwing his hands in the air. "Weekend! Woo!"

Auryn smiled despite himself. Sometimes it was the little things in life that kept him going.

∞∞∞∞

It was Sunday night, and Auryn and Theo were both off work. That, of course, meant only one thing: a horror movie marathon.

As the teenage virgin of their fifth film of the day stabbed the masked killer in the chest on screen, Theo turned to him. "She's gonna do it."

He shook his head emphatically. "There's no way she's that stupid."

The virgin stood trembling, staring at the killer's body lying on the ground before she dropped the knife beside him.

As one, Theo and Auryn groaned.

"Why would she do that?" he gestured around him in exasperation. "It's like she wants to die!"

Theo just gave him a smirk. "Called it."

The killer jumped to his feet, and the virgin squealed in terror, running down a long corridor along which seemingly every door was locked. As they watched, the pair of them once again mocked the usual trope of bras being non-existent in horror-based situations.

Glancing across at Theo, he found her stretching out her hands.

"They going numb again?"

"Yeah. I had to cut a load of chocolate yesterday, so my right shoulder is a mess."

"Here, let me see what I can do," he said, twisting her around and

355

pressing his thumbs in beside her shoulder blade, feeling the hardened knots underneath. "My god, they're everywhere. It's like they're having a knot party."

"No. I'm pretty sure they've claimed squatter's rights at this point and refuse to leave."

"Get out of there, you mangy knots! You're evicted! Get out! Get out!" he exclaimed, massaging harder and harder as he yelled at his new enemy, only pausing when he noticed Theo wincing. "You want me to stop?"

"No, it's good. It just hurts," she squeaked.

Auryn smiled to himself as he continued, the overacted screams of the female protagonist drawing his attention back to the screen. The film really was atrocious: the directing abysmal, the acting barely worthy of the job title. The most painful element, though, was the writing. There were holes in the plot so large you could fit a planet through them, and characters so under-developed he was sure there were more complex amoebas. How anyone had managed to get funding for the project was mindboggling to him, and his mind whirred with his own film ideas as he wandered into the dream world of what-ifs.

He moved down to Theo's arms and finished with her hands as the movie came to an anti-climactic close. The virgin won the day for reasons that didn't make an iota of sense, and the fate of the killer was left up in the air, as was customary. After all, an open ending meant the potential for a sequel, and by some non-sensical twist of fate, this one had several.

As the credits rolled, Auryn kissed Theo on the neck. "Any better?"

"Sore, but better. Thanks," she said, kissing him on the cheek and squeezing his leg. "Bed?"

He smiled and nodded, looking at his watch and realising it was well past midnight.

They snuggled into the covers, Theo tucking herself along his side, her head resting on his right shoulder, her hand on his heart. Auryn listened to her breathing slow down as she drifted off to sleep, and he was left to his thoughts, his eyes tracing the banded moonlight on the ceiling as his emotions crashed like breaking waves against the walls of his stomach. At the moment, he felt disconnected from his life, as if he was an innocent bystander watching his own movie play out from the sidelines.

Theo twitched, and he gently kissed her on the forehead.

The more Auryn thought about it, the more he came to reflect on how much pain he was inflicting on her by simply existing. They were in love, yes, but that love seemed to be causing Theo misery. He was holding her back from her dreams, from the things that would fill her heart with a joy he could not provide.

As he lay there, he couldn't help but entertain the most excruciating of thoughts: was Theo better off without him? Would she ultimately be happier without his emotional and financial baggage? He sighed to himself, trying to force his mind from such negative thoughts. He didn't want to leave Theo; he couldn't. She was the only thing giving his existence meaning.

Theo twitched again, groaning incoherently, and Auryn looked down at her, concerned. When she'd first fallen asleep, she'd looked peaceful, but her body had grown tense, the hand over his heart balled into a tight fist.

He stroked her hair, hugging her tightly to him, when she suddenly jerked around, a restrained whimper escaping her lips.

Auryn went from concern to fear in a heartbeat. "Theo?" he whispered softly.

He'd often heard that waking someone in the midst of a nightmare could do more harm than good, and so, although it went against his instincts, he held off.

Her subconscious just needs to work some things out, then she'll be fine, he reassured himself, holding her and trying to send her all the love he had.

The next second, though, she let out a tortured cry, and he threw all advice out the window, grabbing her arm and shaking her. "Theo?"

She cried out again, the agony in it cutting him to the bone, his heart thundering in his chest. He had to stop this. He had to save her from it.

He shook her harder. "Theo? THEO!"

All at once, her eyes shot open, and she started thrashing around as if she was fighting off some kind of unseen assailant, stray limbs slamming into him as she writhed in the sheets.

"Theo, it's me. It's Auryn," he shouted.

He tried to grab hold of her, but she continued flailing until she was on the other side of the bed. At the last second, Auryn managed to catch her by the wrist, preventing her from striking her head on the bedside table and crashing to the floor.

Eventually, the thrashing subsided, and Theo huddled into a ball, her whole body shuddering, her skin slick with sweat, her breath coming out fast and shallow.

"Theo, it's me," he cooed. "It's okay. You're safe. I'm here."

For a long moment, she remained silent, seemingly in her own world, until she unfurled herself and flew into his arms, clinging to him as though she was afraid he would disappear.

"Theo?" he said, but she only hugged him tighter. "Theo, did you have a nightmare?"

It was a stupid, obvious question, but he was desperate to elicit some sort of response from her. It was almost like the nightmare had rendered her mute.

Slowly, ever so slowly, Theo nodded.

"What was it about? What happened? Was it the Spider again?"

Theo shook her head violently.

"You don't remember?"

Another shake of the head.

"You can't tell me?"

She finally nodded.

Auryn didn't know what to do. He'd never seen someone wake up so violently before. Was he supposed to just give her time? Was he supposed to say nothing? It didn't seem right. He had to say something, so he said the only thing that came to mind, the only thing that truly mattered.

"I love you, Theo. I'm here."

She hugged him closer and looked up at him. "You promise?" she whispered, her voice almost inaudible.

"Of course," he replied gently, kissing her head.

"And you won't ever leave?"

It was a loaded question; at least it would be, normally. Now, though, in that moment, it was the easiest question he'd ever been asked.

"I will never leave you, Theo. Ever."

As he held her, he knew deep down in the depths of his soul that he was telling the truth. He would never let anything happen to her as long as he drew breath. He would never abandon her. He would protect her until the end of his days.

∞∞∞∞

When the sun finally rose the next morning, Auryn woke to find Theo in an amicable mood. She didn't mention the nightmare, and he didn't either, both of them letting it settle into their subconscious like sediment while the clear water of the day passed around them.

As they cleaned away the mess of dinner, Theo suggested they forgo another night in front of the television and instead tread into the uncharted territory of board games: an endeavour he was more than happy to attempt. After all, what better way to learn the deeper complexities of your partner's personality than through the medium of Monopoly? Of course, testing relationships against a game notorious for unearthing people's worst traits naturally called for the involvement of alcohol and snacks. Thus, with cocktails made, chips at hand, money allotted, and the dog and battleship sitting eagerly on Go, the game began.

The next hour was spent around the dining table, buying properties and swilling drinks as they mentally sparred with each other. Eventually, about three margaritas in, Auryn took stock of the situation, finding them at the tipping point of most rounds of Monopoly. Neither of them owned a complete set of properties, and neither of them were willing to trade and give the other person an advantage.

He flashed Theo a grin. "You get super competitive, don't you?"

"So do you," she scoffed, rolling the dice. "We both hate losing."

"True," he said as she picked up the dog and moved it around his side of the board, depositing it to the safety of her own property. "Should we call it a draw?"

She made a face. "No!"

Auryn rolled the dice and picked up the battleship, waggling it at her. "Look, normally I'd agree, but there are plenty of other games we can play. If we fight this out until someone wins, we could be here for days."

359

"Fine," she huffed with mock outrage, trying to stifle the grin tugging at her mouth.

"We both know you would have won anyway," he said, collecting up the cards. "Why prolong my misery?"

Scooping up all the money, she started to fastidiously sort them by denomination. "You're damn right I would have won!"

"Checkers?" he asked, putting the lid back on the Monopoly box.

"Sure. It shouldn't take long to whip you in that one!"

Auryn grinned as he set up the pieces laying the black tokens on his side and the white on hers.

They both started carefully, going for the corners and laying traps the other person never fell into. Miraculously, not a single piece was taken by the time the game fell into some bizarre mirrored deadlock, Theo resetting the board while he fetched another round of margaritas.

The next game ended the exact same way, and she glared at him. "You're supposed to lose, dammit!"

"I'm not going to lose on purpose, just to satisfy your ego."

"Yes, you are!" she giggled.

Shaking his head, he emptied the pieces back into the box. "What should we play now?"

Theo held up her empty glass. "Drink!"

"Fair enough, but after I've made the drinks, what do you want to play?"

Theo glared at him, trying unsuccessfully to keep a straight face. "Drink!"

Auryn chuckled to himself, grabbing the glasses and wandering to the kitchen. "How about chess?"

"Drink!" was the only response.

This one had less of an inflection to it, though, which he took as assent, and delivering her drink, he sat down and set up the board.

Theo took a sip, staring at the pieces. "I'm not very good at chess."

"Me neither. I haven't played in years," Auryn admitted. "That should make for an interesting game. Anything could happen!"

"Prepare to be annihilated!" she threatened, rubbing her hands together with a sly smile.

He laughed as he moved his first pawn.

The game progressed with much drunken tangential conversation and dramatic fights played out between the pieces, including the gleeful destruction of one of his pawns by her queen.

"No!" he cried out, reaching for the sky in exaggerated grief. "Not my pawn. I raised him like he was my own son!"

She laughed maniacally. "The queen rules all! Bow to her will!"

The game continued, neither of them able to gain an edge, pieces falling one by one until they were left in a stalemate, their kings performing an endless do-si-do around the board.

Auryn finally knocked his own king over in disgust. "You know what this means?"

"What?"

"We're so compatible that a draw is the only possible outcome in every situation!"

Theo smiled. "I guess we should probably just team up and whip other people at games then."

"Yep. I mean, it won't be fair on them, but it's the only logical solution," Auryn agreed, holding up his hand, Theo responding with a crisp high five that left them both shaking off the sting.

Setting the game aside, Auryn propped his elbow on the table, resting his unsteady head on his hand and gazing serenely at her.

"What?" she asked.

He leant across, gently caressing her cheek. "Nothing, I just enjoy losing myself in your beautiful eyes."

"Pfft. I'm not beautiful. I'm plain, like a moth."

Auryn shook his head fervently. "No. You're beautiful beyond measure, both within and without."

"You get weirdly poetic when you drink tequila," she chortled.

"I can't help but be poetic. You're beautiful, Theo."

"Oh yeah?" Theo asked, her voice dripping with scepticism. "How beautiful?"

Auryn stood up abruptly, grabbing her by the hand, pulling her up, and twirling her around. "Beautiful enough to dance with."

Theo looked at him incredulously. "You hate dancing."

She was right, of course. Auryn had never been one to feel the rhythm. That night, though, with this amazing woman in his arms and a fair amount of tequila to bolster his confidence, he *was* feeling it.

"I do. But you don't, and you're the exception to all my rules," he said, pulling her close and starting to sway.

"There's no music, you dolt. Shouldn't we put something on?"

Auryn smiled at her, gently leading her around the room in what could only loosely be described as a waltz. "We don't need music. The beating of your heart is enough."

Theo looked up at him for a moment, then punched him lightly on the arm. "That's for being an idiot."

Auryn laughed, her inability to accept his compliments amusing him. It was like she didn't know what to do with them, like they were a foreign object, but he still detected the flicker of a grin on her face as she tried to leer at him.

"An idiot you want to dance with?" he offered.

Theo shook her head with a resigned smile and took his open hand, placing her other lightly on his shoulder. "The *only* idiot I'll dance with."

Together they waltzed around Theo's lounge room to the silent symphony of their love, their troubles falling away with each spin, their eyes only for each other.

∞∞∞∞

Auryn had just left Theo's apartment the following morning, on his way into work to get some of the banal admin jobs out of the way for the week, when he came to a decision. With his confidence bolstered by spending time in love's presence, and Tony's words of support still in his mind, he had decided to back himself and ask for a raise.

There's no harm in asking, he thought as he crossed the road and continued past Fitzroy Gardens. *What's the worst that can happen? They can say no.*

He'd barely walked in the door of Benzin when his phone pinged, a message from Adam beckoning him upstairs making it clear that he'd been watching the cameras, awaiting Auryn's arrival. A small knot of anxiety constricted around his stomach as he headed for the stairs. There was only one reason Adam would be sitting in wait, and he knew it wasn't to tell him he was doing a fantastic job.

Taking a deep breath, he knocked on the office door, opening it to find Adam sitting expectantly at the desk wearing an expensive, crisp white designer shirt, the top two buttons undone to reveal an obscene amount of chest hair.

"Hey, Adam. What's up?" Auryn asked, doing his best not to betray his nerves.

"Sit down, Auryn," he said, gesturing at the adjacent seat. "We had someone post a defamatory comment about the bar on social media yesterday. It said they'd had the worst service they'd ever experienced and encouraged people to boycott us." Adam leant forward. "They described you in exquisite detail."

Auryn grimaced. "Listen, I know who it was. He was extremely rude and was holding up service, so I asked him politely to leave. I'm not sure what else I could have done in that situation. There were other customers waiting, and he was making a scene. He was a being detriment to the business. I-"

Adam held up his hand. "I don't care if everyone there was on your side. Thousands of people have seen that post and won't come here ever again. That is a far bigger detriment to my business."

"What was I supposed to do?" Auryn asked, slinking down in his chair in exasperation. "The guy was one of the rudest people I've ever served."

Adam's eyes bored into him. "You should have been polite and made him a drink. You definitely shouldn't have yelled abuse at him or thrown him out."

"I didn't yell ab-"

"Enough, Auryn. Look, we appreciate everything you do here, but make no mistake, if there's another incident like this, your position will be terminated."

The words hit Auryn like a tonne of bricks, his chest filling with a flurry of despair and rage, words of disgust creeping into his throat. Thoughts of Theo washed over him, though, and he swallowed his words along with his pride, rising to his feet.

"No worries, Adam. It won't happen again."

"Thank you," he nodded. "Is there anything else you want to discuss while I'm here?"

Auryn stared at him like a deer in headlights. There was, of course, something he wanted to discuss, but now was possibly the worst conceivable moment for it.

363

"It's okay. It can wait. I'll go down and start the ordering now," he said before heading to the door.

"No, come on. Tell me now. Let's get it out of the way."

Auryn took a deep breath and turned back around, gripping the back of the chair. "I was just thinking, I've been here for over five years, and it seemed like an appropriate time to review my pay. Seeing as it's not, though, maybe we should talk about it later."

"You're right, this isn't the time, but it is something we should discuss," Adam replied, giving him a small nod of acknowledgment. "Like I said, we do appreciate your work, but if you want a raise, you need to make it worth our while. You need to be saving us more money on stock, and pushing down staff costs, even if that means you're picking up the extra hours. You need to make sure every customer leaves happy and, more importantly, wants to come back. You need to earn it."

"Sounds fair," Auryn nodded, trying to placate him despite the conditions sounding less than reasonable. "Anyway, I should get to work. We can discuss it later."

Adam gave him a half-hearted smile and grabbed an invoice off the desk.

Taking his cue, Auryn left the office, closing the door behind him despondently.

In the aftermath of the meeting, he found himself surrounded by a cloud of depression. In one fell swoop, his confidence had been cut down at its knees, the joy and peace his weekend had provided blotted out and replaced by a storm of destructive emotions.

Even when he arrived back at his apartment in the evening, the feeling did not wane; in fact, it only grew the more he dwelled on his situation. Despite greater responsibility being stacked on his plate at steady and frequent intervals, his pay hadn't risen in more than two years. He'd more than earned his dues already, and yet there sat Adam demanding another pound of flesh. Not only that, he was demanding that flesh be taken from Auryn's already fleeting time with Theo, his most treasured asset.

The night felt darker and the bed colder as he lay himself down to sleep, his thoughts of Theo the only source of warmth to his melancholic heart. When he'd told her of the day's events, she had been supportive, ensuring him they would work through whatever was thrown their way.

Regardless of how soothing her words were, though, they served only to remind him of his promise to make her dream come true no matter what it took. Looking over at the empty pillow beside him, he reached out to the space he wished so desperately she was there to fill, his heart yearning for the presence of her soul. As the weight of his sadness ushered him into sleep's arms, a question drifted into his mind. Was that what he missed when he lay by himself? Her soul, the very essence of her being?

∞∞∞∞∞∞∞∞∞∞∞∞∞

The building was immense, its exterior clad in red bricks laced with clean white grouting, the interior a warren of dimly lit corridors lined with endless rooms, their wooden doors charred by the lick of flames long since extinguished. His shoes clacked on the hard timber floors as he wandered, something compelling him along, calling him to explore behind the doors. Each time he reached for a handle, though, he was met with a faceless figure blocking his way, shaking its head as if his attempt to gain entrance was an act of sacrilege.

The shadows grew longer around him, and he began running, searching erratically for an unguarded door, an escape from the endless labyrinth. Finally, he reached the top of a spiral staircase, its intricately carved railing charred just as the doors were, its delicate details crumbling to ash at his touch. He scurried down, his head spinning from the tightly coiled steps as he reached the bottom. There were no corridors here, only a single metal door, its surface so dark it was almost indistinguishable in the shadows.

Before it, another faceless figure stood shaking its head in disappointment, but he didn't care anymore. He pushed past, plunging into the room, the harsh clang of metal echoing behind him as the door slammed shut.

In the darkness, he could just make out shapes swarming around him, circling like vultures, enraged by his intrusion. He pushed them back, but they only pressed forward with greater intensity, shoving him to the ground, his head hitting the cold, concrete floor and jarring him into unconsciousness.

When he eventually opened his eyes again, he was met with harsh, white light. Blinking into it, he saw a man step into view, his features shrouded in darkness, a cocked revolver in hand, finger on the trigger.

He opened his mouth to scream, but before the sound could escape his lips, he heard a bang, and his forehead exploded.

Râșnov, Transylvania, 1692 CE

The Kingdom of Spain was beautiful this time of year, the sun shining warmly over the fields of sugar cane and dancing on the tips of the azure waves lapping along the southern coast of Castile. Iris tucked a flyaway strand of wavy black hair behind her ear as she looked across the sandy beach to the rugged cliffs rising from the water to the east. Her long, beige wool tunic flapped against her slender frame, her soft olive skin, delicate nose, and gentle cheekbones contrasting with the sharp, earnest look in her amber eyes.

Shifting her focus to the distant horizon, she sighed. There was nothing before her but endless water, yet something still pulled her towards the sea. It always had, ever since she was young.

Her parents seemed forever disappointed in her, embarrassed by the fantastical dreams she would recount to the other villagers with unwavering vigour: dreams of other lands, of adventure, and of a winged figure who sometimes accompanied her. They had no patience for her wild imagination, and even when she would wake from nightmares in fits of terror, screaming about a dark figure stalking her, they would offer no sympathy or comfort.

Amongst her seven siblings, she was the one they simply did not understand; she was the black sheep, the runt, the problem. In her eyes, though, their love came with far too many conditions, and when she rebelled against their wishes, they scorned her for being difficult and ungrateful. The final straw had come when her father betrothed her to the baker in the next village against her will, adamant that she be married and with child before her upcoming eighteenth birthday. In that moment, she had known only one thing: she needed to escape.

In some ways, leaving had been hard, but in others, it had been the easiest thing in the world. Iris did not miss her family or her home. She did not miss her chores or sleeping crushed between her two younger sisters on the floor of their tiny hut, and she certainly didn't miss the future she had been assigned. To the overly critical community that filled her village, Iris was little more than a strange girl with her head in the clouds, a girl who dreamt more than she thought, but they were wrong. Deep down, she knew her dreams were more than just fantasies; they were memories of lives been and gone, and finding their truth, that was her future.

It had been two months since she'd stolen away, slipping out from between her sisters just before the break of dawn, taking nothing with her but the clothes on her back and a few scraps of food. She had no plan, no knowledge of anything outside the village she'd been born in, and now here she stood, staring out to sea with absolutely no idea of what to do next. Finding the bare necessities had proven harder than expected, and she'd been living off the kindness of strangers, for the most part. She took scraps where she could get them and had even spent a week amongst a group of monks who'd taken pity on her.

Looking down at her aching feet, she noticed the blistered skin was beginning to peel away from their raw soles, and she lamented the shoes she had been forced to discard a week ago after the sheep hide finally gave way and fell apart. Tucking the bottom of her tunic up into the rope that cinched her waist, she gritted her teeth and stepped forward. The saltwater stung her wounds as the waves lapped over them, washing away the sand and dirt, but she could not stop here to allow them time to heal, not without food and water. As such, she tore away two strips of fabric from her fraying clothes and wrapped her wounds as best she could.

Iris hobbled back to the dirt track that had led her there, pausing at its edge. She knew following the coast was her best bet, people always lived along the coast, but she had no idea which direction to head. Taking a deep breath, she decided to continue west and see what happened. Hopefully, she would reach a small village or a farm before dusk, and if luck favoured her, she might be able to convince someone to offer her safe haven, if only for the night.

With her stomach growling, Iris bolstered her resolve and wandered off down the track. She didn't know what her future held or where it would lead her, but she knew she was destined for great things in far-off lands, and she was determined to meet that destiny head-on.

∞∞∞∞

The sun was nearing the horizon when Iris began to grow concerned that she was still without shelter for the night. As she contemplated her predicament, the sound of hooves rumbled behind her, and she spun around to see three men cantering down the track. They slowed to a walk as they approached, and Iris moved aside, giving them plenty of room to pass. To her surprise, though, they stopped.

Taking a step back to regard them from a safer distance, she noticed that although they were all olive-skinned with dark hair and brown eyes, the two at the back appeared somewhat unfamiliar. Neither looked older than thirty, and they both sported thick moustaches and tall, brimless, brown felt hats. Their loose-sleeved linen shirts were topped with dark sheep-skin vests embroidered with bright red thread, and their sheathed swords were wide and slightly curved.

The man leading them, however, appeared to her like any other Castilian who passed through her village. His hat was flat-topped and broad-brimmed, his unembellished, tan doublet was half-buttoned over an open-necked linen shirt, and his sword was thin and straight. The trio shared fleeting glances before the leader gently guided his horse forward, removing his hat to reveal a face dominated by a large nose and smattered with stubble, his long, black hair tied in a low ponytail.

"Is your name Iris, young lady?" he asked.

Iris took a step back and nodded mutely. How did he know her name?

The man smiled, his face softening. "Thank God! We have been searching for you for the longest time."

"What are you talking about?" she blurted out after a moment of stunned pause.

"Let me introduce myself," he said, dismounting and walking over to her. "My name is Gregorio. I was tasked with locating you two months ago, but it has proven to be no small feat. You are not an easy person to find, Miss Iris."

"My parents sent you, didn't they?" she snapped, fear gripping her as she realised how large the man was in comparison to her slight frame. "I'm not going back. I won't marry the baker."

"No, I was not sent by your parents, although I did speak to them. If I'm honest, they seemed disinterested in your whereabouts."

As his words washed over her, they brought with them a wave of sadness. She may not have missed her parents, but their rejection stung all the same, leaving her feeling empty and alone.

"The man who tasked me with finding you," he continued, "lives far away, in Transylvania."

Iris remained silent, her mind churning. She had no reason to trust these men, but something within her elicited questions she yearned to know the answer to. Could the man he spoke of be the winged figure from her dreams, the one she believed was her soulmate? Was he out there waiting for her? Of course, there was only one way to find out.

"Who is he? I don't know anyone from there. I don't even know where it is."

"Transylvania is many weeks ride from here to the north-east. As for who he is, I am not at liberty to say. I have simply been instructed to bring you to him," Gregorio replied.

"I have no horse. I don't even have any shoes," she said, looking down at her feet with a pang of shame. "I can't travel that far."

"No need to worry. There has been money provided to cover your needs. You will ride with me to the next town where we will buy you a horse. From there, we will journey from town to town until we reach a castle hidden in the forests of Râşnov in Transylvania. It is there that we have been directed to deliver you."

Her heart raced at the idea of her own horse and a new life in a castle, but although the proposition spurred excitement, a feeling of hesitation remained. The pull on her soul was still calling her south, across the sea, and yet the man who had called for her lived in the opposite direction. What if he wasn't the figure from her dreams? What if she was making the wrong choice?

Gregorio seemed to sense her uncertainty. "Believe me, miss. You are better off with us than alone. We have been instructed to make sure you sleep and eat well until you reach the castle. You will want for nothing."

As she considered another night alone, cold and hungry, the decision made itself. Food and shelter trumped everything else, and riding meant her feet could finally heal. Besides, if she met the mysterious man and didn't like him, she could always just leave.

"Okay," she nodded slowly. "I'll come with you."

"Excellent!" he said with a smile before gesturing at the two men accompanying him. "By the way, this is Luca and Codrin. They work for the man who sent for you, but I'm afraid they don't speak Castilian."

Iris nodded meekly at them and stepped towards Gregorio's horse, noticing as she did that the older of the two men, Codrin, appeared to be missing the index finger on his right hand. She glanced away quickly, a niggle of unease tugging at her as she took one last look out over the waves before shaking off her concerns.

Gregorio climbed into the saddle, his strong, calloused hand guiding her up behind him. "Hold on tight," he said, grabbing the reins and clicking his tongue.

The horse jolted off, and Iris found her arms instinctively wrapping their way around Gregorio's waist, gripping tightly to his solid, muscular frame. As they trotted along, she probed him with questions about the wealthy, enigmatic stranger who had gone to such lengths to locate her, and she was surprised to discover that Gregorio had never met the man himself. Luca and Codrin, he told her, had hired him just east of Madrid to assist with their search. He explained that although the pair themselves did not speak the language, they had provided him with a letter from their employer, written in Castilian, in which her name, age, general description, and rough location had been listed.

Outside of that, he could offer her neither insight nor information to satisfy her curiosity. Still, there was something about going forth into the great unknown that she found intoxicating. In that moment, it mattered very little to her where the journey ended or why it had begun in the first place.

As promised, Gregorio had purchased her a horse at the earliest convenience: a sturdy bay mare she'd named Suerte. When they'd reached a large town a week later, he had also bought her a new dress woven of fine linen dyed a delicate shade of blue, a pair of short, brown leather boots, and a thick, brown wool cloak to keep her warm and dry as autumn marched on. Iris was still no closer to knowing who the man was that had summoned her, but if he offered her a life of comforts such as these, she was sure she could forgive him any trespasses.

The days quickly turned into weeks, then into months. Luca and

371

Codrin occasionally signalled a change in direction but otherwise remained silent and stern, although never disrespectful. Gregorio, on the other hand, was cheerful and talkative, recounting tale after tale of his travels both in the saddle and over a goblet of wine in the evenings. He'd been all over Europe, seeing the kinds of things she'd only glimpsed in her dreams, and she found herself spellbound.

Each night they would stop in a town or a village, and Gregorio would take coins from the pouch he kept at his hip to pay for comfortable lodgings where the beds were warm, and she could wash as and when she wanted. True to his word, he also ensured there was a hot meal set before her morning and night, and she ate to the point of discomfort at every opportunity. In time, the hunger and hardship of her youth became a faded memory, and her usual slender frame began filling out until she no longer resembled a poor peasant's daughter.

Iris found herself dreaming of the winged figure with increasing frequency until he became ever-present each time she closed her eyes. It was as if he was trying to reach her through her subconscious, calling out to her soul from some distant place.

In her quiet moments, she would think about him, assuring herself that this most unexpected journey was leading to his arms. After all, who else would search the world for her?

∞∞∞∞

Eighty-seven days had passed by the time they rode into Râşnov at dusk, the last golden leaves of autumn barely clinging to the stark, silver branches of the birch trees sprinkled between the lush pines. An unfamiliar chill in the air prompted Iris to hug her cloak tight around her, and she found herself longing for the warmth of the now distant Castilian summers she'd run from. As she looked around, she was met with yet more hills. Each one was blanketed with thick forests, and the nearest was topped with a centuries-old fortress, its bright stone walls and towers crowned with rich red tiles.

The town sitting at the foot of the hill was far less grandiose, the wooden houses weathered, the streets quiet, the only movement the cracking of shutters as locals peeked out, their faces painted with wary suspicion. The excitement buzzing in Iris's chest continued despite their sullen demeanours, though. She was not in search of their warm welcome and open arms; she was there to meet her soulmate and to discover if the dreams she'd had over the years were, as she suspected, not dreams but memories. She was there for answers, not approval.

Gregorio reined in his horse outside the inn and dismounted, Iris following suit, landing lightly on the ground and straightening out her cloak. The sound of hooves continued past her, and she spied Luca and Codrin riding off down the road without them.

"Where are they going?" she asked Gregorio as he ushered her inside.

"To tell the man who sent for you of our upcoming arrival."

"Can't we just go there now?"

"Not tonight. We must give him time to prepare. From what I can tell, he's been searching for you for a long time. I'm sure he'll want the opportunity to ensure your lodgings are in order," he replied, placing a comforting hand on her shoulder. "Come on in out of the cold. You'll meet him soon enough."

Her heart warmed as she took one last look down the road before stepping inside, her heart aflutter with anticipation.

"You know, you never did tell me how much they paid you to find me," she said, suddenly interested in her value.

"Enough," he laughed. "Truthfully, though, I did it more for the adventure than the money. Plus, the long journey was made all the more worthwhile by having such a lovely young lady as company."

Iris blushed, looking down at her boots with a small smile, the innkeeper interrupting the tender moment to show them to their rooms.

Later, as she nestled into the heavy wool blankets of her bed, she thought about Gregorio. She'd never considered it before, but in the still of the evening, she wondered what would have happened if she'd refused to join him all those months ago in Castile. With eyes closed, she imagined him grabbing her, lashing her hands, and forcing her onto his horse. She imagined him sitting behind her as he rode, his strong arms reaching around her for the reins, his breath on her ear, riding carefully so as not to hurt her. In her fantasy, he was forceful but not cruel, doing his job as instructed while taking no pleasure in her pain.

Suddenly, a question struck her. What if Gregorio was the man who had sent for her, and this was all just a test to confirm she was the one? The more she thought about it, the more it seemed to make sense. In the months they'd spent together, he'd been kind and protective, and he knew the places she'd seen in her dreams. On top of that, he'd managed to find her on an obscure road with little more than a name and description that surely fit hundreds like her in Castile. The idea entranced her so much that it was well past midnight before she managed to fall asleep. When she finally did, she dreamt of Gregorio, dark wings billowing behind him, his hand outstretched to her.

∞∞∞∞

Iris sprung out of bed as soon as the first rays of dawn crept across the sky, excitement pulsing through her veins and buoying her step. For the first time in months, she ate very little of her breakfast, her stomach filled with far too many butterflies to allow food to settle. Eager and restless, she was spurring Gregorio out the door before the sun had even fully risen, finding Luca and Codrin already awaiting them just outside the door.

Without a word, the ever-silent pair turned and began to lead them into the forest, the horses treading carefully in single file down the barely perceivable track and past the southern foot of the fortress topped hill. Morning mist swirled around them, sunlight piercing the trees and glinting off the droplets as birds chirped merrily all around, the sound of trickling water completing the symphony.

They continued in the same vein for almost two hours before Iris finally spied something through the trees, staring at it in wide-eyed awe as they drew closer. Just across the narrow river they'd been following sat a small, square castle built of dark stone and encircled entirely by ramparts. The gate was hidden from view on the far side, and tall turrets sprouted from the front two corners of the main building, arrow slits offering clear aim at unwanted visitors.

As they reached the riverbank, Iris noticed a series of gargoyles perched along the parapets. Their demonic faces were contorted into pained, open-mouthed expressions, their hunched backs sporting flared wings and long stone spikes down their spines. The place seemed impregnable, and as much as it terrified her, it fascinated her

374

in equal measure.

Crossing the small wooden bridge spanning the river, she peeked behind her to find Gregorio equally as entranced. "The man who searches for you has made an impressive home for himself," he said, meeting her eye, his brows raising in surprise.

Iris beamed as Luca and Codrin led them under the open portcullis, through the thick, wooden gate, and into a wide, gravelled courtyard where they dismounted, handing their reins to the awaiting stablehand. It all seemed so surreal, like she was wandering in a dreamscape she'd wake from at any moment. She was a peasant girl from half a world away; things like this didn't happen to people like her. Taking a deep breath to steady her nerves, Iris straightened her cloak and tried to think of something polite and thoughtful to say to her host as Gregorio gestured for her to take the lead.

Luca and Codrin opened the towering double doors of the castle, and she stepped inside, Gregorio close behind, her heart pounding as she crossed the antechamber and wandered into the great hall beyond. The space stretched the full height of the double-storey castle, and everything about it filled her with wonder. The long, dark wood table running down the centre of the room was notably devoid of chairs save for one at either end, and it was lit by candles set on a massive, circular, wrought iron chandelier suspended from the roof by thick chains. High on the stone walls hung enormous tapestries woven with bright red, geometric shapes on a dark background, and at the far end sat a large hearth alight with crackling logs.

It was only after taking in the rest of her surroundings that she noticed the tall, thin man in the long, bear fur trimmed coat standing beside the fire, waiting for them. Nothing about him was appealing: his shoulder-length grey hair hung limply against his neck, his skin had an unsettling pallor to it, and the gauntness of his clean-shaven face was only accentuated by his sunken brown eyes.

Gregorio responded to Iris's look of trepidation with an encouraging nod, and she slowly walked forward. As they approached, the man smiled, and all at once, the butterflies in her stomach fell still, the joy in her heart evaporating to make way for fear. He did not wear the warm smile of someone who had found their soulmate but instead the malicious smirk of a predator having caught its prey.

The man straightened up, flicking his hand theatrically. "Welcome, child! My name is Garridan," he said, his accent so thick Iris could barely understand him at all. "Let me apologise for my Castilian. I have been learning for a year, but I am still not as fluent as I would have hoped."

"Thank you for greeting me, sir. But where is the man who summoned me here?" she replied, giving him a small curtsy, hoping more than anything that he was not the one she'd travelled so far to meet.

"You mean my master? He is upstairs resting. You will meet him a little later. I am here to help you settle in first. Before I do that, though, I must attend to your friend Gregorio here," he said, turning to regard her companion, his words seeming heavily rehearsed. "After all, he has done my master a great service, and for that, I am willing to grant him the greatest gift I can bestow on another man. A quick death."

Before Gregorio could react, Luca grabbed his arms and pinned them behind him, Codrin stepping up and driving a dagger deep into his chest, nothing but the hilt visible as blood began to seep through his doublet. Looking down in disbelief, Gregorio collapsed to his knees, a trickle of crimson spilling over his bottom lip before he tumbled backwards onto the flagstones and fell still.

Iris's scream echoed around the hall, and she tried to run, to escape the nightmare she'd found herself in, but an icy hand latched onto her wrist. Jerking her arm, she tried to free herself from Garridan's clutches, but his grip held firm, and he flashed her a cold, insidious grin.

"You can't leave yet, child. There is still so much for us to discuss."

With another scream, she yanked desperately at her arm, tears welling in her eyes, terror constricting her chest. Suddenly, something struck the back of her head, and she blacked out.

∞∞∞∞∞

When Iris awoke, her mind was fuzzy and disconnected. She was dimly aware that her hands were shackled and strung up above her head, her shoulders aching from their unnatural position, and as the still, dank air sent a shiver up her spine, she realised she was naked.

Opening her eyes, she could barely make out her surroundings, the

376

only light in the low-ceilinged room being a single candle flickering in a lantern hung on the wall at the far end, its flame struggling to permeate the darkness. All at once, the image of Gregorio's murder filled her mind, and she choked back a sob, panic re-emerging as she began to comprehend the gravity of her situation.

"I love this moment," a voice uttered from behind her. "The moment you finally understand, there is no escape from the suffering. It is inevitable."

Iris moaned, twisting to try and find the source of the words, but they bounced around the space as if to mock her from all sides.

"Oh yes, you will feel the most exquisite pain, child. You will suffer, more than you ever thought possible," the voice continued with a laugh as footsteps sounded to her left, and Garridan crept from the shadows, rolling up the sleeves of his white linen shirt as he did. "Before we begin, I must ask you, who did you expect to find at the end of your journey? Be honest. There are no secrets here."

Iris shook her head, clamping her lips shut and refusing to speak.

"Now, now, this won't do. It's not an unreasonable question, is it?" He strode forward quickly, his face only inches from hers as he grabbed her chin and forced her to meet his gaze. "IS IT?" he shouted, pulling back and striking her hard across the cheek.

Her skin stung from the impact, and her now split lip greeted her with the taste of blood. "No, it's not," she squeaked, hoping her obedience would buy her leniency.

"Good! So, tell me, who did you expect to find here?"

Iris shifted uncomfortably, the chains above her rattling as she tried to ease the pain in her shoulders. "I don't know."

"Then why did you come?"

"Because I had nowhere else to go," she sobbed, her rueful words little more than a whimper.

Garridan shook his head, slapping her again. "No, no, no! We both know that is not the real reason. Now, I'll ask one more time. Who did you expect to find here?"

"My soulmate," she replied, the words feeling like a betrayal as they left her.

"See, that wasn't so hard now, was it? And who is this soulmate of yours, hmm?"

Iris shook her head, looking back down at the floor before Garridan struck her already throbbing cheek once more.

"I can do this all day," he snickered. "Better to tell me now than later through shattered teeth."

Blood dribbled from her mouth as she tried to speak. "I don't know. I see them in my dreams. We have been together before, in other lives, and we will be together again. I know it," she said, her voice growing desperate.

"Your dreams are nothing but delusions, child. Pure fantasy. There is no soulmate waiting for you. You have only me. And pain."

He melted back into the shadows, and she heard him muttering to himself in a language she couldn't understand. His words traced circles around the room until she felt his presence right behind her, his rancid breath hot on her right ear. She went to turn her head, but his icy hand clasped her neck, and she froze.

All at once, the most incredible pain lanced through her as a cold blade ripped open her flesh. She yelped, his hand releasing its grip, her right leg giving out from under her. When she looked down, it was to find a gaping wound running down the front of her thigh, the skin rent asunder, the warm blood cascading freely down her leg jarringly juxtaposed to the seeping cold around her.

Garridan grabbed her by the hair, holding her head in place and forcing her to watch as he raised the dagger again, slicing it across her belly. Iris saw her skin come apart, the muscle bulging beneath, blood sheeting down and painting her trembling body a deep scarlet. Iris cried out in pain, writhing in her shackles, every ounce of her trying to find the strength to fight back. She felt her terror morph into anger, and she compressed it into a tight ball in her chest until it overwhelmed her and exploded from her lungs as a blood-curdling scream.

Energy burst out from her in all directions, and Garridan released her head, flying backwards. The shackles that bound her shattered, and she collapsed to the ground, her wrists throbbing as proper circulation recommenced.

She looked around in confusion, attempting to piece together what had happened, when she heard a groan across the room. Frantic, she tried to scramble to her feet, to escape while she had the chance, but her leg crumpled beneath her again, her head spinning as she lay in a pool of her own blood. Footsteps echoed around her, and a moment later, Garridan crouched down at her side.

"Impressive, child. You're not even aware of your power, and yet you can access it. My master was right to warn me about you."

As he raised his hand, she saw the weak candlelight glinting off steel, and before she could move to stop him, he struck her in the temple with the butt of his dagger.

∞∞∞∞

Iris was roused from unconsciousness by the clinking of chains, blood oozing down her forearms from the shackles biting into her wrists. Slowly opening her eyes, she noticed there were more lanterns than before, their halos of light revealing the walls of the windowless chamber. The rough stone was covered in grime and soot, and something else: blood, caked-on and blackened. Surveying the space, she spied a heavy wooden door in the far left corner and a wrought iron brazier filled with brightly glowing coals a short distance in front of her.

The room felt warmer now, but her bare skin still prickled, although she wasn't sure if it was from cold, pain, or fear. As she looked down, her eyes fell on the wounds Garridan had inflicted on her, and she was surprised to find them stitched and clean. Trying to take the pressure off her aching wrists and shoulders, she straightened her loosely hanging legs only to be met with excruciating pain. She yelped as they gave out beneath her, then yelped a second time as her arms caught her weight again.

In the swill of agony, Iris attempted to clear her mind, to gain control of her faculties, but the pain was overwhelming. Taking a deep breath, she clenched her jaw and tried once again to stand, this time on only her left leg, but it buckled under her, and she cried out. It was then that she heard him laugh.

Following the sound, she squinted through the shadows to catch sight of Garridan watching her from a chair in the corner, the light catching on his teeth as a wide grin stretched across his face. She stared at him in disbelief, a barrage of questions racing through her mind. How long had she been unconscious? Why had he tended her wounds? Had he been there the entire time, admiring his handiwork?

"You know, I was troubled by your power at first," he said, rising to his feet, his calculated footsteps delivering him uncomfortably close to her, his once white shirt now sporting washed out bloodstains. "I was afraid of what you might do. But then I had a revelation. I am the one holding all the power, not you."

Her head felt heavier by the minute, and she peered up at him past her brow, watching as he stepped back and looked her up and down with an expression of twisted pride.

"Have you figured out what I did yet? I've broken your legs, both of them, in several places. Even if they heal, you'll never walk properly again," he said before slinking back into the shadows. "You can't stand. You can't stop the shackles from carving away at your wrists or ease the ache in your shoulders. Even if by chance your power emerged again, it would only serve to cause you more pain."

Iris closed her eyes. Nothing was making any sense. Power? What was he talking about? She didn't have any power.

Suddenly, the dim memory of energy bursting out and freeing her sprung to mind, but as another wave of pain rippled through her body, her thoughts became muddied, the memory fading as quickly as it had appeared.

"Why are you doing this? What did I do to you?" she pleaded, meeting his gaze again. "Where is the man who sent for me?"

Garridan shook his head, tutting at her ignorance. "Foolish little girl, this has nothing to do with you at all. Don't you see? You are just a pawn in this game, as am I. We both have our roles to play. Yours is to stay here with me, and mine is to make your stay as torturous as possible."

Turning his back to her, she watched him approach the brazier and twist a long iron rod protruding from its glowing coals, embers jumping into the air around it.

"You will suffer," he said, regarding her again with a menacing smile, "and you will scream. You will feel agony beyond anything you've ever experienced. And just when you think it's over, that it can't get any worse, I'll do something so unfathomable that even a scream won't suffice."

"I won't scream," she hissed through gritted teeth.

"Oh, you will, child. Firstly, because the pain won't give you a choice.

And secondly, because if you don't, I'll cut out your tongue," he threatened with a laugh, twirling his dagger in his hand, the light dancing off its blade. "But enough of that. You'll get to keep your tongue for a while yet. You have other things to worry about right now."

Slowly, deliberately, he tucked his dagger back in its scabbard and drew the rod from the brazier, its tip glowing a delicate shade of orange. Grinning, he swung the rod, tracing circles in the shadows.

Iris's heart pounded in her ears, and her eyes grew wide as he approached.

"Ahh, this is my favourite part," Garridan said, chuckling softly to himself. "The anticipation."

He stepped forward, moving the rod so close to her skin she could feel the heat radiating from it.

"The female form is such a strange thing, don't you think? So many curves. So many holes."

Spots started to appear in her vision as her breathing became shallow and sporadic. She tried to twist away, to suck her stomach in, to make herself smaller.

"Let's experiment, shall we?" he continued. "Let's pick a hole and see what happens. What about this one?" He brought the glowing tip up to her neck, below her right ear. "Hmm, perhaps not."

Touching the point of the rod to her skin, he slowly ran it down her neck, along her collarbone, and between her breasts before lifting it off just above her navel, a blistering trail marking its journey.

Iris gritted her teeth, the smell of her own burning flesh reaching her nostrils and inducing a wave of nausea. She didn't scream, though; she didn't even whimper.

"No. I have a better idea," he said, the glint in his eyes nothing short of maniacal as he kicked her legs apart with his foot, grabbing her chin and forcing her to look at him.

When the rod touched her again, it was on the inside of her left thigh. Garridan's eyes never left hers as she felt it burn its way higher and higher until it reached its destination. It was then, and only then, that Iris began to scream: ear-piercingly, involuntarily, and unceasingly until, at last, she lost consciousness.

Garridan stood on the parapet of the castle, leaning against one of the gargoyles as the chill, damp air of the evening blustered around him. He looked down at the forest, the last of the winter snow clinging to the branches, shards of ice catching the faint starlight as they drifted down the river, the waxing moon tucked behind a cloud.

There had been times he'd believed his master was wrong, that he'd been naive to follow him. Even in his most faithless moments, though, when he'd considered leaving the castle to ply his gruesome trade elsewhere, Garridan's loyalty had kept him grounded. Deep down, he knew his fidelity would be rewarded in the end. He just had to be patient. He just had to trust in the plan.

The day the girl had arrived, willingly and brimming with boundless optimism, all of his doubts had been erased. She was exactly as his master had described: young, pretty, and convinced she was there at the behest of her soulmate. It had been in that tantalising second, when Codrin had rammed his dagger into Gregorio's chest, and the girl had realised that she was trapped in a carefully laid web, that Garridan had foreseen the fun he was about to have.

Despite his eagerness, his master had been most explicit in his instructions. Once found, she was to be tortured mercilessly, but under no circumstance was she to succumb to her injuries. The orders had made little sense to him, but he knew better than to question his master. The man wielded knowledge like a marksman did an arrow: with control, restraint, and deadly precision. As for his power, Garridan shuddered at the mere thought of it. His master's power was unlike anything he'd ever seen. It was incomprehensible.

The plan had been followed to the letter, and the events had progressed precisely as his master had prophesied. When pushed to the extreme, the girl had unwittingly exhibited her own power, but just as predicted, the more he broke her body and muddled her mind with pain, the weaker her spirit became.

He quivered with pleasure as he thought about what he'd done to her, the look in her eyes as the searing iron rod slid up between her legs flashing before him and painting a contented smile on his face. By his very nature, Garridan was a sadist. Causing pain and suffering provided him with a rush he couldn't find anywhere else, and he relished any opportunity to unleash the darkest parts of his soul.

Something about the screams, the flesh, and the blood, made him almost giddy inside. To him, his work was an art form, an expression of grotesque beauty carved on the bodies of lesser beings that filled a deep desire within him. He was devoid of anything that even vaguely resembled love, compassion, or empathy, and his master had always made clear that his immunity to these weaknesses was what made him so valuable, so perfectly suited to the task at hand.

It had been ninety-three days since he had first strung her up in the dungeon, ninety-three days of uninterrupted and unparalleled joy. There had been days where he'd simply left her there, swinging slowly in the darkness, all alone with her fear and her pain as he revelled unseen in the shadows. On other days, though, on his most treasured days, he'd done things so heinous his body tingled at the thought.

At times, he used his dagger or the searing tip of the rod; at others, he used ropes, chains, and vices. Varying his methods, he would leave areas to heal while working on others, then return to reopen old wounds weeks later. He was meticulous and calculated, slicing, lashing, burning, and breaking whatever it took to elicit the reaction he desired, her screams both vindicating and validating him. Amidst her tortured cries, he knew he was doing his master proud.

As adept as he was at his job, though, there were instances where he lost himself in his craft and was forced, with great reluctance, to stop. When she neared death, he took her down, sedated her with a tincture of poppy, and tended her wounds, waiting until she was just healed before returning her to the dungeon. Looking across at the grotesque stone sentry beside him, he ran his finger up the long stone spikes protruding from its spine and sighed. Although it pained him to admit it, he would have to take her down again soon. He couldn't risk her dying of infection, and her wrists were starting to show signs of festering beneath their iron cuffs.

Pondering the unfortunate reality, he was stirred from his thoughts by a sudden thump on the adjacent parapet. He glanced across, scanning the shadow-drenched silhouette of the roof's far edge for the source of the sound, but he found nothing unusual, only the hunched shapes of gargoyles standing stoically in place. Garridan had always loved them. They gave the castle an instant and irrefutable air of foreboding. They foretold terror and ruin; they foretold death.

He returned to his position, his mind drifting back to the girl as he watched the trees sway in the breeze, and yet something nagged at him. Turning around again, he studied the outline of the distant parapet once more. It was then that he noticed it. There were usually seven gargoyles posted along the western edge, not eight. His eyes traced the finer details of each, one by one, until he reached the fifth. It seemed the right size, with the same hunched back and flaring wings as the others, except ... it was facing inward.

Before he'd even registered the thought completely, the gargoyle opened its eyes, the starlight reflecting off them as it sprung forward, cannoning into him and sending him skittering along the length of the battlement. As the creature stalked towards him, Garridan looked up to see not a grotesque figure but a man.

The shirt and trousers he wore appeared tight and ill-fitting against his rippling muscles like they were made for someone else, the fabric's dark hue melding seamlessly with his skin so that he almost seemed to blend into the night itself. From his back, shafts of pure darkness flowed like wings, dancing with shadows and black lightning. It seemed impossible, and Garridan blinked a few times to make sure he wasn't seeing things. The Phoenix, the one his master had warned him of, he was real!

The Phoenix grabbed him by the hair, forcing him to his feet and marching him to the east tower. Taking the lantern off its hook just inside the door, the man propelled him forward, down the spiral staircase. They came to an abrupt stop as they reached the entrance hall, and he saw the man close his eyes for a moment, concentrating, before opening them and pushing onwards, across the antechamber and down the corridor to the left of the great hall. Finally, they stopped outside the door of Garridan's own bedchamber, and he realised what was happening. The Phoenix was attuned to the girl somehow; he could sense her.

Entering the room, Garridan was thrust to the ground, and the Phoenix slammed the door shut, closing his eyes and running his fingers along the wall until he reached a section covered by a large tapestry. With a single yank, it crumpled to the floor, and Garridan saw the man lift the lantern to inspect the stonework. A smug smile settled on his face as he watched on. Even if the man could find the seam that marked the entrance, he would never find the latch.

Garridan began to slink quietly towards the door, hoping to flee and rouse the mercenaries in the upstairs dormitory, but just as he reached for the handle, he felt the hair on his arms and neck prickle and his ears pop as the pressure increased. Glancing back, he found the Phoenix engulfed in a swirl of dark energy, the lantern sitting on the floor beside him, its candle flickering wildly.

In a heartbeat, Garridan realised what the man was about to do, and he dove to the ground just as an explosion ripped through the air. He felt rubble rain down, ricocheting off the four-poster bed and pelting his back, his ears ringing, the room engulfed in darkness.

Climbing to his knees, he heard the Phoenix lift the lantern from the ground, its hinges creaking as its door opened and a tiny spark appeared, lighting the candle once again. The room came back into view just long enough for Garridan to see the man step through the newly made hole in the wall and disappear down the stairs to the dungeon below, his wings pulsating with power.

As he hurried to his feet, the words of his master echoed through his mind. *Find the girl, torture her mercilessly, keep her alive, and if the Phoenix comes for her, kill it.*

His master had spoken of the Phoenix very little. Garridan was given no description, no age or gender, nothing to identify the being at all except that it would come with dark wings and vengeance in its heart. More importantly, though, his master had been clear on one thing: although powerful, the Phoenix was as mortal as any other.

Lurching forward, Garridan grabbed his dagger from where it hung in its scabbard from a hook on one of the bedposts and hurried over to the stairs. He was sure Luca and Codrin must have been woken by the explosion, and he considered waiting for them to reach him, but he knew there was no time for that. He had to strike while the iron was hot, while the Phoenix was distracted by the girl.

As he reached the bottom of the staircase, he snuck in the open door, creeping silently into the cover of the shadows and waiting for the opportune moment. He watched as the man strode forward, stopping in front of the girl hanging limply in her chains, holding up the lantern as he tenderly brushed her cheek. Wrapping his arm around her waist, he lifted her down, the shallow rise and fall of her chest barely perceptible, a burst of energy breaking her shackles and sending them clattering to the floor.

Garridan seized the moment and charged forward to attack the Phoenix from behind while his hands were full. With one final bound, he leapt into the air, his blade held high, but he never reached his target. Instead, there was an ear-splitting crack, and something unseen slammed into his chest, sending him hurtling backwards, his body sliding across the icy stone, his knife lost to the shadows. Gasping for breath, he looked up in disbelief as the man turned to face him, an aura of dark energy seeming to radiate from his skin.

Weaponless, Garridan's instincts switched to flight, and he scrambled to his feet, racing up the stairs and out of his bedchamber, navigating the dark by memory. His shaking hands fumbled for the key hanging from a leather strap under his shirt, and he pried it out, feeling for the keyhole and locking the door behind him. As he turned from it, he saw Luca appear in the antechamber at the far end of the passage, half-dressed and half-awake, with a sword in one hand and a torch in the other. He heard the shouts of men upstairs, and a moment later, Codrin emerged, lighting the torches along the wall as he marched forward with three other men in his stead, all of them wielding muskets.

Garridan scampered past, shouting at them to kill the intruder as they knelt down to load their weapons and took up their positions along the width of the corridor, their barrels trained on the locked door. Reaching the antechamber, he snatched Luca's torch from his hand as three more mercenaries appeared, all armed with swords. The four swordsmen filed in behind the others, and as Garridan glanced back at them, he knew they didn't stand a chance. In the end, though, the outcome of the fray mattered very little to him. They would either earn their keep, or they would die trying.

Stopping at the door to the west tower, he glanced back, watching with fascination. There was a long, tense pause as the men awaited the emergence of their enemy, and a low hum began to emanate from the bedchamber. Garridan felt the hairs on his arms bristle again as the hum grew louder and louder until it was almost deafening. Suddenly, the pressure in the castle spiked, and the wall of his room exploded, the door splintering, the men ducking their heads to avoid the stone flying out like shrapnel.

As the dust began to settle, Garridan saw the Phoenix step out into the corridor alone in all his glory, silently assessing the threat before him, his black wings billowing in the dim glow of the few torches still alight. Captivated by it all, Garridan watched as Codrin called out, and his men opened fire. Through the smoke, he saw the musket balls fly towards the Phoenix only to hit some invisible shield, kick up puffs of shadow on impact, and drop harmlessly to the floor.

As the men scrambled to reload their firearms, the Phoenix charged towards them, his wings flaring. Codrin thrust his bayonet forward in defence, but his foe simply dodged to the side, grabbing the barrel and forcing the butt of it back into his nose.

With a cry, the Phoenix let out a burst of energy that sent Codrin flying sideways into the wall, where he collapsed into a motionless heap, the other musketeers all sent sprawling to the ground by the blast.

Finding themselves exposed, Luca called his men to arms, taking the lead and darting forward. Before his sword was even midway through its arc, though, the Phoenix lunged at him, and he was hit square in the chest by a ball of dark energy. The force sent him hurtling back down the corridor, blood trailing in his wake, his head cracking onto the flagstones as he landed.

The remaining mercenaries began to advance as one, swords held high, when the pressure spiked and another wave of power exploded from their foe, sending them careening down the passage to join their leader on the cold stone floor.

Garridan watched on as the first three men scrambled to collect their muskets and regain their feet, only to be cut down at the waist as the Phoenix shot forth a beam of shadow, sweeping it through them like a scythe through wheat.

A fragment of stone skittered across the floor, and the Phoenix turned on his heel just as Codrin reached him, dagger raised. Ducking to the side, he grabbed Codrin by the throat and lifted him off the floor with unsettling ease, black lightning lancing from his hand and coursing through his attacker. Codrin let out a guttural scream, his body sizzling like meat over the fire until the Phoenix dropped him to the ground, wisps of smoke gently rising from his corpse.

It was only then, when all of the men lay dead, that Garridan was shaken from his sadistic spectatorship. Panicked, he reached for the handle and yanked open the door to the stairs just as the Phoenix looked up at him, their eyes meeting for a brief moment. He could hear his foe's heavy footsteps as he kicked the door shut behind him in a vain attempt to delay his fate. Taking the steps two at a time, a single thought filled his mind: he had failed in his mission.

A thunderous explosion shook the tower, echoing up the stairwell, but Garridan didn't slow down, taking the steps two at a time until he reached the upper room and scurried inside. Heaving for breath, he placed the torch in the bracket beside him just as its flame flickered out.

As his eyes adjusted, he looked around the shadow-cloaked room, the only illumination that of the moon as it crept in through the arrow slits. The space was deathly cold and completely empty save for his master, who rested on the stone slab at its centre.

Hurrying over, Garridan dropped to his knees beside the slab. "Master, I beg of you. Please help me! I have done your will, and it has only brought destruction and death to us all," he pleaded, hands clasped in desperation. "Master, please. You must help us defeat him!"

Garridan heard the door creak open and turned to see the Phoenix standing there. His looming silhouette appeared like the angel of death he had so often admired in the stained glass of his childhood church. Paralysed by fear and indecision, he watched as the Phoenix approached the other side of the slab, running his fingers along the dust-covered clothes of his master and pausing as he regarded the sunken, desiccated skin of the corpse's face.

Garridan tried to back away silently, but the Phoenix glanced across as soon as he moved, rounding the slab and advancing on him with slow, deliberate footsteps, his jaw squared, his eyes narrowed by vengeful rage. Picking up his pace, Garridan shuffled backwards until he hit the wall just below one of the slits, holding up his arms to shield his face.

"No. Please. No! NO!" Garridan begged as a burst of dark energy exploded past, the wall crumbling away behind him, the dislodged stone skittering down the side of the tower and thumping into the ground far below.

Through the gap in his arms, he saw the Phoenix barrel forward, grabbing him around the middle, his legs swinging wildly as he realised he was being carried into the air like a mouse in the talons of an eagle. They soared higher and higher until he could see Râşnov Fortress perched atop its summit in the distance, its pale walls catching the soft light.

Suddenly, the Phoenix released his grip, and Garridan began to fall, his face towards the stars. The worst part was the anticipation, the fear of not knowing when or where he would land, but he didn't have to wait long. There was a horrific crunching sound, and he glanced down at his torso in disbelief, shock keeping the pain at bay. Three stone spikes protruded from his body, their blood-covered tips gleaming as he raised his hand to touch them. From the corner of his eye, he spied a set of stone wings, and he realised he'd fallen onto one of the gargoyles and been impaled along its spine.

He tried to move, to wrench himself free, but as he shifted, he heard something click in his back. A wave of pain radiated through him, and he felt the warm trickle of blood as it ran along the furrows in the stone beneath him, flowing down the sides of the statue and dripping onto the parapet.

At that point, there was nothing else he could do but scream, the agony-filled call echoing through the forest. Each time he stopped, a wave of pain would crash into him and draw out another cry, as if fate was eliciting from him in death the same sound he had fed on in life. He screamed until his final breath, until the pastel rays of dawn stretched from the horizon and marked the first new day without him in it.

∞∞∞∞∞∞∞∞

As she slipped in and out of consciousness, Iris moved between moments as though outside the constraints of time. Each blink of her eyes snatched away a second here and a day there until she was left with nothing but brief freeze-frames she could not tie together.

She remembered energy coursing around her and strong hands lifting her gently from where she hung. She remembered being laid down on a bed, a loud crack, and the scent of gunpowder. She remembered the soft hug of a blanket and the jolt of agony each time the dark figure carrying her took another step. After that, the snippets grew more indistinct: vague recollections of weightlessness, of blue as far as the eye could see, of warmth like a sunburnt Castilian summer, then nothing.

When she finally came to again, Iris found herself lying on a bed of straw in a small, circular hut, the walls built of woven branches and plastered with crumbling mud. Cheerful birdsong and soft light filtered in around the cowhide hanging over the doorway, and she guessed it was early morning, although she had no way of knowing for sure.

As she looked up at the thatched roof, wondering where she was and how long she'd been there, flashes started to return. Amongst the blurry jumble, she found the image of a gentle hand raising her head, giving her milk to drink, and spoon-feeding her something unfamiliar that she vomited back up almost immediately. She recalled the bitter, woody smell of a paste being spread on her stinging wounds while a feminine voice spoke to her in a language she could not understand.

Then, all at once, she was met with the nauseating memory of her legs being broken again, the pieces moved around like mosaic tiles while a soft hand held hers in comfort. It felt like only yesterday, but she knew it couldn't be as she shifted them slightly. The bones had refused, and the lingering pain was dull if she remained still, as though weeks or even months had passed her by.

Sitting up, her unaccustomed body aching from the movement, her skin pulling taut at its scars, she took in her surroundings. Along the walls of the hut stood stacks of woven baskets and a few earthenware pots, but aside from those, the space was empty. As for herself, she was still naked aside from a small pelt draped over her lap, and although the air was warm on her bare skin and she was alone, she felt vulnerable in her nudity and folded her arms tightly across her chest.

Iris heard footsteps in the dirt outside and her heart pounded as they grew closer, continuing until a middle-aged woman pushed aside the cowhide and stepped inside. She was unlike anyone Iris had ever seen, with dark skin, a wide, flat nose, and black hair shaved close to her head. Just as Iris found herself, the woman was bare-chested, bare-footed, and wore a length of red roan cow pelt from her hips. Around her neck hung an eclectic mix of coloured beads, stones, and shells strung on a thin leather strap, and on her face was painted a stern expression.

Iris hugged her arms closer to herself and stared up at the woman whose entire demeanour suddenly changed, her lips curling into a wide, toothy grin. The woman began talking with great fervour, her hands shooting out in emphatic gestures, but Iris could do nothing but shrug, the words utterly incomprehensible to her.

Eventually, the woman gave up the attempt, waving as if to tell Iris to stay put before disappearing back out the door. Iris looked down at the jagged scars marking her legs and shifted them a little, only to be met by shooting pain that elicited a grimace and a clipped gasp through her teeth. The woman need not have worried; she was fairly certain she couldn't stand, let alone run away.

A moment later, the woman returned, leading in a man with similarly dark skin, shaved hair, and broad features. He looked to be in his mid-twenties, the light shining through the door cutting around his tall, muscular silhouette covered with little more than a cowhide loincloth.

Meeting Iris's eye, the man smiled, crouching down and reaching towards her. The second his hand moved, though, she screamed. It was an involuntary action and one born of pure fear, the gentle gesture splicing in her mind with the impending strike of her torturer. Keeping one hand across her breasts, she used the other to shuffle away from him, her legs lancing with pain, her heart racing.

The man pulled away sharply, his words coming out soothing but unintelligible. He reached out to her again, and again she screamed, this time not stopping until the woman grabbed the man's shoulder and shooed him out of the hut.

The memories flooded back unbidden: the clinking of chains, the glow of coals in the unpierced darkness, the smell of her own burning skin, the taste of blood, and the curl on the lips of the heartless man who'd kept her alive when she'd wished only for death. As the trauma caught up with her, she found herself overwhelmed by emotion, and she collapsed into a tight ball, tears streaming down her face, her panicked breath coming fast and shallow between choked sobs.

She remained in that state as the day slipped into night, the woman sitting beside her, patting her head softly and humming sweet melodies until Iris fell exhausted into sleep's arms.

∞∞∞

It wasn't until late the next afternoon when she finally stirred, swollen-eyed and dehydrated, but she made no attempt to move. As she lay there staring into the middle distance, her heart feeling empty and numb, Iris couldn't help but think that she never wanted to move again. She wanted to just fade away there in that hut, to escape into the peaceful, painless embrace of death.

A week passed around her unchecked, and Iris made no attempt to care for herself. For all intents and purposes, she existed only because the woman who cared for her willed it so, drinking only when milk was poured into her mouth and eating only when fed. If she needed to relieve herself, she just went where she lay, the straw of her bed wicking away what it could.

It wasn't until the seventh day, when the woman came in toting an earthenware pot sloshing with water and began to wash her, that Iris snapped back to reality. With a wave of shame, she realised that this woman, this kind stranger, had been cleaning up after her for weeks, if not months.

Turning to the woman, Iris touched her arm and shook her head. She wanted to help, but as she tried to move off the soiled straw, pain shot up her withered legs, and she collapsed back down. The woman gave her a comforting smile, lifting her waify frame and placing her to the side of the hut before clearing away the straw, scattering down a fresh layer, and returning Iris to her place.

A sense of helplessness swept over her, and Iris waited to be left to her sorrows once again, but instead, the woman sat down at her feet.

"Chau-si-ku," the woman said slowly, tapping her finger against her chest. "Chausiku."

"Ir-is," she responded, following suit. "Iris."

Chausiku pointed at her, grinning. "Iris," she echoed.

Something stirred in Iris's heart, and a brief flicker of warmth sprung up inside her. She had been stripped of her name for so long in that dungeon that the simple sound of it from the mouth of another felt like home. In that moment, she finally felt safe again.

Chausiku patted her on the shoulder, gesturing for her to lay down and rest before picking up the earthenware bowl and leaving the tent.

Left alone, Iris found herself creeping back into despair. As she lay there, she ran her fingers over the scars crisscrossing her skin, tracing the incision across her belly and the burnt path from her right ear to her navel. Switching tracks, she found the burn on her inner thigh and followed its raised line until she reached the mess of disfigured skin between her legs.

Tears trickled freely down her cheeks as she thought about how hideous she must be, how damaged and unlovable. The actions of the malevolent man in that castle had stripped away her hope and beauty. He had torn her apart and sewn her back together most crudely. He had made her a monster in his image. That thought, and that thought alone, rendered her inconsolable.

A few hours later, Chausiku returned, helping Iris to sit up and preparing to feed her when she took the bowl for herself for the first time. Iris ate the steaming stew slowly, her emotions still raging as she wondered where its unique flavour was coming from, and she looked up to see Chausiku watching her with a satisfied, motherly smile. Something about the smile soothed her; it encouraged her; it motivated her. In the presence of that smile, she found the strength to finish her food.

When she eventually placed the empty bowl down beside her, Chausiku stood up, gesturing as she did that she wanted to help Iris do the same. Iris nodded, and with Chausiku's strong arms tucked under hers and a deep, bracing breath, she heaved herself up. Even with most of her weight borne by the woman at her side, Iris could feel her muscles straining to support her, her bones aching as she shifted her feet to try and find balance.

It couldn't have been more than half a minute before her legs began to quake, and Chausiku helped lower her to the ground again. As she landed back on the straw, she felt a smile creep onto her face. It was the first time she had smiled since the day she'd arrived at that godforsaken castle. All of a sudden, she was being bundled into a joyous hug as Chausiku spoke excitedly, and although Iris had no clue what she was saying, she knew there was pride in the words.

393

Every day, they would repeat the ritual, and every day Iris would improve. Her appetite returned, and her muscles grew stronger until not only was she standing by herself, she was hobbling around the tiny hut, circling the room as her hand wore a clear line in the mud of the wall.

There were times when despair caught up with her, though, when her determination wavered in sync with her unsteady legs, and her captor's words haunted her. He was right; she would never walk properly again. She would never run or jump or climb. She would be crippled until her last. And yet, regardless of these truths, she persevered, each step leading away from the reality he had promised her and towards one of her own design.

∞∞∞∞

It was six weeks or so into this endeavour, while Iris was sitting pensively beside a small fire in her hut on a cool, moonlit night, that Chausiku came through the door unexpectedly. In her arms, she bore a folded length of dark brown cowhide and two branches that had been stripped of their twigs and fashioned into makeshift crutches. Iris stood up to meet her, folding her arms across her bare chest as she always did, and with a look of unspoken understanding, Chausiku unfurled the cowhide to reveal a long tunic that she slipped over Iris's head with a satisfied nod. In that one simple gesture, her carer's intentions became apparent: the time had come to venture beyond the familiar walls of the hut.

Holding tight to the crutches, Iris took her first steps back out into the world. The moon was full and bright, the landscape before her lit by its gentle glow. Behind her, she saw the other huts of the village dotted around a central area where a dying fire burned. The space sat empty now, but she knew it was the source of all the sounds that reached her during the day. Singing, music, the constant chatter of women as they worked, the laughter of children: these were the soundtrack of her days, the reminder that life continued all around.

Hearing the lowing of cattle, she turned to find lumbering silhouettes wandering through the expansive grassland that surrounded them. In the distance, she could see the moonlight reflecting off a large lake, a few flat crowned trees dotted here and there the only other features.

394

She stood still for the longest time, looking up at the blanket of stars stretching out to the ends of the earth and breathing deeply. Then, tightening her grip on the crutches, she hobbled over to a nearby tree not more than fifty paces away, Chausiku following close behind her should she stumble.

By the time she made it back to the door of the hut, she was exhausted, her legs and arms aching from the effort. Still, it was with a great sense of achievement that she lay back down on her bed and bid goodnight to Chausiku, knowing the next stage of her recovery had begun.

And so it was from then on that Iris would leave her hut in the quiet of the night, building her confidence unseen as the others in the village slept, her body growing stronger step by step until she could walk without the aid of her crutches anymore. As therapeutic as the endeavour was, though, the sleep that followed was plagued with the same inescapable nightmares, and she woke, more often than not, crying out for help, straw clinging to the cold sweat drenching her skin. No balm could heal the still bleeding wounds in her soul, and in the quiet of the night, when all she had for company were the shadows of her trauma, she longed for death to come and release her.

During the day, when her demons shrunk a little in the sunlight, Chausiku would visit, keeping her occupied by teaching her new skills. Although her legs were shattered and her wrists still bore their shackle marks, her hands had escaped torture for the most part. Whether weaving baskets, preparing food, tanning leather, or sharpening spear and arrow tips, Iris relished the opportunity to lose herself in her work and set aside the ghosts of her past, if only for a while.

Occasionally, one of the children would creep up to the door and peek inside, and Chausiku would wave them in to meet her. They would giggle when she tried to speak to them, and with wide-eyed wonder, they would touch her smooth, wavy hair and pale olive skin. With their tiny, innocent hands, those children helped to heal her fear of being touched.

Chausiku encouraged her to venture out, to meet the other villagers, but her lingering distrust of men kept her bound to the safe confines of her hut. After a while, Chausiku decided to try a new tack and began bringing women to work alongside them instead. Iris knew she was trying her best to integrate her into the community, but as pleasant as the company was, communication remained almost impossible.

She had picked up a few words, but only so much as to fulfil her basic needs, the rest left to hand gestures and a fair amount of guessing. As the women chatted around her, sharing stories and laughing at jokes she could not understand, a feeling of profound loneliness and isolation settled over her. She was welcome here, yes, but in her heart, Iris knew she was nothing more than a visitor, a crippled ward that had come into their charge.

In the evening, when the beat of drums and the chorus of rhythmic singing weaved their way in around her, Iris pondered the same questions she had since her arrival. Where was she? How had she come to be here? Who had rescued her, and how? Was it the man who'd visited her all that time ago? Would she ever see him again?

She would toss and turn, frustrated by it all, and as the music died down and the villagers went in search of sleep, she would take up her crutches and begin her walk in the company of the most vexing question of all. Was this to be her life? Was she destined to live out her days in this village, a world away from anything familiar, with no answers and no one to talk to?

∞∞∞∞

One day, out of the blue, Iris was startled awake by the sounds of commotion, the trample of feet and frenzied voices humming between the huts. Unaware of the meaning behind the words, she strained to discern the tone. It was not fearful or concerned; there was no panic to trigger her own. The voices were laced with excitement: fervent, unmitigated excitement.

Sitting up, she brushed the straw from her hair and tunic and tried to decide what to do. Her curiosity begged her to go outside, but her fear kept her planted on the ground.

Not a minute later, as her internal debate raged on, Chausiku rushed in and knelt down beside her, smiling ear to ear, a new shining bead Iris had not seen before hanging on her necklace. She pointed towards the door, then turned back to Iris, acting out with her fingers on her hand the motion of someone walking. Iris pointed to the ground to ask if the person was walking to her hut, and Chausiku nodded with a grin, tapping beside her eye twice and then pointing at Iris. A pang of anxiety sprung up in Iris's stomach at the thought of an unknown visitor coming to see her. Sensing her discomfort, Chausiku placed a gentle hand on her shoulder, gesturing with a downward hand for her to stay calm, and Iris realised who it would be.

The commotion seemed to be moving closer, and as the chatter died down, a man entered the hut: the same man who had come to see her when she'd first awoken. Staying by the door, he sat down, offering her a small smile. Chausiku squeezed Iris's shoulder and stood up, walking over to the man and saying something in a clipped tone before leaving them alone.

The man seemed to gather himself for a moment, then placed an open hand on his chest. "My name," he said, pausing to take a breath, "My name is Jelani."

Iris sat in stunned silence. It was the first time she had heard her native tongue in the longest time, and she barely knew how to respond. Her first instinct was to barrage him with questions, but she stayed her racing thoughts and instead chose a more cautious approach.

"My name is Iris."

A wide smile stretched across his face, softening his features and soothing the uncontrollable fear lingering in her heart. "Hello, Iris. I hope my Castilian is not too bad," he responded, his accent thick.

"No, it's good," she reassured him, something about the man putting her at ease. "How did you learn it? No one here understands me here when I speak."

"After I came to see you, I knew you would be scared of me until I could explain things. You talked in your sleep, so I decided to learn the words and travel until I found people who understood them. Eventually, a farmer in the south of Castile agreed to teach me his language if I worked with him. He had no sons and needed help with his crops. It took two years to learn enough to return to you, but I'm here now."

Iris stared at him in amazement. "I've been here for two years?"

"No, you have been here almost three years. You were close to death for six months after I brought you here, just conscious enough to give milk and broth to as you healed, and it was many more months before you were awake enough to move and talk."

"Three years," Iris repeated incredulously, rubbing her eyes as the thought of all the lost time sent her world spinning. Just then, his words registered, and she looked up at Jelani again. "Wait, so it *was* you that saved me?"

Jelani nodded and gave her a meek smile.

"But how? How did I get here? I remember being in a –" Memories of torture slammed into the forefront of her consciousness all at once, and she shuddered.

"I know you have many questions about what happened, but I think we should save the answers for another time," he said with a look of concern.

Iris nodded reluctantly, flashes of glowing coals and glinting metal still assaulting her.

Jelani slowly got to his knees and shuffled forward, but her mind spliced his face with the man who had caused her such pain. His name finally shook free of her scattered memories, sending a chill up her spine as it bounced around her head: Garridan. She screamed despite herself, pulling her knees to her chest as she began to hyperventilate.

"I'm sorry. I'm sorry!" said Jelani, scurrying back and disappearing out the door, calling for Chausiku.

Iris gasped for air, clamping her eyes shut to try and quell her fear and halt the flashbacks, but it was no use. Overwhelmed, she blacked out.

When she finally came to again, dusk was fast approaching, and Chausiku was sitting beside her, quietly weaving a basket by the firelight and humming a soothing tune to herself. Seeing Iris stir, she set down her work and smiled.

Iris sat up and looked around the hut. "Jelani?" she asked.

The answer she received made little sense as Chausiku played out the strange motion of wings flying through the air. Shaking her head in confusion, Iris watched as Chausiku seemed to search for the words to explain from the few local phrases Iris actually knew.

"Don't worry. Jelani come back," she said finally, her eyes scanning Iris's face to make sure she understood before reaching for a bowl beside her and handing it to Iris. "Jelani brought Iris. Eat."

Iris's mouth fell open as she saw the bunch of small, dark purple grapes in the bowl: the same grapes she would pick from the vines in

398

Castile as a child. Looking back up, she found Chausiku gathering her things and standing up.

"Eat," Chausiku said again, touching her gently on the shoulder as she retired from her watch and headed back to her own hut.

As Iris picked up the first grape and bit into it, the sweet juice bursting from its skin, a fleeting sense of comfort wrapped around her. In that moment, the innocence of her childhood didn't feel as distant or disconnected. The nostalgic flavour of the past returned her to a time before she became a canvas of scars, before her legs buckled under the weight of her trauma, before fear became her bedfellow. For just a minute, her helplessness slipped away, and she felt brave again.

When the last grape was gone, and all she had left was a bowl of stems, she lay down in the dying light of the fire, the comfort falling away, the cloak of grief she was so accustomed to draping itself over her once more.

Garridan's face was there to meet her when she closed her eyes, just as it always was, and so she opened them again, watching the embers as tears welled in her eyes. The torture he had inflicted on her body had been horrific, but the eternal torture of her mind was his true legacy. The vivid dreams she'd revelled in as a child no longer visited her. It was as though she had lost access to that part of her own mind.

In their place, there were only nightmares of the castle, of the shackles and the dagger and the rod. No matter how hard she tried, no matter how much time passed, the unshakeable memories kept her trapped. Her mind remained stuck in a tortured loop, her will to live pouring from her unhealed soul until she could barely breathe.

Settling into her melancholic nightmind, Iris thought of Jelani. She knew she should be grateful to him; after all, he had saved her from her fate. Still, part of her hated him for it, for the half-life she'd been left with.

Chausiku had said he would return, but she didn't want him to. She wanted him to go away; she wanted all of it to go away. Before she'd stepped through the door of that castle, she'd believed other lives were waiting for her beyond this one, lives full of love and adventure, but she did not long for them anymore. In their place, she longed for death, for nothingness, for oblivion.

∞∞∞∞

Two weeks passed before Jelani returned to the village. Chausiku came to fetch her just after noon, and together, with Chausiku holding her hand tightly, they walked out of the hut to meet him. Blinking into the sun she so rarely indulged in, she looked across to see Jelani standing beneath a tree, grasping the reins of a bay mare and stroking its neck.

Almost instantaneously, a deep fear rumbled within her, echoes of her past flashing through her mind of a bay horse and three men leading her to doom's door. They were about five paces away when the horse snorted, and Iris found herself overwhelmed, pulling her hand from Chausiku's and stumbling back to the hut as panic snatched at her breath.

An hour later, when she'd calmed herself again, Jelani came to the hut to see her. He kept his distance, sitting by the door as Chausiku followed him in and took her place at Iris's side, meeting her with a nod and a comforting smile.

Jelani looked at her, his face etched with regret. "I'm sorry, Iris. I didn't mean to upset you."

"I know. It's just..." she said, her voice shaking as she looked down at the wide scars on her wrists, the freshly unearthed memory sitting raw in her thoughts, "that was how my journey started. Three men found me in Castile. I was tired and hungry, and they told me a wealthy man had sent for me from far away. They bought me a horse just like that one and led me to the castle. Two of them knew what waited for me there. The one who didn't, they killed him right in front of me."

"I'm sorry," he said again, shifting nervously before he continued. "I brought the horse for a reason, though. There are places I need to show you, things you need to see for yourself."

She glanced up at him with a frown, his words stealing her attention away from her darker thoughts. "What things?"

"You are not like other people, Iris. Your soul has been born all over the world at different times, as different people. You have lived many lives, just as I have. We have known each other before."

"No," she retorted. "You're wrong. I'm not special, and I don't know you."

Jelani gave her a soft smile. "Tell me, before all this happened, did you ever have dreams so real they felt like memories?"

"No ... maybe ... no. They were just dreams. Silly little dreams of a silly little girl." Iris spat out the words as if scalding her inner child.

"They weren't dreams, Iris. You know it in your heart. You don't have to be scared of them, though. Things weren't always like this. You weren't always the victim," he said, his voice growing earnest. "I want you to come with me. Let me take you to the places you've lived before. It will help you heal, I promise."

"No! You're lying," she snapped at him, looking across at Chausiku for help. "Don't make me leave! This is the only place I feel safe."

"You will be safe with me. I won't let anyone hurt you," he pleaded.

"I can't," Iris said, shaking her head as she closed her eyes, a tear rolling down her cheek. "I can't do it."

Chausiku said something to Jelani, and he nodded, standing up and leaving the hut.

Gently, Chausiku took Iris's hand, searching for words she would understand. "Jelani good man. Iris safe with Jelani. Jelani help Iris be happy," she said before gesturing from Iris's heart to her own. "Chausiku want Iris happy."

Iris remained silent for a long moment, her mind replaying Jelani's words. They rang true, but she knew they couldn't be. The fantasy of past lives had just been a way of escaping her unhappy childhood, and following that fantasy had brought her nothing but pain. He was trying to trick her, to manipulate her. What if the man who'd sent for her was still out there? What if Garridan was still out there? What if they had sent Jelani?

Her anxiety spiked, and she was about to refuse again when something in Chausiku's expression gave her pause for thought. There was an honesty in the curve of her lips and the dip of her eyebrows like she knew something Iris did not, and all at once, she knew she had to go with him. She had to find out the truth.

"Iris go tomorrow," she said with a sombre nod, leaning over and wrapping her arms around Chausiku. As she squeezed tightly, she grappled with the fear of leaving the woman who had nursed her back to life, the woman who had been more of a mother to her than her own. "Iris love Chausiku."

With a smile, Chausiku kissed her on the head, hugging her to her chest. "Chausiku love Iris."

Even with Chausiku by her side, it took all the strength and courage Iris could muster to approach the horse. When she finally did, though, and her hand brushed its nose to the sound of a soft whinny, her fear yielded its throne. In the dark depths of the mare's eyes, she saw only goodness, trust, and safety.

With one last tearful hug, she bid farewell to Chausiku, and, taking a deep breath, she allowed Jelani to boost her into the saddle. As he began to lead the mare away, the villagers shouted their goodbyes, the children following in their stead until their parents called them back.

She took one last look at the cluster of huts she'd called home, spying Chausiku's shrinking shape amongst the crowd, and a pang of sorrow struck her. This place, these people, they'd saved her just as much as Jelani had, and with each step away from them, she knew part of her soul had been left behind. It lingered between the huts. It was woven into the baskets. It danced amongst the flames of the fire.

Home never stops being home, she thought to herself with a sigh. *No matter how far from it you wander or how long you leave it for.*

Turning back in the saddle to the unexplored expanse ahead, her mind turned to the future for the first time in years, a burst of anxiety striking her in the process.

"Where are you taking me?" she asked, looking across at Jelani.

"I need to show you things. Things to help unlock your memories," he replied, his eyes fixed on the horizon.

"I don't want to remember anything. Not from this life or any others you might think I've had."

"Not all memories are painful, Iris, and the ones that are, need to be faced and understood. Otherwise, when you die, you won't have the will to return."

She paused, dark thoughts creeping forth against her will. "When I die, I want to return to dust, not to life."

"And that is why we must make this journey," he said, glancing at her before returning his gaze to the road ahead. "To change your mind."

They travelled slowly north, stopping often to allow Iris's body time to adjust, her legs tiring quickly from their forgotten position astride the horse, her skin growing red in the harsh and constant sun. Jelani tried to engage in conversation, to unravel her story from this life, but her answers were short and reluctant, and in the end, he gave up. They ate in silence and slept in silence, Iris spending her nights alone with her nightmares in a small tent they carried with them while Jelani slept under the stars beside the fire.

Almost six months passed by the time they made their way beyond the Red Sea, through the Ottoman Empire, and to the eastern edge of Europe. Jelani carried a small pouch of coins with him, doling out its contents in exchange for more conspicuous clothing as they moved through changing landscapes without incident, although the odd pair did gain more than a few sideways glances and unwelcoming glares.

After a while, Iris began to recognise the flora and fauna, and she began to fear she was being led right back to Râşnov and the hell hidden in its forest. Despite Jelani assuring her otherwise, her unease continued until, on a snowy mid-winter day, they reached the coast of the North Sea in Ostend, the water assuring her that the castle and the nightmares held within it were far behind her.

Here, they traded their horse for passage to England, and as Iris leant against the railing of the small merchant ship headed for Dover, breathing in the salty air, she allowed herself a quiet moment of introspection.

The trip had taken its toll on her, stripping away any glimmer of hope she'd once had that she might learn something to help her heal. Jelani had promised her the journey would unlock lost memories, and yet her mind remained filled only with the shadows of Garridan and all he had put her through. She did not know where they were going, nor did she care anymore. Her trauma had left her hollow, and in doing so, she had become apathetic to her fate.

When they reached the shores of England, Jelani left her to rest on the beach, and she settled onto the sand, looking out at the boats bobbing on the water alongside the towering white cliffs. She was enviously watching the seafoam dissipate on the sand, wishing she too could dissipate from the world, when he returned with a piebald mare in tow.

With their dwindling funds, she was baffled how he had managed to acquire the beast at all. Still, with a permanent limp marring her gait and draining her even in short stints, she was thankful she would not be forced to continue the journey on foot.

Back in the saddle, Jelani began the march again. As always, he seemed to be leading them by memory, as if following an invisible trail of footprints he'd left himself, but nothing felt familiar to Iris regardless of how many times he asked her.

They wound their way north down muddy roads and through quaint towns until they reached the sprawling expanse of London. Passing through the narrow streets, Jelani's eyes flitted from building to building, searching for absent landmarks. He stopped passers-by here and there, miming out what he was looking for in the hopes they could help, but it was all for naught. From what she could gather, he sought a well, hidden amongst the warren of streets, but hours passed, and their hunt remained fruitless. Eventually, the crush of people and buildings left Iris feeling claustrophobic, and Jelani was forced to concede defeat.

"It's all so different from my memories," he lamented as they left the bustling metropolis behind. "Everything is so new. It's like the whole city has been replaced, and nothing of the past exists there anymore."

"Maybe it has been replaced. Maybe the past has finally found somewhere to rest where the present can't disturb it anymore," she replied wistfully before the two of them fell back to silence.

∞∞∞∞

A week later, just after dawn, Iris woke to the sound of drizzle on her tent, her breath escaping her mouth as a wisp in the crisp air. With great reluctance, she pulled up the hood of her cloak and crept out to continue yet another day of relentless travel, her companion already dampened by the dismal weather.

Their path seemed as indistinct as ever, and she found herself on the verge of refusing to continue, her body spent, her mind convinced the trip was a pointless endeavour. Still, as she looked over at Jelani, a sense of duty sprouted in her chest. Not only had this man saved her from the violent hands of Garridan, he was now doing all he could to repair the damage those hands had wrought.

His face had weathered dramatically, his feet bloodied and bruised from the rough terrain and immeasurable distance they'd traversed, and yet he did not complain, nor did he ever request to share the horse with her. With a determination and conviction she could not understand, Jelani had walked half the world in search of a remedy for her woes, to try and fix her shattered soul, to prove she was more than she believed herself to be. It was in that moment, as she watched him wipe the mix of rain and sweat from his brow, she found a deep respect and gratitude for all he'd done for her.

Shifting in the saddle, Iris allowed the feeling to settle within her, and it was then that she realised something that struck a chord in her heart. That feeling of thankfulness, that profound appreciation for his existence in her life, was the first familiar thing she'd felt on the whole journey.

As the sun reached its zenith and the rain eased, they came to a town where a river met the sea. Left alone on the banks, she waited with the horse for Jelani to return, watching the water lap softly, each wave bringing with it a sense of anticipation she could not explain.

When he did finally reappear, he led her down to the docks, helping her off the horse and handing the reins to one of the fishermen, who gave him a satisfied nod and pointed at a small wooden boat moored on the pier.

"Where are we going now?" Iris asked as he guided her to the boat.

"There is a small island not far from here we need to visit."

The crossing from Ostend to Dover had been rough, and she was more than a little worried how the tiny boat would fare on open water, but Jelani seemed confident, and so she warily climbed into the rickety vessel. As he threw in their packs from the horse and slid the rope from the pier, she gripped the ageing wood tightly, her muscles tensing as he pushed them from the safety of the shore with one of the oars.

"How did you get this boat? You don't speak their language," she asked him as they made their way towards the mouth of the river.

"Trade doesn't require words, only willing people," he replied matter-of-factly. "He got the better end of the deal, though. That horse was worth far more than this boat."

Iris didn't reply, instead turning her attention to the horizon in the hopes of quelling the seasickness growing in her stomach as they slipped out onto the sea, the waves growing choppier.

After an hour or so, her dull worry morphed into alarm. Water was slowly pooling in the base of the boat, seeping in through the planks, and she began to fret it would sink long before they reached land again.

"We're not going to make it!" she exclaimed, scooping out the water inching closer to her ankles with cupped hands in a futile attempt to fend off the inevitable.

"Don't worry. I won't let anything happen to you," Jelani reassured her, glancing over his shoulder at the still distant island and pulling harder on the oars.

The water was halfway up their shins when he suddenly stopped rowing, and Iris could feel the boat sinking lower, bucketfuls splashing in over the side as each wave hit them.

"We're going to drown! I can't swim!" she said with a look of desperation.

She had wished for death for so long, and yet when faced with the dark, fathomless depths beneath her in that moment, she knew this was not the way she wanted to leave the world.

Jelani took a deep breath and grabbed her hand. "Iris, I need you to close your eyes and trust me."

"No. I can't!" she shouted as cold panic set in.

"Please. It's the only way. I won't hurt you."

Iris closed her eyes, panting for breath, the water lapping against her thighs, the boat almost level with the sea. "What are you going to do?"

"Something we've done together once before," he whispered, his breath warm on her ear as he wrapped his arms around her waist.

Suddenly, the hairs on her neck and arms prickled, her ears popped, and her stomach seemed to drop to her feet. She could feel herself being lifted upwards and out of the water, the cold air chilling the dripping tunic clinging to her legs as it flowed past them, almost as though they were flying.

The sensation confused her, so she cautiously opened an eye, peeking over Jelani's shoulder to see the white-tipped waves far below. Suppressing the urge to scream, she clamped her eyes shut again, clinging tighter to him until, much to her relief, she felt the ground under her feet.

He let go of her, and she found herself standing safely in a meadow at the centre of a small island. Turning full circle, she took in her surroundings: the long, yellowing grass and swaying bluebells that rippled in the whistling wind; the broad, shady hazel tree at the far end; the rocky border protecting them from the raging sea; and the small stony beach to the north. As she reached the end of her rotation, her eyes fell on Jelani, and she stumbled back a few steps in surprise. Large black wings stretched out behind him, dancing with ethereal dark energy and black lightning.

"I've had dreams ..." she said, pausing as she stared at him in disbelief, images of the winged figure from her childhood returning in flashes. "I've had dreams about someone like you."

"Not *like* me," he replied with a smile, his wings dispersing into the wind.

"I don't understand. What are you saying?"

Jelani gestured for her to follow. "Come with me."

Iris walked with him across the meadow until they reached a jumble of overgrown ruins beside the hazel tree. The toppled stones sat battered by wind and sea spray, but it was clear enough that a small house had once existed there, the base of the walls still standing to knee height, although they seemed on the verge of collapse.

"We lived here together once, twice actually, a long time ago," he said, looking over at her.

It seemed as though he wanted to say something more, but he left his thought unfinished and led her over to a solitary, vertical shard of stone poking up from the soil beside the ruins like a headstone. Shifting the long grass out of the way, she knelt down, tracing the faint outline etched on its weathered surface with her finger. She couldn't quite make it out by sight, but as she followed her finger with her eyes, she realised it was the image of two wings.

"These look just like your wings. Did you do this?" she asked Jelani, who had crouched beside her.

"No. I have no memory of this stone," he replied. "Do you?"

She turned to it again, a dream she'd had as a teenager tugging at her, but it was hazy and indistinct. The more she tried to grasp it, the more it slipped away, its whisper growing fainter until it faded entirely and was replaced by the everpresent swirl of more tortured thoughts.

Slowly, Iris shook her head. "I ... I don't think so."

A brief expression of defeat crossed Jelani's face, but he stifled it with a forced smile. "That's okay. Let's camp here for a couple of days. You can explore the island and see if anything comes back to you. Then we'll leave."

Iris nodded, sensing a disappointment in him that mirrored her own as she retraced the wings, wishing more than anything she could retrieve the buried dream from her mind. Still, this mere glimmer of remembrance had finally given her hope that the trip was not pointless. It inspired her to believe there was a chance that what Jelani had told her, what her innocent heart had known all those years ago, was true.

∞∞∞

In the days that followed, the pair came together only to eat. Jelani whiled away most of his time in pensive thought on the stony beach, and Iris spent her time exploring the island in its entirety. No matter how much she searched, though, she could not conjure up anything more than a vague feeling of familiarity or a fleeting sense of déjà vu.

Regardless, something about the island made her feel safe for the first time since she'd left her hut. As such, she was gripped by a pang of sadness when she woke on the fourth morning to find Jelani packing up their things.

"Do we have to go?" she asked with a frown.

"We do," he nodded, rolling the tent up and tying it with a leather strap. "We are almost out of food, and there are other places we must visit. The sooner we leave, the sooner we arrive."

Iris watched as he kicked dirt over the dying coals of the fire and shouldered the pack. "How will we get back to the mainland, though?"

Jelani opened up his arms. "The same way we got here."

Iris was petrified of flying again, but there was no alternative, and so she gripped him tightly and clamped her eyes shut, her breath bated until she felt her feet touch the ground.

"Stay here. I'll be back soon," Jelani whispered as he released her.

There was a thud and a whoosh of air across her face, and she opened her eyes to find she was alone in a forest clearing, the packs resting unattended at her feet. Turning her attention to the sky, she caught sight of Jelani high above, his black wings just visible against the looming clouds as he banked towards the south and disappeared.

It was almost dark when Iris heard rustling amongst the ash trees and peered between the trunks to see Jelani emerge into the clearing on a horse. As the piebald mare stepped out from the shadows, she realised it was the same horse they had sold to the fisherman.

"Hey, isn't that –"

"It is," replied Jelani, dismounting and starting to gather tinder for a fire.

"But how did you get it back? It's not like you could return the boat."

"I took it," he shrugged nonchalantly.

"You mean you stole it?"

"Depends on how you look at it. The fisherman gave us a boat he knew would sink as soon as it hit open water, so I see it more as a refund than stealing." Crouching down, he struck a piece of flint with a small knife he'd pulled from one of the packs, sparks showering down over the jumble of kindling, a small flame springing up in the waning light. "Come, warm yourself. We'll make camp here tonight, and tomorrow we'll begin our journey to the north, to a place where there is little warmth but hopefully plenty of answers."

Sitting down in silence, Iris shivered at the thought, and in the growing flames, her mind recreated the warm interior of her hut and the gentle smile of Chausiku she missed so much.

∞∞∞∞

The month that followed was laborious and tiresome as they travelled north into Scotland in search of passage across the sea to Norway. By a stroke of luck, they managed to find a Norwegian timber merchant docked in Aberdeen who spoke a little Castilian, and they managed to negotiate a place aboard his ship.

The merchant was less than enthused about the idea of allowing a woman aboard and seemed perplexed as to why they wanted to travel from one country in the midst of famine to another. Still, he was desperately understaffed and so agreed on the proviso Jelani help his crew during the voyage.

They sailed at dawn, the pair boarding the ship without their horse, having traded it for a few sacks of grain, two pairs of worn but solid leather boots, and a bundle of warm clothes. All around them, brawny, hardened men scurried across the deck and clambered up the rigging, Jelani leaving her side to join them.

Their unwelcoming leers triggered a sense of crippling vulnerability in Iris, and so, looking to escape, she confined herself below deck, the horrors of the castle creeping out from the dark, creaking corners and plaguing her in sleep and waking. In need of a distraction and hoping to ease the distrust of the men on board, she did her best to help where she could, filling her three days at sea by washing and darning their clothes and assisting in meal preparation.

By the time they finally docked in Bergen, after a journey graced by fine weather and favourable winds, the merchant's concerns about her had fallen away. As such, he gifted the pair a small pouch of coins as he bid them farewell.

Walking down the gangway, they found themselves amidst the bustle of the port. Burly men shouting in thick, guttural accents lugged goods along the road and flitted in and out of the brightly-painted, gabled buildings running parallel to the water's edge. Seeing her grow agitated by the chaos, Jelani shouldered their packs, took Iris by the arm, and ushered her away. As they wove through the streets, the gaunt, sombre faces of the locals passing by served as clear evidence of the famine they were enduring.

Jelani and Iris reached the edge of the city soon enough, buildings yielding to farmland, snow still clinging to the ground despite it being late spring. A short distance out of town, they stumbled upon a despondent farmer standing beside a stocky, tan gelding at the edge of a freshly sewn field. After a series of spirited hand gestures between the men, Iris watched the farmer hurry off with a sack of their grain as Jelani threw the packs over the horse's hindquarters and boosted her onto its back.

A week of slow, gruelling travel came and went, and although the mountains and fjords that surrounded them were breathtaking, Iris found the freezing temperatures difficult to endure. The seeping cold made the bones in her legs ache, and her teeth chattered ceaselessly as they trudged along.

On the seventh day, Jelani drew the horse to a stop amongst a copse of pines just past a quernstone quarry. Iris watched him as he paced between the trees and crouched down to inspect the fragments of rock dotted here and there. They appeared to be tool marked, their edges too unnaturally shaped to be carved by nature's hand, but if the area had once been part of the quarry, she reasoned it must have been centuries ago. Without a word, he returned to her side, took the horse's reins, and led them onwards. She wanted to ask him what he was searching for, but it was clear from his pained expression that whatever memory was buried there was a wound she would be best served leaving closed.

A few hours later, the road they were following delivered them to the edge of a field.

"What's wrong?" Iris asked, turning to see a look of dejection on Jelani's face.

"It's nothing. There used to be something here, but" –he spun full circle– "it's not here anymore."

Glancing around, Iris spotted a small village a short distance away and the silver trunks of a birch forest undulating up the slope of a mountain beyond the field. None of it looked familiar, and yet something tugged at her, an indecipherable message echoing from an unknown place deep inside her soul.

Jelani watched her for a moment before pulling the reins and leading them towards the village. "Let's see if we can find lodgings here. We need a good rest out of the weather."

That night, nestled happily into the rare luxury of warm furs and a soft straw mattress, Iris was met with the most incredible dream. In it, she found herself standing in a ring, clad in jet black leather armour, a blonde braid resting over her shoulder.

Boisterous spectators called out from the edge as a fearsome, bearded warrior swung a massive axe at her, and with an agility she no longer possessed, Iris danced around him. Dodging his advances with ease, she nimbly cut him down with two long knives, wielding them as though they were extensions of her own hands. As he fell defeated into the dirt, she opened her eyes to a brand-new day, her heart full with a joy she had not experienced in years.

Just like when she was young, her dream felt more akin to memory than fantasy, and as she lay there, soaking in the warmth of the bed, Iris finally allowed herself to truly believe once again that she had lived before. After all, if the winged figure she'd dreamt of as a child was lying in the next room, surely it wasn't too farfetched to believe the rest of the images were also real.

As Jelani led them out of the village, Iris told him of what she'd seen, her words laced with the same emphatic vigour she'd had as a child. Unlike the dour expressions her father used to pull at her stories, though, she instead found a broad smile stretched across Jelani's face.

"Why are you so happy?" she asked.

He opened his mouth but caught himself before he uttered a word, pausing as he rethought his answer. "I wasn't sure if we should continue, but now I am. I want to take you further north, to a special place hidden in the wilds. It will be a long, hard journey, but once we arrive, I believe you will understand why I smiled."

His words sounded more like a riddle than a response, and Iris sat confused by their meaning. It didn't really matter to her if she understood or not, though, nor did it matter how arduous the journey might be. For the first time, she was excited by the prospect of a trip that might actually hold some answers, and as the horse clopped along the dirt road, Iris noticed a change within herself.

This dream, this tiny snippet of forgotten bravery, had restored in her soul the resolve she'd bled out on the dungeon floor, and in doing so, the seeds of healing began to sprout.

∞∞∞

Five weeks passed, and the days grew longer until the night was only signalled by a slight dimming of the sky, summer slowly thawing the stubborn blanket of snow, although the chill remained. As they travelled, Iris became more vocal, creeping further out of her shell until her conversations with Jelani morphed from the stilted exchanges of acquaintances to the playful chatter of friends. With each word, smile, and laugh, the pair grew closer, and Iris no longer felt lonely.

The further they ventured from civilisation, the more the landscape began to resonate with something deep inside her. The winding rivers, the snow-capped peaks, even the curious animals rang a bell she recognised the sound of and yet could not place. To her, each dense forest seemed like a maze she had already deciphered, and when Jelani paused to decide on a direction, she could swear she knew the way before he did, the sensation akin to the pull she had once felt drawing her across the ocean.

One afternoon, as the gentle sunlight filtered in through the pine needles, they reached the edge of a majestic lake, the mountains beyond reflected on its surface, its banks dotted with tiny, white wildflowers.

"This place seems so familiar," Iris said as she admired the landscape.

Jelani bent down and plucked a stem of flowers, handing it to her with a smile. "Come on. We're almost there," he said, tugging the reins and leading them back into the trees.

Iris brought the flowers to her nose, their herbaceous scent mixing with the heady aroma of pine needles. As she tucked the stem into the clasp of her cloak, she could have sworn her hands were paler, the horse's tan coat exchanged for ivory. Blinking in surprise, she found everything to be as it should, and she shook the idea out of her head with a laugh.

Only a short while later, they stepped out from the trees to find themselves at the base of an embankment that ran up to meet the mouth of a cave cut into a large crag of rock. Helping her down from the saddle, Jelani tied the horse to one of the pines and returned to her side with the packs.

"Just wait here a minute. I need to check it's safe first," he said, scurrying up and disappearing into the cave.

Iris was just starting to grow concerned when he emerged again, returning to her side with a grin and gesturing up the embankment. She was barely four steps in when her right leg gave out from under her, and she yelped in pain.

"I've got you," Jelani said, catching her before she hit the ground and acting as a crutch.

"Thank you," she replied as they reached the top, peering past him to see a fire already burning at the far end of the cave. "How did you –"

"I came here several years ago while searching for my own memories. There were still a few logs left," he replied, reaching out his hand to her. "Here, let me help you. The rock is slippery in places."

Sitting down beside the fire to warm her icy fingers, she watched as Jelani set about fixing them a meal from their meagre grain rations and a small animal he's managed to catch and kill the previous day, although Iris could not identify what the strange beast was. As the smell of cooking meat filled the cave, an overwhelming feeling of déjà vu swept over her and remained there until she fell asleep, warm and satiated.

That night, Iris was visited by another vivid dream, this time of a long journey through blinding snow and of a young man close to death. When she awoke, something within her beckoned her to the mouth of the cave, and she staggered over.

Images flashed through her mind one after the other: battles and victories, long talks and melancholy moments, lights dancing across the sky. Finally, the scenes faded to black, and she was left with the feeling of deep love followed by overwhelming loss, and she dropped to her knees under the weight of the emotion.

"Iris, are you okay?" Jelani asked, hurrying over.

"I don't know. I was dreaming, and then there were all these flashes. I don't understand any of them, but they feel like memories," she replied, disorientated by it all. "It feels like I've been here before."

"You have," he replied. "We were here together, just like on the island."

"What are you talking about?"

Jelani took her hand gently in his. "Hundreds of years ago, in another life, you saved me. You brought me here and put me back together."

"I saved you," she repeated, the face of the young man from her dreams replacing his for a split second.

"Yes. You pulled me back from the abyss. The same way I'm trying to pull you back now."

"No, that can't have been me," Iris said, shaking her head and frowning. "The woman in the dream, in the flashes, she's strong and fearless."

"She was you. She *is* you. You've just forgotten who you are. What happened to you in Râşnov fractured your mind. It broke your connection with your soul. You need to let go of your past in this life to find your past in others. It's the only way you can reclaim who you really are."

"I don't know if I can," she said, her shoulders falling in defeat. "The memories of Garridan, of the torture, they never go away. It all still feels like yesterday."

Jelani tilted his head until she met his eye again, and he gave her a soft smile. "There are some wounds that time can't heal, but you can grow around them, Iris. You can make them smaller by making other

414

parts of you bigger. It might take years, it might take the rest of our lives, but it will be worthwhile if it helps you to discover your true self again."

Iris was pensive for the rest of the day; in fact, she spoke very little over the two weeks they spent at the cave, instead spending her time exploring the area in search of answers. Jelani accompanied her, lost in his own silent reflection as they ventured back to the lake or through the forest.

The more she looked, the more she seemed to see, fragments of the life they had shared coming back to her. Some fragments were filled with joy and love, others with profound sadness, but whether good or bad, each memory, each emotion, did just what Jelani said. They grew inside her, flourishing, filling the empty spaces until the trauma she carried felt smaller; not absent, but smaller.

One afternoon, Jelani found her sitting under a pine not far from the cave, mindlessly stroking the rigid bark and humming one of Chausiku's favourite songs.

"Am I disturbing you?" he asked, crouching down beside her.

Shaken from her thoughts, she looked over at him with a calm, serene smile. "No, no. I'm just taking it all in. It's still hard to fathom that all of this is true. Everything I believed when I was younger, I was right all along."

Pausing, her mind led her back to the shores of Castile and the pull that had lured her there on that fateful day five years ago.

"Have we shared every life together?" she asked.

Jelani grinned as if it was the question he had been waiting for. "We have both lived many lives, me more so than you, but they have not always been together. There are many things we do not have control over: when we will die, where we will be reborn, how soon our memories return to us. No matter where we end up, though, from our first life together to this one, there has always been a bond between our souls, a pull that draws us towards each other and to the places that mattered to us. Sometimes, if we're lucky, we are able to reunite before fate intervenes, just like we have in this life and just like we did in the life we shared here centuries ago."

"You must have been disappointed when you found me this time," she said, looking down at the scars on her wrists.

Running her fingers over the marks, the image of her equally scarred face reflected in the placid waters of the lake came back to her. Iris had so often thought herself ugly in her youth, her skin too dark, her hair too unruly, her forehead too short, but when she'd looked in the lake, when she'd finally seen the true extent of what Garridan had done to her, she'd mourned the beauty he'd stolen.

"Disappointed? You are everything I want in this life and more," he said, his expression laden with guilt as she glanced up at him. "I just wish I'd found you sooner."

She wanted to reach out and take his hand, to ease the blame he'd burdened himself with, but something stopped her, her trauma remaining a steadfast barrier to the next stage of her life. In that moment, once again paralysed by her past, Iris came to realise an irrefutable truth, a truth Jelani had tried to instil in her on the very first day of their journey. Until she confronted the source of her pain and disarmed it, she would never be free of her shackles.

Steeling her resolve, she announced a desire she never imagined possible. "I want to go back."

"Back where?" he asked.

"To where my pain began."

∞∞∞∞

The waxing gibbous moon hung high over the forests surrounding Râşnov when they finally landed by the river outside the castle walls. It had been fifteen days since they'd set their horse free and left the cave. Fifteen days of travelling by night. Fifteen days of Iris facing her fear of flying wrapped in the arms of the only man to ever offer her a feeling of comfort and safety. Looking across at him, his wings dissipating into the mild, late-summer breeze, she could see that he was weary, but there was a hard edge to his expression that resonated with her own pounding heart.

Before them, the castle cut a sharp outline amongst the soft, swaying edges of the forest, but no sound or movement came from the monstrous place. It sat abandoned, ivy slowly enveloping its walls, forgotten by all except the two who now stood in its presence once again. As they drew closer, Iris looked up to the gargoyles lining the parapets, her eyes flitting from one to the other until they reached the fifth and stopped. On the back of the grotesque sentry, trapped in place by the stone spikes running along its spine, sat what appeared to Iris to be a ribcage, the bones stripped clean and catching the light on their ivory surface.

"That was the fate of the man who tortured you," Jelani said, his voice cold.

"Garridan," Iris replied. "You killed him?"

"And all those who served him. None survived that night except you."

"Even the man who sent for me, Garridan's master?"

"He was already dead long before I arrived. He rests in the west tower."

All at once, a firm resolve took hold of Iris, and she hobbled off, rounding the corner of the castle. She heard Jelani call after her, but she didn't stop, passing through the open gate and across the courtyard until she came to the towering wooden doors. Reaching for the handle, she stopped, images of Garridan flashing before her, his limp hair shining in the firelight, his rehearsed hospitality, his predatory smirk.

"Are you sure you want to do this?" Jelani asked, catching up to her.

She stared at her shaking arm, fighting back the fear clawing at her. "I have to," she said, her hands curling into defiant fists.

Jelani just nodded, shouldering open the door, its rusting hinges creaking as it swung inwards. Disappearing inside, he fumbled in the dark for a moment before Iris felt the hair on her neck prickle and saw a light spring up. Appearing with a flickering lantern, he held out his hand to her.

"Will you show him to me?" she asked, stepping inside. "The man who sent for me, the man in the tower. I need to see him for myself."

"If you're sure," he replied.

Jelani led her across the antechamber to the tower, each step reverberating around the space, the smell of dust and mildew heavy in the air. Gritting her teeth to help bear the pain, Iris ascended behind him until they reached a room high above, the candlelight catching on the dust of the almost empty space as it was kicked up by their sudden entrance. It was through the dance of dust that she saw him, the desiccated corpse of the man who had orchestrated her torture, the master of a game of chess she'd never wanted any part in.

417

Limping over to the slab of stone upon which he lay, she took in his grim features in the dim light. His skull was hugged tightly by a mask of dry, blackened skin, and his frame was so frail and skeletal it was almost inconceivable that he had ever been capable of anything at all. As she touched his threadbare clothes, she finally found a place to lay her blame.

"When you were young, when you used to dream of someone like me, did you ever have nightmares of a dark figure?" Jelani asked, stepping to the other side of the slab. "Someone who stalked you from the shadows, who hunted and killed you again and again?"

Iris frowned, trying once more to access the dreams from her youth only to find them blocked. "I can't remember. Why?"

"There is a man who has lived more lives than us, a man who does not want to share the power we have, and so he taunts us, he hunts us, he tries to do all he can to make us want to never return to life. He does not have wings like me but blades that sprout from his back like the legs of a spider. I believe this is him," –he looked down at the corpse– "was him. I believe he wanted to break your soul. I believe that it is why he ordered for you to be tortured. His name, the one he takes with him, is Anasazi."

As soon as the words met Iris, a deep sense of dread sprang up in her chest, as if he'd just spoken to a part of her she didn't even know existed. She had never heard the name, yet it triggered an inexplicable fear that shook her very being and contorted her face.

"Don't worry, Iris," said Jelani with a reassuring smile. "Even if he is alive somewhere out there, it will be a long time before he remembers who he is and comes in search of us again. Time will keep us safe for now, and when it can't anymore, I will be there to protect you."

Iris nodded slowly, the name still sitting uncomfortably in her mind as she tried to bury it again. "Will you take me to the dungeon now?"

"Follow me," he replied, ushering her back down the stairs and towards a long passage to the left of the great hall.

About halfway along, her foot hit something, and she looked down to find a sprawled skeleton devoid of everything except a decaying pair of leather boots and a rusted sword. Hearing a rattle, she peered past Jelani to spot seven more ill-fated souls dotting the corridor, the skull of one about ten paces ahead moving of its own volition. Suddenly,

418

there was a squeak, and a rat peeked its head out of one of the eye sockets before scurrying out, Iris's arm flying out to grab Jelani as it scampered past.

Picking their way between the bodies, the pair continued, coming to a stop outside the last room, the wall that had once held the door laying in rubble around them. As she stepped tentatively inside, Iris found herself beside a four-poster bed, its sheets nothing more than moth-eaten shreds, the down stuffed mattress riddled with holes from the plague of rats she knew must nest within it.

"This is where you left me," she said, touching the post gently.

"I couldn't leave you strung up down there, so I put you here while I dealt with the men," he replied, his voice choked with anger.

Iris reached out to him, taking his hand in hers, his rage seeming almost tangible on his skin. "Thank you," she said softly.

Jelani nodded at her, his eyes moving to the large hole in the far wall. "You don't have to go down there."

"I do," she replied, taking a breath and letting it out slowly to steady her nerves. "I have to see it, to enter it on my own terms."

She took the lantern from his hand and made her way to the top of the stairs. Clenching her teeth, she plunged ahead before she could stop herself, Jelani right behind her as she reached the bottom and stepped into the inky black space.

The familiar smell of stale, musty air met her at the door, and her heart quavered. With shaking hands, she crept inside, the candlelight catching on the metal brackets lining the walls and the single chain hanging from the roof, the hook at its end sending a shiver down her spine.

Jelani stood silent at the door, and she wandered to the centre of the room, each step bringing with it echoes of the past, as if her screams were trapped within the very stone itself. Stopping beside the brazier, her hand gently touched the metal rod sticking out from the undisturbed pile of ash at its base, tears welling in her eyes. Tortured memories flashed before her uninvited until she could swear the smell of her own burning flesh still lingered in her nostrils.

Shaking the thoughts away, she walked across to the hook that had held her hostage for so long, crouching down to find her broken shackles laying on the flagstones, her blood still upon them like macabre black paint. The sound of their clinking chain triggered something deep inside her, and in an instant, she was completely overwhelmed. Her tears transformed from a trickle to a flood as she sobbed uncontrollably, the shackles falling back to the floor beside the lantern.

A strong hand guided her to her feet, and she collapsed into Jelani's embrace, crying into his chest as all of her pain, all of her trauma, poured out.

When the emotion eventually ebbed, she lifted her head. "How did you find me that night? How did you know I was in trouble?"

Jelani's face grew distressed, as though he were reliving the events again in real-time. "I was travelling the world, searching for the places from my past, searching for answers, when I was struck by the most intense pain. I didn't know what it was or where it had come from, so I ignored it. It came and went in waves for months, growing in intensity each time until I finally realised it was not a physical pain but something much more profound: a signal, a beacon."

He frowned before continuing. "After that, I began having different dreams about my past. The blank spaces that had once been there were suddenly filled with images of a soulmate I had forgotten about. One night, I dreamt of a girl with chestnut hair and green eyes, the same girl I had shared the island with. In the dream, the same intense pain pulled at my soul, and I followed it until I found her being attacked by a group of bandits. When I awoke, I knew the pain I was feeling wasn't mine; it was my soulmate's."

Taking her hands in his, the weight of his guilt forced him to his knees, tears streaming down his face. "It's all my fault, Iris. I should have figured it out sooner. I should have known. I'm sorry. Please forgive me."

Iris knelt in front of him, enveloping him in her arms, her heart breaking in empathy for the undue guilt he had carried with him all this time. "The blame is not yours to bear," she whispered. "You saved me."

For a long moment, forehead to forehead, nose to nose, the pair cried not for themselves but for one another, each tear love in liquid form.

Sitting back, Iris wiped Jelani's cheek with the edge of her cloak, realising as she did that the trauma she'd been choked by for so long had finally lost some of its grip, its claws filed down.

"We should go. There's nothing left for us here," she said, picking up the lantern and rising to her feet, her words resolute.

Jelani followed suit, but as she tried to take his hand and lead him out, he pulled away. "I can't leave yet."

"Why?" she asked, feeling the hair on her arms and neck prickle.

He looked down at the broken, blood-smeared shackles, then turned to Iris again, rage sharpening the angles of his face. "There's something I need to do. Something I should have done the day I took you from this place," he said, a low hum starting to fill the air, wisps of dark energy drifting off his skin like smoke.

Iris backed up against the wall as his wings appeared from his back, their shafts alive with black lightning. Holding the lantern up to illuminate his face, she saw something foreboding flicker in his eyes and her heart began pounding in her ears.

A single word escaped his lips. "Go!"

Without a second thought, she turned on her heel and limped as fast as she could to the door, ascending the stairs with gritted teeth, the pressure rising behind her. She was just stepping back into the bedchamber when she heard an explosion, the door of the dungeon slamming shut and then shattering into a thousand splinters. Widening her halting gait, the candle barely alive in the wildly swinging lantern, she used the wall to steady herself as she hobbled towards the front door.

Iris was halfway across the courtyard when she felt the ground begin to rumble, the hum replaced by an ear-piercing whine, but it wasn't until she reached the safety of the treeline that she finally turned around. In the moonlight, she saw blocks of stone tumbling down from the parapets and thumping onto the dirt. A whirlwind of energy began whipping around the castle, picking up leaves and debris as it sped up. Then, all at once, the chaos came to a crescendo, and there was a thunderous detonation, the castle torn asunder, stone catapulting outwards.

Iris threw herself behind a tree, crouching down and covering her head as debris shot past her, a few of the larger fragments snapping off tree branches or lodging themselves in trunks.

In the aftermath, when everything fell still, Iris opened her eyes to find the head of one of the gargoyles lying beside her, its tortured expression seeming somehow more apt in that moment. Standing up, her ears ringing, she peeked cautiously around the tree and blinked in disbelief. The castle was no more, its once-imposing silhouette demolished save for the eastern tower, which, as she watched on, groaned momentarily before toppling to the ground to join the rest of the rubble.

As she crept from the trees, Iris searched the settling debris desperately for movement, for a sign of life. She was just about to call out his name when she saw Jelani emerge, marching towards her, his face grim, his skin almost ghostly white from the layer of dust clinging to him.

"You didn't have to do that, you know," she said as he approached.

Jelani held out his hand, gently brushing her scarred cheek with the backs of his fingers, the tears welling in his eyes catching the moonlight as one broke free and cut its way through the dust. "Yes, I did."

∞∞∞∞

The journey had returned to Iris not only her sense of self but her soulmate as well, and with its purpose served, they made their way back to the East African village they'd left behind.

Their arrival was met with joy, the pair enveloped in the kind of genuine embraces Iris had never experienced from her kin. Of course, there was one face she sought more than any other. Hearing a familiar voice, she turned around to find Chausiku, a pang of sorrow lancing through her as she saw the eyes she knew so well clouded over, the hands that had brought her back to life reaching for her blindly.

"Iris?" said Chausiku, patting along Iris's arm and up to her cheek.

Feeling the scar on her neck, Chausiku smiled and bundled her into a bone-crushing hug that melted away Iris's sorrow in an instant. Jelani appeared beside her, and all of a sudden, they were both in the arms of Chausiku as she burst out in a jumble of words Iris could not understand but knew were full of love.

Escaping her grasp, Jelani fumbled for something in one of the packs and presented Chausiku with a small pebble just like those that lined the stony beach of the island. Watching on with a smile, Iris saw him slip Chausiku's necklace over her head, undo the knot, and poke the leather strap through the hole he had carved in the pebble. As he draped it over her once again, Iris realised that each one of the beads, shells, and stones was a promise of return fulfilled.

After that, their life settled into some form of normality. Iris and Jelani lived together in the hut she had longed for so often on their travels, the feeling of cautious affection between them evolving each day into a deep, comfortable love. Only in his arms could Iris find true peace, only in his arms were the nightmares of the castle kept at bay, and although there were physical aspects that weren't possible, their bond never faltered.

And so it was for sixteen years, their days spent in service of their community, Iris picking up the language enough to finally converse fully with Chausiku as they worked side by side. In the quiet of the night, their time was dedicated to refining Jelani's power and trying to unlock Iris's. Despite the attempts, though, Iris struggled to harness her energy, as if the scars her trauma had left on her soul remained as clear and immovable as those on her skin.

One morning, Iris awoke later than usual, Jelani still snoring at her side, and a sudden jolt of panic pierced her stomach like a dagger. Each morning she was reluctantly stirred by the perky sound of Chausiku at their door, and yet the sun shining in around the cowhide covering was not the gentle hue of dawn but the bright light of day.

Scrambling to her feet, she limped outside, what she already knew in her heart confirmed by the huddle of people crowded at Chausiku's door. The group parted as she approached, her heart shattering as she stepped inside the hut to find Chausiku lying lifeless but peaceful on her bed.

Iris fell to her knees with a yelp, gently lifting into her lap the head of the woman who had been nothing less than a mother to her. Weeping inconsolably, she stroked the deep laugh lines of Chausiku's face, longing more than anything to see the smile that had made them, Jelani appearing by her side and closing her eyes one last time.

Chausiku was buried beside the lake the next day, wrapped in cowhide, her necklace still resting on her chest as Jelani helped the other men fill the hole, the villagers coming together to mourn their most beloved elder.

Music, dance, food, and drink filled the night in celebration of her life, and as Iris sat beside the fire watching the festivities, Jelani joined her.

"How are you?" he asked gently, taking her hand in his.

Iris shrugged. "It doesn't feel like home without her."

"Maybe it's time we leave then."

"Where would we go?"

Jelani lay back on the still-warm earth, pulling her into the nook of his shoulder and looking up at the stars. "The island. If we're to leave here, that's the only other place I would like to be. This village has been our home for this life, but the island is home for our souls."

Iris stayed silent for a moment before nodding slowly. "Tomorrow. I've said enough goodbyes today."

∞∞∞∞

Dark clouds were approaching from the south when they landed on the island, the wind whipping across the water and sending the waves crashing into the rocks around its edge. Despite the wild weather, Iris breathed a contented sigh as Jelani's wings dissipated into the air. They were home.

Salvaging what he could of the ruined foundations, Jelani reconstructed their former cottage, using pieces of their past to surround them in their present. When he was finished, he carefully carved a butterfly into the stone above the hearth as a mark of his affection: a reminder their love lived within its walls.

As for Iris, she procured some seeds from the mainland and set about resurrecting their once-bountiful garden around the wing carved headstone. The constant smattering of spring rain was a boon to the venture, and when coupled with the nuts from the hazel tree and Jelani's newly discovered aptness for fishing, they were more than self-sufficient by the end of the summer.

In the evenings, when the temperamental weather allowed, they would visit the stony beach and watch the sunset together, immersing themselves in the soothing sound of the waves rolling in. It was on one such evening, as they stood on the stones, swaying gently in each other's arms to a tune only they could hear, that Jelani grew sentimental.

424

"Iris, my beautiful butterfly," he said, waiting for her to look up at him before he continued, "You are a marvellous creature. There is a power inside you that I can see as clearly as the sun's light. You are the strongest person I have ever met, a treasure that I am honoured to hold as my own." With a smile, he leant in and kissed her gently. "I love you, Iris. I always have, and I always will."

Iris looked up at him, stroking his cheek, the hairs on her neck prickling as deep emotion swelled in her chest. "I love you too. Promise you'll find me again in the next life."

Jelani squeezed her hand gently, holding her out at arm's length to admire her in the golden hues of the sunset. "I pro-"

Suddenly, Jelani's body jerked unnaturally, and blood sprayed over Iris's face. He stared at her, his eyes wide and unfocused, four black blades protruding from his torso.

As she opened her mouth to scream, she felt something slam into her back, pain lancing through her like hot knives. Looking down in shock, she saw the same black blades extending from her own body, each one pulsing with a power she could feel beneath her skin. She lifted her hand, trying to touch them, but as she reached the one piercing her sternum, she realised they were not made of steel. In fact, they weren't tangible at all, her hand passing straight through them like smoke.

Croaking for air, a trickle of blood spilling from her mouth, Iris turned to see a young man at their side. His skin was a deep olive, his black hair short and curly, his features strong, his eyes so dark she could not see where his pupil stopped and his iris started. He grinned at her viciously, and as her focus drifted past him, she realised that he was the source of the blades, each one arching from his back like the legs of a spider.

All at once, the blades disappeared, and she felt herself stagger for a moment before falling to the ground beside Jelani. Warm blood flowed down her skin, soaking through her clothes and filtering into the pebbles beneath her as Jelani reached out and took her hand, his mouth gaping like a fish out of water.

The young man crouched down, leaning over her. "It wasn't hard to find you again, Iris. As soon as I rediscovered my memories and my power, I came for you," he hissed, his words Castilian but his accent

425

unfamiliar. "Did you really think you'd escaped? That it was over? Foolish girl. I am Anasazi. There is no freedom from me in this world. There is nothing here for you except pain. Spare yourself the torture. Release your soul to the aether."

Iris coughed, blood splattering the pebbles as she heard Anasazi stand up. Her eyes remained fixed on her soulmate's, the life slowly draining from them as his hand fell limp and slipped from her faltering grasp. In the edge of her fast-narrowing vision, Iris saw two blades descending, and then there was nothing, only darkness.

Theo

Streaks of light rained down like shooting stars, their mesmerising beauty illuminating the night and calming her anxious heart until the decision became the easiest she'd ever made. She walked over to the edge of the balcony, peering down to the ground far below, the cool evening breeze running its fingers through her hair, beckoning her with the scent of flowers and freshly turned earth.

Tying the rope to the railing, she slipped the noose around her neck and climbed over, leaning out to arm's length. It would be better this way, for everyone; she knew it in her heart. The world would spin smoother unburdened by her presence, her family would no longer have to waste their time pretending to care, and Auryn would finally be free to live the life he deserved.

With one final breath, she closed her eyes and stepped out into oblivion, willingly and without regret.

Mist swirled around her, the weight she had carried for years lifting from her shoulders, and she found herself standing in a cemetery beneath the sprawling branches of an oak tree. The sun shone bright overhead, birds chirping merrily as she looked across to see a coffin topped with purple flowers poised above an open grave, her own name etched into the headstone beyond: Theo Shaw. On either side, she found her mother and father, their faces resigned but otherwise unaffected, each checking their watch in turn before walking away.

Suddenly, a third figure appeared, and her heart skipped a beat. From the shade of the tree, she watched Auryn fall to his knees beside the coffin, his shaking hands resting on its lid, his head bowed, a single tear falling to the ground. She wanted to comfort him, to tell him that she loved him and it was all for the best, but as she took a step forward, something appeared beside her, reaching out to block her way.

Glancing across, Theo was met by a being shrouded in energy, tendrils of purple light stretching from its back, latent power surging through its body and charging the air until her skin began to prickle. Despite its haunting appearance and unclear purpose, the being filled her with a feeling of calm and comfort. She searched its face for discernible features, for a way to read its intentions, but she found only empty eye sockets, its sightless gaze boring through her as though to look upon her soul.

Again, she moved to pass, and again, it blocked her.

"Please, I need to speak to him," she said in earnest.

The being shook its head. She could offer Auryn no comfort, not anymore.

"Can I watch over him at least? I need to know he's okay."

After considering her request for a time, the being finally nodded.

Theo went to thank them, but before she could, they dissipated into the air like smoke, the breeze whisking them away.

For decades, Theo followed Auryn, the years slipping past like minutes. She had only planned on lingering until he filled her absence with a happier life, but that time never came. Instead, he existed as a mere shell of the man she had left behind, adrift and joyless. He sought no new connections, wrote no stories, played no music. Encased in his grief, he wandered the world as little more than a ghost.

Eventually, when age had drained the colour from his hair and time had stolen the life from his eyes, he settled into the indented cushion of his couch, Theo unseen at his side, and took his final breath. She expected him to appear as she was so they could move on to the next life together, but as his body fell limp, she remained alone, as though his soul had simply dispersed into nothingness.

For two weeks, Theo paced that room, watching his body decay, waiting to hold him in her arms again, until finally, she accepted the unimaginable. She had lost him forever.

∞∞∞∞∞∞∞∞∞∞∞∞∞∞

Jolting awake with a gasp, Theo opened her eyes to the empty left side of her bed, the banded moonlight creeping through the curtains and falling across the sheets like the bars of a cage. A squinting glance over her shoulder revealed it was barely four o'clock, and as she lay there for a moment, her heart aching, she knew she wasn't going back to sleep, not yet.

428

The dream crashed loudly around her head, knocking into the delicate supports she propped herself up with until she was left trapped in the rubble. As the dust settled, she found herself alone with a thought she had been playing host to for some time now, and one her dream only served to amplify: the thought that Auryn would be better off without her. In spite of her best efforts, Theo couldn't seem to shake the feeling she was a burden on him, that if she removed her emotional baggage from his life, she would clear the path for happiness.

As her mind settled even further into its morbid musings, Theo found herself growing restless, and so she rolled out of bed, heading for the balcony in search of fresh air. The night was crisp, and as she stepped out onto the cold tiles, she wrapped the blanket from the couch tighter around her shoulders, ambling over to the wrought iron railing and gazing out at a world asleep to her sorrows.

In the quiet, her thoughts returned to other occasions when, in her darkest of nightminds, she'd contemplated death by her own hand. Her suicidal ideation had led her to consider many routes over the years, but she always seemed to find flaws in them. Jumping in front of a train was too messy and inconvenient to others, overdosing was too much of an exact science, slitting her wrists was painful and slow, and shooting herself required access to a gun.

When she eventually snapped back to the present, it was to find herself staring over the railing at the protruding balcony of the apartment three storeys below. As her eyes traced the blurred grout lines of the tiles, she acknowledged for the thousandth time that a fall from where she stood was likely to cripple but not kill.

With that option off the table, her mind once again circled back to the benefits of hanging herself. It would be fast, effective, clean, and if she got it right, entirely painless. Of course, there were still things to consider: the length of rope needed to ensure her neck snapped, the best knot to secure it to the railing, the ideal time of day to ensure no one would try and stop her. Beyond those details, there was also the aftermath to contemplate. If she did it inside, it would be Auryn who found her, and she couldn't bear that to be his final memory. Out here in the open, though, she would be taken down long before he had a chance to see. In a perfect world, she'd just disappear, and no one would have to deal with her body, but the world wasn't perfect, and thus she could only choose the lesser evil.

Auryn would be upset when he found out, that was sure enough, but he would be better off in the end. In her absence, he would soon move on to someone who filled his days with unmarred joy, and in the midst of that joy, he'd realise her death had been the best possible outcome for their relationship. When it all came down to it, he would be grateful for her sacrifice, her act of selfless love.

Out of the blue, the image of purple tendrils and eyeless sockets reappeared in her head, and she found her last train of thought rocking on its tracks, her certainty wavering in the presence of this phantom. Turning back to the balcony door, she peered inside at the familiar silhouettes of her furniture, and from somewhere beyond the tempest of her depression shone the warm memories of her time with Auryn.

In her mind, they were dancing once again to a tune only they could hear, his face alight with a love she struggled to comprehend. What if her dream was right? What if her death condemned him to an existence devoid of love, hope, and happiness, where there was no light in his eyes and no song in his heart? What if, in sacrificing herself, she wasn't saving him at all?

Theo's hands shook as she scrambled desperately to organise her swirling emotions, to find safe ground amidst her internal battle, but her entire being was at odds with itself. Agitated, she returned to her room to grab her phone before sinking into the cushions of the couch. As she sat in the dark with her thoughts, the screen suddenly lit up like a beacon over stormy seas, guiding her to safety. Auryn was on his way over from work. She just had to survive until then.

∞∞∞∞

When he'd finally arrived, Theo had kept the night's events to herself, acting as best she could as though she'd been asleep only moments before, roughing up her hair and mumbling a sleepy hello. As she'd slipped back under the covers, she'd snuggled into them like they weren't cold from her absence, faking sleep until Auryn's breath eased into a smooth, shallow rhythm. Only when dawn began to creep through the curtains did she manage to find rest again, the light of a new day offering respite from her melancholy machinations.

430

As they chatted over lunch, she did not divulge the details of her dream, and as they debriefed on the week's happenings, she made no mention of her thoughts of suicide. She did not want to burden him with the weight of her sorrow, and determined not to, she masked it all beneath the rehearsed smile she had learnt to don more than a decade ago. Between scenes, in the backstage of the bathroom, she removed the mask for a moment, sobbing silently away from prying eyes before returning for the next act dry-eyed and buoyant. It was a performance rehearsed so often that it had become second nature to her, polished to the point of flawlessness.

None the wiser to her plight, Auryn had, with a satisfied smile on his face, announced that he was taking her out for dinner, although he would not tell her where. Such secrecy played havoc with Theo's anxiety, but she didn't have it in her to dampen his mood, so she did her best to rebrand her apprehension as enthusiasm.

With her hair straightened and pinned back, Theo slipped into the same strapless, black dress she'd worn to every vaguely formal occasion for the past eight years. Pulling it up, she couldn't help but feel like its fabric was woven with the heavy threads of social expectation. Sewn into each stitch were the remnants of every family event she hadn't quite felt welcome at and every party from which she'd longed only to escape. As uncomfortable as those memories were, though, she refused to buy into consumerism's assertion that each event required its own unique garment, and so it retained its position within her wardrobe.

As they stepped out the door, she pleaded with him once again to tell her where they were going.

"Just a little place I've been wanting to visit for a while now. Don't worry. You'll love it. They have the best desserts in Melbourne," he said, intertwining his fingers with hers.

They were halfway down the block when she realised where he was taking her: Porphura. In an instant, Theo's anxiety increased tenfold, her heart pounding in her ears at the thought of having to face her colleagues outside the familiar confines of her section. When clad in the armour of her chef's jacket and wielding her knives, she had the confidence to handle whatever Porphura threw at her, but with bare shoulders and loose hair, she felt unprepared, exposed, vulnerable.

She wanted to object, to insist they go literally anywhere else, but as she looked over at him, she saw on his face an excitement she could not bear to trample.

"Here we are!" said Auryn, opening the door for her.

Forcing a smile, she stepped in to be greeted by her least favourite co-worker.

"Theo!" said Craig, swanning over with a level of smarm that made her skin crawl. "I barely recognise you out of your whites. You look like an actual girl."

"The booking is under Auryn Berenger," said Auryn, appearing beside her and cutting Craig off before he could say anything else.

"Ahh, yes. I'm Craig, by the way. I'm sure Theo's told you all about me," he replied, his hand touching the small of her back as he ushered them across the restaurant, every part of her yearning to punch him.

As they sat down at their quiet corner table, Auryn watched Craig disappear to harass another table of unfortunate souls before turning to her with raised eyebrows. "Wow. You weren't kidding, huh? That guy is ... something."

Theo couldn't help but chortle. "Don't say I didn't warn you."

"It's a small price to pay to finally try your masterpieces. You know, I'm tempted to skip mains and just order the entire dessert menu," he said with a playful wink.

Suddenly, Craig appeared beside them again, handing them menus and clicking his pen ceremoniously as he pulled a pad of paper from his apron. "Drinks to start? I can suggest some fabulous wines."

"Can I get a Kraken, ginger beer, and lime?" said Auryn before turning his attention to Theo. "You want a drink, beautiful?"

Part of her wanted *all* of the drinks, but she was acutely aware she would have to face everyone here in a couple of days, so she decided to play it safe and pass on the offer. Besides, in her current mind frame, there was a fair chance that alcohol would lead her to a darker place.

"Just water, thanks."

"You okay?" Auryn asked as Craig scurried off.

"Yeah, I'm fine," Theo nodded, producing the most reassuring smile she could muster and standing up. "I'd better go say hi. I'll be back in a sec."

As she walked through the dining room, dispensing polite waves to the bartender and other waitstaff on the way, she couldn't help but notice how different the place seemed through the eyes of a customer. Amongst the soft house music and glinting polished stemware, Theo felt a stark disconnection from the pressurised world she was used to on the far side of the pass.

To her, Porphura was everything the dining room wasn't. It was glaring fluorescent light bouncing off stainless steel to the sounds of broken plates, clanging pots, and crashing cutlery. It was chefs shouting over the incessant chirp of the docket printer as the searing heat doused their jackets in sweat. It was three minutes, two minutes, one minute. It was adrenaline to the last. There was calm waiting for her in that chaos, but here, in the company of congenial dinner conversation, sipped drinks, and paced food consumption, she felt out of place.

Reaching the warm halo of the heat lamps, she peered across the pass to find Peter wiping the rim of a plate and pushing it forward.

"I didn't know you were coming in tonight," he said, catching sight of her as he rang the bell.

"Either did I," she shrugged with an awkward laugh.

He nodded knowingly, his eyes flitting to the new waitress who had just appeared beside her. "Table thirty-three. Two eye fillet: one medium-well, no charred onions, cover one; one bleu, mash instead of Pommes Anna, sauce on the side, cover two."

Theo stifled a grin as the poor girl just blinked at Peter, who unapologetically rolled his eyes.

He pointed past her to a table across the room. "You're going to that table there. This one is for the man, and this one is for the lady," he said slowly, pushing the plates forward one at a time as he spoke.

"Yes, Chef," she said meekly, taking the steaks and scurrying off.

Peter sighed and turned back to Theo. "Don't worry about the menu. I'll sort you out. No allergies, yeah?"

"No allergies. Thanks, Chef," she said before catching Ruth's eye and giving her a quick nod.

Sitting back down, Auryn looked up from the menu. "Everything sounds great on here. What's your favourite?"

"No need to pick," she replied, taking the menu from his hands and placing it on the side of the table. "Peter said he'd organise it."

433

"Awesome. I knew coming here was a good idea."

Internally, Theo was anything but enthused about eating the food she spent every day surrounded by, but as the candlelight caught in Auryn's eyes, she found in them a genuine joy that melted her annoyance. It was then that she understood. To him, coming to Porphura was a well-intentioned show of support; it was, of its very essence, a display of love, and one that not a single other person in her life had ever made.

All at once, an overwhelming feeling of melancholy swelled in her chest again, a frightening realisation materialising from the darkness. Everything she had in the world was, at that very moment, contained within the walls of Porphura. Her place beside Auryn and her place at the bench just across the pass were the entirety of her existence, the dishes written on the dessert menu her only tangible legacy to the world should she cease to exist. As the gravity of the thought settled on her shoulders, she suddenly felt utterly insignificant.

"What's wrong?" Auryn asked, his words dragging her back to reality.

"Nothing," she replied.

"You sure?"

"Uh-huh," she nodded, tearing a corner from the slice of baguette that had appeared on her side plate without her noticing. "Just lost myself for a second."

Before he could press the issue, the first of their dishes arrived, and she let out a silent sigh of relief for the distraction.

Auryn devoured each morsel with gusto, asking her a million questions as he went, and Theo, finding herself stripped of an appetite, used her in-depth answers as a way to hide the fact she was eating very little. Of course, part of her felt guilty for only picking at it all, especially given that Peter and Ruth had clearly put in extra effort to deliver off-menu dishes for her benefit. There was rare roasted duck with Jerusalem artichokes and brandied cherry jus; pepper-crusted beef carpaccio with fresh peas and horseradish crème fraiche; and pan-fried scallops with charred corn puree and chorizo. Every plate was immaculate, and yet it seemed to Theo that her depression had muted all their flavours, every listless mouthful a cruel denial of a pleasure she held dear.

When the desserts came out, she could tell by the plating that Ruth had taken the reins. Each dish was almost identical to Theo's own handiwork, albeit lacking an iota of her finesse. Her mind picked up on microscopic differences no one but her would notice, from the marginally askew jug of dark chocolate sauce with the mandarin soufflé to the minutely oversized quenelle of burnt honey ice cream beside the port poached pear.

Disinterested in eating food she'd prepped only the day before, she pushed them over to Auryn, who seemed to inhale them with great fervour, only taking a breath to sing her praises before hoeing into the next plate.

Excusing herself to bid her farewells while he scraped up the last few skerricks, Theo popped her head into the kitchen to see Ruth packing down her station.

"Hey, Theo," Ruth said with a smile, twirling a roll of masking tape on her finger as she spoke. "What did you think? I tried to spice it up for you."

"Yeah, thanks for that. You know how it is when your family wants to visit your work," she replied, taking herself off guard with the realisation she'd just referred to Auryn as family for the first time.

"Ergh, yeah. Remember that week I came in twice because my sisters wanted to try the food with me, but they refused to eat together?" Ruth empathised. "So, was everything okay?"

"Duck was a bit salty," Theo jibed.

"Salty!?" snapped Ruth with mock outrage, plonking down the gastro tray she had taken from her fridge. "I'll have you know that duck was perfectly seasoned!"

"If you're a cow looking for a salt lick, maybe."

"What about your desserts then? Did I get a passing grade on those?"

"I don't know. The stem of the poached pear was facing out instead of in. I'll give you a B-," Theo replied with a wry grin. "No, they looked great. Can't say I felt like eating any myself, but Auryn's currently out there going to town, probably contemplating if it's socially acceptable to lick plates in public."

"So, you guys going out after this? We still haven't caught up for that drink, you know," Ruth said, swearing under her breath as she ran her fingernail around a roll of cling wrap for the third time, trying to find the end.

"Maybe another time. I'm still pretty drained from yesterday. Anyway, I'll let you get back to it. Is Peter in the office?"

"No, he left before you even got your desserts," Ruth replied, rolling her eyes. "He said to say bye."

"Of course he did. Well, have a good one, yeah. I'll see you Tuesday."

"Night, babe."

Wandering back across the restaurant, Theo found Auryn putting on his jacket.

"It's all paid for," he said, flashing her an innocent smile as she opened her mouth to protest. "I know, I know. I'm supposed to be saving, but I thought you deserved to be spoilt, just this once. Besides, they didn't even charge us for the desserts."

"Just this once," she echoed, her mind once again not knowing how to process his act of kindness and so turning it into the usual mix of sadness and guilt.

"Did you want to grab a drink somewhere or just go home?" he asked as he walked her to the door, escaping into the cool night air before Craig could peel away to accost them.

"Home, please."

Theo remained quiet on the walk back, Auryn continuing his praises and trying to elicit a smile to no avail. As much as she wanted to appease him, her mask of false joy had grown too heavy to lift now they were without an audience, and by the time they arrived back, his face had dropped a little.

As they stepped into the comfortable privacy of the apartment, he took her hand in his. "I did bad, didn't I? I'm sorry."

"It's okay. I just ... I don't know. Work is work. It's hard to relax there. I'm glad you got to see it, though, and I'm glad you liked the food."

"And here I thought I was doing something for you when in reality I was doing it all for myself," he said with a grimace, squeezing her hand. "I don't know why you keep me around."

As his last sentence reached her, the insecurity it carried threw her for a loop. Her entire day had been filled with feelings of inadequacy, a sense that she was a burden to him. She'd stood convinced that it was him keeping her around against rhyme or reason. With that one sentence, though, with that one vulnerable admission, the mortal thoughts that had been clawing at her returned to the dark and distant corners of her mind.

Cupping his cheek in her hand, she kissed him. "Because the darkness would win if you weren't."

Auryn

"Oh, for fuck's sake," Auryn muttered to himself as the stem snapped off the wine glass he was polishing.

The doors to Benzin hadn't even opened for the start of what was sure to be another absurdly busy Saturday night service, and he already knew it was going to be one of those days. His shift had started with the grim discovery that the glasswasher wasn't turning on, and everything had spiralled downwards from there.

True to form, Adam had refused to organise someone to fix it until Monday to avoid paying weekend rates to a repairman, and Auryn's rational explanation about potential lost revenue had fallen on deaf ears once again. When coupled with the twenty minutes he'd spent unclogging one of the toilets and Janet calling in sick less than an hour before the start of her shift, Auryn was already close to the end of his tether before the first customer had stepped through the door.

As he wrapped the broken glass in paper towel, tossed it in the bin, and began polishing the next one, he could feel the ball of anxiety in his stomach growing heavier, the feeling of entrapment adding to his simmering rage. In the past few weeks, his usual annoyance with the bar had transformed into a deep loathing, every fibre in his body becoming ever more sensitive to even the most minor irritant. In spite of that, though, he had doubled down, picking up extra hours and poring over the bar's numbers in an attempt to secure a raise.

When he struggled to find the will to continue, he would conjure up Theo's face in his mind and repeat the promise he had made her. Looking down to the end of the bar, Auryn sighed, his imagination painting her into the scene, placing her gently atop the stool on which she'd captured his heart. The next day would mark six months since she had walked into his life and changed it completely: six months of arched eyebrows and impish grins, of laughter and tears, of feeling like he'd known her forever.

While the thought of her usually propelled him on, in that moment, with his temper close to flashpoint, a tiny part of him blamed her for his predicament. In promising to fulfil Theo's dream of travel, he had become burdened with the weight of obligation. No matter how much he wanted to quit, to just walk out and leave the chaos of Benzin behind, he couldn't. To leave would be to let her down and worsen a depression he knew was already begging her deeper into its embrace.

As he turned the wine glass beneath the cloth, he found himself awash with a swirl of emotions: helplessness, guilt, shame, despair. Not knowing what to do with them, his mind did what it so often did; it converted them all to anger. And with that, he felt the stem of a second glass break in his hands.

∞∞∞∞

It was just after one in the morning, and the bar was three deep with customers. Auryn was up to his elbows in soap suds, washing glasses at reckless speed, drying them, and sliding them down the bench to Tony and Olivia, who scrambled to keep up with orders. As fast as his hands were moving, though, his brain was outpacing them, his body running almost robotically as his mind continued seething at the message he had received from Adam an hour before.

In the middle of a service he himself had wantonly made harder, Adam had mustered the gall to send an abusive text chastising Auryn for using petty cash to purchase toilet paper after their supplier had failed to make their delivery. Mumbling profanities under his breath, Auryn dumped the next stack of glasses into the sink. The entire situation was utterly ridiculous. Carlos was drinking the place out of business, and instead of confronting the real issue, Adam was questioning whether toilet paper was a necessary business expense.

As ludicrous as Adam's behaviour was, though, the appearance of Carlos in the venue inspired far more dread amongst the staff. Auryn didn't really care if the man drank himself to death, but his alcoholism had reached new depths, and as a result, his actions were becoming more reprehensible by the day. Most nights, he rocked up completely plastered, then proceeded to hand out free drinks like it bore no consequences, insisting they stay open past their licence just so he could keep partying.

Despite his demands breaking several laws, there was no reasoning with him. If anyone dared to refuse him service, he simply pulled the 'I'm the boss' card, marched behind the bar, and served himself.

The few jobs he was actually responsible for were either abandoned or shambolically executed, with two DJ's almost getting into a fight the previous night when they'd both turned up to perform at the same time. This was, of course, due entirely to the fact that drunk Carlos had booked one and failed to tell even drunker Carlos, who had then booked the other.

To top it off, he was growing increasingly sleazy with the female bartenders, making derogatory comments, forcing shots on them even if they were driving, and touching them inappropriately whenever they were close by. Every instance made Auryn bristle, but with his job security in the hands of the perpetrator, he was handicapped in what he could do beyond trying to intercept Carlos before he got anywhere near them.

Just when Auryn was starting to think they'd dodged having to deal with his antics for the night, Tony appeared at his side, unloading two towering stacks of glasses beside the sink.

"Hey, man. I know you're not in the mood for this right now, but Carlos just rocked up."

"Of course he fucking did," Auryn said with a grimace. "Where is he?"

"He grabbed a beer from the fridge and disappeared to the courtyard. I don't think he has anyone with him, but I'm sure he's out there trying to make friends."

Auryn took a deep breath and dried his waterlogged hands. "All right. Can you man the fort for a minute while I go touch base?"

"No troubles, bubbles. Good luck!"

Why now? Auryn thought to himself as he stepped out from behind the bar, wading through the gyrating masses on the dance floor towards the courtyard at the rear of the venue.

Stepping outside, he was robbed of the night's refreshing chill by the gas heaters dotted around the sparsely lit space, the air thick with the suffocating smell of smoke wafting from the bleary-eyed patrons reclining on the wooden benches. As he scanned the courtyard, his heart pounding with an acute anger he was desperately trying to

441

wrangle, Auryn spotted Carlos sitting with a cigarette and a half-finished beer between two couples he was clearly making uncomfortable.

"Auryn!" Carlos shouted, flicking his butt onto the concrete, his eyes glazed. "Hey, everyone. This is my manager, Auryn!"

Smiling politely, Auryn stamped out the still smouldering cigarette under the watchful eyes of the unwitting bystanders who'd turned to observe the spectacle. "Can I speak to you for a moment, Carlos?"

"Sure thing, buddy," Carlos replied, wavering a little as he stood up and followed Auryn inside.

Leading him over to the relative quiet beside the storeroom door, Auryn scrambled to think of something to say, knowing full well that he couldn't tell Carlos he was saving the customers from his unwanted company. At times like these, distraction was far more tactful than honesty.

"So, what did you need to tell me?" Carlos slurred.

"Umm, yeah, I ..." Auryn fumbled before remembering something perfect for Carlos's level of inebriation. "I just wanted to let you know we refused entry to a group trying to sneak in someone underage, and they called the cops."

"*They* called the cops?" Carlos asked incredulously, finishing his beer.

To be fair, it wasn't a lie. A bunch of teenagers had tried to get into the club earlier, and when security discovered one of them had a fake ID, they'd confiscated it and refused entry to the entire group.

"Yeah. The cops rocked up to see what the deal was, and when we handed the officer the fake ID, the kids cracked and confessed. They got off with a stern warning and disappeared pretty quick. It was hilarious. Anyway, the cops praised the security and told me we were one of the best-run venues in Melbourne."

"Really?!" Carlos replied, raising his eyebrows in amazement.

"Yep, just thought you'd want to know."

Carlos clapped him on the shoulder. "Good work, Auryn! Come on. I think this calls for a shot." And with that, he marched off towards the bar, the desire for more alcohol seeming to steady his gait.

Auryn hurried after him, swearing to himself as he cut through the crowd, reaching the bar just before Carlos, hoping to mitigate the damage. Grabbing two shot glasses, he reluctantly took down a bottle of top-shelf tequila, waving it at Carlos and luring him away from Olivia, who appeared to be shaking her head and miming the act of driving home. As he poured the shots, he spotted Tony arriving back behind the bar with another stack of glasses and gestured with his head for him to join them.

"Bottoms up, boys!" shouted Carlos, sloshing his drink.

"Cheers," replied Auryn and Tony in unison, giving each other a knowing look before downing their shots.

"Chuck us another Estrella, will ya, Tony," said Carlos, pointing wildly at the beer fridge until his wish was granted before wandering off into the crowd again.

Letting out a slow, measured breath, Auryn allowed the burn of the tequila to empathise with his anger and returned to the sink, which was now overflowing with glassware, all of his previous progress undone. If nothing else, he just wanted Carlos to refrain from doing anything stupid for the remainder of the night, or even better, remove himself from the venue entirely.

Auryn's wish was not to be, though. When he finally turned the house lights up at three o'clock, it was to find Carlos appearing from the courtyard with four heavily intoxicated older women in tow, the group making a beeline for the bar. All of them looked to be in their mid-forties, clad in dishevelled, slinky dresses designed for women half their age, and sporting smeared make-up and voluminous hairstyles as loud as their voices.

Sidling over beside Tony, Auryn soon discovered Carlos had just ordered a swathe of cocktails, once again playing gracious host at the expense of his staff, who were clearly trying to pack up the bar.

"I've got it, man," said Auryn, relieving Tony from the hassle and setting about making yet another round of free drinks for people Carlos had likely known for the whole of ten minutes.

With the order finally complete, Auryn carried the drinks over to the booth they had plonked themselves down in. As he slid the glasses to their gaggling recipients, he explained in his most upbeat customer service voice that the bar was about to shut, gesturing at the last few stragglers making their way out the door and the DJ packing up her gear.

Ignoring his sentiment, Carlos simply waved him away and turned his attention back to the women without a word.

Twenty minutes later, as Auryn placed the last clean glass onto the rack to drain, he looked over at the booth again, a loud cackle of laughter exploding out from one of the women and echoing around the otherwise empty venue.

Clenching his jaw in his frustration, Auryn moved to exit the bar.

"You want me to do it?" Tony asked.

"No, I'll do it," he replied with a sigh. "That's why they pay me the big bucks, right?"

Tony gave him a half-hearted chuckle, picking up a cloth and settling in to polish the endless array of glasses awaiting him.

Before he'd even reached the booth, Auryn could hear the women giggling like schoolgirls and pestering Carlos for more cocktails. Finding himself between the same rock and hard place he'd been forced to endure more times than he could count, Auryn readied himself for another heavily rehearsed performance of diplomacy.

His mission was to convince Carlos to leave the venue whilst simultaneously making him believe it was his idea: a task he already knew was about as easy as convincing a hyped-up toddler that they actually wanted to go to bed. Of course, after years of having to deal with the same scenario over and over again, he'd picked up a few tricks to help things along. As much as Carlos loved to flex his authority and show off his bar, he was, at his core, a people-pleasing attention seeker. All Auryn really had to do was get the women to bat their eyelids at Carlos and egg him on a bit; after that, his superiority complex would do the rest.

"Hey, Boss," said Auryn picking up their empty glasses with a forced smile. "What are your plans?"

"Dunno. What do you girls want to do?" Carlos asked, looking around the table.

"WE WANT TO DANCE!" one of the women shouted.

"Well, we can't play any more music here because of the noise restrictions, unfortunately. We can't afford another visit from the police," Auryn said, glancing over at Carlos, who was nodding sagely, "but I'm sure Carlos knows somewhere you ladies can dance, and I'm sure he'll happily shout you all a round of parting shots."

The women already looked eager without the bribe of alcohol, but he knew it would take a tipple to entice Carlos from his seat.

"Can you take us somewhere, Carlos? Pleeaassee," the woman beside him begged, squeezing his leg as the other three scooched out of the booth and stood up, tugging at his arm and adding their pleading whine to the chorus.

"I might know a place," he replied, throwing a smug grin in Auryn's direction in a bizarre attempt to elicit envy.

Oh, if you could only see this without the beer goggles, Auryn thought to himself, trying not to laugh as he walked back to the bar and set up a row of glasses, filling each one with Cafe Patrón.

"OMG, this tastes just like espresso martinis," one of the women groaned with pleasure as she took her shot alongside the others. "I looove espresso martinis. We should have espresso martinis. Carlos, take us somewhere with espresso martinis."

"Sure thing, babe. Whatever you girls want," replied Carlos, giving Auryn and Tony a quick wave before wrapping his arms around the shoulders of his entourage and leading them out the door.

"Do you think she likes espresso martinis?" Auryn asked Tony with a smirk, both of them bursting into laughter as a high pitched 'Woo!' filtered down the laneway from their still departing guests.

Tony flashed him a tired smile. "It's like herding cats. How you haven't committed bloody murder in this place, I'll never know."

"Welcome to management, my friend. One day, if you work really hard, you too can become a professional adult babysitter," Auryn replied before surveying the mess revealed by the unflattering glare of the house lights. "So, do you want me to do the cash or clean up?"

Tony shook his head. "Neither. Go home, man. You've done too many hours this week already. Me and Liv will sort it out. Go see your missus and have a rest."

"I can't leave you with all this. It looks like a bomb's hit the place. Besides, Adam will –"

"Fuck Adam," said Tony, batting away his concern and grabbing him by the shoulders. "Dude, I don't want you to take this the wrong way, but go the fuck home."

Auryn let out a relieved laugh. "Not all heroes wear capes. Thanks, man."

"Go on, get outta here."

With Tony shooing him out, Auryn grabbed his bag, waved goodnight to Olivia, and stepped out into the cool night air. The distant sounds of thumping music and drunken reverie carried on the breeze reminded him that the city was still very much alive despite the quiet roads, and he began his weary trek towards Theo's apartment.

As the details of his day played out on repeat in his mind, he found each step leading him further from the redeeming kindness of his co-workers and back to the contemptible behaviour of his employers. In the dark of the pre-dawn sky, Auryn could almost swear the swiftly burning fuse of his patience was visible before him, drawing closer with each shift. Typing fifty-three into the dial pad of the building, he asked himself a question he did not know the answer to: how long could he continue to fend off the inevitable implosion of his situation?

∞∞∞∞∞∞∞∞∞∞∞∞∞∞∞∞∞

For once, there was no darkness, no shadows to offer hidden refuge for lurking creatures, but although there was light here, it felt like the brightness of the world had been dimmed.

He stood behind the bar, but nothing seemed familiar. The space was large, open, and steeped in a thousand shades of washed-out grey, but there was no industrial feel to it, no polished metal or welded art pieces to denote an attempt at modern monochrome design. No, the place was cold and corporate, devoid of life and joy. It was the kind of establishment put together by accountants and middle management using a formula they didn't understand: an attempt at replicating art by people lacking the soul required for artistic endeavour.

There were very few customers, but they all painted the same sorry silhouette, each one sitting alone and sporting a crumpled suit, loosened tie, and scrappy stubble. On their weathered faces, they wore an identical look of hopelessness, like life had beaten them into submission long ago.

Pouring a shot of whiskey into a glass, he slid it towards the man sitting hunched over the bar top, his head propped up on his hand, his eyes distant. As he watched the man down the drink in one gulp, he silently assured himself that this was not his job; it couldn't be. Was he doing a shift to help someone out? Was it just for some extra money?

446

He couldn't remember. All he knew was that every fibre of his being was revolting against his forced attendance.

He polished and re-polished glasses as though he were caught in some twisted time loop, an NPC trapped within the limitations of his circumstance until his shift finally came to an end and the next pitiful employee came to take his place. Leaving his towel on the bench, he walked to the office in search of his pay, but when he opened the door, he was met with a disinterested shake of the head from the man behind the desk. He lashed out, screaming and yelling, but his words seemed to escape him like the muffled drone of distant conversation, the man's only response a flippant wave.

Slamming the door behind him, he stormed out, kicking over chairs as he went, passing through the bar like a tornado. As he stepped outside, though, he stopped in his tracks; there was nothing there. It was as if the bar had been dropped in the middle of nowhere. The only landmark in the otherwise barren landscape was a dusty road bereft of cars disappearing towards the horizon in either direction, the sky blanketed with looming clouds. Around him, melancholic men wandered aimlessly, and he paced in a circle until he found himself facing the bar once more, the man from the office standing in the doorway, beckoning him.

He had two choices: stay amongst the lost souls in this desolate purgatory or go back to work. Staring at the man, he wished for another option, but there wasn't one. He was trapped.

Faced with an impossible decision, he closed his eyes for the longest time, his anger threatening to overwhelm him until eventually, he opened them again. Looking at the dust swirling across the road, he sighed, shaking his head and walking slowly back inside.

∞∞∞∞∞∞∞∞∞∞∞∞∞∞∞

Auryn had already been awake for an hour when he heard Theo roll over.

"You're up early," she said, reaching over and booping his nose. "Everything okay?"

He looked across at her with a sleepy smile. "Yeah, I'm fine."

Of course, he wasn't fine. He'd been woken up by his anxiety and had proceeded to continue his microanalysis of the previous day,

447

stewing in his anger until his muscles had tensed and his chest had grown tight. Not wanting to disturb the light but seemingly peaceful slumber Theo had been basking in, he'd tried his best to remain still despite his restless body. Thankfully, though, she was awake now, and he shifted onto his side to face her, flexing his legs to dispense with some of his pent-up agitation.

"You sleep okay?" he asked, trying to distract her from any deeper questioning.

Theo pointed to her face. "Tired."

"That's not what I asked," he replied, smiling despite himself.

Again, she repeated the movement. "Tired."

"I see. Would tea help?"

Theo nodded, brushing his cheek with her hand, his heart melting a little under her touch.

Swinging himself out of bed, he shuffled off to the kitchen, setting up two mugs with peppermint tea bags before filling the kettle and flicking it on. As he waited for the water to boil, his thoughts moved back to his dream, the remnants of it still lingering between his seething over Adam's toilet paper offensive, the glasswasher debacle, and the shitstorm that was Carlos.

His dreams were usually nonsensical and difficult to decipher. Last night's, however, had left no unanswered questions, his feeling of entrapment wheedling its way into his subconscious in a most dystopian fashion. The irony was that he would likely be far better equipped to deal with the stresses of his work if he could actually get a good night's sleep, but apparently, his brain had misplaced that memo somewhere along the way.

With the two mugs in hand, he returned to the bedroom, placing one on the bedside table beside Theo, who was mindlessly scrolling the annals of the internet as she attempted to reboot her brain.

"There you go, beautiful. I'm just going to drink mine on the balcony," Auryn said with a half-hearted smile that he was reasonably sure she couldn't see without her contacts in anyway.

"I'll come join you."

"No, it's okay. You enjoy the lie-in," he replied.

Theo frowned a little, tucking her leg back under the covers. "Oh. Okay."

Stepping out into the late morning air, he could smell a storm coming, the clouds visible in the limited sky view seeming unsettlingly similar to those in his dream, dark and foreboding. He sat down at the table and leant back against the wall, cupping the mug with his hands and breathing in the wafting aroma of mint. Normally, his moments of quiet calm on Theo's balcony would soothe away the stress of the week, but he found himself in an unshakable funk, his arms and legs twitchy with bound-up emotion, his mind flitting between feelings.

Losing himself in his existential crisis, he became deaf and blind to the world around him until he was shaken by the sound of the chair opposite him grinding against the tiles, the scent of lemon demanding his attention shift back to the here and now.

"Earth to Auryn, come in, Auryn," said Theo sitting down across from him, waving as if she'd been calling him for quite some time.

"Hmm?" Auryn replied, his sights finally refocusing on reality as he looked down at his now cold, half-drunk tea to see a plate had appeared beside it bearing blueberry pancakes smeared with lemon curd.

"Ahh, there you are. I was starting to think you'd left your body to eat Turkish delight with Tilda Swinton," she said with a laugh before gesturing at the pancakes. "Happy six-month anniversary!"

"Sorry, I was off in my own world," he replied.

"Yeah, I could tell you were out of it when the smell of pancakes didn't lure you inside. So, what's going on? Did something happen at work?"

"It's nothing. I'm just tired."

"And terrible at lying. Something is clearly bugging you. Come on. It's an Auryn and Theo day. We let the bad stuff out and put the good stuff in," she said, taking a bite of her pancakes and prompting him to do the same.

He opened his mouth to rebuff her again, the protective part of him wanting to shield her from his troubles, but something in her eyes made him feel safe, their glint reminding him she was stronger than he gave her credit for. All of a sudden, the previous day's events came tumbling out of him, the weight of his anger slipping off his shoulders as Theo listened to every word: no look of judgement, no interruptions, just silent empathy. As the words escaped, he felt the

449

insurmountable obstacles of his work shrink until they were little more than twigs beneath his feet, his fuse growing longer again, his rage losing its grip.

When at last his rant came to an end, Theo reached across the table and took his hand. "Do you feel any better now?"

"Yeah, I do," he replied, taking a deep breath and letting it out slowly. "Sorry if it was a bit much. I know you have a lot on your plate already without worrying about my crap."

"Honestly, knowing I'm not the only one with a full plate is strangely refreshing. Is there anything I can do to help? What do you need? Solutions? Sympathy? Sarcasm?"

Auryn laughed, lifting her hand to his lips and kissing it gently. "You've already done plenty just by listening. Sometimes talking to Adam and Carlos makes me feel like I'm talking to a wall. It's just nice to be heard, you know?"

Out of nowhere, the sky flashed bright, and a rumble of thunder rolled past, the heavens finally releasing their baggage as if to follow his example. With a smile, he watched as Theo jumped up in childlike excitement, reaching her hand over the railing and catching a smattering of raindrops on her palm. As she looked back at him, beckoning him to her side, he couldn't help but think how unlike all of his exes she was.

Standing up, he wandered over to her, and Theo placed her head on his shoulder. "I love thunderstorms," she said wistfully. "I don't know what it is about dark clouds and lightning, but they feed my soul. Can we stay out here till it passes?"

"Of course, beautiful. As long as you want," he replied, kissing her head and wrapping his arm around her waist.

As the next wave of thunder vibrated through his chest, he savoured the simple pleasure of her hair dancing in the wind, the intoxicating scent of petrichor surrounding their embrace. Theo reached her hand out again, catching the rain with a soft smile, and as the water pooled there, he imagined the drops to be all the vulnerable parts of himself: his fear, his insecurity, his inadequacy, his anger. In the hands of this imperfect woman, this wonderous creature built of broken pieces and glued together with spite and spirit, the parts of him that pushed others away found a soft place to land.

It was in the presence of this thought that he discovered something he had, up until then, failed to see. In the three long term relationships he'd had before Theo, he had purposefully sought out partners who were his opposite, searching for women full of colour and sunshine in the hope that they would deliver clear weather to his stormy soul. No matter how bright their sunshine was, though, the clouds above him had always remained far too thick for their rays to shine through.

Theo, on the other hand, was not made of the glaring light or garish technicolour he had tried to force into his life time and again. Instead, her portrait was painted with the same darkened shadows and lustreless greys that depression had chosen for his palette. Despite this, though, she brought a sense of peace and joy to his life that he'd never felt before.

In that moment, as the rain grew heavier and the lightning closer, he realised something most profound. He didn't need someone to change the weather; he just needed someone who wasn't afraid of the storm.

.

Chester, England, 1810 CE

It was silly, really. She didn't know why she did it. Still, when life suffocated her with the weight of its expectations, sitting atop the weathered, old tree stump at the crossroads brought Viola a peace she couldn't find anywhere else. To her left, the road led to the bustling port city of Chester, and to her right, it led to Hobbes Manor, her home. In the other two directions, a small, potholed track provided access to the farmhouses dotted amongst the rolling fields, although she rarely saw anyone pass down them. In fact, she would often sit for hours on the stump and never see a single soul coming or going, and today was proving to be no exception. Aside from her grey mare, Storm, who she'd tethered to the oak tree beside her, and the cattle grazing in the adjacent paddock, she was alone.

The late-spring sun shone brightly overhead, its dappled light filtering through the leaves, but a lingering chill in the air prompted Viola to pull her shawl tight around her shoulders. With a puff, she blew aside the stray ringlet of mousy-brown hair that flicked across her porcelain cheek, and prying a pin from her carefully constructed bun, she anchored it back in place with no real finesse. After all, it was sure to shake loose again on her ride home.

As she stared longingly down the road, a sudden gust of wind sent the hem of her brand-new morning dress flapping against her leg, and she turned her attention to it with a sigh. The combination of its heinous shade of pink, absurdly high waist, and irritating ruffled neckline had swiftly catapulted it to her least favourite item of clothing. As such, finding a way to ruin it had taken top spot on her list of minor rebellions, narrowly beating out freckle acquirement through wanton sun exposure, deliberate lapses in etiquette during dinner parties, and obtuse treatment of parent-assigned suitors.

She knew her mother was going to have a conniption when she found out she'd worn the dress riding, but Viola was anything but contrite. The woman was driving her crazy of late, and it seemed only fair that she repay the courtesy.

Barely two months had passed since she had made her debut at the first round of spring balls, and at sixteen, she had been one of the youngest debutantes in attendance. Still, her mother's inexhaustible insistence had secured Viola's place as an early bloom amongst the other girls, and she'd been pushing for a match with one of the eligible bachelors ever since. The search for a son-in-law consumed her every waking moment, and going by the way she paraded Viola around like a prize peacock, it would seem like having a spinster for a daughter was fast becoming her greatest fear.

When her father had last graced the halls of Hobbes Manor, Viola had pleaded with him to see reason, but he was no help, lazily deferring to his wife's judgement and reminding his daughter of her duty. As much as she had wished for a different result, his actions did not surprise her. With most of his time spent in Liverpool increasing the size of his merchant fleet and building his trade ties in the East, he was relying on an auspicious match to secure an heir for his legacy.

Naturally, Viola protested her use as a pawn in her parent's game of social chess, but her dissent fell on deaf ears no matter how fervently she expressed it. She wanted so much more for her life than to wither away in some pompous manor with nothing to fill her years except pandering to her husband's whims and attempting to avoid death by childbirth. She wanted a future of her own design. Above all else, though, she wanted someone to share her time with who in no way resembled the stiff, boring men being foisted on her week in and week out, especially not her mother's current favourite.

Mr William Johnson, as she was constantly being reminded, was a highly reputable and wealthy gentleman who would offer her a life of security and comfort. Of course, Viola knew perfectly well that she wasn't being set up with the thirty-two-year-old, heirless widower for her own benefit. William's father was the sole proprietor of Johnson & Son, an influential trading company in Liverpool with far-reaching connections across India and the Far East. More importantly, though, he was nearing retirement, and with the company soon to pass into his son's control, marriage offered the potential for an advantageous business merger with her own father's business. In short, Viola was a bargaining chip being shined up by her mother in the hopes of purchasing a refill of the Hobbes family coffers.

As the image of William sprung into her mind, she grimaced. She had met him half a dozen times already, and he had failed to impress her at any point. On top of the fact he was twice her age, he was also everything she hated about the men in her family's social circles. He was officious, courteous to a fault, and about as charming as a sack of potatoes. Speaking to him was only marginally more engaging than speaking to a blade of grass, and the content of his conversation rivalled her former governess for sheer mundanity.

Stirred from her thoughts by the sound of hooves, Viola turned to see a carriage slowly trundling down the road in her direction. A smartly dressed coachman sporting a top hat and a black tailcoat with shining silver buttons drove the pristine green and white landau, its top down so that his passenger might enjoy the fine weather. As it approached, Viola heard a bell ring, and the coachman pulled on the reins, the two chestnut horses coming to a stop right in front of her.

Leaning over the side of the landau, an older lady wearing dainty, white lace gloves and a broad-brimmed, beige hat fastened with a green silk ribbon waved her over.

Viola stood up from the stump, straightening her dress, walking to the road, and curtseying politely. "Good morning."

"Good morning," the lady replied, tilting her head in greeting. "Are you, perchance, Viola, the daughter of Gareth Hobbes?"

"I am."

"You may not remember me. My name is Edith Frost. My husband hunts with your father sometimes. Our estate is a few miles past yours."

Viola did not remember the lady in any way, shape, or form, but to say as much would be the height of bad manners, and so she let etiquette pave the way. "Of course I remember you, Mrs Frost. It is lovely to see you again."

Edith regarded her sceptically for a moment before looking her up and down with a knotted brow. "Whatever are you doing out here on your own? You are without hat, gloves, or chaperone. Has something happened?"

"No, no. I was just out for a morning ride and decided to stop and rest here before heading back," Viola said, her cheeks flushing red with embarrassment as she scrambled to craft an explanation for her deplorable state. "I must seem quite the mess. My riding habit is being laundered, and I was so eager to enjoy the sunshine that I was halfway from home before I realised I'd forgotten my hat."

Mrs Frost gave her a knowing smile. "I understand, dear. The fresh air is wonderful for one's constitution. Anyway, I must be off. Do say hello to your dear mother Agnes for me, won't you? And let her know that she must pop by for tea sometime soon."

"Of course, Mrs Frost," she replied, stepping back from the landau. "Have a safe journey."

"Good day, dear."

Viola curtsied once more as Mrs Frost settled back into her seat, and with a snap of the reins, the landau jolted forward, heading once more towards Chester.

What a strange encounter, Viola thought, turning back to the stump.

All at once, her hopeful mood gave way to despondency. She was not there to be stumbled upon by old ladies, but it was clear she was not going to find what her heart sought, not today at least. With a sigh, she waded through the swaying grass and untethered her horse, who whinnied as she stroked her neck.

"Come on, Storm," she said, climbing into the saddle. "I don't suppose we can avoid mother forever."

∞∞∞

Agnes came rushing out the front door of Hobbes manor just as Viola was dismounting. "Viola Charlotte Hobbes, where have you been?" she screeched, throwing her arms in the air.

Viola handed the reins to the stablehand, flicking the same stray ringlet off her cheek before turning to her mother. "I was out for a ride. I met-"

"You are sixteen years old, Viola. You need to start acting like an adult, and adults do not just disappear for hours on end without telling anyone where they are going. What would your father say?" snapped Agnes, stopping to regard her daughter's appearance, her anger palpable. "Good Lord, you went riding in your new dress. Look at it. It's absolutely covered in dust. And where are your hat and gloves? Please tell me no one saw you out so underdressed."

Agnes wasn't a tall woman by any means, barely the same height as Viola, but she had an uncanny ability to loom over her daughter when she was displeased. When coupled with her tight, greying-brunette bun and sharp features, she usually exuded the feel of a severe matron far more than a caring, effeminate mother. That day, however, Viola was surprised to find her clad in an expensive, midnight blue gown edged with ivory lace, her hair curled and pinned into an elaborate chignon, two tight ringlets framing her face.

"What's going on, mother?" Viola asked, sure she had not forgotten any occasions that would call for such formal attire.

Taking a deep breath to compose herself, Agnes forced a tight-lipped smile. "Mr Johnson has called in to see you again. I have stalled him for as long as I can. Now, go upstairs and change into something presentable. And for goodness sake, Viola, fix your hair and put some gloves on. We can't have him seeing you like *this*."

"Mother, he will have to see me like this eventually if you are to have us marry. It's only fair he know what to expect beforehand," she replied, rolling her eyes.

With a casual smirk, Viola made a show of polishing the dirt off her riding boot, rubbing it on the back of her leg and further soiling her dress.

"And what *should* I expect?" a voice asked from beside them, both women whirling around to find William standing there.

He was hardly the most handsome man in the world, but he certainly wasn't the ugliest. In truth, he resembled almost every other suitor her mother had thrown her way. He had short, brown, neatly-styled hair, unnecessarily long sideburns, a button nose, and thin lips, which were currently curled into a bemused smile. As for his clothing, it was just as unremarkable as the rest of him. His black, double-breasted tailcoat was buttoned over the usual combination of white shirt and waistcoat; his beige breeches were tucked into his polished riding boots; and his silk top hat was as straight and spotless as his necktie.

Agnes, caught off-guard, began to splutter, but William held out his hand. "Forgive me, Mrs Hobbes. I found myself growing idle and decided to admire the grounds whilst you searched for your rather capricious daughter," he said, turning to Viola. "I see you managed to find her in the end."

457

"Indeed I have, Mr Johnson. I must apologise again for all of this. The silly little thing went for a ride and forgot to inform anyone where she was going or when she would return," Agnes said with a polite laugh before glancing back to her daughter, her face stern. "Viola, run along and have Molly help you change into something more fitting. Quickly now. You have kept this fine gentleman waiting long enough."

Viola propped her hands on her hips, opening her mouth to argue the point, when William stepped forward. "That is really not necessary, Mrs Hobbes," he said, retrieving his pocket watch and checking the time. "I'm due back in Chester before six to attend a dinner party with some important business associates, so I only have a short while left to spare. Would it be all right if Miss Hobbes and I share a quick spot of afternoon tea by ourselves? I feel as though I have imposed on your day quite enough."

"Of course. I will have Alice fetch some refreshments and bring them to you in the garden," Agnes said, beaming with self-satisfaction as she scurried off into the house.

William turned back to Viola, holding out his arm to her. "May I, Miss Hobbes?"

Viola yearned to tell him that he absolutely may not, but given her already questionable behaviour for the day, she decided it best to play nice. Reluctantly, she slipped her arm into his, sighing as she looked up at the house. Hobbes Manor had been in her family for generations, and it was a beautiful place, but Viola found herself increasingly resenting her position within it. In the past, she'd admired the ivy clinging to the red brick facade, but these days, its creeping tendrils seemed as suffocating as her mother.

William led her across the manicured lawn, and as they passed the front garden beds, Viola looked down at the purple pansies sprouting there and regarded them in a different light. Each delicate bloom felt like a reflection of herself: trapped, defenceless, and waiting to be stripped of their colour and joy by forces beyond their control.

Pausing for a moment, William leant down and plucked a stem from the bed, holding it out to her. "Alas, it pales in comparison to your sapphire eyes," he said, his words sounding so rehearsed it was jarring.

Taking the flower with a half-hearted smile, Viola stared at it with pity. *And just like that, its life was plucked away by a hand it did not*

458

choose, she thought as she twirled it in her fingers.

Wanting nothing more than for their time together to be over, Viola tightened her arm around William's, snatching the lead from him and marching them into the hedged rose garden and over to the white, wrought iron table beside the fountain. As she released his arm to pull out one of the chairs, he hurried forward and, with exaggerated movements, completed the task for her, Viola rolling her eyes as she took a seat.

To her mind, men performing basic tasks for women was nothing more than an unnecessary assertion of dominance. Each chivalry-dressed act served as nothing but a cold reminder that she had no control: not over her life, not over her future, not even over a chair.

Of course, she felt more than a little alone in her desire for independence, furniture-based or otherwise. Her mother, along with her peers, seemed to relish every opened door and pulled-out chair, perpetuating their perceived feebleness by acting as though functioning a doorknob was beyond their capability. Each one of them solidified the status-quo and secured the subserviency of their entire gender in the process.

Sitting the plucked pansy down on the table, Viola closed her eyes for a moment and turned her face to the sun, trying to dig out her manners from beneath her frustration.

"I do apologise if my unannounced visit has inconvenienced you at all, Miss Hobbes. I was just eager to see you again," said William, brushing a stray leaf from his chair and sitting down.

"This is your seventh visit in as many weeks, William. Surely we are on first name terms by now," she replied, opening one eye and glancing over at him.

"Of course, Viola," William said, smiling with satisfaction. "So, what shall we talk about whilst we wait for our tea? Is there anything you would like to discuss?"

Viola shrugged. "Not particularly. You may pick a topic if you like."

William chuckled to himself. "Well, I could tell you about the exciting growth of our imports this spring at Johnson and Son, but I fear I would bore you. The last time I spoke about business, your eyes completely glazed over, and you appeared on the verge of sleep."

Viola let out a snort of unflattering laughter. "Was I really that bad?"

"It was actually quite adorable."

The compliment left an awkward tension lingering between them, and Viola let out a sigh of relief as she looked up to see Alice, Hobbes Manor's long-serving housekeeper, approaching with a shining silver tray in hand. As she placed it down on the table between them, Viola smiled at the spread: a fine china pot of Ceylon tea beside two matching cups, a plate of warm scones, and a small jar of clementine marmalade, her favourite.

"Can I get you anything else, Miss?" the housekeeper asked.

"No, thank you, Alice."

With a small curtsey, she tottered back to the house, leaving Viola once again to the stiff company of her guest. Without a word, and likely to the disgust of her mother had she been present, Viola did not pour William a cup of tea or offer him refreshments. Instead, she took one of the scones on a small plate, cut it open, slathered it with marmalade, and took a bite, sitting back in her chair with the plate held under her chin.

"I get the sense you did not make time to eat before heading out on your ride this morning," said William with a grin, pouring them both a cup before taking a sip.

Viola did not speak, shrugging her response as she crossed her legs and continued devouring her scone with great gusto. When she had finished not just that scone but another in quick succession, she placed the plate back on the table and nonchalantly brushed the crumbs from her lap, watching as a sparrow flitted down to retrieve them.

An uncomfortable silence filled the air, but she made no effort to break it as she took her cup from its saucer and cradled it in her hands. She was more than happy to be entertained by her own thoughts whilst waiting for their time to dwindle. Still, after a few minutes, Viola could sense William growing restless and decided to intervene.

"Speak your mind, William. You clearly have something you wish to say," she said, placing her cup back on its saucer and turning to him.

William cleared his throat, removing his hat and setting it on the table. "As you know, I have declared my intentions to your parents. They, along with my own family, are overjoyed by our match and openly give their blessings. The only person not excited by this turn of events appears to be you."

"Well, I cannot help that," snipped Viola. "This was not how I envisioned my life turning out, and I will not pretend to be joyous for the comfort of others."

"And what did you envision for yourself, if I may be so bold?" he asked, sitting forward in his chair.

"I imagined I would meet my soulmate without the guiding hand of my parents, and our union would not be constructed to fulfil some ulterior motive. I care very little for marriage or children, William, and I do not wish to spend my life cooped up in a house with no one but the staff for company: comfortable but utterly miserable. I want an equal to share my life with. Someone who will travel the world with me and weigh my opinion with the same scales they use for their own."

William mused on that silently as he took his final sip of tea and slipped his gloves back on, Viola avoiding his gaze by watching the fountain.

"What is it that calls you to travel, Viola? This is not the first time you have mentioned it. I remember standing outside your father's office in Liverpool last October, waiting to meet with him about a business venture, and I could hear you spouting a rather animated monologue on the subject through the door. You were quite insistent you didn't want to spend the rest of your life in this," he paused, smirking, "backwater, I believe was your exact choice of words."

Viola's stifled a laugh as she recalled the incident. She had been in Liverpool with her mother to be fitted for her debutante gown, and, in a fit of frustration, she had marched into her father's office demanding to board his next ship to China. In truth, when she had marched back out after his denial, she had paid no heed to the man she'd almost collided with outside the door.

"I have wanted to travel since as far back as I can remember," she said, her voice growing spirited. "My father would always tell me stories of the wonders of the Far East and bring me home little trinkets. I would read Gulliver's Travels relentlessly, to the point my mother tore it from my hands and tossed it in the fire as punishment for neglecting my embroidery, of all things. And at night, I often dream of distant lands, of oceans and deserts, and dense forests filled with strange creatures and wild adventures. I want to see those places with my waking eyes. I want to breathe them and smell them and feel them."

461

William watched her speak with a smile. "Do you know what I want most in my life?" he asked when she'd finally finished.

"What?"

He tilted his head to one side. "To travel the world."

"What about your work?" she asked, sitting up straight at the sudden turn of events.

"That's the best part. My work offers the perfect excuse to fulfil the urge to travel. To expand a business, one must venture to new places to seek out new products and trades, and when I take over Johnson and Son next year, that is precisely what I plan on doing," he replied with a grin. "We are more alike than you think, Viola, and I could offer you all the things you have dreamt of. However, I fear you have discounted me as a suitor simply because our pairing serves to benefit your father more than you believe it would benefit you."

Viola bit her tongue as she pondered his words. They did not sound like the stiff, formal conversations he usually engaged in when speaking to her in the presence of others. Instead, away from the social pressures and inquisition of her mother, William seemed almost ... likeable.

She turned back to him with piqued curiosity. "May I ask you something?"

"Anything," he nodded.

"There are hundreds of eligible young women out there. Why have you chosen me?"

"Well," William said, scratching his sideburn, "if I am honest, you are the first one who does not see me as a ticket to an easy life. I have met scores of women since my wife passed and my father announced his upcoming retirement. Almost every merchant and businessman in Liverpool has tried throwing his daughter at me, but as soon as your mother introduced us at your debut, I knew you were different. You did not fawn or pander. In fact, when we danced, you were barely amiable. As I recall, you excused yourself before the song was even over."

A wry smile flickered across his face before he continued. "You are a challenging person: smart, headstrong, and overflowing with opinion. You are the complete opposite of everything I should be looking for in a wife, and yet these traits are exactly what makes you so refreshing to me. I can be the person you are looking for, Viola, even if it was our parents who guided us to one another, and I think, in time, you will see how fulfilling a life together could be."

It was a stirring speech, she had to grant him that, and the fact he returned even after her countless bouts of bad manners and unladylike behaviour showed great dedication to the cause of courtship. As enticing as his promise of travel was, though, he did not inspire love in her heart. Still, he was a fine gentleman, and she couldn't bring herself to cut him down any further, so she tried to add a little warmth to her response, as false as it felt.

"Your kind words have left me with much to consider, William. I promise to think on them at length before we next meet."

A triumphant smile appeared on his face, softening his features. "You wish to see me again?"

"Yes," she replied with a flicker of hesitance. "At the very least, it will make mother happy, and perhaps we can speak further about our shared desire to travel."

"I would enjoy that very much," he said, rising to his feet, re-donning his hat, and offering his hand.

Of course, Viola didn't need his help up, but she accepted it gracefully.

"Shall I escort you back?" he asked.

"You know, I might stay and enjoy the sun a little longer."

"Well, I must be off. It has been a pleasure, Viola. Until next time," he said, kissing her hand gently, the warmth of his lips surprising her as they touched her bare skin.

With a tip of his hat, William took his leave, and as Viola watched him go, she noticed his step to be more lively than once it was. Frowning, she looked down at her still hovering hand to find her feelings muddled. That morning, she had been so sure of her distaste for him and the life he offered, but now, in the afterglow of their surprisingly pleasant encounter, that certainty wavered.

Before she could consider the change in herself, though, her mother appeared across the garden, waving her over to what was sure to be an in-depth interrogation and subsequent scolding. And with that, Viola swept her emotions aside for later contemplation.

∞○○○∞

It wasn't until after supper that Viola managed to steal herself a moment of introspection, sitting in the armchair beside the fire in her room. A book lay open in her lap, its pages filled with stories of far-off places, yet its words remained unread as her thoughts returned to William. He seemed a kind soul, the sort of considerate and courteous man she should be flattered to have garnered the attention of. So why was she so reluctant to embrace him?

As she pondered the question, her mind drifted back to her place atop the tree stump at the crossroads, and it was there she found her answer. William was a fine man, someone with whom she could travel the world, but he was not the person she was destined to spend her life with. Her true soulmate was still out there, and given time and patience, they would find her; she knew it in her heart. Unfortunately, her mother would not be as willing to wait, and therein lay the crux of her troubles.

Startled by a sudden knock at the door, she looked up to see Alice peeking in.

"Apologies, miss. I'm here to turn down the bed. Molly is feeling out of sorts this evening," she said with a curtsy.

Viola nodded her acknowledgement before turning her attention back to the fire once more.

Alice was a fussy woman in her late fifties with a stern face, portly figure, and grey hair that was always perfectly pinned under her cap. She was an ever-present figure of comfort and reason in Viola's life and had been a trusted mainstay of the Hobbes family for years. One of Viola's earliest childhood memories was of being wiped down by Alice after she'd escaped the house and dived into a puddle of mud. Alice, who had been her nanny at that point, had spent the entire time muttering to herself as if she couldn't believe a little girl would do such a thing, only for Viola to wriggle free and dive face-first into the puddle again with glee. It had taken three servants to get her out, kicking and screaming, and she would likely have jumped right back in if her mother hadn't locked her in her room.

Viola smiled at the memory as she watched Alice turn down the covers, fill the copper bed warmer with coals from the hearth, and run it along the sheets, her movements precise and expertly quiet.

When she had finished, she emptied the coals back into the fire, hung up the warmer, and turned to Viola. "Goodnight, miss."

"Alice?" Viola called after her as she begged off.

"Yes, miss?"

"How long have you been in my family's service?"

Alice thought for a moment, her hands folded neatly in front of her. "Twelve years, I believe. I arrived just after your fourth birthday."

"So, you have known me a long time?"

"Yes, miss," Alice replied with a warm smile.

Viola looked away, her eyes moving to the window and the bright crescent moon peeking out through a hole in the clouds. "Do you think I should marry Mr Johnson?"

"It's not my place to say, miss."

"I am making it your place, Alice. Please, answer me truthfully," Viola said in earnest, looking back to the level-headed woman whose presence had always offered her such calm.

Alice studied her face before responding. "Do you love him?"

"I barely know him," said Viola, shaking her head. "He seems kind enough, and he speaks willingly of a desire to travel, but I feel no affection for him beyond friendship." Viola closed the book on her lap and clasped her hands atop it. "Do you think it childish to believe a soulmate waits for me out there somewhere? Should I just give up on that fantasy and fulfil my duty?"

Alice paused for thought, her brow knotted slightly. "If you seek my honest opinion, miss, marriage is a meaningless construct of society. It is designed purely for men to grow richer by exchanging women as currency. Love is rarely considered in the trade, and more often than not, it is pushed aside in favour of fortune," she said, the sharp edges of her features softening and giving way to a look of hard-won wisdom. "If I could give you only one piece of advice on the matter, it would be this: finding true love is the only worthwhile endeavour in this world. If you abandon your search for it, if you sacrifice love for duty, you forsake happiness and bind your soul to unrest. Wait for love, child. Wait for peace."

"Thank you, Alice," Viola said, looking down at her hands, her mind a blur.

"You're welcome, miss. Good night," Alice nodded, leaving the room.

Viola leant back in her chair and looked up at the ceiling as she weighed Alice's advice. Her words had confirmed a truth Viola had known all along and bolstered her resolve. No matter how long it took, no matter what it cost her, she would persist with the search for her soulmate. To settle for less would be to sell her heart short.

∞∞∞∞

The next few weeks were tedious, to say the least. Viola stayed true to her word and made an effort to spend time with William, much to the delight of her mother, but the faint flicker of interest he had sparked that day in the garden had blown out as soon as she fanned it a little. The more she grew to know him, the more boring and tiresome he seemed to become.

He spoke almost exclusively of import price fluctuations, company expansion, and, just to spice it up a bit, the weather. On the rare occasion she actually managed to engage him on the topic of travel, she discovered he neither wanted to see nor do anything remotely interesting. His idea of adventure was to sail past the jungle and observe it from the safety of the deck, whereas Viola wanted to row to shore and march right into the heart of it. She longed to immerse herself in everything her life wasn't, to find answers within the unknown, and her admission of that drew nothing but shock and confusion from her stiff suitor.

If nothing else, Viola had hoped her efforts would placate her mother somewhat, but it seemed to only worsen the situation. After seeing the pair spending more time together, Agnes grew convinced she could hear wedding bells fast approaching, and her actions morphed from irritating to downright unbearable. She would hover around them constantly, eavesdropping on their conversations and throwing out obvious hints at every opportunity. As soon as William would take his leave, Agnes would critique Viola's every move, blaming William's lack of marriage proposal on everything from the parting of her daughter's hair to the way she folded her hands between sips of tea.

Each morning, Viola would seek respite from the chaos by taking up her post at the crossroads, and although Agnes tried her best to forbid it, Viola always found a way to sneak out. That being said, she was fast running out of believable excuses to elude her mother and was left relying on a mix of speed and distraction to get the job done. On that particular day, for example, Viola had only managed to escape because her mother had felt it necessary to spend ten minutes berating one of the laundry maids for daring to hang the sheets to dry vertically. Seizing the opportunity, she had swiftly saddled her horse, sworn the stablehand to secrecy, and galloped off before anyone noticed.

With Storm tethered to the oak tree just like every other day, Viola plonked herself down on the well-worn stump she'd made her own, pulling her legs up beneath her dress and crossing them. Running her fingers along the tree's rings, she wondered what the world had looked like when it had been a sapling and what secrets it held within the grain of its timber.

She gazed out at the familiar scene surrounding her, sighing as she watched tiny white butterflies flit between the swaying clover flowers, the shadows of dappled clouds painting the paddocks piebald. Flapping her dress and attempting unsuccessfully to push up her slender, full-length sleeves, she squinted up at the sky in annoyance.

The sun was harsher than she had expected when she left, and the flask of barley water she'd managed to secretly fill at the breakfast table was already running low. On top of that, her dress was hardly suitable for riding or warm weather, and as she shifted uncomfortably, she cursed her mother's insistence on appearance over practicality. She may have appeared every part the lady, but the pastel blue silk she was encased in was absorbing heat at an alarming rate. Furthermore, the lacing of her stay was fastened a little too tightly against her still sprouting chest, and she was left feeling suffocated.

As she dabbed the sweat from her forehead with the back of her sleeve, wishing a breeze would spring up to ease her discomfort, she pondered heading home early. She felt foolish making the same fruitless pilgrimage every day, but at the same time, something within her compelled her to do it. Of course, there was no way of explaining it that didn't sound entirely insane. The closest she could get was that the stump at the crossroads offered her a feeling of hope, as though she were closer to her soulmate when perched atop it.

Stirred by a sound in the direction of Chester, Viola glanced down the road to spy a carriage trundling towards her. For a second, she feared it might be Mrs Frost again, and she considered hiding behind the oak tree to avoid having to explain her mother's lack of visitation. As she regarded the approaching carriage, though, she noticed it was not the green and white landau she expected but rather an elegant red stagecoach trimmed with gold and drawn by four majestic, buckskin draught horses.

The two men driving the carriage were clad in matching livery, their tailcoats crisp scarlet and so finely made that Viola suddenly felt terribly underdressed. Never in her life had she ever felt frantic about missing her hat and gloves, but in that moment, a pang of anxiety sent her stomach aflutter, and once again, she considered hiding.

The nearer it drew, the more her curiosity kept her fixed in place, and as the intricate detailing of the coach came into focus, she wondered why on earth such a wealthy passenger was travelling down such an obscure road. If nothing else, she knew it wasn't to visit Hobbes Manor. Her mother would have been in a tizzy for a week beforehand if such a visitor were on the cards.

Before she could muse on its destination any further, it ground to a halt in front of her. Viola scrambled to her feet, brushing out the creases in her dress and straightening her sleeves, her heart racing as every etiquette lesson she'd endured flooded back all at once. She watched the coachman on the right alight from his seat, folding down a step for his passenger and opening the carriage door. From the plush interior of the stagecoach emerged the most handsome man she'd ever laid eyes on. Removing his silk top hat, he placed it on the seat behind him, and as he did, Viola felt her breath catch in her throat. Everything about him drew her in. He was tall and looked to be in his mid-twenties, with fair skin, steely blue eyes, a dimpled chin, and a clean-shaven jawline so chiselled she was almost certain she could cut herself on it. The colour of his hair matched the coffee her father was so fond of drinking, and as he ran his ungloved fingers through his short, wavy locks, she couldn't help but think him equally as intoxicating.

Just like his carriage, the man's clothing oozed wealth and refinement. His crisp white shirt was topped with a black damask waistcoat and matching silk cravat, and his fitted black trousers, which clung to his muscular legs, were tucked into polished, black, knee-high Hessian boots. The otherwise monochrome outfit was completed by

468

an impeccably-tailored, rich maroon tailcoat with gold embroidery on its cuffs and lapels, its two rows of gold buttons gleaming in the sun.

As their eyes met, a smile crept onto his face. "At last," he said, his voice deep and silky smooth.

Viola stared in stunned silence as he approached, her tongue seeming to have lost all ability in his presence.

"Where are my manners," he said, stopping before her. "Allow me to introduce myself. My name is Richard Chase."

"V-Viola Hobbes," she stammered, bobbing a small curtsy as she felt her cheeks flush. She didn't know what it was, but something about the way he gazed at her made her almost giddy.

"A pleasure to meet you. May I call you Viola?"

She nodded mutely. If she was honest, she didn't mind what name he called her at that point, so long as he didn't turn out to be some heatstroke-based hallucination.

"I did not mean to interrupt your solitude," he continued, "but I was led here by something I can scarcely explain. You see, I have been scouring this country for months, searching."

"And what is it you seek, Mr Chase?" she asked, regaining her faculties.

"Please, call me Richard. Mr Chase was my father," he said with a grin.

Viola's heart performed the most acrobatic of backflips. "Of course, Richard."

Stepping forward, he took her hand and pressed it against his chest. "I seek the only thing of importance in this world: the person who will give my life meaning."

"I don't understand," she replied, his heart beating hard beneath her fingers.

Richard smiled, lowering her hand, taking the other, and holding both lightly. "May I ask you why you are here, sitting all alone by the side of the road on an unseasonably warm day?"

"I –" she paused, looking away in embarrassment, "I was just getting some air, I guess."

Ducking his head, he caught her eye. "I find that hard to believe. What is the real reason? It's all right. I won't judge," he said with an encouraging nod.

"I was waiting," she replied meekly.

"For whom?"

She was hesitant to share her flight of fancy, but as she opened her mouth to lie, she found herself too captivated to do so, the arch of his brow and endless blue of his irises drawing the truth from her lips. "For my soulmate."

"Then our goals are one and the same, Viola," he said, stepping closer until she could feel his breath. "Don't you see? Something called us both here, to this very spot. What else could it be if not fate?"

He couldn't be ... could he? Viola asked herself, scarcely able to believe what he was saying.

The wave of emotions that flooded over her mixed with the still-rising heat of the day, and she found herself feeling suddenly light-headed. Taking a deep breath, she fanned her face, fighting to stay upright as Richard's expression changed to one of concern.

"There is so much I wish to tell you, but I fear I have overwhelmed you already," he said. "Perhaps we should wait until you are not at risk of fainting before we speak further. Please, allow me to escort you home."

"Thank you," she replied, tucking her arm in his as he guided her to the carriage. "It's really not that far, only a mile or so. The red brick manor with the wrought iron gate."

Shifting his hat off the seat, Richard helped Viola up, and with a sense of relief, she settled down into a cushion so soft it put her own bed to shame. As she heard him command his coachmen to tether her horse to the carriage, she took in the opulence of the interior: the luxurious, red velvet upholstery, the rich mahogany facings, the gold trim. Every inch of it spoke of a level in society she was not privy to, and she blinked a few times just to make sure it was real.

Bundling himself inside, Richard sat down opposite her, rapping his knuckles on the roof when he was ready, the wheels crunching in the dirt as the stagecoach pulled away. Aside from checking she was comfortable, the pair journeyed along in amiable silence, exchanging glances from time to time before their eyes flitted back to the passing scenery and the pensive contemplation it played host to.

Something about Richard made her feel like she'd known him for years, his forward actions and intimate dialogue only serving to make him more endearing, although all common sense told her they should not. As the fields rolled by, Viola basked in the buoyant new feeling swelling in her chest. Glancing over at him once again, she dared to entertain a possibility she had, up until then, only dreamt of: that she had finally found her soulmate.

∞∞∞∞

When they eventually pulled up outside Hobbes Manor, Viola couldn't help but grin as she watched the staff begin to scramble, Alice appearing at the door before scurrying back inside.

"Allow me to apologise for my mother in advance," Viola said with a smirk. "She can be ... well, you'll see."

When the coachman opened the door a minute later, Viola peered out from the safety of the shadows to see Agnes rushing over, trying desperately to compose herself as she went. With a wink, Richard slipped on his gloves, donned his hat, and stepped out, offering his hand and helping Viola down.

It took everything within her not to laugh as she saw her mother's mouth drop open at the sight of her daughter on the arm of such an unexpected and esteemed visitor.

"Please, forgive the intrusion, good lady," said Richard with a tip of his hat. "I stumbled upon your daughter caught out on this unseasonably warm day and felt obliged to escort her home in comfort lest she faint on her ride back."

"That is very kind of you ..." Agnes paused, realising she did not know her guest's name.

"Oh, how dreadfully rude of me," he said with a flourish. "My name is Richard Chase."

"Welcome to Hobbes Manor, Mr Chase. I am Agnes Hobbes, and you've obviously met my daughter, Viola. Would you care to join us for some refreshments? I was just about to sit down for afternoon tea."

Viola knew she was about to do no such thing, but when a guest arrived, announced or otherwise, the only polite thing to do was to invite them for tea. It was the English way.

Richard turned to Viola, a sly smile tugging at his lips. "What do you think?"

"That would be most enjoyable, Richard," she replied, tucking her hand in the crook of his outstretched elbow and eliciting a dumbfounded look from her mother in the process.

Following Agnes to the conservatory, the three of them took their seats around the small, round oak table at its centre, the heady smell of roses filling the space with their sweet fragrance. Richard placed his hat down on the spare seat beside him and removed his gloves before shuffling a little closer to Viola. Hidden out of sight of Agnes, he took her hand and squeezed it gently, her skin prickling with excitement at his touch.

Not a moment later, Alice appeared, placing a large silver platter between them all and giving a polite nod to the guest who had so ruffled her staff. Viola marvelled at the spread, astonished at the speed and skill with which it had been constructed: perfectly cut finger sandwiches filled with smoked salmon and cucumber, raisin studded scones with raspberry jam and clotted cream, a delicate, golden cake topped with glistening wheels of candied lemon, and a large pot of tea with all its accoutrements.

Alice moved to begin serving, but Agnes shooed her away, doling out the cups herself and picking up the pot. "So, what brings you to our corner of England, Mr Chase?" she asked, pouring him a cup of tea with the polished precision of a woman boasting twenty years of hostess experience.

"I was in Liverpool on business and decided to make my return journey through Chester and this picturesque slice of countryside," he replied, nodding as she offered to add sugar to his cup.

Agnes stirred in a spoonful and handed it to him. "What business has you travelling to our bustling port? If you don't mind me asking."

"Truth be told," said Richard, taking a sip and setting the cup casually back on its saucer, "I was in Liverpool on behalf of the Crown. With His Majesty King George's failing health, I was asked to attend to some matters on his behalf."

"You travel on royal business?" Agnes asked, her eyes growing wide.

Richard shrugged. "It is somewhat of a family obligation. You see, my full title is Lord Richard Chase, Earl of Cromartie, Viscount of Wick, and seventeenth in line to the throne."

It took every ounce of strength Agnes could muster to keep herself upright as his words reached her, and Viola had to admit she was impressed at her mother's fortitude. That being said, there was wild amusement to be had in watching her try and keep her composure, and Viola had to take a sip of her tea just to keep herself from laughing.

"Seventeenth in line to the throne?" Viola asked with a suppressed grin.

"Indeed. Only sixteen people stand between me and the crown," he said with a laugh before leaning in close. "What say you, Viola? Would you like to be my queen?"

She blushed, taking another sip as her mother stood up abruptly.

"Do excuse me, won't you, Lord Chase," said Agnes, clasping her shaking hands in front of her. "There is something I must attend to."

Richard chuckled as she scurried out of the conservatory, running his fingers through his hair again.

In the absence of her mother, Viola's mind began to whir, and she allowed her ingrained etiquette to take over while she arranged her thoughts, sliding a slice of the cake onto a plate and offering it to Richard. With her offer turned down, she took it for herself, winkling out a morsel with her fork and eating it eagerly.

About halfway through the slice, when she had finally processed the gravity of Richard's admission, she placed the plate down and turned to him. "Are you telling the truth?"

"About being a Lord? Of course. Why would I lie about something like that?" he said, almost offended by her scepticism.

Viola shook her head. "No, not about that. About something pulling you here."

"My dearest Viola, I have spent years searching for meaning and purpose, for something that might make me feel whole. Money has not filled that void, nor has power. In the end, I realised it was not some*thing* I was missing, but some*one*." Richard took her hands in his. "I believe there is someone in this world made just for me. Someone I have loved in the past and whom I am destined to love again. Someone whose soul is tethered to mine beyond the sense and reasoning of man, beyond mortality, beyond the constraints of time itself."

"Do you ... do you think *I* might be that someone?" Viola asked, her heart fluttering so fast she was sure his hands were the only thing keeping her from flying away.

"I have felt a constant pull all my life, a pull leading me towards my soulmate, and today, at that crossroads, it finally stopped." Richard lifted her hand, gently kissing her forefinger. "I do not think you are that someone, Viola. I *know* you are."

Viola let out a laugh as she choked back the tears welling in her eyes. "I always thought I was crazy waiting there every day. I had almost abandoned all hope, and then out of nowhere, you appeared."

"Tell me," he said, brushing the side of her cheek with the back of his fingers, "do you ever have dreams so vivid you could swear they were memories? Do you ever dream of an island surrounded by rocks with a perfect pebble beach and a meadow of golden grass and swaying bluebells, an island that feels like home?"

The question hit her with such force she felt her stomach in her throat, her face answering his question without words. She had never told anyone of that island. It had been her own private joy. How could he know of it? How could he recount every detail?

"I have dreamt of that same place, my love. It is not your memory; it is ours," Richard said with a smile, drawing his chair closer until his knees enveloped hers. "It may have been duty that sent me to Liverpool, but it was fate that guided me to the crossroads. We were meant to find each other, Viola, just as we have in the past and just as we shall in the future."

∞∞∞∞

In the days that followed, despite Agnes's insistence he stay in the guest room, Richard set himself up at an inn near Chester. Each day, he rode the thirteen miles to Hobbes Manor to visit Viola, the pair spending their time lost in private conversation as they strolled the grounds or picnicked beside the nearby lake, the hours slipping by unnoticed.

When they were not discussing travel or planning outlandish futures for themselves, they shared their dreams. Her fragments of memory matched his like puzzle pieces until, at last, Viola allowed herself to believe she had lived before, her soul bound to Richard's for eternity. As soon as she'd accepted that knowledge, she had felt a weight lift off her shoulders like she'd shaken loose the shroud of ignorance and found enlightenment.

With each passing moment, her affection grew, her once restless spirit quelled by the love Richard instilled in her heart. He promised her the world, and in his embrace, she knew he would not fail her. At his side, she finally felt like she had found her place, and in the depths of his eyes, Viola saw her entire life laid out before her. For the first time, her heart felt full.

It was not only Viola who found joy in Richard's presence either. Agnes was so elated by the turn of events that her usual temperamental nature gave way to an almost fawning adolescent excitement, her good mood trickling through the staff and brightening the manor. At first, Viola simply put the change down to her mother's pleasure that she'd finally taken a fancy to someone. As it turned out, though, the catalyst had been the sudden possibility of marriage into the aristocracy.

Agnes had been so convinced of such an eventuality, in fact, that in the brief interim when she'd excused herself from the conservatory, she had managed to dispatch a letter to her husband in Liverpool calling him back to meet 'his future son-in-law'. Her father had arrived the very next day full of eagerness and charismatic conversation. After all, nobility meant not only wealth but professional opportunities beyond any he could achieve through local suitors.

As positive as the change in her mother was to Viola's own existence, it did not serve everyone so kindly. Two days into the courtship, William had turned up unannounced, seeking an audience with Viola, only to be sent away by an uncharacteristically tactless Agnes. Catching sight of his horse through the window, Viola had requested to speak with him herself, but her mother had expressly forbidden it, barring her way until he left. Whereas only a short while ago she'd seen William as the key to marrying her daughter off, Agnes now viewed him as a nuisance and a threat to her comfortable future.

In the aftermath, Viola had been racked with guilt. As tedious as William was at times, he was a good man and deserving of an explanation as to why he'd been so abruptly set aside. In the quiet of her room that night, she had written him a letter filled with regret and goodwill in equal measure, but come the morning, she had found it in her mother's hand. Without an ounce of remorse, Agnes had torn the envelope in two and tossed it in the fire, scolding her daughter for wasting time and ink on such a frivolous pursuit.

Viola had been furious, storming out without a bite of breakfast, slamming the door of the morning room as she'd strained under the weight of her conscience and her mother's heartlessness. As she'd stepped out the front door, though, her skin bristling with outrage, she had spied Richard riding through the manor gates, and her anger had melted away. A smile had crept onto her face, and all at once, she'd wondered if perhaps there was some sense to her mother's actions.

After all, she did not owe William anything. He was not her suitor anymore; Richard was.

∞∞∞∞

Twenty-seven days came and went in the blink of an eye. Twenty-seven days of joyous morning greetings and bittersweet evening farewells. Twenty-seven days of finding herself in the depths of Richard's eyes. Twenty-seven days of falling in love with her soulmate all over again.

It was on the morning of the twenty-eighth day, however, when she was coming down for breakfast, that Viola stopped outside her mother's room. Through the closed door, she could hear the familiar voices of Alice and Hattie, her mother's chambermaid, as they stripped the bed of its covers for their weekly wash.

"What do you think of Miss Viola finding the man of her dreams?" Hattie asked. "I can't half believe he's a lord. And to just stumble upon him on her morning ride; what are the chances? It's like a fairytale."

"Man of her dreams?" Alice scoffed. "He's just a rich man who's found a pretty little bauble he can polish into a perfect wife. He doesn't love her, just like the one that came before him didn't. He's a vulture, not a valiant knight."

There was a billow of sheets before Hattie replied. "How can you say that? He rides all the way here from Chester every day just to visit her. And haven't you seen her after he leaves? She practically floats around the manor. I've never seen her so happy."

"Neither have I, but my reservations remain." Viola took a silent step back from the door as she heard Alice's voice grow nearer for a moment before moving away again, the patter of footsteps denoting the housekeeper's journey around to the other side of the bed. "Nothing ever comes that easily, Hattie. True love doesn't just come driving past to find you waiting by the side of the road. You seem to

476

have mistaken coincidence for fate."

"You've grown bitter, Alice. Sometimes life *does* work out for people," Hattie asserted.

"And sometimes life doesn't work out, and you end up alone," Alice said in a low tone clearly meant more for herself than anyone else. There was another billow of sheets, and Viola heard a scurry of feet. "Oh, for goodness sake, be careful, Hattie! You almost knocked over the vase."

"Stop fussing. It's fine. You know, you're just projecting your own worries onto the young miss. Let her be happy. She'll marry, move away to Mr Chase's lordly estates, and start a family of her own. She'll live a charmed life and never want for anything. Isn't that what we've all dreamt of? I know I have."

There was a long silence before Alice answered. "Perhaps. I don't want her to be trapped in a miserable marriage, is all. Heaven forbid she end up as unfulfilled and pernickety as Mrs Hobbes."

"You're such a dear," Hattie chuckled. "You care more for that girl than her own mother does, I swear! Come on, let's finish this bed. There's still plenty of work to do."

With that, Viola scurried off down the corridor, straightening herself before she stepped into the morning room to find her mother already seated at the table with a cup of tea. Taking a sip, Agnes nodded towards Viola's usual seat with a tight-lipped smile, where a letter sat waiting on her plate.

Sitting down, Viola turned the envelope over to find Richard's name noted as the sender, and without a care for table manners, she took her butter knife, slipped it into the fold, and pried the letter open.

It read simply:

My dearest Viola,

There is a pressing errand I must attend to this morning but do not despair, my love. I shall return to your side come the afternoon bearing a small gift and a most important question.

Yours always,

Richard

Viola could feel her cheeks blush as her heart began pounding in her ears, rereading the letter twice over to be sure she was not misinterpreting it. When she was certain of its meaning, she read it a fourth time just to bask in his words, her eyes tracing the loops of his perfect penmanship and imagining the hand that wrote them.

Finally, she looked up to find her mother on tenterhooks, her face making it clear she had asked of the letter's contents several times already, although Viola had been deaf to her pleas. Handing it over, she watched as her mother's expression changed in an instant, a clipped shriek marking the moment she realised her hopes would soon be fulfilled. Richard was to propose.

In an instant, Agnes was on her feet, hollering orders at full volume as staff ran in from every direction and dispersed again just as quickly to carry out their commands. The parlourmaid began cleaning up the entirely untouched breakfast before joining in the frantic cleaning alongside the other maids. The butler scurried off to inform the cooks of the sudden need for a meal fit for a lord come the evening. And Viola had barely stood up when Alice appeared to escort her upstairs to begin preparations for Richard's still distant arrival, her mother hurrying along behind.

The next three hours were a whirlwind. A copper bathtub was carried into Viola's room and promptly filled with scaldingly hot water and rose petals. She was then ushered into it and subsequently scrubbed to within an inch of her life under her mother's direction. Her hair was washed with egg whites and rose water, and when she was finally allowed to escape her lobster pot of a bath, she was dressed in her finest linen chemise and plonked down in a chair at her vanity table.

As her mother fussed over the details, Molly and Hattie painstakingly pinned her hair into a tight chignon and wove tiny purple wildflowers into it before taking the curling tongs to the locks framing her face. When they were done, her mother set an intimidating chest of cosmetics on the table and began painting her with so many creams and powders Viola swore she was being transformed into a doll.

With lips rouged and freckles hidden beneath a facade of ivory, Viola watched her mother carefully pack away the chest and exit the room. Left to her own thoughts, a pang of anxiety lanced through Viola's stomach. She'd been longing for this day since the moment Richard had stepped out of his stagecoach at the crossroads, and yet, when faced with its enormity, she found herself feeling wholly unprepared. All of her dresses suddenly seemed too paltry and plain for such a momentous occasion, and her mind seemed unable to string together a single response to the question she was about to face that didn't sound either stilted or unnatural.

As the floor clock down the corridor chimed midday, Alice appeared bearing a corset and a look of resignation. Molly and Hattie worked in tandem to pull the laces tight, and as the whalebones constricted around her waist, Viola's concerns only grew. Regarding herself in the mirror, she couldn't help but notice how grown up she looked, her blossoming figure reminding her she was no longer the free-spirited child of Hobbes Manor but a woman in her own right.

Attempting to take a deep breath, she heard the lacing strain in its eyelets and watched as her breasts rose until they threatened to spill out of the corset entirely, her lungs still begging for air.

"Mother, I can scarcely breathe," she said, catching sight of Agnes in the reflection and spinning around. "Is this really necess-"

Viola stopped in her tracks. In her mother's hands lay a breathtaking gown sewn of deep purple silk and trimmed with delicate ivory lace. It had a tight-fitting bodice, sweeping neckline, slender half sleeves, and a full skirt with intricate lilac embroidery and tiny glass beads decorating the hem. It was, without question, the most beautiful dress Viola had ever seen, and yet it was clearly not new.

Staring at it, her mouth agape, Viola stepped over and ran her hand along the fabric. "Mother, where did you get this?"

"Your father bought it for me twenty years ago," she replied with a sentimental smile. "The first time I wore it was at the party your grandparents threw to celebrate our engagement." Agnes unfurled the dress and held it up against Viola's frame. "I know it's a little old-fashioned, but the colour brings out your eyes. Richard is sure to be overcome when he sees you."

"Do you really think so?"

"If he is not, then he is a fool. I am so proud of you, Viola," Agnes said with tears in her eyes, stepping forward and kissing her on the forehead with a tenderness she'd not shown since her daughter was a child. "Now, quickly, put it on. He'll be here any minute."

∞∞∞∞

As it turned out, it was seventy-three and a half minutes before Viola spied Richard's stagecoach trundling through the gate, not that she was keeping track. The footman let him in, taking his hat and gloves, and Viola listened just out of sight as her mother swanned down the master staircase and welcomed him with polished conviviality.

Taking one look back at Alice and the chambermaids, Viola clasped her shaking hands in front of her and stepped out to the top of the staircase, pausing as her eyes met Richard's. He was, as always, dressed impeccably, with brown ankle boots, tan breeches, a white shirt, waistcoat, and necktie, and a dark blue tailcoat. As he smiled, the stubbornly disobedient wave of hair that melted her heart fell onto his forehead, and she couldn't help but smile back, placing her hand on the banister and beginning her descent.

With each step, the beads on her dress glimmered, rainbow dots dancing across the walls until she reached the bottom and stopped, dipping into a curtsy. "My lord," she said with a grin.

Richard stood spellbound. "My love, I have always considered you the most wondrous creature on this earth, but there are no words to describe your beauty in this moment."

Walking over, he took her hand in his and kissed it gently before fumbling in the inner pocket of his tailcoat. With something hidden in his closed fist, he bent down on one knee as Viola's heart began to race, her hand shaking.

"I wanted to do this later, down beside the lake," he continued, "but I feel my heart will burst if I wait a second longer. My dearest Viola, your voice is my soul song, your smile the balm that soothes my wounds, your eyes the ocean that washes away my sins. I want to wake up with you every morning and fall asleep with you every night. I want to make memories with you, and I want to remember them with you. I want to explore the past, the present, and the future with you. You are my greatest treasure, Viola, and losing you is my greatest fear."

Looking up at her in earnest, Richard held out the ring he had tucked in his hand, its delicate gold filigree band set with five dark purple amethysts. "I promise you my heart in this life and all that come after it. Viola Charlotte Hobbes, will you do me the honour of being my wife?"

Choked by emotion, all Viola could bring herself to do was nod, both of their hands shaking as he slid the ring onto her finger with a boundless smile.

She knew decorum would have her wait until he stood up to embrace him, but adhering to the rules of etiquette had never been her strong suit. Thus, tossing aside her inhibitions like unwanted layers on a summer's day, she leapt into his arms, both of them crashing to the floor in a bundle of joy and bursting into laughter.

"I love you, Richard," she said, brushing the wave off his forehead with a smile as he propped himself up on his elbow beside her.

Leaning in, he kissed her gently, his eyes seeming all the bluer as the sun streamed in the window and fell across his face. "And I you."

∞∞∞∞∞

The weeks following their engagement passed by in a haze of euphoria. Richard finally agreed to stay in the guest room, and Viola spent every waking moment by his side planning their future.

The wedding ceremony, at Richard's insistence, would be an intimate affair held at Hobbes Manor. With no immediate family alive to share his joy, Viola's parents would be the only witnesses, but if she was honest, she had never wanted a grandiose celebration anyway. No part of her desired the false happiness of her peers and the stilted conversations their attendance would require. All she needed was her soulmate, and the day would be complete.

After the wedding, they were to move to Richard's family estate in Scotland, where she would take up her place as Lady Viola Chase, Countess of Cromartie and Viscountess of Wick. As she rested her head on his knee beside the lake one day, he described in great detail the castle she would call home. It was, as he told it, located near the coast and surrounded by farmland on one side and dense forest on the other, with over twenty bedrooms, a ballroom large enough for two hundred guests, and sixty members of staff.

She knew she should be enamoured by the thought of such a grand residence, but as it materialised in her imagination, she found herself terrified. Viola barely knew how her small family manor ran, and the stress it caused her mother was plain enough to see. The idea of being charged with an entire castle seemed far beyond her capabilities, and despite Richard's assurance that it practically ran itself, her fear of disappointing him remained.

It was only when they spoke of travel that her concerns were finally eased, his promise of taking her in search of their pasts reminding her that she would rarely be at the castle at all. To her surprise, over tea in the conservatory one afternoon, Richard revealed he knew the location of the island from their dreams, having stumbled upon it as he'd followed the pull on his soul. Naturally, it was agreed then and there that no better place existed as a starting point for their adventure, and this agreement saw Viola dancing around the room like a child as Richard watched on with a satisfied smile.

When she had finally finished her dance and fallen breathlessly onto Richard's lap, he had, much to her delight, suggested that they marry as soon as possible so that they might begin their journey. As such, the date was set for a fortnight later.

Tasked with her daughter's most important day, Agnes became an unstoppable whirlwind of vim and vigour, dispatching multiple letters calling her husband back from Liverpool and organising everything from the priest to the napkin rings. As the details of her wedding fell into place around her, Viola, for the very first time, found a deep sense of gratitude for her mother. After years of resentment, the pair had finally discovered a bond they had been so sorely lacking, and with the next stage of her life about to begin, Viola couldn't help but be thankful that she would leave behind her a home she no longer despised.

∞∞∞

It was late on a sunny Monday morning, five days before the wedding, when William appeared unannounced at the manor. Viola's father was yet to return from Liverpool, so it was left to Agnes, once again, to greet him. After a brief conversation, she went to find her daughter, who was, at that moment, sitting in the conservatory with Richard, chatting over tea and shortbread.

"What is it, mother?" Viola asked, looking up to find Agnes standing at the door holding a neatly wrapped gift, her brow knotted.

Agnes walked over to the table, nodding politely at Richard before handing the gift to her daughter. "Mr Johnson is here. He has asked that I give you this as a gesture of goodwill. He has also requested to speak with you, to ask you a few questions and wish you luck in your new life."

"And what did you tell him?"

"He remains an important contact of your father's, so I could not turn him away again, especially considering it is a reasonable request," Agnes replied. "I told him he may see you on the condition that myself and Richard are present, and he has agreed to that. The footmen are rearranging the furniture in the parlour in preparation for the ceremony, so he is waiting for us upstairs in your father's study."

Viola nodded, carefully unwrapping the gift in her lap and staring at it in amazement.

In her hands lay a first edition copy of Gulliver's Travels, the small, handwritten note resting on top of it reading:

May this spark fire in your heart, not in your hearth.

As the sentimentality of it settled over her, she found herself a little choked up. She had not spoken to William since Richard had come into her life, and faced with his gift and his sudden arrival, she found herself playing host to a slew of mixed feelings. He had never held her affection romantically, but she did have a soft spot for his kind-hearted nature and a deep sympathy for his ill-fated search for lifelong love. As bittersweet as the meeting was to be, Viola was glad she would have the opportunity to smooth things over with him and move forward without animosity.

Placing the book down on the table, she stood up and brushed the creases from her pale blue dress, and Richard rose along with her, offering his arm and giving her a warm, bolstering smile to soothe her apprehension.

"Come on, dear," said Agnes, turning on her heel and leading them out. "The sooner we speak with him, the sooner we can all get on with our lives."

As Viola stepped into her father's study, a room she was very rarely permitted entrance to, she found a sense of familiar comfort in the air.

To the right, his large mahogany desk sat topped with a neatly stacked pile of paperwork flanked by a beautiful glass inkpot and his favourite black swan feather quill. Above the desk hung the Hobbes family's most sacred heirloom: Leviathan, a longsword dating back some five hundred years that had been passed down through the generations. Along the inner wall ran a series of floor to ceiling bookshelves stacked with countless tomes, and to her left sat two brown leather armchairs, between which stood a small wooden side table topped with a crystal decanter and two matching glasses. To Viola, the room smelt like her father, like whiskey and leather, knowledge and stoicism.

Looking over to the window, Viola saw William peering out over the gardens, his light grey tailcoat and black breeches as perfectly pressed as ever, his riding boots polished.

Agnes took the lead, walking over to William to stir him from his thoughts.

Glancing up, he met Viola with a sincere but forlorn smile, his eyes flitting briefly to Richard before returning to her. "Good day, Miss Hobbes. I had wanted this to be a private meeting, but seeing as this seems the only way to gain an audience, I guess it will have to do."

Ever a woman of etiquette, Agnes attempted to cut the tension by fulfilling her social responsibilities.

"Why don't we start with a cup of tea, Mr Johnson?" she suggested, whirling around and spotting Alice, who was quietly dusting the bookshelf in the corner. "Alice, go and fetch us a pot of tea. Quickly now!"

Alice nodded and went to leave, but William held out his hand. "That's very kind of you, Mrs Hobbes, but unnecessary. If it's all the same, I would rather say my piece and be on my way. I do not wish to take up too much of your time," he said, turning to address Richard. "Firstly, I would like to congratulate you on your engagement, Lord Chase. Viola is a fine woman, and I dare say she will make an even finer wife."

Richard nodded his thanks as Alice quietly returned to her dusting, doing her best not to interrupt the awkward situation she had found herself cornered in.

With the pleasantries over, William met Viola's eye again. "Miss Hobbes, if I may be frank, I have come in search of closure. I had been under the impression our relationship was progressing well, and yet I find myself dismissed. So, I must ask, did I do something to offend you?"

"Of course not, Mr Johnson. Quite the opposite, in fact. You are and have always been a true gentleman. The problem lies not in you but in my heart. I'm afraid I just –" she paused, taking a deep breath. "I do not love you."

Viola's gaze fell to the floor, her heart heavy with the guilt of hurting a man who had done nothing but care for her.

"And you love Lord Chase?" William asked, turning back to the window, his pain evident in the curve of his shoulders and the furrow of his brow.

"I do," she replied, looking across at her future husband, who took her hand and squeezed it gently. "With all my heart. He is my soulmate." There was a moment of silence before she continued. "Your soulmate is out there too, Mr Johnson, I know it. You must not give up the search."

William's focus did not shift from the window, the middle distance a canvas for his memories. "Alas, I fear fate snatched away my soulmate as she endeavoured to bring our first child into the world," he said, his voice heavy with resignation. With a sigh, he regarded Viola again. "Thank you, Miss Hobbes. Your words, although difficult to hear, have helped me a great deal."

As the tension lifted, Agnes released her anxious grip on the desk and looked around the room with a practised smile. "Well, now that's all out of the way, we can finally get back to the preparations for the wedding on Saturday."

William raised his eyebrows in surprise. "So soon! You two really are destined for each other, aren't you?" he said, doing his best to sound happy for the couple. "So, tell me, where are you headed after the wedding? Travelling abroad, I assume."

"Indeed. My desire for adventure has only grown since we spoke last," Viola replied, unable to hold back a grin. "We have made plans to visit Richard's estate in Scotland first, then we shall head off to explore the world. That reminds me, I must thank you for your gift, Mr Johnson. It will make for an inspiring read on the journey."

"You are most welcome," William said with a nod. "I wish you nothing but luck and good weather. Why, we may even run into each other in some distant land if we are lucky!" There was a titter of polite laughter around the room. "And where might you be starting your adventure, if you don't mind my asking? Rome, perhaps, or Vienna? Maybe somewhere further afield?"

"A small island just off the coast near Hull," she said with glee as she laced her fingers between Richard's and looked across at him, smiling.

Behind them, Alice froze, her duster falling to the floor with an unceremonious clatter.

William held out his hands, ignoring the clumsiness of the housekeeper. "An obscure choice, I must say, but I wager any destination may offer adventure so long as you are there, Miss Hobbes. May the wind be ever in your sails, wherever you end up."

Viola opened her mouth to thank him when a voice rang out from across the room. "Let go of Lord Chase's hand, my child, and come to me."

Turning, Viola found Alice facing her, arms outstretched.

"Alice, what on earth has gotten into you!" Agnes snapped. "Leave this room at once."

Alice took a step forward, ignoring Agnes's commands and beckoning Viola with a wave of her hand. "Please, Viola, you must come to me. You have no idea of the danger you are in."

Agnes stamped her foot sharply and pointed at the door. "Alice, get out of the room this instant!"

Alice glanced across at her employer, her expression devoid of its usual deference. "I will not. Your daughter is in grave danger, Agnes, and I will not leave her alone to her fate," she said before imploring Viola once more. "Please, child, come to me."

Viola frowned, looking first at Richard, then at Alice. "Why? I don't understand!"

"I have cared for you for twelve years, Viola. I have watched over you and kept you from harm. Now, I need you to trust me. Come here, and I will explain everything," she pleaded.

Viola let go of Richard's hand but stood frozen by indecision. Alice was right; she had cared for her more than anyone else, more than her own mother, but her sudden plea made no sense. There was no danger in the room, and even if there was, Richard would protect her from it.

486

Finally, Viola shook her head, stepping away from Alice until she felt Richard at her back, his reassuring hand coming to rest on her shoulder.

Realising with a pang of panic that Viola would not obey her, Alice drew herself up. "This island you spoke of, the one near Hull, was it you who mentioned it to Richard?"

"No," Viola replied, smiling up at him for a moment. "It was he who mentioned it to me. That is how I know he is my soulmate. I have dreamt of that island for years, and so has he. Isn't that amazing?"

The blood drained from Alice's face as she beckoned frantically. "Please, Viola, you must come to me, now. You are in terrible danger. PLEASE!"

Agnes took a step forward, pointing at the door again. "Enough, Alice. Leave. Now. You are relieved of your duties, and you are no longer welcome at Hobbes Manor."

Alice's eyes never left Viola as William stepped forward. "Don't worry, Mrs Hobbes. I shall escort her out myself. Consider it a gesture of goodwill to your family."

Agnes nodded her thanks, and William marched over, grabbing hold of Alice's arm and trying to usher her towards the door, but she wouldn't budge.

"Please, my child," Alice begged, yanking her arm free. "You must listen to me!"

William took hold of her again with both hands, pushing her towards the door as she struggled to stand her ground, her voice distraught as she shouted to Viola. "Do you dream about a figure of darkness? A spider who haunts your nightmares?"

Silence filled the room as William paused his attempts to expel the housekeeper, his hands still holding her firmly as he looked over at Viola.

As all eyes fell on her, Viola frowned, images of the creature crawling from the dark recesses of her mind: a figure with blades sprouting from its back like the legs of a spider, a figure that had chased and tormented her since she was a child. She had never told anyone about the Spider, not even Richard.

"How do you know about that?" Viola asked, her voice wavering slightly.

"Because I dream of him too, only he is not a figment of your imagination, my child. The Spider is real. Just like that island is real. Just like all the other places you have dreamt of are real."

"That is impossible, Alice. Places exist. Islands exist. Giant spider people do not," said Viola, growing ever more frustrated.

A look of distant sadness crossed Alice's face. "I wish that were so."

"If this Spider *is* real, if he is such a threat to me, where is he then?" Viola challenged with a look of disdain, her skin bristling with annoyance as she gestured around the room. "Is he hiding under the desk, Alice? Behind the bookshelves, maybe?"

"My sweet Viola, the Spider"–Alice grimaced, lifting her finger to point–"he stands behind you."

Viola shook off Richard's hand and spun around, taking a step back as she stared up at him. "Who are you?"

"You know who I am, my love," replied Richard with a gentle smile before reaching out and enveloping her in a warm embrace, his mouth beside her ear.

∞∞∞∞∞∞∞

Alice didn't hear what Richard whispered to Viola, but then, she didn't need to, the look in his eyes dropping its warm facade and turning cold in the space of four syllables. Before he'd even finished the last, she released the energy she'd been holding in her chest, the power exploding out of her with a crack and sending William flying across the room, his body hitting the wall beside the family sword and falling out of view behind the desk.

With heart pounding, Alice gauged the distance between her and Viola. Six steps, she just had to make it six steps, and yet each one felt as though she was stuck in slow motion, the horror around her speeding to its end at a pace she could not match. Richard met her eye as her second step landed, a grim half-smile stretching across his face, eight black blades emerging from his back. By the time she launched into her fourth step, it was already too late.

The blades arched around Viola, impaling her in a perfect line down both sides of her spine, piercing her bowels, stomach, heart, and

488

throat, her body jerking from the impact. In that moment, Alice felt the pain as if it were her own, and as her foot landed, her leg buckled under the weight of her loss. Crumpling to the floor, she heard a thud as Viola's lifeless body fell beside her, the eyes of the child she had loved as her own snuffed of their flame.

Hearing a cry, Alice looked up to see Agnes leaping towards Richard wielding her husband's quill, its pointed nib glinting in the sunlight as she aimed it at his neck, her maternal instincts overriding her fear. Time seemed to stand still all around her when suddenly, Richard retracted the blades back into his body, energy erupting outwards from him in a sphere and sending Alice careening backwards into the bookcases. As for Agnes, she was flung out the window, her back breaking the wooden frame and shattering the glass, her scream trailing behind her until she hit the gravel far below and it stopped abruptly.

With a groan, Alice struggled to her feet, sucking air into her winded lungs as she hoisted herself up using the bookcase for support. Looking around the room, she took in the devastation: the plaster of the ceiling cracked, the decanter shattered, the pile of papers strewn across the floor, the ink from the well splashed across the wall like blood splatter.

"That was very rude of you, old friend. Very rude indeed," Richard retorted, wandering over to the window and wincing as he peered down at Agnes's body. "She really should have thrown you out earlier. Then none of this would have happened."

Alice stammered towards Viola, but before she could reach her, Richard turned with a grin that made her stop short.

"Well, Little Phoenix, we meet again," he said, his once soothing tone replaced by one of smug satisfaction. "It's been such a long time since we've had a proper battle, just the two of us. I'm eager to see how your power has grown compared to mine."

He took a step forward, running his finger across the corner of the desk, its tip cutting a line through the plaster dust as he looked over at Viola. "My plan really wasn't that complicated, you know. A variation on an old favourite, really. Your sweet, innocent butterfly; she was so young, so ... malleable. Silly little thing was convinced I was her soulmate, although she barely knew what it meant. I was to marry her, take her away to some quiet corner of the world, coax out all of her memories, and groom her to love me as her phoenix. Then, when she grew assured beyond all doubt that I was you, I was to torture her, to grind her mind to dust until the aether swept her away. Imagine. Imagine the agony of such a betrayal. Soul destroying, wouldn't you say?"

"It never would have worked," Alice replied through gritted teeth, her muscles tensed, the air around her starting to shimmer. "She would have returned in spite of your best efforts. Her soul is stronger than you know."

Richard glanced back up at her, his expression darkening, his blades slowly emerging from his back once more. "Perhaps. But it is of little consequence now, isn't it? Come, Little Phoenix, the dance is over. Let us end this!"

It was at that moment, as Richard readied himself for battle, that Alice let out a laugh. "You think yourself so clever. You stand convinced you hold the winning hand, and yet you have not once looked over your cards long enough to even realise who your opponent is. You are not playing against the Phoenix, Anasazi," she said, watching with a satisfied smirk as ten purple tendrils of light crept out from her back, undulating in the air behind her. "You are playing against me."

Richard took an involuntary step back, a look of disbelief cutting through his confidence as Alice flexed her hands, blades of purple energy shooting down from the inner side of her wrists. She charged towards him, but he managed to put up a shield of his own dark energy just in time, the impact forcing them both back a few paces.

Without hesitation, Alice lunged forward, the blades at her wrists cutting through the air like steel despite their ethereal nature. Richard tried to counterattack, sending a bolt of dark energy to meet her, but she dipped out of the way, ducking low and slicing him across his calf. He screamed out in pain, his leg buckling and causing him to topple sideways as his energy exploded outwards and sent him skittering away to the far wall where one of the armchairs sat upturned. Alice, on the other hand, was propelled along the floor until she hit the wall behind the desk, her wristblades dissipating into the air as she went.

The pair rose in unison, Alice shaking her head to regain clarity and looking up to find Richard ready to strike, his eight blades poised behind him once more, darkness dancing off them like smoke. He made the first move, leaping through the air, his blades arching. Before he could reach her, Alice struck him with a ball of energy that sent him sliding back, his boots scraping across the floorboards as he struggled to stay upright, his injured calf quavering slightly.

He'd barely come to a stop when Alice brought up her hands in front of her and flexed them, the wristblades not only reappearing but shooting towards her foe like arrows. Richard barely managed to evade them, the second slicing his right arm near the shoulder, his perfectly tailored coat gaping open, the fabric staining with blood. Alice stood with a defiant glare as she watched him grimace in pain and clutch at the wound, her arms at her sides, her wristblades once again creeping down into place.

Richard glanced over at her and suddenly smiled, his blades retracting back into his body before he flung his bloodied left hand forward, dark energy streaming out and engulfing Alice. Her body stiffened as if she had been struck by lightning, the power holding her upright as her muscles spasmed uncontrollably, the pain immeasurable, the taste of blood flooding her mouth. As he released her from his phantom grip, his blades re-emerged to finish her off, and Alice collapsed to her knees.

With her eyes closed to steady her mind, she placed her fingertips on the floor and focused her energy into the floorboards. Suddenly, there was a sharp crack, and the wood gave out from beneath Richard. In an instant, he disappeared into the morning room below, and Alice heard the breakfast table break as he landed, the plates and cutlery clattering as they were sent airborne.

Heaving for breath, she crawled on hands and knees to the edge of the hole, hoping more than anything to find him lying prone and vulnerable so that she might strike one final blow. As she peeked over, though, a blast of energy barrelled towards her head. With barely an inch to spare, she yanked herself away, toppling over onto her back as Richard leapt up into the room with inhuman agility, his silhouette resembling a spider more than ever.

As he descended, blades poised to strike, Alice raised her forearm, a semi-sphere of energy springing forth to shield her. Landing at her feet, he swung his right blades around to strike but found her defences impenetrable. With a shout, he swung again, left and right, Alice shuffling backwards as she endeavoured to hold off his mounting attack. Finally, with a burst, she pushed the shield away, sending Richard staggering towards the centre of the room and scrambling to regain her feet.

Panting for breath, her eyes fell on Viola's lifeless form for a moment, a profound sadness rippling beneath her skin as she glared up at him.

"Well, well," he said, meeting her eye and stretching his neck from side to side. "You have indeed grown formidable, haven't you? I see my efforts to destroy you have only served to make you stronger. No matter, though, your power is still nothing compared to mine."

"We'll see about that," Alice hissed through her teeth, her tendrils flaring.

With a deep, bracing breath, she conjured every ounce of strength and sorrow within her and poured it outwards, the unbridled torrent crashing into Richard as he tried to defend himself. Alice did not relent, her energy continuing to pummel into him, slowly pushing him back towards the shattered window. Just before he reached it, though, the blades on his right side arched up, suddenly shooting forward, detaching from his body and lancing towards her like spears.

Alice refocused her energy into a shield, and although she was quick enough to send the first three blades ricocheting away, the fourth escaped her defences. It pierced her abdomen clean through, blood splattering out behind her onto the bookshelf, her tendrils disappearing in an instant. Collapsing to her knees, she absently felt the entry wound, and as the pain registered, she keeled over onto her back, hitting the floor with a thud.

Her mind called her to rise, to keep fighting, but her hands began to shake, a warm pool slowly expanding beneath her. She coughed, blood and spittle flying from her lips, and she sucked in a laboured breath through her nose. Hearing footsteps, she looked up to see Richard limping towards her until he stopped at her side, a victorious grin painted on his face.

"I must thank you for the inspiration. I'd never thought of using my blades in such a way until today," he chortled. "Surely you see now, no matter how powerful you become, no matter what new tricks you add to your repertoire, you are destined to remain inferior, inadequate, and wholly insignificant. I cannot be killed by you or anyone else. Your choice to suffer this same fate life after life serves no purpose. You serve no purpose." His blades flexed behind him. "Think on this as you die."

Richard reared up to strike, but before he could, his body jolted forward, the point of a sword bursting through his chest, his blades vanishing in an instant. Staring down at it incredulously, mouth gaping, he watched as the sword disappeared back through him, and he crumpled to the ground.

With her eyes still trained on where her foe had just stood, Alice blinked at the sight of William, standing in the sunlight, Leviathan's bloody blade hanging in his hand.

The sword dropped to the floor with a clang, and William knelt down beside her. "I'm sorry, Alice."

She laughed, the sound quickly transforming into a racking cough. "I should be the one apologising, Mr Johnson. It's my own fault," she croaked.

William looked over at Viola before meeting her gaze again. "I don't understand any of this. Who are you? Who was she?"

Alice took his hand and squeezed it gently. "I have lived countless lives. She was the one who showed me how. She is my soulmate."

"I ..." he trailed off, shaking his head in confusion.

"Remember this, William," she said, taking a slow breath and swallowing hard. "If our souls are strong, we can all return. Even you."

William's final words reached her muffled and indecipherable like she was hearing him underwater, and as her vision began to blur, she looked across at Viola with a smile. There was no sadness or regret in her final breath, only peace as she slipped from one life to the next, hope taking her hand and leading her into the aether only a few steps behind her soulmate.

Theo

The forest was hauntingly beautiful in the moonlight, the pine needles bristling in the breeze, the shadows mottling the moss-blanketed rocks, the roots of towering trees arching from the ground like claws. It was the kind of place that would normally fill her with wonder and calm. So why, in the midst of such tranquillity, was she so afraid?

As she stood in the moon-drenched clearing, she heard an owl flutter from its midnight perch and a twig snap somewhere behind her. With racing heart, she whirled around, her eyes flitting from tree to tree in search of movement, but she found nothing. Letting out a sigh of relief, she moved to continue onwards when she noticed light glinting off a pair of glassy black eyes. Who or what they belonged to remained unclear, the creature indistinguishable from the darkness surrounding it, and she stared at them in frozen trepidation, the wind seeming to hold its breath alongside her.

After what felt like an eternity, the creature melted out of the shadows, its true form revealed as it stepped into the clearing. Before her stood a human figure with legs like those of a spider stretching from its back, its features shrouded by a swathe of black energy that hung around it like fog. The pair stood motionless, each waiting for the other to make the first move, when suddenly, the Spider's legs twitched.

Turning on her heel, she darted into the pines, twigs whipping across her cheeks as the branches seemed to close in with every step. Then, just like that, the forest ended, and she found herself standing on the edge of a barren plain. She knew leaving the trees would mean exposing herself, but she had no choice, and so she ran onwards, the dust of the plain catching on the wind and drying her mouth.

Two hundred paces from the treeline, she dared to pause, a cough racking her lungs as she looked back. In the dim light, she could just make out the creature standing at the edge of the forest, but it made

495

no attempt to pursue her, almost as if the result of the chase was a foregone conclusion.

Spitting the dust from her mouth, she took off once more, fear quickening her pace as she scanned the horizon in vain for somewhere to hide. The grit scratching at her eyes was beginning to send tears streaming down her cheeks when, out of nowhere, a small beam of light sprang up in the distance. With nothing else to aim for, she sprinted towards it, closing the gap quickly, a door materialising ahead of her.

As she yanked it open and plunged through, she found herself no longer on the plain but in a narrow, doorless, concrete corridor. Fluorescent lights flickered on as she progressed, each one revealing more of the same until she reached a solid wall and stopped. It was not a passage; it was a dead-end. Realising her mistake, she turned around to find the Spider standing in the doorway, her own ragged panting echoing off the walls as they faced off. Her only chance of escape lay in getting past him, but as she tensed up in preparation to charge, she felt the ground move beneath her like quicksand.

Glancing down in horror, she saw the concrete begin to liquefy, her feet sinking quickly out of sight. She tried to lift one leg, but it only served to plunge the other knee-deep. The sudden shift caused her to lose her balance and topple forward at the hips, her left arm submerging into the floor as she tried to break her fall. Starting to panic, she reached for the wall with her free hand, but it offered neither grip nor stability as she sunk further.

Desperately, she tried to thrash her limbs, to propel herself through the unset concrete, but it was no use. As it began to engulf her chest, she felt the pressure squeeze the air from her lungs, her shallow breath coming out as little more than a wheeze until she was neck-deep and completely paralysed.

The last thing she saw before the floor swallowed her up was the Spider, its silhouette traced in the frame of the door. In her final seconds, as the concrete crept over her nose, the shroud of dark energy around the creature cleared for just a moment, and through tear-filled eyes, she saw its lips curl into a hideous, satisfied smile.

∞∞∞∞∞∞∞∞∞∞∞∞∞∞∞∞∞

496

Theo woke with a jerk, drenched in sweat and tangled in her covers to the point of restraint. Frantically, she tried to release herself, her mind still in a panic, her heart hammering in her ears, her lungs gasping for air. Flailing her limbs, she managed to throw aside her doona and swivel her legs off the mattress, sitting up and leaning her head over her knees to try and calm herself. The image of the Spider's smile remained in her head, though, and she found herself beginning to overheat as her panic attack worsened, her hair clinging to the sweat on her neck.

With shaking hands and still unable to catch her breath, she slid off the bed and crawled to the bathroom, sprawling out on the floor in search of cool relief. As she lay there, her excess heat seeping into the tiles, she stared up at the ceiling, the soft morning light creeping through her curtains and casting shadows around the light fixture. Focusing on the sounds of her own body, she tried to displace her fear with long, controlled breaths, distracting herself by mentally naming all the shapes she could see in the blur around her. Scales. Toothbrush. Comb. Bathmat. Towel. Toilet roll. Showerhead. When she'd run out of things to name, she began to count the tiles along the wall, the numbers growing further apart as her chest began to loosen, her temperature stabilising.

Sitting up, Theo reached over and grabbed her contact lens case from the edge of the basin, putting them in and bringing the waking world back into focus. As she looked out into her bedroom, she noticed the flecks of lint dotting the carpet, the bedding she hadn't washed in weeks, and the thin veil of dust covering the lampshade on her bedside table.

Each day off, she woke with every intention of tidying up, and yet her depression consistently robbed her of the energy and motivation to do so. That morning, however, her situation offered her the unique set of circumstances she required to rectify things. For the first time in months, her anxiety had managed to overtake depression as the driving force, and in her current state, her brain demanded she seek order amidst the chaos. Luckily, cleaning provided the necessary outlet.

That's not to say this was an unfamiliar position for Theo to find herself in. In fact, she'd been this way as far back as she could remember, her overloaded emotions forcing her childhood self to seek control through the studious sorting of her physical surroundings. It had been the reason her bedroom had always sat spotless without prompting from her mother, the reason her clothes had been folded precisely, and the reason the stationery on her desk remained perfectly aligned. It was why, at ten years old, she had taken to writing out the dictionary of her own volition and straightening the products on the supermarket shelves during their weekly grocery shop. And, it was the reason she had been scolded more than once for sorting out her closet at three in the morning on a school night after waking from yet another nightmare.

Taking one more deep breath, she rose to her feet, batting away the encroaching replay of the Spider's unsettling smile and her slow descent into a concrete grave as she marched into the kitchen and collected the cleaning supplies stashed under the sink. Six hours stood between her and the start of her evening shift, and every single one of them was filled with fastidious cleaning.

Each completed task had a knock-on effect as the things around it appeared comparatively dirtier. Washing her bedding led to the dusting of the washing machine itself, which, in turn, led to the detailed scrubbing of the bathroom. Of course, she couldn't finish the bathroom without mopping the floor, which naturally meant she had to mop the kitchen too. All of a sudden, she was sorting the jars in the fridge and vacuuming under the couch cushions, losing herself in the work until the clock neared three and the Spider was back hiding in the dark recesses of her mind.

Once she'd packed everything away, Theo stood in the centre of the lounge room and admired the fruits of her labour, her apartment immaculate. Tomorrow marked her twenty-seventh birthday, and she found solace in the fact she would enter her next year of life without the dirt of the last encasing her.

As soothing as that knowledge was, though, the fast-approaching celebrations she had planned at Benzin the following afternoon left her grappling with a possibility she had tried her best to ignore up until that point. With the distraction of cleaning no longer available, the year's most dreaded question finally took its place at the forefront of her mind: what if no one came?

Escaping her control, her memory ran through each post-high

school birthday party, one after another. The number of attendees had dwindled with the passing of time, friends falling away into the realm of acquaintances, their eager yeses yielding to soft, polite maybes, and eventually, to no response at all. Those she had once trusted as her dearest companions were now tethered to her through nothing more than the impersonal lines of social media. It was as if the currency of their friendship had been converted to Monopoly money by their own hand: superficial and of little use in the real world.

In that moment, as she checked her watch and wandered to her room to pack her uniform, she wished she could let them go, to cut the ties and free herself of the weight of their rejection. She had never been good at giving up on people, though. In her heart burnt an eternal flame for all those who had brought some good to her life, no matter how small, its fire stoked by the hope they would return to her one day. As masochistic as it was, she knew it was not in her nature to change that facet of herself. Her love was a door willingly left ajar, even when it meant parts of her were stolen.

∞∞∞∞

Work was a fairly uneventful affair. The late start meant she had little time to prep anything, and having swapped shifts in order to take the next three days off, she was unable to start anything substantial. Still, not wanting to accommodate her intrusive thoughts more than humanly possible, she whiled away the time before dinner service with in-depth planning for the following week's jobs.

As she leant over her bench, endeavouring to calculate how many macarons she'd need to cover all the upcoming functions, she saw a figure out the corner of her eye. Glancing over, she spotted Peter approaching, one hand tucked behind his back.

"It's going to be a quiet one tonight, I think," he said casually.

"Looks that way, unfortunately. Bit weird for a Saturday," she replied, tapping her pen on her list and standing up. "I'm just planning for next week's functions."

"You're off tomorrow, aren't you?"

Theo nodded, quietly amused once again that the man who wrote the roster seemed entirely incapable of remembering it. "Yeah. I'm having drinks for my birthday."

"I did hear that through the grapevine. Happy birthday," he said, placing a bottle of champagne on her bench before pausing theatrically. "I guess *my* invitation must have been lost in the mail."

Theo regarded him as she scrambled for a response, unsure if he was genuinely hurt. Of course, she couldn't exactly tell him the real reason for his exclusion: that being, his attendance would stifle the age-old pastime of ranting about one's employer over drinks.

"I didn't think you'd want to come. Besides, you're not missing out on much. It's just a small get together with a few friends," she finally replied, trying to minimise the situation. "Plus, you know, you're my boss."

Peter sighed. "Well, I'm a little disappointed, I won't lie. I mean, I have to work tomorrow, so I can't come anyway. Still, it would have been nice to be asked." He let his words hang for a moment before abruptly clapping her on the shoulder and turning to go. "All right, I'll let you get back to it."

"Thanks for the champagne," she called after him, his only response a quick nod as he disappeared around the corner.

Theo turned back to her bench, shaking her head as she tilted the bottle to read the label, her brain still trying to decipher whether or not he was being facetious.

"Peter doing his whole passive-aggressive thing again?" Ruth asked, popping her head around.

"Yeah. He gave me this"–Theo held up the bottle–"said he was disappointed he wasn't invited to the party, then proceeded to tell me he couldn't come anyway."

"What a fucking weirdo. The penis sure does do some weird shit to the brain," Ruth laughed.

"I think his crippling insecurity is more likely to be at fault for this one."

"You're probably right."

"The man gives me emotional whiplash, I swear," Theo said, rolling her eyes. "You still coming tomorrow?"

"For sure, babe! I'm having dinner with some friends beforehand, but I should be there around eight." Ruth took a step forward, peeking around the combi oven at larder before looking back at Theo. "My mission is to get Captain Teetotaller down there so drunk we have to wheel him home!"

"Hey! I heard that," said Justin, looking up from the crab beignets he was quenelling. "You're not getting me drunk. I'm driving."

"Just get a ride like a normal person. I want to see some more of those dance moves you pulled out last time," Ruth replied, breaking into a bout of what could only loosely be described as krumping, Justin cringing at the sight and getting back to work.

"Neither of you are drinking if it's going to end in *that*," laughed Theo.

"Fair call," Ruth replied. "I'm serious about getting him plastered, though. The boy needs to unwind."

"He'll be your responsibility if you do. I'm not dealing with that mess."

"Agreed," said Ruth with a wink as she scurried off to see why Peter was yelling her name from the office.

Theo smiled, pushing the bottle aside and returning to her calculations.

As with most weeks, Ruth and Justin shared at least one day off with her, their shifts covered by the crew of chefs Ruth affectionately dubbed 'the B team'. It seemed a bit cruel on the surface, but her assessment of them wasn't entirely false. They were rarely trusted to work busy shifts unless someone was on leave, and aside from section handovers on half-days, the only sign of their existence appeared to be the sub-par prep they left scattered around the coolroom. In fact, Theo's counterpart, Jordan, who Peter had hired in a fit of desperation despite his obvious lack of qualifications, was so useless that Theo was left doing the work of two people just to prevent him from destroying the pastry section in her absence.

As she clicked her pen on the bench, Theo found a deep sense of gratitude for her colleagues' willingness to sacrifice their private time for her, especially given its scarcity and value. Glancing down the bench at Justin, she felt the weight on her shoulders lightening as the image of a guestless party slunk away. For the first time, she allowed herself to contemplate something she had long denied: dropping the word 'work' from 'work friends'.

∞◌◌◌∞

Theo rose late the following day, her fitful slumber stripping her of the motivation needed to venture out of bed before midday. Instead, she simply lay starfished under her covers with her eyes closed, resting but not restful as the first half of her birthday slipped away without her participation.

Eventually, she gave up on her pursuit of further sleep and rolled onto her side, reaching for her phone to find a wildly impersonal message from her mother sitting in her notifications.

Happy birthday

That was it; that was all it said. Those two words were her only gift from the woman who'd brought her into the world.

As she read it a second time, Theo felt a mixture of sadness and anger swirl in her gut, their volatile reaction causing her chest to tighten. Even the bots running social media bothered to put her name alongside their greetings. Hell, there were distant acquaintances she barely spoke to in her inbox who at least put in the effort of adding an exclamation mark or a novelty emoji. Of course, she was thankful *one* of her parents had managed to remember, but she'd be lying if she said the half-hearted message didn't bother her all the same.

Shaking her head, she flicked the notification aside and swivelled out of bed, putting on some music to soothe her nerves while she readied herself for her party. As usual, though, the more put together she became on the outside, the more fractured she felt internally, her mind unable to distinguish whether it was excitement or anxiety setting her on edge.

It was almost one o'clock by the time she stood in front of the mirror to assess herself, taking a deep breath as she did so. She was a year older, but she neither felt nor looked any different, her appearance as stagnant as the life she lived, her reflection the same familiar shape wearing the same familiar dress and hairstyle. In fact, aside from a slight deepening of her laugh lines, she was basically interchangeable with any version of herself on any birthday for the past ten years.

Torn by the feeling that realisation brought, Theo frowned. Her soul longed for change, its claws scratching at her, refusing to be ignored. It demanded a life where monotony was exchanged for adventure, yet

502

around her heart was wrapped the warm, comforting blanket of routine, the security of sameness. It was in that moment of introspection, as she met her own gaze, that she experienced a profound burst of clarity. All these years, she had thought it a blanket, but it wasn't; it was a straight jacket.

Before she could fully come to terms with the epiphany, her phone buzzed, and she glanced over to see a message from Auryn, a smile softening the crease in her brow as she read his love-filled words. Once again, he was the light that guided her to safety, coaxing her out of depression's cold embrace with sweet nothings and quelling the storm battering her spirit.

I'm not the same, she thought to herself, peeling off her dress and marching over to her closet.

Theo hadn't worn it in almost a year, not since the day she'd found out her ex had cheated on her. Digging the knee-length, black and white striped, A-line dress out of her belongings, she slipped it on, and as she took in her reflection once again, she found it no longer turned her stomach. She was right; she wasn't the same insecure woman who had once stood broken and unlovable in that dress. Auryn loved her, and she was worthy of his love. For now, that was all the adventure she needed.

∞∞∞∞∞

Auryn was standing behind the bar when she walked through the door of Benzin, and as he looked up, she couldn't help but smile.

"Happy birthday, beautiful," he said, hurrying over to hug her before stepping back to take in her appearance in its entirety. "You look stunning!"

"Thanks," she said, looking around the bar, a small group huddled on the red velvet banquettes the only other people in the room. "Been busy?"

"Not really. Had a few people in, but that's something at least," Auryn replied, glancing back at the group of customers who'd burst into a cackle of laughter. "When Tony gets here, I'll knock off, and we can start the party. He shouldn't be long."

Theo nodded. "Sounds go-"

"Wuzzup, motherfuckers!" said a familiar voice from behind them.

503

"Speak of the devil," said Theo as she turned to see Tony sauntering over with a grin.

"Hey, bro," he said, clasping hands with Auryn before wrapping Theo in a big, if slightly awkward, bear hug. "Happy birthday, kiddo. You ready to get drunk?"

"Am I ever *not* ready?" Theo laughed.

Auryn gestured over at the bar with his head. "You cool to jump right in? I've gotta get changed."

"All good. You go pretty yourself up," replied Tony, shooing Auryn away and ushering Theo towards the booths that had been reserved for her. "Drink?"

"I knew there was a reason I liked you," she replied, settling into the corner as Tony tottered off to the bar, appearing a few minutes later with a cocktail and putting it down in front of her.

"Voila! Coconut margarita. Enjoy," he said with a flourish.

"Thanks, Tony," Theo replied with a grin before taking a sip.

As he disappeared back to his post behind the bar, Theo looked up to see Auryn crossing the room. Just like almost every hospitality worker, he looked almost unrecognisable when sporting his own style, but even Theo had never seen him quite so dressed up. His familiar work look had been set aside in favour of black pants, dress shoes, and a dark purple shirt she'd never seen before, the sleeves rolled up to reveal his tattoos. To top the transformation off, he even seemed to have run a little wax through his hair to tame its usual dishevelled state.

"What do you think?" Auryn asked, holding out his hands as he reached the table.

Theo smiled. "You scrub up all right, Mr Berenger."

"Well, you know, I thought I should put in a little extra effort. It is your birthday, after all."

Theo pointed at his shirt. "Where did you pull that from? I've never seen it before."

"I bought it last week. I had to go to seven different stores before I found one in a decent shade of purple," he grimaced sheepishly as he ran his hands down its front. "It was a little pricey, but I thought you deserved a decent-looking boyfriend for your party."

"You look good regardless of your clothing choices," she said, patting the seat beside her.

"I know," he replied, sitting down and kissing her on the cheek, "but now I look good in purple. Besides, I have an important announcement to make."

"And what might that be?" she asked, taking another sip of her drink.

"As of yesterday, I am officially debt-free!"

Theo felt her stomach flip with excitement as the words reached her. "That's amazing! I'm so proud of you."

"I told you, I'm not going to stop until we're both on that plane," he said, fumbling with something in his pocket before pulling out a credit card and a pair of scissors. "Will you do the honours?"

"I thought you'd never ask," Theo replied, taking them from him and proceeding to cut the card into smaller and smaller pieces.

Auryn hopped up from the table. "How about I get us both a drink while you finish that?"

Nodding, Theo downed the rest of her margarita and slid the glass over to him before continuing the gleeful massacre of his final credit card. Although it shamed her to admit it, she had grown ever more convinced she was on another slow march towards disappointment and heartbreak, and yet in her hands lay the evidence that proved her fear false. While she had been busy stressing over the twelve-year age gap between them and worrying he would want to settle down by the time he paid off his debts, Auryn had been busy scrimping and saving. He'd spent months bending over backwards to try and earn a raise, and his sacrifices were beginning to pay off. Now, for the first time since they'd met, he was out of the red, and Theo felt her dream of travel catch alight from its dying embers.

Time passed inexorably, but no one else showed up, not that it surprised Theo much. Instead, the hours were whiled away beside Auryn, their conversations tangential and all-consuming as he tried to divert her attention from their lack of company. Taking it as a personal challenge, Tony played his own part in the entertainment by ensuring each cocktail was different from the next and challenging the pair to guess the ingredients by taste alone. Despite their ardent attempts, she soon gave up on the idea of anyone coming at all, her phone devoid of messages no matter how many times she checked.

It wasn't until it began to grow dark that Justin finally arrived, apologising for his lateness as he sat down and regaled them with his

505

parents' attempt to prevent his attendance by loading him with chores.

Soon after, three of Theo's former colleagues rocked up, Erin, Amber, and Danny adding to the chorus of amusing kitchen stories and tales of troublesome customers being batted around the table. Just when she was beginning to feel like her hopes were not lost, though, the trio headed to the bar under the guise of buying another round of drinks and took it upon themselves to disappear without a word. When Theo noticed their absence, she found an all too familiar wound open in her chest, their sudden abandonment leaving her floundering in a mix of embarrassment and obsolescence.

Luckily, Ruth arrived a few minutes after their departure, her already alcohol-soaked personality distracting Theo from fixating on her emotions. In perfectly predictable fashion, Ruth immediately ordered four margaritas, sliding three of them to Justin and proceeding to hound him until he took a sip, his face recoiling as the tequila soaked his uninitiated palate.

Fortunately, Theo managed to occupy Ruth just long enough for Auryn to secretly swap out Justin's unwanted drinks for non-alcoholic versions, saving his sobriety whilst preventing a future ribbing. Of course, at that point, Ruth turned her flitting attention to Auryn, asking an endless string of probing questions about his intentions with Theo, much to her amusement. The lengthy interrogation continued until, rather abruptly, Ruth disappeared to the bathroom to vomit, eventually admitting defeat and allowing Justin to bundle her into a cab as he took his own leave.

As the door closed, Theo and Auryn found themselves alone again, the party over despite the clock barely reading ten, an air of disappointment lingering in the booth.

Appearing beside them, Tony began to clear the empty glasses. "Hey, do you mind if I close? It's just you two left, and I'd love to have a few drinks with you before I start cleaning."

Theo looked up from the rings of water catching the light on the tabletop to see Auryn nodding happily and Tony scurrying off to lock the door. Feeling her phone buzz, she looked over at it to find a new message in her inbox. After rereading the text she'd sent when her former colleagues had disappeared almost two hours earlier, her eyes fell on the lacklustre reply she'd just received in return.

Hey Danny. Where are you guys? I can't see you. Everything okay?

Erin and Amber were bored. Went to Revs. Forgot to say bye. Lol soz.

As she read the response for a second time, the levity of it hit her hard. Tucking her phone away before Auryn could catch a glimpse, she dabbed the tears welling in the corners of her eyes as discreetly as she could manage.

"You okay, beautiful?" Auryn asked with a frown.

She forced a smile as she met his gaze. "Yeah. Stupid contact lens won't sit still," she lied, poking at her left eye to try and quell his concerns.

Before he could ask again, they both heard clinking and glanced up to see Tony approaching with a laden tray.

"I didn't want to go back to the bar, so I just made a whole bunch. Have at it," said Tony with a grin, plonking the tray down between them all to reveal a plethora of drinks. Dispersing them, he lifted a shot of clear liquid, nodding at them to join him in his toast. "Happy birthday, Theo!"

A soft smile crept onto her face as she clinked her glass against Tony's and downed the shot. The familiar flavour of her favourite gin soothed her woes, diluting the sour taste the evening had left in her mouth, if only for a minute. Amidst the delicate notes of finger lime and ginger, her inebriated mind shook forth the memory of meeting Auryn over the same drink, and she felt a sense of relief wash over her. As she rested her head on his shoulder, his lips bestowing a gentle kiss on her hair, a single thought offered her solace. If she had no one else in the whole world besides him, that would be enough.

∞∞∞∞

The walk home was a quiet one, Theo's drunken state moving from placated to melancholic with each unsteady step, her mind replaying the night's events as the frigid air heightened her awareness. By the time they stepped into the halo of light on the landing outside her apartment, she was trapped in a loop of intrusive thoughts, the noise in her head a deafening echo of self-doubt and deprecation.

As the door clicked shut behind them, her thoughts reached a crescendo, and, overwhelmed, she crumpled onto the couch. Tears rolled down her cheeks, and she hugged her knees tight to her chest, her face buried behind them.

"What's wrong, beautiful?" Auryn asked as he knelt in front of her.

Theo didn't look up, instead just silently shaking her head.

"Come on," he said, stroking her arm. "Tell me. Please."

After a long moment, she peeked up at him, folding her arms on top of her knees and balancing her chin on them. "I'm just"–she gasped a little between sobs–"sad. I invited thirty-two people, and only five turned up. Ruth probably won't even remember it. Plus, she made Justin uncomfortable. And look," she said, showing him the message from Danny, "the others were so bored they went to Revs."

"What the actual fuck?!" said Auryn with a look of disgust. "I already thought those three were fuckheads for not saying goodbye but fuck me. 'Lol soz'. What kind of bullshit response is that? What a bunch of cunts!" Shuffling forward, Auryn wrapped his arms around her, kissing her on the forehead. "I'm sorry, beautiful. You deserve so much better than that. I think you're amazing, and I love spending time with you, even if those fuckers don't."

His words pried a tight-lipped smile from her, and as her self-doubt struggled to reconcile his compliment, she found herself responding on impulse with a snipped jibe. "That's because you're an idiot. You'd hang out with a giant stuffed toy if it looked at you the right way."

"Well deflected, beautiful, but it doesn't change the fact I love spending time with you," Auryn replied with a laugh before standing up. "I'll be back in a sec, okay? I'm just going to get changed."

"But I like you like dressed up," she pleaded, not wanting to be left alone with her thoughts.

"You want me to wear my dress pants and good shirt to bed?"

Theo posed a thinking face before nodding. "Yep. I expect you to do that from now on. Sophisticated sleepwear is the new dress code."

"I don't know, my love," he said with a grin. "I'm not sure that's a great idea. They'd get all crumpled, then where would we be?"

"Fine!" Theo pouted as she tried in vain to suppress a snicker. "I just think I deserve a dapper boyfriend, even in bed."

Auryn chuckled. "How about I make an effort to dress up more when we go out from now on instead?"

"I suppose so," she replied with a look of resignation.

"Oh, before I forget," said Auryn, rummaging around in his backpack for a moment, then returning to her with something tucked in his hands. "Now I know you told me not to get you anything, and I won't from now on, but I saw this, and I couldn't resist."

As he opened his hands, Theo was met with a small jewellery case, and she scowled. "I said no presents. Bad Auryn!"

"I know, I know," he shrugged, his smile completely devoid of regret. "Too late now, though. Go on. Open it."

"Hmm," Theo said, pursing her lips and glaring playfully at him before crossing her legs and taking the case in her lap.

Inside sat a necklace looped through a delicate, silver butterfly pendant, its wings laced with filagree so fine she was almost afraid to touch it. Something about it stirred a feeling deep in her chest that she could barely fathom, let alone name.

"Where did you find this?" she finally asked.

"Just some random shop I stumbled upon in my wanderings. I saw it in the window, and it made me think of you."

Theo picked up the pendant carefully, running her thumb across the wings, her mind spinning as a thousand thoughts and images vied for her attention. "Why a butterfly?"

Auryn leant forward, his head touching hers as they both stared at it. "A few months ago, on that night we were playing chess, you told me you were plain like a moth, but nothing could be further from the truth." He sat back on his heels, reaching up and caressing her cheek as she met his gaze. "You're my beautiful butterfly, Theo. You're the most amazing person I've ever met, and this tiny gift is my small, insignificant way of trying to show you that. I love you."

A tear tumbled down Theo's cheek, but this time, it was not from sadness but gratitude. Lifting her hand to the side of his neck, she guided him towards her until they were forehead to forehead and nose to nose, both of them breathing deeply as their souls resonated with one another, energy flowing between them.

"I love you too," she whispered.

The road stretched as far as she could see, each direction pulling at her for different reasons. Behind her lay her past, a place filled with boundless joy and deep sadness. Before her, however, lay her future, the great unknown bringing with it hope and anxiety in equal measure.

For the first time since she'd arrived here, she found herself alone. This land had been her home for ten years, and yet her dark skin sat as a reminder that she was still an outsider, her presence unwelcome amongst the superstitious locals. Adjusting her pack, she glanced around cautiously, but there was no one to be seen in either direction and no movement in the fields. She let out a sigh of relief, and with one final look back over her shoulder, she continued on her journey.

As she carried on, the sound of trickling water drifted to her on the breeze, and knowing her waterskin to be nearing empty, she followed it into the dense copse of ash trees lining the road. After a few minutes, she found herself emerging beside a small brook, its crystal-clear water babbling a playful melody over the rocks. Kneeling down, she cupped her hands and splashed her face, the chill eliciting a sharp gasp before she dabbed herself dry with the edge of her cloak. She pulled out her waterskin, drinking the last mouthful before refilling it. After downing another long draught and topping it up once more, she sat back on her haunches, her mind wandering to her soulmate, his love now alive only in her heart.

Suddenly, a rustle on the other side of the brook stirred her from her thoughts, and, looking across, she saw a tiny, pointed nose poke out from beneath a low bush. Entranced, she watched as the small creature waddled out and began to quench its thirst from a dip in the opposite bank. It almost resembled a large mouse, with dark, beady eyes and fluffy, rounded ears, and although its face and underbelly sported pale fawn fur, its back was covered in a blanket of white-tipped spines with rich brown roots. She held her breath, worried she would frighten it away, but it paid her no heed until it finished drinking. As it licked the last drops off its lips, the creature peered up, studying her warily for a long moment before turning around and disappearing back into the bushes.

Standing up with a smile, she returned to the road, finding herself newly energised by the silent encounter. The sun dipped below the horizon, painting the sky orange, but it did not bother her; instead, she quickened her pace. She would always look back on her past, that much was certain, but it was time to move on. Her whole life stretched before her now, her future full of adventures just waiting to be had, and she strode towards it with purpose. The world was waiting, and she was eager to meet it head-on.

Auryn

Auryn stopped at the intersection, waiting for the light to go green, and took a deep breath. He had spent a week worrying that Theo would be angry at him for violating her no present rule, but he'd been unable to resist. The butterfly pendant had seemed to almost call to him, stopping him in his tracks on the way to work one day and compelling him to buy it, as if his actions were guided by a force greater than himself. Fortunately, and much to his relief, she'd loved it, and in the afterglow, he couldn't help but feel their connection had somehow grown stronger.

As warming as that memory was, though, it sat at the wayside for the moment, replaced instead with an icy pang in the pit of his stomach as he marched towards the inevitable. His shift didn't start for another hour, but there was something else at Benzin that demanded his attendance: a meeting with Adam and Carlos to hear the final verdict on his raise. He'd done everything they had asked of him and more, and the time had come for an answer, but as he walked, he knew in his gut they would say no.

Running a hand through his hair as he reached the door of the bar, Auryn took out his key and opened it. There was no sign of either owner aside from Carlos's jacket lying on a table beside an empty beer bottle. That could only mean one thing: they were both already upstairs waiting for him.

The tension of the imminent confrontation only served to twist his insides into tighter knots, and before he'd even reached the bottom stair, he had resigned himself to the worst-case scenario. With one last deep breath, he trudged up to the office and knocked, Adam's familiar voice summoning him inside. Pushing the door open, he walked in to find Adam leaning forward in his chair, his elbows propped on the desk, his hands clasped in front of his mouth. Carlos, on the other hand, was sitting casually on the edge beside a pile of invoices he'd likely never even thought to look at. Both of them flashed him a tight-lipped smile as he entered, each one seeming almost commiserative in nature.

I'm screwed, Auryn thought to himself as he closed the door, turning back to them with the most optimistic expression he could muster.

"Hey," he said, receiving only a nod in response. "So, what's the verdict? I've done everything you asked. Revenue is up, costs are down, and customers are happy. Am I getting a raise?"

The pair looked at each other before Carlos turned to face him. "Look, Auryn, you've done an awesome job the last couple of months. More than we asked for, really. And you're right, revenue *is* up, and costs *are* down. It's just …"

Carlos glanced over at Adam, who drew back his lips before speaking. "Unfortunately, we're still not making enough money to grant you a raise. Times are tough, and the venue isn't as profitable as we'd like it to be. Carlos is trying to put together some events to increase our profits, and hopefully, we'll have a busy December with Christmas functions, but at the moment, a raise is just not feasible. I think the best thing to do is re-evaluate the situation in six months and see how we're tracking then."

Auryn tore his eyes from Adam's and looked down at the desk, not trusting himself to speak. A barrage of emotions swirled in his chest, but one thrust itself to the forefront and quickly quashed all others: rage. It was profound and all-consuming, boiling beneath his skin until he could feel the hairs on his arms and neck bristle.

Clenching his jaw, he swallowed the lump in his throat. He wanted to flip the desk and scream that *they* were the reason their business was failing. He wanted to make it clear that Carlos's drinking was the reason they couldn't make a profit, and that Adam's penny-pinching and micro-managing was handicapping service and strangling team morale. He wanted to remind them how much he'd done for them over the past five years, and how loyal he'd been, even when they gave him no reason to be. Above all else, though, he wanted them to know how unforgivably insulting it was for them to look him in the eye and tell him they weren't willing to pay him what he was worth.

Just when he felt like he couldn't hold it in any longer, something stopped him, and from amidst his swirling rage emerged the image of

Theo when he'd handed her his final credit card. All of this had been for her, and the thought of having to tell her he'd failed hit him so hard in the stomach he almost doubled over. As much as he longed to leave and never come back, he knew he had to persist. He would start looking for something else, but he couldn't afford to be without a source of income, even for a week; not now he'd come this far.

Eventually, Adam broke the silence. "I know this is disappointing for you, Auryn, but I can assure you this is not a decision we made lightly. Is there anything you wanted to say?"

"No," replied Auryn, avoiding eye contact as he continued to grapple with his emotions. "Thanks for considering it, at least." He paused, the tension in the air almost tangible. "I guess I'll go start the ordering."

Carlos and Adam nodded, and Auryn turned and left the room, quietly closing the door behind him. Each step felt like a marathon, his legs burdened by the weight of his failure until, about halfway down the stairs, he stopped, unable to go any further.

There, in the only blind spot of the security system, he crouched down, cupping his head in his hands, his fingers pulling at his hair as he let out a silent scream. Taking in long, deliberate breaths, Auryn felt his rage yield to an emotion far more crippling: guilt. Despite his best efforts, he had failed the only person in the world that mattered, and that knowledge destroyed him.

∞∞∞∞

The hours after the meeting passed around Auryn in a haze, his actions mechanical as he performed his job on instinct. In the inbox of his phone, Theo's messages remained unopened, his mind too shell-shocked to even think about breaking the news to her. Besides, he knew he needed to tell her in person, to be there to catch her when she fell. Before he could do that, though, he had to make it through another night of serving endless drunken uni students, and in his current mental state, that prospect was nauseating.

Adam and Carlos had slunk out of the venue in the early afternoon, leaving Auryn to wrestle with his grief alone, and he remained in that solitude until Tony arrived just before the doors opened at five.

"How's it hanging, man?" Tony asked in his normal jovial mood as he sauntered over to the bar.

Auryn shrugged, putting the polished glass down in the rack.

"I take it you didn't get the raise, huh?"

"They said they'd re-evaluate in six months," Auryn replied, his hands balling into tight fists around the polishing cloth, the fabric straining from the pressure. "After everything I've done for this fucking hellhole!"

"That's fucked. What are you gonna do?"

"I don't know," Auryn said, his shoulders suddenly slumping in futility, his arms falling to his sides. "Stay here, I guess. Maybe look for something that pays more."

Tony scanned the room. "Fuck it. Get out of here. We can handle tonight without you."

"What are you talking about? What if it gets busy?" asked Auryn.

"Meh. It's been a while since I've had my arse handed to me," Tony shrugged.

"You sure?"

"Positive. If I can't handle a Tuesday without you, I deserve to drown. Now, get the fuck outta here," Tony said with a sympathetic half-smile. "You need some time with your girl anyway. She seems sensible. Go talk to her and work out your next move."

Auryn stood torn. On the one hand, he felt guilty ditching the team on a night that had the potential to be insanely busy. On the other hand, though, Tony was right; he needed to go and talk to Theo.

"All right," he finally replied, "but if you get slammed, I'll come back in. Just let me know, okay?"

"Like hell I will," said Tony, shooing him out from behind the bar.

"I owe you, man."

"De nada," Tony replied, waving his words away. "Get out of here, you bum!"

Without another word, Auryn grabbed his backpack from the storeroom and left, his headphones already blaring his favourite songs before he reached the end of the laneway.

∞∞∞∞

To say Theo was puzzled by his early arrival was an understatement, and as she opened the door to let him in, he could see the concern written all over her face.

516

"What are you doing here?" she asked, closing the door behind him. "Did something happen at work? Are you okay?"

Auryn gave her a quick kiss on the cheek as he tossed his bag down and headed for the couch. "Tony has it under control. Come sit down. I have to tell you something."

The furrow in her brow only deepened as she sat next to him. "What happened? Did you get fired?"

"No. I -" he said, looking down at his hands, unable to meet her eye as he delivered the news. "I asked for my raise today. They said no."

"I'm sorry," she said, bundling him in a tight hug before sitting back. "Did they say why?"

"They said despite all the work I've done, the place wasn't making enough money to justify it."

"What a crock of shit! Carlos drinks more than you make in a week most nights," Theo scoffed.

"I know," he said, flopping back on the couch and clasping his hands on top of his head, "but I couldn't exactly say that, could I?"

Theo opened her mouth to disagree but thought better of it, placing a comforting hand on his knee instead. "So, what are you going to do?"

"Stay and see what happens, I guess. Maybe start looking for something else in the meantime."

Theo stared at him dumbfounded, her eyebrow arched. "You mean to tell me that after the way they've treated you, you're just going to accept it and go back! You realise they're never going to give you that raise, right? They're just stringing you along. This is some carrot on a stick bullshit."

"Yes, I know that, Theo!" Auryn snapped, immediately lowering his tone as he saw her face drop. "I'm sorry, beautiful. I just don't know what else to do. I need to save money so we can travel, and I can't do that if I don't have a job."

She sat up straight, her eyes growing stern. "No! You need to do what's right for you, Auryn. That place does nothing but make you stressed and miserable all the time. I can't stand it."

"But if we can't travel, then *you'll* be depressed, and I refuse to be the cause of that," he replied, slinking further down the couch.

"Look at me, Auryn," Theo said, leaning forward. "That's not for you to decide. I am responsible for my own life and my own emotions, just as you're responsible for yours. I forbid you from being a martyr to misery in some ridiculous belief that you're protecting me! And if you think I would be happy travelling the world with the shell of the man I love after he drained himself of life for my benefit, you are sorely mistaken."

Auryn threw his arms up in frustration before letting them fall listlessly to his side. "Well, what should I do then!"

"I can't make that decision for you," she said, the earnestness of her voice melting to a soothing coo. "What do *you* want to do, honestly? Give them an ultimatum and demand the raise?"

He thought about it for a moment, then shook his head. "No. What I really want," he said, hesitating before the last part came spilling out, "is to leave. I want to quit and never go back."

Taking a deep breath, Auryn found a sense of relief in having admitted the truth, not only to Theo but to himself. Glancing over at her, waiting for her response, a small tremor of anticipation shook his insides. He expected her to yell at him or fall silent for the rest of the night as she came to terms with the gravity of his failure, but instead, she squeezed his hand and smiled gently.

"Don't you feel better now?" she said.

"I do, but it doesn't make any difference. I can't just quit."

"Of course you can. They don't hold the power here; you do. I think you should go in tomorrow and quit on the spot. You can live on your annual leave payout while you look for something else."

Auryn grimaced. He had to tell her, but he knew it wouldn't go down well.

"What?" she asked.

"Adam and Carlos don't believe in annual leave or sick pay. They don't think it's fair to have to pay someone if they're not actually working," he answered, his face screwing up as he waited for her response.

Theo stared at him for a second, her eye seeming to twitch as she processed. "Why the fuck are you still working for these people!" she exclaimed, punching him in the leg. "I take it back. This *is* up to me now. You fucking leave! Tomorrow! Non-negotiable. You hear me? You find a proper job with reasonable bosses who pay you what you deserve, *with* annual leave *and* sick pay. Got it?"

"All right, all right. First thing tomorrow," Auryn said, holding his hands up in defence and smiling for the first time since he'd kissed her goodbye that morning. "You know, I was so scared to tell you all of this, but I actually feel relieved now."

"We're a team. You should never be scared to tell me anything. Good or bad, we face the world together."

"I don't deserve you," he said, pulling her into his arms and kissing the top of her head. "You're the best thing that ever happened to me."

"Okay, enough of that mushy stuff," she said, squirming out of his embrace and standing up. "We've got things to do. First, I'm making dinner, then we're going to discuss you moving in here."

"What? Live here? Are you sure?" Auryn asked, sitting up in shock.

Theo nodded. "After you quit, give notice on your apartment. You basically live here half the time anyway, and this way, we'll both be paying half the rent."

"But all my stuff won't fit here," he said, looking around the apartment.

"It'll be a tight squeeze, and we might have to get a little creative, but we'll sort something out," she said with a smile before disappearing into the kitchen and starting to rustle up dinner.

As Auryn digested the sudden turn his life had taken, his mind began to whir. If he was honest, Theo's apartment had been more of a home to him than his own for months, his soulless abode now nothing more than a temporary place to sleep during his working week. Still, he'd always assumed that they would shift to a larger apartment when the time came to move in together.

Wandering around as Theo cooked, he tried to visualise his own belongings in the limited space, although it was clear not everything could find a new home here. Of course, there were things he could sell; after all, they hardly needed two beds. Plus, there were things like his couch that were well and truly on their last legs that he could simply purge from his life altogether.

They discussed the finer details over their meal, the conversation continuing until he was convinced it would work. By the time he stood brushing his teeth, though, he found himself filled with a mix of competing emotions. The idea of waking up with Theo every day filled him with joy, and the thought of working somewhere that didn't make

519

him want to tear his hair out was an exciting one. Still, there was a doubt-fuelled sense of doom sitting in the pit of his stomach.

As he allowed it to fill his mind, he imagined not being able to find a job, the weight of his financial burden grating on Theo until she grew to resent him. In his mind, he saw her depression flare as she was forced to abandon her dreams, then he saw something that threatened to break him; he saw her walk away.

"Hurry up. I need someone to snuggle," Theo called from the bed.

Shaking his head to dispel his fears, he ran the tap, splashing his face with water. "I'll just be a sec," he called back, looking at himself in the mirror once more before he flicked off the light and slid into bed beside her.

"What would I do without you?" he said, tracing her cheek with his finger in the darkness.

He heard Theo scoff playfully. "Walk off a cliff, probably, you damn lemming."

"Nah ah," he retorted. "I have an excellent sense of direction!"

"An excellent sense of direction, but no common sense," she laughed, kissing him before nestling into the nook of his shoulder. "Now, get some sleep. You've got a life to turn upside down tomorrow."

"Good night, my love," he said, kissing the top of her head and laying back on his pillow with a sigh.

She's right, he thought to himself.

He'd let his unspoken concern for her interfere with his entire life, and yet only through discussing those fears with her had he been set on the right path. In that moment, he realised something profound. She was not his to protect from the flames of life; she was his to walk through the fire with.

∞∞∞∞

Daylight came, and with it, a relentless churning in Auryn's stomach. To say he was nervous would be a gross understatement: petrified was probably a more apt assessment. Still, he tried not to fixate on it as he swung out of bed as quietly as he could, grabbing his clothes and phone before making his way into the lounge room. He gazed around as he slipped on his jeans and t-shirt, picturing all of his belongings interspersed with Theo's, and couldn't help but smile. The thought of being able to come home to her every day provided him with a welcome sense of relief.

Auryn held his phone before him, staring at it with trepidation. It was now or never. With adrenaline stinging his stomach, he messaged Adam and Carlos, requesting a meeting at their earliest convenience, before stepping out onto the balcony to pace away his dread, his phone still clutched in his hand. There was a brisk wind blowing, but it didn't bother him. In fact, the bluster seemed to empathise with his anxiety as he reached one end of the balcony, checked his phone, then turned on his heel and marched to the other end, only to do the same there.

Finally, after twenty-two and a half laps, his phone buzzed, and with shaking hands, he unlocked the screen to find Adam had responded.

> *Carlos and I are both at the bar if you wanted to come in now. What's this about?*

With no desire to explain the purpose of the meeting and give them time to do damage control, Auryn simply ignored the last part of the message. Instead, he replied only with confirmation that he would be in to see them in half an hour.

Slipping his phone into his pocket, he gripped the rail of the balcony, his knuckles turning white as he prepared himself for the confrontation.

For the future and for Theo. For the future and for Theo, he repeated to himself before sneaking back to the bedroom.

Auryn opened the door quietly, not wanting to wake Theo, but as he peeked in, he found her lying there scrolling through her phone.

"Morning, beautiful," he said, wandering over and perching beside her. "I just messaged Adam and Carlos. They're both at the bar, so I'm going to head down now and get it over and done with."

"Okay," she nodded, looking up at him sleepily. "What are you going to do afterwards?"

"I'll go to mine and start sorting my life out: look for a job, give notice on my apartment, list some stuff online, and pack my shit. You sure you're okay with me moving in straight away? You don't want a few more days of freedom before I come and ruin it?"

"I'm sure. I've had quite enough time alone here. Besides, it'll be nice to have someone to come home to," Theo replied with a grin, her eyes flicking to her phone before looking back at him. "I emailed the building manager last night about a new fob. He said it'll be ready by tomorrow afternoon. Aside from that, you'll just need to get my key copied, and you'll be good to go. Why don't you swing by Porphura tomorrow and pick it up so you can get a copy made while I'm not using it? You can borrow the car too if you want, so you can start bringing things 'round."

"Sound good, beautiful," he said with a smile, his anxiety going quiet for a moment as he savoured the idea of waking up beside his soulmate every day. "Anyway, I'd better go. Wish me luck."

She rolled her eyes. "You don't need luck. You're quitting, remember? Just be firm and don't let them make you feel guilty or change your mind. And let me know how it went when you're done."

"I will," he said, leaning over and kissing her, keeping his forehead pressed to hers as he lingered. "Thank you."

"For what?"

"Everything."

∞∞∞∞∞

Auryn could barely hear his hand knocking on the office door over the sound of his heart hammering in his ears, and he entered to find Adam and Carlos standing behind the desk, talking quietly.

"What's going on, Auryn?" asked Adam, gesturing for him to sit.

Ignoring the offer, Auryn took a deep breath, letting it out slowly before answering. "I took some time to think about my position within Benzin after our meeting yesterday, and I've come to the decision that it's time for me to make a change in my life. I wanted to let you know that I am formally resigning, effective two weeks from now."

A deafening silence filled the room as Adam blinked at him in shock before looking across at Carlos with raised eyebrows.

Carlos, in turn, looked over at Auryn, holding his hands up. "I don't know what to say. I'm a little stunned."

"I understand it's a little out of the blue," Auryn replied, clasping his shaking hands behind his back, his palms slick with sweat, "but after putting in all the extra hours and effort and still not getting the raise, I

522

don't think working here is a viable option for me anymore. My heart won't be in it, and that's not fair on any of us."

Carlos nodded in resigned agreement, but as Auryn glanced at Adam, he was met with a cold stare.

"So that's how you thank us after all these years? By quitting?" said Adam, shaking his head in disgust. "I expected better from you. You're leaving us in the shit here, and I, for one, don't appreciate it."

Auryn gritted his teeth, swallowing his anger before he replied. "I'm sorry you feel that way, Adam, but you must have known this was a possibility when you denied the raise."

Carlos opened his mouth to speak, but Adam cut him off before he could get a word in. "I guess we can see where *your* loyalties lie. There's no point in you staying for another two weeks if you hate this place so much. I think you should leave."

"I don't hate this place," Auryn retorted. "Some of my best memories are here."

"I don't care," Adam replied, his voice eerily calm. "I want you to walk out of here and never come back. I don't want to see you in this building again."

The words stung Auryn, and he felt his heart sink as they reached him. Even though he had secretly wanted a clean break, hearing that he was no longer welcome in a place he'd dedicated half a decade of his life to cut deep.

Auryn turned to regard Carlos but found him looking down at the ground like a scorned child. "Fine," Auryn said, nodding slowly, unhooking the key to the bar from his keychain and placing it on the desk. "Thanks for everything. It's a shame it had to end this way. I wish you both all the best."

Adam waved his words away, turning his back as Auryn headed for the door. As he shut it behind him, he felt a mixture of relief and bitterness, the weight lifting from his shoulders only for a leaden ball of hurt to settle in his stomach. If nothing else, the feeling perfectly summed up his time at Benzin.

When he reached the bottom of the stairs, he looked around the empty bar, ingraining it into his memory, his mind playing out the best and worst of it in flashes. Then, with a sigh, he strode across the room and out the front door, closing it one last time. He would miss the good times, but there was something freeing about leaving it behind.

He was almost at the end of the laneway when he heard the door swing open again.

"Auryn! Wait a second," a voice called out, and he turned to see Carlos popping his head out, gesturing for him to stay where he was before disappearing back inside. He returned a minute later, walking towards Auryn with an apologetic expression on his face. "Hey, look, I'm sorry about Adam. He doesn't take rejection well," Carlos said, handing him a bulging envelope. "Consider this your severance package, okay? I know this isn't how either of us wanted it to end, but I'm glad you worked with us for so long, and I appreciate everything you did for us. We wouldn't have made it this far without you."

Auryn peeked in the unsealed envelope to see no less than a thousand dollars worth of fifty-dollar bills. "Thanks, Carlos. That means a lot," he said with a half-hearted smile.

"Hopefully, once the dust has settled and you find a new job, you can come back and have a drink with us," Carlos replied, holding out his hand.

"We'll see what happens," said Auryn, shaking his hand firmly, despite knowing in his heart that he would never set foot in Benzin again.

He turned to leave, but suddenly, a thought sprang to mind, and he stopped. "Oh, and Carlos. You do whatever you think is best, but if you want my advice, you should promote Tony. He's more than capable of taking over."

"Thanks, Auryn. Good luck!" said Carlos before waving and heading back inside.

Auryn took one more look at the envelope and stuffed it in his jacket, continuing down the laneway. As he reached the end, he paused for a moment, letting out his breath through puffed cheeks and allowing his shoulders to relax. Then, without looking back, he turned the page to the next chapter of his life and walked away.

Tunguska, Siberia, 1908 CE

The sun was shining, but little of its light reached the ground, the towering pines and larch trees surrounding them so densely that the rays pierced through as mere pinpricks. Each breath brought with it the smell of moss, pine needles, and fertile soil, and on the breeze floated snatches of bird calls and the rustle of small creatures in the undergrowth. Larger animals roamed the forest as well, thriving in the unadulterated wilderness of central Siberia, but they spotted them only sporadically and from a distance. For all intents and purposes, they were completely alone, but that was the way they liked it. They didn't need anyone else.

As they wove between the trees, Emilia glanced across at Rurik with a smile, reflecting for the thousandth time on the events that had brought them together. It had been two years since they'd stumbled upon one another in Saint Petersburg. She had travelled from her home in Italy, seeking the source of a pull that had tugged at her soul her entire life, and Rurik, following the exact same pull, had ventured from his home near the Urals. They had been perfect strangers, but the second they'd seen each other, they'd known.

When she'd first arrived in Russia, she'd found the people to be harsh-spoken and unwelcoming, although their distaste for her seemed to stem from the fact they mistook her for Romani rather than Italian. Of course, she could see where the misunderstanding might have come from: she had olive skin, brooding brown eyes, dark wavy hair, and was travelling nomadically. On top of that, she could neither speak nor read Russian, and thus she'd had difficulty finding anyone willing to offer her lodgings or help in any form.

Eventually, after many months of rough travel, the pull had led her to the streets of Saint Petersburg. It had been there, on a rainy autumn morning, that she had spotted three young ruffians harassing a tall, burly man with pale skin, scruffy brown hair, a bushy beard, and tattered clothing. Almost instantly, her skin had begun to tingle, her stomach leaping into her throat, and although she could not explain it, it felt like she was seeing an old friend after a lifetime apart.

The ruffians had hustled the man off the street and down a narrow alleyway, and, despite her better judgement, she'd followed them. Before she'd reached the corner of the alleyway, though, she'd heard a shout followed by a blast, stone skittering out onto the road. Carefully, she'd peeked around the corner to find the three young attackers sprawled unconscious on the ground, the man standing between them, emanating an aura of dark energy.

As she'd stepped forward, her shoe had caught one of the loose stones and sent it skipping across the ground. Looking up at her, the man's aura had disappeared, and he'd stared at her in shock. Then, all at once, his expression had changed, a broad smile appearing on his face.

"Rurik," he'd said, pointing at his chest, and Emilia had responded with her own name.

Walking closer, she'd gestured to ask if he was all right, and he'd nodded, motioning for her to follow him. Now, normally, the notion of following a stranger anywhere, let alone one that had just single-handedly dispatched three thugs with supernatural forces, would have petrified her, but in that moment, she had felt nothing but serene calm. There was something about the light in his soft blue eyes that spoke to her soul in an intimate way, and it was then that she noticed the pull was gone. Her destination was not a place; it was him.

In the days that had followed, they'd spent their time beside Lake Lagoda, just outside the city, where Rurik had set up his chum amongst the trees. It was there, in that small, conical tent of reindeer hides and wooden poles, that they'd grown to know each other and understand the history they shared.

Communication had been hard at first, but they'd persisted, and through a mix of hand gestures, drawing in her notebook, and pointing, they had worked through it. Over time, they'd managed to learn snippets of each other's language, her native Italian melding with his regional Russian dialect until they had their own hybrid of the two. More often than not, though, they could communicate with very few words at all, a knowing look expressing far more than their language barrier allowed. Despite the challenges, their bond was as strong as ever, and they would often lose themselves in conversations about their dreams, their nightmares, and their lives, past and present.

Of all the things they remembered, it was the Spider that haunted them most, tainting their joy with a constant undercurrent of fear. Each time Emilia closed her eyes, she was tormented by images of her death at his hands, his name echoing in her mind: Anasazi. It was not those memories that cut her the deepest, though, but rather her memories of Rurik's death. Night after night, she watched on as her soulmate fell to the Spider, unable to change the outcome. At times, she saw a fair-skinned, dark-haired man gasping for breath on the edge of an island that felt like home. At others, she saw a young woman with mousy-brown hair and sapphire eyes dropping lifeless to the floor beside a desk, unaware of her own power.

When Emilia had first drawn the Spider in her notebook and showed it to Rurik, only three days after they'd met, his face had told her all she needed to know. It was then that they'd made a vow: they would not allow history to repeat itself. Anasazi would not separate them, not in this lifetime.

Gathering what they needed to survive, they'd turned their back on civilisation and began their trek into the heart of Siberia, seeking refuge and anonymity amongst the trees. They convinced themselves that if Anasazi couldn't find them, if he couldn't reach them, they would be safe. As much as they wanted that to be true, though, it wasn't long before they realised that hiding was not enough to quell their fears. Their choice might serve to protect them in this life, but it would not neutralise the threat to their future selves. To do that, they needed to find a way to defeat him. As such, they spent the majority of their time training, building and refining their powers so that one day, in some future life, they might destroy the Spider once and for all.

Rurik stopped as they reached a small clearing, the roots of the trees surrounding it pushing up from the soil like the claws of some ancient monster.

"Here?" he asked, turning to her with a smile as she stopped beside him.

Looking around, she assessed the space. "Perfect."

"Rules?"

"Why?" she asked, untying the green silk ribbon from her hair and running her fingers through her thick locks to dislodge the sweat before tying it back in a high ponytail. "You always cheat anyway."

Rurik guffawed, the sound frightening a bird from its perch overhead. "Every time I win, you say I cheat, but every time *you* win –"

"It's because I beat you," she retorted, casually brushing a twig from where it had snagged on her trousers and poking out her tongue at him, dimples appearing on her cheeks as she grinned.

Shaking his head, Rurik tossed his pack down at the base of a tree and stretched his arms across his chest, his white shirt sweat-stained from the long walk. "Back to back?"

"On ten," she replied with a nod, tossing her own pack down and rolling up her shirt sleeves.

Taking up their positions in the centre of the clearing, Emilia could feel the heat radiating from Rurik's back, his shoulder blades gently touching hers as she flexed her hands at her side, eager for combat.

"Ready?" he asked.

"Ready."

She felt energy build up behind her, the hair on her neck prickling, the air pressure rising. Closing her eyes, she concentrated on her own power. It was difficult to describe, more of a feeling than something tangible, but it was always there, dwelling deep inside her. She could summon it at will these days, but it hadn't always been that way. The first time she'd used her power, it had been completely involuntary.

At seventeen, she'd been walking beside Lake Como in her hometown of Argegno when a man had begun harassing her. At first, she'd ignored his sexual remarks, her fear and anger rising as she quickened her pace and headed for home. The man had followed her, though, and as she'd turned onto her street, he'd reached out to grope her. That's when it had happened. Emilia had lunged forward to shove the man away, but as soon as she'd touched him, her anger had burst out through her hands, and he'd been sent flying across the road, slamming into a wall and falling to the ground in a daze. It had all happened so fast, she'd barely understood it herself, and in the aftermath, she hadn't told anyone.

As the years had gone on, she'd learnt to harness the power, practising when and where she could, although living in a family of ten meant time to herself was hard to find. Now that she could practise freely, though, her control over it was growing exponentially, and she was fast discovering skills she'd never even dreamt of.

Emilia felt movement at her back as she reached the count of ten and opened her eyes. There was a crunch of footsteps, and she turned on her heel to find Rurik gone, a single tremoring branch the only hint of his direction. Scanning the trees, she stayed the power in her chest and allowed it to swell, ten tendrils of purple energy appearing from her back and undulating in anticipation. A rustle of leaves came from her right, and she spun around to see a sprinkling of pine needles falling slowly to the ground. As she crept forward, a branch snapped behind her, and, wheeling around again, she searched for the source of the sound amongst the trees. Instead of her soulmate, though, she was met by a small bird shooting up from the undergrowth in a flutter, chirping as though it had frightened itself.

With each passing second, it was growing harder to contain her power, and she clenched her stomach, closing her eyes again and trying to locate Rurik by other means. It was then that she felt it. The air pressure was higher on her left, her ear on that side popping, a whistle like wind coming from overhead.

Turning her face skyward, she opened her eyes to see Rurik streaking towards her, dark energy blazing behind him, his wings outstretched. At the last moment, she stepped to the side, dodging his attack and releasing a burst of her own power into his back that sent him slamming into the ground with a grunt. Unable to stop his momentum, Rurik tumbled across the clearing, eventually coming to a stop in the tangle of roots at the base of one of the pines.

Emilia brought her arms down at her sides, producing two blades of ethereal, purple energy from her inner wrists, power emanating off them like ink in water. With a smirk, she leapt at Rurik, raising her right arm and slashing through the air, wanting to capitalise on the situation while she had the upper hand. Before she could reach him, though, the earth exploded beneath her, the force of the blast sending her careening sideways.

She tried to catch herself as she landed, rolling onto her stomach to stand up, but he was too quick. Grabbing hold of her shoulder, Rurik flipped her back over, straddling her torso and pinning her to the ground by her wrists.

Trapped and unable to use her blades, Emilia lashed out, releasing a burst of energy from her chest, but Rurik twisted his torso out of the way, the orb of purple just missing his face as she watched it dissipate into the air behind him.

With one of her arms now free, she grabbed the front of his shirt and pulled him in, kissing him hard on the lips. The sudden distraction was all she needed. As she felt him melt into it, she seized the opportunity and shoved him off her, a quick blast of energy sending him rolling across the clearing as she scrambled in the opposite direction.

Emilia was halfway to the trees when she felt the air behind her move upwards, Rurik taking off into the sky again. Pulling up short, she turned just in time to see him descending towards her, black energy dancing around him as he stretched out his hands to release an attack.

Her first instinct was to create a shield to deflect it, but she decided to stand her ground instead. Unleashing her own burst of energy, she struck him square in the right shoulder, forcing him into a spin that ended with him landing face-first in the dirt.

Taking a two-step run-up, she leapt into the air, her wristblades reappearing, but Rurik arched his spine, a semi-sphere of energy exploding from him and sending her flying. She managed to land on her feet but stumbled back until she was pressed against the trunk of a pine, her head hitting the wood and disorientating her for a second.

Winded, she heaved for breath, lifting her arms to defend herself. As the world stopped spinning, though, she found Rurik already standing in front of her, his raised fist swirling with dark power. He held it there for a moment, then pulled back, his energy dissipating harmlessly away.

Rurik flashed her a grin. "Let me guess. I cheated?"

"No. You won," Emilia replied with resignation, frustrated by her thirty-second loss in a row. "I just wish ..."

She left her thought hanging, but he understood all the same. "It doesn't matter who wins, butterfly. In the end, we'll have to fight together to defeat Anasazi. He's stronger than both of us," he said, trying to comfort her. "You're improving every day, and you took me by surprise when you didn't use your shields. That was good."

Emilia slunk down the tree into the dirt. "Not good enough, though."

He bobbed down beside her, putting a reassuring hand on her shoulder. "My soul is much older than yours, my love. I've had more time for my power to grow. Don't lose hope," he said, dipping his head to catch her eye, a cheeky grin creeping onto his face. "Maybe we could win if you kissed him. It worked on me."

Despite the disappointment weighing on her, Emilia couldn't help but laugh. Rurik was a man of few words, and he had about as much tact as a lamppost, but he always managed to find a way to make her smile.

"Again?" he asked, standing up and offering her a hand up.

"Again!"

∞∞∞∞

By Emilia's reckoning, it had to be after midnight, but the sky wasn't dark; it never got dark this time of year. Instead, she lay beside the fire, looking up at the pastel blue and soft amber of the sky, the sun tucked below the horizon but never straying far enough for her to see the stars.

In the trees above, an owl hooted, its call alternating with the snores weaving their way out the flap of the chum. Rurik had gone to bed straight after dinner, both of them having gorged on a hearty stew of sable meat cooked with freshly foraged mushrooms, the meal rounded off with a glut of berries they'd stumbled upon after their day of practice.

Their meals weren't always as satiating as that night's had been. In fact, during the winter months, the forest often left them struggling to find enough food to survive. Regardless of whether she was starving hungry or burstingly full, though, she found herself missing her mother's risotto with fried perch and the bready, buttery goodness of her nonna's miascia cake more every day.

As she lay there, the sweetness of the last berry lingering on her lips, Emilia's mind wandered back to her family. Leaving her home had been the hardest thing she'd ever had to do, and not a day went by that she didn't think of them. The deep, bellowing laugh of her father, the warmth of her nonno's hugs, the bright eyes of her younger sister, Gaia: she yearned for it all.

531

She'd wanted to tell them, to explain why she had to go, but her parents would never have approved of her wandering the world alone. Nor would they have understood if she'd showed them her power or explained her memories. In the end, the pull of destiny had overtaken her sense of duty, and although it caused her much guilt, she'd slipped away in the dead of night, the note she'd left on her pillow her only chance at goodbye.

A tear ran down Emilia's cheek, and she wiped it away, dragging her mind back from her sombre thoughts. In an effort to distract herself, she sat up, holding her hands in her lap and directing her tempestuous emotions into them, the regret and sadness prickling under her skin as it moved down her arms. When it reached her palms, she allowed the energy to spring from her skin and hover before her as a soft purple orb, its surface swirling like stormy seas.

Mesmerised by the movement, she directed her mind back to the discussion she'd had with Rurik over dinner every night for the past week: a discussion about where their powers came from and what made them grow over time. Despite hours of conversation and debate, they continued to have opposing views on the topic.

On the one hand, Rurik believed that their powers came to them in death. To his mind, each time their souls passed through the aether, they drew strength from all who'd dispersed and carried it with them to rebirth. On the other hand, Emilia stood by her own theory that their powers came to them in life. In her opinion, it was the emotions and memories they gained during each mortal existence that accounted for their growth. She believed that because they could hold their souls together, they could bind the strength of all their experiences to their eternal being and carry them forward.

When it came down to it, though, it didn't really matter where their powers came from or whether they were influenced by internal or external forces. What mattered most was learning how to bind their knowledge to their souls so that they might carry it with them into the future. If they couldn't figure out how to do that, then all the training they did in this life, all the skills they'd honed and refined, all the truths they'd uncovered, would be for naught. Every life they had to relearn their abilities from the fragmented memories of their past was a life they started steps behind Anasazi.

Emilia heard the flap of the chum open, the orb of energy dispersing as she turned to find Rurik poking his head out, his eyes bleary.

"Why are you still up?" he asked, opening the flap wider and waving her over. "Come to bed."

Standing up, she stretched out her legs, taking one last look up at the sky before she crawled in beside him. Nestled in his arms, all her anxiety and fear seemed to melt away. Each beat of his heart brought with it the comforting reminder that, should they fail in their task, there would always be a next life, a next chance. No matter what happened, whether they kept all of their knowledge or none, their love would endure, as it always had. They would find each other again.

∞∞∞∞

"Where are we going?" Emilia asked as Rurik shouldered his pack early the next morning and tugged her in a new direction.

"I want to show you something," he replied with a grin.

"Aren't we going to the clearing to practise?"

"After," he said, leading her through the trees. "There's somewhere I want to take you first."

About an hour or so later, they emerged from the trees beside a river, its clear waters cutting a winding path through the landscape, the warm sunlight glinting off its surface.

"How did you find this place?" she asked, crouching down on the bank and letting the current flow through her fingers.

Rurik sat down next to her, kicking his boots aside, peeling off his socks, and plunging his feet into the water to cool. "I went flying while you were still asleep and spotted it. I wanted to show you. You deserve to see beautiful things."

"You know, for someone so big and scary, you sure are soft-hearted," she laughed.

Rurik lifted a finger to her mouth. "Shh. Don't tell anyone," he retorted with a wink.

Emilia mimed locking her lips, tossing the imaginary key into the river before settling down cross-legged and resting her head on his shoulder.

"The river is just like us. Powerful and constant," said Rurik, kissing the top of her head and sighing as he always did before he was to say something sentimental. "When it faces obstacles, it either moves them or is moved *by* them. Over time, it changes the world around it, cutting new paths in the earth. It's never the same, but it's always there. The river will always exist, just like our love."

A contented smile sprung onto her face, and she gazed up at him. "I love you, Rurik."

"And I love you, my beautiful butterfly," he said, lacing his fingers through hers. "Today, tomorrow, and forever."

Suddenly, a sound startled them, and they both sat bolt upright. From behind them came slow, deliberate clapping, and they turned to see a sinewy man in tattered, ill-fitting clothes emerging from the trees, a wide smile on his face. He looked to be in his twenties, with brown skin, cropped dark hair, and a black tattoo of accentuated lines almost resembling stitches that ran across his cheeks from either earlobe to his lips and encircled his mouth.

Emilia and Rurik climbed to their feet, their gaze never leaving the man as he drew a few steps closer and stopped.

"Who are you?" Emilia called out, reverting from their usual mishmash language back to Italian in the hopes he might understand. "What are you doing here?"

The man drew his lips back in an unsettling grin, his eyes seeming to bore into her as he spoke a word that made her blood run cold. "Anasazi."

Feeling the hairs on her arms start to prickle, she realised Rurik was amassing his power, readying himself to strike. She reached out to grab his arm, but he held up his hand, an unfamiliar emotion crossing his face: fear.

"Run," he said in a hoarse whisper.

"No," she snapped back, Rurik's latent emotions serving only to strengthen the power swelling in her chest. "We fight together, remember? It's the only way."

Rurik opened his mouth to argue but stopped as he finally met her unbending gaze. "Together."

With a nod, they both turned their attention back to Anasazi to find he hadn't moved, his expression almost amused, like he was watching two children squabbling. Taking a deep breath, Rurik released his pent-up power around him, wings of black lightning appearing at his back, dark energy swirling at his hands. Emilia followed his lead, her purple tendrils creeping out as she threw down her wrists, her blades emerging, the wind seeming to almost buzz as it flowed around them.

"This ends now," growled Rurik through gritted teeth, flexing his shoulders as he spoke.

Anasazi let out a mocking laugh in response as eight blades emerged from his back.

Rurik didn't waste a second, lunging forward and thrusting out his hands with a shout, bolts of energy shooting from his palms as he threw everything he had at the Spider. The outward explosion that accompanied the attack was immense, and Emilia was forced to crouch into a ball to avoid being thrown off her feet, trees shaking from the force, birds taking flight.

Lifting her head as the air fell still again, Emilia looked across at their foe, blinking twice to make sure her eyes weren't deceiving her. Anasazi appeared completely unharmed, not a single hair on his head out of place despite the ferocity of Rurik's attack. As she watched, though, a trickle of blood oozed from Anasazi's nose, and he wiped it away, his lips curling into a wry smile.

All three of them stood in a frozen moment, then Anasazi let out a gleeful laugh and Rurik charged towards him, black energy trailing in his wake like smoke. He was about ten paces away when Anasazi lifted his hands and discharged a burst of darkness into Rurik's chest. The impact sent him flying backwards, his body skipping off the water like a stone and coming to rest on the far riverbank.

As much as she wanted to run to Rurik, Emilia knew her best chance of protecting him was in mounting her own attack, and she sprang towards Anasazi. He turned quickly, but not quickly enough, and she slashed her wristblades across his side and up his chest, the tattered fabric of his shirt flapping open as he stuttered backwards, blood seeping from the wounds and painting his skin crimson.

She tried to press her advantage, but as she lunged forward, she realised she'd fallen into his trap. The blades on Anasazi's right side swung around with unnatural speed, and she was forced to duck to avoid being decapitated. Seeking the safety of distance, Emilia shifted her weight to her back foot and rammed into his left hip with her shoulder, knocking him off balance as she backed out of his range.

Across the river, she saw Rurik clambering to his feet, but before he could fly back to her side, a bolt of dark energy hit him square in the stomach, and he toppled to the ground once more.

A second later, something moved in Emilia's peripherals, and she whirled to find Anasazi, the blades on his left side slicing through the air in front of her as she leapt back. Bringing up her arms, Emilia tried to slash at him from both sides, her wristblades aimed for his chest, but Anasazi flung out his hands, grabbing hold of her forearms. She tried to wrench herself free, releasing a ball of energy from her chest into his, but it simply glanced off him and dissipated harmlessly into the air with a crackle.

As she met his eye, she saw a smile tug at his lips, and it was then that she began to feel the energy he was building up around her, the hair on her neck bristling, the rise in pressure making her ears pop. The world around her darkened as an eddy of black began to engulf them, and a burning sensation surged up her arms and into her chest, her skin afire. In that moment, Emilia felt fear in its purest form. The power he possessed was incomprehensible.

Without warning, Anasazi unleashed a blast of energy outwards, the explosion cannoning into her and sending her past Rurik to a bend in the river some two-hundred metres away. She landed flat on her back, the air knocked from her lungs despite the power she'd tried to use to cushion her landing. Groaning, she propped herself up, heaving for breath as a sudden realisation struck her. Of all the power Anasazi had at his disposal, it had only taken a fraction to defeat her. This wasn't a battle for him; it was a game.

Emilia felt the air ripple again, and she held up her arm, drawing in all of her strength and creating a shield around herself. Squinting into the sun overhead, she saw the silhouette of the Spider descending, her foe landing a few paces away.

Before she could move, energy exploded past her, her shield glowing with fire as she tried to withstand the onslaught. As it began to falter, she sent a stream of energy towards Anasazi, trying to catch him off guard. Although it did succeed in halting his attack, he dodged the strike with ease, landing lightly on his feet and smirking.

With little strength left, Emilia prepared herself for the end when, out of nowhere, Rurik swooped in at high speed, his wings blazing. He hurtled into Anasazi at full force, carrying him to the nearby forest edge and slamming him into a tree. Bringing his fist up, Rurik struck him in the jaw with a loaded blow, and Anasazi twisted to the ground and tumbled away.

"Come on!" Rurik called out to Emilia, looking back over his shoulder. "This is our chance!"

Scrambling to her feet, she ran over to him, taking his outstretched hand. He didn't need to speak for her to know the plan. It was something they'd only ever talked about, but it was their only hope. They needed to combine their powers into one thunderous attack.

Emilia's heart pounded in her chest as the energy built between them, a deafening hum pulsing outwards as the air began to whip around them like a whirlwind. Through the gale, she saw Anasazi rise to his feet and barrel towards them, his blades poised behind him, fire in his eyes.

"Ready?" Rurik asked, lacing his fingers through hers.

With a small nod, she squeezed his hand, both of them raising their outer hands in front of them, Rurik waiting until Anasazi was five steps away before he gave the signal.

"NOW!" he shouted, clasping Emilia's hand tightly, power flowing between them as though they were one.

In an instant, the air fell still, and the pair released their energy, the two streams coming together before them, black and purple intertwining and ploughing into their foe with a force far beyond anything they'd achieved before. Anasazi tried to deflect the attack, to shield himself from it, but it cut through his defences like paper, hitting him full-on and eliciting a scream of pain. In desperation, he slammed his hand into the ground, blasting the earth beneath his feet and sending himself hurtling into the air, his form a dark spot in an otherwise cloudless sky.

Tracking his trajectory, Emilia realised too late that he was not careening out of control; he knew exactly where he wanted to land. Before she had a chance to turn around, though, Anasazi hit the ground behind her, four of his blades ripping through the right side of her torso, lifting her up like a skewered carcass, blood spurting into the air. She looked down, her mind seeming to swap the grassy riverbank for a pebbled beach for a split second before the blades disappeared, and she landed back on her feet. With a wheezing breath, she felt at her wounds, blood oozing beneath her fingers, its metallic taste filling her mouth. It was then that her legs buckled, and she crumpled onto her back.

As she looked up, her eyes met Rurik's. "Run," she croaked, but he didn't move. "Run!"

Rurik took a step towards her, hesitated, then ran backwards, leaping into the air, his wings flaring behind him as he took off and disappeared into the sky.

∞∞∞∞∞∞

Anasazi shook his head as he watched the Phoenix shoot into the air, a judgemental tsk escaping his lips.

A coward in this life, he thought to himself. *How pitiful.*

A laboured breath drifted up to him, and he looked down at the girl lying at his feet, smiling as he admired his handiwork. Casting his mind out, Anasazi reached into her subconscious, her language transferring across to him without her knowledge, the information stimulating memories from his own past. His brain adjusted quickly, fusing the fragments together seamlessly until speaking her language became as effortless as speaking his own: a trick he had perfected over the millennia.

"So, here we are again. Another life, another death, another failure. Will you never learn?" Anasazi said, circling her, watching as she tried to rally her strength. "You've lost the battle, and you will lose the war. I would tell you not to bother returning, but I won't waste my breath." He lifted his foot, digging his heel into the puncture wound in her chest. "I'll see you again soon, Little Butterfly."

Twisting his heel, he revelled at the grimace on her face, the girl's pained expression morphing to a plea for mercy. He tilted his head, blocking the sun from her eyes so that she might see him clearly as the aether took her, but instead, her gaze flitted over his shoulder. It was then that he heard a high-pitched whine cutting through the air like a comet screaming towards Earth.

With a smirk, he turned from the girl, lifting his hand to block the glare as he searched the sky for his foe. There, amidst the pastel colours of the morning, Anasazi spotted a bluish streak of light as bright as the sun, hurtling towards him, a thin trail of energy left in its wake.

"You should have run," he said, crouching down, drawing in his energy and focusing it into his legs.

The power within him grew as he judged the distance, counting down to the opportune moment in his head. Then, glancing one last time at the girl, he leapt into the air.

The two eternal enemies met head-on, fury striking fury, their bodies colliding with such force that it sent a pillar of fire into the air, the landscape doused in a deep red glow. The impact stopped them short, and they hovered midair, each grasping the other's shoulders, wings and blades alike flaring as they grappled.

A maelstrom of raw power began to swirl all around as they fought for the upper hand. Arcs of lightning discharged outwardly with thunderous cracks, the pressure rising until Anasazi became deaf to the world. Suddenly, a sphere of pure black energy sprang up in the space between them, absorbing their powers and combining them into a volatile mix of rage and revenge.

In its glassy surface, Anasazi could see his own reflection, his blades shining in the light, and he allowed the image of his glory to feed his strength. Inside the sphere, the darkness danced like smoke until it ran out of room to move, and as he met the Phoenix's eyes again, it began to expand, engulfing them entirely.

Time slowed to a crawl, the veil between the aether and the mortal world seeming non-existent within the confines of the sphere, and Anasazi blinked at the sight before him. His human form remained locked in battle, but his soul was no longer present within it. Instead, both he and the Phoenix lingered in the space behind themselves, their form now ethereal, their outline appearing pencil-thin. Then, just like that, the sphere burst, the pillar of fire splitting in two and fading to black.

As the barrier broke, the energy surrounding them imploded, dissolving their human forms and crushing their souls together, compacting them until their combined essence reached critical mass. At the centre of their conjoined souls, a tiny spark ignited, and with that, an almighty explosion tore the sky asunder and sent a flaming wind rippling outward. It flattened the trees as far as the eye could see, every trunk scorched, every branch stripped of its leaves. From the epicentre of the blast, a ball of black energy shot out, racing towards the bend in the river and slamming into the ground, the impact so immense it forced the water back upstream for more than a kilometre.

The next thing Anasazi knew, he was standing in the centre of a crater. Holding his hand in front of him, he regarded its ethereal outline in shock, looking through the translucent, intangible darkness that composed his current form to the scorched earth below. He'd done it. He hadn't even known it was possible, but he'd done it. At long last, after all these years, after millennia upon millennia, he had transcended mortal existence. He was a soul untethered, a being unaffected by the limitations of the physical plane. Finally, he was free to explore the cosmos, to escape the bindings of Earth and discover what lay beyond.

As he stood there, he flexed his blades, basking in the limitless energy surging through him. It was far beyond anything he'd felt before: a power stolen, born from the destruction of another. Throwing his head back, he let out a triumphant cry, the sound disregarding the laws of physics and bursting towards him like an echo in reverse.

From the corner of his eye, Anasazi caught a flash of purple, and he glanced across in horror as the third blade on his right side fell away and faded into the aether, his exultant shout cut short by an indescribable pain ripping through him. Dark energy seeped from the stump like smoke, power bleeding from the wound and lingering in the air. As he wheeled around, he saw the girl collapse to her knees behind him, her wristblades faltering before disappearing as she heaved for breath.

The pain inside him grew until it became excruciating, his very soul tearing in two. As he looked down at his hand again, he saw himself begin to disperse. In his final moment, only one thought flooded his mind.

This paltry little girl, this sapling soul, she has stolen my one chance at freedom.

It was the first time she had ever seen panic cross the Spider's face, and as Emilia watched his soul begin to disappear, she saw him as he truly was: vincible. He opened his mouth to scream, but no sound came out, his form fading faster and faster until nothing remained in his place but the mass of black energy leeched from his severed blade.

Feeling her strength draining, she sat back on her feet, her breath becoming fast and shallow, her skin growing clammy and pale. She wanted to close her eyes, but something about the black mass pulled at her soul, and she squinted, trying to focus her swirling vision.

Slowly, the cloud began to coalesce, condensing until it fused into a familiar form. In the space her greatest enemy had just departed, now stood her greatest love, her Rurik. He was not as he once was, though, his silhouette fractured as if his soul had been damaged, his features distorted in pain. He reached out to her, pleading, but as she lifted her hand to him, his essence caught on the breeze and drifted away.

As the last wisps of her soulmate disappeared, Emilia toppled onto her back, her head hitting the ground with a jolt. Spots started to dapple her vision, and she closed her eyes, a sudden realisation sending her heart racing. Gathering what energy she had left, she searched within herself for the pull that had always been there, but all she found was emptiness. The unseen string that had connected her to her soulmate had fallen loose, as though he'd disappeared not only from the mortal plane but the aether as well. She'd lost him.

To her left, she heard trickling and felt the cool waters of the river as they returned, slowly filling the crater around her and washing away the blood of battle, the chill soothing her wounds. Rurik had been right; the river always found a way. It would always exist, no matter the obstacle.

In that moment, as Emilia's life began to ebb, she felt her shattered heart come back together, and with her last breath, she made a solemn vow. Even if she had to pluck every wisp of him from the aether one by one and sew him back together with threads of her own soul, she would not forsake their love. No matter how long it took, whether it be a century or a millennium, one life or a thousand, she would find her soulmate again.

Theo

The river lapped against the shore, its force constant and inevitable. In the distance, she could see where it met the ocean, fresh and saltwater swirling together in a turbulent and never-ending battle as the sea forced its way upstream on the incoming tide.

Above her, circling gulls squawked before diving into the water in search of food, and half-hidden by the horizon, the sun hung amidst a glow of deep amber, its warmth giving way to a chill that rode in on the coastal wind. Despite the cold, she continued to wait, hugging her cloak tight around her shoulders and tucking her wavy, chestnut locks behind her ears.

As the sun ducked out of sight, she heard water slap wood, but when she looked up, she was disappointed to find its source to be a lonely log adrift on the waves, its seabound direction marking the turn of the tide. Sitting down with a heavy sigh, she pulled her knees up to her chest and wrapped her cloak around them. As the cold settled in, a sudden feeling of defeat crept into her mind, but she swatted it away like a bothersome fly. She knew he would come eventually, and she wanted to be there when he did, no matter how long she had to wait.

Finally, as the last hues of sunset yielded to starlit navy skies, she heard the dipping of oars, her heart leaping at the sight of a small boat appearing from the shadows. He'd returned at last.

∞∞∞∞∞∞∞∞∞∞∞∞∞∞

Theo opened her eyes, her lips bearing a residual smile as she rolled onto her back and looked up at the ceiling. The river seemed as vivid as any memory, and teetering on the cusp between sleep and waking, her mind sat almost convinced it was such. She could swear the smell of salt lingered in her nostrils, the lapping of water echoing in her ears. Beyond that, though, it was the deep emotion still surging through her veins that made it hard to separate her dream from reality.

The sense of déjà vu followed her as she climbed out of bed, clinging to her with a persistence she'd never experienced before. Something about the dream felt unshakably familiar, and as she packed her uniform into her bag and walked out the door, a sudden realisation struck her. The joy she'd felt at the sight of that boat was identical to the joy Auryn inspired in her each time he arrived home.

As critical thinking regained its hold in her mind, Theo found herself rationalising the dream, putting it down to nothing more than a mix of lucid imagination and a reflection of her excitement over Auryn moving in. She knew her hopes of travel were even further from fruition now that he was without income, but, strangely enough, the resentment she expected to find in her heart was not present. Instead, the weight that had lifted from Auryn's shoulders when she'd given him her blessing to quit his job had sparked a happiness in her that she was not used to bearing. It was a happiness born from seeing the one she loved find peace.

Walking through the back door of Porphura, she discovered the lesson hiding within her dream. Things would be harder for a little while, but travel would come to her in the end, just as the boat had come. All she had to do was be patient.

As she slipped on her uniform and stuffed her backpack into her locker, Theo couldn't help but smile. Closing her eyes, she took a deep breath, basking for one last quiet moment in the images of her dream and the thoughts of her future. When she arrived home, it would be to *their* home, not hers. That night, she would fall asleep in his arms, and when the morning came, she would wake up in them. From that day forward, her life would be different, better, and for the first time in a long time, she felt the light surrounding her.

Her workload for the day was monumental, but with the darkness at bay for once, she found no animosity towards it. On top of her usual prep, there were three large functions booked for the upcoming weekend that begged her attention. Before she could offer them any thought, however, she needed to craft a plethora of savoury tart shells for Peter's newest addition to the menu.

With the recipe for sour cream pastry open beside her, Theo began weighing out the flour, looking up as she saw Peter appear.

"You got my note about the tart shells, yeah?" he asked in an uncharacteristically chirpy tone.

Theo nodded towards the recipe as she poured the flour into the sieve. "All over it."

"Excellent," he replied with a smile. "How was your weekend? Have a good birthday?"

A ball of sadness caught in her throat, but she swallowed it and chose a more neutral response. "Yeah, it was good. Auryn quit his job yesterday, though, so it was a pretty hectic weekend overall."

"He doesn't want a job as a chef, does he? I'm still looking for someone to work larder with Justin," said Peter, scratching his stubble.

Theo scrunched up her face. "The kid can make a mean margarita, I'll give him that, but cooking is definitely *not* his forte."

"Well, it was worth a try," Peter laughed, turning to go before stopping short and spinning back around. "I need those tart shells ASAP, yeah? They're already on the menu."

"Yes, Chef!" she called over her shoulder, suppressing the urge to throw something at him and returning to her measurements.

The morning passed in its usual flurry of expertly timed oven coordination, frenzied preparation, and miscellaneous chaos. Peter got his precious tart shells with time to spare. Justin copped an earful for leaving a stray container on the wrong shelf in the coolroom. And Ruth, well, she was nursing a hangover so epic it took four coffees, three trips to the bathroom, and a slice of dry toast for her to cobble herself into a functioning chef in time for service.

Luckily for everyone involved, there were only a handful of tables booked for lunch, the majority of which consisted of suits with company credit cards splurging on expensive wine but skipping dessert. As such, Theo revelled in the luxury of extra prep time afforded to her, midday coming and going with little interruption to her careful balancing act of completing three jobs simultaneously. As she slid her second batch of macarons into the oven, she heard her phone buzz on the shelf above her bench and looked over to see a casual message from Auryn.

She was just setting her phone back down when she heard footsteps behind her and turned to find Justin standing there.

"Hey, Theo," he said with a nervous smile. "Have you seen that box of lettuce that came in this morning?"

"Aren't you the one who put it away?" she asked, arching an eyebrow.

Justin grimaced. "Yeah. But it's not where I put it."

"Well, I don't know. I'm the last person using lettuce in this place. Have you looked behind the other veg boxes? Someone's probably moved it."

"I'll look again," he said, scurrying off as Theo rolled her eyes.

It couldn't have been more than twenty seconds later when she heard a triumphant cry filter out from the coolroom, Justin returning to his bench with the box of lettuce tucked under his arm.

"Was it in the 'open your eyes' section?" she quipped with a smile as she strained popcorn ice cream base into a bowl and placed it in an ice bath to cool.

"I don't know what you're talking about," he replied, pursing his lips and getting back to work.

Theo chuckled to herself, walking over to the dehydrator and checking the pineapple crisps she had placed in there the day before. Justin lacked common sense at times, but he was a good guy at heart. More importantly, though, he was becoming a better chef by the day: a valuable trait in a world with far too many restaurants and not nearly enough experienced people to staff them.

She rarely had to pick up his slack anymore, and in the busier times, when she was by his side to push entrées out, the pair of them had grown harmonious in their actions. Of course, the day would eventually come when one of them would leave Porphura, and they would be forced to retrain their steps around another. Until then, Theo was glad to have him as a benchmate and a friend.

As she peeled the crisps from the paper and tossed them in sherbet powder, she saw Ruth wandering over with an apologetic look on her face.

"What do you need?" Theo asked with a sigh, her words annoyed but not accusing.

Ruth propped her hands on her hips and bent over for a second, obviously still battling the effects of her hangover. "Peter told me to tell you he needs a triple batch of those tart shells tomorrow. He doesn't want to run out. Sorry."

Theo groaned. "I already have a full prep list."

"Don't shoot the messenger," Ruth shrugged sheepishly.

"I think you're in enough pain today without me shooting you," Theo laughed. "I told you not to go out drinking with the waitstaff.

You're not in your twenties anymore."

"Yeah, yeah. I know," said Ruth, waving her comment away and standing up straight, trying to look more put together than her pallor allowed. "It was fun hanging out with you and Auryn the other night, by the way. We should do it again sometime. When I don't have other shit on beforehand, obviously."

"Sounds great. Auryn's moving into my place, so it'd be nice to go out and celebrate."

"Moving in? When did this happen?" Ruth probed, her eyebrows raised.

Theo was about to elaborate when a shout from Peter reached them from the other side of the kitchen. "Ruth! RUTH!"

"Oh, for fuck's sake," said Ruth, rolling her eyes before glancing back at Theo. "We'll discuss this over staff meal."

As Ruth scurried off to a third bellow of her name, Theo packed away the pineapple crisps, labelling the container and marking the job off her list. Scanning the remaining tasks, she decided to get a start on the cake order for Sunday, taking out the request form and rereading it, marvelling for a second time at the wild budget of the client.

Not only had they ordered a three-tiered cake, but they'd also booked out the entire venue for their exclusive use. That in and of itself wasn't unheard of. They'd had several wedding parties fork out the five-digit sum required to secure the booking, but this was undoubtedly the first time someone had done so for a second birthday party. No part of her understood forking out tens of thousands on an event the child wouldn't even remember. Then again, she'd never had tens of thousands of dollars to throw around in the first place.

It seemed strange to her that just across the dining room sat people who made her entire year's salary in a month, and she'd be lying if the thought did not embitter her somewhat. They frittered away money on expensive wine and complained when the prices went up by a dollar or two. All the while, they wantonly ignored the fact that the people serving them were often working themselves into the ground to ensure they could afford both food *and* rent.

Her mind was just beginning to venture down the rabbit hole of all the good she would do if she shared the wealth of those she cooked for when the docket printer sprang into action beside her. As she listened, she recognised the sequence of noises it was emitting, her trained ear identifying it as a dessert docket without looking, and a long one at that.

Tearing it from the printer, Theo looked at the order in surprise: a table had ordered every dessert on the menu. She frowned as she saw the table number, wandering over to the pass and surveying the room. It was not the group of six businessmen who had placed the order, as she'd initially suspected, but rather a man seated alone at a table in the centre of the dining room.

Confused, she waved down Craig as he walked past. "I think you put the table number in wrong on this one," she said, handing him the docket.

"No, it's right. The guy said he'd heard about the desserts here and wanted to try them all," Craig replied with a snort. "He's a weird unit. He didn't order anything savoury. Didn't even look at the menu. Just sat himself down, called me over, and told me he wanted one of every dessert."

"Does he want them staggered at least?" she asked.

"Nope. He said to send them as they're ready."

Theo raised an eyebrow and took the docket back. "Umm, all right then. Whatever the customer wants, I guess."

As Craig hurried off towards the beckoning table of businessmen, Theo looked across the room at the man, who was sitting casually in his seat, legs crossed and sipping an espresso. He looked to be in his forties, with jet black, wavy hair that hung to his shoulders and a neatly-trimmed box beard.

Before she could regard him any further, he glanced up, and Theo hurried away. Pulling her finished macarons out of the oven and sliding them into the racks below to cool, she took a moment to mentally organise the steps of service in her head. With the soufflé made and baking, she set about plating up the remaining desserts, sending each one in quick succession. Finally, the oven timer buzzed, and she called for service one last time. Satisfied with her handiwork, she watched as the soufflé was set beside the other five plates on the table, the man taking a spoonful here and there, trying them in no particular order.

Not wanting to get caught staring at him, Theo returned to her prep bench, her mind moving its focus to Sunday's cake. She'd barely finished upscaling the recipe's measurements when Craig called her over to the pass, a sigh escaping her lips as she once again stepped away from a job she just couldn't seem to start.

"What's up?" she asked as she reached him.

"So, I've got an odd request. That guy just demolished all those desserts, and now he wants to meet you."

Theo raised an eyebrow. "Me? Why?"

"I don't know. Probably wants to thank you," replied Craig, leaning across the pass, his voice a whisper. "I think he might be a food blogger."

Peter sidled up beside Theo. "What's going on? Is there a problem?"

"No problem. A customer just wants to talk to Theo, that's all," Craig said with a shrug.

"The one who ordered all the desserts?"

"Yeah, the guy on twenty-three."

"You comfortable doing that?" Peter asked, looking across at Theo. "You don't have to if you don't want to. I can tell him you're busy."

Theo considered the request for a second before she answered. The thought of speaking to the man made her queasy and anxious, but she felt a sense of duty given the fact he'd come to Porphura just for her desserts. Besides, a little praise was always a nice way to break up the monotony of a fifteen-hour shift.

"It's okay. I'll go."

"Excellent!" said Craig, clapping his hands together.

Untying her apron, Theo set it down on her bench, brushing the flour from her jacket and straightening the creases. With a deep breath to calm her nerves, she walked out of the kitchen, meeting Craig at the pass and following him to the table.

"Sir," said Craig with a deferential nod. "May I introduce our pastry chef, Theo."

The man stood up to greet them, running his fingers through his hair to sweep it off his face before offering her a smile.

"May I clear these out of your way?" asked Craig, moving to collect the near-empty plates.

The man waved him away with an air of nonchalance. "No, thank you."

Craig gave another obliging nod and turned to go, mouthing the word 'weirdo' at Theo before swanning off across the room.

"Nice to meet you," said Theo, meeting the man's eye. "You wanted to speak with me?"

The man gave her another small smile and gestured at the seat opposite him. "I did. Please, sit."

Theo glanced back at the kitchen, her stomach churning. She'd thought he would just say a quick thank you and send her on her way. As Peter met her eye, he gave her an encouraging nod, and so, with a sense of apprehension, she sat down, taking a moment to regard the man in greater detail.

He was well dressed, sporting polished leather loafers, dark brown chinos, an expensive watch, and a crisp white shirt with rolled-up sleeves and an open collar. From his accent, rich tan, and strong features, she assumed he was Spanish, and as she looked closer, she noticed the darkness of his eyes and the grey flecking his beard. The thing that perplexed her the most about him, though, was his build. He was a large man, broad-shouldered and muscular with barely a shred of fat on him: the kind of man who most certainly does not eat dessert regularly, especially not six at a time.

The man straightened his watch, then clasped his hands in his lap. "Thank you for coming out to meet me. I know you don't like these kinds of situations."

His comment caught her off guard, and not knowing what to say, she simply laughed politely, reasoning that he was probably just reading her body language.

Staring at her intently, the man shifted in his seat. "I must say, Theo, your desserts are quite something. When you've lived as many lives as I have, food becomes such a meaningless thing. A way of nourishing your body, nothing more. But what you've created here" -he spread his arms over the remnants of his meal- "magnificent." Picking up his spoon, the man used it to point at the black plate to his left. "What was this one, might I ask?"

Theo took in a quiet breath. The man was starting to freak her out, but she felt trapped and obliged to answer. "Coconut parfait with roasted pineapple and kaffir lime sorbet," she replied, praying to gods she didn't even believe in to save her from the awkwardness.

"Of course. It reminds me of a trip I took to Cuba to see an old friend. Wonderful!" he laughed before pointing at the bowl beside his right elbow. "How about this one?"

"Rose crème caramel with lychee foam and raspberries."

The man nodded before gesturing at another plate. "And this one?"

"Salted caramel soufflé with popcorn ice cream and passionfruit coulis," she said, thinking to herself that all of this was clearly written on the menu, had he actually bothered to read it.

The man smiled to himself, placing the spoon down and leaning back in his seat. "You know, after everything we've been through, I'm surprised I've never noticed what an amazing cook you are!"

Theo froze. He was talking as if they'd met before. "I'm sorry. Do I know you?"

"My apologies. I'm confusing you," the man said, holding his hands up in a gesture of regret. "My name is Ambrosio Moreno."

"I don't believe I've ever met anyone by that name before," she replied, anxiously wringing her hands together under the table.

"That doesn't mean we do not have a long and rich history together, does it?"

Theo could feel her heart thumping in her chest. The man was clearly insane. She glanced over her shoulder, trying to catch Craig's eye, but he was busy schmoozing the businessmen with his back to her. With little other option, she turned back to Ambrosio, deciding to engage him in the hope of making some sense out of what he was saying.

"I'm sorry, sir, but I still don't have any idea what you're talking about. I think you may have me mistaken for someone else."

Ambrosio cocked his head, a bemused smile tugging at his lips. "I find it so fascinating, the differences between us. Whereas I have trained my soul to carry my memories and knowledge unfettered into each new life, you remain unable to achieve such a feat. You waste your time on pointless emotions instead. Such a pity."

"Look, Mr Moreno, I'm glad you enjoyed the desserts, but I'm afraid I have to get back to work now," said Theo, rising to her feet, her mind so loud with her anxiety's call to flee that she wasn't even registering his words.

"Nonsense," he said, gesturing towards the chair again. "Please, sit down. There's one more thing I must tell you."

Every fibre of her being wanted to run away, but her fear of making a scene forced her back into her seat against her better judgement.

Leaning forward, Ambrosio placed his elbows on the table, resting

551

his chin on his clasped hands, his eyes boring into her. "Now, what I'm about to tell you might seem ridiculous, crazy even, but I need you to listen carefully. This is very important." He paused, waiting for her to nod before he continued. "My name is Ambrosio Moreno, but that has not always been my name. My soul has lived for thousands of years, in different bodies and at different times."

"What, like reincarnation?" she asked with a sceptical frown.

"Not exactly," he replied, tilting his head from side to side. "There is no grand plan, no gods, no karma to dictate my fortune in the next life. When most people die, their souls dissolve into the aether, their unbound energies mixing and forming fresh new souls, devoid of any remnants of their past. Mine, however, does not. When my body withers and my life ends, my soul remains complete, travelling through the aether in search of a new body to inhabit." He paused theatrically. "Just as yours does."

Theo sat silent for a second as she tried to reconcile what he was saying, but none of it made any sense to her. The aether, past lives, it all just sounded like the ramblings of a madman.

"With all due respect," she finally replied, "I don't believe in that kind of thing. We are who we are; there is nothing beyond that. We live, we die, we rot, and if we're lucky, we manage to do something of value in the interim."

"You don't believe?" he asked with a puff of laughter. "You've grown cynical in your old age, my dear. It's a wonder you've made it this far at all." Ambrosio sat back in his chair again, brushing a few crumbs off his lap and crossing his legs. "Tell me, Theo, do you ever have dreams so vivid you almost think them real?"

His question stopped her short, the image of the boat on the river flashing through her mind, begging for answers. Her common sense knew better than to entertain the coincidence, though, and thus she swept the thought aside. "Everyone has dreams like that."

Ambrosio regarded her with a smile. "That's simply not true, I'm afraid. The dreams of ordinary folk fall into two categories: those that help them sort through the trials and triumphs of their lives and those that offer whimsical entertainment for their idle subconscious. Of course, we have those as well, but people like us, we have dreams of another kind, dreams fed by the memories we carry with us from times long since passed. We dream of who we once were, the places we saw, and the people we knew. We dream of our joys and our sadnesses, our successes and our failures."

Theo remained silent as she allowed his words to settle over her. Something in them drew forth images from her dreamscapes: gazing at a castle from the edge of a forest, walking down a road with weapons hidden beneath her cloak, dying of thirst in a desert, hanging in a dungeon wearing nothing but her fear. As her rational mind regained the driver's seat, she clenched her teeth, scorning herself for her childishness.

"I know you don't believe me, Theo," Ambrosio continued, "but I can prove it. I'm going to tell you something now that will convince you I am speaking the truth. A single word that will unlock all you have tried to deny."

"What word?" she asked, raising an eyebrow.

Ambrosio propped his elbows on the table again. "My true name. The one I take from life to life. The namesake of my soul." He gestured for her to come closer, and as she leant in, one whispered word escaped his lips. "Anasazi."

Theo's first reaction was one of confusion as he presented her with yet another unfamiliar name. A mere heartbeat later, though, a second reaction sprung up. As the name wove its way into her mind, it seemed to spark a deep-seated fear in the very pit of her stomach, and although she did not understand it, it threatened to overwhelm her all the same. With her pulse racing, she looked up to find Ambrosio watching her with a satisfied smile, the smile of a predator.

"You know that name, don't you?" he said, reclining back in his seat, his voice ice cold. "You have no memory of hearing it, yet it stirs an innate fear deep within you, clawing at your soul, opening old wounds. It is a fear born from a past you can barely remember, but you bear its scars, nonetheless. You have lived before, Theo, and I was there with you. You can see that now. It's written in the furrow of your brow, in the rise and fall of your chest, and in the squareness of your jaw."

As she sat in the aftermath of his words, she found her initial fear ebbing, leaving in its place an unease that gnawed at her. What he was describing was utterly ludicrous: defiant of all sense and science. Yet, for reasons beyond her comprehension, despite her mind's rejection of all he'd said, her heart and gut knew he was telling the truth. She *had* lived before. Her soul knew it, even if she didn't.

Theo felt her world begin to spin as though she was losing control of her own existence, all she'd ever known seeming to unravel around her. She needed time to process what he was saying, but in the absence of such a luxury, she did the only thing she could think to do; she sought answers.

"Why are you here?"

"I won't lie to you," said Ambrosio, looking past her into the middle distance. "I've been having somewhat of an existential crisis of late. My entire existence has been centred around power, both increasing my own and quashing it in those around me. A selfish endeavour, I'll admit, but one I committed myself to long ago. Recently, though, I've begun to question my choices. I used to relish my life's work, but I feel as if I'm simply going through the motions these days."

He paused, picking up the spoon again and swinging it lightly between his fingers as he pondered. "You know what I think the problem is? A while back, I found a different path for my life, one that would offer me true fulfilment. Of course, I should have discovered it centuries ago, but I was too caught up in my own youthful hubris to see it," he said, chuckling to himself before his expression changed to one of rueful sadness. "Unfortunately, that path is lost to me now, and I fear my motivation to carry on has been lost with it."

"What happened?" she asked, something about his loss stirring her empathy. "How did you lose your path?"

"What happened?!" Ambrosio snapped, his eyes flaring with anger. "You should know. You –" He stopped, taking a steadying breath before giving her a wry smile. "Of course. You don't remember anything about Siberia, do you?"

"No, sorry. I've never been to Russia. I've never even been overseas."

"Not in this life, dear." Ambrosio pointed the spoon at her. "Don't worry, they all come back in the end, the memories. Even I am not immune to losing them from time to time. It happens to the best of us. When we are faced with trauma, mental and physical, our connection with our past becomes blocked. We don't forget, as such, but we remain cut off from our memories until the pain recedes and the fog clears. Sometimes they drift back to us slowly like gentle snowfall, and sometimes, if we face a sudden shock, they surge back like an avalanche."

"Is that what happened in Siberia? Did we face a trauma together? Is it why I don't remember? Is it why you lost your path?"

"Uh-uh-uhh," Ambrosio said, shaking his finger at her. "You have to remember that for yourself. Me telling you won't accomplish anything."

There was something in the way he was looking at her, the way he smiled, that sang of a man holding all the aces. He knew what had happened, yet he withheld the information from her willingly, teasing her with fragments of the truth. He was playing with her for sport and loving every second of it. It almost reminded her of –

No, Theo thought to herself. *Past lives, fine. But not that.*

"Can you at least tell me *how* I've managed to come back?" she asked, finding herself determined to pry what information she could from him regardless of his wanton secrecy. "Is it something you're taught?"

Ambrosio chuckled at her question as though she were a child. "It is not something that *can* be taught. It is, for the most part, the luck of the draw. If fortune favours you, your soul will be strong enough to hold together in death, and you will return to new life unchanged. After a soul has achieved this once, it continues to do so almost on instinct. The more it does, the easier it becomes. Only great despair can stop the cycle. Only in stripping the soul of its strength of will can the cycle of death and rebirth be stopped."

"This aether you keep talking about, what is it? Is it like purgatory or something?"

"To be honest, I have no idea," Ambrosio replied with a shrug. "I met a theoretical physicist once, German, I think, lovely guy. Anyway, it turns out he himself had been born before. We spoke in length about the aether before we parted ways. He speculated that it's another dimension that exists all around us, although we cannot detect it. A dimension for the soul, if you will. Much of his life was dedicated to its study. He even had a name for people with souls like ours, souls that remain unaltered. He called us Children of the Aether."

Theo weighed his words. "And you believe his theory to be the truth?"

"His guess is as good as anyone's, I suppose."

For the first time in the conversation, Theo finally had a lead towards someone else who might help her understand all of this, someone who might offer her more clarity than the titbit talking stranger across the table.

"Where is this man now?" she asked with a pang of hope. "Is there any way I can reach him?"

"He's dead, I'm afraid. A shame, really. He was a truly remarkable man," Ambrosio said.

Putting the spoon down, he sat back and scratched his chin. "Now, where was I? Ah, yes. My existential crisis." He straightened his watch again before continuing. "The crux of my problem occurred to me only recently. I've realised that culling all those who are born again is no longer sustainable. There are more than seven billion people in the world now, and the number of souls that have learnt to return is increasing exponentially. I simply can't keep up anymore."

The feeling of unease in Theo's stomach spiked at the word 'cull', adrenaline flooding her system. There was no way of misinterpreting such a word, and given how calculated the man had seemed thus far, she knew well enough he had placed it there with purpose. All at once, the things he had said before found new meaning: quashing the power of others, visiting old friends, parting ways with the physicist.

As surreptitiously as she could, Theo scanned her peripherals for something to defend herself with, but she found nothing. Short of gouging him with the spoon or throwing a plate, she sat unarmed.

"Is that what you do then?" Theo asked, her voice quavering with a mix of anxiety and scorn. "You go around the world killing anyone like you?"

"None of them are 'like me'," Ambrosio said, taking umbrage at her comparison. "And I can't just kill them; that's far too myopic. If I did, their souls would simply return again in a new body. Haven't you been paying attention to anything I've told you? The cycle can only be broken by great despair. They must suffer before they die."

Theo took a slow, bracing breath, her mind running a million miles a minute to process his words. Not only was the man a serial killer, but he appeared to be an immortal and highly sadistic one to boot.

"But why?" she asked. "Why kill them? What purpose does it serve?"

"The power born from the aether is mine by right. It is not for them to have, nor is it yours."

In that moment, only one thought stopped her from falling into a blind panic. "You said you couldn't keep up, though. You said you'd lost your motivation to continue on your path."

Ambrosio gave a short mocking laugh. "Indeed. My life's work has become an endless game of whack-a-mole, so I've decided to give it up and pursue a new path."

"And what is this new path you've chosen?" Theo asked, swallowing the knot of fear in her throat.

"Of that, I am still uncertain," he replied. "I once stood with two choices before me, but I now stand at a dead end. I must take some time to contemplate what I wish to achieve with my existence." He fiddled with his sleeve and let out a sigh. "It's a sad day when you realise that as powerful as you are, you're still ignorant as to how the universe truly works."

His answer brought her some modicum of relief, and she loosened the white-knuckle grip on her knees ever so slightly. Still, for all the talking they'd done, he still hadn't answered her original question.

"So why are you here then?" she asked again.

"Simple," said Ambrosio, smiling broadly. "I'm here to kill you."

The blood drained from Theo's face, and she felt her heart drop.

Despite his threat, Ambrosio made no move towards her. Instead, he watched her with a look of calm amusement. "I know what you're thinking. I said I had forsaken that path. There are always exceptions to the rules, though, aren't there?" he said, his eyes narrowing. "The thing is, Theo, I have a hatred for you that burns unrelenting. I may have given up hunting the mewling miscreants, but I will never stop hunting you, if only to see the expression on your face as I end your miserable existence, again and again and again."

The venom in his voice made Theo queasy, and her mind reeled as it see-sawed between fight or flight, her thoughts jumping from one plan to another and finding none of value. She sat without a weapon, her knives were far from reach, and her colleagues remained out of earshot and eyeline. With no other option, she decided to keep him talking, hoping in vain that something or someone might miraculously appear to save her.

"I don't understand. Why do you want to kill me? I haven't done anything to you."

"You have, though," he replied, reaching across his body and touching his right side. "You have stolen something from me that cannot be replaced, and in doing so, you have sealed your fate. You will pay for what you did, in this life and all that come after it."

Theo sat frozen and silent. He was going to kill her for something she didn't remember doing, in a life she had no recollection of.

"Originally, I'd planned on dispatching you in my usual way, wielding despair as a weapon to convince your soul to disperse," he continued, clasping his hands in his lap and peering out the window as if bathing in wistful thought. "I was so sure it would work this time too. You see, Theo, I've been following you for years now. When I found you in this life, you were just a teenager, sitting alone in the schoolyard, your depression already alive and well, your mind barely treading water without my intervention. Circumstance provided me a job half done, and from there, the rest was easy. Every shred of misery you have endured from that day onward bore my fingerprints, in one way or another. Your family's disinterest, your friends' abandonment, your partners' betrayal, even your own self-doubt: all of it was my doing."

Ambrosio let out a small sigh of contentment. "It really is deceptively simple, you know, entering the minds of others and persuading them to follow their own selfish desires. We're all just a whisper away from enacting our own doom."

With his words came flashes of all those who'd walked away in her hour of need. Theo felt a wave of melancholy wash over her, and for a moment, her soul shrank back into the shape of the lonely teenager she'd once been. Finally, the wave ebbed, and Auryn appeared in her mind.

"If your plan was to isolate me, to murder me with misery, I'm sorry to break it to you, but you failed," she said, her voice growing defiant. "I am not unhappy, and I am not alone."

"Ahh, yes, you have a new flame now, don't you. Auryn. That's his name, isn't it? I found no need to bother with that one. He has enough problems to sabotage himself without my help. Besides, he's inconsequential," Ambrosio replied, a grin creeping onto his face. "In the end, it doesn't matter who you try and fill the space with. Boy or girl, it makes no difference. None of them will fill the void. None of them will change the truth. Your soulmate is gone."

"Soulmate?"

"Surely your dear little phoenix has visited your dreams. Or have you forgotten him too?" Ambrosio asked with a tilt of his head.

A thousand images of the Phoenix raced through Theo's mind. The dark figure with wings like lightning; he couldn't really exist.

"You must be awful at poker, my dear," Ambrosio snickered. "Your face gives you away every time. The Phoenix exists, or at least he *did* exist. It's ironic, isn't it? I spent so long trying to destroy him, but I really need not have bothered. When it came down to it, his destruction was his own. That was always his problem, of course. Whereas I enter each battle having considered every possible outcome, he entered with reckless abandon. A headstrong but ineffective hero."

A spark of hope sprung to life in Theo's head as she found the flaw in his final sentence. "If you consider every possible outcome, how is it that I stole something from you?"

"All this time, I believed the Phoenix to be my penultimate threat, but his power was too similar to my own, born of the same rage and hatred. Your power, on the other hand, is born of emotions I once considered to be your greatest weaknesses, emotions I do not share: empathy and love. I underestimated you, Theo, and it cost me dearly. It is not a mistake I will make again."

"What power? I don't have any power," said Theo, scrambling for a way to dissuade him. "I'm just a pastry chef. I pose no threat to you."

"As long as you draw breath, Theo, as long as your soul endures, your power remains. Whether you're aware of its existence or not is irrelevant. The threat you pose is not dependent on your knowledge."

"So, what happens now then?" she asked, her hands shaking as she waited for an answer she didn't want to hear.

"In a moment, you're going to stand up, and the manager will come over to see what the problem is. After all, I've kept you far longer than he expected," Ambrosio said, his gaze darting over her shoulder towards Craig for a second. "When he gets here, I will kill him and lay waste to the restaurant. I will kill every person here: every customer, every chef, every waiter. Then, when you have seen all those around you fall to my power, I will kill you."

Theo did not respond. Instead, she sat paralysed by her fear, holding her breath like it was the only thing keeping the inevitable at bay. Ambrosio basked in her terror, savouring the indulgence until finally, he winked at her and raised his hands theatrically.

"Let's get this started then, shall we?" he said before slapping the table as hard as he could, the plates between them clinking, the spoon clattering to the floor.

Jolting out of her seat in surprise and stumbling to her feet, Theo felt the hair on the back of her neck begin to prickle.

In a flash, Craig appeared beside the table, looking from Ambrosio to Theo in search of an explanation. "Is everything all right here?"

"Run!" Theo snapped, waving him away, but he didn't move.

As they both turned their attention to Ambrosio, Theo saw the air around him begin to shimmer. Ever so slowly, black blades emerged from his back like the legs of a spider, their colour like night distilled.

Faced with the creature of her nightmares, Theo felt everything she knew begin to fall away around her. As spine-chilling as his silhouette was, though, it wasn't the blades that made her blood run cold but rather the gap on his right side: the gap where an eighth blade should have been. In its absence, in the space left behind, Theo found the proof of his honesty. It was true, all of it.

Craig opened his mouth to react, but before he could make a sound, Ambrosio's hand shot out and clamped around his neck. A split second later, the three blades on his right side sliced through the air, piercing Craig's torso. Ambrosio let him dangle there, blood dribbling from his mouth, before the blades drew back, and Craig slumped lifelessly onto the table, the plates crashing to the floor.

Every instinct in Theo's body told her to run, but as she looked at Ambrosio, his very being pulsing with unseen power, she knew any attempt at escape would prove futile. Instead, she decided to make a stand, hoping that in going against his expectations, she could catch him off guard.

She lunged at him, her intention to knock him to the ground and buy herself enough time to reach the front door, but it wasn't to be. His icy grip clasped her throat just before her hands connected with his chest, her feet lifting until she stood on her tiptoes.

Through bulging eyes, she watched as his blades retracted back into his body, his stern expression yielding to a vicious smile as her skin began to prickle again. "Ahh, the memories," he said, hoisting her higher until she was left flailing for a foothold.

Suddenly, Theo felt something slam into her chest, the force sending her flying backwards and crashing into the wall above her service window. She collapsed to the ground, gasping for breath as she crawled across to the metre-high divider that separated the three nearby tables from the service space beside the pass.

Pressing her back hard up against the divider, she looked across at the businessmen scrambling from their seats in terror. She felt the air pressure rise, and a beam of pure darkness sliced across the room, indiscriminately striking down all six men, their blood spraying across the wall behind them.

With her head still ducked out of Ambrosio's sightline, Theo sidled along the divider in the direction of the side door that led to the foyer of the apartment building. When she reached the edge, she peered around, spotting Ambrosio's feet amongst the table legs, his back turned. As she went to move, Theo heard a scuttle and spotted Katie, the blonde waitress, bolting out from under one of the tables and rushing behind Ambrosio in an attempt to reach the same side door. Just before she passed him, though, he spun on his heel, his left four blades reappearing in an instant and slashing into her as he completed his turn.

Stifling a scream at the sight of her colleague's mangled form tumbling to the floor, Theo shuffled to the other end of the divider in search of an alternate escape route.

As she surveyed her fast-shrinking options, she spied Luca, the new bartender, crawling out from behind the bar and heading for the function room door only a short distance away. He was just beginning to slide it open when she felt the air pressure rise again and saw a blade trailing with wisps of smoke-like energy shoot across and lance through his chest, blood pooling on the hardwood floor beneath him.

Theo had barely pressed her back to the divider again when she heard Ambrosio's slow, deliberate footsteps drawing closer. Not wanting to be caught on the floor, she moved to stand up, but before she could, he grabbed her collar and hauled her to her feet.

"You taught me that little trick, you know," he said, nodding towards Luca's blood-soaked body before tossing her backwards over the divider.

Slamming into the top of a neatly-set table, Theo slid off and crashed to the floor in a mess of crockery, glassware, and upturned chairs. She propped herself up, expecting him to attack again, but as her hand crunched into the broken ceramics at her side, she saw Ambrosio vault over the pass and disappear into the kitchen.

A second later, she was met with the sound of knives clattering to the floor and a gargle of pain, followed by a shout from Peter that cut off abruptly. Theo tried to find her feet, but she slipped on the blood-slick floor and fell hard on her backside again.

There was a scream, and as she glanced up at the pass, she saw Ruth reaching for its edge. Her face was splattered with blood that was not hers, and she met Theo's eyes with a look of pleading before she was dragged back out of sight.

A stillness settled over the restaurant, the hum of the exhaust fans and the gentle beat of the lunchtime playlist the only sounds remaining. Suddenly, Theo saw a figure fly through her service window and land to her left with a thud. Recognising Justin's shape in the huddle of crimson-stained white fabric, she crawled over, taking hold of his shoulder and rolling him onto his back. Her eyes darted along the series of puncture wounds peppering his torso until they fell on his lifeless face, horror contorting her features as she realised she was the only one left.

Again, she heard footsteps and glanced across to see Ambrosio striding out of the kitchen, his blades poised eagerly behind him, blood splatter streaking his shirt. "See?" he said with a grin as he walked towards her. "It all went exactly to plan. This is your future, Theo. Death and despair. Torment and suffering. It doesn't *have* to be this way, though. You can join your little phoenix in the aether. You can find peace there. You need only let go."

Theo scooted backwards, her shoes fighting for traction in the blood as she passed Craig's table-top resting place, the afternoon sun glistening off the trail of red left in her wake. Eventually, she felt the warm glass of the front window against her back, and she pressed herself against it, using it as leverage to regain her feet.

Ambrosio stopped his approach and brought his hands up, his blades retracting as black energy swirled between his fingers, coalescing until it became a sphere of darkness. "Goodbye, Little Butterfly. May we never meet again."

As Theo stared into the abyss of the sphere, her racing thoughts fell silent, and she was left faced with one incontrovertible truth: she was going to die. All of a sudden, the image of Auryn kneeling beside her coffin appeared in her mind, and she felt her heart sink. The scenes of his joyless life in her absence replayed in a millisecond, the last frame clearing just in time to see Ambrosio throw out his hands and send the sphere of energy racing towards her.

She raised her forearms to defend her face, peeking between them as she braced herself for the inevitable impact, but it never came. Instead, she watched in shock as the sphere seemed to hit an unseen barrier, its power absorbed, the kinetic force it expended sending her flying backwards through the window. Shards of glass followed her, smashing into the asphalt and skittering away as she landed amongst them, rolling to a stop in the middle of the road.

Theo blinked, her vision a mix of blinding sunlight and dizzying spots. With a groan, she drew her arm under her shoulder and propped herself up, coughing as she struggled to take a breath, her body aching, the taste of blood on her lips. The park came into focus, its lush green lawns devoid of people, and she was struck with a fresh surge of adrenaline. She didn't know how she'd blocked the sphere, but there wasn't time to contemplate the mystery. She'd delayed her death, not stopped it.

There was a crunch behind her as Ambrosio's slow steps ground the broken glass into the concrete of the footpath, and she froze, weighing her options. Running would be futile, even if she could muster the strength and clarity to stand. As for any hope of assistance, that disappeared in the passenger seats of the cars halting at the nearby intersection before quickly driving away.

With no other option but to fight, Theo pulled her legs in and bundled herself into a crouched ball, readying herself to attack. She clenched her fists, and as the footsteps stopped behind her, she sprang into action. Spinning around, she thrust herself upwards, a sharp uppercut aimed at Ambrosio's jaw. Once again, he outmatched her speed and grabbed her wrist, a grim smile meeting her as they faced off.

"You always did have a knack for shields," he mocked, his breath hot on her face.

Suddenly, Theo felt his fist collide with her cheek, and she crumpled, the back of her head connecting hard with the concrete. Wincing in pain, she blinked up into the sun to see Ambrosio standing over her, his blades re-emerging from his back and twitching in anticipation.

"It was pure instinct that protected you in there, Theo, nothing more.

563

It won't be enough to save you, though," he said with a smirk, placing a foot on her chest and pinning her in place. "Even at your most powerful, you could never defeat me."

Theo groaned, shifting her shoulders and gritting her teeth, her fear yielding to defiance as if she'd discovered long-forgotten bravery in the face of certain death. "I'm sure I'll figure it out eventually."

"Perhaps," he laughed as the three blades on his right reared up, poised to strike, "but not today."

Theo closed her eyes tight, turning her head away as she waited for the end. Then, out of nowhere, she heard someone cannon into Ambrosio, his foot leaving her chest as he crashed to the ground. She scrambled away, standing up and cradling the back of her head with her hand until the spots cleared from her vision.

Blinking in shock, she recognised the familiar features of her saviour as he regained his feet. It was Auryn, his stern gaze fixed on Ambrosio, who was picking himself up off the asphalt, his blades gone, his silhouette once more that of a perfectly mortal man.

Before she could call out to warn him, Auryn charged forward, ramming his forearm into Ambrosio's chest and marching him backwards into the side of the black Audi sedan parked outside Porphura.

"Stay away from her, you piece of shit!" Auryn hissed through his teeth.

Ambrosio responded with a smile, grabbing Auryn by the throat and lifting him into the air. A burst of energy smashed into his torso, and he was propelled onto the lawn, a good ten metres away.

"And who might you be, my good samaritan?" Ambrosio asked as he strode past Theo to the edge of the park. "This is a private matter, and if you have any sense of self-preservation, you'll leave. Now."

Auryn stood up, brushing the grass from his t-shirt. "Not gonna happen. That's my girlfriend, you sick fuck!"

Ambrosio glanced over his shoulder at Theo before turning back to Auryn. "Ahh, yes, the new attempt at happiness," he snickered as he strolled forward, his hands clasped calmly behind his back, the air shimmering around him. "And here I thought I wouldn't get the chance to kill you in front of her. Impeccable timing, my friend."

Ignoring the comments, Auryn raised his fists, throwing a sharp right hook at Ambrosio's face, but he sidestepped it with ease. Theo saw dark energy spring to life in Ambrosio's hands, and before she could react, Auryn was sent flying backwards, skidding across the grass and rolling to a stop.

Regaining her senses, she tried to run over to help, but two steps in, her vision began to spin. She collapsed to her knees, the back of her head throbbing, the pain making her nauseous. All she could do was watch on helplessly as he approached Auryn, who lay flat on his back, still gathering his wits.

Bending down, Ambrosio grabbed him by the shirt, hefting him up before hitting him with another blast of energy that sent him careening towards the road and crashing into the footpath, barely three paces from Theo.

Ambrosio strode over to his prone body, glancing across at Theo with a smug smile. "You know what? I think I'll have a poke around in his head before I kill him, find out what fears and secrets he has rattling around in that brain of his. Maybe he was cheating on you like your last one," he said, raising his eyebrows. "Let's find out, shall we?"

Auryn was barely on his knees when Ambrosio reached down and clamped his hand around Auryn's throat, forcing him to his feet and driving him back three steps until he was pinned against the boot of a silver SUV.

"I have to warn you, my friend," he said, his booming volume clearly chosen so that Theo would hear every word. "I can perform this trick so painlessly you wouldn't even feel it, but where's the fun in that. No, for you, it will be agony beyond your wildest nightmares."

"No! Wait!" Theo protested, trying to crawl towards them but finding her arms still too weak to bear her weight.

Her plea went unheeded, and as she sat back on her heels, she saw Ambrosio clasp Auryn's forehead with his left hand, his right still tight around his throat. Taking a bracing breath, Theo tried to boost herself onto her feet, but before she could move, she felt the air fall still. The next second, an ungodly scream burst from Auryn's lips. Ambrosio stumbled backwards with his head in his hands, his own scream coming out in unison. Released from his chokehold, Auryn collapsed into a crouched huddle, his palms pressed to his face as he cried out over and over.

Theo looked from one to the other, frozen by indecision. Part of her wanted to go to Auryn, to cradle him in his pain, but the other part of her knew this was her only chance to get the upper hand on her opponent.

Before she could decide, Ambrosio lifted his head, his eyes trained on Auryn, disbelief staining his face.

"No!" he bellowed. "It's impossible! How did you survive? HOW DID YOU SURVIVE?!"

Glancing across, Theo watched as Auryn pushed himself away from the SUV and staggered across to the edge of the park lawn, his cries growing so intense she could feel it tearing at her heart. As his next cry escaped him, her skin prickled, and she looked down to find the hairs on her arms standing on end. The air pressure began to rise, her ears popping as she turned her attention back to Ambrosio, expecting an attack. To her surprise, though, she found him still staring at Auryn.

All at once, the pressure plummeted, and a sound akin to a bass drop rippled outwards. Auryn let out a deafening, drawn-out cry, throwing his head back as a whirlwind of black energy sprung to life around him, funnelling upwards into the sky like a tornado. Clamping her hands to her ears and curling into a ball, Theo peeked across to see the branches on the nearby trees contorting, leaves dislodging and catching in the updraft. At the centre of the chaos, she watched shafts of energy dancing with black lightning slowly stretch out from Auryn's back like wings, and her breath caught in her throat. The Spider was wrong; the Phoenix was alive.

Another thousand questions joined the chorus in her head, but there was no time to ponder them. The vortex dissipated until all that was left was Auryn, his form encased in a translucent fog of black energy, his wings flowing behind him. Forcing herself to her feet with a groan, Theo called out to him, but Ambrosio was faster than her words, lunging towards Auryn with inhuman speed. Without warning, Auryn threw up a hand, a bolt of energy cannoning into Ambrosio's chest before he could strike, blasting him backwards into a tree, the trunk cracking as he hit it.

Despite the force of the impact, Ambrosio did not give his foe the chance to gather his bearings. Instead, he sent his power into the ground beneath him and leapt towards Auryn in a three-metre-high arc, his fist blazing with black energy. The punch struck Auryn in the sternum, the power behind it detonating and sending him tumbling through the air and landing on the other side of the lawn with a thud.

Theo ran towards him as fast as her unsteady gait would allow, adrenaline propelling her unwilling muscles, but Ambrosio outpaced her, reaching Auryn as he scrambled to his feet, the two grappling fruitlessly. Without a second thought, she vaulted onto Ambrosio's back, her right arm locking around his throat as she tried to peel him off. He twisted sharply in response, the jerk breaking her grip and sending her stuttering away as Auryn toppled over.

Ambrosio backed up a few steps, his focus flitting between the two of them. Holding his gaze, she watched his expression glaze over like he was watching something play out in his mind's eye. Seeking to seize the opportunity, Theo moved to charge at him, but she'd barely landed her first step when he snapped back to reality with a smile. Suddenly, a ball of energy slammed into her chest, and she felt herself fly through the air like a ragdoll.

She heard Auryn call her name as she struck the ground, her ribcage screaming with pain as she drew in a shallow, wheezing gasp. In the sky above, she saw the silhouette of Ambrosio leap high into the air in the direction of the city, landing somewhere beyond the park.

Auryn appeared at her side a moment later, dark energy hanging around his wings like smoke and shading the sun from her eyes as she propped herself up with a grimace.

"Are you okay?" he asked, crouching down.

"Fucking spectacular," she replied, her sarcasm eliciting a half-smile from him that softened the concern on his face.

Meeting his gaze, Theo saw something in Auryn's eyes that hadn't been there before: the reflection of a soul as familiar to her as her own. He placed a gentle hand on her shoulder, and she felt a spark of energy pass between them like static electricity, the feeling energising and reviving.

"Stay here," he said, leaning in and kissing her forehead before rising to his feet, the air crackling around him, his wings flaring with power. "I don't know what's going on, but he won't hurt you again. I promise."

Theo reached up her hand to stop him. "Wait. You ca-"

Releasing his power downwards, Auryn took off into the sky in pursuit of Ambrosio, and Theo found herself left alone, her unfinished warning still clinging to her tongue.

Auryn

A ray of morning sunlight crept across Auryn's face, stirring him from his restless slumber, the unwelcome visitor squeezing through the paper-thin gap between his makeshift blackout blind and the wall.

I won't miss you, he thought, letting out a huff as he rolled to the other side of the bed.

No part of him was ready to be awake yet, but as he stared up at the ceiling, he found solace in the fact he had just weathered his final night in his soulless apartment: his final night without Theo beside him. As joyous as the thought of moving in with her that afternoon was, Auryn found his stomach churning with anxiety, although he couldn't put his finger on the source. It was not his financial woes or lack of employment clawing at him, nor was it the stress of breaking his lease or moving. In place of his usual feelings of instability and impending doom, he found a ceaseless pull, tugging at him as though he was needed elsewhere.

Unsettled, he swung himself out of bed, heading for the shower to seek the calming caress of scalding hot water. Auryn stepped in with a sigh, breathing in the steam, hoping that it might soothe the tightness in his chest. Showers had always been his sanctuary: a place where his mind was free to wander, where problems were solved and answers were found. Amongst the droplets and suds, he searched for peace, for a way to placate the pull, but his new strain of anxiety seemed indelible. Only when the water began to run cold did he notice the passing of time, and he cursed the tiny water heater that had come to ruin so many of his showers.

I won't miss you either, he thought, turning off the faucet for the final time.

Roughing himself dry, he wrapped the towel around his waist and stood in front of the mirror, its fog clearing as he began to shave. With each stroke, he searched his mind in vain for a reason for his restlessness, scouring his thoughts for forgotten responsibilities or unfinished tasks but finding none. In the absence of a cause, the pull worsened, and by the time he placed his razor beside the sink, his jaw was clenched so tightly his teeth were beginning to ache.

Auryn wandered back into his bedroom with a sigh, slipping on a pair of jeans and selecting a black band t-shirt from his collection. The slowly crawling ray of morning light reached his bedside table, catching on the face of his watch and casting a rainbow ribbon along the ceiling. Picking it up, he felt his anxiety tugging harder with each tick, and as he clicked the clasp shut on his wrist, he headed into the lounge, his need for distraction swelling.

A pile of flattened boxes leant against the wall, and he grabbed the roll of packing tape off the kitchen counter and set about condensing his life into a jumble of cardboard cubes for the umpteenth time. Moving from room to room, he packed like with like until a stack of boxes began to line the wall beside the couch. Eventually, he found himself kneeling in front of his bookcase of DVDs. There was ordered comfort to be found in the straightforward stacking of uniform shapes, yet it offered no balm to the leaden weight in his stomach.

He took down each row in order, reading the alphabetised titles as he slid them into the box. When he came to the fourth shelf, his hand fell on the case of the first movie he'd watched with Theo, and he stopped, standing up and carrying it over to the couch. Something stirred in him as he looked at it, and it was then that he felt the pull become a yank. Following it over to the window, Auryn looked out at the city in the distance, an unheard chord vibrating in his chest as though he'd struck one of his heartstrings. All at once, he felt a deep fear lance through him. It was Theo; she was the source of his anxiety.

His rational mind tried to pacify him, combating his doubt with promises that Theo was safe at work and that he simply felt out of place because his life was in transit. Still, the pull did not ease. It was a day like any other outside his four walls, peaceful and pleasant, but in his soul, a storm brewed. Seeking more absolute confirmation, Auryn grabbed his phone off the arm of the couch and messaged Theo, keeping his tone casual.

How's work going, beautiful?

Her response came swiftly, and although she assured him all was as it should be, Auryn found his chest tightening nonetheless, his heart pounding in his ears. He'd told Theo he would pick up her key around three, but as he looked down at his watch, his angst demanded he reconsider. He needed to see her. He needed to be sure.

Before fully registering his actions, Auryn had pulled on his shoes, slipped on his jacket, plugged in his headphones, and closed the door behind him. His feet matched the heavy beat in his ears as he marched towards the station, the five-minute wait for the next train seeming to pass at a snail's pace. With restless feet, he shifted his weight from one foot to the other until it finally pulled up, and he plonked himself down in a seat by the door.

For the first time, he found no relief in the music, the once soothing melodies sounding discordant when mixed with his swirling thoughts. As such, he tore his headphones out in frustration and tucked them in his pocket. His racing heart was making him feel claustrophobic in the confined space of the carriage, so he unzipped his jacket, tying it around his waist as he moved his focus out the window. The stations came and went, and Auryn bounced his leg unconsciously as he counted them down. Eventually, the bright day yielded to the subterranean darkness of the City Loop, and his train arrived at Parliament Station at long last.

Weaving through the glacially-moving masses, he took the escalator stairs two at a time, hustling through the gates and out onto Spring Street. Auryn felt the pull grow firmer, and he allowed it to quicken his step as it led him past Parliament House to the edge of Fitzroy Gardens. The park sat serene and tranquil all around him as he started along the path, the soft sough of the wind and the chirping of birds providing a soundtrack in stark contrast with his own state of being. It was then that he heard a loud boom and the sound of shattering glass travelling through the trees from the direction of Porphura.

In a heartbeat, Auryn broke into a run, taking off across the grass and up the hill, the few other park-goers scampering past him in the opposite direction. His jacket shook loose from around his waist, and he tore it free, tossing it aside as the restaurant came into view up ahead, panic gripping him at the sight.

The front window was completely shattered, the sun reflecting off the fragments scattered across the road, and at the centre of the mess, he discovered the justification for his morning's dread. Wrapped in a blood-soaked uniform stood Theo, her back turned to him, her wrist clamped in the hand of a man he did not recognise. The man raised his fist and struck her in the cheek, Theo crumpling to the ground, and Auryn saw red, his gait widening to a full-pelt sprint.

He barrelled forward as the man pinned Theo to the ground with his foot, cannoning into him and sending him sprawling to the ground. Auryn felt the skin on his hand graze across the asphalt as he tried to catch his own fall before scrambling to right himself. Heaving for breath, he charged as the man regained his feet, ramming his forearm into his chest and marching the man backwards until he slammed into the car parked outside the restaurant.

"Stay away from her, you piece of shit!" he hissed through his teeth, meeting his opponent's cold, dark eyes.

The man just smiled in response, and Auryn felt a hand clamp around his throat, his feet lifting off the ground. What happened next made no sense. Out of nowhere, something unseen slammed into his chest, and he was sent flying through the air, landing on the lawn of the park some ten metres away. Coughing as he tried to fill his winded lungs, Auryn saw the man striding towards him, his hands clasped casually behind his back.

"And who might you be, my good samaritan?" the man asked, his accent foreign but clear. "This is a private matter, and if you have any sense of self-preservation, you'll leave. Now."

Auryn pushed himself to his feet again, brushing the grass from his t-shirt as his adrenaline surged anew. "Not gonna happen. That's my girlfriend, you sick fuck!"

He'd expected the man to back down, but instead, he glanced back at Theo before offering Auryn a look of amusement. "Ahh, yes, the new attempt at happiness," he snickered. "And here I thought I wouldn't get the chance to kill you in front of her. Impeccable timing, my friend."

Auryn stood dumbfounded. He felt like he'd just walked into a movie two-thirds of the way through. He didn't know who this man was or how he knew Theo, but in the end, it didn't matter. Protecting her was his priority; he could search for explanations in the aftermath.

As the man reached him, Auryn swung his arm back, aiming a sharp right hook at his jaw, but his strike was sidestepped. He felt his skin begin to prickle, but before he could analyse it, the man threw his hands out and, once more, an unseen force slammed into him. Skidding across the grass, Auryn rolled to a stop on his back, his head spinning.

He was still trying to gather his wits when the man appeared over him, grabbing his shirt and hauling him up, a third inexplicable blast hammering into him. Careening through the air, Auryn slammed into the concrete footpath face down, the impact leaving him stunned.

"You know what?" Auryn heard the man say somewhere to his left, although his words were clearly directed at Theo. "I think I'll have a poke around in his head before I kill him, find out what fears and secrets he has rattling around in that brain of his. Maybe he was cheating on you like your last one. Let's find out, shall we?"

Auryn had barely managed to hike himself onto his knees when he felt the man's hand on his throat again. With a yank, he was pulled onto his feet, his unwilling body driven backwards until he was pressed against the boot of an SUV.

Through spotted vision, he saw the man's face come into focus only centimetres from his own. "I have to warn you, my friend," the man said, his voice booming in Auryn's already ringing ears. "I can perform this trick so painlessly you wouldn't even feel it, but where's the fun in that. No, for you, it will be agony beyond your wildest nightmares."

Theo called out from behind the man, but Auryn did not hear her words as he tried to writhe his way free, the man's left hand rising into view and clasping his forehead. All at once, a stabbing pain lanced through his skull, eliciting a scream from his lips and drawing time out until it almost stood still.

Without warning, a barrier seemed to collapse within his consciousness, breaking like a dam and sending a tidal wave of information surging forth, the force ousting his mind's unwelcome intruder.

The man released his grip, and Auryn crumpled into a crouched huddle, but the pain in his head did not dissipate. Instead, it intensified, images flashing before him too fast to discern their details but leaving a sense of familiarity in their wake all the same. Although he could not explain it, it felt like he was reconnecting with a part of himself he didn't know existed. The sensation came in waves, each more overwhelming than the last, and he pressed his palms to his face,

573

crying out over and over, all other sounds muted by the noise in his head.

As the pain grew, something else grew alongside it: a power he'd always felt in his darkest moments, a fire in his soul stoked by hatred and rage. It was the same power that had stood with him on the stairs at university all those years ago. Back then, he had sworn it was an immaterial wish for vengeance and nothing more. In that moment, though, it finally felt tangible, simmering beneath his skin, begging for release.

Pushing himself away from the SUV, Auryn staggered across to the edge of the park. The pressure within him reached a crescendo, and he threw his head back, one last cry bursting from his lungs as he finally unleashed his power. Wind rushed around him, and he looked up to see dark energy surging from his skin and funnelling upwards, the sky visible through its centre as though he was standing in the eye of a tornado. The pain yielded to elation, and in turn, to ecstasy. For the first time in his life, he no longer felt helpless.

As the vortex continued, the release point of his energy concentrated into his back, and in his peripheral vision, Auryn saw shafts of darkness stretch out behind him like wings, black lightning dancing around them. The sight should have frightened him, and yet it didn't. Instead, the wings brought him a sense of sentimental comfort, like seeing an old friend after a lifetime apart. Allowing the feeling to join the chaos in his mind, a single name filtered to the forefront, one that connected him to Theo in a way he did not expect and brought with it far more questions than it did answers: Phoenix.

Slowly, he began to find an equilibrium, harnessing his energy and wrangling it as though his ability to do so was innate, the swirling darkness around him fading. As it cleared, he was met with a sight he could not explain. Before him stood the shadow of a young lady, curls framing her face, her silhouette dressed in a gown from some bygone era. Her form seemed unstable, as though she was an echo of the past, and as he looked at her, he realised that some new part of him recognised her, her name coming unbidden to his lips.

"Viola," he whispered despite himself.

The shadow brought up her hand, turning to point behind her. Following her finger, Auryn's focus snapped back to the present just in time, the shadow dispersing like smoke as his opponent lunged towards him. Without a thought, Auryn threw out his hand, a bolt of dark energy shooting from his open palm. It struck the man square in the chest, the force sending him flying into a tree across the lawn, the trunk cracking audibly as he connected with it.

A feeling of rapture filled Auryn as he stared at his hands, dumbfounded by his actions. He didn't know where this sudden power had come from, but in truth, he didn't care. If it meant he could protect Theo, that was all he cared about.

As he gathered his bearings, Auryn heard a sound, and he peered across to find the man gone. A shadow streaking along the grass caught his eye, and he looked up just as the man descended from above, his blazing fist sending a shock wave into Auryn's body. The world spun in his vision as he tumbled through the air, coming to a stop with a thud and clambering to his feet in anticipation of another attack. A split-second later, the man was upon him again, and before he knew it, the two were locked together, grappling for the advantage but finding their strength evenly matched.

Over the man's shoulder, Auryn caught sight of Theo running unsteadily towards them, launching herself onto the man's back and wrapping her arm around his throat, trying to pry him away. The man twisted sharply in response, and Auryn toppled to the ground. Climbing to one knee, he readied himself for the next strike only to see Theo charge at the man before being thrown backwards by a ball of pitch-black energy to the chest.

"THEO!" Auryn cried out as he watched her body strike the ground, the sound of the air leaving her lungs tearing at his heart.

Adrenaline propelled him as he sprinted over to protect her, but instead of attacking again, the man leapt high into the air and disappeared towards the city. As Auryn neared Theo, a kaleidoscope of images flashed through his mind at speed, each as vivid and familiar as a memory, although they were not of his life.

"Are you okay?" he asked, crouching beside her as she propped herself up, his heart pounding in his ears.

"Fucking spectacular," she replied, the sound of her sarcasm bringing with it a wave of relief.

As she met his gaze, Auryn noticed a light in her eyes that he'd never seen before, a light that stirred something in his soul for reasons he could not understand. Placing a gentle hand on her shoulder, he felt a spark of energy pass between them, the barrage of images subsiding until only one thought lingered. He couldn't let her die, not this time, not again.

"Stay here," he said, kissing her forehead before rising to his feet. "I don't know what's going on, but he won't hurt you again. I promise."

Straightening up and turning towards the city, he was faced with another shadow, its outstretched wings identical to his, its name once again recalled like a memory long buried: Ingram. The figure nodded his acknowledgement, then forced his hands down at his sides, shooting into the air and disappearing.

Auryn saw Theo reach for him from the corner of his eye, pleading for him to wait, but he couldn't. As his power swelled again with his heart's newfound resolve, he knew there was no turning back. The shadows were there to guide him, to show him the way; he knew that now.

Pressing his own hands down, Auryn released his energy into the ground and ascended into the sky. His determination to save Theo was so all-consuming that he didn't question how or why he was suddenly capable of defying every law of physics. Instead, he allowed instinct to take the wheel, soaring towards the city in pursuit of the man.

As he approached the fringes of the CBD from lofty heights, he heard a commotion and spotted a group of cars stopped at the intersection of Russell and Lonsdale Street. The asphalt at its centre was fractured as though something had struck the ground with great force. Swooping down, he attempted to land elegantly, but he pulled up too late and succeeded only in tumbling head over heels and stopping in the middle of the impact zone, his wings disappearing in the spill.

Auryn hurried to his feet, peering through the fog of dark energy obscuring his features to find scores of faces pointed in his direction. The footpaths were filled with shell-shocked onlookers startled from their comings and goings or drawn away from their late lunches and early drinks at the surrounding restaurants and bars. Those caught in the traffic jam craned their necks in search of the cause of their delay. As for the curious office workers and residents in the buildings above, they pressed their noses to the glass or leant over their balconies.

Auryn scanned the sea of strangers, but nowhere could he locate the man he sought. Spinning full circle for a second time, he caught sight of a shadow standing amongst the crowd and stopped short. As he watched, the figure his soul recognised as Einar lifted his finger and pointed at something over his shoulder. Before Auryn could turn his head, though, the man seized him from behind, pinning his arms to his side. Pain lanced through his body as if he was being electrocuted, his back burning as the man's grip grew tighter.

In desperation, Auryn fought to focus his energy inwards, drawing it into a tight ball before unleashing it, the air around him exploding and leaving his ears ringing. The detonation dislodged his foe, and as he pivoted, he saw the man hit the ground and roll to a stop a few metres away. Auryn took a few deep breaths, and the pain subsided slightly as he regained his concentration, his wings reappearing in his peripherals.

The man rose to his feet slowly, glancing across at Auryn with a wry smile as a cloud of dark energy danced around him. "You know, at first, I was angry at your reappearance, old friend. There's nothing more irksome than a vanquished foe rising from the ashes. After a moment's thought, however, I'm starting to reconsider," he said, beginning to circle Auryn like a predator sizing up his prey. "Maybe this is how it was always meant to be, our powers finally revealed to the world. Maybe it's time we change the script and show them who we truly are."

"I don't know who you are or what you're talking about," said Auryn, holding his ground, his head swivelling to follow the man's movements.

"Come now, Little Phoenix, you know who I am," the man said, stopping several paces in front of Auryn and flexing his back, seven blades as black as obsidian emerging behind him like the legs of a spider.

Gasps from bystanders mingled with the sounds of phone cameras snapping, their primal fear overtaken by more modern compulsions as they sought to capture proof of the impossible. At the centre of their focus, still shrouded in his own swirl of energy, Auryn stood frozen by the sight of his newly transformed foe. Images flitted through his mind of hard-fought battles and untimely ends. Then, all at once, he realised he *did* know who the man was.

"Anasazi," he said, the name rolling off his tongue of its own volition, its aftertaste bitter and astringent.

"Well done," Anasazi mocked, clapping slowly before looking around at the crowd encircling them with a smirk. "Now that the formalities are out of the way, what do you say we get this show on the road? The stage is set, the cameras are rolling, and it seems we have a full house. Needless to say, I think this fight might actually make the history books for once. Of course, you won't be around to see it" -his lips curled with malice- "nor will your precious butterfly."

It was the word 'butterfly' that pierced Auryn's soul, Theo's lifeless form suddenly flashing before him as Anasazi's barbed threat lodged in his heart. Reason abandoned him in an instant, and in its place, he allowed the reckless hands of rage to seize control.

Raw power surged through his veins, and he charged forward, his wings flaring, a booming war cry bursting from his lips. Anasazi rushed forth to meet him, and Auryn channelled his power, stretching out his hands and sending a stream of black energy into his opponent's chest.

Forced to his knees, Anasazi dipped his shoulder, slashing with the blades on his right side, but to no avail. Auryn jumped out of reach, bolstering his stance and unleashing another attack as his foe tried to stand up. The blast carried Anasazi over the heads of the onlookers and into the second storey wall of the old Greek restaurant on the corner. The impact cracked the facade and shattered the windows, Anasazi's blades slicing through the awning as he tumbled to the ground below.

Auryn watched the crowd part, people screaming as they scattered away, self-preservation finally trumping social media. Taking a deep breath, he refocused his power and marched towards Anasazi, determined to finish off his enemy while he had the upper hand.

Auryn was five steps away when there was a loud crack, and he shot backwards, his chest numb. He skidded across the asphalt, grunting in pain as he rolled to a stop on his back. Before he could get up, Anasazi descended from above, landing on top of him and pinning his arms.

"You're fast, Little Phoenix, but not fast enough," Anasazi said, tilting his head with derision. "I must say, I'm somewhat disappointed. I thought you a more worthy adversary."

Auryn struggled under his opponent's weight, but Anasazi only tightened the grip on his wrists, smiling sadistically. "It seems your efforts to save your soulmate have fallen short yet again. I'll be sure to let her know of your failure between the screams."

Rage consumed Auryn, the power lingering beneath his skin racing back to his core. "NO!" he roared.

There was an explosion, and a sonic boom rippled outwards as the unbridled energy burst from his chest, flinging Anasazi into the air, darkness trailing after him like thick smoke, his blades flailing.

Auryn was on his feet before his opponent had even landed, building up his power for a final strike. Before he could, though, the shadow of Nergüi appeared, his hand outstretched to stop him. Something about the gesture sparked a feeling of hesitation in his soul, as if to approach his grounded enemy would be to step willingly into harm's way.

Heeding the advice, Auryn halted his advance and glanced around. The crowd had thinned out to a few camera-wielding individuals of questionable good sense and a handful of innocent bystanders hobbling away to join the retreating masses after being toppled by his last attack. The front few rows of cars gridlocked at the intersection sat open-doored and abandoned, the ones further back locked up tight, their occupants slunk down in their seats to hide from the escalating fray. More curious figures appeared in the windows overlooking the intersection, their phones pressed to the glass, and as he scanned their gawking faces, he saw one of them point at him. No, not at him, behind him.

Auryn turned just in time, his power springing forth to create a shield that deflected the black energy streaking towards him. Ricocheting off, the torrent slammed into one of the forsaken vehicles, the force flipping the car back onto the one behind it. As the sound of distant sirens filtered through the screams, the last few remaining onlookers at ground level finally fled.

A second later, Anasazi was in front of him, the three blades on his right side slicing through the air. Auryn dipped back, the blades barely missing his cheek as he twisted out of the way. He tried to counterattack, his right fist charged with energy, but Anasazi seized his wrist, holding it fast as Auryn swung with his left to the same result.

"Tsk, tsk," scolded Anasazi with a smirk. "Where is your finesse? You've grown weak."

"I'm stronger than you think, you psychopathic fuck," Auryn hissed through clenched teeth as he struggled in vain.

Gathering his power in his chest again, Auryn unleashed it into his opponent, but as the swirl of energy between them dissipated, he blinked in disbelief. The attack had done nothing, his wrists still firmly restrained in the hands of Anasazi, who stood unscathed, not a hair out of place.

"Even after all this time, you still have no idea what true power is," Anasazi chuckled to himself, his grip tightening until Auryn could feel his wrist bones grind together.

The air began to vibrate around them, and Auryn felt his ears pop as the pressure increased, a low hum emanating from his foe.

Without breaking eye contact, Anasazi retracted his blades and narrowed his eyes. "Let me show you."

There was an explosion of darkness, and Auryn's wings disintegrated instantly, his chest afire as he was propelled upwards. His vision faded to black for a moment before he struck the upper storeys of the skyscraper on the north-west corner of the intersection. Snapping back to reality as he glanced off the side, he saw window after window shatter from the shock wave that carried him, the sound deafening. He felt his speed slow as his arc reached its peak, and he realised he was on a collision course with the ground.

His mind battled to stay lucid, and he closed his eyes, images flashing before him of dune-filled deserts and snow-capped peaks, castles of sorrow and an island that felt like home. It was the final image, though, that seemed to stop time.

In his mind's eye, he saw Theo sitting at the bar at Benzin, a wry smile tugging at her lips as she raised her glass to his. He saw the shadows catching in the hollows of her collarbones and the light glinting off her grey-blue eyes like the sunset off the ocean. She was the centre of his universe, the fulcrum around which his whole world moved. Before her, he'd wandered aimlessly through life, but because of her, he had purpose. She was his whole heart, his soulmate, his beautiful butterfly.

Suddenly, his eyes flew open, rekindled power surging through him and making his skin prickle. He felt his wings emerge once more, and he began to glide, watching as the storm of glass in his wake fell away. Turning to face the unbroken windows of the building he was now alongside, Auryn finally saw himself as he truly was. In the reflection, he found his body engulfed in dark energy, his wings stretched behind him and alive with black lightning.

There was something else too. Beside him flew the shadow of Jelani, his head up and shoulders back as though heading confidently into battle, sure of his place in the world. Auryn adjusted his posture to match, and as Jelani disappeared in the wind, he discovered a feeling of self-assurance deep in his soul, a reminder that great strength lay within him.

Banking to his right, Auryn wove between the buildings, staying low to keep out of Anasazi's sightline, cutting a wide loop and approaching the intersection from the south. He remained amongst the safety of the buildings until the last moment, swooping silently out over the road and soaring towards his foe, who stood with his back turned. Before Anasazi could move, Auryn rocketed into him at full speed, his blades dissolving like smoke upon impact.

With his arms clamped around his foe, Auryn redirected his power downwards, and the pair shot up into the sky. The wind whistled as they rose past the now windowless tower, the air growing thinner as they left humanity behind and approached the thin wisps of low-hanging cloud drifting lazily overhead.

Auryn felt Anasazi struggle, writhing to free his arms from where they were pinned, and as his grip began to loosen, he did not tighten it. Instead, as Anasazi tried to twist and attack, Auryn simply let go, stopping in mid-air and watching as his opponent fell earthward.

Anasazi picked up speed, plunging towards a pair of beige skyscrapers at the eastern edge of the city that played host to a five-star hotel. The towers were identical, over fifty storeys tall and offset so that the south-west corner of the front tower sat a stone's throw from the north-east corner of the rear. Auryn hovered in place to witness the death of his enemy, but as he looked on, he saw Anasazi begin to angle his body until he was aimed at the gap between the skyscrapers.

Suddenly, a barrage of black energy erupted from Anasazi, and he hurtled towards the rear tower, his blades reappearing just before he struck its north-east corner. Sparks and rubble flew outwards as the blades bit into the concrete siding like talons, his descent slowing before he sprang across the gap to the adjacent corner. He slid down further, cutting through the facade as he leapt between the two towers to slow his momentum. Nearing the Perspex roof of the atrium below, Anasazi sent a barrage of power downwards, tearing it asunder as he leapt free and disappeared through the gaping hole and into the sunken courtyard.

From his lofty position, Auryn could see people fleeing, the sounds of screams and sirens mixing with the frantic ding of a tram at the far end of the block cut off by cars as they tried to speed away. Gravity began to tug at him when something caught his eye, and he looked up to find the shadow of Ashur. As they hung there, face to face, Ashur placed his hand on Auryn's shoulder, the connection making his skin prickle. All at once, Auryn felt the weight of responsibility fall on his shoulders, and deep in his soul, a forgotten truth came to light. He had to finish things no matter what it took, not only to protect Theo but every other innocent life in Anasazi's warpath.

Ashur dropped his hand back to his side, and in perfect unison, they both flipped their bodies backwards and dove down, Ashur dissipating into the air like a comet breaking up. Auryn sped towards the ground, and as he drew closer, he spied Anasazi in the centre of the tram tracks that ran down Collins Street, poised and unflinching, his face skyward.

Doubt flooded Auryn's mind, but he pressed on, adrenaline bolstering his nerve as he streaked towards his target. Gathering his power in his chest, he braced for impact, closing his eyes and unleashing all of his might in one explosive blast as he collided fist-first into his foe.

The detonation rocked the city, the resulting shock wave shattering every remaining window within a five-block radius while concrete and asphalt alike cracked underfoot. Every tree in sight stood stripped of its late-spring foliage, and the few people who had not managed to retreat in time lay sprawled on the ground where they'd toppled or hid crouched behind parked cars.

As for Auryn, he was sent careening sideways towards the atrium. He slammed into a series of broken metal pipes that had once supported the Perspex roof but now hung at the entrance like twisted wind chimes, his wings disappearing as he struck them. Hitting the ground hard, he felt the air shoot from his lungs, and as he tried to catch his breath, he heard muffled screams begin to filter past the ringing in his ears.

Slowly, he picked himself up and stumbled back the way he came, coughing as he glanced around to find the space filled with a thick cloud of dust. Above him, shards of glass hit the roof like rain and skittered across the ground as they fell from the towers. His hair began to stand on end, and he looked up to see black lightning lancing

582

between the dangling metal pipes as if the energy released by his attack had taken on a life of its own.

Auryn weaved through the concrete benches and desperately retreating stragglers until he reached the road, hoping for a clearer view, but the low hanging dust cloud was just as thick out on the street. Overhead, the same autonomous lightning arced between the buildings as if jumping between Tesla coils.

There was no sign of Anasazi as he turned on his heel, and part of him hoped the nightmare was over, but as he came full circle, Auryn was faced with the shadow of Madkodi, spear in hand. Pointing its tip to something unseen to the right, Madkodi's message was unequivocal: Anasazi would not be so easily defeated.

Despite his heart pounding in his ears, Auryn stood his ground and peered into the dust, glass and rubble continuing to fall as the surrounding buildings settled into their new injured state.

"Well, that was entertaining, wasn't it?" a voice called out. "We've fought many battles over the millennia, Little Phoenix, but we've never brought a city to ruin in the process."

Bracing himself, he watched as the silhouette of seven blades appeared in the haze before him. A gust of wind funnelled down the street, and Anasazi was revealed, a trickle of blood running down the side of his head and seeping onto his collar, his clothes torn and tattered from the explosion. Auryn gathered his power again, his wings reappearing and sending a shiver down his spine as they reacted with the latent energy all around.

"This ends now!" he shouted defiantly.

"Indeed," replied Anasazi, glancing around before meeting his eyes again with an approving smile, his blades flexing behind him. "The time has come."

Anasazi rushed forward, and Auryn swung at him with a cross punch, his energy increasing its force tenfold. Before it connected, though, his foe dodged, ducking under his arm and continuing ten paces before turning back to face him.

"Is that the best you can do?" Anasazi asked with a laugh.

Without hesitation, Auryn sent a burst of energy at his face with a grunt, but again, Anasazi deflected the attack as though it were nothing. Instead, the dark mass shot upwards to join the swirl of power feeding the lightning arcs.

"Your feeble attempts are barely worth my time," mocked Anasazi. "Paltry and pathetic."

Auryn felt the words claw at him, digging into the scars his childhood bullies had left behind decades earlier. Glowering at his opponent, he was met with a grin, and he stumbled upon a sudden realisation. Anasazi was goading him on, trying to manipulate him into striking with mindless rage.

He closed his eyes, ignoring Anasazi's ongoing barrage of taunts, and redirected his focus inward. Overhead, Auryn could hear the crack of the lightning, the energy surrounding them moving like the tide, ebbing and flowing with equal force. It was so thick he swore he could feel it washing over him, waves of darkness that threatened to engulf them both in an eternal night.

Taking a deep breath, he gathered his anger and channelled it to a place deep within his soul. As he allowed it to swell, he couldn't help but feel like a dam just before it burst, the force building up until it threatened to consume him if not unleashed. When he opened his eyes again, it was to find Anasazi silently waiting for his first move, revelling in the calm before the storm.

An arc of black lightning cracked directly above them like a starting pistol, and the pair barrelled headlong towards their uncertain fate. Auryn's wings blazed behind him, the thought of Theo filling his mind. He was only a step away when he swung his right fist, seeking the connection of flesh that would serve as a conduit through which all his power would flow. An inch from his opponent's face, though, he felt his hand stop short, Anasazi grasping his wrist and holding it firm while attempting to connect with a punch of his own. Auryn seized his foe's wrist in return, the pair locked in a mirrored stance, equally matched and equally unyielding.

They remained that way for what seemed like an eternity, the air crackling like fire as they stared each other down, their powers meeting at each point of contact but finding no release. As they grappled fruitlessly, the smoke-like energy around them began to swirl and darken, snaps of lightning discharging from it and joining the maelstrom above as though they were standing in a storm cloud. The pressure rose with each passing second, and a low hum emanated from both opponents, the two sounds resonating until Auryn became deaf to the world.

Suddenly, a sphere of pure black appeared in the space between them. Its interior churned with ever-growing darkness, and Auryn felt the swirl of energy engulfing them begin to condense as though being absorbed. In its glassy surface, he saw his reflection, his wings billowing behind him, but there was something else. Over his shoulder, he saw the fractured shadow of Rurik reaching out to him, and an overwhelming feeling of sadness and loss filled his soul.

Glancing up through the encroaching haze, Auryn saw Anasazi watching him with a malevolent smile, and as the sphere began to expand, he realised the gravity of his mistake. The power held within it would not only destroy them both but the entire city as well.

Before such a doom could come to pass, though, a fist encased in purple energy appeared, rising upwards in an arc and shattering the sphere. The blast it caused sent the two enemies flying in opposite directions, and as Auryn hurtled backwards, his mind stuck in slow motion, he played witness to the most incredible sight. Standing there in the lingering cloud of darkness was Theo, her form encased in an ethereal aura of purple energy, ten long tendrils flowing from her back like wings, her eyes smouldering with determination.

Beyond her, he saw Anasazi crash into the side of a parked car, its doors crumpling from the impact, his foe collapsing in a heap. Auryn hit the ground with a grunt and rolled to a stop on his back at the foot of one of the concrete benches. Blinking a few times, he looked up to find Theo standing over him. All traces of her majesty were gone, her visage returned to normal, her chef's jacket discarded somewhere along the way to reveal her familiar black singlet, her arms scratched and bruised.

"Come on!" she urged, reaching out her hand to him.

He took it, heaving a breath and standing up. The dark energy that filled the air had changed, and as he regarded it, Auryn noticed that it had taken on a deep purple hue, as though Theo's singular strike had altered it somehow.

She squeezed his hand, his grazed palm stinging as he turned to her with a frown. "What are you doing here?" he demanded.

"What do you think I'm doing here?" she replied, raising an eyebrow. "I'm saving you, obviously."

"I didn't nee-"

"Yes, you did."

"Fine, maybe I did, but that's beside the point," Auryn said, tilting his head with resigned acceptance. "Do you have *any* idea what the fuck is going on here?"

"No, nor do I care. All I know is that this nutjob showed up at work, and it's been a clusterfuck ever since."

A groan reached them from across the road, and they peered through the haze to find Ambrosio propping himself up on his elbows and spitting blood onto the asphalt.

"You need to get out of here. I'll finish him off," said Auryn in earnest.

"Are you insane?" she snapped back. "Last time I checked, *I* was the one who just saved *you*."

"And *I* saved *you* before that, remember? Now go."

Theo shot him an indignant glare, letting go of his hand and poking him in the chest with her finger. "Let's get one thing straight. I'm not going anywhere. We face this together."

Auryn opened his mouth to argue, but the image of Theo ablaze with power flashed before him, and he knew she was right. "Okay," he replied with a small nod. "Any ideas?"

"I don't know! Hope the military turns up before he recovers?"

Auryn spotted movement and glanced across to see Anasazi slowly rising to his feet. "I don't think we're gonna be so lucky."

"Well, do *you* have any bright ideas that don't involve hand-to-hand combat with Shelob over there?"

"Nope," he said, holding out his hand and giving her a half-hearted smile. "Together?"

Theo smiled back, interlacing her fingers in his, her eyes steady and assured. "Together!"

Auryn's skin prickled as their energies coalesced, soul connecting with soul, purple fusing with black before his eyes. As he tightened his grip on Theo's hand, he felt something pass between them: a hardened resolve that the monster they faced would not prevail, coupled with a deep-seated love that defied all boundaries.

Anasazi didn't bother with words this time, leaping towards them, his face cold and jaw square. Before he could reach them, though, a forcefield of interlaced energy enveloped the pair, and he was knocked onto his back. He righted himself quickly, but he did not attack again, instead staring in disbelief.

The shield of energy pulsed around Auryn and Theo, growing in intensity until the surrounding world was almost obscured from view. As its limits warped and undulated, Auryn felt a low hum start up again, vibrating through his chest on a wavelength that seemed to match his emotions. Theo's fingers squeezed tighter between his, and in unison, they raised their free hands, palms forward, and took a bracing breath. Auryn drew his power into a tight ball in his chest, and without need for word or signal, he released it outwards just as Theo did the same.

There was a sound like a bass drop, and the dome of dark purple energy protecting them began to expand. As Auryn peered through it, he saw their foe leap into the air again, his blades flared behind him. Anasazi unleashed a stream of darkness at the dome, trying to penetrate it, but as his power collided with theirs, he seemed to freeze in place. He screamed out with rage and pain as streaks of purple surged up the stream towards him, creeping across his skin and dissolving his blades. Auryn saw Anasazi's eyes widen with horrified realisation as the dome reached him, and the sound that escaped his lips on contact defied explanation: guttural yet ear-piercing. His gaze never left the soulmates as he was engulfed inch by inch, his entire being turning to ash. What little remained of him caught on the swirling surface of the forcefield before dispersing into nothingness, his essence wholly obliterated.

Despite the defeat of their enemy, the dome did not stop. It expanded like an atom bomb in slow motion, absorbing the dark lightning overhead and clearing away the haze of dust and debris. In the calm of its protection, Auryn could feel Theo's pulse between his fingers, her heart beating in time with his, their souls seeming to intertwine further the larger the dome became. A deep sense of empathy flowed through her palm into his, and he felt the rage boiling in his heart simmer down until it fell still. The darkness of the dome paled to a softer purple, and as the sun's rays shone through it, a rainbow band of light was cast across his face.

He watched the dome continue on its course, shimmering wherever it touched a new surface, gently washing over cars and buildings without damage. It swelled until it encompassed the entire city, hanging there in all its glory for a long moment, cradling every hidden laneway, towering skyscraper, and unsuspecting soul in its embrace. Then, just like that, it popped, wisps of purple energy dissolving into the air.

As the breeze off the bay swept through the streets once more and the sounds of the city returned, Auryn looked across at Theo, her hand still held lightly in his.

"What the fuck just happened?" he asked.

Theo raised her eyebrows and shrugged, peering around in incredulous awe at the altered state of the city they knew so well.

"I just ... I have so many questions," he said, rubbing his eyes as his mind tried to process the events, barely convinced they'd happened at all.

"You and me both," Theo replied, letting out a long breath through puffed cheeks.

"So, what now?"

"I don't know," she said, taking one more peek at the ruined atrium, "but I don't think we should hang around here to find out. I don't know if you've noticed, but you destroyed a decent portion of the city when you decided to 'save' me."

She grinned at him with the impish expression he adored so much, and he couldn't help but laugh as he pulled her instinctively to his chest, embracing her lightly. "I love you, my beautiful butterfly," he whispered.

"I love you too."

The sound of distant shouting reached them, and Theo grabbed his hand, gesturing towards home with her head. "Come on. We need to go before someone sees us."

The two of them scurried down the block and away from the epicentre, but it wasn't until they reached the edge of the city that they encountered another person. As they turned the corner onto Spring Street, a little old lady with a dishevelled puff of pure white hair and a dust-covered, pink cardigan tottered towards them, her brow furrowing in concern.

"Are you two all right?" she asked in an endearing British accent, looking their battered figures up and down before brushing the dust from Auryn's shirt with a fuss.

"We're fine," he assured her, finally taking in his shambolic appearance, his hands bloodied, his clothes tattered. "Are you okay?"

"Well, I must say, this isn't what I was expecting on my first visit to Australia. I was awfully frightened with all the explosions, but then there was that wave of purple light," she said with a contented sigh.

"Did you feel it? Wasn't it wonderful? It made me think of all my most treasured memories."

Auryn glanced across at Theo with a grin before nodding at the lady.

"You know what it made me think of?" she continued in fervent tones. "My daughter. We've been estranged for such a long time. I disapproved of her husband, you see. But that light. Oh, it made me think of all of the fun we used to have together. How foolish of me to let such a silly thing get between us." She beamed up at them both, her eyes welling with tears. "Do excuse me. I have a long-overdue phone call I need to make."

Auryn smiled at her warmly.

"Take care of each other, won't you?" she said, reaching for each of their hands and squeezing them. "Life is so awfully short."

With a serene smile, the old lady bustled away, fussing with her cardigan as she went.

Theo watched her go, then met Auryn's eye with a raised brow. "What was that all about?"

"Beats me," he shrugged. "What the fuck did we do?"

"No idea, but she seems pleased about it," Theo replied, chuckling to herself before clutching at her side with a wince. "Ooo, that's gonna hurt in the morning," she said as the sound of sirens drew closer.

"Come on, beautiful," he said, kissing her on the forehead. "Let's go home."

Taking her hand, they crossed the road and wandered into the gardens, passing between the avenue of tall trees swaying in the breeze. As he watched a wisp of Theo's hair dance across her face, his mind an addled mess of unanswered questions, a truth as sure as the day is long surfaced in his soul. Whatever the future held, they'd meet it together.

Acknowledgments

From Benny

First of all, I'd like to thank Alex, my love and my muse. This novel would literally not exist without her. I love telling a story, but Alex loves the written word, and her beautiful phrasing and poetic turn transformed this novel into something far greater than what I could have done myself. Her strength, energy, and patience helped bring this novel into being, and my life would be but a pale shadow without her.

I'd also like to thank:

My father, David, for his intelligence, foresight, passion for life and enduring love of the Western Bulldogs.

My brother, Tim, for always being there when I need some advice, and for his music, which is always an inspiration.

My brother Daniel, for always being such a great sound board, and for helping me take my mind off things when times were stressful.

My sister Emma, for always being my adorable baby sis, for your ample supplies of chocolate, and your strength as a person.

Anthony (and Wilson) for the late night/early morning chats about every nerdy topic imaginable.

And lastly, to my mother, Maureen, for always taking the time to listen to my problems, for always being the voice of encouragement, and for always championing my writing, even when most others would have tried to persuade me otherwise. I love you more than anything, and I wish you could have lived long enough to read this.

From Alex

First and foremost, I would like to thank my mum, Judy, for showing me the importance of being a strong woman in a man's world, even if that intimidates others. For teaching me that sometimes soldiering on through the hard times is all you can do. And for patiently sitting through all of my rants and knowing that I didn't need you to try and fix things; I only needed you to listen.

Secondly, I'd like to thank my brother, Steven, for reiterating to me that without risk, there can never be reward. For teaching me that betting on yourself is the only bet worth making. For showing me that outside your comfort zone isn't necessarily uncomfortable. And for reminding me that it is better to have tried and failed than to have never tried at all.

Next, I would like to thank my honorary aunty, Kerry, for sharing with me her love of literature. For reminding me that writing what you believe in is more important than writing a crowd-pleaser. And for teaching me the power of the handwritten word and its ability to harm or heal.

I'd also like to send a special thank you to my best friend and wife from another life, Alicia, for her unwavering enthusiasm, excitement, and encouragement. And for teaching me that soulmates come in all shapes and sizes, but more importantly, that they're always there when you need them most.

Last but in no way least, I'd like to thank my life and writing partner, Benny, for allowing me to share this adventure with you. For not stabbing me while we strained under the weight of our attempt at perfection. And for reminding me through your writing of the complexity and boundless nature of your heart. You have written us down, and in doing so, you have made us and our love immortal.

From Both of Us

Finally, we'd both like to thank everyone who has helped us on our journey:

Judy, for letting us live with you while we finalised the novel. We're sorry it took as long as it did.

Tony and Lisa, for letting us stay in your house in Surrey while we finished the third draft at the end of our first travelling adventure.

Anthony, for letting us borrow your larger than life personality.

Debbie, for your expert copy-editing and proofreading despite being faced with a heart-wrenching family emergency.

Xenoyr, for producing our amazing cover art, which has finally given a physical image to the figures who have lived so long in our mind's eye.

About the Authors

Benny Charles

When he's not transferring his boundless story ideas from brain to keyboard, Benny is a bar manager and Alex's loyal travel companion. He loves film, music, literature, video games, and basically any other outlet for turning pain into productivity.

If broken down into his base elements, he would be composed of 65% imagination, 25% heavy music, 7% disappointment at the failings of mankind, 2% common sense, and 1% pure stubbornness.

Alex Robinson

If gallivanting around the world, eating to excess without consequence, and booping dogs was a career path, Alex would have picked that. In the absence of such a choice, she can usually be found polishing Benny's rough drafts, plying her trade as a pastry chef, or taking a year off here and there to answer the call of her wanderlust.

If broken down into her base elements, she would be composed of 50% song lyrics, movie quotes, and dessert recipes, 25% sarcasm and disdain, 14% unwilling compromise, 10% spite, and 1% insistence that Oxford commas are necessary.

When they're not being nomads, they live in Melbourne, Australia, with their absurdly large plush Yoshi, very little spare time, and a feeling that writing this in third person is a little weird.

Follow Us

www.childrenoftheaether.com

Facebook: www.facebook.com/childrenoftheaether

Instagram: www.instagram.com/childrenoftheaether
@childrenoftheaether

Twitter: www.twitter.com/children_aether
@Children_Aether

Printed in Great Britain
by Amazon

13649299R00347